Copyright © 2018 by Kim Wedlock
All rights reserved.

This book, its cover image or any portion thereof may not be reproduced or used in any manner whatsoever without the express written permission of the author, except for the use of brief quotations in a book review or scholarly journal.

First Printing: 2018 Amazon Publishing
Bristol, UK

www.KimWedlock.com

@KimWedlock

The Devoted
Book One

The Zi'veyn

Kim Wedlock

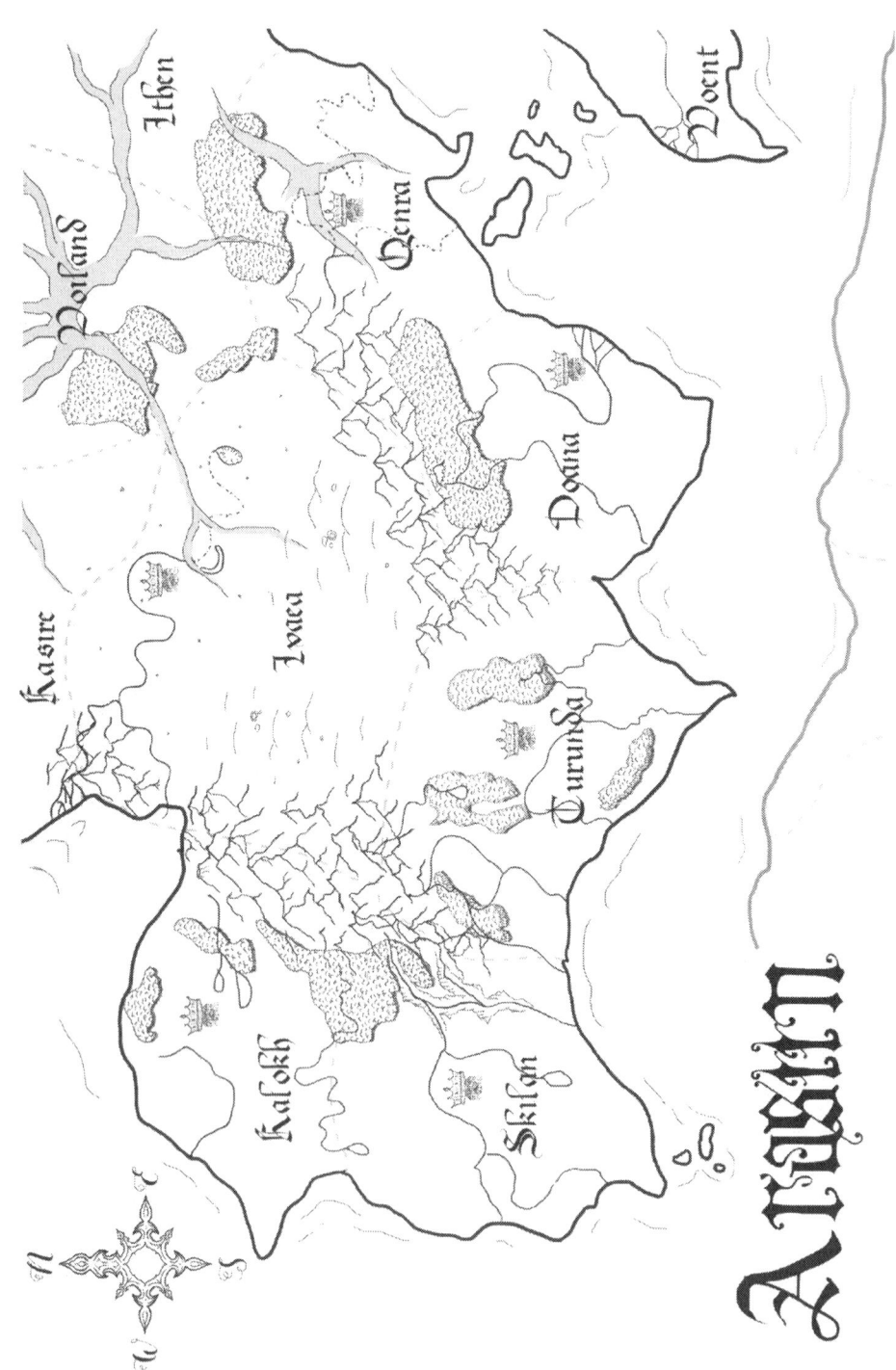

Chapter 1

It was a quiet evening. The sun had fled the Scowles hours ago, plunging the jagged, rock-studded forest into an early dusk, the green of the leaves and the red of fox coats washed out in the numb, blue-grey light. There was a thin scent on the chill air, of moss and loam, and a hint, when the young, spring breeze shifted, of thyme and sage that lured the noses of foraging beasts. Aside from the gentle pad of their feet moving haltingly through the undergrowth, there was little but tousled leaves to be heard.

Until a scathing curse ricocheted through the labyrinth.

Rathen scrambled around the cramped little kitchen, rubbing the top of his head where he was sure a lump was already forming, and continued his hunt for the spoon he was *certain* had just been in his hand.

He cursed a second time when a pot of peppercorns fell from the table and scattered across the floor, and a third when he dove to collect them and thumped his head again, this time on the underside of a drawer the wretched cupboard had once again caught and dragged open.

He muttered indignantly, moved well back to avoid any more malicious storage, and rose with a huff in the midst of his mess while the room continued to spin. The cheerful bubbling of the pot over the fire suddenly took on a mocking tone. He shot it a spiteful look, and only then noticed the whittled spoon hanging brazenly on the iron rail beside it. And the fallen bottle of wine on the shelf above.

He watched helplessly as the last few drops dribbled straight down into the stew. The pot gurgled in amusement; his shoulders slumped in defeat. "Thin stew it is." Assuming, of course, that it hadn't destroyed the flavour entirely, but at least the bottle had already been almost empty.

The one toppling on the opposite shelf, however, was not.

Panic flashed through his veins. He rushed towards it, muttering threats as he stumbled between strewn pots, lids and linen sacks, ignoring Oat's agitated bleat from just outside the window. But he knew he would never make it in time. He cursed once more, raised his hands, and rapidly contorted his fingers.

The bottle froze.

Slowly, it stood itself upright, as though it had caught its balance all on its own. It made no effort to fall again.

His hands dropped back to his sides and he puffed a long sigh of relief. Kicking the box of carrots out of his way, he returned to the cooking fire and retrieved the blasted spoon at last, adamant that it hadn't been there before. Then, after finally giving it a good stir, breaking the stew's thickening skin, he began tossing in the dumplings.

Until a knock rattled the door.

He fell perfectly still.

Steam licked up and around his hand while a deep, confused furrow creased the perpetual misery lines in his brow. Slowly, his head craned around towards the door.

The knock came again, along with the goat's protest from the window. His frown grew even deeper. He hadn't imagined it...

Slowly, tentatively, he stepped away from the chortling pot and wove quietly through the kitchen on the lightest of feet. Whoever it was hadn't arrived by accident. The land outside was a maze - it was the whole reason *he* was here. No one would venture into the Scowles if they had even an ounce of sense. And the calm knock didn't suggest that it was someone who had gotten lost...

He stopped silently beside it, listening carefully and thinking. He had two options, as far as he could see: he could either pretend he wasn't home and wait for them to leave, hoping they were suffering from the nasal blockages of a cold, or...hope they didn't knock again.

Both were equally genius, but before he could make his choice, his own accursed curiosity got the better of him.

His hand moved before he could stop it, snatching the door open at speed, as though he thought a show of aggression might frighten the visitor off, but instead he found only a pair of gloved knuckles raised and ready to rap again, this time upon his face, and a startled look on that of the man behind them.

After blinking at one another for a confused moment, the hand hastily withdrew, and Rathen's eyes passed just as quickly over his neat, black uniform and the sword at his hip. With a single glance at the white hammer insignia on its pommel, he stepped back inside and closed the door, interrupting the man's cordial greeting.

A moment later, the knock came again.

Rathen pointedly ignored it as he returned rigidly to the dumplings, just as he did when it came a second time, and a third. His name was called between the bangs, but he scorned those, too, and took his growing frustration out on the stew instead, setting down the spoon and pot lid both with unnecessary force.

"I have the authority to enter at will," the man outside declared with only the slightest annoyance, "but I would prefer to start on civilised terms."

Rathen scoffed even as he continued to feign ignorance, and began cleaning up in the hope that simply keeping busy would be enough to shoo the man away. *'Civilised terms.'* He shook his head vehemently to himself as he collected the pots and utensils he'd strewn about the place. How anyone could consider coming to someone's home unannounced, making a racket against the door and demanding to come in as 'civilised', he would never know. The world must have changed for the worse in his absence.

"Sahrot Rathen Koraaz!"

His patience finally snapped. Fired by either anger or insult, he slammed down the pot lids, stormed back towards the door, tore it open and stared coldly at the thirty-something man, the usually unpleasant lines on his face made only worse by the fury he fought hard to restrain. "There is *no one* here by that name," he snarled through his teeth, but, though he wanted dearly to slam the door in the officer's face, he found himself suddenly quite unable to. So he used himself to block the way and prevent him from just striding on in instead.

The barely ruffled officer had already collected himself. "Perhaps not by title," he replied, standing straight and composed beneath the threatening glare, "but you *are* Rathen Koraaz, are you not?"

"No."

The man breathed in minute exacerbation and closed his eyes. Rathen watched him closely. They opened again a moment later and he offered a smile of apology. It didn't seem sincere. "Then I'm afraid *you're* mistaken, and I'm also afraid that I need a moment of your time."

Rathen's aggression slipped as his accursed interest elbowed its way forwards. "...For what?"

"A proposition."

Rathen blinked.

"May I come in?"

He decided that he did feel both anger and insult after all, and yet he found himself stepping to one side anyway, confusion adding to his middle-aged wrinkles. The officer left him no chance to change his mind.

"This is a very unusual home," he said with careful politeness as he slipped past him and looked about the small, cluttered space. "You're making dinner; I won't keep you long."

Rathen's lip curled in defeat, but he said nothing. Closing the door behind and keeping the man fixed firmly in his sight at every moment, he gestured reluctantly towards one of the two dining room chairs. Whatever his business, he wasn't inclined to entertain him for long enough to warrant the softer seats of the equally cramped sitting room. The sooner it was done, the sooner he'd leave.

"I am Inquisitor Garon Brack," he said at last, sitting only once Rathen had and keeping his sword at his hip and his hands away from the laid table settings. "I've come on behalf of the Hall of the White Hammer - so you can appreciate that I'm not here on trivial matters."

Rathen said nothing. He merely watched him through impatient eyes.

"There have been reports of strange occurrences around the country," he continued, unperturbed, "unnatural sights and sensations, unusual weather patterns, creatures that don't fit description - creatures that have 'changed', the reports state - all isolated to otherwise unimpressive locations. It's causing disruption to the trade routes that pass through them and the people who live nearby, and making the general protection of the populace difficult, especially in these uncertain times."

Still, Rathen didn't react.

The inquisitor's eyes grew weighted. "I believe it may be the result of magic. If it is, it also reinforces the possibility of, and need for action against, a rebellion of mages within the Order."

Suddenly, Rathen couldn't help but laugh, and he made no attempt to stop the bitter chuckle from tumbling out. This time, the inquisitor stared. "'Rebellion'," he shook his head and looked back at him in disbelief. "And this was a *commissioned* investigation?"

"I have the approval of my superiors."

"'No' will do, Inquisitor."

His grey eyes were as hard and unreadable as stone. "It has taken a great deal of pestering on my part," he admitted with no trace of shame, "but my superior has allowed me the matter. I've come to believe that it's far more significant than anyone else wishes to acknowledge, the Crown included. It can't be ignored any longer."

"And you believe that the *Order* is at fault - rebelling, just like in Qenra?" Rathen folded his arms and sat back in his seat, maintaining his acrid, calculated stare. "The mages in the east were treated poorly, Inquisitor, their reaction was *far* from unexpected. But the Order is like *royalty* by comparison. They're not rushing to join them. And I daresay there are more effective ways to rebel than doing strange things to the weather or infecting cattle. And anyway," his eyes narrowed down the length of his nose, "I'd have thought the Hall of the White Hammer would have more pressing matters to deal with than baseless paranoia - especially in these 'uncertain times'."

"Usually, you'd be right, but rest assured that we're handling all we've been given and the guard force and military are taking care of the rest."

"Then you're either underworked or overstaffed." His unfriendly smile turned to mockery. "Your superior doesn't think anything will come of this, does he?"

"...If I am correct in my concerns, and magic *is* to blame, then it needs to be stopped as soon as possible."

"If you are correct, then I agree. But why are you telling *me* this? How do you know I'm not a part of this 'rebellion'? That I won't go and tell the others that you're onto them?"

A smile twitched across the officer's thin lips. It only further unsettled Rathen's stomach. He doubted any humour had *ever* graced those eyes. "I know. You've been out of touch with the world for eleven years; you're not a part of any rebellion. That's why I've come to you. I need the expertise of a mage to determine whether or not magic is involved, and I'd like that mage to have no affiliation with the Order. I'm sure you're aware that you're the only one who fits that criteria."

Again, a venomous taint darkened Rathen's eyes as he cocked his head to the side. "Then it seems you have a predicament."

"Oh?" The inquisitor sat forwards then, a flicker of something in his eyes at last, though it was not for the better, and his voice dropped and hardened with that granite glint. "Chasms have been torn open in Hin'ua and Ithen to the north-east. Even now, they continue to grow - the emergency is so great that it's even overriding their war and forcing it to a close. Whole cities have been wiped off of the map, arid land has flooded, marshlands have dried out, farmland has frozen; the very landscape *itself* is racking up the death toll all across the north. And in *all* of these cases, *magic* has been to blame. I'm sure you can imagine the scale of such devastation - with your understanding of magic, you may well know better than most just what it can do."

Rathen fought down the sharp insult to keep the blood from draining from his face.

"The cases reported in Turunda have been minor, so far, but if it *is* magic, it needs to be stopped before it takes hold. Turunda has avoided being dragged into war while the rest of Arasiin has succumbed, but if this is the first stage of a foreign attack or the start of a strike from within, then it *needs* to be addressed. And for that, as I said, I need a mage. I need *you*."

"And yet, all you've brought to try to convince me are vague and desperate conclusions, a notable lack of evidence and more 'if's than I can count." His dark eyes shifted calmly towards the window where the thick forest rolled away beyond. "I don't see why I should care all the way out here - and, frankly, if the cases are so minor and people are that inconvenienced, then they should just avoid those areas. Problem solved. Evacuate, divert the roads, and fence off cattle from infected wildlife. Hin'ua and Ithen are both a very long way from here and we have no problems with either of them - I highly doubt that they're striking out at us."

The goat grunted outside as its hooves stomped lazily through straw. The officer didn't turn. Rathen's sceptical eyes drifted back onto him. "Have you got any proof that suggests magic *is* involved in Turunda's cases? Or did someone just mention it once, offhandedly? Because I'm sure a man of your intelligence knows that that's all it takes for the finger of blame to fall upon mages as a whole *any* day of the week, alleged uprising or not."

The inquisitor's eyes narrowed. "You're quite adamant that the rebellion isn't happening here."

"Does my denial alarm you?"

"No." He was irritatingly confident. "I told you that I know you're not a part of it. I wouldn't be here if I thought that was a possibility."

"I still wonder why you're here *at all*. And you've still not told me why I should care."

"Because whatever is happening out there could be *serious!*"

Rathen's eyebrows rose at the shattering of the man's composure as he thundered to his feet and slammed his hand down upon the tabletop, rattling the cutlery.

"If this *has* been created by mages, then as tame as it may seem right now, it *will* get worse, and you won't want to be around when it does! Whether anyone else has realised it or not, events like these were the precursors in *every* other country where mages have rebelled, successfully or otherwise. It may seem to be a little bit of unseasonal wind and rain here at the moment, but this could easily go the same way, and there's no telling just where it could happen - these very scowles could close up and swallow your home with you still in it! And who knows what it's ultimately building up to?!"

"Once more: what does this have to do with me?"

The inquisitor leaned upon his fists and stared down at him fiercely, reining himself in with clear effort. "You took an oath to use your powers to protect the country."

"Hah!" Rathen stormed to his feet and squared ominously towards him. He may have only been a fraction taller than the officer, and only about seven or eight years older, but the past decade had made him bitter and his menace easily outmatched authority. "That oath was rendered obsolete the day I was banished and left to die from my wounds."

"I can order you to come with me," he informed him sorely. "If your help and knowledge can benefit my task and bring it to a swift close, then it is more than within my authority to forcefully place you in my custody and drag you out of here by your collar. But, as I said before, I'd prefer this to be civilised." He took a step back and straightened, a composure returning to his voice though his eyes remained aflame. "It would take only a few days at most, and the task is simple.

You cared about the country and its people once, and no matter what you might tell yourself now, you still do. You are the only mage who isn't under suspicion, and I know you're not affiliated with either a rebellion or the Order. I *need* your expertise."

Rathen's jaw began to knot. The inquisitor stared back at him, the weight of his words hanging in the air.

Finally, Rathen straightened.

Though his eyes blazed, he steeled himself and doused his temper, taking a step back and a steadying breath while a rigid distance fell over him, dulling the weight of the officer's gaze. "A man can change in a decade of forced isolation," he said with notable restraint. "Even if - *if* - a rebellion is happening here, there won't be that many involved. A small fraction of the Order at best. If you go to the Order House in Kulokhar, you're bound to find a mage more than willing to help and much more qualified than I am, and the chances are *very* slim that they would be a renegade."

The inquisitor began to protest, but Rathen shook his head, his eyes still firm if injected now with a note of apology. "Though I may disagree with it, my banishment was an order from the Crown, and I must obey it for everyone's sake, regardless of what permission you've been given or whatever it is you were prepared to offer me in return. I can't help you."

"Sahr--"

"I'm not 'Sahrot' anymore. Now please leave."

The inquisitor stared at him, trying to read his stern, pale face, to find something he could work with. But Rathen had walled himself up. No matter how hard the man searched, there was no evidence of his thoughts.

His jaw soon tightened in frustration, and after a slight and rigid bow, the officer did as he was asked, stepping over the boxes of vegetables still scattered across the floor and disappeared out into the thickening darkness.

Rathen released a long, shaking breath as the door clicked shut behind him. He sank heavily back into his chair while his head dropped into his hands. The atmosphere left in the inquisitor's wake continued to press down on his shoulders. It took him several long minutes to wrap his head around the fact that the encounter had actually happened. Either that, or he'd finally gone mad out here in the woods and had started imagining more than just noises.

A soft and careful creak soon rose from the far end of the kitchen, followed by a light patter that pricked at his ears. In that moment, the weight on his heart relented, forgotten as suddenly as his rage.

He looked up, brushed his long, raven hair from his face, and held out his arms as a warm smile shattered his miserable countenance. The little girl hurried into his embrace, her eyes wide both with caution and curiosity.

"Who was that, Daddy?" She asked quietly, her gaze fixed on the door as she wrapped her little arms around him as far as they would go. Her doll was still clutched tightly in her hand, and though he squeezed her in reassurance, her giggled protest was disappointingly brief.

He sighed and stroked her curls, grateful for the simple reminder of what a true priority was. "No one important, little one."

"I heard shouting..."

The controlled fright in her voice stirred a sharp pang of guilt. He squeezed her again. "I'm sorry - but it's nothing to worry about. Someone just got lost and wanted directions, and when I couldn't help them, they got a bit upset."

She nodded slowly as his hold softened, but looked back at him as they parted with eyes too suspicious for an eight-year-old. He knew what was coming, and smiled sheepishly ahead of it. "You're lying."

"Do you want to know the truth?"

She stared at him for another long, sceptical moment. "No," she said eventually. "You wouldn't lie if it was something you wanted me to know."

He chuckled and planted a firm kiss on her forehead. When he looked back into her eyes, her worry had been replaced by her usual, beaming cheer. She sniffed the air, giggled and hurried towards the steaming pot. "It smells delicious!" She declared, reaching up to lift the lid.

Rathen was there in an instant to deflect her bare hand. "You say that about toast," he reminded her, ushering her quite pointedly to the other side of the kitchen.

"But toast *is* delicious! How long do I have to wait?"

"Not very."

"Good! My tummy's rumbly."

Rathen shook his head with a smile and resumed his tidying, but as Aria dutifully stepped forwards to help, he noticed the thin strip of cloth wrapped around her wrist, and the small wooden flakes speckling her clothes. "Oh, Aria..." He took her wrist as she reached out to lift a small sack of potatoes, and she returned his disappointment with a foolish look, realising she'd forgotten to keep it hidden. "Slipped, did you?"

"I did," she admitted, "but I'm fine!"

"I know you are," he replied wearily, and sat her down at the table before unravelling the makeshift bandage to find the cut across the heel of her hand. It wasn't too deep, but it certainly needed a clean, and after taking quick and all-too-practised care of it, they tidied the kitchen together before sitting down to dinner. Aria declared that, aside from a strange, sour, fruity pang, it was indeed delicious, and proceeded to tell him all about her evening.

"Everywhere, you say?"

"*Everywhere*," she assured him. "I chased it all around my room - it hit the floor, then the box, then the wall, then the ceiling, then me, then it hit the floor again, and it all started all over! I called it, ordered it, but it wouldn't stop bouncing!"

"How strange. Wooden balls don't usually bounce that much, do they?"

"No, they don't." Her big, blue-grey eyes narrowed. Despite the smile he fought down, he met her gaze levelly. Finally, she pointed at him. "You know what I think?"

"What's that?"

"*You* did it."

"Would I do such a thing?"

"Yes, you would. You cast a spell over it. I know wood doesn't bounce."

"I could be very hurt by all these accusations, you know."

She huffed in frustration, but though she seemed intent on keeping quiet, certain in herself that he was guilty, her dedication in his punishment was fleeting. She looked back at him barely a moment later, the cheer suddenly evaporating from her eyes. "Was that man *really* lost in the woods?"

Rathen paused mid-chew. "I'm sure he found his way out."

She gave him her familiar slow, unconvinced nod. "He needed your help, but it wasn't with directions, was it?"

"...No." He found himself suddenly unable to meet her gaze. "But I couldn't give him what he needed."

"Are you sure?"

"Quite."

She nodded again, but asked nothing more. She knew that tone. He didn't wish to speak of it. "Well," she said, giving in to his stubbornness, "I hope someone else can."

"So do I." For the third time that evening, he wrestled away the irritating thoughts the encounter had stirred. Fortunately, while Rathen was one to endure a heavy atmosphere, Aria was not, and she quickly began telling him another story about her suspicious trials with uncooperative toys.

She kept his mind mercifully occupied throughout the remainder of the evening, singing silly songs, running around and, of course, forcing him to play with her. But her efforts inevitably wore her down, and though she assured him that she wasn't tired at all, even while stifling a yawn, he soon ushered her to bed with the very honest excuse that he, at least, was exhausted.

But no sooner had he tucked her in, closed the wooden hatch in the floor and slumped down in a chair beside the fire than his still-reeling thoughts tumbled back to the forefront of his mind, dragging him into a deep, dark well of fret.

He discovered as he stared into the dancing flames that he was still furious. His confusion had abated, but the sudden arrival of the inquisitor and subsequent upheaval of his comfortable seclusion had quite distressed him. As far as the world was concerned, he was dead - not by his own choosing, perhaps, but certainly for the best - and pushing aside his past life to try to make a new one had been the hardest thing he'd ever had to do. Every thing, every one and every privilege he'd ever known had been thrown quite suddenly well beyond his reach.

And yet, in time, and in spite of both himself and the Crown, he'd grown rather fond of his modest life and its few expectations - Aria was easy to handle in comparison. And this little home in the Scowles was just that: his. This was a life that the Crown *couldn't* take away from him if just because it was small enough to hold on to.

But then, all of a sudden, out of the blue, without a *hint* of warning, he'd been found. And not by mistake.

Some small part of him had expected such a day to come somewhere down the line, but he'd never expected it to come bearing a proposal. A death sentence, perhaps, but not a plea for *help*...

A twig snapped and popped in the fireplace. A brief but wild tongue of flame licked out, and a small scattering of embers rolled down onto the worn stone hearth. The glow didn't reach his eyes.

Instead, his tired and twisting mind wove deeper into pondering the lengths the resourceful White Hammer must have gone through to find him, and who else must have known besides. After all, he was largely left alone; the usual travelling traders that made a tidy profit from his isolation didn't know who he was, and neither Aria nor Kienza, the only two who *did*, would ever betray him.

He also wondered, in deepening dejection, just what would happen now that his whereabouts *had* been discovered. Surely it wouldn't just be disregarded - but what would they do with it? Warn people and traders away? Wall him in and introduce some obscure tax? Or would they re-evaluate his position and finally correct his unjust punishment? He *hadn't* died from his wounds as they'd expected him to...

He adjusted his seat, turning further towards the heat of the flames, absent to the intensity of the knot in his brow. Spring hadn't quite arrived; the nights were still cold, and the tiny stone house seemed to trap the chill even in the summer.

A sigh seeped from his lips for the lick of warmth a stirring of the air passed his way, but it dropped into hopelessness all too soon.

Though he actively shunned the thought, he couldn't seem to look past the detail that plagued him the most: of all the authorities in Turunda, it had been the Hall of the White Hammer that had knocked upon his door.

A far cry above the department of guards, the royally-appointed organisation of intelligent minds and problem-solvers were only mobilised to deal with the more severe matters of the country's safety - insurrections, organised crime, mass murderers. All within its ranks were experts capable of tracking, gathering evidence, confronting directly their deadly quarry and making the arrests themselves. In short, they *never* needed help.

Except now, apparently, they did, and this Inquisitor Brack was adamant that it had to come from him...

And then there was the fact that this wasn't actually the first he'd heard of wild magic causing trouble out in the world. Kienza herself had mentioned it a handful of times, and though he so often stuck his fingers in his ears whenever she brought mention of the world beyond these trees and limestone mazes, he knew she'd been troubled by it. And she wasn't one to be troubled by insignificant details...

His mind slowed as he watched her glide through his thoughts. Not for the first time, he wondered just where Kienza was...

A small bleat outside ripped him from his musings and his heart suddenly pounded in hope. There were only two people Oat would greet like that, and one of them was asleep in the basement.

But, when there came no rustle of hay, patter of hooves or answering coo, he realised he'd imagined it. Clearly, the events of the evening had exhausted him; he should have known better. Kienza never came at the answer of a thought. Not unless that thought was hers.

He growled to himself and thundered to his feet, seeking sleep at last if just to hurry in the next morning.

He abandoned the dying fire and threw off his clothes, tossing them aside with unnecessary aggression, and pulled back the curtain that hid away the bed that stood in a nook a few feet from both kitchen and sitting room. *'These very scowles could close up and swallow your home with you still in it!'* He shook his head as he dropped onto the bed and pulled the covers up over himself. It had been a nice try, but even disregarding how foolish it was for him to be around people, he hadn't even the slightest interest in returning to the fickle world that would ignore his

existence one minute, then send a messenger with a bag of tricks to summon him to its aid the next.
   'Scowles could swallow my home...'
   What a preposterous notion.

Chapter 2

Tall, sheer rock faces loomed like sentinels over the narrow passes, making the dark, wild lanes seem even more tight and unnatural. Their faces were so perfectly flat that a roof was almost expected overhead, but instead it was the trees that grew atop them that blotted out the sun and plunged the labyrinthine landscape into perpetual dusk, even at mid-morning.

But the inquisitor paid no mind to the claustrophobia. He traversed the hostile, dew-dampened ground as best he could, taking care with every treacherous step and steadying himself against the moss-covered walls whenever the ground dropped abruptly through the ferns. It was no wonder the mage had survived unknown for so long. Only the truly desperate would wander willingly into these woods.

Garon conceded that, in a way, he was one of them. And just as he'd navigated the natural fortress the previous evening, so would he again now. There were no two ways about it: he needed Rathen's help, and he would get it, one way or another.

The path eventually moved uphill, and after shuffling through a few more careful squeezes, he stepped out from the ominous shadows and into what was probably the closest thing the labyrinth had to a clearing. The trees overhead were thinner, offering some relief from the stiff darkness, and the dramatic, rocky growths that made the maze so forbidding stood much further apart. There was room to breathe here, to gather one's bearings. And room, apparently, to live.

He dusted himself down, deciding once again that the filth from the ordeal of reaching this place would only compromise his authority in the face of a difficult individual, and started towards the largest of the studding rocks, itself about the size of his superior's office. Just as the previous evening, he heard the offended bleat of a goat long before its pen came into sight, and passed by a small vegetable garden that looked extremely out of place in the otherwise wild terrain, both nestled neatly between the shortest pillars.

He circled around the enormous, moss-covered rock until he found the door set into its flattest face. Once again, he couldn't help marvelling at the extraordinary housing the mage had made for himself.

He raised his hand to knock, preparing himself for another strenuous encounter, when the door suddenly swung open and the same pale, unfriendly face framed with raven-black hair stared back at him, just as it had last night. Once again, Garon thought he looked ill and long-suffering upon that initial glance, but the man's stoic bearing and dark, lively eyes disproved it just as quickly, especially when they looked back so wide and startled.

Then, the mage's expression turned suddenly serious. "Good," he said before the inquisitor could speak, "I was afraid I'd have to scout all around the woods looking for you."

Garon frowned in growing confusion as he stepped back and out of the way while the mage continued out of the door with a bag slung over his shoulder. Both of them ignored the goat's ongoing protest from the other side of the rock house. "What are you--"

"You said you only needed a mage to determine if it's magic or not," Rathen reminded him pointedly, "so this shouldn't take long. Then you can either go home at ease or find some way to deal with it - either way, *I* won't have to worry about you knocking on my door every day - an assumption it looks like I was right about. *And*," he gave him a direct look, "I wouldn't mind finding out just what it is I stand to gain. You've come a long way, so I presume you have something to offer - how far *is* the nearest Hall, anyway?"

"About three days' ride," Garon said, nodding to himself in satisfaction and choosing not to ask what had changed his mind, accepting his easy victory instead. "And you will be paid enough to cover your living expenses for five years. However much or little that might be."

Surprise broke Rathen's severity as his step faltered. Clearly, he hadn't expected that much - which only made Garon wonder further at what had convinced him in his absence. But those thoughts were silenced when the mage's face sobered again, and a dark gravity hardened his eyes. "You knew where to find me. And you know who I am. So you must also know--"

"I know all the details of your banishment," Garon interrupted, raising a gloved hand both to silence and reassure him. "I know of the Order's previous expectations of you and that you failed to meet them, I know you had only a brief childhood, I know about Elle - I know everything I need to know about you, including that this wasn't a matter you would turn away from." His eyes softened a fraction as he noticed the flash of grief in Rathen's at the mention of the woman's name. "I've read your file. You were perfect for the position of Sahrot. And I believe you still could be. But," his eyes hardened again, though not unkindly, and he held the mage's gaze with heavy assurance, "should the need arise, I am prepared to take any action that is necessary."

Rathen said nothing. He stared at the officer for a long moment, scrutinising his eyes for any trace of misunderstanding, any hint of underestimation. But there was nothing beyond a dauntless tenacity. This man was more than aware of the weight behind every detail he'd presented. He was an inquisitor - of *course* he was aware.

Rathen sighed and gave a single, satisfied nod, though his body stiffened despite the easing of his shoulders.

"I'm readyyy!"

Garon jolted in shock at the small, sudden, sing-song voice, and spun around to find a child hurrying out of the door, a bag much like Rathen's slung over her back, though it seemed distinctly empty. She jumped to a stop between them and beamed. His eyes flicked searchingly to Rathen, but the mage simply returned her smile and pulled the door closed behind her.

"What--who is this?!" He managed as he fought to reclaim his composure, but the girl's grin only widened.

"I'm Aria!" She declared. "Are we going to be out for long? I don't want to be back before dinner, I want a *long* adventure!" But her expression dropped into a pout as Garon shook his head, vigorously, and turned urgently back to Rathen.

"She *can't* come with us. It isn't safe!"

"She'll be *fine*," Rathen promised, at which Aria's expression suddenly lifted again, and he offered the inquisitor no explanation despite knowing full well that he wanted one. He privately felt rather smug about it. 'Everything he needed to know about him' indeed. But this was one detail he wasn't at all surprised had slipped by. "I won't let her out of my sight for a moment. And anyway," he added tactfully, "I can hardly leave her here on her own, can I?"

Garon sighed as his eyes dropped back to the girl. He thought quickly, but knew there was little point in asking if there wasn't someone else who could take her. If there was, she wouldn't be here at all. "Fine," he yielded at last, and turned back to the mage stepping past him, already setting off away from the house with the child on his heels. "What about the goat?"

"Oat will be fine."

He frowned at the careless tone, as well as the name, but chose not to object to either. The sooner they were on their way, the better.

Half an hour later, they finally broke through the edge of the scowles. It would have been sooner but Rathen had slowed down to accommodate the inquisitor who, he suspected, believed he was doing a graceful job in manoeuvring through them.

Now, however, faced with simple, sloping woodland and no towering rock faces in sight, Rathen's confidence collapsed. His steps faltered, hesitation gripped him like a iron vice, and he felt himself begin to sweat. Aria must have sensed his change because she wriggled her hand into his and squeezed.

Her reassurance was forgotten a moment later, however, when Garon untethered two horses from the shadows nearby.

Rathen frowned at the beasts. "You were that sure I'd say 'yes'?"

"I told you this wasn't something you would turn away from, and I was prepared to argue you down."

The over-confident inquisitor handed him the reins to a grey-dappled mare while Aria approached the tan with both caution and awe. A smile flickered as he watched her, but discomfort quickly set back in.

His eyes then flicked onto the officer. "You said 'ruins' - where are we actually going?"

"Silverwood," he replied, hoisting himself easily into his saddle as Aria reached out to gently pat the horse's nose, wary of its tusks as she did so. She giggled as it huffed against her skin. "But we're stopping in Edam, first. We need an expert."

Rathen's frown became dubious as he ushered Aria over to what was apparently his horse. "Expert in what?"

"History."

His commitment to his hard-fought decision to join the inquisitor had been weak to begin with, but as he lifted his daughter up into the saddle, he found it was only further unbalanced by this cryptic new detail - a detail he'd been suspiciously quiet about the night before. But, though he opened his mouth to question it, or perhaps even to revoke his involvement altogether, the words caught in his throat and he found himself climbing up into the saddle behind her instead.

His heart hammered as the inquisitor urged his horse forwards, and when his own obediently followed, as it probably had all the way here, he watched, paralysed, as his last opportunity to turn back slipped away.

"It's fine, Daddy." He looked down at Aria as she turned him one of her beautiful, encouraging and almost magical smiles. "I'm here. You'll be okay."

He managed, somehow, to smile back. "Promise?"

"I certainly promise." She grinned, then snapped forwards and grasped the reins as the horse carried them away from familiarity.

He forced a deep, steadying breath as he took a hold of them from behind her. It had been his choice to come out here, to step back into the world. The decision hadn't come lightly - he'd thought over everything a thousand times that past night - and though he remained far from convinced, in the end it had all boiled down to one simple fact: he was never going to let anything happen to Aria if it was within his power to stop it. And if leaving the safety of his home for a few days was necessary towards that end, then so be it. She was and always would be the only thing that mattered - even if stepping back into the world after eleven years of isolation terrified him.

It was mid-afternoon by the time Edam's old, cobbled walls rose further along the road, though doubt, anxiety and the silence broken only by Aria's singing and cooing to the horses had made that time drag by to the point that it surely should have been midnight.

Rathen had sat rigid throughout the entire journey and endured that discomfort without a word, but now that they rode towards the stables standing just outside the town - the busy, populated town - he somehow managed to grow only tenser. Fortunately, though his head already throbbed, he discovered that he didn't have to think. His body followed the inquisitor's actions and dismounted from the horse on its own, catching Aria as she insisted on getting off of the giant beast herself, and followed him away from the stable hands for a quiet word once she'd said goodbye to the horses and promised them they wouldn't be long. He smiled at her sadly. She, at least, was enjoying herself.

They were brought to an abrupt stop just beside the gates, where Garon turned upon them a look of such command that they *both* could have been unruly children. His harsh tone did nothing to correct it. "Listen to me: you are to stay at my side at all times, unless I say otherwise - *both* of you. Though you have accepted the task, you are here under the Crown's agreement, and in my custody. I am personally responsible for your every action and anything that may come of your presence. You are not to wander, cause trouble or stray from the task at hand, and if there's anything you need to do, you will ask me first. Do you understand?"

Rathen stared at him flatly.

"I'm obligated to make this clear."

He cocked a single eyebrow. "I understand. Tell him you understand, Aria."

"I do, I understand. I'll stay with you both." She crossed her heart.

He looked back and smiled with satisfaction.

The inquisitor didn't respond. He turned away and led them both silently through the gates.

A sigh of reluctance escaped Rathen's lips as his eyes roved over the town ahead. The sooner they found this historian, the sooner they'd be away from people and back in sweet, peaceful, empty woodland.

It didn't take long for the group to be swallowed by Edam's bustle. It was market day, to Rathen's misfortune, so the streets were far busier than they should have been, but though he concentrated his efforts on remaining calm as they moved deeper into the throng - recalling, in Kienza's voice, that 'panicking would only make it worse' - he was surprised to find Aria's face somehow still alight with wonder.

There were people everywhere, of all kinds of sizes, buying and selling a rich variety of wares from pots and vases to clothing and jewellery, and more colours than she'd ever seen before assaulted her sight. Food was the most popular product, and a jumble of aromas tangled in the air, some wafting from stalls selling fresh cuts of meat, others from those offering carefully baked breads and cakes, and the most fragrant drifted from the most colourful stalls, which supplied expertly picked and ground herbs and spices imported from the tribes.

Aria pulled this way and that as she wrenched herself around to see absolutely everything, to follow every scent, and she pointed, shouted and giggled every few moments, all while maintaining her tight and certain grip. Rathen would have enjoyed her merriment had he himself not been so knotted inside.

But Garon paid neither any attention. He led them doggedly through the crowds to wherever he sought to find his next 'expert', just as keen to get them away from the market-goers as Rathen was to escape them. The streets were still busy when they were finally free from the packed square, but at least Rathen felt a small sense of ease at the transition - though it wasn't to last, he discovered, and vanished entirely when they began turning down darker, narrower streets.

The buildings weren't tall, but so tightly packed that they eliminated sunlight and made the alleys and backstreets seem all the more hostile, and though they were still far more spacious than the routes within the scowles, at least he could be certain that no one was hiding within dense rock faces. That was the trouble with buildings: they concealed people. Streets may appear empty of bodies, but never of watchful eyes, be they bored or malicious, and though many might view the scowles with the same fear and uncertainty, they were Rathen's own definition of sanctuary.

He tightened his hold on Aria's hand and looked down with a reassuring smile when she squeezed it back. But it waned as he noticed the familiar anxiety that had suddenly crept over her. Only then did he realise how quiet she had fallen, and how close beside him she walked.

He frowned sadly. Of course. She'd never been in a place like this. They only ever met traders in the open, waiting at specific points along forest roads just beyond the edge and safety of the rocks; they never ventured into populated areas. She had no experience in a world like this, and he felt a sudden punch of shame for worrying mostly about himself.

Mercifully - though he was surprised to consider it that way - they soon stepped back out into wider streets that glowed once more in the reach of sunlight, where the buildings became almost welcoming and the people were in less of a hurry. Their leisure eased the two forest-dwellers, allowing them both to breathe a little easier and the smile to return to Aria's face, which soon widened into a grin when she heard lilting music in the distance. He knew she wanted desperately to find wherever it was coming from but she didn't dare to ask, so instead she returned to spinning around while squeezing his hand, looking this way and that, trying to find it so that, perhaps, they could go back when they were done.

He silently wondered how she'd managed to hear it at all over the din of the city. He had to strain to notice it - and so it was in that concentration that he didn't notice the clamour of raised voices and hurried footfalls growing louder from the opposite direction, nor that Garon had stopped to pinpoint their source. It was only when he came to a sharp halt behind him and was struck by something both heavy and red that it was brought to his attention, and by that point he was already on the ground.

The haze that muddled Rathen's head took an age to pass, during which he heard Aria shout 'Daddy', another female voice utter a curse, and Garon's voice booming above them both. When he finally looked up, he found the inquisitor wrestling a much larger man to the ground while a young woman pushed herself up from the cobbles beside him. There was a smile on her face, even despite the patches of crimson smeared across her skin and soaking into her clothing.

"Get back here, wench!" The man growled from face-down on the road. "You set me up!"

"It was a fair fight," she declared as she rose, "you just underestimated me."

Though Rathen's head still spun, and his confusion only slightly abated when he realised he'd stopped at the mouth of an alley, he pushed himself up with Aria's help, whose eyes remained glued to the woman, her blood-red hair and the sword sheathed at her hip.

"You *tricked* me!"

"I did no such thing," she informed him. "You knew who you were challenging."

The man bellowed and bucked so suddenly that he threw Garon off of him. He scrambled madly to reach her, seizing his opportunity, but she didn't recoil from his furious advance. In fact, she showed little concern for it at all, even though she was clearly struggling to stay on her own feet. As he leapt and reached out for her in a swift and powerful movement, she took an easy step back and slammed her knee up into his jaw, just as Garon descended back upon him.

The attacker dropped to the ground like a sack of bricks and howled again as the inquisitor wrenched his thick arm behind him. After being imparted a few choice words, he reluctantly calmed down.

The woman straightened and turned her attention briefly onto her rescuers, apologising first to Rathen, then thanking Garon. But, as she turned to limp away, satisfied that her pursuer was unable to continue, her knee buckled beneath her. Rathen was close enough to catch her, and saw the extent of her wounds as he did so. He frowned in concern, his daze forgotten as guards finally arrived to take control of what little remained of the situation, inclining their heads respectfully to Garon. "You need medical attention."

The woman shielded her eyes from the sun and looked up at him to reply, but her expression twitched into hesitance as she noticed the unfriendly creases in his face.

"I can help."

"I'm fine, thank you." She pushed herself up and out of his arms with such haste it was as if she believed he could only worsen them. "I can manage."

"There are no medics here," Garon said as he walked over to look at her wounds himself, "and you do need patching up." He turned his stern, grey eyes to hers. "I suggest you let him help."

The young woman looked back at him dubiously until Aria spoke up from beside her. "It's okay," she smiled shyly, the cheer usually so present in her young voice replaced instead by caution, "my daddy looks mean and scary, but he isn't. He's fixed lots of cuts." She showed her the bandage still wrapped around her hand. "See?"

The woman smiled back at her with puzzlement, but as her gaze drifted carefully back to Rathen, her hesitance returned.

"Fine," she said eventually, though he suspected she'd been convinced by pain alone. "Thank you."

Though she sought either to spare her pride or simply keep a wary distance from him, she had little choice but to accept Rathen's help and lean awkwardly on his shoulder as Garon lead them away.

A tavern stood on the corner of the street, one surprisingly empty for that time of the day; there were no more than a handful of people within and each kept to themselves, barely paying any attention to the slight creak of the door nor the spilling light as they entered. They chose a quiet corner table, and Rathen began to look over the wounds while Garon asked the barkeep for necessities.

Her bared left arm was easily his priority; three cuts marred her skin, two superficial and one fairly deep, while the blood-beaded line across her cheek needed only a clean. Her right arm, covered by a long, loose sleeve, seemed uninjured if the unmarked fabric was any indication, but blood had soaked into the side of her blouse and Rathen couldn't yet tell if it was from her wounded arm brushing against it or from another injury beneath. Otherwise, none of it was beyond the reach of his experience.

"This may hurt," he warned her as Garon set clean cloth, alcohol and a basin of warm water down on the table beside him, and she nodded and gritted her teeth as he gently wiped the blood away. A heavy silence descended as Rathen concentrated.

When he reached for the alcohol, the woman deliberately turned her head away and looked towards Garon instead. "You're an inquisitor, right?"

"I am." He didn't look back from the window.

"We don't see many of you out in small places like this. What are you doing here?" The curiosity in her eyes intensified. "Are you after a murderer?"

"I'm afraid it's classified," he said with the same note of superiority that Rathen knew came with all such statements, and the subject was brought to a very swift close.

"What's your name?" Rathen asked instead, touching the soaked cloth to the deepest wound, at which she immediately winced.

"Petra," she replied once the sting began to pass.

"Care to tell us what happened, Petra?"

"Just a bad loser, that's all. I was looking for a fight, he challenged me, I beat him, he didn't like it, then he tried to attack me." She shrugged. "It happens."

"You were *looking* for a fight?"

"You're a duelist, aren't you?" There was a very clear note of disapproval in Garon's voice, and it sat even plainer upon his brow.

The woman rolled her eyes as though she knew precisely what he was about to say, but suddenly flinched as Rathen touched at the bloodied tear in the side of her blouse. He scratched his head and returned her frown uncomfortably. "It's, um..."

To his surprise, she needed little coaxing, and removed the cinch tied about her waist and set it on the table. Her sword followed. Then two smaller blades joined it, along with a length of coiled chain ending with two steel balls. Rathen stared at her arsenal in surprise, and even Garon's eyebrows rose, but both lost interest when she raised the side of her blouse just high enough to reveal the wound beneath her ribs. She peered over to look at it herself, and though her eyes were troubled, her sigh didn't relay any astonishment.

Rathen's brow dropped gravely. Brutal burns warped the skin of her left hip and reached around to cross her lower back, and though their extent was concealed by her clothing, they were too severe to be so kindly isolated. So severe, in fact, that the senses of the affected area must have been dulled when it had happened - years ago, he guessed. He shortly spotted two more scars hidden within it, no doubt sustained from previous duels and gone as unnoticed as this one would have been, if their rough healing was anything to judge by.

"And what does it matter if I'm a duelist?" She demanded as Rathen silently turned his attention onto the injury, flashing her eyes defiantly back to Garon as she put it from her mind. "I'm not hurting anyone who didn't literally *ask* for it."

"Duelists cause disruption and injury, they encourage gambling which leads to violence and theft, and they put themselves and those around them at undue risk with undue reason." Garon looked down at her from beneath a stern frown, his arms folded tightly across his chest and his presence imposing enough to make the rebellious young woman shift and Aria, who had spent the while staring transfixed from the other side of the table, finally move away to stand close beside her father.

"I know," she replied flatly. She'd likely been given the speech many times before. "I have to make a living somehow, though, and this is what I'm good at."

Garon shook his head and another long, weighted silence descended. Fortunately, and not a moment too soon, Rathen declared that he was finished and the duelist rose quickly to her feet, eager for the opportunity to leave, and flashed him a grateful smile.

"Thank you. I'm sorry there's nothing I can give you in gratitude, but I only just got here and--"

"It's fine," Rathen interrupted, "just take care of yourself."

Garon frowned at the softness of his voice - it was still rough enough to make most hesitate, and indeed the young woman did, but beyond its usual abrupt edge, there was also the same softness that emerged whenever he spoke to Aria.

"I always do," she assured him. "This was just an unfortunate occurrence, and I'm going to pay for it."

"What do you mean?"

She indicated the very wounds he had just dressed. "I won't be able to fight for a while. But I'll get by; I have in the past." She returned the cinch carefully about her waist and slipped her weapons back where they belonged. "Thank you again," she said with another grateful smile. "I'd definitely be much worse off without your help. It's nice to know there are still good people out there, even if they're few and far between."

Rathen couldn't help a bewildered, self-effacing smile.

"Wait a moment," Garon said as she turned to leave, and she stopped rigidly in preparation for another condescending speech. "You wouldn't happen to know where we could find a man named Anthis Karth, would you?"

Her eyebrows rose in surprise. "No, sorry, I--"

"Just got here," Garon nodded. "Thank you anyway."

Rathen shook his head after her as she limped away and vanished outside, absently taking hold of Aria's hand and giving it a similarly thoughtless squeeze.

Then he turned expectantly towards Garon. "Lead on."

Chapter 3

The barkeep had been of equally little help, but the inquisitor appeared unperturbed and set a purposeful path back through the maze of streets. Though he seemed disinclined to share his plan, Rathen and Aria trustingly followed him into every lane, road and building all the same, the mage's spirit curiously calmed despite the uneasy darting of his eyes. Before too long, as the sun began its descent, they stepped into the third and final of Edam's taverns, where music and the smell of cooked and spiced meat filled the stifled air.

Of all the town's public houses, this was probably the most pleasing, and though it was busy for that fact, the far less hostile atmosphere managed to offer at least some comfort against Rathen's tension. Here were not drunkards or layabouts, but friends and colleagues laughing, unwinding and enjoying private conversation - and, most importantly, a number of old and learned-looking men, some reading, some in discussion, and others simply smoking in peace.

"This looks promising," he said quietly to himself as they headed towards the bar, keeping Aria close all the same, and sure enough, no sooner had the inquisitor mentioned the name to the tavern-keep than he pointed off towards the far corner of the room.

Rathen followed the gesture to sparsely occupied tables, and his eyes fell immediately upon one elderly gentleman in particular, sitting much like the others: alone, book in hand, pipe in his mouth, with a glass of what looked like port on the table beside him, and cloaked in an undeniably scholarly air. In fact, he looked just as Rathen had expected him to, for despite his seclusion and lack of interest in the subject, even *he* had heard of Anthis Karth. Kienza had mentioned him more than a few times in the past, gushing over his academic discoveries of the long-passed age of the elves. He remembered that one of those occasions had actually caught his interest, though he couldn't presently recall the details - and there was something about the man himself he felt as though he was forgetting, too. He doubted it was important, though.

That aside, this man, highly respected within historical circles, wore his reputation for passionate fascination well; it was evident in a single glance, from the way he pursued the book in his hand, his eyes transfixed as though being transported back in time by the words on the page, all the while picking apart every minute detail and storing it for future reference.

Garon thanked the tavern-keep and started towards the corner while Rathen and Aria followed close behind him, picking and weaving their way through the chairs. Those who noticed them - or rather the inquisitor's dark uniform - stepped aside or tucked in their seats to make as much room as they could, and a few inclined their heads as they passed. Rathen noticed how respectful each gesture was; not like those most mages received, stiff and steeped in fear.

The old man at the table didn't notice them approach, nor even glance up from his book as Rathen stopped beside him. Nor even as he lingered, without a word, frowning after Garon who had simply continued on past. Aria turned him a questioning frown while pulling on his hand for him to hurry up and follow along as she was trying to do.

His confusion only deepened when they stopped instead beside another solely-occupied table, one at which the man seated was surely no older than twenty five. Like the others, he was absorbed in his work - his nose in a book and a quill in his hand while papers stood in a disorganised stack on the table in front of him - but in less than a moment, Rathen was struck by the unmistakable and peculiar hunger in the young man's eyes, one that informed him in no uncertain terms that, never mind anyone else, *this* was the scholar they sought.

He stood momentarily dumbstruck, glancing back towards the older man and wondering if they weren't actually mistaken - but Garon had known where to find *him*. He was surely right on this count, too.

"Excuse me, Mister Karth," the inquisitor began, standing in the same passively official manner he had when he'd first visited Rathen, and the young man reluctantly dragged his attention away from the pages of his book to smile expectantly up at him. "Might I have a moment of your time?"

"No, please, goodness, go ahead, Inquisitor, certainly," he replied hastily, slightly flustered as he made an attempt to tidy the table top, and he gestured to the chair beside him before turning his remarkably friendly gaze then upon the others. It lingered curiously first upon Rathen's bemused expression, then on the very presence of the child before returning to the officer. Despite the shift of his thoughts, however, his cheer never once faltered. "I apologise for the mess, I was just comparing notes from today's work - nothing that can't wait."

"That's actually what I'd like to talk to you about." Garon seated himself, though he didn't look like he expected to stay for long, and Aria, her little legs having grown quite tired, quickly followed suit. "The site you're presently studying is in Silverwood, isn't it?"

"Yes, yes it is, the ruins." A single blonde eyebrow dropped a fraction as concern crept over his young face, and his eyes flicked briefly up towards Rathen. "Why?"

"I wondered if you'd noticed anything strange about the place at all? Or in others?"

"Oh for *goodness sake*..." His friendly demeanour abruptly collapsed as he groaned and rolled his head back in weary frustration, before leaning suddenly forwards, his cheer replaced by defence. "None of that has *anything* to do with me," he told him quite precisely. "Regardless of what *some* 'distinguished' individuals might claim, I didn't trigger *any* kind of spell or whathaveyou in my 'tramping around' the ruins. It's been happening outside of Turunda, even in places I've *never been*, so how could I *possibly* be involved with it?"

"We're not here to accuse you of anything," Garon assured him, raising his gloved hand passively, "we're just investigating the situation. We have a few suspicions regarding the nature of the phenomena and we were hoping you might be able to help us."

The young man paused. "Oh..." He smiled apologetically while his cheeks reddened, and his posture eased with a sigh. "I'm sorry, it's just that I've had the unfortunate honour of being the first to witness a few of these 'phenomena' and some people have assumed I was somehow to blame." He shook his head to himself then raised his tankard, half-full with ale, and drank another half of what remained.

Rathen frowned at the lively young man with lingering scepticism, wondering whether the reputation he'd earned as one of the finest scholarly minds was really deserved or if he wasn't in fact, and far more likely, an imposter. The only facts that gave him thought to concede was that Garon seemed convinced, and he was too young to have earned it in any ordinary way. So either he truly would be able to help them, however Garon intended to use him, or he was simply a very convincing fake.

"Could you tell us what is happening in Silverwood?" Garon asked, putting the matter back into focus.

The young man nodded, but he kept a rein on his quickly returning enthusiasm and took a moment to collect his thoughts. When he spoke again, he did so carefully. "There's a great beauty about the place," he began slowly, "but you must understand: I *don't* mean the landscape. It's like there's a blanket smothering that part of the forest, and once you step beneath it, your whole perspective shifts. Approaching the site, you'd see only the trees, the roots, the mud and eventually the ruin itself, and, even speaking as someone who is admittedly no happier than when I'm surrounded by crumbling walls, the site is basic and doesn't have much aesthetic value - and yet," he leaned further forwards, excitement colouring his green eyes even as his voice tightened in secrecy, "when you cross a certain point in the trees and the sun breaks through, they suddenly become majestic pillars holding up the sky, and the roots become seats to sit upon and stare at the incredible world around you and the ruins of one passed, as if it was a portal through time. But," now he shook his head and squinted, squeezing his hands as though he could will an image of the place into being, as he couldn't possibly convey it in words, "but it's *more* than that. You could sit there for days - *weeks* - completely enraptured if you let yourself, and...and you'd..."

But he sighed and shook his head again, staring down at his papers though he didn't truly see them.

A long moment later he looked back up to Garon, then to Rathen, whose own expression had been touched by interest even despite his relentless scepticism. His voice hardened. "Silverwood isn't the only place I've seen this. It was in Loggerhead, too, and when I got there the village was at a stand-still. If it wasn't for the fact that it sits along a main road, I really do think people could have died - starved to death, sleep deprivation or something." His eyes grew haunted. "The danger is too real - but I don't understand it at all."

"Why do people think you have something to do with it?"

"Well, that one they don't," he admitted, but though he looked at Garon as he spoke, his mind was still elsewhere. "It was already happening when I got there, but a few people trying to discredit myself and my theories have leapt upon the unfortunate fact that I was the first to stumble upon them, and as I'm much younger than most of my peers, some of them have put it down to me being careless and setting something off - which is preposterous anyway because elven traps are *far* more sophisticated than that, it's not like snagging a tripwire! And why would anyone even create a trap like that? Do you know, some people have even been saying that I've hired a mage to do it *for* me, to keep people away so I can fabricate evidence to support my theories!"

Rathen watched him carefully. "Do you believe they *are* spells?"

The young historian's eyes lost their incredulous edge as they flicked up to him. He opened and closed his mouth for a moment, but not a word came out. He hadn't missed the weight behind the question. "I don't know," he said at last. "I wouldn't be surprised, but I also can't justify why such spells would have been put in such places, nor indeed why they've only just become active."

"You're assuming the elves made them."

He looked back to Garon, his eyes turning momentarily blank, as though the point should have been obvious, but realisation slowly dawned on him and his mind was pulled back to the present. "Force of habit," he replied sheepishly - then alarm flashed across his face and his voice hushed again. "You think *mages* have done it?! So they *are* rebelling?!"

"We don't know yet," Garon replied, raising his hand to calm him once more while Rathen bit his tongue, hard, "nor if it's even magic. That's why we're investigating. We need to know what's causing it, why, and, more importantly, how to stop it. Whether mages are involved or not, it can't be allowed to escalate."

"I quite agree - but if you think it could be mages, why are you coming to *me?*"

"Because all the reports mention elven ruins of one kind or another, and we want to know why."

"We need someone with an understanding of the sites," Rathen clarified, solely for his own benefit. On further thought, Kienza had mentioned that detail, too.

The historian grinned eagerly, his alarm forgotten as quickly as it had arrived. "I see. Well, count me in! I've almost finished studying the place and I'm not currently on commission, and I'm certainly curious about the matter - I'd be honoured to work with you and help where I can, Inquisitor." But then his keen smile faltered, and he lowered his voice one last time as he glanced furtively around the tavern. "But won't we also need a mage?"

"We have one."

He stared at Garon for a long moment, then looked carefully to Rathen, and then to Aria. "Who?" He followed the inquisitor's discreet nod and his eyes widened in horror, though whether it was for the mage's presence or for his own recent words, it wasn't clear. Rathen assumed both. "Forgive me," he said quickly, "you're not-- you're not wearing your cloak. Is - forgive me - is that allowed?"

"It is." Not for any *other* mage, it was true, but he at least was exempt. A fact for which he was glad, as the Order's rank-issued and emblazoned cloak would have certainly earned him unwanted attention.

"Oh... Okay, that's good. Well, in that case, um..."

Aria frowned as the historian nodded vigorously. "Are you all right..." Her pastel voice, so out of place, immediately grasped their attention, and her eyes widened in her hesitation as she tried to recall what was evidently an extremely important detail. "...Mister...?"

The young man's alarm swiftly vanished, swept away by a broad smile so handsome and infectious that Aria instinctively smiled in return, forgetting her timidness in the busy, alien setting. "Karth - but call me Anthis, please." Finally, he gave in to his wondering and turned to face her directly. "I'm curious: why are *you* here?"

"Because my daddy is," she replied quite simply, pointing proudly towards Rathen.

"...I see... Well, I suppose that's as good a reason as any." Anthis looked to the inquisitor and the mage, the latter having yet to take a seat. "What approach do you intend to take with this?"

"There's only one we can: we have to see the ruins themselves, and the sooner the better."

"Of course - but, though I assure you I'm keen, spring hasn't quite set in yet." He nodded towards the desk. "There are a few rooms available and I'm well-liked by the keeper; I can get you some good rates for the night, and we can set out in the morning."

Rathen felt his heart sink. Though he had to agree that it would probably be a little too dark to see very clearly by the end of the next hour, he'd hoped they wouldn't be staying in the town a moment longer than necessary. The thought of spending the entire night here set his heart hammering. Aria must have heard it for she rose and hurried to his side to take his hand, even while beaming with her own renewed excitement.

Garon thanked him and accepted rather presumptuously on everyone's behalf, and after the historian had quickly drained what was left of his ale, folded the page of his book and pulled together his papers, they followed him to the tavern's desk, some more willingly than others.

Rathen frowned despite the smile that pulled at his lips as he tucked Aria and her raggedy doll into bed - one far bigger than any she'd ever seen, let alone slept in before, and she kicked her feet about beneath the sheets to take full advantage of that fact. "What are you grinning at?"

"Our adventure!" She giggled as he moved aside to pull the curtains together, leaving the room to the weak reach of a single candle.

"Staying in an inn and going to a ruin is an adventure, is it?"

"It *is!* Oh I hope we see a big, rocky stendjur in the forest!"

"I don't think you do. And anyway, Silverwood is too close to people for anything like that to live out there." Suddenly he was quite grateful for the town and its populace, but as he sat down on his side of the double bed, for it was all that had been available, Aria's smile weakened and her eyes grew sad.

"I know you're not happy," she said softly, her feet still kicking about despite her seriousness, "but try not to dwell. It really will be all right."

"You sound like Kienza."

"And she's always right," she reminded him, "which means that if I sound like her and say the things she says, then I'm right, too." She nodded matter-of-factly. "So that means you should listen to me - but *not* like you listen to Kienza. I mean actually *doing* what I say, not just hearing me say it."

Laughter finally shattered his discomfort, and the only lines the candle light caught were those of good humour. Aria grinned victoriously and squeezed her eyes shut tight. "Keep smiling until I fall asleep, or I'll have bad dreams."

"I will," he said, his smile persisting.

"Promise?"

"Cross my heart."

She murmured in satisfaction as he blew out the candle, and snuggled down into the sheets, holding her doll close and wriggling in comfort. He chuckled again and kissed her forehead, wishing her sweet dreams before settling down himself.

As comfortable as the bed was, he'd known even before he'd climbed into it that he wouldn't be getting any sleep that night. Now, minutes were moving like hours - he wasn't sure how long he'd been staring up into the black ceiling.

He couldn't douse his mind; he tumbled through a pointless train of fretful thought, and each time he caught himself and forced his mind to clear white in favour of rest, it would just start right back up again and his muscles tied back into knots. One thought collapsed into another, coalescing into a heavy mass that squeezed his suppressed tensions right back to the surface. When he reached the point of wondering if the ceiling was even still there any more or if it hadn't been lost to the ravages of time, he finally gave up.

He slipped out from the sheets as quietly and carefully as he could, stepped over to the window and pulled aside the curtain, oblivious in his fatigue to the night's cold. He wasn't sure why looking out over the streets below would ease his mind, but at least it would give his thoughts some direction. Staring into blackness, there was nothing to guide them but his fears.

There was little to see at that time of night, but he settled against the windowsill anyway, and after five minutes he'd spotted only one pedestrian, presumably hurrying home, and a guard making his rounds. He watched lanterns go out in some windows, light in others, and there was hardly a sound but for a couple of dogs barking in the distance and a few patrons laughing in the tavern below. But as dull as his view was, it did, somehow, settle his mind enough to get his thoughts in order.

Now that he was out there, there was no going back, and he'd begrudgingly discovered a growing interest besides his concern that further entangled him into the matter, especially with the sudden involvement of the eager young historian. But he seemed just as convinced as the inquisitor that magic was to blame, and surely such preconceptions would only muddy the water.

Not that the assumption surprised him. People had a tendency to accuse magic of anything they didn't understand - miraculous healing despite magic being incapable of such a thing, sudden overnight freezing due to an unexpected cold snap, or even infestations of frogs around lakes in the summer following a particularly damp spring. None had anything to do with magic but people cried it all the same, fearfully or jovially, whichever and whenever it suited them. And as for this historian's examples, it sounded as though Silverwood could be put down to simple romanticism; the light striking just right, or a personal fascination with the place. For someone with no such care for the past or for wandering through a forest, they might well disagree with his description. And as for Loggerhead, the village stood near a pipe weed farm whose product was known to be more than simply 'calming'. If a fire swept through it and the wind blew just right...well, who was to say what affect it could have across a village so small?

Put simply, his doubt hadn't been swayed and his presence felt even less necessary.

He looked around at the small noise behind him, and smiled to himself as the moonlight brushed over Aria's soft features. He thought children were supposed to have fitful dreams, but the only peep Aria ever seemed to make while she slept was laughter.

And that was another fact he couldn't deny: Aria was enjoying herself, even if she was daunted at the same time. Of course she was excited, and of course staying at an inn overnight and visiting a ruin was an adventure. She'd been in that little corner of the forest for most of her life, and she'd been too young to remember when she *had* been beyond it. The latter was undeniably for the best, but there was no harm in letting her see a small part of it for a few days. She'd never said anything to suggest she was curious of the world beyond, but she probably knew he wouldn't approve. This was a unique opportunity for her, and one she was able to embrace with enthusiasm. In fact, for her sake, he almost regretted that it would be over so soon.

Almost.

He sighed heavily and looked back out of the window, folding his arms and tapping his fingers absently against the metal band clasped tightly about his left bicep. He watched a figure leave the tavern below, pause in the middle of the street and then head decisively down the western road. No, it was too late to turn back now, and five years' worth of expenses was too much to refuse.

His concerns would be laid to rest as soon as they were back in the Scowles, but for now all he could do was sleep. When the morning came, he would do his job and set his curiosity at rest. If it turned out that magic really *was* involved, word would be sent to Kulokhar and the Order could be mobilised to counter it, and the idea of rogue mages within the organisation would also be taken more seriously. Neither Sivaan Rosh nor any of the grand magisters would allow a few renegades to force the Order into greater disrepute, so no rebellion within their borders could last for long.

A small knot formed in his brow as he wondered if Rosh was even still in command of the Order's military wing. It had been a long time, after all...

He shook his head, rattling the thought away, and stepped back from the window to draw the curtain decisively back into place. His head was organised and that was all that mattered. He headed back to bed, a yawn finally stealing over him and weighting his eyelids. The matter would conclude tomorrow and then he and Aria could head safely home; the adventure would be over as suddenly as it had started, and life would return to normal.

Chapter 4

Salus paid little attention to his surroundings as he marched through the darkened corridors, his purposeful stride weighted by frustration and weariness as he returned from yet another debriefing. People stepped aside as he approached, respectfully making way and never once looking directly at him, and while he wouldn't usually ignore his subordinates or their formal gestures, this time his mind was turned too far inwards to notice them.

The world was in turmoil. War was raging all around them, and while Turunda had managed to avoid getting sucked into the furious affairs of other countries so far, their luck was about to run out. Everyone could feel it.

No one could recall either why nor when their long-standing tensions with Skilan had formed, but they'd been dutifully maintained by at least one of the two reigning monarchs ever since, and though King Thunan seemed disinclined to fan the flames like his father had - dark times when *both* monarchs had been at each other's throats - it appeared that Skilan's King Jalund had his bellows close at hand and polished for the occasion. The tensions were more than ready to snap.

General Moore had begun laying out pre-emptive plans in response, and large bodies of soldiers were moving across the country. Salus couldn't argue with this course, but, when factored in alongside the wars that had erupted in surrounding lands, his people's work was made much more difficult. Above the other challenges, intel was harder to collect and verify, and without solid information, the military would be unable to act quickly or effectively. But the country couldn't risk holding the army back while they worked.

His people could handle it - if the tasks the Crown issued them were easy, other people would be doing them - and he had little choice but to work around it just the same. Setting an example was just as much a part of leadership as directing his subordinates and assigning their orders, and he'd managed a fine job over the past eight years. What was a little more complication?

Unfortunately, though such interference could be anticipated and negated, the mysterious movements of the Order could not. Strange arcane things were happening in the world, and a handful of mages had been found in such affected locations within their own borders, snooping around and refusing to reveal when questioned what they were up to. But the moment the Arana detained them pending investigations, the command for them to be released into the Order's custody was issued over his head without explanation, and he couldn't do a thing to stop it. It felt as if there was a tumour growing within Turunda itself, and how he was expected to do his part to protect against it if he was denied information from another body of the land's authority, he was beside himself to discover.

He growled in increasing frustration as he neared his office door. It had been a long day, and at that moment all he wanted was to finish up, file away the last few reports and get home for a long overdue cup of tea.

But when he opened the door and his eyes fell upon the finely dressed man already sitting in the chair before his desk, his shoulders sagged in weary defeat. This was just what he didn't need.

He forced his feet to keep moving as the door closed behind him, watched all the while by his esteemed guest. Though he did a perfect job of keeping it from his face, he was far from pleased to see the king's liaison. But he wasn't surprised. He had been avoiding him and cancelling meetings all week, and with how his day had been going, *of course* it would catch up to him now. But the king needed to be kept apprised of their findings, so he was well aware that he'd brought this on himself. Not that that made the situation any more bearable.

"I'm sorry to drop by so late, Salus," the old man said mildly, choosing as ever not to address him by his title of Keliceran, "but I had a moment and I didn't think you'd be busy at this time of the night."

"No, of course," Salus replied with a brief smile, the ease of biting back his sour tone coming with great practise, and he offered him a neatly bound folder from a pile on his desk as he went about finishing his own work despite the company. But the old man waved it away with a bony hand.

"I've already read it."

Again Salus bit his tongue at the man's brazen impertinence. The Arana - 'Crown's Fang' as it was referred to by the few more common members of the king's advisory privy to its existence - was hardly open to being snooped through on a whim, by king's decree or not, and that went doubly for the keliceran's own office an hour away from midnight. The information contained within its walls went beyond 'sensitive', and if any of it were to fall into the hands of Turunda's enemies, it could spell certain disaster for her people. The office - the whole *building* - was under close guard for that reason. But, of course, the liaison had free access and the guards were under the king's orders to stand aside when his representative arrived. So it was, quite irritatingly, all too easy for this man to waltz right on in and do just as he pleased.

Salus straightened and forced the fact aside, as he always did, and placed the king's monthly account back on the table. It took notable restraint not to slam it down.

"Your latest detainee has been released into the Order's custody."

Salus's jaw tightened as he lowered himself with even greater control into the chair behind his desk. *'What a surprise.'* But such had been the case with all three mages so far, so why not the fourth? He turned his blue eyes, devoid of kindness, back onto the man and his voice emptied into formality, turning to business so that he might leave sooner. "King's orders?"

"Anything new you can give me on the ever-changing state of the wars," he replied, crossing his legs beneath his fine robes and quite deliberately making himself comfortable.

"Neither Antide nor Dweron are making any headway against one another," he replied dutifully, "that much hasn't changed, however we do know that Doana will be ready to sail east to Voent in two days, and that they've recruited mercenaries to bolster their numbers. They'll be heading over in the first wave. Ivaea has begun brokering a treaty with Kasire, and Skilan's war with Kalokh is spiralling to a close, as I'm sure you're already aware. My people have been doing what they can to shift the favour towards the weaker Kalosians, but it doesn't seem to be working. It won't end well for them."

"Nor for us, it seems." The older man sighed, running his hand through thinning hair.

"I intend to pull back for the most part - prepare for the worst rather than continue to use up resources. If Skilan does turn their attention our way when they're done with Kalokh, they'll be so low on resources and man power that they'll only be securing their defeat, but lives will still be lost in that battle, brief as it may be. I'd prefer to focus on reducing those losses."

The liaison nodded. "The king would agree. Approved."

"Thank you." Salus hid his surprise. He hadn't expected an immediate answer, let alone approval, and especially not without further questions. "I've issued the order for operatives stationed in the west to increase their observations over Skilan's forces. They can calculate the plans of any approaching force based on number, direction and supplies, and, as you know, there are already a few deep-cover agents planted in Skilan's force itself."

Again he nodded, but a thoughtful crease had deepened in his brow. "Keep a few of your men in Skilan," he suggested. "Have them hassle the force and give the deep-cover agents a chance to pass on what they can, and then have them do whatever they can to delay any movements towards Turunda."

"Block passes, burn bridges, pay off dockworkers and captains," Salus clarified.

"Indeed. Otherwise, all we can do for the moment is reinforce our borders and safeguard our assets and trade routes. Guard patrols along main roads and around farmland are already being increased."

"A wise idea. And I'd also like to increase the Arana's presence along the borders--"

Now the liaison shook his head. "No. That will only distract the soldiers and the watchmen already stationed there."

"The soldiers are only patrolling," Salus argued carefully, "and the watch don't have the eye for such detail, not to mention that the watch towers themselves are extremely obvious. No one would approach from those points unless it was a bluff or distraction. I don't think I need to remind you that if a single detail is overlooked, we could be opening the door to their vanguard."

But he was already shaking his head again.

"My Lord Malson, forgive me," Salus said calmly, though his confused and irritated frown sharpened, "but the soldiers stand out like a sore thumb! They're the perfect distraction for the enemy; they won't be looking for my people if their eyes are caught by glinting armour or peering up at watch towers - and I'm sure I don't need to remind you, either, that the spots the soldiers and watch can't reach always provide the better intel."

For a long, silent moment, the old man simply stared at him in thought. Then, finally, he sighed. "I'll pass it on to the Crown for deliberation, but I'm quite sure they'll agree that you would be better off keeping your attention *over* the border, not along it. Spies gain their greatest intel from the enemy, not from their fellow soldiers, and the men you have along the border already are surely enough."

Again, Salus bit his tongue. He knew that was the best he was going to get. Lord

Malson's approval for withdrawing the majority of his operatives was already more than he had expected to get that night. "You're right, of course," he replied politely. "Thank you for passing on the request."

"My pleasure." His smile didn't reach his eyes. Salus noticed long ago that it never did. There always seemed to be an ulterior motive lurking somewhere within them - or perhaps it was just the intensity of his scrutiny. Either way, those strangely youthful eyes had never displayed anything good.

The king's envoy rose to his feet, his rich burgundy robe falling about his legs as neatly as if it had just been pressed, and Salus stood, bowed and followed on formality as he turned towards the door.

"Oh," Lord Malson added, pausing and turning back as though the thought had only just occurred to this far from forgetful man, "and the king is mobilising a greater portion of the army to take up position near settlements in the west."

"What? Why? To frighten people? More chaos isn't going to help *either* of us, my lord."

"But it *will* help us to move quicker should the Skees manage to take us by surprise." He turned away, and darkness finally descended over the face of the Arana's leader. "Keep up the good work, Salus." Then he left the office, quite unaffected.

Salus's gaze burned into the door as it closed in front of him, his lip curling into a snarl, baring his tightly gritted teeth. The foul man hadn't forgotten that last detail at all, he'd kept it as a parting gift, along with the suggestion that he and his subordinates weren't doing their jobs as well as they should have been. But if that was truly the case, how had they managed to avoid war for so long while it had consumed everyone else around them?

Unless that was exactly it: the inevitable shadow of war had finally began to draw in, and rather than being taken as an unavoidable occurrence, it was seen as a failure on the Arana's part that it had come to pass at all.

Or perhaps the liaison knew this very well and was simply looking for a jibe.

He couldn't know for certain, but he favoured the latter.

He growled and shoved it wearily from his mind. It was just too late for that.

Salus turned back to his desk, stacked up the remaining reports and made a note of the exchange, insults aside, before finally making his escape. But though his mind continued to turn over matters as he hurried back down the corridors, he was aware of another man falling into step beside him. The building was always remarkably quiet, despite the bustle of bodies in even the smallest hours - a clock's hands had little impact on the Arana's activity - but it was enough to overshadow the perfectly silent, feather-light footsteps. And yet he had still heard him arrive.

"I'm getting quite tired of that old fool, Teagan," he said quietly without looking up. "And of these damned mages going to the king over our heads. I feel like a knight who has sworn an oath of protection, been given a sword and then had his hands tied behind his back. How are *any* of us supposed to do our job if everything has to be deliberated and no one will co-operate? It's as if every authoritative body in the country is acting independently." Now he looked at him, though he paid no attention to the man's empty expression, nor his averted eyes. "We're supposed to be responsible for gathering crucial information, but the king seems to want to keep us outside of the country rather than knowing what's going on within it." He shook his head. "And *another* of my requests has been promised the attention of the king, but all that means is that I'll have to *wait* for the refusal, assuming he even passes it on at all."

"You still suspect him." Teagan's voice, when he finally spoke, was just as plain and free of judgement as it always was, and his eyes remained forward.

"It's hard not to when he refuses almost every proposal I make."

"But what do you suspect him of?"

Salus shook his head while his lips pursed. "Being a vile old man, I suppose." He sighed and ran his fingers through his overgrown hair. "I know; you don't have to say it."

Teagan cocked his head. There remained little emotion in his expression, just the ever-present hardness to his calculating brown eyes that most operatives of his highest rank bore, and though few others were given leave to look directly at him or any keliceran who came before him, the eight-year bond between them allowed him now to do so, if for half a moment, as well as ask his following question, even if that, too, had been delivered dispassionately: "Are you all right?"

"I'm fine. Just tired. And frustrated."

"You're frustrated more and more often lately. Is this situation affecting your sleep?"

"No," Salus frowned thoughtfully to himself, "I slept fine..." Unbidden, the images of rolling streams and drifting leaves that had filled his dreams returned, as did the sense of peace that had driven their winds and currents. "Just fine."

He shook it off and looked back to the portian-ranked operative with serious eyes. "Report."

"The tribes are still fighting amongst themselves," Teagan replied orderly as he stared straight ahead, "and it looks like they're finally coming to blows. They're on the equivalent of martial alert and their territorial patrols are on the rise. Our own have been tightened along their borders to keep them away from any settlements should it spill over, but as long as they remain focused on each other, they won't be a problem, no matter how savage they might get."

Salus nodded in approval - then cast him a dubious side glance when he sensed his hesitation. "And?"

"He has moved again."

Now Salus sighed in all too familiar irritation.

"But regarding certain details, are you sure you want *his* help?"

"I'd rather not take on *any* help from outside of the Arana, *least* of all from someone like him. But if associating with his likes is what it takes, then so be it."

Teagan nodded. "And if we can't find him?"

"Then we settle for second-best."

"Tem Drassa?"

"Yes. With access to our resources, he'll catch up and exceed him in no time. In the end, first or second choice won't matter." He cast him another sidelong glance. "What about the matter from *our* end?"

"No news. But it's difficult to gain solid intel on such a subject, regardless of war."

Salus sighed once more as he felt his meagre hope slip closer to extinction, and watched absently as a number of his subordinates made their way across the foyer, every one of them bearing silent purpose in their step. A dark-haired woman brushed past them to head back the way they'd come, her eyes averted as though she hadn't seen him, as was polite. His own gaze lingered on her as he thought. He looked back to Teagan when they drew to a stop a moment later. "Keep looking for him," he said decisively. "He'll surely pop up again sooner or later. In the mean time, have a phaeacian watch Drassa, and we'll continue our own search."

Teagan inclined his head. "Understood. Is that all, Keliceran? Then I'll let you get home. Good night."

"Good night, Teagan."

The two parted ways, Teagan heading to where he would find an idle phaeacian, the lowest of the three Aranan ranks, while Salus finally moved towards the atrium doors to reach his home in the private grounds beyond, focusing his efforts on silencing his incessant thoughts. "I just hope we have enough time..."

Chapter 5

Morning just couldn't come soon enough. Rathen had barely gotten more than three hours of sleep, but as the long overdue dawn finally approached and he lay waiting for the softest glow of sunrise to brush the back of the curtains, his thoughts were too alive to notice any weariness. He rose moments before the light hit, bored of waiting.

The others weren't far behind him. Aria was particularly eager; she'd been awake longer than he'd realised but had lay patiently still until he got out of bed, at which point she all but sprang out after him, and after a quick breakfast the four were on their way. No one seemed inclined to waste any time, and Rathen wasn't about to complain.

The forest was an hour and a half's ride north and, in that time, barely a word was exchanged. Rathen wasn't in a talkative mood, Aria was suddenly too shy, Garon was just as rigidly official as the day before, and the still-cheerful Anthis was clearly burdened by the silence but too uncomfortable to break it. So they rode without a word, and Aria spent her time looking all around herself from within Rathen's saddle, staring with the same awe as she had on their way to Edam. He'd wondered for a while what it was that enraptured her so - after all, there was little to see - but he eventually realised that it was the very openness itself. The sight of the distance, rounded by hills and dotted with trees; the ability to see more than ten feet ahead was so new that she drank it all in with hungry eyes, and indulged the need to sniff the air and stretch her arms out around her whenever the fancy struck.

But as the trees began to close back in on either side of the tattered road, she soon became enamoured by the slowly transforming forest instead, for at least half of the dense trees were not actually green.

Aria peered up at each bouquet of pendulous limbs as they rode beneath them, but not for their bloom of small, white flowers. Instead, it was their long, slender, silver leaves that gripped her attention. She squinted at them thoughtfully, and finally broke the silence. "Silver wood..." She looked around at Rathen. "Are they really made of silver?"

"No, little one," he smiled, "they're just coloured that way. It's a pear tree."

"Oh I love pears! ...The trees all look like they're covered in spider webs, don't they? But in a *good* way."

Anthis chuckled from beside them. "They do make for quite a sight."

Rathen frowned as a thought crept up on him. While Aria continued to sing the trees their praises, he looked around critically, assessing the setting and carefully considering every detail. But the longer he analysed the forest and its silvery complexion, the less certain of his opinions he became. He turned to the young historian as he continued to pick the forest apart. "Are we under that 'blanket' yet?"

Anthis shook his blonde head. "Trust me, you'll know it when we are."

Ten minutes later they left the road and veered west by Anthis's lead, at which point the forest itself confirmed his promise. Roots reached up to trip any who would try to walk across its already uneven terrain, while the once charming weeping branches sought to ensnare and blind them before turning them around. It would be all too easy to get lost in this forest; the silver trees would have been markers if not for their great number, but in their abundance they offered only confusion.

They'd been away from the safety of the road for only five minutes when Garon abruptly reined in his horse. It snorted in protest, but he paid it no mind as he looked around them with eyes alert and studious. Rathen sat taller in the saddle as caution equally descended, and urged his horse to slow. He strained his eyes and ears, searching for whatever had set him on edge, his grip on the reins tightening in apprehension as he focused - and so he was somewhat startled when Aria gasped in front of him, and just as he was about to ask what she'd seen, his own breath was snatched away.

Anthis was the only one unaffected by the sudden transition. He simply smiled with satisfaction while his horse continued its lead. "*Now* we're under the blanket."

Mouth agape like a broken window, Rathen stared around himself in open shock while his horse carried him deeper. The forest hadn't changed - it *hadn't* - and yet, somehow, it *had*. The thick roots reached up not to trip weary walkers, but to offer them a seat should the ground be too sodden, while the silver, draping leaves were like curtains or folds of hanging silken cloth, giving the forest a welcoming softness that invited wandering even into its darkest and most tangled depths. It was only now that Rathen noticed the scent of the place - damp and earthy, but also clean and fresh, and it offered peace, tranquillity and the promise of safety. It was, truly, the most wonderful place Rathen had ever been.

And that unsettled him greatly.

"How far are the ruins?" Garon asked just as Rathen collected himself to do so, a frown of caution still firmly entrenched upon both of their faces even as they looked around in awe.

"A few minutes ahead."

The historian continued easily through the weaving woods, his immunity no doubt a result of his frequent trips, and pulled to a halt when they reached the edge of a small clearing. There was little to see among the rocks that studded the ground; the only notable feature was that of a single smooth, stone pillar that curved over to one side at the top. It had once been part of an archway, though to what was anyone's guess. But, curiously, that single, crumbled arc had an incredible allure, one that conjured the thought that, once, it could have been a portal to a whole other world, or that one could step through it right now and find themselves back in the time of the elves who had built it. Just as Anthis had said.

"Are we almost there?" Rathen asked, staring warily at the displaced doorway, unease rising in his bones.

"Actually," he replied, slipping easily out of the saddle, "this is it."

Rathen blinked in surprise as Garon followed the young man's lead, and Aria wriggled to try to get down herself. How could this be it?

"You said 'ruins'," he reminded him as his feet touched the ground, catching Aria once again, though she scolded him quietly for embarrassing her.

"I did, but I also said it was basic," Anthis replied, then began rummaging through his saddle bag, setting the issue aside.

Rathen shook his head and looked about himself. The air to this place was beyond peculiar. He could feel his guard rising.

He approached the crumbling structure as Aria eagerly hurried past him, and looked closely at the time-worn carvings on its surface in case they were somehow relevant. But the few images he could see were too decayed to make out, and the rest were runic letters and numbers that, for the most part, bore no meaning to him. And there was nothing at all to suggest that any mage of the Order had been here at any time in recent months, either.

As Anthis joined them and turned his attention immediately upon the fallen fragment, half-buried in the earth beside it, Rathen's focus shifted onto the sensations that surrounded them.

"This ruin isn't secluded," Garon stated as he stood back and let his two experts look around, "but there has been little impact on anyone living nearby. There has been no volatility in the weather patterns or the earth, it's not caused anyone harm or caused anyone to *cause* harm, but other sites have started out this way and all have grown steadily worse. I've gathered what I can on them in my preliminary investigation, both within and out of Turunda, and while those that stood near populated areas are known to have exhibited this strange...beauty, there was nothing documented anywhere to suggest why some affected weather, others the land, and others remained like this, if with growing intensity."

He turned towards Anthis, who was peering very closely at the markings on the shattered stone and sketching them quickly into a small book, while Aria peered over his shoulder and made constant, scrutinous comparisons between his depiction and the real thing. "Mister Karth, is there anything you can tell us?"

"As far as I am aware," he began, his eyes never straying far beyond either paper or rock, "every mention of this phenomenon has been from an elven ruin, and every one of those affected sites have been significant in elven history."

"Significant how?"

Aria pointed towards the rock, then a portion of Anthis's drawing, and he promptly adjusted the detail. "Places of worship or simply sites with some kind of connection to their gods; all revered. This place, for example, is where they read funerary speeches before burying the dead."

"It's a graveyard?" Rather than being troubled by the suggestion, Aria simply glanced up and about for headstones. Rathen, his back already turned, took a further step away and removed something small from his pocket.

"No," Anthis smiled, finally sparing a glance her way, "just where they honoured the dead and their memories and asked the gods to accept their arrival." He rose to his feet and hurried around to the still-standing portion of the arch and began to carefully dig the earth away from one side of its base, removing just enough to make out the next rune and compare it to his drawing of the other. "Pre-magic elves were buried in places of significance to each family, so they were unmarked. Unfortunately, such burial sites are extremely rare, most have been built over by humans and elves alike. But that's what happens when you don't mark a grave..."

"Um, what does 'pre-magic elf' mean?"

"Before they were gifted magic by the gods. They were good and reverent initially, then, when they gained their powers, their culture underwent a change - as it would - and they became more sophisticated and artistic. Then, once they realised just exactly what they could accomplish with it, they changed again to become *exceedingly* lazy and arro--"

"How does this help us?" Garon interrupted, bringing Anthis's wild attention back to the matter at hand.

"I don't know yet, but elves of this age connected the gods to greater power than they did in later times. Magic is consistently mentioned in the same breath - well, stone," he corrected, gesturing to the arch, "as the gods even long before They gifted it to the elves. And the elves built these kinds of monuments in the strangest places, sometimes within their settlements and sometimes far, far beyond them in what would have been uninhabitable terrain, and no one has been able to uncover any viable reason for it. But there *must* be one." He shook his head. "I believe they may have some kind of magical significance which they linked to the gods, but...I have no means of analysing magic to explore it."

"'Magical significance' is right," Rathen agreed from further across the clearing, turning at last to face them.

Garon's bearing tightened as he noted the concern in the mage's eyes, and while Anthis mirrored the inquisitor's sudden worry, his expression was riddled quite openly with interest. "What is it?"

"I can't speak for the other places," he made a point of stating quite clearly, "but *this* place has strong magical magnetism." He opened his hand and showed them a tattered copper coin. Then, after he'd curled and flexed the fingers on his right hand with astounding speed - coating the coin in energy, he told them, though they both suspected it wasn't as simple as that - he tossed it up in the air and caught it as it dropped. But though he'd thrown it straight upwards with surprising accuracy, it moved slightly towards the left at its apex. He tossed it again, and it pulled to the left once more. He offered the coin to Garon and Anthis, and though they each flicked it straight upwards, tried it in both hands and Anthis even took a moment to face the direction opposite the coin's consistent pull before giving it a final attempt, it always resulted in the same eastward shift.

They frowned, bemused, as he put the coin back in his pocket. "Somewhere over there is the central focus of the magnetism, and the energy I wrapped around the coin was drawn to it. It's a very, *very* slight pull, which is why the coin only moved a fraction, but it's enough to affect a spell with a sensitive construction like this one so close to its focus. If I created a blanketing spell of energy over this area, it would be fractionally stronger here than, say, back on the forest road, and if I created a scattering spell of energy, one or two more clusters would gather here than elsewhere over the forest. In short, magic is drawn to this point."

"Magical magnetism..." Anthis mused, his eyes brightening with intrigue. "So what does that mean?"

"I suppose, if the other sites are the same, it means you could have your answer regarding magical significance for the elves and their gods, whatever good that would do you. For mages, though, it means little; studies have been made and it's quite possible some are still ongoing - I'm not exactly in the loop - but as far as I'm aware, there is nowhere within the magnetic field, at the edge or dead centre, where either magic or spells have been truly strengthened or weakened, spell range increased or decreased, or anything truly helpful or hindering occurring. And as magnetism can't be created, even if magic *was* affected in a useful way, it would only be affected where it was naturally occurring." He shrugged. "Honestly, despite all the studies, it's proven to be of little significance. It's just one of those things - like cows lying down when it's going to rain, or Aria's milky hiccups."

The girl blushed and pursed her lips.

Garon turned him a level stare. "And what does this mean for *us?*"

Rathen's deep brown eyes met his gaze, and both inquisitor and historian saw the growing haunt within them. "The magnetism itself doesn't mean much, but there *is* magic here."

Garon's shoulders straightened rigidly while Anthis looked thoughtfully off into the distance. "'Ongoing studies'," the officer repeated, "so it could be mages after all. They've found a way to use magnetism to their benefit and they're setting up--"

Rathen was shaking his head, his frown twisted into a strange mixture of confusion and certainty. Only then did Garon notice that that puzzlement had been there since he'd begun.

"It *is* magic," Rathen assured him, "but it doesn't feel...*right*."

"What do you mean? And be clear, please."

He breathed a faintly helpless laugh, but he would do his best. "This magic is chaotic; it's wild - almost *raw*. I know what you were thinking, Inquisitor, but this is no spell. It's not woven, there's no construction or purpose to it at all...but..." his frown deepened as he looked around at the clearing, as if hoping an explanation would fall from the top of one of the trees, loosened by a foraging squirrel. Aria followed his gaze. "It shouldn't be possible..."

"Could the magic not have been put here?" Anthis asked, "like you coating that coin in energy? ...Or was that just a simpli--"

"Simplified explanation, yes. Look, I've been out of touch with the Order for some time, I don't know what they've learned to do or what they've been working on. I suppose it's possible that this *could* have been put in place deliberately, perhaps as some kind of large-scale defence against the wars, or as some kind of power reserve...but what it does, how they could have managed it, or why they would risk it, I haven't a clue."

Aria smiled privately at the power of the concern in his eyes.

"You were right, Inquisitor: this is serious - even dangerous. There is something *far* from right about it, and whatever the reason for this...this pool of magic being here, it *needs* to be removed. If this magic is the same as the other places you and Karth have mentioned - and I suspect it is - then it's not surprising that it's affecting the world and weather around it, and it could get much worse than even you, Inquisitor, suspect."

"Can you do it?"

Rathen blinked at the officer's question, and wondered for a moment if it hadn't actually been a joke. The intensity of his grey eyes told him otherwise. "No," he replied without a trace of doubt. "*No one* can. I can't even fathom how they managed to put it here in the first place, or *whoever* it was that did! Magic *cannot* exist unchained, it's like the blood it mixes with: it's formed by and used within the organisms that made it. When spells are created, the raw magic is drawn out of the mage's body and given structure and purpose, and when the spell is released, the magic does *only* what it was woven to do; there are absolutely *no* effects beyond what was intended. And when a spell disintegrates over time, the weave falls apart and the magic gradually disperses and fades away, like spilled blood evaporating and drying. It no longer has a purpose and it can't maintain its form - and no, before you ask, this *isn't* the gathering of disintegrated magic, either. It doesn't take very much magic to form a spell, even a big one, and it disperses so slowly that it has no effect except the ending of the spell because the intention behind it is lost." He shook his head as Anthis frowned, likely chewing over his messy explanation though he'd delivered it as simply as he could. "And yet this magic is so raw it's as if it was formed right here, out of nothing, all on its own."

"Is the structure of the magic any different from that within people?" Anthis asked, his thoughtful expression unchanging as his eyes refocused from the distance and back onto the mage. "As in, its...well its actual existence here compared to its existence in your...blood...?"

"No, not as far as I can tell. The magic here feels as if it's ready and waiting to be shaped into a spell, but there's nothing and no one to contain or direct it so it *can't* be used. It's purposeless. And there's much, much more of it than *any* single mage could ever possess."

"So to further your analogy, it's as if blood has formed on its own in a puddle somewhere with nothing to give life to." Anthis folded his arms. "Then won't this magic disperse like the blood would dry up?"

"If it would vanish so easily then I don't see why it would have appeared at all."

"You're concerned," Garon observed.

Rathen had felt the inquisitor's eyes drilling into him for some time, and at the man's vaguely victorious tone, his shoulders tightened as though a steel rod had been shoved through them. He deliberately looked away. "No," he lied, "I'm confused. I can't see why or how raw magic would be here like it is, nor what could come of it."

"Back to basics," Anthis said decisively, shaking his muddled thoughts away. "Can no mage remove this magic from this place?" Rathen shook his head, his eyes pulling around at the clearing. "Then, with the elves having died out centuries ago, that means *no one* can." Anthis raised a finger before Garon could protest. "But perhaps some*thing* can."

Rathen frowned sceptically, but the speed with which he'd turned betrayed his intrigue.

"There are legends that the elves, near the end of their reign, created something that could take *away* someone's magic."

Garon's eyes sharpened. "That's possible?"

He gave a non-committal bob of his head. "Legends say so."

"Legends say a lot of things." Rathen folded his arms and regarded him with increasing scepticism. "Like some men turn into wolves on a full moon, or that if you look a harpy in the eye, you'll see your death."

"That is true," Anthis nodded, smiling even despite the mage's challenge, "but legends actually make up a good deal of history, and they can be quite insightful into extinct cultures - stories and superstition can reveal what they considered important in life, which can shed light on the purpose of buildings, keepsakes, artefacts and relics - and where those mentioned but not yet discovered are likely to have been kept."

"But is that still the case when the very item in question is also a legend?"

His smile inexplicably broadened. "Sometimes. I certainly wouldn't put it past the elves to have created such a thing - they had the knowledge, and the means, and the arrogance."

"Did legends lead you to that conclusion, too?"

"Nope, their very history did, and it doesn't take much to get there when you think about it: humans were servants to the elves, so they must have had quite a sense of superiority to put themselves above a whole race. Then there were their increasingly grand buildings and the increasingly useless and fanciful possessions they created and accumulated, and *then* the fact that they eventually deemed themselves so far above everything that they wouldn't even *touch* things anymore and wore gloves all the time instead."

Rathen raised an eyebrow. "Arrogant, then?"

"Eventually, yes," the excited young man replied, "Extremely. Which worked out well for us because it meant that our knowledge and skill in building and crafting increased under their instruction; they taught us so we could do it all instead."

"Then this artefact would have been a means of maintaining their standing above humans? By removing their magic?"

"Of those few who had 'stolen' it from them, yes - or perhaps as a weapon against each other."

Surprise fell over even Aria's face.

"Remove the magic of the enemy and hit them with all you've got," Rathen mused.

"But would that not also cancel out their own magic?"

"Elves were very contextual," the historian replied, "they weren't the type to generalise when it came to their own people, and in the case of a weapon such as this, they would have been *especially* precise."

"And against magic, steel would have no effect."

"Steel wouldn't have been a likely resort anyway, Inquisitor. No weapons from post-magic elven civilisation have ever been uncovered; once they'd gotten to grips with their magic and let it go to their heads, they turned away from other forms of attack and defence and relied exclusively on that. I know *I* would."

Rathen silently conceded to the fact that he didn't really know how to swing a sword.

"Do you have anything solid on these legends?" Garon asked cautiously. "Or is it just another theory?"

"Oh no, I've *definitely* done my research," he assured him eagerly, with such enthusiasm, in fact, that Rathen only shrank back further in doubt. "Among the many vague mentions of magic suppression my colleagues have already chased to dead ends, I've found several strong associations between magic removal and an item of some kind that could achieve it...but I admit that there has been no hard proof and certainly no recovery of such a thing. *But*," he added, raising another quick finger to silence the inquisitor's impending frustration, "given the variety of sources containing these mentions, and the consistency of the noted locations, I and many others believe it's very likely to have existed."

"Wait," Rathen suddenly growled, "exist*ed?*"

"Well unless a mage was in its presence its magical potential wouldn't be sensed," Anthis replied quickly in fear of invoking the mage's wrath, and stumbled back a step, raising his hands defensively as he noted Garon's expression similarly darken, "so if it *has* been recovered, I've heard nothing about it. So much gets bought and sold privately by treasure hunters that only about half of it actually reaches the attention of historians..."

"I'm a treasure hunter!" Aria suddenly declared, her cheerful voice startling them all. Rathen and Anthis both spared her a brief, lopsided smile, while Garon expressed only further irritation. It was difficult to know if it was aimed at her or at Anthis. "I found a spoon in the garden! It was really, really old and dirty! My daddy said it was left by *garden* elves!"

Rathen couldn't help a brief chuckle, but his severe expression rapidly returned as he looked back to Anthis, who seemed disappointed that the distraction was so brief. "No ordinary mage would sense magic in an inanimate object," he told him plainly, "and besides, you're conveniently forgetting one detail: it, *if* it ever existed, is lost. Which means no one has been maintaining whatever spell is within it, so it has certainly broken down by now - *irreparably* so."

"I'm not so sure. This was an object of great importance to the elves."

"You're assuming."

"Aside from a potential weapon, it was also a landmark accomplishment, a great advancement in their use of magic. I think the magic within it could well have been...safeguarded, sealed or something."

"You're still assuming!"

"If it was truly that important, then it could have been, couldn't it?"

Rathen shifted beneath their hopeful gazes, then sighed reluctantly, "I *suppose*, b--"

"So magic *does* work that way?" Anthis asked, surprised.

"As I understand it, the spells holding elven cities together are still mostly elven, they've just been patched up by the Order. Some spells take longer to fall apart than others depending on what they were designed to do."

"Yes," Rathen began, "but--"

"Well that backs up my theory! It should still be salvageable!"

Rathen shook his head in exasperation. "*If* such a thing were to have existed," he pressed, his voice edged, determined not to be interrupted again. "But, as I've said, no ordinary mage would notice the magic! It would take someone with *potent* magic themselves to react to such a thing - no one below the rank of sahrakh would notice it."

"Which is one thing that has been holding me back from exploring the matter further," Anthis explained with a sigh, though Rathen hadn't missed the suddenly bold trace of hope in his voice. "Having someone versed in magic wouldn't just help to detect the artefact itself, or reach it if it's been put behind some kind of magical defence - it would also help me make much quicker sense of some of the more technical details of my research."

Rathen narrowed his eyes, very aware of the fact that Anthis's eyes hadn't grazed him once throughout that last statement.

"But regardless," he continued tentatively, "I'm confident that something like that wouldn't be found anywhere treasure hunters could go. If it can silence the magic of elves, it wouldn't be kept anywhere so easily accessible by their *own* kind, let alone by humans."

"So where *would* it be kept?"

Anthis smiled impishly. "That's the question, isn't it?"

Rathen shook his head and finally turned away, heading back towards the horses in dismissal. Aria frowned and hurried after him, pausing momentarily to glance uncertainly back to the others.

"I would feel much more comfortable knowing for certain that it *hasn't* been found."

"Then perhaps you should contact the Order, Inquisitor," Rathen suggested as he began adjusting his dappled mare's bridle. "One of the scholars might know something. Otherwise, I think you're wasting your time with this man."

Anthis suddenly stammered and blustered, his expression twisting into a frown for the first time that morning. "I've got a better idea of what's going on in this matter than any of your colleagues do!"

"Then tell me," Rathen shot back, turning away from the horse, "besides not having a mage to follow you around, what *else* has stopped you from pursuing this subject? Because I thought you were supposed to be some kind of genius among historians, but it sounds to me like you're working with nothing but 'legends' and guesswork."

Anthis glared back at him, his previously bright green eyes now tainted by insult, and a defence that fit him as perfectly as a well-used suit of armour suddenly fell over him. "I've got *plenty*," he managed not to snap. "Over the past three years I've followed numerous leads to dead ends - leads that have cost others their careers - whittling the matter down from 'legends' to as close to fact as it can be without solid proof. Because that's what this job *is*. We read, we compare, and we think; we *rarely* have solid or physical evidence to work with. We make connections using information and findings from past research and create a gradually bigger picture that provides answers to *thousands* of questions, some of which haven't even been *asked* yet while others have for decades, and yet often *never* to the question you're actually trying to crack!" He stormed forwards before his caution managed to restrain him short, though neither his anger nor offence could hold a candle to Rathen's seething impatience. "I've had no choice but to put this research on the back burner *countless* times, despite my desperation to bring it to fruition, because, if I don't keep working on other more promising discoveries and theories, I'll be cast out from the Fellowship of the Historical Society, and without the money I make from their contacts and independent commissions for my work, I'll have no way to support myself!"

Aria shrank beneath the weight of the atmosphere as the two stared daggers at one another.

Finally, with a tense sigh, Anthis loosened the knot in his jaw and forced himself to reel his offence back in. "I've done all the leg work for this already," he assured them both, carefully, "and since the last time I had to push this aside, a number of notes in my research have begun to stand out. I've made an educated guess and finally found a next step, I just needed the opportunity - and the help - to get it moving."

"'An educated guess'," Rathen turned back to the horse. "Then you have no real leads. This is just a convenient partnership."

"What is this next step?" Garon asked, snatching the reins of the conversation before Anthis could respond, even as the young man appeared again to boil over.

His furious eyes snapped back onto the inquisitor and once more fought to pull himself together. "The city of Mokhan. That's where all my research seems to point."

"And you think the artefact will be there?"

Anthis managed a weak smile. "We should be so lucky. At best I'll find more information."

"What do you know already?" Aria asked, her presence once again surprising all gathered as she took a careful step towards them and away from her father. "Do you think you can find it?"

Anthis blinked down at her. "...Well," he began slowly, wondering if it was worth simplifying his thoughts for her benefit, "from elven documents, journals and the like, there's reference to the ability to silence magic as a 'significant advancement', and that 'with further research and greater understanding of magic, endless possibilities could arise', along with the idea of 'ascension'. There's also more consistent mention of a 'great magical advancement' having been conceived in Mokhan, but I can't tell yet if that's in terms of someone having an idea or someone actually *creating* something. Many elven words have multiple meanings - like I said, elves were all about context - but in this case, while both meanings fit, they're also both promising. And, finally, there's a name that keeps popping up around references to an object of cultural significance dated around the same time, and I know from past research that the individual is associated with the same place as the 'magical advancement'. I've believed for a long while that this 'advancement' is the artefact."

Rathen shook his head at the vague, almost desperately gathered threads, but this time he said nothing about the likeliness of none of them being related.

"I admit it's a bit of a stretch," Anthis said as he glanced towards Rathen's back, "but I've been thinking about this for a while, and I usually have only a little more than this to work with at the beginning of most studies anyway."

Garon nodded slowly, chewing it over for a long moment.

Rathen fiddled with the mare's girth straps, making a show of adjusting the saddle while he waited to see just how the inquisitor of the distinguished White Hammer would respond.

"If Rathen is right," he said, finally, "and mages can't remove this, then perhaps the elves can help us from the grave."

Rathen's shoulders dropped in disappointment. He began fixing the saddle now in earnest.

"It feels like a long shot, but it's either that or we sit out the effects of this magic and hope it resolves itself, and it will undoubtedly get worse before it gets better." He turned to the historian and inclined his head, his calculation replaced once more by formality. "Mister Karth, I thank you for your help, you and Rathen have certainly given me valuable insight. But, as this matter does directly involve magic, it can't be repaired overnight, so I'm afraid I must ask if you would be willing to lend me your continued support. You will be paid." He glanced to Rathen. "Both of you."

Rathen froze just as he prepared to fetch Aria, mount the horse and be away from this nonsense, while a smile of disbelief crept across the historian's face. A moment later the young man was nodding eagerly and beaming like a fool.

"Certainly! Yes! I'd be honoured to continue helping your investigation, Inquisitor - for the good of everyone, of course," he quickly amended, but though his smile vanished momentarily in seriousness, he couldn't prevent it from creeping over him again. "But I admit I'd be lying if I said I wasn't excited by the opportunity to work on this artefact, at long last."

"It may take some time," Garon warned him, but Anthis was already nodding his understanding, grinning still, and again his infectious enthusiasm had fallen upon Aria as she bounced on the spot between them and her father.

Satisfied, Garon turned then towards Rathen, but the mage was already climbing up onto the horse.

Aria slouched, disappointment abruptly filling her eyes, but though Rathen wanted to call her over, lift her up in front of him and leave the others to their wild goose chase, he found himself reluctant to denounce their quest. Reins in hand, ready to put the ruin behind him, he was suddenly racked with doubt.

Try as he might - and try, he did - he simply couldn't shut out the voice of concern in his head. What Garon had told him of the lands to the north-east, and Kienza before him, had set him on edge already, but as he'd investigated this magic, the words had begun ringing in his ears and a strange sensation had moved through him, a tingling through his veins as if his own magic was protesting its very existence. This was true, raw magic, somehow completely disembodied, and if the Order *had* found some way to manipulate the magnetism, it was a reckless and foolish thing to do whatever the reason. But even that theory was becoming less and less likely with every passing moment, as the magic's presence felt equally less intentional.

His eyes dropped to Aria as she approached him, dragging her feet, clearly unwilling to leave but ready to do so all the same, and the corners of his mouth pulled downwards in further indecision. Silverwood was only half a day's ride from the Scowles; if the situation here worsened as it had in the north, it could come to affect them directly. The Scowles *could* swallow his home, with the *both* of them still in it.

And right here, right now, he was being handed the ridiculous, half-baked opportunity to fix it. Because if this lone man from the Hall of the White Hammer was truly the only man investigating it, then he himself may have been his own home's single hope.

And Aria's.

He hung his head and sighed feebly, then looked towards the inquisitor who had been staring at him all the while he'd been lost in thought. Anthis had wandered off to get another final look at the ruined arch. He sighed again, and his voice dropped in defeat. "What is it you think *I* can do in a search for an old relic? Stand there idly, waiting for someone to show me a brooch or something and sniff it for magic, then patch it up like an old maid? I was only a sahrot, I can't detect that kind of thing, and I have very little experience in repairing elven spells."

"You heard Anthis," the inquisitor replied patiently, taking a step towards him, "your knowledge would help in his research; you could shed light on his findings and the matter would be dealt with all the quicker for it."

"But I was a soldier, not an academic."

"Even so, you are still our best chance, and your knowledge of magic is most certainly superior to any of our own - and likely to most other mages. You were, as you said, a sahrot. That's equivalent to colonel, isn't it? It may not be sahrakh, but it's close."

Rathen sighed again, and though he thought he'd come close to making a decision, he was discovering otherwise. It was nothing short of a fool's errand. "I've told you that this is magic. I've done as you've asked. Just what is it you expect from me now?"

"What I would like from you," he began simply, "is to help us identify the artefact, repair it--"

"I hasten to add that I was not a preserver, either. I can't say how much I'd be able to do until it's in front of me, and I may well not be able to do *anything*."

"I realise that, but I'm confident you'll manage. And I would also like you to find a way to remove the magic *without* the use of the artefact, in case we *can't* find it."

Rathen's eyes suddenly flashed. "*Remove raw magic?!*" He cried, startled, confusion spilling over him and making his first ridiculous request seem suddenly quite reasonable. "It would be like taking magic from a *mage!* If the artefact *did* exist and *was* capable of such a thing...well, there's a reason the elves would have gone through the trouble of making a *vessel* for the spell rather than just casting it directly themselves! It would be *far* too complex to weave, if anyone even had the magical capacity to complete it--in fact it probably took *several* elves and quite some time to even get it *into* the artefact in the *first* place!"

"But they had to create the spell itself before it could be stored inside it."

Rathen merely blinked. "Well...yes...of course they did," he conceded, "but--"

"Then, in theory, such a spell *is* possible."

Despite all of his preliminary investigations, this inquisitor clearly hadn't bothered to do much reading on how magic actually worked. He spoke of it as if they were discussing the best placement for sewing on a new button. "The *spell*," he specified, rubbing his increasingly aching head, "yes, but, as I said, there's a reason the spell was stored in an object."

"Part of that reason would have been elven flair and arrogance, remember," Anthis said from nearby, still studying the worn stones. Rathen fired him a bitter look. He was quickly deciding that he did not like this man.

"How would the spell work? In theory? Would it cause spells to disintegrate faster than natural? Stop magic from responding to the caster? Catch and trap released spells?"

"Spells aren't butterflies, Inquisitor," the mage replied wearily, "and I really can't tell you how it could work. I suppose any of those could be possible, but it would be a very, very, *very* tall order; it would take a lot of time, a lot of study, and a lot of experimentation."

"But," Garon said again, "it's a *possibility*."

Rathen sighed. "Yes. It is - for the right person."

"Well, I'm afraid only you can be that 'right person'."

"Somehow I thought you'd say that." Rathen sighed again, then mumbled 'I was only supposed to confirm it was magic' before looking down at Aria, who peered back up at him with eyes that revealed a muddle of a thousand thoughts. There was one among them, however, that he couldn't mistake: the hope that he wouldn't disappoint her. *'Or anyone else.'* He cursed as he realised he was only adding more weight onto his own shoulders.

His eyes shifted back onto Garon. "The Order--"

"War is on the horizon, Mister Koraaz," he told him plainly, though his voice dropped against the others. "Rebels aside, the Order answers to the Crown, and the Crown will direct them where it sees fit. The Crown does not recognise this as a priority. It took my *own* insistence to get this moving. If anything, the Crown believes this to be the Order's *own* doing, in which case, they won't be allowed anywhere near it. They are not investigating, and they are not about to start. Banished, as you are, you are the *only* mage capable of stopping this."

Though the inquisitor's gaze gripped like a steel fist, Rathen's eyes dropped to Aria on impulse. The inquisitor noticed.

They were resigned when they returned. He shrugged helplessly. "I really don't know how you expect me to achieve this..."

"You'll manage. The Order predicted great things from you."

Rathen winced at that.

"So you're with us?" Anthis asked hopefully as he rejoined them from his study. He'd either forgotten their previous clash, or now viewed Rathen as merely a means to complete what would apparently be a ground-breaking study.

But even as his mind continued to turn under the burning stares of three pairs of eyes and their varying degrees of hope, Rathen slowly nodded. "Yes..." His gaze turned reluctantly onto the inquisitor. "*If* all previous conditions still stand."

"Until you're safely back home," Garon assured him.

Rathen sat a little taller in the saddle and gave a single, decisive nod. Even so, he couldn't believe the words had come out of his mouth. "Then...I suppose I'm with you."

Aria squealed in delight and hurried over to be helped up onto the horse at last, but though Rathen smiled, glad at least that she was pleased, the weight that settled upon him as he lifted her into the front of the saddle was uncomfortably familiar. It seemed he was once again facing another's heavy expectations for him to exceed himself.

He deeply wished Kienza was around to offer a suggestion.

"Most of my notes are at my home in Kora," Anthis informed them as he hurried over to the horses, tucking his little book back into the tattered satchel before climbing onto his own, "but I can work without them for now."

"Kora is only three days away, it would be worth heading over. You surely can't recall every detail from memory."

"You'd be surprised," Anthis grinned, "but I suppose I can't know what I'd need to cross-reference. Plus I've not been there in...seven weeks?"

"How can you call it a home if you haven't been there for seven weeks?!" Rathen asked, stunned, and Aria stared back, open-mouthed at the absurdity.

But Anthis only smiled. "It's part of the job."

Chapter 6

It was late; midnight had come and gone, but Salus continued to pace up and down the length of his office, his movements so constant that the candles seemed to predict them, flickering back and forth with him in perfect synchrony. But the shadows shifting along the walls were of little distraction; instead, they lulled him deeper into his worries, and his arms folded tighter across his chest.

He was wasting time by fretting, but though he knew there could be only one outcome, he still wrestled with the what-ifs and worst case scenarios, wondering almost desperately if there wasn't still something he could do to change it. Only the steady knock at the door managed to freeze his feet, but he equally knew that he didn't need to hear his visitor's tidings.

"Come in," he said anyway, moving around behind his desk with a sigh, and Teagan silently stepped inside to stop rigidly in the centre of the room as the door clicked shut behind him. Salus waved his hand for him to begin, but he didn't sit. This wouldn't take long.

"The decisive blow came three hours ago," the portian told him dutifully, neither wasting a moment nor delivering the words with any trace of caution. "Kalokh's numbers were already weak, and when their general was killed, their morale shattered. They've fled; Skilan is victorious."

Salus growled and slammed his fist into the desk despite his identical expectations, but he said nothing, and Teagan didn't react. The keliceran leaned upon his knuckles and stared down at the table for a long while, his eyes surely boring a hole through the polished wood, while the portian waited patiently, keeping his hard eyes fixed respectfully to the wall. Perfect silence enveloped them until Salus finally sighed.

"The world is a mess," he said at last, his shoulders slumping, "and even though we can see what's coming, all we can do is defend against it." He shook his head and pushed himself upright, folding his arms and pressing his fingers into his biceps again. "The Arana can stop most things before they're even set into motion, but for some reason, as soon as something *does* manage to begin and the public gets wind of it, the Crown holds us back..."

"The Arana is adept," Teagan agreed, "but we can't stop everything. And at least by allowing things to happen from time to time, the Arana is kept out of public knowledge. That makes it harder for enemies to know where to find us, or to know when we're involved. The military is a public force; if they were never put into action, Turunda would seem suspicious even in the view of its own citizens."

"As true as that may be, I wish there was no *need* for the Arana *or* the military. Lives are lost in service to *both*." Salus shook his head again and finally dropped into his seat, calmed by his own frustration. Though he gestured for Teagan to do the same, he, as always, declined. "If only there was a way to safeguard the country *without* it costing any lives..."

Teagan's gaze slipped to rest briefly upon him, and noted the distance in his superior's eyes. He was already staring a thousand miles away from beneath the frown that had plagued his face for the past few weeks, and it took ever longer for the keliceran's attention to return.

"Inform the general," he said eventually, fully intending to provide suggestions to the Crown for the Arana's usage though he knew they'd be pushed aside, and leaned back wearily into his chair as he, too, pushed the matter out of his mind. "How many agents are still out?" He asked, moving on to his next thought.

"Six of those recalled are still to arrive."

"I hope they *do* arrive. Dead men can't exactly send word of their demise, and we can't do without them."

Teagan continued to study him. "When did you last sleep?"

The papers on his desk suddenly screamed for his attention. "Two nights ago."

"Then perhaps you should go and get some rest."

"You're dismissed." He rearranged the reports, setting them in a tidy stack without dignifying Teagan with a glance. But, of course, his favoured operative didn't react to the attitude. A portian could never take insult, it was beyond what little of their humanity remained after their extensive conditioning. Instead, he inclined his head, bid the keliceran goodnight and left on silent feet, his report concluded.

Salus stared down at the now jumbled folders as the door clicked shut, but he quickly stopped seeing them. His attention was lost again to his equally muddled thoughts.

Despite all of his best efforts, war was finally falling upon them, and certainly for no good reason. It was little more than a grudge being indulged while high on winnings, and the Crown would surely reject any proposals to stop the situation before Skilan even began marching their way - just like they had his request to increase the Arana's presence along the borders. But he couldn't help wondering if, despite how patient King Thunan had been with King Jalund's attempts to stir up trouble over the past few years, he equally yearned to clash with him. In fact, he'd found himself wondering from time to time if the king didn't actually seek the country's downfall himself with each of Salus's proposals he turned away - but on each of those occasions, as he did now, he was also forced to concede that they'd had worse rulers in the past, individuals who must truly have made his own predecessors wonder if *their* efforts weren't for nothing.

The more he thought about it, the easier he realised his job must have been compared to that of the keliceran in charge under King Ellory just twenty five years ago - not that that changed the weight of his present ordeals.

In the end, he could only do so much, and if the king held the Arana back, he surely had a reason beyond a childish desire to respond to the Skee King's constant jibes and insults - and keeping the organisation out of public knowledge was certainly not something Salus wished to change. Ultimately, whatever came of it, the Arana *would* be prepared to handle it from the shadows while the military maintained the public's attention, offering the simpler folk pride in their country's sense of honour to handle issues face to face, while the more grisly tasks were left to 'ghosts'.

A tired spasm forced his leg to jolt upwards, tearing his mind back to the office as his kneecap struck the underside of his desk. His lip curled resentfully at the brief, dull pain, but he sighed to himself and sat straighter in his seat rather than concede to his weariness, and looked back down at the reports. He still had work to do.

He sorted through them once again, returning them to their previous arrangement by the date and time stamped in the corners and the colour of the ink drawn along the bottom, but no sooner had he begun reading them than the words started to blend together. It didn't take long before he found himself reading the same line four times over.

By the third report, his eyelids had grown heavy, his mind began to flag, and the words made less and less sense - so he accepted without thought the nonsensical accounts of Doana's hired 'mercantile' force sailing eastward to bring war to Voent, and of the 'dessert' tribes maintaining a tenuous peace with those of the mountains while those of other regions fought tooth and nail. As his mind ran away with the increasingly vivid images, his work grew equally distant, along with his concerns.

When his chin slipped out of his hand and the sense of falling invaded his thoughts, he noticed that, somehow, in the space of only a moment, two of the candles set upon his desk had burned down.

He blinked at them, wondering sluggishly how it could have happened, then sighed for the hundredth time that night and finally surrendered to his state. Not only had he not slept for forty eight hours, he hadn't even laid eyes on his bed. But there had been just too much to do. And while he still believed he could hold on to that excuse, this time he didn't have the focus to achieve it.

Defeated, he pushed himself to his feet. The usual thought to tidy his office didn't present itself; he extinguished the candles, left the papers to be revised in the morning, and fled the quiet darkness on graceless feet. He couldn't get to his quarters soon enough.

It was quieter outside in the chill, and he moved through the grounds quickly before the cold could steal away his fatigue. Though he'd resented it half an hour before, now he wanted nothing more than to indulge it. Hopefully the sun would bring good news - at the very least, it would provide opportunity to speak with the king's representative.

The fact that he considered that a positive thought proved just how delirious he was.

When he reached the small house concealed within the trees of the Arana's grounds, their reach far more extensive than any who looked upon the apparent stately house would guess, he headed straight for his bed. He wasted no time with candles; he knew the way, and only moments after he fell upon his sheets and wriggled lazily out of his clothes, his body racked by a burning manifestation of fatigue, sleep leapt upon him.

He'd expected his dreams to proceed as the last, to be assaulted again with the images of war and the pressures to do all within and beyond his power to stop it, but instead he was carried away to a world in which danger could never possibly rear its head. The softest, greenest grass covered the hills and the land as far as he could see, tousled by a warm, gentle breeze and speckled with tall and wonderful trees. Rivers meandered torpidly, given permission to weave and wend this way and that by the land itself rather than carving its own indiscriminate path, and large red and golden leaves drifted on the wind to land upon the clear waters, ferried away to whatever lake or ocean the river met. And through it all, an overwhelming sense of peace finally, mercifully, slowed and soothed his heart.

Chapter 7

Five days had passed on horseback. Roads closed and rerouted by martial order had delayed their arrival at Kora by two days, but with every night's stop-over in various settlements along their way, the reason was repeatedly made clear.

Neither the presence of the military nor the news of the impending war had come as a surprise to the officer or the historian, and though Rathen had been aware of the unprecedented number of conflicts raging across the continent, he was surprised to find Turunda finally succumbing. Aria, meanwhile, had visibly shrank in the saddle at the first sight of the armoured men.

But her alarm didn't shackle her for long; the sight of the tall, sloping city breaking through the forest-lined road ahead of them soon rekindled her enthusiasm. In the evening light, it looked almost like a fairytale: creeping ivy coated the old, stone walls, while grey watch towers rose up above the trees with merlons carved into similar leaves along the parapets. From there, they seemed to peer out over the land beyond for pleasure rather than defence, while the backdrop of forest-topped cliffs bounced the late sun back from countless glinting grains. But those quartz-studded cliffs coaxed from her a greater gasp of astonishment, as the back of the city seemed to be carved straight from the rock face itself.

This was a city of ages, Anthis had told them; its foundations built by the hands of the most ancient reaches of elves long before they'd gained their magic, it had been expanded as needed, and then abandoned when they'd become corrupted by their powers and sought to build newer and more aesthetic abodes elsewhere, far from their origins. When the elves as a whole had mysteriously disappeared, humans branched out and took their place, charmed by the craftsmanship of the rock and the absence of any ostentatious gilding - the lack of what most knew as 'elven'.

Rathen wasn't at all surprised that a historian would choose to live in such a place, and following the brief recount of the city's history, even he felt a fascination for it.

But when they reached the top of the inclining road, the gates that rose ahead of them weren't as welcoming as they'd hoped.

Six guards stood to attention on either side, watching the new arrivals closely while others stood at regular intervals further along the walls. An order could be heard barked from somewhere nearby, perhaps on the other side, perhaps behind the trees, carried on the wind that tugged at the ivory military standards hanging over the walls. They dwarfed the ochre pennants of the city's ruling family; they were not merely passing through.

Rathen tightened under the hawk-like stares.

"They've almost tripled their number," Anthis noted in a careful, disapproving whisper once they'd left their horses at the stable and were permitted an uneasy entry to the city. "I doubt the Marlands are happy. They do a lot to ensure the guards can take care of this city without military interference. Oh, but I suppose war is war." He looked away, murmuring 'damn Skees' under his breath, and paused beside one of the city's bulletin boards before taking the lead of the group.

In that moment, Rathen's eyes fell searchingly upon the cascading selection of bounty posters, half-certain he'd find an image of himself amongst them. He knew full well that it was unreasonable, and he'd finally begun to identify that fact - there was, after all, no cause for his face to be there - but though over the past week he'd also gradually grown a little more comfortable outside of the safety of the Scowles, his tension always returned upon entering a settlement. It made no difference if it was a crowded city or a small and pleasant village with a three bedroom inn and no sign of even a single minor theft having taken place for years.

But, while each bout passed a little sooner than the last, this time he sensed it wouldn't move on too quickly. It was too large a place with too many probing eyes, and soldiers were known to cause trouble in such numbers, be it by their own restless hands or by their presence upsetting more temperamental locals.

Fortunately, he wasn't given the time to stop and fret. Anthis led them through the city by its winding uphill roads, straight through the lower and busier districts and towards the more impressive stone-carved buildings at the back. After twenty minutes, the cliff faces began to loom above them.

Anthis drew to a sudden stop at a fork in the road, a point surrounded by large and pleasing buildings, including a rather grand and ivy-laced inn. From here, one of the two routes continued up towards the top of the city, while the other disappeared around a corner to loop back down towards the crafting quarter where smoke presently rose from the smithy. But though they each thought he'd stopped to gather his bearings as he frowned and muttered to himself, instead he delved into his bag, withdrew a key and started down the short garden path beside them.

Rathen's eyebrows rose as he peered up at the large and rich building at the end of it, a home that had apparently not been lived in for several weeks despite its well-tended garden, and Aria didn't hesitate to give voice to her matching thoughts as they followed after him.

"This *can't* be your house!" She declared as she charged past Garon to get a look inside as soon as possible, which she repeated with even greater certainty as she discovered it to be as spacious as any of the larger taverns they'd recently taken lodging in - though instead of being cluttered by tables and chairs, it seemed fit to burst with books. Some volumes had been left open on any flat surface, others were stacked beside chairs, and countless collections stood along shelves beside unusual trinkets of exquisite detail, but no obvious function. She shook her head as she spun around, her eyes growing in astonishment. "It's too *big!*"

"Historical research paid for this?" Perhaps Rathen had joined the wrong wing of the Order. Even as a previously respected officer, his home had never been this grand...

He closed the door behind him as Anthis pulled open all of the curtains, loosing not a flake of dust, and only then did he notice the extent of the trinkets displayed in his cluttered sitting room as they caught the golden light. Some were impressive, relics presumably dated from the later age of the elves, while others were little more than carved stones and hardly worth acknowledging. Evidently it took a trained eye to see their value.

"It did, but I do also have the favour of the ruling family here. They employ me from time to time to act as a consultant for the masons when the elven district needs repairs, as well as for general research into the city's history." He stopped beside a well-worn armchair and began rummaging through a pile of books that stood a fraction taller. "I admit I've gotten quite lucky here. They even employ housekeepers for me while I'm away."

"They don't do a particularly good job," Rathen observed as he looked about at the mess. "Either that or they've been looking for something."

"Actually," Anthis chuckled, "they're just very good at replacing things exactly where I left them."

"Where is everyone else?" Aria asked, peering up the stairs and listening carefully, but Anthis turned and frowned.

"There, uh...there *is* no one else..."

"There *must* be," she insisted, mirroring his puzzlement, "this house is too big for just one person, there must be at least seven others..."

He blinked and looked to Rathen. "Did she grow up in a tree house or something?"

"Something like that. I presume we're staying in the city tonight?" He fetched Aria quickly from the foot of the staircase, his tone weary, though not quite as laden as it had been.

Anthis pulled a book victoriously from the bottom of the stack, but his brow dropped a moment later as he glanced at the cover. He dropped it back down and turned instead towards another pile. "Yes and no. There's room here, as your daughter pointed out, so there's no sense in sending you out to an inn and emptying the inquisitor's pocket if it can be avoided." Garon inclined his head gratefully. "In which case," he continued, turning back to everyone and offering them his usual cheerful smile, "make yourselves at home."

He'd barely finished speaking before Aria kicked off her shoes and ran off to begin climbing the stairs, and Rathen hurried after her just as quickly, telling her he hadn't meant it literally. Anthis simply chuckled to himself.

"Odd pair, those two," he observed as they disappeared and Garon looked around at the trinkets in passive interest. "Where did you get them? And will Aria be staying with us? She's no bother, of course," he assured him quickly, "in fact I rather like her - she balances her father perfectly - but Mokhan is probably three weeks away with all the redirected roads, and that's likely to be just the first stop of many. Not to mention that we're going to have to sneak into the old district, what with all the superstition..." He frowned in growing concern. "And then there's the war... I can't say how long or how far we're going to have to search, but we're quite likely to be travelling through some unwelcoming regions. It won't be easy going. Or quick."

Garon sighed and shook his head. "She was somewhat unexpected," he admitted, "but Rathen insists that she'll be fine, and if there was anyone else who could take her off of his hands for the duration, he would have said so. And anyway," he added, even as they glanced towards the ceiling as a thump came from the room above, "I don't believe for a moment that he'll let any harm come to her."

"As a father shouldn't." Anthis's eyes narrowed speculatively as they fell back upon him. "What did he mean when he said he was 'out of the loop' with the Order, anyway? In Silverwood? And despite what he says, I'm quite certain that he *should* be wearing a cloak..."

"He isn't a part of the Order."

Anthis blanched, his eyes widening in shock, and he dashed frantically over to the inquisitor, several books still in his hands. "He *isn't* with the Order?!" He asked in a strangled whisper. "How?! *Why?!*"

"He has his reasons, and should he choose to give them to you, he will. But I'm not at liberty to divulge anything, myself."

Anthis grunted doubtfully and peered over to the staircase. "I'll never find out, then. That man is a closed book."

"And I'm not?" Garon asked, a lopsided smile pulling at his face as it did from time to time, under moments of irony or curious humour that often seemed to reveal itself to no one else.

"Well," Anthis smiled carefully, "yes, but I don't believe it's by choice. Inquisitors have a difficult job; being easily read surely can't help when you're investigating something sensitive. But him," he shook his head. "He chooses to be that way, I'm quite sure of it. He keeps to himself - he's barely said a word in days, he just listens to conversations and tightens up with nervous glances when he's around other people. No offence to you, Inquisitor, but if Aria wasn't here, I think I'd have gone mad by now."

Garon frowned. "It's been a week."

"Yes, and I like to talk," Anthis replied simply. "But, all right. As long as he's aware of what's ahead of us..."

"He is. I've made sure of it."

Anthis nodded and shrugged the matter away before making his way back across the room, looking through the tomes in his hands as he went. "I hope he loosens up," he added to himself as he set them down and looked through another collection spread across a table. "I don't think I can stand the atmosphere for much longer."

Curiosity satisfied, Aria eventually came skipping back downstairs, trailed by her weary father, and by which point Anthis had recovered only one of the books he sought. But he set his search aside as a number of stomachs grumbled, his own surely the loudest, and with so little in the pantry, a simple meal didn't take long to prepare. Then, as had become a nightly routine, Garon left to look around the city and find out what he could about nearby areas and rumours of strange happenings. Anthis had followed ten minutes later, taking the opportunity to see to other personal matters since he was there anyway, leaving Rathen and Aria alone in the large, unfamiliar house.

They sat for some time in the living room, Aria busying herself by looking carefully through the books in search of more of Anthis's sketches, which she replaced quite meticulously back where she'd found them in the hope that he wouldn't notice when he returned, while Rathen sat in silence, scowling in thought. He was brought out of it only by Aria loudly sighing right beside his ear.

He turned and looked at her expectantly.

"Welcome back," she beamed. "Can I have my knife?"

Rathen sighed, but rather than ask if she didn't ought to go to bed instead, he obliged, and she followed him with the ceaseless skip in her step over to their bags by the door. It didn't take him long to find it in her near-empty satchel, nor the single piece of wood with an unnatural shape nestled beside it. She all but snatched them and hurried back to the living room.

"Don't do it in there," he called after her, at which she came to a sudden stop and turned on her heel, then followed his finger towards the kitchen and clambered into a chair. "Make your mess over this." He set on the table a smooth oak trencher he'd taken from a sideboard, and she immediately got to work cutting away small flakes and strips of wood with supreme dexterity to further her image of whatever it was she was creating.

"Anthis wouldn't mind," she sang as he dropped heavily into the chair beside her and sleepily watched her work. "He's a nice man."

"How can you know that?"

"Because I can see it," she replied with a grin. "And he smiles all the time." She gave him a knowing look. "You don't smile all the time, but that's okay, because I can see it in you, too, in other ways."

"Such as?" He asked as his curiosity sent a smile creeping across his face.

"Such as you saying 'yes' and coming out here, even though you'd rather be at home, because, even though you say you don't, you do actually care."

"About some things, yes," he conceded, and he leaned back in his seat, his eyelids growing heavy as he watched her manipulate her knife to quite precisely carve away long, slender slivers, creating wonderful curves and contours with minimal strokes.

"Do you think you can fix the thing if we find it?"

"The artefact?" He asked, stifling a yawn. "Perhaps. I won't know until I feel whatever of it is left."

"And what do you plan to do about this spell you have to maybe make?"

"Not a clue."

Her eyes crashed upon him in shock, though her hands continued their work. "But you've had five whole days to think!"

He managed a tired smile. "Five days isn't enough."

"Well, can I help?"

"No, little one. I wish you could, but I haven't the faintest idea where to even begin." He leaned forwards, resting his folded arms on the table, and lay his head down upon them. "The whole thing is ridiculous."

"You keep saying that. So why did you agree?" She gave him a deliberate sidelong look when he didn't answer. "*I* know why."

"Oh?"

"Because you're a nice man, just like I said. You can't let the world end."

He chuckled. "The world isn't going to end."

"No," she beamed, pointing her knife towards him, which he carefully nudged away, "because you said *yes!* Which means you'll find the arty-fact, or you'll make the spell. You just need to think."

"It's not like I *haven't* been thinking..."

"You'll just have to think more, then." Her grin softened as her heart slipped into her eyes. "I know you'll manage."

Rathen breathed a laugh while a doubtful smile moved over his lips. "At least one of us does."

Neither Garon nor Anthis returned while Rathen was still up that night, but after a surprisingly comfortable and quiet night's sleep, all were present and accounted for, and they set out early before the city awoke. But though most residents still slept or took their breakfast at home, aside from those few whose work began with the crowing of cockerels, the military presence near the city gate was no less prominent than it had been the previous evening. Armoured bodies glinted in the morning light, standing among the guards who sent them bitter sideways glances while they watched the drowsy city, but for the most part they'd taken up positions along the walls, replacing a number of the stationed guards who'd been reassigned to simple city patrols.

Soldiers and guardsmen alike watched the group as they passed, their gaze touched by curiosity rather than suspicion, surely for nothing more than the inquisitor's involvement, to whom a few inclined their heads. And it was also, no doubt, only for Garon's presence that they went unhindered and their bags unsearched. But he and Rathen carried only food and supplies between them, and Anthis's old satchel was filled exclusively with the books he'd finally managed to locate in the chaos of his living room, though he'd somehow managed to injure his forearm while 'rummaging'.

Once they'd fixed their loads to the horses at the stables, noting as they did so the military tents pitched in between the trees just beyond the walls, they finally set out, and Rathen breathed a long sigh of relief as the city and its residents fell away behind them.

Anthis glanced towards him in curiosity, the elated smile that had been on his face since he'd risen barely weakening. But he said nothing, pondering instead what Garon had told him the night before, as well as how Rathen's apparent social anxiety might fit in.

But though it didn't take long for the usual silence to descend - aside from the little girl's humming, whose own enthusiasm made Anthis's heart even lighter - he chose not to give voice to those thoughts just yet. But that didn't mean he was prepared to put up with the atmosphere.

"So," he began, turning his smile towards Garon. "You said you've worked out our route?"

The inquisitor nodded from the lead. "I gathered what I could in the city last night about military movements and redirected roads, and there are two ruins affected in similar ways to Silverwood between here and Mokhan. I've taken delays into account and planned the shortest route to the city that will still take us by one of the sites. Rathen, you said the magic felt different, so perhaps if you feel it again, it will help you figure something out. The other site is too far out of the way to consider; it would add two more weeks onto the journey, so this one will have to do."

Rathen nodded. "It should help," he replied, managing to keep his doubt from entering his voice.

"But," Garon continued, "this and the redirections mean that we'll be straying from the road a few times, and we may well be too far from settlements to spend the night comfortably for a few days at a time. I've already procured enough supplies to last a little over a week; we shouldn't need to stop for more until just before we head into the hinterlands."

"Which site is it?" Anthis asked curiously.

"Wrenroot."

"Then we should be there in a week."

"Closer to a week and a half," Garon amended.

"Is anything there different to Silverwood?" Rathen asked, even while keeping his horse at a slightly less than social distance from the others.

"I can't honestly say. From what I've gathered, people don't go there often; traders who pass nearby are drawn in, presumably by the same thing we all felt in Silverwood, but they don't go too far because they say they feel like they're being watched."

Rathen frowned. "Watched?"

"Well if the magic that shouldn't be there can make a place look and feel like the pinnacle of beauty, why could it not also instil the feeling of being watched?"

Rathen bobbed his head in concedence, though he frowned at the level of cheer with which Anthis had spoken. He was more boisterous and excitable that day than they'd seen him yet.

"You're interested, aren't you?" Aria whispered from in front of him, and he couldn't keep the smallest of smiles from tugging at his lips. He was; there had been no structure to the magic he'd felt before, but if there was an alternative effect, he might be able to find some subtle differences now that he had something to compare it to, and that might well lend him the beginnings of understanding. Of course, whether that understanding would ultimately help him or not was another matter. The structure of the magic, or even its source, could play no part at all in the creation of the spell he'd been coerced into attempting.

Fortunately, though little more than a legend, the artefact still seemed to be the inquisitor's priority, and while Rathen questioned the likelihood of Anthis's success, he felt that it was still a more hopeful solution. Anthis had something to work with, after all, even if it was just 'educated guesses'; Rathen, however, had absolutely nothing.

"What about Mokhan?" He asked the historian, shifting attention away from his certain future failing. "What do you expect to find?"

"Well, it's an old elven city," Anthis replied, his smile broadening as a touch more enthusiasm entered his voice - clearly he was very excited about the whole matter. But then, that passion was what he was known for. "Long post-magic, about a hundred years old by the end of their age, eight hundred from now, but because people keep to the newer reaches of the city, the elven district is abandoned and the Order doesn't maintain it. The people are a bit...superstitious about it. It collapses from time to time as the spells that hold it together fall apart, but people think it's ghosts, traps and curses."

"Spells hold the city together?" Aria asked with a frown as Rathen rolled his eyes at the gullible tendencies of common folk.

"Elves got lazy," Anthis reminded her, "so their grandest cities were constructed and held together with magic rather than by hand and mortar."

"Which means the spells disintegrate over time and the Order's preserver wing steps in and repairs them to hold it together," Rathen finished. "But it's a time-consuming process, identifying every little hole in a spell and patching it with a replacement, so it's only done if it's necessary, like when people still live in the area and there are too many of them to relocate."

"So will it be safe?" Aria asked with a frown.

No one answered right away.

"It will be fine," Rathen eventually replied, offering her a smile.

Her face lit up and she gave him a single, reassured nod.

"Anyway," Anthis continued in an almost sing-song voice as Aria giggled, "although the elven district will be quiet, it would still be best if we weren't seen going in at all. There's a back gate, barely manned - we can use that."

"You've been there before, I take it?"

"Yes, Inquisitor, but I was there on other research so I didn't hang around for long. Which brings me to what I expect to find: information. Everything I already have converges at Mokhan, but it isn't enough, it just suggests that someone either had an idea or made something in the place, but that doesn't mean that whatever it's referring to will be kept there."

"'Whatever it's referring to'?!"

"Don't go getting the wrong idea, Rathen," Anthis sighed mildly. "You said yourself that this is guesswork, but you'll just have to trust my expertise on the matter. And anyway, I know what I'm looking for; this won't be like walking into a library and having to filter through every single book - for starters it won't be so organised. But I know where to find it."

"Is it *possible* that it will be there, though?" Aria asked, her voice a mixture of hope and disappointment. "At all?"

"Well," Anthis replied slowly, "I suppose there *is* a small *sliver* of a chance, but I find it unlikely." He cast her a sideways smile. "And it would be a bit boring if it was that easy, wouldn't it?"

Aria nodded vigorously, grinning. "Over too soon," she agreed.

"But we *will* find it," he assured the others, neither of whom seemed to share in their enthusiasm for the hunt, "and every piece of information we find will bring us one step closer."

Rathen shifted doubtfully in the saddle, but he did his best to feel the hope the others shared in. After all, if they didn't find it, it would all be resting on his heavy shoulders.

The silence shortly returned, and the clop of the horses' hooves became deafening. Rathen wouldn't usually have noticed nor cared, but this time its weight only seemed to add to his grim mood. Fortunately he didn't have to think on how to break it, as Anthis began nattering about the history of their destination, providing a one-sided conversation with little need for additional input to keep it going. But even so, Aria asked lots of questions, and Rathen found himself quite unsurprised by her interest. She was astounded by the world presently around her, so why not the past? After all, stories of people who once were must have seemed to her like fairy tales.

Salus drummed his fingers on his knee as the carriage bumped leisurely along the uneven road. He stared impatiently out of the window, his face creased in intense thought, and seemed to have forgotten Teagan's presence in the opposite seat. He didn't react to the dry and monotonous rustle of unrolled parchments, nor the weight of the silence in which his subordinate read them, and his eyes didn't graze him for a moment to try to discern their contents from his expression. It would have been futile anyway; portians, never gave their thoughts away so easily.

"They're marching, aren't they?"

Teagan looked up from a report scrawled onto an unreasonably small strip of paper, and if he was startled, he didn't show it. Salus hadn't moved. His chin remained in his hand and his eyes fixed, unseeing, to the hills rolling by in the distance. "They are."

"They'll lose through exhaustion," Salus mumbled critically. "I can't believe Jalund doesn't see that, it's *screamingly* obvious... Mm. Perhaps it's a king-thing. His arrogance has blinded him." He puffed with resignation and finally sat back in his seat, dragging himself away from tiresome thoughts and his blue eyes away from the window. "What of us?"

"The detachments at the western border have begun forming a defence, but it's too soon to tell where Skilan will launch their attack from, so they're not setting permanent posts just yet. They need more information."

Salus merely nodded.

"The rest of the military is waiting for the order to advance, which will certainly follow our report. Otherwise, the military is prepared, and General Moore has drawn up a number of strategies for various scenarios, all of which have the Crown's approval."

He nodded again. "And the Order?"

"They're equally prepared to move to defend the military against foreign mages and counter any magical attacks. They've been included in a few of Moore's plans, but for the most part, he seems to be allowing Sivaan Rosh the room to form his own responses."

Salus clicked his tongue. "I don't like that."

"He has a better idea of his mages' capabilities than the General does, as well as that of the opposition," Teagan reminded him. "But I admit that it gives the Order too much freedom."

"And freedom is the *last* thing the mages should be given." Salus shook his head and growled, his eyes drawn back at the world outside. "Magic," he all but spat. "The world would be better off without it. And these reports of new mages are alarming - I thought magic was supposed to surface no later than the age of eighteen, and now there are people at twice that suddenly discovering that they possess it!"

"It is possible for magic to surface at a later or earlier age," Teagan reminded him with the same absence of emotion, "but for six such cases to occur within a month, it is a highly unlikely situation."

"As well as suspicious. And reports of strange activity near elven ruins keep coming in, and despite denying any involvement, the Order is moving too quickly and in very small numbers in response to it - or to *cause* it." He shook his head again, the curl of his lip worsening. "It's *all* suspicious, but they're too damned good at covering their tracks for us to get any information by our usual measures, and whenever we catch one of the damned things the Order takes custody almost immediately and we hear nothing more of it!"

"You've said this before."

"And yet nothing has changed because no one who can do anything about it, like the Crown, does so!"

Teagan stared at him. "What are you suggesting?"

His fingers resumed their irritated drumming, his jaw convulsed, and he gripped the changing scenery beyond the window with another burning, consuming scowl. But his heat abated a moment later with a sigh, and he shook his head in defeat. "Nothing. I simply can't believe that the king would be in on this. Whatever it is, it's all mage. We just need to find one and *keep* one."

"That's easier said than done with the Order keeping better tabs on their people than we can."

"Which is *also* suspicious!" Salus leaned his head against the carriage's plush wall in further thought, biting back a curse as it struck the edge of its gilded metal frame. "Increase surveillance on the Order," he said eventually, "and keep a closer eye on previously-detained mages in particular. It's all we can do at present, for whatever little good it might do us, at least until we have what we need to stop whatever it is they're up to."

"What of the magic-users in the Arana?"

"Keep them at their posts. Their magic may not be as strong as that of the Order, thank goodness, but they have a better understanding of what they're seeing than the rest of us - and are we any closer to finding this blasted artefact?" Teagan shook his head, as Salus expected. "Ugh. And we still haven't located Karth..." His eyes dragged themselves heavily back to the window as the carriage finally rolled to a stop, and he brushed down his uncomfortably regal attire. "Well, let's hope Drassa lives up to his reputation instead."

The carriage door swung open from outside, and as Salus stepped out onto the cobbled road in a suit as fine as any noble's, his grim expression shifted seamlessly to one of dignified importance and his bearing straightened to match. Teagan followed in the similarly elegant vestments of a personal aide, and two others joined them outside, flanking them at two paces with the stoic, hawk-like eyes of accomplished bodyguards. The transition of attitude that each undertook was so effortless, so well-practised that no one would ever suspect that the four were anything other than what they appeared to be.

Teagan took the lead down a short garden path and knocked commandingly upon the door at its end. It was not a large building, though it was a grander house than that of any common man, and the entourage undoubtedly appeared out of place to any onlookers. But theirs was not a social call, and the owner's profession surely attracted the occasional well-to-do stranger.

No answer came, so Teagan knocked again just as firmly, while Salus displayed the same touch of impatience any nobleman would who was kept waiting by someone inferior, and after a third attempt, the call was finally heeded. A middle-aged man appeared in the doorway, looking quite put out, and was already demanding what his visitors wanted before he'd even taken a look at them. He hesitated only when the glint of gold snatched his eye, and fell abruptly silent when he noted the finery and official bearing each of them held. He dropped into a deep and apologetic bow, his thinning hair slipping forwards.

"Presenting the Lord Baymont of Adin," Teagan announced in a well-seasoned tone, a fraction louder than necessary yet no quieter than any other such aide would, and stepped to one side so that his master may be looked upon in his deserved glory. "He has travelled for seven days and nights to reach your respected presence, so you may oblige him with your time and hear his proposition."

Such a formal introduction pushed the balding man even lower. "My Lord Baymont, it is an absolute *pleasure*," he gushed. "I did receive your message through the historical society's channels, I apologise for my manners - please do come inside and out of this dreadful wind."

The Lord Baymont inclined his head and strode in through the door as his host stepped obediently aside, leaving behind the gentle breeze that had barely tousled his neatly combed hair. His guards followed closely, and his personal attendant after them, and as he took a seat in the finest chair the sitting room had to offer, they took up rigid positions on either side of him, their eyes alert even as they scanned the empty room, while his attendant waited to one side, out of the way and quietly forgotten until his service was next needed.

"My Lord Baymont, allow me to introduce myself personally," the man said as he hurried in after them and quickly set about tidying up, tossing cushions around and moving books out of sight so as not to offend his guest by his clutter, but the nobleman raised his hand for silence.

"I don't need another introduction, Mister Drassa," he said with barely a smile, his expression kept taught and superior in a manner that appeared quite natural. "I know well who you are; I would not have sought you out if I didn't."

Drassa bowed low once again. "Please, My Lord, call me Tem. And may I say that it is a great honour to be sought out by one of such high standing, such as yourself." He straightened slowly and looked at him with anxious eyes. "May I find you anything to drink? To eat?"

"No, thank you."

"Then, may I ask what has brought you to me? Forgive me, but your message was a little vague..."

"Your skill, of course," he replied with a fleeting upward twitch of his lips that couldn't quite be called a smile. "I require your expertise."

Tem's thick, grey eyebrows rose in mild surprise. "You require research, My Lord?"

"More specifically, I require an item."

Now they dropped in confusion, but before he could give it voice, the false nobleman continued.

"There is mention of an old elven relic that is said to be able to suppress the magic of another caster - I believe you have put some work into the subject over the past few years."

His eyebrows rose once again, and now his eyes came alive with excitement. "Goodness, My Lord, yes I have! An item that can suppress the magic of humans - created by the elves to keep--"

Lord Baymont raised his hand again. "Yes, that. I would like you to recover it - you will be paid for your time, of course."

The historian grinned as he did his best to ignore the jewels that decorated the nobleman's rich fingers. "Of course! It will be an easy matter! There is plenty of mention of such an object, and I've uncovered much through other projects as well as some leads others have abandoned. In fact, I believe the items to be quite numerous - a number of elven households supposedly possessed them - so I'm certain a few have already been uncovered by individuals who have little idea of what they truly are! I shouldn't even need to travel to uncover what few details I still require, I can just call in a few favours with some friends and colleagues, and once I know precisely what we're looking for, I can reach out to collectors - of course," he stalled suddenly as doubt replaced his excitement, "convincing an elven collector to part with even an *insignificant* piece will be expensive, even if they aren't informed of its nature..."

"I am willing to pay whatever is asked," the nobleman replied firmly, and Salus kept conscious control over the hope he felt rising within him at the historian's own enthusiasm. Clearly some things took a truly expert eye, as his own people - people finely trained in gathering information, among other things - had had little luck uncovering anything promising on this subject.

Tem nodded vigorously, and though he tried reining in his own excitement, he was far from as successful. "May I ask," he began carefully, the brightness of his eyes unchanging, "for what reason do you wish to find such a specific relic?"

Lord Baymont's expression suddenly softened. The tight line of his lips turned upwards, curving into an affectionate smile, and though he appeared to fight it initially to maintain his regal bearing, he soon gave in. "My grandmother, may she rest in peace. History was a passion of hers - she was one of the first to decipher the mention of such a relic. She always spoke of its significance to elven culture, that its creation was a turning point for them and their society, as unfortunate as it was for us humans, and she deeply wished to find it, but...but she fell ill and was unable to maintain her search." The smile faded as his eyes dimmed in thought. "Her hunt ended before it could truly begin, and for the last five years of her life she obsessed over it. She uncovered what she could from her sickbed, but the torment of being able-minded enough to continue the theoretical work and research, yet broken-bodied and unable to physically leave, to search for it herself or uncover more crucial information still locked away in old ruins...I believe that was what truly killed her."

His eyes, still distant, dropped to his hands as he fiddled with what seemed the oldest and least impressive ring from the array across his fingers. Tem watched his bearing weaken, sadness lining his own ageing face, and he found that even the attendant displayed some degree of grief when he glanced up at him, while the guards remained professionally unaffected.

"I wish," Lord Baymont continued as he straightened and, with some effort, forced the sorrow from his face, though it lingered in his blue eyes, "to recover the artefact so that her torment may not be for nothing. I struggle already to bear the thought that the artefact being out of her reach was what drove her to the grave, and though I do not believe for a moment that its discovery will undo her suffering, I hope that it will at least soothe her spirit."

The historian nodded in understanding, and he smiled sadly. "I understand completely, My Lord."

"I am glad. It is hard to speak of; I do not wish to do so again." The nobleman rose to his feet, his finery falling about him perfectly once again, draping as though he was made for it as equally as it for him, and the two guards immediately stepped forwards to attention. "Needless to say that anything you need to complete this task, you shall receive, be it money or resources," he continued, apparently unaware of the sudden movements of his entourage, nor the brief panic they evoked in the historian. "I am also more than happy to provide you with my grandmother's findings, though I don't know how much good they would be to you. You've undoubtedly uncovered a great deal more than she managed to..."

"I thank you, My Lord. I would be honoured to receive any and all help from your esteemed grandmother, may she rest in peace, and I dare say that putting her work to direct use and bringing it to fruition would give her spirit greater cause to settle."

Lord Baymont inclined his head and graced him with an appreciative smile, then gestured to his attendant who stepped forwards and offered their host a folder. "This is everything. I hope it will be of use - but please be careful with it. Even these papers have great sentimental value to me." He moved towards the door, the guards and attendant following him in perfect time, as though they'd had years of practice, while Tem stepped hurriedly after them. "Though I deem this of extremely high priority, I am nonetheless a very busy man and as such I may well be difficult to reach from time to time. As such, I must ask that you report your progress to a representative of mine in town. His name is Daryl Vakh. You can find him in the Harpy's Nest tavern near the town centre on Tuesday evenings. He'll be waiting for you."

Tem quickly rushed the last step ahead of them and opened the front door, bowing just as clumsily. "Thank you, My Lord, I shall most certainly report every week."

"Thank you, Mister Drassa, I deeply appreciate your help - it means a *great* deal to myself and my family." He glanced towards his attendant and gave the slightest nod of his head, and without waiting for any final questions, offering any further details or the exchange of farewells, he stepped outside and made his way back up the path towards the waiting carriage.

Eyes flashing in panic and his tongue burning with one last question, Tem quickly started after them, but his path was immediately blocked by the attendant. A small pouch of coins dropped into his hand. "You will be paid with every report," he informed him, "and a greater sum when your task produces results. Consider this an incentive." The attendant then inclined his head and, without waiting for any thanks or query as to the weekly amount the historian could expect, he turned on his heel and climbed into the carriage with the same dismissive attitude as his master.

Tem couldn't help peering inside, and as the perfect, shining gold within caught the midday sun, a grin swept across his face. He turned back through the door and immediately set to work.

"You should rest," Teagan said as they stepped back into the Arana's grounds some hours later, but evening had barely set in, and the suggestion had lost its impact after being repeated for the umpteenth time.

"I'm fine," Salus sighed roughly, rolling his eyes while stifling another yawn as discreetly as he could. He was unsuccessful.

"You aren't. Twice this afternoon your true emotions showed themselves."

Yes, Salus was well aware. His eyes had flashed with hope, and he'd had to truly force sadness into them when speaking of Lord Baymont's poor, deceased grandmother. Tem had been completely unaware, of course, but it was shoddy work nevertheless. "Look," he replied, brushing it off, "I've not had the chance. I had a proper sleep about four nights ago, maybe five, but since then all I've had is one or two hours of dead sleep and the rest has been fitful. If I'm honest, I think that did more damage than if I'd just stayed awake."

"Even so, you didn't go to your quarters at all last night."

Salus blinked and looked back at him in surprise as they stepped into the atrium. away from the cold, spring drizzle. "You're spying on me?"

"No; your office light was never extinguished."

He groaned in annoyance, but as he looked away to dismiss the point, his gaze fell upon a brown haired woman walking in their direction. She didn't look at him, as no one ever did, but he was certain he'd noticed her before. He gave it little conscious thought as he looked back to Teagan to protest, but his irritation had subdued despite a touch of tension passing throughout his body, and he found himself oddly aware of the fact that she had just brushed inches by his shoulder.

Teagan noticed his subtle change. "Keliceran?"

"I'll rest tonight," Salus sighed, his attention falling back on his favoured, the moment slipping as suddenly from his mind as it had begun, "but I appreciate your concern - or whatever it is. In the mean time, inform the general of Skilan's movements, and send a moth to 'Daryl' to let him know that Drassa has accepted - and have the necessary funds unlocked in his name while you're at it. We've got our historian, now we just have to hope he can get somewhere before the mages get too far ahead of us. And as for the war...well, I'll speak with Malson and do what I can to convince the king to let us try to obliterate the matter, but I think it's already a little too far out of our hands. Dismissed."

With a nod of acceptance, the portian operative turned and left to carry out his orders, leaving Salus to continue to his office, dropping his boxed nobleman costume with all the others along the way. As always, he had plenty more to do that evening before he could dare trying to sleep, and while he wasn't keen to attempt it for fear of what an awful night he may have, he begrudgingly knew that Teagan was right to pester him. One of his best operatives he might be, but he was also Salus's second in command and the one who dealt with most of his subordinates on his behalf. It was part of his job to ensure the keliceran was at his best, and there was little better than a portian agent to provide the kind of unbiased counsel and occasional prod Salus needed to stay on top of his job. After all, it was far from an easy one, and its stresses seemed to have been hitting much harder and faster as of late.

But he would handle them, with or without a good night's rest. Because that was his job.

Chapter 8

Dawn had broken less than an hour ago, and the early sun was just beginning to weave its way between the surrounding trees, casting long, cool shadows across the camp. Rathen had been awake for only a few minutes, making a very welcome change, and for the first time in almost two weeks, he wasn't skittish with the need to leap out from beneath his blankets and escape beyond the latest town's walls. Instead he lay content on his bedroll, staring up at the underside of the oak tree that had sheltered them through their first night in the hinterlands, his nerves as calm as if he was waking in his own bed.

The nearest settlement was a day behind them, marking their abandonment of the roads, and ahead lay the promise of several days of peace and little chance of contact with people. They'd reached such wonderful seclusion three days sooner than expected thanks to roads reopening as the soldiers acted on new orders, and Rathen had breathed a sigh of relief the moment the clop of his horse's hooves turned to muffled thumps across the grass.

Roused by the warmth of the sun as it found them, the others shortly rose, and though the hard and uneven ground had managed to impede their night's comfort, as the slowly rising sun began glinting off of the drops of rain the leaves had caught around them, no one saw fit to complain. The sheet of cloud that had shadowed them since leaving Kora had finally moved off, leaving nothing but blue sky to peek through the canopy.

The still air was broken only by birdsong and Anthis's own soft, cheerful whistling as he set about preparing breakfast. His incessant chirpiness had barely discoloured, but Rathen suspected he was probably quite accustomed to sleeping in the wilderness while exploring isolated ruins, and after a few minutes, Garon, too, appeared unaffected, though he probably took it in his stride just as he did everything else. Aria was the only one still under the tug of sleep, but when Rathen discovered her damp clothes strewn beside the fire, he understood why. She'd stayed up and run off into the rain.

"But it smelled so *nice*," she explained as he dried her clothes with a twist of his fingers, distinctly unruffled by the preceding scolding. "Besides, I didn't go far, just to the edge of the big tree. There were birds flitting about in it, like they were dancing. I just wanted to watch them."

"You should have woken me first."

"Not when you were finally sleeping so well." His eyebrows rose at her sudden objection as he straightened her pinafore, and the twenty-year ageing of her voice. "You've tossed and turned every night so far, but last night was the *first* time you seemed at peace since we left home."

"That's not a good enough reason, Aria."

"It's a *very* good reason."

He sighed in silent agreement even as he pushed aside his shame at the fact. He couldn't afford to be so useless a father when they were out in the open world like this, especially with a magically-affected ruin so close by.

But even so, he gave her a very stern look, and she finally shifted under his gaze, her own disapproval melting away. "Next time, Arenaria," he told her firmly, "you either wake me, or you go back to sleep. Understood?"

She sighed in defeat and nodded her head. "Fine."

"Good." He combed his fingers quickly through her fair curls, untangling the rain-teased knots, then they joined the others at the fire for breakfast.

The atmosphere was far from as dense as it had been in the past; the previous five days of travel had allowed them to adjust to one another, and though Rathen and Garon continued to keep out of conversations for the most part, Aria and Anthis were lively enough to keep the whole group's spirits up by themselves. Silences became mercifully less frequent, if no less uncomfortable.

And so, as one such silence crept upon them a few hours later, Anthis fidgeted in his saddle. Rathen was staring off into the trees, his eyes seeing for miles and his mind just as distant, while Garon maintained the lead, concentrating on their route through the woods to avoid getting turned around. This was little different to usual, except that Aria had fallen asleep, so there was no one to ask abrupt questions nor to be kept entertained.

He sighed to himself and his eyes fell upon the mage. They narrowed thoughtfully as he revised the past two weeks, and finally decided that his curiosity needed satisfying.

"So, Rathen," Anthis began casually, pretending not to notice that he'd startled him, "I was wondering about your connection to the Order."

Rathen didn't turn to look at him. "What about it?" He was quite uninterested in having such a conversation, but he also found himself too relaxed to want to offend him by rudely brushing him off. So he settled for a flat and unfriendly tone that did nothing to discourage him.

"What do you do? You're a soldier, you said?"

"I was, a while ago."

"Why did you leave it?"

Rathen noticed Garon turn his head ever so slightly in interest of how he would answer, but he merely shrugged. "I had a change of heart."

"Really?" A touch of surprise coloured Anthis's voice. "What happened?"

"I...found I didn't fit the position anymore." His brow lowered as he stared ahead. "It was mutually decided that I step down."

"I see... And did you stay with the Order after that?"

His brow dropped further as he cast him a suspicious glance, but the historian missed it as he looked down at a small ditch his horse had stepped in and out of. It turned then onto Garon, but he seemed intently fixed to the path, suddenly no longer listening. Rathen sighed to himself. Evidently Anthis had been told something, otherwise he would never have had the thought to ask such a question. And Rathen found himself angered by the inquisitor's impertinence. He straightened in his saddle. "No."

"Oh... I...didn't know that was allowed..."

Rathen's eyes narrowed at his tactful tone. "Not all mages are part of the Order."

This time the surprise on the young man's face was genuine, and, to his satisfaction, even Garon twitched. "There are a few who use their magic for the good of the country in other ways. You just don't hear about them."

"I-I didn't know that," Anthis said more animately than he had his careful questioning. "Is *that* allowed?"

Rathen nodded, unaware of the darkening of his own expression or the brooding in his eyes. "The Crown is aware of it, though the Order disapproves. It's kept out of public knowledge."

"...And are you one of them?"

"No."

"...Oh..." Anthis's wary eyes flicked towards Garon, but he, as ever, kept himself out of the matter, and as he looked back to the mage he found himself more unsettled in his presence than he had when they'd first met. No further questions seemed willing to leave his tongue. Whatever more he thought he wanted to know, he decided that he probably didn't.

"What about you?"

Anthis's startled eyebrows rose further. "Me?"

"You're in the mood for sharing," Rathen replied, though not unkindly as Aria began to stir, "so share. Why do you travel so much? From what I hear, you've been all over."

"Uh, yes." He recovered from the unexpected interest, as meagre and stilted as it was. "Well, field research - and, to be honest, I've never liked to keep still."

"Why do you do so much field research? I thought most historians locked themselves in libraries or exchanged notes in taverns and relied on other, bolder people to carry out that sort of thing for them."

Anthis smiled warmly. "I thrive on it," he admitted. "I want to see things for myself, find things - learn as first-hand as I can. There's little excitement in libraries or like-minded meetings in familiar surroundings."

"I suppose I can understand that - it must get expensive, though."

"It does," he hesitated, "but I'm given what I need on commission."

"And that covers everything, does it?"

Anthis looked away. "It covers enough."

Rathen frowned at his sudden evasiveness. His voice was still kind, but there was an abruptness to it that was out of place - one, he realised, he would have missed had they only just met - and another conversation was brought to a sudden end. Though it had annoyingly caught his interest, he let the matter lie. Rathen had his own secrets; Anthis was entitled to his own. He wasn't about to pry.

"I like learning," Aria half-sang, half- yawned, "but I learn at home."

"Oh?" Anthis asked, suddenly unclamming as his cheer returned, and Rathen found himself oddly pleased for the smile he gave her, as well as the attention. "Have you learned anything interesting?"

"Well, I learned to read," she began, raising her fingers and counting things off as she thought of them, "I learned to make eggs, I learned to pull carrots and dig for 'tatoes, I learned to ride a goat - they can climb *really* high - I learned to whi--"

The sudden whinny of Garon's horse interrupted her as he pulled it to a short stop. Rathen's snorted in protest as he jerked the reins a second later to avoid trotting into him, but he raised his hand for silence before Rathen could bite off a curse. The inquisitor looked around, slowly and carefully, his grey eyes sharp as he strained his ears to listen into the depths of the forest, and Rathen and Anthis equally raised their guard as they moved up quietly beside him, scanning for whatever had put him on alert. But they were met by silence, broken only by the song of a few nearby birds. It took a long moment for any of them to ease in their saddles.

"What was it?" Rathen asked as Aria continued peering about, her recital forgotten, and Garon pointed towards the roots of a tree ahead of them.

"Ditchlings."

They followed the inquisitor's finger and promptly spotted the small footprint stamped in the mud amongst the tangle of the tree base.

"There's only one print," Anthis noted warily, "and it could be a child's."

Rathen shook his head. "It's not a child's."

"Do you think it's a trap?"

"No." He looked to Garon, who stared at it a moment longer before agreeing. "It's too close to the tree, and look: the bush beside it has been snapped. It was an accident, and it doesn't look too recent. But..."

"Ditchlings don't roam," Garon finished. "For there to be a single footprint, there will be a sett nearby. We need to be away from here."

"What are ditchlings?" Aria asked, her voice a mixture of concern and interest as she looked about to spot one.

"Monsters. Creatures that look like children with a reputation for being more than just a nuisance on their own. In groups they're a real menace. We'd do well not to run into them."

Aria frowned at the concern on her father's face. "But they're *not* children?" She asked. "Because they *sound* like children..."

"They're wild and they're dangerous," Garon stated firmly before Rathen could answer with more delicacy, "with a reputation for kidnapping and 'changing' children, stealing anything they can get their hands on, and attacking lone travellers in groups whenever they get the chance. Your father's right: we don't want to risk crossing their path."

Rathen sighed and shook his head as Aria's eyes widened in fear, and even Anthis frowned at the inquisitor's thoughtless response - he had yet to display much finesse when dealing with her.

"Now, from what I can tell from the direction of the print and the damage to the trees, this one was heading west. Ditchlings don't typically move like this close to their homes, so they were likely out hunting for something."

Anthis squinted into the dark forest. "I can't see the damage, where is it?"

"What do we do?"

Garon gestured east. "We take a detour. The forest is denser to the west, so that's where they'll have made their home. If we skirt around through the thinner parts of the woods we can avoid them. It will add a few hours onto the journey, but it would be for the best."

"Daddy, I'm scared."

"We'll be all right," he assured her softly, wrapping an arm around her to usher the fear from her voice, "I'm here."

"You'll be fine," Anthis agreed. "Not even Garon would let anything happen to you."

"I know he wouldn't," she said, though her voice was still small, "he's a good person, too."

Garon ignored her and turned his horse towards a new heading. "Let's move."

The group remained silent as they focused on putting distance between themselves and the single track, but after ten minutes, even as the others began to relax and the trees began to thin, Aria hadn't remotely eased. Anthis was as aware of it as Rathen, but her father seemed more interested in keeping her safe than calm as he constantly scanned the forest, and it didn't take long for her big and fearful eyes to weaken the historian.

"What--"

"Why do you like elves so much?"

Anthis blinked in surprise as she snapped towards him and posed her sudden question, interrupting his attempt to revive the last conversation. But as it served the same purpose of taking her mind off of the forest, he answered: "I grew up near ruins. I used to climb on them with my friends, but I never gave them much thought. I must have been just a little bit older than you when the word 'ruin' really dawned on me; before then I'd just assumed someone had built them to look that way, but I asked my parents about it and they told me that, thousands of years ago, they looked as tidy as my own house did."

Aria's jaw dropped. "A *thousand?*" She looked around to her distracted father. "Daddy, how old are you?"

"Not a thousand."

She spun back to Anthis, amazement flaming in her eyes and searing away her distress. "Then it must have been a *really* long time ago!"

"It was," he grinned once his laughter subsided, "and it fascinated me. I wanted to know more, but when my parents exhausted their knowledge of it, I struck out to discover more on my own."

"But why elves? Why not people?"

"Because the elves aren't around any more."

She cocked her head and frowned. "Where did they go? Did they all die?"

He considered her for a long moment as he decided how to answer, but his choice was made for him when he recognised the potency of the interest in her eyes. He smiled. "No one knows."

Her expression snapped into a frown as her confusion and intrigue swelled, just as he hoped it would. "How can no one know?"

"Because the elves were here one day, gone the next."

"It can't be that simple," Rathen mumbled through his study of the forest, but the historian's smile only grew.

"And yet, that's what happened. There were no remains - the only ones that have ever been found are those that were formally buried or entombed by other elves - and while human servants wouldn't have been privy to direct information, war is a hard thing to hide and they *would* have been aware of it. There were tensions between nations, as there always have been and always will be, but there was no hint of a war, no sudden attack, nor any survivors from any such thing. And nothing was gathered to be taken to another land, either - homes are still being discovered full of belongings even now." Against possibility, Anthis's smile had broadened even further in endless fascination. "They really do seem to have just *disappeared*."

Despite Rathen's increasingly sceptical frown, he found himself unwilling to challenge him, or try to devalue his excitement. Everything the learned young man had just said was true; the very foundations of the mystery that fuelled so many of his colleagues, and one that perplexed even Rathen enough to want an answer, even if he only spared it the briefest of thoughts while his mind drifted towards sleep. Now, however, he regarded Anthis curiously. "What's *your* theory?"

"My theory? The Craitic legend. Zikhon got to them. Slipped past Vastal and destroyed them all, just like the legends say, and Vastal swooped in to save the rest of us just in the nick of time." He grinned. "After all, gods destroying them is just as unlikely as all the other ideas floating around, but by far the most colourful. Living among the stars comes a close second, but there's simply no way they would have changed their appearance to live among humans, given their disdain for them."

"What about packing up the bare essentials and just leaving?" Rathen suggested. "Magic originated with the elves; they could easily have used it to disappear overnight, and to conceal their new home. Perhaps they hated humans enough to just drop everything and get away from us once and for all."

"And yet there's no mention of such a thing. No plans or concerns in journals - nothing at all. Businesses and possessions were abandoned, social plans were half-made, and every single elf vanished. A world-wide change of heart is just as unlikely as divine intervention." His grin suddenly broadened again. "And that's why it's such a fascinating mystery! But one I doubt will ever be answered. That's why I like the idea of gods destroying them - that the God of Death finally overpowered the God of Life in an epic struggle and managed to lay waste to Her creations: because it could never be proven anyway. I find it easier to live with."

"Why can't you find out?"

"Rathen."

The mage looked towards the inquisitor as Aria chimed in with more questions. He'd kept his voice low enough that the others wouldn't hear; rather than ride up beside him, the mage simply nodded. "I feel it," he murmured as his gaze sharpened and movements softened, searching subtly through the forest for the eyes they could feel upon them, "but we're not under any magic yet."

"If the elves were still alive, would you still want to know so much about them?" Aria asked, oblivious to the concerns exchanged over her head.

"No," Anthis admitted with a smile, "I probably wouldn't."

"Hmmm... Daddy says that sometimes I don't appreciate something until I don't have it anymore. Maybe it's the same thing."

"Maybe."

Aria leaned forwards in the saddle. "Do you like to learn, Mister Inquis'tor?"

"When it's relevant," he replied flatly.

"I can teach you something," she offered. "It's a song."

"I'm fine, thank you."

The little girl pouted. "But it's about a goat."

"No--"

"*We* wanna hear it."

A clamour of curses and startled neighs broke out as all around them came dozens of sudden footfalls and only the slightest rustle of leaves. Hooves clattered over embedded rocks as they hastened their horses into a tight group over Garon's barked orders, and Aria's short, sharp scream pierced the air as she spun around in the saddle. Within only a moment of the rough voice's interruption, almost twenty pale children had sprung out and surrounded them, many having dropped from the treetops. They were markedly wild; their hair tangled and skin caked in dirt, clad in roughly-stitched skins, though a few wore dirty shirts or trousers stolen from washing lines, and every one of them was armed, some with slingshots, others sharpened sticks, but none to be taken lightly.

But despite his alarm, Rathen quickly noticed that not one of the ditchlings had readied those weapons. Their spears stood beside them, rock-slingers held limp, and they stared closely back at them with oversized eyes that weren't quite silver, nor quite green, absorbing every detail with a critical harshness. Then they each fixed upon Aria.

He barred a protective arm across her, and though she clung onto it, she must also have noticed their passive manner, for she simply frowned back at them with caution.

The inquisitor straightened in his saddle and eyed their ambushers carefully. "Let us go," he began, trying to decide which of the inhuman children might be the leader, "and we'll leave you alone. We have no business with you, and nothing you want."

The creature who wore the tidiest shirt - or the least distressed - turned its sharp orbs onto him and cocked its matted head. The gaze of the others shortly followed. "Why?" It asked, its voice curious but harsh, as though manners and proper speech were completely alien concepts. "What're you doing?"

"That is none of your business."

"Never said it was," it replied, its impish eyes never leaving him, just as none of the others' did. "Still wanna know, though."

Aria looked up at her father. The lines in his face were deep and stern, and his unblinking eyes were vigilant, but they only gave her pause for a moment. "It *might* be their business," she said thoughtfully, but she was spared only the briefest frown of confusion before his attention snapped back to their apparent captors.

Then, upon an unknown cue, all silver-green eyes shifted suddenly away from Garon and turned onto Rathen instead. He became rigid in his saddle beneath their abrupt attention, but he didn't otherwise react - though he ensured his right hand was empty of the reins, should he need it.

"Is it you?" The child-thing asked him with a great degree of suspicion.

"Is it me, what?"

"All the hocus pocus," it replied, twisting its slender white fingers ridiculously in demonstration. "It's doing something to the Tree. We want you to stop it. Now."

"That's why you've come out, isn't it?" Anthis asked carefully, though only the shirted ditchling looked back to him. "We wouldn't have seen you for even a moment if you were going to target us. You would have followed us, waited for us to get distracted then taken what you wanted - no one ever knows a ditchling was there until they've already gone."

It grunted and exaggeratedly rolled its giant eyes, and now the group's attention fell upon him instead, and they all seemed to share the same insult and ego. "We're *not* 'ditchlings'," it drawled, "we are *Arkhamas*."

Anthis restrained his amusement from touching his lips. "'Lords of Mischief'. How is that any better?"

"'Cause it's our name," it pointed out, then grinned suddenly, revealing chipped teeth, "and it's the truth."

"What's going on?" Rathen asked, though he regretted speaking when all eyes snatched back to him.

"'Arkh' is elven for 'mischief'," Anthis replied quietly, "and '-amas' means 'superior'."

"It was them elves what started calling us 'ditchlings'," it grumbled, folding its arms across its narrow chest as if having one of Aria's sulky turns. "They used to show us respect, but they turned away from us just like they did everything else when they reckoned they were 'too good' for us, and called us that stupid name instead. What does it matter if we play in the mud?! It ain't no harm!" It looked abruptly back to Rathen and jabbed a dirty finger towards him. "And you never answered our question."

"I'm not doing *anything*."

The creature's shoulders suddenly dropped in a huff. "It's only a question!" It complained. "It's not hard! Just answer it!"

"I..." Rathen frowned. "No, I meant I'm not responsible for the magic..."

"Where is this tree?" Anthis asked slowly, dismounting cautiously despite Garon's order, and Rathen shortly followed, sensing the same lack of threat though he kept his guard all the same, and remained close to Aria's side.

"If we tell you, you might go and make it worse."

"How could we make it worse?"

"'Cause you might be lying." Its gaze gripped the mage with open suspicion. "I can't see your head's insides. If we tell you, and it's you what's done it, then you could make it worse. And then we'll *all* be in trouble."

Anthis glanced towards Rathen who looked back with the same brush of concern, and they both came to the same conclusion. "You'll just have to trust us," Rathen replied. "We're out here to try to put a stop to it."

It shook its head again. "Could still be lying."

"You're not very trusting."

"We can't see your head's insides."

"You said that before."

"'Cause it's still true."

"They're telling the truth."

All eyes, including those of the adults, shifted onto Aria as she dangled from the horse. Rathen caught her as she let go, but rather than set her feet on the ground, he lifted her back into the saddle.

"Daddy, let me down," she ordered him quite firmly.

"You're safer up there."

"Do you promise?" The ditchlings' collective eyes remained glued upon her, but their distrust had been replaced by doubt, as though they were still disinclined to believe but at least willing to listen to her, if not to the others.

She sat taller in the saddle, as she'd seen Garon do, and gave them a single, certain nod before slipping back down with Rathen's reluctant help.

The lead ditchling stared at her closely. "What's your name?"

"Aria."

"I'm Nug." He stepped away from the circle of ditchlings and approached her. Anthis shuffled closer and Garon finally dismounted, his hand gripping his sword hilt, but Aria didn't shrink back. Nug stopped in front of her, and as she smiled at his earthy scent - he smelled like home - he stared studiously into her eyes. "I can't see inside your head," he began slowly, "but I can see your eyes. And that's the next best thing where hoomans are concerned." He gave her a nod, and the surrounding circle of wild children finally moved, shifting their weight with ease as if they'd all been holding their breath since they'd gathered. "We believe you. We'll take you to the Tree - but *only* you."

"Absolutely not," Rathen growled, snatching her back towards him.

"What's wrong?" Nug frowned, then rolled his eyes again. "Ohhh, it's them rumours, ain't it? Well, we don't take kids like you think. Some live with us sometimes, yeah, but only 'cause they wanted to. We don't turn 'em away if they're lonely or lost, but we also don't *make* 'em lonely or lost." His eyes narrowed fiercely at the mage. "It's a load of horse dung you folks made up about us 'cause we're not like you."

"Stop it," Aria demanded, stomping her way between Nug and her father just as he inhaled to respond, "*both* of you. Now, Nug, I'm sorry, but either they come with me, or none of us go at all."

"Why?"

"Because there's no use just *me* seeing it, I won't know what to do. They're the only ones that can help it." She offered him a reassuring smile, which he duly scrutinised. "Trust me, they won't make it worse."

His silver-green eyes flicked to Rathen, Anthis and Garon in turn. "We don't trust *them*...but..."

"But you have no choice."

Nug hung his head in defeat, and a few of the ditchlings smiled. "*Fiiine*," he groaned as he looked back up to her, "but you have to make sure they don't cause any trouble."

"They won't," she promised with a grin, "cross my heart."

"This don't mean we trust you, mind - we won't take you there for nothing."

"What do you want?" Anthis asked carefully.

"Dunno," Nug shrugged, then turned around and beckoned them to follow as he and the others began disappearing into the trees.

The three adults glanced at each other in bewilderment, and after Aria had turned and ordered them with a look to do the same, they took their horse's reins and trekked obediently behind her, Rathen keeping so close he almost stepped on her heels.

Anthis lowered his voice to a whisper. "It's funny, I thought we were moving *away* from their territory."

"Well it seems they were looking for us," Garon replied just as quietly, ignoring his condescension. "You said yourself that if they'd wanted anything from us, we would never have known they were here - and at least we've discovered why people feel like they're being watched."

"If they're leading us to the ruin, they probably expect us to fix it," Rathen pointed out in concern.

"Well, then they're going to be disappointed."

"What's this tree?" Aria asked Nug as all but a few of the other ditchlings clambered dexterously up the surrounding forest to follow through the treetops. All four of them marvelled at how silent they were as they jumped from bough to bough - no leaves rustled, no branches creaked or snapped; their movements were so practised and so natural that the trees themselves barely seemed to notice them. Clearly, the single bare footprint and few broken twigs that had given them away served as substantial evidence to a catastrophic accident, one that had quite probably ended in a splinter.

"It's where the Lady lives," Nug replied. "She used to live nine and a half days north of here, but hoomans started getting too close, so she moved and we followed her."

"Who is the Lady?"

Nug frowned as he looked at her, surprised she didn't know, but as he glanced towards the pale-skinned, black-haired and unkind man who walked barely half a pace behind her, he seemed to remember why. "She looks after Arkhamas spirits," he explained. "She keeps us alive with joy, mischief and laughter, and when we go to sleep forever, she takes our dreams and carries them with her so they're always safe. She makes everywhere she goes beautiful - trouble is, she goes lot of places, so it's not easy to follow her when she leaves 'cause she never leaves a map."

"She sounds wonderful," Aria smiled, "but is that what the problem is? That the magic will make her leave?"

He nodded, his dark blonde, dishevelled hair falling in his face. "It's too beautiful, and it ain't her doing. If it keeps going on, she's going to get angry and jealous, so she'll either leave or destroy the place."

"Destroy it?" Aria frowned. "Why?"

"'Cause it's prettier than what she could make it. Her sisters have done it before." His lips pulled down at the corners, and as Aria watched him, she saw tears forming in his now haunted, oversized eyes. "One place crumbled when the ground shook, and another was set on fire. It's not a nice place to go to sleep."

Aria nodded in understanding, and as she watched his expression worsen, sorrow tugged at her own lips. She soon noticed that the few of his kind still around them wore similar looks of anguish, but before she could say anything naive to try to soothe them, she yelped in surprise and stumbled over a rock.

A strong grasp caught around each of her arms before her knees hit the ground. She puffed in relief and looked up to smile in gratitude, but was surprised to find her father holding only her left arm, and Nug holding her right. Together, they pulled her back to her feet. "Thank you," she smiled, then glared down at the curiously attractive rock that had tripped her.

"We're here."

Rathen needn't have made the dubious statement; the four were well aware of the fact as they stared out at the grove of carved and scattered rocks sprawling ahead of them. The trees that studded the area were spaced almost evenly enough to have been placed intentionally, like pillars in a hall, and the ceiling of leaves let soft fragments of light through like high, glassless chapel windows. But the stones seemed to have come from another world, one overlapping the forested realm that nature tried to maintain. Amongst the weathered rubble that tree roots imprisoned, portions of wall still stood, some covered in a vertical carpet of moss much like the rock faces in the scowles, and others pierced by trees that had somehow wended their way through cracks as they grew, continuing through them rather than finding another way around. But rather than swallow or smother the remains, the forest appeared to be trying to preserve them, adding itself as foundations to prolong the architecture's already ancient life, as though it belonged there just as much as the trees and the grass did.

As they stared at the light-dappled stone and the shining diamonds of rain on the leaves, Anthis suddenly blustered past them, having snatched a notebook from his saddle bag and forced the reins into Garon's hand. He made immediately for the nearest standing fragment of wall while Nug called a warning after him. He made no motion that he'd heard him.

The ditchling turned to Aria in exasperation, clearly already regretting his decision. "Anything he does--"

"He *won't* make it worse," she promised once again, but she hurried after him all the same, shouting for him to be careful and not to upset the Lady, while Rathen promptly rushed off after her, calling for her to be careful in turn.

Only Garon remained, and as Nug turned and looked at him and the three sets of reins in his hands, he grinned cheekily before skipping away.

As Aria peered over Anthis's shoulder, torn between making sure he behaved himself and watching him flick quickly through his sketchbook, urgently comparing the stone before him with illustrations from other sites, Rathen stood behind them and studied the surroundings. He paid particular attention to the ditchlings that had gathered to watch with the same interest as Aria, and Nug even more so as he joined them. But despite his caution at their present situation, he couldn't keep his mind from being dragged away by the unmistakable magic. Once again they were surrounded by beauty, and every gentle breeze brought with it a curious sense of peace. Standing there in that perfect grove, he could forget every worry he'd ever held, every grudge that had ever formed, and he could watch the world pass him by without a thought of time - *if* he let himself.

But how the others didn't immediately succumb and stand there dazed, staring off for miles, Rathen had little idea. His own magic gave him enough natural resistance, and the ditchlings weren't human, so who was to say how resilient they were to the effects? But how Garon, Anthis and Aria managed to stave off the desire to envelop themselves in the tranquillity of the place and let their minds vanish from the world, he couldn't begin to ponder. Perhaps their minds were just that strong - and yet the temptation of the peace was almost too much for *him*.

He folded his arms and pinched himself to shove the matter aside, and turned his attention back to the magic itself, ignoring the lure as best he could.

And the very moment he turned away, Nug took Aria by the elbow and led her off into the grove.

She frowned and looked uneasily back towards the others, but just as she began to protest, he brought them to a stop at the foot of another tree.

"This," Nug smiled, peering up at it, "is where the Lady lives."

Aria's eyes snatched away from the adults, bright with sudden fascination. The tree was not a giant; it had no pure white staircase leading up to a home hollowed out within, no white balconies to oversee the grove and its visitors, nor a garden of flowers and fruits planted along its branches. But its reality was no less enrapturing.

It was no bigger than those around it, but unlike the others, its chaotic boughs seemed to have grown with a precise intention, as misplaced as it may have been. They haphazardly reached and crossed one another, creating what looked like a twisting ladder up and around the tree's wonky trunk, sometimes leading vertically, other times horizontal, but always reaching the dense leaves in the end, and from the outermost branches hung baskets and bottles constructed of grass, twigs and leaves, nests to small, speckled weaver-birds that seemed not the least troubled by the creatures that moved through the surrounding trees and the grass below. But the ladder served no purpose beyond leading to the highest reaches, and there seemed to be little more than owls living within the hollowed knots of its trunk.

"She lives in the tree?" Aria asked, captivated by its wonderfully misshapen form.

"Kinda. She's in there, somewhere."

"Is she an owl?"

Nug laughed, a joyful cackle, and Aria smiled at the curious sound. "*No!* She ain't an owl! She lives in the leaves, in the sap, in the bark - but she ain't the tree, neither. She's sorta like what you hoomans call a ghost, I guess."

Her eyes grew wider in slow understanding, and when she looked back to it, she no longer saw just a tree, nor the home of eighteen birds. She saw a living, thinking being that seemed to have suddenly become a giant within the forest. "I get it," she nodded as she heard the tell-tale footsteps of her father approach behind her, and though she expected him to scold her when he stopped, he said nothing at all. She smiled to herself. He was surely as enraptured by the tree as she had been. "Then how do you know when she leaves?"

Nug cackled again. "'*Leaves.*'"

Aria grinned.

"We know when she's gone 'cause she tells us in our dreams, but she don't tell us *where* she's gone. It's like a game - if we love her enough, we'll find her. If we don't...well we'll probably find one of her sisters instead."

"But that won't do?"

"Nuh-uh." He shook his head vigorously, his giant eyes so wide and severe it was apparent that the very thought was blasphemy. "We want *her*, not her sisters. They might look after our spirits in sleep like she does - least I *hope* they would - but it wouldn't be the same."

Aria nodded, and as Nug looked back to the spirit-tree, his eyes shining in reverence, trust and absolute adoration, she pursed her lips and regarded it thoughtfully herself.

Chapter 9

With movements Anthis once believed physically impossible, he managed to save himself from stumbling over the gaggle of childlike creatures that scurried about like mice beneath his feet. But though they, too, scrambled to get out of his way each time he darted suddenly through the half-standing ruins, studying its every inch, they remained obliviously glued to his heels. So it had been for ten minutes; the ditchlings - the *Arkhamas* - followed him everywhere, nattering to each other as they went, talking about his blonde hair and how it wasn't as long as anyone else's, about his drawings and how they were better than what most of them could do, but 'squirrel nuts' compared to others, and about his clothes and how they were nicer than *everyone* else's - though he wasn't quite sure what to make of that last point as he glanced at the skins and torn and sodden shirts.

But between discreet glances and keeping one eye on his belongings all the while, he did his best to ignore them. He knelt in the damp grass whenever he found half-buried fragments of stone that were not, to a trained eye, like the others, or runes carved into the stone as pre-magic elves often laid into their structures, be they homes, workshops or even just kilns, and he focused himself on sketching them out with a quick hand, reading their almost entirely eroded shapes as easily as if the rock spoke them aloud. And as he turned a corner in search of his next subject, his unwanted entourage dutifully in tow, excitement stalled his feet.

The lines were sheer and delicate, but they gripped him immediately. Etched almost imperceptibly down the inside corner of two intersecting walls, protected by chance from the elements for centuries, hid a string of runes that released a rabble of butterflies in his stomach. He blustered over, almost stumbling over the ditchlings as he went, and pressed his pencil so urgently into his notebook that he almost pierced the page. He scribbled feverishly, only fractionally disheartened by the thought that the top half of the passage was surely shattered and lost forever in the rubble behind it.

He managed to copy only two edges before the nib snapped.

The ditchlings around him gasped; Anthis only tutted. But though his hand twitched towards the hem of his shirt, he quickly thought better of it. He could sharpen it later. He had at least a dozen others in his saddlebag.

He feigned an itch instead and looked up to see who was nearest to the horses, but sighed with mild irritation when he spotted Garon at the other end of the grove, though he was sure he'd been beside the beasts just a moment ago. The inquisitor's bearing hadn't changed, though; he still stood rigidly, his arms folded across his chest, while his eyes somehow tracked every single ditchling's movements at once.

He looked about for Rathen or Aria instead, but he noticed them just as quickly, several feet away and standing at a bizarre-looking tree where other ditchlings sat uncharacteristically quiet amongst its roots.

He sighed. Clearly, he had no choice but to get it himself - but as he rose and turned to do so, a young, silvery-eyed girl suddenly stopped in front of him, her hand outstretched. Within her grasp was a pencil.

He frowned. It was one of his; the end was covered in familiar chew marks.

"Thank you..." he said with confusion as he took it, then noticed that she hadn't been one of the throng to have spent the last fifteen minutes following him around. At least, he hadn't noticed any around him with small sticks like antlers tied into her hair. Leaves and flowers, yes, even a bird's nest, but these curious adornments were a detail he was quite sure he wouldn't have missed. "How did you--?"

"They told me," she said, her voice and manner just as common as the others she pointed towards, but as he looked around at the thirteen gathered behind him, they each looked just as innocent as the next.

"But they never said a word..."

Frowns of shared confusion muddled their faces.

"We don't need to," one of them said, as if he was stupid, and tapped the side of his head. "We just thunk it - oh yeah! But hoomans can't do that, can they?"

"No!" Said another. "They need to speak out loud."

"But *you* speak out loud," Anthis insisted suspiciously, looking from one round face to the next while trying to decide just how deceptive they looked, "so how can you..."

The girl giggled. "Look! He's confused!"

"*So* confused!"

"But he's so smart! I liked him when he was smart!"

Anthis frowned tightly and shook his head as their voices clamoured around him. "But you're so *loud!*"

"*Course* we're loud!" The one with a crown of leaves and shattered bird eggs laughed. "'Cause we don't need to be!"

"We don't like the silence, see, so we like to talk loudly!"

"And shout!"

"And sing! And laugh!"

"And *roar!*" The boy promptly demonstrated.

Anthis was still shaking his head, fighting to get his thoughts in order over the cacophony, unable to deny the brief but screaming evidence. "Telepathy..." he said quietly, very much to himself rather than trying to be heard over their din, "that would make you highly organised - good at raiding, stealing things..."

"We *are*," the crowned one nodded as the others suddenly fell silent, though they all continued grinning widely. "But we're also good at spying and learning. One of us learns something, then we *all* do. That's how we know where the best stuff is."

"Is it immediate?" He asked, wondering why he was indulging their lies.

The girl beside him bobbed her head about indecisively. "Kinda. Depends where we are. If we're far away, it takes a while. A few minutes, I reckon."

"And how far is 'far'?"

She pursed her lips. "Ten days away?"

Anthis's eyebrows rose in surprise, then dropped just as quickly in doubt.

"He doesn't believe us," one of them said sadly.

"Well he can't see *our* heads' insides neither, so how *could* he trust us?"

Anthis's shoulders dropped and his frown similarly weakened as Nug's previous statement repeated itself in his mind. "...He meant it literally..."

They each frowned at him. "It's annoying not knowing what he's thinking."

Anthis dropped his wide eyes back to them. "So," he began carefully, still wary of being caught in a trap, but he couldn't deny his fascination, "you can exchange thoughts to each other, information...but how do you know when the thought is your own, or another's?"

They stared at him blankly.

"You're right, he ain't smart."

One of them suddenly picked up a stick and drew three lines in the mud, and the others immediately began nodding in approval. "This," said the girl with the pencil matter-of-factly, pointing at the top line, "is the top of our heads. Like the top branches, right? The wind can reach it. This," she continued, pointing at the middle line, and he peered at it with growing interest, "is the middle of our heads, the main bit, like the meat of an animal, not the skin - yeah, the skin is the *top* line."

"Why not the top line is the leaves," Anthis offered, "and the middle is the branches? Or is it the trunk?"

"Yeah, it's the trunk. It's both."

"He is," one of them agreed, though Anthis wasn't sure what to.

"And this," she said, finally pointing to the bottom line, "is the roots. Now, we have thoughts and feelings and ideas - we make them on our own, right? Like if I fall out of a tree, it hurts. The hurt is mine. The 'mine' bit happens at the roots."

"Because you're the one that feels it," Anthis nodded slowly, kneeling down beside her.

"Yep! But this bit, the trunk, that's where the decision that it's pain comes from, and the curses that fly out with it. It's where the thought forms, but the fact that it's mine comes with it, like the trunk comes with the roots. You can cut a tree in half, and the roots and trunk will still stand, right? But you can't have just the top of the tree standing with no roots, can you?"

"No, you can't," he agreed, frowning thoughtfully.

"Right? So the roots can exist on their own without anything else, the trunk can only exist with the roots--"

"So every thought and idea is sort of stamped with 'you'."

"Yeah!" She grinned as the others began murmuring excitedly around him. "And everything at the top, where the leaves are and the wind can carry things, is what we tell everyone else. Just like a trunk can stand without the leaves, I don't *have* to tell anyone else that I fell out of a tree if no one saw it, but if I *do* tell anyone, it *has* to come all the way from the roots."

"So you choose what you share," Anthis clarified, "and you share it at the leaves, on the wind, and it comes with your identity, because the leaves can't stand without the trunk *or* the roots."

"He gets it!"

They all cheered, and Anthis found himself feeling quite pleased with himself. "So that means you always know who a thought came from?"

"Usually."

He frowned at the girl.

"Sometimes some of us can let the tree stand without the roots."

"But...but you just said--"

"Yeah, crazy ain't it?" She grinned. "Shouldn't happen, like a tree shouldn't stand without roots, right? But some can, like sometimes a brown bird is white. So sometimes we might get sent a thought by someone and not know it ain't ours, 'cause we don't feel the roots give our thoughts 'me' when we have them, it just happens, it's like the roots are just there for the sake of whoever gets the thoughts, right? So if we get a thought without no roots, sometimes we think it's ours."

Anthis's frown grew, touched in concern as well as a battering confusion. "So a few of you are able to manipulate everyone else's thoughts?"

"Yup," she smiled simply.

"But..." his brow knotted tighter still. "That's not a good thing."

"No, it ain't really, is it?"

"We don't do it, though," said the crowned one, "'cause it ain't right. I mean, no, stealin' ain't right, I s'pose, but sometimes a pie smells too good. But this is a different kind of 'not right'."

"So...you've never been inclined to try it? To see if you can do it?"

"O' course we have," said another cheerfully, as if it was nothing. "Just like you've been inclined to choke someone. Difference is, we *don't* do it, just like you don't. Probably."

"And you *can't* do it to other races?"

"No, it's..."

"Biog..."

"Bi-bibilo.."

"Biochemical?" Anthis offered.

"*Yes!*" Several of them cried, and suddenly all fourteen pairs of eyes - and others beyond, he noticed - looked to him with relief. "We been tryin' to remember that 'un for *ages!*"

Anthis couldn't help smiling in amusement, but it shortly dropped in fascination as his doubts finally began to subside. "So do you know when something is fact, not just an idea or a random thought?"

"We do. Fact is fact, you know? It's..."

"It's fac--no, you said that."

"Yeah but that's what I *mean*. Fact is fact, and we know it's fact because it's fact."

"Because it's true?" Suggested another.

"I get it," Anthis assured them. "Does *that* have roots?"

"It has roots of fact."

He nodded very slowly. "I think I can appreciate that."

"He gets it." They all grinned.

"So," he turned back towards the corner, "can you pass on thoughts a while after you've had them? Such as, if one of you found somewhere you could stash food, but it wasn't relevant at the time, you could pass it on when it *was* relevant even if it was, say, six years later?"

"We have good memories," one nodded, "so yeah."

"And if it wasn't used, that one could pass it on after another six years?"

They nodded again.

Anthis frowned thoughtfully at the runes. "Then does your collective knowledge know anything about *this* place?"

Now, to his disappointment, they all shook their heads.

"No Arkhamas has been here before us, and we didn't get here that long ago ourselfs," one of them replied. "Aside from the Lady, it's just rocks and trees and grass to us." He narrowed his giant eyes as he peered at the notebook in Anthis's hands. "But *you* know more, don'tcha?"

"Would you tell us?"

He had little choice as twenty eight silvery-green eyes swelled in hope, so he indulged their wonderful curiosity as he resumed sketching out the runes with the pencil the deer-girl had brought him. They asked almost constant questions throughout, mostly 'why didn't they just...?' and 'what was the point?' and he learned - upon everything else he had in the twenty minutes they'd spent in the grove - that curiosity wasn't necessarily a happy thing. These creatures seemed more interested in passing judgement than truly learning anything, but from what he gathered, they didn't care all that much for the elves. Evidently just as they had the remarkable ability to pass on memories after time, they could pass on grudges, too, and their insult at the elves' conceit seemed not to have lost its novelty even after unknown centuries.

Once he'd told them all he knew of the place, and answered a few other strange questions that seemed entirely irrelevant - as far as he could tell, unable to 'see their heads' insides' - they decided to go and play a game and finally leave him in peace. Of course, typically, he'd finished by then, but at least he was able to indulge his own curiosity at what his unlikely colleague had learned without being interrupted.

"Rathen," he began quietly as he stepped beside him into the shadow of the tree, glancing warily around at the nearby ditchlings and subsequently missing the mage twitch in fright, having startled him out of a daydream, "did you know ditchlings are telepathic?"

"Yes," he sighed, shaking it off until his shock was replaced by panic at the fact that neither Aria nor Nug were any longer in front of him. He spun about and spotted them a moment later climbing over nearby stones instead, and Garon appeared to be keeping an eye on them. Relieved, he only passingly noticed that she seemed to be having a great deal of fun with the child-creature. "I also know that they're impulsive and over-imaginative," he continued with a definite tone of disapproval, following Anthis as he walked slowly towards the tree. "They up and leave everything because they have a dream that a spirit has moved and told them to seek it out. It's madness."

"You sound almost concerned for them."

"Not concerned," he corrected carefully, "just confused."

Anthis slipped him a sideways glance, then looked around at the ditchlings as they interacted with the grove, noticing again that they either kept a respectful distance from this particular tree despite its very climbable trunk, or quietly sat at the foot of it. "Not a very faithful individual, are you?"

"Faith?"

He returned his frown mildly and lowered his voice. "I'd say this 'Lady' is as good as religion to them, and who are we to say what - or who - does and does not exist? If they really do believe this spirit protects them then of course they'd follow her if they thought she'd left."

Rathen's eyebrow twitched. "I prefer to rely on my wits. It's proven *much* more dependable than divine intervention."

"'It's a troubled man who would view the world through the harsh light of truth than entrust himself to a little faith.'"

Anthis's blood turned cold as Rathen's eyes crashed upon him. A strange and abrupt darkness swarmed within them, one frighteningly different from his usual acidity, and as the lines in his face deepened and twisted, they revealed the traces of a demon. "Don't quote scripture to me," he hissed. "Vastal has had *little* good to give me throughout my life, so don't you, or anyone else, blindly tell me that I should 'have more faith'. *My* decisions are what keep Aria and I safe, *not* the will of a god." His contemptuous gaze gripped the young man for an eternity, his eyes as sharp as the teeth of a steel trap.

When he finally looked back to the tree, Anthis managed to stifle his gasp for breath. He watched him fester in his anger, studying the sourness in his eyes and the curl of his lip, both of which were so intense it was clear he'd bitten back a great deal of venom.

So there was a grudge here, too, but this time Anthis had no intention of indulging his curiosity at its nature. Wondering at his broken ties with the Order was one thing, but prying into the history of a man with so perpetually miserable a countenance was quite another. Whatever weight he carried, it had little relevance to their collaboration.

He shifted uneasily under such a fuming presence, but Rathen's eyes soon began to soften, and as they gave way to some unknown and grievous thought, Anthis's discomfort passed along with it. Now he wasn't so sure that his faith was as weak as he made it out to be - or perhaps wished it to be.

A small smile touched his lips and he looked away, following the mage's gaze back to the tree. "You have Aria."

Rathen's eyes flashed towards him again. Anthis saw the movement, and though he didn't look, he knew it was a shameful realisation at somehow having forgotten to count that detail as 'something good'. "Faith is funny, really," he continued lightly, cocking his head and looking at the hanging bird nests as he toyed with a fine chain that hung about his neck. "Early elves believed the gods were responsible for all the good that happened in their lives, and that the bad was just a passing detail, a stepping stone to the next good thing. They truly embraced the idea and devoted themselves to the gods and believed they were in such safe hands. That devotion vanished when they became aware of their own power, of course, but even in their conceit, they still thought of the gods. But, in time, their views degraded and they took to the idea that the gods weren't omnipotent, They were just living beings like themselves, albeit powerful, and that everything that befell the elves - good or bad - was of their *own* hand. And while that's not necessarily untrue, I believe pushing their faith and reliance aside like that was ultimately their undoing. They fell from grace to become selfish and arrogant, and whatever *actually* happened to them was a result of this, be it the manifestation of Zikhon's natural hate for everything of Vastal's creation because the loss of their faith disempowered Her, or simply something magic-related that we have yet to discover.

"But," he continued before Rathen could protest to the suggestion that he was leading himself to his own downfall, "humans are different. We each carry our own degree of faith, and we utilise it for different purposes. For some, it's a way of telling themselves that everything bad that befalls them happens for a reason, that there's some kind of plan and there is good still to come to them, they need only get through it. For others it's a feeling of safety, that they're always in good hands and that whatever happens to them was something Vastal allowed, whatever Her reasons, and that they will overcome it because Vastal is still with them. And for some, like me, it's a way of maintaining perspective. Given all the war around us - now and in the past - and never mind the troubles in dark alleys or behind closed doors, the idea of a higher power, grander designs and wider intentions makes everything awful feel a little less significant. After all," he shrugged, "a war *will* be won - who by doesn't matter in the end because we'll all make the best out of whatever hand we're dealt - but a god's wrath?" He shook his head. "That, we can't do a thing against. So it's best to take care of what we can, where we can--"

"And rely on our own wits."

Anthis's small smile widened, and he found Rathen looking back at him with the slightest smirk of his own. "I suppose that *is* what I said, but I didn't mean it so absolutely. But in the end, every single one of us chooses our own priorities and we do what we must for them, whatever that might be."

Aria and Nug suddenly hurtled past them, dashing towards another ruined structure held together by a weaving tree, and began climbing its anchored limbs like chipmunks. Rathen smiled after her. "That we do."

"Gentlemen." They straightened at the sudden dampening of authority. "Any luck?"

"I have all I'm going to get on this place," Anthis replied assuredly as they turned to face the inquisitor who followed the two as they continued their games, but as Rathen quickly agreed, Garon stumbled to a halt. "Parts of this place are in remarkable condition, so I can say with confidence that it was an important place of craft."

Hope faded as the two older men frowned dubiously. "So it's *not* a religious site?"

"Oh, no no," Anthis quickly amended with a frantic wave of his hands, "it certainly *is*. Places like this were dedicated to the God of Hands, and there's a very clear inscription stating as much - it's *remarkable,* really," he stepped absently towards it as if to lead them over to marvel at it themselves, but Garon raised his hand to stop him. "Sorry."

"The God of Hands?"

"Yes - sorry, Vastal. I said before that elves were very contextual and, irritatingly, that extended to the way they viewed the gods as well. Vastal was given new names and new faces in different circumstances." He released a long-suffering sigh. "For example, as we know, Vastal is the God of Life, but in some situations She was named the 'God of Death' when 'death' referred to the simple and inevitable end of a life cycle rather than anything dark or evil, just as Zikhon, the God of Death, was called the 'God of Life' when referring to legends of dark creatures that lived forever." He scratched his head and puckered his lips distastefully. "They did it on purpose to confuse us, I'm sure of it." He shook it off as he looked back over the ruins, a small, faraway smile playing over his lips, oblivious to the others' growing impatience. "Here, a few craftsmen would have created family talismans and images of Zikhon and Vastal's various faces and associations, and crafting those kinds of things in a place the God of Hands watched over was believed to ensure their creations were not only wonderful, but also appropriately blessed, whichever god they may have been dedicated to or purpose they were to serve--"

"Wait, they would have crafted *blessed* images of Zikhon here?" Rathen asked, horrified, as he finally managed to interrupt Anthis's explanation which was delivered with ever increasing speed. "The God of *Death?*"

"Yes," he blinked, "they needed effigies of them both in all contexts and in equal spiritual weight. Stone masons still carve Zikhon with detail equal to Vastal in our temples even now, though our own depictions aren't nearly as varied." He sighed sadly as he looked around himself again. "It's a shame that there are no tools left here, no half-finished works - at least, not to be found without digging the ground up--*oh!* But there *is* a kiln!"

"So," Garon summarised before Anthis's excitement could overtake him again, "this is also a religious site."

Anthis blinked. "Yes."

The inquisitor then turned to Rathen, and Anthis shortly followed with similar expectation. Neither of them posed the question. There was no need.

The mage nodded. "There is magnetism here," he confirmed, "and focused around this tree, but it's a bit weaker than the last site."

"We know that the feeling of being watched isn't related," the inquisitor reminded them, though his tone remained hopeful, "but is anything else different here? Anything that could help with understanding how this magic got here? Where it came from?"

He shook his head regretfully. "Nothing. It's the same as before: just as beautiful, just as peaceful..."

"Peaceful?" Anthis suddenly frowned. "Silverwood was beautiful, but not necessarily *peaceful*..."

"I'd have said almost disturbing, myself," Garon agreed. "Uncomfortable, at the very least. None of it sat right with me. In fact I feel the same here."

"Me too, now you mention it."

Rathen's brow knotted as he thought back to the ruined archway, wondering if he'd just forgotten or grown confused by his present surroundings... No. He knew as a fact that he hadn't. Silverwood may have been almost two weeks behind them, but its tranquillity was unmistakable, and it was one perfectly mirrored by that which tried to tempt him now.

Perhaps these two simply didn't sense it. Perhaps the lure was a result of his own magic; the tingling in his veins was there again - which, of course, was *another* detail he still couldn't begin to explain. "Either way," he frowned, pushing it out of his mind with some effort for the time being, "this place feels no different to Silverwood. But feeling the magic again may have helped a little, I think. I've had time to think on it since, so hopefully something will come to me..." He held absolutely no confidence.

"Well?"

The three turned together at the demanding grunt and found Nug marching towards them, an air of superiority about him that was neither successful nor out of place, while Aria skipped hurriedly behind him with a cheerful grin on her face.

"'Well' what?"

Nug narrowed his eyes at Rathen. "You're rude. And 'well' have you fixed it yet?"

They each frowned at the expectation. "We can't stop the magic's interference right here and now..."

"But we *can* learn from it," Anthis quickly and tactfully added while Aria reminded Nug that she 'did tell him'. "We're working on a way to stop it - even reverse it, if it's possible."

"And how long will that take? A day?"

Anthis frowned carefully.

"*Two?!*"

"We don't know," Rathen snapped, feeling the weight on his shoulders double, "it's unlike anything any of us has seen before, but we're...going to find a way to stop it."

Nug turned to Aria accusingly. "You said they'd fix it."

"I said they'd fix it *eventually*," she replied, rolling her eyes. "You just have to give them time."

The ditchling sighed as he looked back to the three adults, and each duly fell under his scrutinising gaze. Anthis's eyes flicked past him to those of a few others, and as he found them all staring back with the same studious regard, he wondered just what they were all thinking - *together*. He shifted uncomfortably.

"You're clever," Nug began at last, startling Anthis as he looked towards him; "you're clever, too," he continued, turning to Rathen, "not as much, but you do have magic. And you," he finished, glancing to Garon, "well, I dunno, but you watch things and you got thinking-eyes." He looked over the three of them again and a frown took hold of his young features, growing so tightly knotted it was as though he was wrestling with something quite severe in his head. Finally, he gave a single nod. "You might be able to do it, together. But if you do, you've gotta fix this place *first*." He blinked. "No - you gotta fix this place *second*. Don't want you to mess up your first go and make it worse."

"And we certainly *will* fix it second," Anthis promised him. "In fact, the sooner we're off, the sooner we'll be back to do so!"

"Wait wait wait wait wait," Nug stepped towards them, eyeing them seriously. "If you ain't fixing this now, you're *definitely* not walking in here for nothing."

"Ahh," Anthis hesitated. "Right, yes. What...what did you want?"

Giant eyes fell on each of them while Nug's seemed to glaze over, and silence filled the grove again. There were no spoken suggestions; it was as if the question hadn't been heard. They exchanged wary glances between watching the little wildlings, and in those few long moments, thoughtful gazes were gradually dragged onto other targets, until they all finally settled upon Aria.

Rathen's heart leapt. "*No--*"

"We wanna know how to do that."

Aria grinned knowingly as he pointed towards her, and as Rathen continued his absolute refusal, she lifted the plait she'd tied into her hair at breakfast that morning.

Anthis frowned in confusion and put his hand on Rathen's shoulder to subdue him.

"That's it?" Garon asked, just as bewildered.

"I thought all kids knew how to do that," Anthis remarked. "Or, girls, at least."

"We're *not* kids!"

"Which I suppose explains it."

"That's really all you want?"

They nodded eagerly.

Aria didn't need to be asked. She stepped forwards and lifted another hank of her long, fair hair, and as several ditchlings gathered around her, their eyes wide and surely ready to absorb whatever they saw, she began to demonstrate. They quickly began to copy her actions, clumsily at first and perfectly only a moment later, and soon both boys and girls had twisted their knotted hair into elegant braids. As Rathen watched suspiciously, he spotted a few further back, too far to have seen for themselves, begin to join in.

Once she and the others had licked the ends to seal it, she grinned and stepped back in satisfaction, but rather than rejoin her father, she stopped in front of Nug and put her hands behind her back in a particularly polite manner that Rathen recognised was about to be followed by a 'please may I?'

"Please may I be so rude as to ask you for something?"

"For you," Nug grinned, "anything."

Anthis's eyebrows rose. Rathen's only lowered.

"I would like," she continued quite graciously, doing her scowling father proud, "if it isn't too much trouble, a piece of wood from your forest. A branch would do."

Nug rolled his head. "*Easy.*"

Three ditchlings promptly scurried up a nearby tree as easily as if they'd been squirrels, and out along a branch surely too thin to support them. It did, though only just, and they lined up along its length. Each of the adults expected them to hold onto a higher branch for safety and jump up and down to break the one beneath them, but clearly that was too obvious, for instead they each bent down, took a firm grip of the wood between their feet and, presumably after a silent count of 1-2-3, jumped off backwards together and ripped the branch free with their momentum.

They landed hard on their rears with the limb sprawled across them, and they cackled with great enjoyment at their senseless lack of self-preservation, even as they winced. The others howled around them as they shared in their joy, and it became gradually more evident that the safer method *had* occurred to them, they'd just purposely decided against it.

"Why ever would she want a branch?" Anthis asked quietly as Aria squealed in delight and thanked them all profusely, but as she began analysing the wood, touching at the knots and kinks in its length, Rathen only smiled.

"Thank you," Aria gushed once again, "it's perfect - what do you want for this?"

Nug waved it away. "Nothin'. It's only a branch. We have plenty."

She turned and grinned at her father, then bowed gratefully to Nug before heading over to the horses to have her father fix the three-foot branch to the side of the saddle.

Anthis shook his head as he watched the two struggle. "Strange child." He and Garon duly followed, and after subtly filtering through the saddle bags to ensure nothing had been taken - Anthis paid special attention since he knew the deer-girl had been in his - they mounted the horses and followed the ditchlings as they led them off through the trees and away from their curious grove. They took sudden turnings from time to time, for no apparent reason but to ensure the humans were suitably lost, and warned them as they went of where a few others of their kind had made their homes and that they should only 'storm in' if it was 'absolutely, positively necessary.' Ditchlings gradually peeled away from the party the further from the grove they moved, leaving so silently that none of them noticed until only three of the wild children trailed behind them. When they finally drew to a stop, only Nug was left.

"Keep going that way," he told them, pointing towards the east with a dirty finger, "and you'll get to the edge of the forest. Then you'll be out of our way. Oh, and there *shouldn't* be any traps out there, but sometimes animals don't set 'em off so we forget about them."

"Thank you, Nug," Aria smiled, sitting tall in the saddle as she relished in the authority of speaking for the group. "We'll see you again when we come back to fix the tree."

"I hope so," he grinned back, "on *both* counts." He looked to Rathen, Garon and Anthis, then back to Aria. "It's just as well you're with them. Make sure they keep out of trouble."

"I certainly will."

"And you," he said, his weighted eyes suddenly flicking towards the rest as they stifled themselves at the thought, "look after *her*. I don't want her to be one of them lost kids that comes and lives with us 'cause they ran away from rubbish parents."

Rathen frowned sadly as he dragged his mind away from the thought. "She'll be fine," he promised Nug, as well as himself. "I'll never take my eyes off her."

"Good."

And with that, the ditchling turned away and started back through the forest without even a wave, leaving the group to continue along in silence, still slightly bewildered by the whole experience. Aria took the matter in her stride, however, and Rathen wondered if she truly understood much about the world around her, or if she viewed the whole 'adventure' as an exciting and harmless event like a story safe on the pages of a book. Entirely unfazed by an encounter that many would still have the shakes from, she leaned over from the front of the saddle and reached for her bag, twisting her way around Rathen though he told her to sit still and wait until later. She couldn't reach it comfortably, but that didn't seem to matter, so she ignored him and rummaged around blindly, her tongue sticking out in her concentration.

Rathen frowned down at her, wondering what she was doing as he knew how little was in the satchel, but just as he was about to ask what was wrong, she demanded they stop.

"We have to go back!" She wailed. "It's gone!"

"What's gone?" Anthis asked worriedly.

"My knife!"

He and Garon exchanged a perplexed look while Rathen's head hung in defeat.

He knew he should have checked her bag; she'd been too infatuated by that stick to do it herself, never mind what she'd told him. "We're going to have to go back," he sighed, and though he offered them a glancing look of apology, no explanation followed. "She's not going to leave the matter."

"What knife?" Anthis pressed. "Why does she have a knife?"

"Whatever reason, we can't turn around," Garon assured them. "The ditchlings likely took it, and if they did, it will be trouble to get it back."

"No," Aria insisted, her eyes wide in horror, "but I *need* it!" She spun around and turned desperate, tearful eyes onto her father. "Daddy!"

"We have to go back." Without waiting for an argument, Rathen turned his horse around and urged it back along the trail. "I'll make sure it doesn't take long."

Anthis sent Garon an uneasy look, but he shortly turned and followed, leaving the inquisitor no course but to do the same. "They were obliging enough the first time," Garon reminded them quietly as he trotted up behind, "but they didn't want us there in the first place and even escorted us out. They're not going to take kindly to us walking back in."

"We have no choice."

They rode quietly at Rathen's lead, looking about with even greater caution than they had the first time. They scrutinised shadows, picked apart shapes in the branches, listened to the sounds of scurrying and tried to judge the size of those unseen creatures. And yet, despite having been in the company of a dozen ditchlings just moments ago, they encountered none at all. Whether that was because there were suddenly none around or because they saw no threat in the four, it was hard to say, but amongst the array of childlike qualities the ditchlings had already exhibited, fickle interest seemed far from unlikely.

They made it all the way back to the grove without crossing a single one, and found not a trace of the child-things even there. It was as though they'd all collectively decided to leave and do something elsewhere, abandoning their present activity on a whim, as Aria herself often did. But they didn't drop their guard.

"If they have it," Anthis began ever so quietly, looking around carefully as they drew to a stop where they'd left their horses the first time, but before he could finish his dubious thought, Aria pointed to the ground, declared she'd found it, and Rathen dutifully dismounted.

It was no wonder no one had noticed it when they'd left. The small pocket knife was nestled in amongst the long grass beside the horse's hoof, hidden well enough that it would never have been spotted without someone actually looking for it. But though it seemed it had simply fallen, she assured them that she hadn't been near the bags, let alone taken it or anything else out. So the others dismounted and checked their belongings once again, just in case the ditchlings had managed to snatch a moment to nose even while they'd been on the move.

But as Rathen sorted through his own, counting off the food, changes of clothes and other bits and pieces, his ear pricked at the briefest squeak nearby. He paused, his attention sharpening, and surveyed the grove with diligent eyes, picking carefully through the boughs of the trees they'd seen the ditchlings move through skilfully already, and then deeper into the forest around them.

"What is it?" Anthis asked quietly, following his gaze.

"I'm sure I heard something..." His dark eyes were fixed to the depths of the forest, and as Anthis prepared to ask him what it had been, the sound came again, louder and clearer than before, a short cry riddled with panic. And it was close.

Caution thickened the air, and they had to strain all the harder to hear through it. But while the others remained still and thoughtful, picking their surroundings apart, Rathen wasted not a moment. By the time they looked back to him he was already running through the trees, calling back for Aria to stay exactly where she was, but of course she didn't listen, just as he didn't when Garon ordered him to stop. She was on his heels just as quickly, leaving the others to follow suit and chase him through the thick woods.

Another pained and frustrated shout rose to the east and his course adjusted sharply towards it, and when an ear-piercing screech followed, not one footfall hesitated. Rathen hadn't even come to a stop when he began contorting his fingers, releasing his quickly-formed spell the very moment the muddy ditchling was in his sight, a sudden gust of dense wind battering the grey-dappled eagle off of her just as it raised its talons to break through her braced spear and slash through her neck.

The instant she was able, the ditchling leapt to her feet and readied her bloodied spear once again, unconcerned with what had thrown the creature off of her. But as the great bird, twice the size of the forest dweller, shoved itself back up from the ground and turned to face her, its yellow eyes flashing in rage, Rathen stopped between them and released another spell before it could recover its bearings. Stones suddenly began to pummel its pelt as Aria skidded to a stop behind a nearby bush, and as its sights flicked onto her instead, Garon appeared to one side with his sword readily drawn, and Anthis on the other, unarmed but at least providing another body to outnumber it.

The grey eagle shrieked furiously, its feathers smattered with its own blood from the ditchling's previous defence, but though it glowered at each of them with eyes flaming toxic yellow, it spread its enormous wings and, with a single powerful pump, rose up above the trees and set off over the forest.

"Yeah, *fly away!*" Aria jeered needlessly after it as Rathen turned towards the ditchling, but she only stared back up at him, her silver-green eyes made brighter by the mud she'd covered herself in. They widened further as he knelt beside her and asked if she was all right.

"I'm fine," she said with wonder, though her hand rose to her collarbone where blood was mixing with the dirt as she spoke, and he gently pulled it aside to have a look.

A sudden rustle came from the forest behind her and the others stepped forwards in response, but the girl wittingly ignored it. A number of ditchlings burst out from the trees, their own weapons at the ready, but they stumbled with the same surprise as she to find humans rather than a beast. Concern struck the four of them that the halfling arrivals might misunderstand, but the facts quickly and silently spread, and as three broke away to hurry through the forest after the eagle, the others stood down.

"Thank you," said one of the girls who was just as filthy as the rest, but half-covered with leaves. Rathen noticed as he pressed a handkerchief against the other's wound that while two more shared those adornments, the rest had decorated themselves in bits of bark and lichen. All the better to blend in with the forest.

"You're a real friend."

His eyebrows rose. "I only got rid of a bird."

She shook her head, revealing the twigs tied in amongst her brown curls. "No big 'uns have ever helped us before. Just screamed and cursed and hit us with brooms - if we were lucky."

"Nah," another spoke up, "one old biddy did throw bread at us once - I think she thought it was a rock or summit."

Another grinned and laughed. "It was as good as helping!"

"It was nothing." He rose to his feet once he was satisfied that the wound wasn't serious, but they shook their heads in absolute disagreement as the injured ditchling rejoined them. Without another word, they began to melt back into the forest, those covered in patches of green scurrying up to the treetops where they leapt from bough to bough, while others kept close to the trunks and hurried soundlessly from one to the next. Only the girl lingered behind, and for that moment she looked at Rathen with eyes far older than she seemed. "It *wasn't* nothin'."

Then she, too, turned and vanished into the trees.

The three adults blinked after them while Aria smiled proudly at her father's back, and she shortly started back through the forest herself, apparently just as unaffected. The others were slow to follow, bemused even by this second encounter, but Rathen shook it off first and hurried after her, while Anthis looked up into the trees around them as they followed, musing quietly to himself. "What an unusual morning..."

Chapter 10

The gentle scent of apples and lavender had trailed the rolling streams down from the perfectly rounded hills, riding the warm air that swept out across the flower-studded fields sprawling beyond. He'd followed those waters in leisure through woodland and plains, his bare feet treading the soft grass while unseen birds warbled in the boughs around him. He didn't recognise their calls, but he felt no pressing need to discover their identities; their lilting songs were lullabies composed to soothe the spirit, and he had contently decided that that was enough to know they meant no harm. They were as harmless as everything else around him.

Salus had experienced four such dreams now, imagined journeys through a place - he was *sure* it was the same place - unspoiled by the hands of villains nor of those who would need protecting from them. A place where he was free of the impossible expectations placed upon him by others or by himself. A place where he could breathe figmented air that was clean and bracing, yet comforting, and wander for miles while contemplating nothing at all, for, at those moments, nothing was more important than embracing that peace.

Never had he slept so well than in the cradle of that place, and it was a welcome novelty to wake feeling so refreshed, focused and hopeful, especially in the looming shadow of war. Even as he sat patiently behind his desk early that afternoon, awaiting the Crown's liaison for another routine meeting, he was still absorbed in that serenity, as if he was still sat beside the crystal-clear river, watching the clouds roll by on its surface.

When the stillness was interrupted by the familiar musical rap, he didn't grunt in frustration as he usually would have, and he found it easy to turn his unknotted mind towards the heavy matters that followed when he bade the old man to enter. He even rose and smiled in greeting.

"Afternoon," Lord Malson said with a slight but wary frown as he closed the door behind himself, and eyed him with a brush of suspicion as he slowly took his usual seat in front of the desk. "Is everything all right?"

"Yes, just fine, thank you," Salus replied, sitting back down, and though his smile promptly vanished in favour of professionalism, his usual hard edge didn't follow. "Any news?"

Intrigue narrowed Malson's eyes a fraction further. "The military is moving west. They'll be set up with time to spare before the Skees reach the border, and the forces stationed in the cities and most western towns have been given their orders to hold, but prepare a portion of their forces to join the main body at a moment's notice.

"Evacuation plans are being drawn up but we don't wish to put them into effect if we don't have to. It will be a great strain on nearby settlements, so we only want to move who we must, when we must. Stored supplies are also being prepared for transport; some will be rationed to the settlements most impacted by the military's movements, and the rest to the military itself."

Salus nodded, though it wasn't anything he didn't already know. He didn't let that on, of course; spying on his own people would be a crime, especially the military, but what they didn't know wouldn't hurt them and it seemed to be the only way he could know for certain what was happening. If he didn't have all the details, the Arana would be unable to act quickly enough if a situation called for it.

He straightened expectantly. "And new orders?"

"Yes," Malson continued, finally shifting his musing gaze, "secure what you can of Skilan's crops closest to the border and burn the rest - barring those that feed immediate settlements. Our feud is with King Jalund and those he sends against us, not the civilians. And when you meet your standing orders of uncovering the most likely attack point, head deeper in that direction and burn more. They're already weak; this can only help our position."

"It will be an unmistakable act of war on our part," Salus warned him mildly.

"They're already heading this way," Malson replied with a touch more weight, "and war is *already* upon us; there is no risk in antagonising them."

"As long as the king is aware."

"More than."

"Jolly good."

The Crown's envoy frowned again. "And have the spies in Skilan's army uncovered anything helpful?"

"Standard reports are due to come in later this afternoon," he replied, no less mildly, and handed him the usual summary file of Aranan activity. The old man began to flick through it as Salus continued. "There have been no spontaneous reports, however, so I don't expect anything ground-breaking. Our planted brigadier general was the one to have reported their intention of marching this way after their victory, but he was killed in the northern war during Kalokh's last-ditch attempt to win by shattering Skilan's chain of command. None of the others have managed to creep high enough in the ranks to be privy to the details of such plans so soon, and while we're working on changing that, whatever we uncover will almost certainly come from the agents closer to home first."

The finely dressed old man nodded slowly, still reading. "And the tribes?"

"They're increasingly determined to keep each other out of their respective territory so they've expanded their patrols to the farthest reaches of their land. They all work in small groups of five to eight, however, so there's no way their bickering will hinder military movements, and I have people prepared to push them back if they get too close to our settlements. The only dispute that may become an issue in time is that between the wind tribes of the Flat Mountain and the earth tribes in Bleakfalls Canyon, but they're keeping to their own territory for now."

"Precautions?"

"If the need arises, we're prepared to block off certain access points from the mountains, flood the White River where the Bruuva meets it, and burn parts of the Green Hills. We can force them further north and west if we need to, and they may unwittingly help to delay Skilan a little while longer in the process."

Malson nodded again and finally closed the file. "Excellent thinking."

"Thank you, my lord."

The old man eyed his smile suspiciously once more. "You're in a good mood today," he said at last, finally defeated by his curiosity, and Salus's blonde eyebrows rose at the casual statement.

"Well things are going well," he replied, "given the circumstances."

"I suppose so... Or has something changed?"

He frowned "Changed?"

"Yes - with you." Malson cocked his head thoughtfully. "Perhaps you're seeing someone."

Salus couldn't hold back the brief burst of laughter. "I'm afraid not," he smiled easily, "I'd never have the time."

"Married to the job, yes." But Malson leaned forwards in his seat, and as he turned a suddenly sober gaze upon him, Salus saw something in his eyes that he'd never seen there before. It was still judgement, of a sort, but there was something different to it, something more...human. But of course it was human; he was not of the Arana. "Perhaps you should *make* time."

"My lord," Salus began carefully as his brow knotted, though his smile remained, if a little confused, "I really do think there are other, more important matters at hand than *romance*--"

"That may be the case," he pressed, "but your job is not an easy one, and you're often extremely tense. More so, as of late. Given the situation as it is, you may find it easier to relax and think straight if you had an...outlet."

Salus shook his head, his smile gradually vanishing as confusion began to win out. "I'm fine, thank you, Lord Malson. I've been in this position for eight years now; I've handled everything up to this point, and I will handle what comes next."

"Yes, but you're, what, forty?"

"Thirty eight."

Malson raised an eyebrow. "And you're counting the years." His voice grew weighted again. "Take it from me, Salus: don't let your work become your life. It will make you narrow-minded, bitter, and above all else it will fill you with the greatest regret for having missed your opportunity to experience what life is all about." Salus couldn't miss the intense remorse that invaded his eyes as he spoke. "No amount of praise for a job well-done - whether it be for deflecting war or winning it, and whether it comes from the king himself or every single man and woman in Turunda - will ever match up to the comfort and ease of being around that one person who truly knows your heart and your mind. Never mind that theirs is the *only* praise that matters, you need to know first hand what it is you're fighting to protect." He stared at Salus for a long moment, either trying to see how far his words had reached, or trying to push them that little bit further with a piercing gaze. But as Salus simply stared back at him with a ponderous frown, Malson rose carefully to his feet, his old joints slowing him down, and patted the folder in his hands. "The king would like to see this report, if you don't mind," he said, his tone abruptly lightening. "There's little in here he's not already aware of, but he's particularly keen to be kept up to date with every single movement Turunda makes in the face of this war."

Salus nodded absently as his brow fractionally relaxed. "Yes, of course, yes."

"Thank you." Malson inclined his head and turned towards the door. "I hope you continue to have a good afternoon, Keliceran."

Salus's eyebrows rose again, and as he disappeared into the hallway, a confused smile crept across his face. He shook his head at the old man's strange turn, wondering what had provoked it, and his thoughts lingered even as he returned to his work.

But what he'd said was true: he had no time. Even now he was trying to determine what could be done about the magic that seemed to be swelling and multiplying around him, as not only had another person well over the average age discovered magic out of the blue, but two mages within the Arana had also grown in strength just as abruptly. They were loyal individuals and had volunteered the information to him themselves, to their credit, but though they'd both assured him that they hadn't sensed an increase in strength from any of the other few mages in their ranks, that didn't offer him much comfort. These two, up until a few days ago, had been deemed only just too weak in their power's capacity to join the Order in any military fashion, despite each of their proven tactical abilities. But that fact now seemed to have changed. The Order could not have them, of course, they were too valuable for that, but their strength made him uneasy. They knew well how to wield that magic - after all, they'd been taught by the Order itself.

He'd always loathed that the Order had any involvement in his people's training, but it couldn't be helped. Their tuition was necessary. One couldn't simply work it out on their own; spells didn't happen by accident, and neither were they instinctive. Magic required guidance, and only the Order could provide it - fortunately, that demand made them picky. They didn't train just anyone who arrived at their gates. It would be a waste of their time to indulge those who were too weak to be of any real use in their service, so, given that untrained magic was as good as a kettle without a spout, those they deemed to have magic below a certain standard were simply turned away.

That fact had never sat well with him, either, nor with many others, but the Order kept a close and vigilant eye for any unauthorised training - which was presumably also how they always knew when the Arana had one of them detained. But the Order was also quite aware of the distrust people held for them and they didn't seem to want to worsen it. Unfortunately the possibility of a rebellious sector of their organisation threw that sentiment right out of the window, and that unsettled Salus about the increasing magic all the more.

But at least these two individuals had already been a part of the Arana when their talent had surfaced. It was only upon the Arana's wish and the king's consent that the Order had trained them and any others without enrolling them into their own ranks or keeping tabs on them, which they resented as much as he did their involvement, and Salus relished the smug sense of victory that came with each occasion. These were the only trained mages to exist outside of the Order, and their loyalty to him was absolute.

But...even so, he couldn't help mistrusting the influence of such power. Magic was capable of far too much, and while he was glad to have a handful of mages and their talents under his command, the idea of betrayal through arrogance had, occasionally, popped into his mind. But he had conceded then, as he did now, that if he was going to start thinking along those lines, any of the phaeacian agents could do the same.

The Arana's lowest rank received no mental conditioning; they carried out their duties without question, but they still thought for themselves and that meant that temptation could creep in, or a change of heart take hold. As it was, it was only the virtue of the individual that kept a phaeacian devoted.

It was possible that a few of the phidipan could go that same way, too, albeit less likely. The half-course of conditioning they were subjected to limited their individuality enough that such thoughts didn't come as naturally, and while many still possessed identity and their own thoughts, they knew when it was right to indulge them.

When it came right down to it, only the loyalty of the portian agents was truly unconditional. Their full conditioning meant that they lived only for their duties, thought only tactically, mathematically, and that the 'life' Malson had just whimsically spoken of could not compromise them. They had no identities, no pasts, so those they were stamped with upon receiving new orders couldn't be exposed by their own thoughts and feelings; they could successfully fulfil the most grisly and necessary commands, the tasks which under no circumstances could fail. There was no room for a change of heart in such crucial work, so they removed it completely. It was the greatest gesture of devotion an operative could make. Unsurprisingly, portians made up less than ten per cent of the Arana.

But, as strong and relentless even they were, they could not stand against magic without possessing it themselves. No one could. It took magic to fight magic and that was another detail that frightened Salus. It was why the Order had a military wing - perhaps even why the Order existed at all.

He sighed and leaned back thoughtfully in his seat. No, he didn't like magic's growing presence, but it was better to have a few mages on his side than none at all, and at least if a few of his own grew stronger, the Arana had a better chance of standing against renegades.

A sudden knock at his door coaxed him away from his thoughts. "Come in," he said, softer than he'd intended, but as he began again and forced a little more authority into his voice, the woman had already stepped inside and closed the door behind her.

She stopped in the centre of the room, her hands clasped respectfully behind her back, eyes fixed immediately to the wall behind him. "Keliceran. You summoned?"

"Yes..." An ever so slight and thoughtful frown creased his brow as he paused for a moment to look at her. She seemed familiar, but he couldn't recall ever giving her direct orders. "Captain Rulan," he began, brushing it off and turning straight to business as he unlocked a long, slim drawer concealed just beneath the surface of his desk. "We have what we need to move on him, and you're the most capable who knows the layout of the palace." He handed her one of the many folders that were sealed away within, safe from prying royal eyes. "This is his activity, gathered over the last three weeks. He doesn't deviate."

Her eyes quickly scanned the documents, soaking up every word and committing them to memory. She closed the folder a moment later and handed it back to him, her gaze returning to the wall. She had no questions. There were never any questions. "It will be done, Keliceran."

He nodded and dismissed her, the matter closed, and her eyes never once grazed him as she turned to leave. His eyes, however, were quite riveted to her as his thoughtful frown returned, and as the door closed behind silent footsteps he finally recalled the dark haired woman who had passed him twice in the corridors, the one with the brown eyes that bore both focus and kindness, and small lips that seemed almost constantly pouted in thought.

So she was one of the handful of phidipans stationed in the palace. He hadn't requested anyone by name - indeed he didn't *know* her name - but had left it to Teagan to direct to him the most capable for this task. He was more informed of individuals' abilities as it usually fell to him and a few other portian agents to hand out the majority of jobs, leaving Salus, often too busy to brief everyone personally, to hand out only the most serious - such as the assassination of one of the Royal Family's personal guards.

But what a funny coincidence that it should be her...whoever she was... He thought her almost too attractive to be an operative. They were supposed to remain unnoticed, and average hair, average build, and average faces certainly helped in that regard - but then, a courtesan was capable of obtaining particularly sensitive information that no other position could have gained, and certainly much quicker. Perhaps a pretty face and narrow waist weren't undesirable traits...

His frown deepened as he became aware of his lingering thoughts, and again as he pondered on what they might imply. But he was only being observant - clearly the liaison's recent turn had gotten into his head.

She was a highly efficient operative, nothing more, and only a phidipan could be planted somewhere so official. The surveillance was crucial, both to the safety of the royal family and the Arana's work, but it wasn't a movement sanctioned by the Crown so not one of them could afford to be caught. Not only would the Arana fall out of favour and become a rogue faction, but portians were trained to take any measures necessary to complete their task - if some deemed it truly necessary to maim or kill to maintain their cover, it would only complicate things. Portians weren't thoughtless, but they were tenacious, and they would always achieve their goal. Salus knew this all too well. He was a portian - *had been* a portian, until the day his mind was freed and he'd gained this new title in its place.

But a phidipan, they were more likely to out-think the situation. A portian could spin a flawless story and become any new identity they were given, but a phidipan still had enough heart to create almost genuine relations they could press on for mercy, and enough confidence in themselves not to put their characters above begging. In some ways, they were the most deceptive; they could truly smile, even while wearing another's face. They were almost perfect.

Warmth brushed his cheek and drew him gently out of his thoughts. The persistent clouds that had smothered the afternoon sky had finally shifted, allowing a shaft of sunlight to leak in through the window, spilling across the desk. Its warmth and brightness soothed his contemplative mind. It felt so pleasant that his body rose from the chair and approached the large, ornate window so he might grow a little warmer. He hadn't noticed the chill in the office.

He took a deep breath and relaxed as he studied the view, feeling his few tensions slip away again as the influence of his good night's sleep stole over him once more.

The large, stately houses of nobles were the first things to catch his gaze. They were difficult to miss; extending a good deal towards the north and east, the facades of each building were covered in various ornate mouldings depicting animals, spirits and family crests, while their vast and richly cultivated grounds exploded in spring colours and shrouded their residents in privacy. The Arana's house looked much the same, hiding in plain sight among them, and its own gardens were dressed with similarly mature trees and hedges. But unlike the others, the rear of the Arana's grounds reached into the dense Blackbrush Forest, its edge only just visible from the window as it arced around the outside of the district. It was precisely this detail which allowed so much coming and going to occur unseen. Even during the winter it hid their activity, concealing the exit to a tunnel that reached beneath the length of the gardens, and though only a small part of the woods was considered private land, the spells set up along that perimeter, cast by Aranan mages with the begrudging approval of the Order, subtly deterred trespassing.

The richly carved Craitic Temple stood further to the north, out of sight of his office window, a detail some might think inauspicious but one he'd never given much attention to. If anything, he was probably glad of it. The Arana did what had to be done. They didn't need divine judgement hampering the decisions. But the royal palace to the far north was also beyond the window's range, and it was from there their orders were issued, there where the judgements that mattered. But he was glad he couldn't see that, either. Theirs was a glare he didn't need.

But the palace itself was a sight that begged curiosity, an unnatural mix of elven and human architecture but built entirely by the latter. Unlikely details had been, by Salus's over-critical eye, poorly copied into stone, including the elegant twists and braids that usually stood in metal. But the masons couldn't truly be blamed for the poor resemblance - in fact, though it was far from perfect, they had to be commended for making by hand and skill what elves had forged entirely from magic. That fact made it worthy of not only the king, but of everyone else as a monument to hard labour and learned skill, and that was a detail Salus *could* respect. Mages could have made it, or at least tidied up rough edges, but they hadn't been asked to, and that was all the better for everyone. There was already too much magic in Kulokhar.

His eyes dragged unbidden to the west. Beyond the reach of the rich, royal and temple districts, far plainer buildings clustered densely where the capital city sprawled unstoppably, and the three tall, spiralling elven buildings that rose from the modesty at its centre were clearly visible from two miles away. Their exquisite gold, silver and ebon exteriors contrasted to the plain stone that tried to smother its fascination, and caught the brief sunlight to cast dazzling, warped reflections from city wall to city wall. And when it rained, the water struck its sides and ran down pipes to create a wonderful melody whose misplaced charm befitted the remnants of a people long since extinguished.

Despite Salus's distaste for magic, he supposed that Kulokhar, too, was an impressive sight. The elven towers were some of the grandest still standing, no doubt thanks to the Order's strong presence in the city, and it had even maintained its elven name where most others had been lost. 'Ebon Star Rise', it meant, though so few were aware of it. The fact meant little to him, either, but it was his job to know the details.

But the towers' gaudy presence, and with it that of the mages, set himself and surely everyone else on edge. From that central point, the mages patrolled the capital city like a sub-force of guards, and while they were an undeniably effective deterrent against crime, he wasn't at all happy with their roaming. Magic was their responsibility, so while a number were out watching the streets and presumably also searching for any magical threats, a few 'preservers' from another wing of the Order were out repairing elven spells that were supposedly about to fail. Salus had always found that suspicious. Who but another mage could tell what spell had actually been cast? They could have all kinds working through the city with all sort of motives, and none but they would ever know of it. And given that the Order was the only authority he had no eyes within, he had no way of easily uncovering the information, either. The Order was watched, he made sure of that, but it wasn't the same as having one of his own moving amongst them.

His eyes narrowed at the parchment he stared right through as he wondered if his own mages might now be strong enough to identify the myriad of spells they'd cast throughout the city, and his brow knotted further as Drassa's research popped into his mind.

But he chose to push both thoughts away before they could take root. If his own mages were strong enough, they might be able to uncover the spells' nature but certainly not counter them, and as for Drassa, his first report was due in a couple of days. All he could do on that front was wait.

He sighed deeply, tired of there being so little he could do himself. Since becoming Keliceran, he'd given up the ability to see to matters directly. Only brief tasks that required moving openly while in disguise were within his reach, as just as he was too busy to give every task to every operative, no matter how simple a job that might be, he was especially too busy to carry any of them out himself. He'd had to remind himself countless times that, as the keliceran, he was in the ideal position to do what was best for the country, to truly protect it...but knowing how often his hands were tied by the Crown or Lord Malson himself, he couldn't help thinking he was actually doing less.

The task he'd just sent the woman on would have been well within his abilities, and quick enough that he could have taken the time to handle it. But if he happened across Malson's path in the palace - and so soon after their meeting, he could well be - he would be recognised immediately. It was a chance he couldn't take. He couldn't allow the liaison or the Crown to find out that an operative from Skilan had gotten into the palace - presumably years ago for him to have gained enough trust to be put in charge of the guards protecting the king's immediate family. To say that the Arana would look foolish would be an understatement. Not only was it their job to gather intel from across the borders, but also to safeguard and protect their own. But just as they changed their tactics in order to remain undetected, so too would their enemies, and that meant that both sides would make their winnings, and take their losses. It was an ever-evolving battle. But the Crown wouldn't see it that way. They never saw *anything* that way. The world was black and white; to their eyes it would unequivocally be the Arana's fault because subtlety and deception was their domain, and it would cast them into unreasonable disrepute.

In the end, the only thing the Arana could do was ensure that the other side failed more often than not, and that, should the enemy manage to get the information they sought, they rendered it useless by uncovering the plans made in response. In such cases, the Crown would never have to know - and, indeed, they never once had.

But despite his pride in that fact, for the first time that day he felt the familiar hopelessness begin to creep through him. He rubbed his head to try to suppress it, but as he took a deep breath and envisioned his river, hoping it might help to soothe him again, his stomach growled and he was suddenly aware of just how empty he felt.

He sighed in defeat and pushed himself away from the window, leaving the city behind as the sun was consumed by the returning cloud. It was three o'clock, and while there were still a few papers on his desk, his good mood that morning had allowed him to get plenty done and leave him with a quieter afternoon. He'd taken to accidentally skipping meals lately - he'd been too busy to remember to eat - but now it seemed he had the time to notice, and he suddenly found himself stuck firmly on the thought of a thick, sweet and tangy tomato soup with warm, crusty bread. It was a simple meal and all his imagination seemed able to muster, but at that moment, it sounded to him like the bounty of a god.

As his stomach growled in zealous agreement, he left the office and all of his tensions behind, urgency and an unpleasant moment of light-headedness and nausea powering his steps. He couldn't recall if he'd even eaten breakfast that morning.

Chapter 11

The sun had only just dipped beneath the south-western horizon, but the steep valley had cast its shadows long before, plunging the region into an early dusk despite the glimpses of lighter sky above them. The setting was eerie, still but for the hoot of the occasional owl that had risen early to take full advantage of the darkness, or the scuffle of leaves as its prey dashed for cover. And when the black fingers between the trees began to merge into a perpetual sheet of night, Aria's complaints joined the disturbance. She was cold, hungry, sleepy and uncomfortable in the saddle, and while the others were inclined to agree on all counts, there was simply nowhere to stop and pitch camp. The horses' tired hooves churned up the muddy ground as they followed what was little more than a narrow trail, carved and trampled more likely by animals than hunters, and the only grass that grew flecked the steep slopes to their left while a wide river ran along their right.

They were forced to ride on through the thickening darkness, and when rain began to fall, their spirits dropped with it. Mercifully, only a light drizzle reached them; the towering trees took the brunt, but the cheer in that fact was not easily seen. The path ahead appeared endless, the landscape unchanging, and none of them had any clue how long they'd been riding when the conclusion that flat ground was an impossibility finally struck.

But just as they began to resign themselves to the idea that they'd be travelling all night, the slope to their left began to lower and a near-level gulley cut through it. It was little more than a dried out, seasonal stream - a month from then the channel would surely flow across the trail and feed into the river, but as it presently stood, it was little more than a path, and the small stones that littered its length provided a drier surface as the rain filtered through them to the ground beneath.

It wasn't ideal, but it was the best they were going to get; none were about to turn their noses up at it. The trees would protect them from the worst of the rain, there was grass for the horses to graze, water to drink and wash in, and the small pebbles would keep them, their bedrolls and their blankets from getting much more than damp as they slept.

But as they led the horses to the top of the river bank and began unhooking their belongings, something grasped Rathen's elbow and tugged him suddenly to one side, back towards the trail.

"Don't you *dare* do that again," a close voice hissed, and Rathen looked around to find Garon's weighted grey eyes burning into him. He snatched his elbow away, but the inquisitor took a short step closer and glowered at him before he could respond. "I told you you were to stay with me *at all times*," he continued harshly, his voice just low enough that Anthis and Aria wouldn't hear. "I told you not to wander, I told you not to stray--"

"I am not a child," Rathen hissed, turning squarely towards him and keeping his voice just as low and just as venomous. "And just *what* would you have had me do? I--"

"I would have had you do as you've been *ordered!* Inform me of the situation, by all means, but don't you *dare* run off by yourself! I am responsible for every move you make and every single thing that comes of it. You might be feeling more comfortable now we're in the middle of nowhere again, but this *isn't* your home. Anyone or *anything* could be out here, and aside from what could have happened to you, you abandoned Aria when you ran off!" He ignored the mage's already enraged expression darken. "What if neither I nor Anthis had noticed you leave and something had happened to her? We were in *ditchling territory!* What were you *thinking?!*"

Rathen opened his mouth to spit a response, but Garon cut him off with another half-step closer. "*I* am in charge here," he growled menacingly as Rathen equally stood his ground, "do you understand that? I'm not just providing you with an excuse to step back into the world for a little holiday - you would not have been called upon *at all* if the situation didn't demand it. This whole matter will require co-operation on a number of different fronts, and that means we need clear leadership and someone with the authority to override the rules to get us where we need to be. And that is not *you*. Not anymore. You will not compromise my authority in front of anyone, nor the success of this matter, again."

Rathen scowled at him, his dark brown eyes shadowed by fury, but his lips remained tightly closed, as though he might spill every single hateful thought he had at that moment if they parted even a fraction.

Garon stared at him, unaffected by his rage nor his efforts to hold his tongue, and even if Rathen had been inclined to try, none of the inquisitor's thoughts were clear to read in his eyes. "I understand why you did it," he said a long moment later, though he didn't take that half-step back even as he straightened, and his voice barely softened despite his intent, "I don't disapprove of that. But you want my protection just as much as I need to provide it. Don't forget that, for anyone's sake." Then he stepped past the silently seething mage, having said all he had to on the matter, and left Rathen clenching his fists as a fire erupted in his core.

"I told you you still fit 'Sahrot'."

Rathen's eyes flashed and he whirled around to shoot another venomous look towards the officer. But though there were plenty of things he'd like to say - such as reminding him that he'd not agreed to anything in any official capacity and that, should he wish, he *could* just turn around and leave - he remained silent, his lip curling. He doubted his tongue would even work in such a rage.

Aria approached him tentatively as Garon began unhooking his blanket, and while Anthis sent a curious glance towards them both, he didn't present either with his question.

"Is everything okay?" She asked as he forced his face to relax, though he succeeded only in weakening his snarl.

"Fine," he said, managing at least not to snap at her, and he finally pulled his eyes away from the inquisitor's back to the river bed, noticing immediately that Aria - it could only be Aria - had set her bed roll on the slope of the bank instead.

He couldn't help a smile. "You'll roll out of that."

"It's *raining*," she explained, as if her logic was flawless, "I don't want to get swept away with the river when it comes, so I set it on the river bank. I tried to tell Anthis to do the same, but he said he was heavy enough not to get washed away, so I think you'll probably be fine, too."

"Well, that's good to know." He followed her back up the slope to lay out his own, stepping as carefully through the mud as he could to maintain what little dignity remained after his scolding, but faltered as a wave of panic flooded his chest at the shrill, avian screech that pierced through the air, stopping him dead as soon as he reached the top. A thick silence followed, blanketing the area even as the eerie sound trailed and reverberated through the trees. Everything around them fell still in its wake.

They turned sharp eyes to the leaves high above them, searching quickly for the source, and even the horses froze.

Rathen snatched Aria close as her eyes flicked about feverishly. "What was that?"

"I don't know," he replied quietly, still searching the boughs, "but it's big, and it's close."

It came again, splitting the stillness, and the sound of shattered branches and whipping leaves joined the cacophony behind them.

They spun in a flash and stared up at the dark shapes silhouetted against the night's sky. Garon immediately drew his sword and spat. "Harpies. Gather everything and mount up - quickly!"

They knew there was no time, but they tried anyway, throwing the bedrolls and blankets back over the saddles without sparing a moment to fix them down. But by the time Rathen had gotten Aria up onto the horse and the others were prepared to move, the winged beasts were almost upon them, the moonlight glinting vividly across their fierce, yellow eyes and flesh-rending beaks.

Shooting a glance over his shoulder, Rathen knew he had little choice. With a curse, he flexed his fingers, forming the seals and signs in a expert moment even as Garon ordered him not to, and from nowhere a gust of wind swept across the flight and sent all seven spiralling away, a din of squawks rising in a mixture of fury and surprise.

"Get on the damned horse!" Garon yelled as he and Anthis kicked theirs into a gallop, but Rathen was already half way up and urging it after them before he was even in the saddle.

The harpies recovered from the blast disappointingly quickly, catching themselves in the momentum and arcing back around, but the horses had still gained enough of a head start to keep out of their reach. They pounded down the stream before fleeing up into the forest, wending through the trees in a panic as they carried themselves to safety, and their riders only by chance. All eyes were fixed to their heading. Only Aria dared a backward glance, and though hers widened in horror at the sight of the dark creatures, torsos of humans and the wings of eagles, she didn't loose a scream. "They're getting closer, Daddy," she warned him fearfully, her voice shaking and higher pitched, "do something, please!"

Another shrill screech rent the air, drowning out his response. A second followed, then a squawking voice screamed over the thumping of the horses' hooves: "you step into a war you do not belong!"

"And chosen your side too easily!" Shrieked another.

None of them looked around nor questioned their meaning. They remained focused only on escaping their savage pursuers, but in their fixation they had no chance to work out where they were going. They could be riding towards open ground where they would be free to run in a straight line, but their assailants would be just as free to attack them from above; or perhaps towards a lake or a sudden drop or rise where they would certainly corner themselves.

Rathen cursed and began to form the seals to another spell, but a small blue light caught his eye from up ahead, a flame that had flickered suddenly into existence, suspended in the air like a burning torch bug.

He dropped his hand at the sight of it, abandoning his endeavour as Aria gasped and pointed hopefully towards it.

A shout of alarm rose from the lead as Anthis yanked the reins to force his horse around it, and Garon quickly mirrored his actions. But while they fought to avoid it, Rathen did not. "Follow it!" He yelled, already pulling his horse in the direction the tiny blue light began to float, and offered no explanation to the confused glances shot back towards him. "Trust me, just follow it!"

He ignored Garon's growl of frustration as the two bowed around, falling in alongside him while weaving through the trees, and the harpies similarly followed suit. But the light led them into denser woodland where their aerial pursuers couldn't manoeuvre so easily, and they were soon forced above the treetops. If they could track them through the leaves, they could easily get ahead of them and cut them off - but here there were no breaks in the canopy, and the ethereal flame's chaotic turns confused them all too easily.

The next shriek that froze the air came from a distance, and only then did any of them dare to look above and behind them, and upon the last, a final wail of defeat, they pulled in their horses' frantic pace with thudding hearts.

The light slowed with the animals' exhausted trot, and when it burned out of existence as suddenly as it had appeared, Rathen breathed a heavy sigh of relief and finally pulled his mount to a stop.

"What was that?" Anthis whispered, his eyes still glued to the treetops despite little to no light to see by.

"That," Rathen sighed as he slid off of his horse, "was our salvation."

Another, larger flame sparked alight a few feet away, startling both Anthis and Garon, and its eerie light reached across the rough and notched bark of the surrounding trees, as well as the woman who stood beside it.

Garon watched her carefully while Anthis's eyes widened in further surprise, riveted by her shapely form, the picturesque mess of dark waves, curls and ringlets that fell over her shoulders, and her confident stance that only further accentuated the curve of her hips. His fright was forgotten. "I had no idea salvation was so beautiful," he murmured to himself.

"You," Rathen declared as he walked towards her, noting as he did so a weave of sensory spells form a protective dome over the area, "are a life saver."

Her perfect lips curved into a smile and she accepted his firm kiss, leaning into his grip as he slipped his arms around her waist. Garon and Anthis stared at the two in another wave of bafflement, while Aria bounced over excitedly.

"How did you know we were here?"

"Oh, Rathen," she tutted, rolling her dark, emerald eyes and stroking his rough cheek, "the same way I *always* know. Though," she added, peering past him to the others, "I do have to wonder at why." Her eyes narrowed as she stepped leisurely forwards, pausing to flash Aria a familiar childish grin, and she approached the two men as her lips pursed thoughtfully. She stopped in front of Garon first, her sharp gaze studying him closely though her eyes revealed nothing of what she was thinking. She noted his sword, his clothing, his stance, his size, but as they lifted and pierced his eyes to analyse them just as deeply, an uneasy frown creased his brow and he shifted uncomfortably. Rathen would have been surprised by his response had he not been just as familiar with that unnaturally studious gaze.

A long moment passed before her attention suddenly flicked towards Anthis, leaving Garon with still no hint as to her thoughts, and though he stared back widely, enraptured now by the lively depth of her eyes, he soon received that same scrutinising stare. Her eyes penetrated his as if looking into his soul, and he quickly began to fidget as nervously as Garon had.

Then, as abruptly as she had from the officer, she turned away from him, apparently satisfied, and walked back towards Rathen with her slender hands resting upon her swaying hips. "Well?"

"Magic!" Aria beamed. "Daddy's fixing it."

Her fine eyebrows rose in surprise. "Really?" She asked with genuine disbelief.

"Apparently," he sighed, feeling that tiresome weight on his shoulders again.

"Uh-huh...and the ditchlings?"

"That's why the harpies attacked us?" He frowned, thinking nothing of how she'd known about that morning's encounter, and she sighed and hung her head, her long, forest-brown curls bouncing forwards.

"I did tell you that the harpies and ditchlings have been warring with each other for a few months now, but you never listen to me, do you?" She looked to Aria helplessly. "Is he at least listening to you?"

She shrugged. "It's hard to tell."

"Isn't it just."

"I'm sorry," Garon spoke up from behind them, his voice coloured by almost genuine apology in his confusion, "but just exactly who are you?"

"This is Kienza," Rathen replied, stepping forwards, "Kienza, this is Anthis Karth and Inquisitor Garon Brack."

Her eyebrow twitched curiously at the subtle emphasis Rathen had put on the latter's title, and he knew she'd noticed it. "Pleasure to meet you both," she said graciously, pulling her long, dark skirt to the side as she curtsied, ignoring the detail, "especially you, Mister Karth."

"Me?" Anthis asked in what seemed to be perpetual surprise.

"Indeed!" She grinned up at him as widely as Aria would have. "I've followed your work eagerly, and I'm *particularly* fascinated by your theories on pre-magic elven religion."

"My..."

She nodded enthusiastically, disregarding his stunned confusion. "Your suggestion that elves believed they *weren't* the first intelligent life the gods created is truly a wild claim, but it appeals to me - perhaps I just like the idea that the elves were once truly so modest. But tell me: do you think humans came first? Or something else?"

"Well, I, uh...I can't honestly say for certain..."

"That's why I said 'think'," she smiled, "not 'know'."

Anthis blinked and a smile equally crept across his flushing face. "I think it's possible," he replied slowly, the familiar note of interest in his voice joined with a restraint meant gauge the extent of her own curiosity, an approach he'd used a handful of times with Aria as an attempt to encourage her, "but I have had other ideas."

"Such as?"

Rathen shook his head and smiled as Kienza exhibited her usual enthusiasm, but Aria tugged at his sleeve, pulling his attention away. "I'm hungry," she reminded him quietly, her eyes wide and sad, and he recalled that she had first mentioned as such almost two hours ago.

He squeezed her shoulder apologetically and glanced around for Garon. He was still beside the horses, having warily not left their side, and even now he kept a careful eye on their rescuer.

Rathen still bristled at their previous confrontation, as brief and irritatingly one-sided as it had been, but he was begrudgingly aware that the inquisitor had had a point. "We'll be fine to make camp here," he said as he approached him, making an effort to sound respectful though he couldn't help a little acid from shortening his tone.

Garon didn't seem to notice, however. "Is it safe?" He asked, his eyes remaining on the mysterious woman.

"It is. Kienza led us here, and if any one of us standing in this forest can be trusted absolutely, it's her."

He turned his eyes upon him. "She's a mage."

"Yes," Rathen sighed with restrained impatience, knowing what was coming, "and she isn't affiliated with any secret and rebellious movements either. She *can* be trusted."

"She's with the Order?"

His lips pursed slightly as he hesitated, and turned towards the horses to begin removing the blankets and bedrolls that had been strewn over their saddles. "No."

"Then she's with--"

"She is with no one but herself," he said firmly, interrupting Garon's alarmed conclusion. He looked back towards her as she continued talking animatedly with Anthis, catching the words 'god-like', 'wild man' and 'lesser' from their excited conversation. "I don't know why, and I don't know how. That woman has been an enigma to me since day one and I learned long ago not to bother asking questions." And yet he spoke without a single trace of curiosity, as though it had been beaten out of him after countless vain attempts to encourage her to reveal her mysteries. "She has her secrets, and she's entitled to them."

Garon frowned at him, but it was clear from his tone that he honestly couldn't shed any light on just who she was no matter how hard he might press. He was less accepting of his eyes' suggestion that they had little to fear from her, but, reluctantly, he left the matter alone. Though when he turned his suddenly disapproving eyes back upon him as another issue stepped into his mind, Rathen was already shaking his head.

"I know what you're going to say, but it was either follow the light or run for who knows how far. I had no intention of 'undermining your authority', I was just doing what was best for all of us."

Garon looked around at the looming dark and empty forest. "In this case, you were right to. I wouldn't have followed the light." He looked back to him, and though the criticism in his eyes had faded, the superiority remained. "But next time you will suggest, not order."

Rathen swallowed his rising irritation. "Yes, Inquisitor."

The two of them began laying the bed rolls over the comparatively flat and dry grass, and Anthis soon joined them to lay his own while Kienza made a camp fire behind them, presumably out of nothing, before leaving with Aria to collect fresh water while food was heated over the flames.

"She's remarkable," Anthis said excitedly as he sat down beside Rathen who tended the meagre meal. "She really *has* been keeping up with my work - she even suggested other avenues of research I'd never thought of! Do you know, she said that if I were to go to the highest point of the southernmost reach of the Olusan mountains I'd find a semi-ruined - *semi*-ruined - house of the God of Mind!" Anthis's eyes were brighter and wider than Rathen had yet seen them, and he was shaking his head either in amazement or some kind of fit. "There are no known standing houses to Nara!"

"Nara?" He frowned mildly, poking at the contents of the warming pot.

"Vastal," Anthis corrected, waving his specifics away, "faces, faces; always Vastal. I wonder how she knows of it." He shook his head in wonder again, then looked to Rathen with calmer but certainly more envious eyes. "You're a lucky man, Rathen."

"I suppose so."

"And I can see the resemblance."

His thoughtful frown twisted into confusion. "Sorry?"

"Her and Aria."

"Oh." He chuckled easily, and his expression relaxed as he turned back to the fire. "She isn't her mother."

"...Oh...sorry, I just--"

"It's fine," Rathen assured him, placing the lid over the pot Kienza had conjured, and as he cast him an amused and casual glance, Anthis began to ease.

"Did you meet her in the Order, then?"

Rathen absently wondered at the young man's unrelenting interest in his past, but he didn't voice it. Instead he sat back from the flames and turned critical eyes upon him. Anthis shrank back beneath them, but what he'd seen as a warning had in fact been calculation. The mage turned away a moment later to look through the dark forest that sprawled endlessly beyond the reach of the firelight. "No. She saved my life."

The words hung in the air while Anthis stared at him in astonishment, and even Garon looked up from a short distance away. But though both foolishly hoped he might continue, as usual he seemed disinclined to divulge anything more. Anthis's brow dropped a fraction in suspicion, wondering if it was even true. Rathen had yet to reveal much about himself, after all, and he was still a little uneasy about that fact.

But neither of them pressed the matter. They let silence fall until Aria came back, filled waterskins bundled in her arms as she relayed the message that Kienza would be back shortly, that she'd already eaten and they shouldn't wait for her. Which was just as well, because the rationed meat had just finished cooking and none of them could ignore their rumbling stomachs.

Aria finished within minutes, and as her sated hunger chased fatigue away, she dashed over to the saddles piled on the ground to tug at the ditchlings' branch. The knots held fast and seemed even to tighten as she struggled, but before she could turn and call frustratedly for help, Rathen was already reaching over her.

He trimmed the wood down with a quick spell following her meticulous instruction, then she rushed back to the campfire - carefully, as her father called behind her - and sat down beside Anthis as he looked over the notes he'd gathered that day, while Garon pored over a map to locate their position on the other side of the flames. They both frowned at her as she giggled quietly to herself in excitement, but as a glint of light caught their eye from the blade she hacked through the thin bark, Anthis gasped in alarm.

"Should she be doing that?!" He stammered, twisting towards Rathen with dismay in his gaping eyes, but Rathen waved the concern away, assuring them a little too mildly that she was fine, and returned without another word to his spot by the fire. But despite how easily her father had redirected his attention, they couldn't tear their eyes away, and their breath tightened as they watched her hands move faster with the knife than any parent should have been comfortable with, yet with more control than either of them yielded to notice.

Moments later, Kienza appeared from the black forest. All eyes turned towards her, but she looked only to Rathen. "Walk with me," she said softly, half turning back towards the woods as she beckoned him, and the others silently and curiously watched him rise and follow her off into the tangled darkness.

They walked quietly, side by side to nowhere in particular, far from the reach of the firelight, and said not a word until Kienza cast a backwards glance towards the meagre glow of the camp. "So," she began, satisfied that they were beyond earshot, "how are you finding your new friends?"

Rathen groaned and rolled his eyes, folding his arms huffily across his chest, but she was already laughing.

"Oh you're *loving* it, aren't you? I bet you've been laying the misery on really thick."

"I haven't," he frowned, a touch insulted.

"No more than usual," she corrected. "And I expect you've clashed with both of them. The inquisitor seems to be in charge, so I'm sure you intentionally don't listen to him, and Anthis is young and excitable - you *really* must hate him."

"I don't *hate* him," he objected said slowly, determined neither to suggest she was right nor admit otherwise, "he's just...more lively than I'm used to."

She smiled and cocked an eyebrow. "Sweetheart, you're 'used to' Aria and I. He can't be more lively than the two of us."

"No, he isn't I suppose, but he's more lively than I'd like a stranger to be."

"Well," she sighed, "he thinks highly of you, at least."

Rathen frowned, surprised, and stepped down the ledge ahead of them and offered her his hand. "He does?"

"Yes," she replied, accepting his help. "I mean, he didn't say as much, but I thought it was quite obvious in his manner, and he was quicker to follow my flame than the other one was. He's very curious about you, too - but I suppose anyone would be."

"And about you," he added.

"Well," she grinned, flicking her stormy hair, "who wouldn't be?"

Rathen shook his head, but he smiled all the same. "You are certainly something else."

"Aren't I just?"

He stopped and caught her waist, kissing her more affectionately than the last, and she smiled warmly when they parted.

"So," she continued, conjuring a blanket which she lay across the muddy ground, while Rathen narrowed his eyes curiously at the fact that she hadn't formed any seals. But, as usual, it was a detail he chose not to question. "How exactly do you plan to 'fix' this magic?"

Hopelessness suddenly twisted his face as he dropped down heavily beside her. "I honestly don't know. Garon wants to hunt down some elven relic that can supposedly remove or suppress magic, but I have severe doubts that it even exists, let alone that we can find it. And the matter seems just too severe to rely on nonsense like that, but--"

"Why do you think it's serious?"

Rathen frowned and looked into her eyes. The moonlight that managed to leak through the leaves above revealed their powerful interest; they bore no doubt or scepticism, and he knew she was asking him plainly for his thoughts, not making a rhetorical remark.

"Because the magic is already affecting other countries. Lands are being torn apart, there have been floods, droughts, and people have been killed in the process. It's only just started to affect Turunda, but, if left alone, it would certainly go the same way. And as for the magic itself... I don't know, but I fear it has the potential to be used as a weapon. If mages somewhere have figured out how to pool it, or at least draw on it, then they have what are essentially *wells* of raw power just waiting to be drained all across the continent. I can't think how they could possibly manage it, but you told me yourself there was something unnatural about it."

"There certainly is." Her eyes sharpened peculiarly, sending a chill right through him. "But you've not touched on even half of it. Never mind the drying of marshes, flooding of forests and *floating hills*," she continued, ignoring the alarm that suddenly flashed in his eyes, "the chasms are *continuing* to deepen and lengthen, and already Dolunokh is set to split in half if any more of the tears meet. People have died, as you've said; villages to cities have been destroyed, and there are locations in Turunda primed for exactly the same thing. The sites of magnetism are spaced together *just close enough* that, if a tear formed at one in every four, the whole of Arasiin could be torn apart."

Rathen stared at her, his eyes alight with growing dread.

"Then there's the danger this magic poses to mages," she continued just as intensely. "The rebellion in Qenra was the only real one, but the events that encouraged them were tied to it. At first, everyone thought they were attacks made as a show of strength to frighten people into mages' submission, but the truth is far from as simple. Just as magic is being forced to the surface of people well past their prime, and even strengthening some who were already fully instructed, a few have been driven mad by it, losing control of their minds and their magic. They've killed themselves - some accidentally, some not - and killed others along with them, mages and otherwise. And while only a *few* individuals seem to be at risk, a single mage can cause a *lot* of damage and there's no way of knowing just who is vulnerable.

"Mages in other countries have already succumbed, and just as the state of affected land is worsening, the number of affected mages also continues to grow at an alarming rate. If left unchecked, who's to say what more this impossible magic could do? It could begin to affect spells already woven, or cause elven-made cities to collapse, killing thousands the country over - and none of this is even mentioning the social upheaval for anywhere lucky enough to remain untouched! Mages are already seen in a bad light, and they won't stand for the oppression that would come of this. Then it won't be a small faction within the Order people should worry about rebelling, it would be *all* mages, because they would have no choice but to fight tooth and nail for their freedom."

Rathen hadn't blinked. His heart had sank so low it now sat in his stomach, even as he felt it hammering in his throat. But she seemed not to notice his horror - or perhaps she had, but had decided that he needed to hear everything anyway.

"Not only that," she continued, her severity unwavering, "but this magic *should not* be here. You've been through Wrenroot, you've felt it yourself, and I'm sure you've come to the same conclusion, which is presumably why you're still out here."

"But *what* is so *wrong* about it?!" His voice finally burst free from his strangled throat as exasperation took over; in her own special way, she'd told him so much and yet nothing at all, and rendered his panic so clear in his eyes he couldn't have hidden it if he'd tried with all his might. "Where has it come from?!" He demanded. "And why?! I can see in your eyes that you *know* something, Kienza! *Tell me!*"

She shook her head calmly. "I only *suspect* something; I have nothing to back it up with. At this point it's little more than a guess, and I won't distract you with what may well turn out to be a falsehood."

He stared at her, his desperate plea still burning in his haunted eyes, but she returned his stare levelly, unmoving. His jaw tightened. His task had suddenly quadrupled in weight, and he was more than prepared to fight whatever she knew it out of her. But...he knew her too well. If she had decided to keep a secret, not even the threat of death could free it from her lips.

He sighed roughly and turned away, suddenly certain that he wouldn't be sleeping that night, then felt a familiar wash of comfort as her hand came to rest upon his shoulder. She smiled softly. "I'm sorry. Give me time, first. Now, do continue: 'too severe to rely on nonsense like relics...'"

Rathen sighed again, only now understanding the true weight behind his own words. "As we've established," he continued, making an effort to calm himself, though it came easily as hopelessness gripped him and turned his whole body to lead, "it's serious. And some kind of elven relic probably *could* do the job *if it exists,* but if it doesn't...if it doesn't, then it's all down to me."

"What is it they expect you to do?" She asked with that same interest again.

"Repair the artefact--"

"Which you could do; it would have been a complex spell, few elves would have been able to maintain it, so those who cast it would have safe-guarded it against disintegration. I'd think there'd be enough left to work with."

"That's what Anthis said, but I'm more willing to trust your word on it over his. And..." he chuckled humourlessly, "Garon thinks that if the elves could create a spell to suppress magic, then so can I." He shook his head helplessly. "It's like the Order all over again."

"The Order may have had a point - perhaps you *do* have untapped power. They wouldn't have kept pressing it if they didn't truly believe it."

Rathen's brow flattened at her boldness. "Don't. Start."

She turned him an impish grin and his temper dissipated readily. "Sorry. But either way, who's to say you can't do it?"

"Who--wh--*every single thing* we know about magic!" Rathen blustered, aggravation quickly spilling back over him, and he wondered despondently if perhaps he was the only one who actually understood magic after all. "I would have thought you of *all* people would know that!"

She pursed her lips, bobbing her head thoughtfully, then looked up at the stars as a light wind moved the leaves above them, creating a brief window to the night sky. "Yes and no." She turned her dark, mysterious eyes back onto him with a simple smile. "No one's really tried."

"Oh, people have tried," he assured her.

"Perhaps, but not with any pressing need to succeed, which you certainly now have. And, as a side note, given the present situation, I don't think we can rely too much on 'everything we know about magic'. Now, tell me: what have you come up with so far?"

"On the magic or this pointless spell?"

"Both."

He took a moment to collect his thoughts and shortly realised with another painful wave of failure just how little he truly had. "Well," he began anyway, "the magic is raw, like that within mages, but with no container to direct or contain it, and it's gathering at magnetic sites - that much I worked out for myself."

"No, *I* told you about the magnetism," she corrected him with a weary sigh, "but at least you've confirmed it for yourself. Anything else?"

He looked at her flatly. "And that there is no construction to the magic at all. It's not part of any spell, and there are no traces of any spells in the areas that could have possibly caused it by some insane circumstance either. As far as I can see, it's just appeared out of nowhere." She continued watching him expectantly, and he rolled his eyes. "And I have no idea where to start with the spell whatsoever. I have no clue how to fix it and I'm quite positive that I *can't*."

"Then why did you accept the task?"

He blinked. "Well...because..."

An irritatingly knowing smile spread across her face as she looked away and up towards the shaft of moonlight, and Rathen's brow lowered again in defeat.

'Because I care.'

She leaned back on her hands and crossed her slender legs. "If it's 'raw', then it should behave as normal magic," she mused, "and if an elven relic can remove or block the magic of a mage, it could do the same with this. That's assuming of course that the spell in the relic affects the target's magic, *not* the target's body. If it just affects the heart and stops magic from either forming there or joining the bloodstream, then it would be quite useless in this case."

"Right," Rathen nodded slowly, his mind now suddenly quite open to the possibility of the artefact, and he waited impatiently for the 'but' that would follow.

"But if the spell affects the magic itself, then with enough information on the relic and understanding of how it would have worked, you could, in theory, find a way to make something similar."

He shook his head, disappointed by her vague response and lack of any helpful suggestion. "Just like everyone else, you're forgetting about the amount of power it would have taken for the elves to make such a thing. *No one* has the magical capacity to do that, and certainly not me - even if I *did* manage to tap into this rumoured power of mine. It isn't possible."

"Hush, Rathen, I'm just thinking out loud, running through the bottom line." She turned contemplative eyes onto him. "What you need to do is take it step by step. Forget the magnitude of the task, that will just distract you and make you feel hopeless."

"I already do."

"What you need to do before anything else is just *understand* the magic; familiarise yourself with how it feels, how it moves and flows, what form it's sitting in - cloud, puddle, brick, whatever. Once you've got that, you can try to affect it as a whole - push it, compact it, expand it - and if you can do that then you can go further and try to interact with it which would *eventually* broaden into removing it. That's it. No grand shows of what a magnificent mage you are, no trying to solve the problem in as few steps as possible. Don't try to run before you can even sit up by yourself. And if you can't get that far, you're not going to be able to do anything about it at all, in which case you can put it out of your mind with the satisfaction of having tried."

His jaw tightened as he shook his head. "It isn't going to be as easy as that."

She took him suddenly by the chin and turned his head towards her, and as her dark, beautiful eyes gripped him, eyes the colour of the maturest summer leaves, he saw within them a flame of confidence. But it was not the confidence which she unfailingly carried for herself - it was in him. "You haven't tried it yet."

His frown softened and his heart similarly melted, and he found himself surprised by how much her faith meant to him. "Where did you get this wisdom of yours?"

"I was born with it," she grinned, and leaned in to kiss him. "So, remind me: what should you do first?"

"Understand the magic."

"And how are you going to do that?"

"By going to another ruin and feeling it again, I suppose."

"Exactly. And how are you going to feel it?"

He frowned. "What do you mean?"

"You're going to close your mind, stop asking 'where has it come from' and getting bogged down in specifics, and just *feel it*. And," she added as she rose to her knees, "I suggest you try somewhere influenced by more than just beauty. Try somewhere more chaotic. It might feel different."

He nodded in understanding, but his eyes suddenly flashed as an urgent thought swept across him, and he reached out to grasp her wrist. "Wait - *you've* been to these places."

She frowned. "I have..."

"And did any of them feel...peaceful to you?"

She took a moment and pursed her lips in thought, her frown barely marring her perfectly smooth face. "Not really, no. Why?"

The lines in his own brow deepened. "No reason."

She cocked her head curiously but didn't pose her question, and rose the rest of the way to her feet. "Anyway, I must be off."

"You're leaving already?" He asked as he followed her up, though only a touch of disappointment found its way into his voice.

"I found you by chance," she told him softly, "a happy coincidence, but I was out here taking care of other business, and I really must get on." She stepped forwards and pressed her lips against his, softly, warmly, her kiss radiating a greater affection than any other that night. They remained there for an endless moment, and when she pulled away, he almost moved with her. She smiled apologetically as she began to take slow steps away, leaving him to catch his balance. "I promise I'll give you more time when we next meet. For now, try not to upset anyone else. This won't be the last time the harpies set upon you, so you'd better keep your eyes open and your hands free, as much as you might hate it. And," she added, smiling widely, "try to *enjoy* yourself. An opportunity like this won't come along for you very often."

"I would rather it hadn't come along at all."

"Trust me, Rathen: you're in good hands. Just try to keep calm. And be nice."

"And don't pull the horses' tails?" He raised an eyebrow and cast her a childish grin, which she returned with one much the same.

"Exactly." And with a final step, she vanished into the darkness. Rathen's heart sank as he found himself suddenly standing alone amongst the trees, and again a little further as he heard her disembodied voice call 'I love you' through the night. He looked down at the blanket that still lay beneath his feet, but even that shortly disappeared, and then no trace remained of her ever having been there.

A breeze picked up around him. He folded his arms tightly against the invading chill that dragged him sharply back to the world, and sighed sadly as he looked up towards the shaft of icy moonlight. Then he turned around and trudged back to camp, alone. He fought hard with every step to push aside the sense of loneliness that assaulted him every time she left, and the longing for the simple, normal life he'd left behind, both of which seemed easily able to overshadow his heavy and far more immediate concerns.

But that existence had gone, and nothing good ever came from indulging its memory.

Chapter 12

The warm glow of the campfire slipped off into the darkness to drape itself softly around Rathen's shoulders. It ushered along his heavy footsteps, welcoming him back to the camp with an encouraging nudge while its heat set to work warding off the persistent chill. But he made no show of noticing. He didn't spare a moment even to wonder if its hospitality had been his imagination. His mood remained bleak and inverted as he stopped silently beside Aria, who continued to whittle while Anthis watched openly beside her, and he dropped heavily to sit in the dirt in front of the fire in the hope that its hypnosis would chase away his gloom if he stared deeply enough into its writhing depths.

Aria looked up sadly at his distant eyes, and the pause of her blade stroke encouraged Anthis's gaze to follow. But Rathen felt neither of their stares upon him. His mind was lost in burning thought.

As if it would really be so easy to push such despair aside. He was assaulted by memories - memories he desperately wished never to relive, and yet clung to so dearly; memories he'd never forgotten, had never even faded, but now seemed to weigh upon him as heavily as they did when they were fresh. Being back in the world had given them a new, stinging vitality, and he found himself asking the same questions he had when his world had first turned upside down: why him? Why did his life have to turn out this way? Why did he have to lose everything? And why by his *own hands?* That was the true torment: everything that had befallen him had been by his own doing, and even now, after the passage of so much time, he still had no idea why, how nor when the curse had befallen him.

But though those questions had eroded him ever since, he had long ago stopped trying to answer them. They had no meaning; even if he could get his answers, it wouldn't reverse a thing. So instead he had turned to bitterness, and he'd nursed it alongside a hate for himself and a greater loathing for the Crown. He'd turned into a dour, resentful man, and how Kienza or Aria could love him like they did, he still couldn't fathom. And what would Elle have said if she could see him now? If she were to peer out from the black and ghostly forest around them, what would she see? Would she see the man she'd loved? Or would she see only his shell?

The thought pummelled him. His heart swelled and dropped, turning to lead as familiar grief surged over him like a tidal wave, and his jaw was clenched so tightly that he became aware of it and had to force it to loosen. But his eyes didn't move. The campfire that Kienza had created, the fire he swore he could hear her voice in, smell her scent within, held his gaze as if it stared right back, and he found himself struck just as violently by guilt for pining over his past after everything she'd done for him.

'That is not my life anymore,' the voice in his head chided him for the thousandth time, and he knew, painfully, that no amount of sulking would change

that. He straightened and forced himself to breathe, inhaling so deeply it almost hurt, and exhaled his thoughts away with the long-practised technique. Others quickly spilled into their place, and though they were far more weighted, he found himself more inclined to deal with them than he had been five minutes ago.

He inhaled slowly once more, suddenly grateful for the distraction, and focused his mind purposefully so that he might, at least for the moment, keep these thoughts from being clouded by severity.

Understand the magic. Kienza was probably right; he hadn't once tried to look at the matter in smaller pieces, he'd just kept obsessing over the enormity and impossibility of it, became frightened and pushed it aside. *'And sulked,'* Kienza would have added. But, alongside telling him more than he'd wanted to hear, she'd also handed him a solution, as he knew she would, and quizzed him to make him think for himself in the process. He hated it when she did that, but it always helped him get his thoughts in order.

For what felt like an age, he turned his mind back, doing his best to recall all he could of the magic that permeated the ruins in the hope that he could make some use of the meagre experiences so far. But no matter how hard nor how long he tried, nothing returned to him beyond the beauty and apparently non-existent peace. He hadn't been paying attention to distribution or accumulation at the time because he hadn't thought to. No, he'd been thinking of that bottom line: that he was expected to form an impossible spell to remove it, and just how much of it there was to remove.

That damned bottom line.

He finally gave up, another rough sigh puffing through his lips, and he drew his knees into his chest while a voice he wasn't fond of and yet was very much like his own chastised him for being so easily overwhelmed. But what could he do when he had so little to work with?

'There will be other sites...' If Garon expected him to achieve his task, there would have to be, and then he could find something of use. But for now, he was decidedly useless in the matter.

He watched the flames flicker back and forth, his thoughts shifting with them as his tired mind grew sluggish, his eyelids heavy, and he became slowly aware of just how deeply his back and thighs ached from being in a saddle for so long. The soreness only worsened the longer he let himself notice it, and soon his whole body felt rigid and sleep seemed mockingly distant. His mind looped around, returning to depths he didn't wish it to, and again he had to force it into silence.

But before he could get a rein on his thoughts himself, he was torn quite suddenly out of them. His heart stopped, shocking his mind into a blank slate, then leapt to race faster than the winds and thud louder than the hooves of a thousand horses, each of which seemed to have kicked him as they'd passed.

He looked up, wide-eyed, as Aria fell quiet, her gentle humming silenced, and he found her staring back at him with an equally wide gaze. But hers was one riddled deeply with guilt, though she seemed unsure as to why. "Why do you look so sad?"

"I don't," he replied quickly, though he noticed even as he spoke the strong downturn of the corners of his lips, and it took much more effort than he expected to smile. But he knew even as he managed that it hadn't been worth it. The way her young brow knitted together made it clear that it wasn't convincing.

Her fringe shadowed her face as she looked down at the half-shaped wood in her hands. "You do. More than usual." She turned her big blue-grey eyes back up at him. "Is it the song?"

He blinked as his heart settled back into its normal rhythm, and though he opened his mouth to lie, he knew there was little point. She was too perceptive; he rarely got away with it. He sighed in defeat instead. "How did you know?"

"Because that's all that changed. You didn't look like that two minutes ago, and two minutes ago you were still sat there with the same clothes, the same fire. And Anthis was sat just here then, but I didn't think it would be that because you've never looked like that when Anthis *wasn't* sat near you before." She shrugged in disappointment as Rathen noticed that the young man had indeed left her side. "What's wrong with the song?"

He sighed again, suddenly feeling guilty himself, and managed another weak smile in an attempt to reassure her. "There's nothing wrong with the song. A woman I know--...knew, used to sing it."

"A woman? Was she important? Of course she was, you wouldn't remember if she wasn't important." Her curious frown softened as a thought occurred to her, and her eyes widened a fraction in wonder. "Was it your mum?"

He breathed a brief laugh, but the half-smile that came with it was just as fleeting. "No," he replied. "I don't recall much about her."

"Was it...*my* mum?"

His sad frown returned. "No."

The flames of the campfire flickered at the edge of his vision. He felt their draw once more, luring his mind back into desolate thoughts. He steeled himself. He wasn't going to let himself succumb to Elle's memory again that night.

Oh, but if only it was that simple. He already had. It wasn't so easy to push her from his mind once she'd made an appearance. He knew this well - he'd spent the last eleven years trying to move past her in order to build a new life, and he'd managed with no small effort.

But that tune...that lilting melody he tied so specifically to her... It seemed it still had the power to knock him sideways. He'd never heard anyone else sing it, and even as Aria had hummed it a moment go, it was recited in his mind in Elle's voice in perfect time. A canticle sung by a shade of the past.

He dragged his gaze from the fire and back onto Aria. She was watching him patiently, her guilt for being the cause of his sorrow still clear upon her young face. "Where did you learn it?"

"I heard one of the Arkhamas humming it. I thought it sounded pretty."

Ditchlings...he wondered where they'd gotten it from. "It *is* pretty," he smiled.

"Do you want me to stop?"

"...No. Yes."

She smiled sadly then rose nimbly to her feet, placing her knife and wood carefully in the grass amongst the strips and shavings she'd worked away from it, and stepped over to wrap her arms around him. "I'm sorry for making you sad, Daddy."

He chuckled and held her tightly. "I'm fine," he assured her. "I promise."

"I'll sing you something else."

"You don't need to do that."

"It's okay, it's one you like."

A hesitant smile forced itself upon him. "Ah. Must you?"

She nodded vigorously, already stepping back in preparation, and following a deep breath and no opportunity to object, she dove into a much-rehearsed rendition of 'Oat, The Lovely, Miserable Goat', complete with a silly and quite irrelevant dance. She put her usual effort in to try to cheer him up, and though it worked, both for the entertainment and the shameful reminder that he had other things he could pour his heart into, she was already tired and her performance finally wore her down.

She didn't object when he put her to bed, and he didn't have to remain at her side for too long before she drifted off. Five minutes after he'd pulled the blanket over her, she was sleeping peacefully, and he returned to his spot by the fire with a much easier heart.

Anthis shortly joined him after tucking his books away in his saddle bag, and as Rathen tossed Aria's mess of wooden shavings into the fire, the young historian smiled fondly towards her. "She's dedicated to you, you know," he said softly.

"And I to her." He lifted the wood she'd been working and ran his thumb carefully over the surface, admiring the almost perfectly rounded edges. There was little to it yet, but though she'd only been working on it for about half an hour, he already had a hunch.

He wasn't at all surprised that she'd asked the ditchlings for a branch from their forest. She was a sentimental girl, and though he deeply disapproved, the ditchlings seemed to have made an impression on her. But then, they were the closest thing to another child she'd ever met.

Anthis watched him handle the wood with great care, trying to work out what it was himself. "What is it?" He asked eventually, and Rathen breathed a quiet laugh.

"If I had to guess, I'd say it was a ghost."

Anthis frowned and peered at it more closely. "Why a ghost?"

He stroked the long, featureless edge that had been only partially freed from the rest of the wood. The carving was so smooth compared to the natural roughness of the branch that it seemed as if the tree had consumed the form in growth, and Aria had merely released it. "Just a guess."

Anthis shrugged it off while Rathen rose and tucked the wood and knife back into her bag. "Where did she learn to whittle? She's remarkably skilled with the blade."

"Kienza taught her."

"Did you not object?"

"Yes, but Kienza is a good teacher, and Aria's a good learner. She loves it, she says learning is like a collection you don't need to find a box for - I'm sure you've noticed her enthusiasm."

Anthis smiled. "I have."

Rathen sat back down beside him while a weary Garon returned from the river, but he didn't speak to either as he moved towards his bed roll and prepared himself for the night.

"She's a...curious girl," he said quietly, the two ignoring the inquisitor just as he ignored them. "She's got such a hunger for everything around her all the time - it's like she's never been to a city before. Every time we stop she acts as though she's stepped into a new world. Even when it's the woods. She has such a zest for everything, even for a child. To be honest, I envy her. I don't think even I was that enthusiastic."

A soft frown descended as another finger of guilt prodded at Rathen's heart. "It's because she hasn't."

Anthis looked back to him expectantly. "Hasn't what?"

"Been to any cities, seen many woods." He noticed Anthis's confusion. "We live an isolated life," he explained. "This is the first time she's ever been more than half a mile from home."

"Well it's a dangerous world, especially now. There's nothing wrong with sticking to what you know is safe - it's responsible parenting."

Rathen twitched and mumbled: "I'm not so sure I'm a responsible parent."

"Sorry?"

"I said," he replied, speaking up, "it's nothing to do with being a responsible parent. She's only ever met a handful of people. To be honest, I'm surprised she's not more intimidated."

"A handful of people? You mean formally?"

He shook his head, wondering why he suddenly felt the need to speak of it. But among everything else that plagued him lately, regret had also been shadowing him for exactly this reason. She was so excited, so happy - even when she'd been frightened or unsettled, her fascination with each situation had stood right alongside her trepidation. But he'd kept her locked up, concealing the world from her, telling himself all the while that she knew no different so it wouldn't matter, that she couldn't miss what she never had. But now he was realising just what he'd hidden from her, and it wasn't just the sight of horizons, hills and properly-constructed buildings.

But it also couldn't have been helped. He was banished, and there was no one else to care for her. She had little choice but to share in his sentence.

He looked thoughtfully back to Anthis. "I think you're good for her."

His eyebrows rose in surprise at the statement, but more so at the implication of a compliment. "In what way?"

"Encouraging her curiosity, helping her understand the world around her. Garon doesn't seem to have much tact with that side of things, and sometimes I think I'm too out of touch to be of much use, either."

"Oh, well, thank you," he smiled proudly. "I'm glad to be of help."

They both threw a glance over their shoulders as a slight giggle came from Aria's direction, but she didn't make another peep as she lay bundled beneath the blankets, lost in whatever amusing dream she was having this time.

Rathen smiled and shook his head, while Anthis turned his eyes upon him in consideration. "Can I ask you a question?"

He looked back to him dubiously, but found he was too curious to say 'no', and even as he cast over him another evaluating gaze, his decision was made on impulse rather than calculation. "Go ahead."

Anthis paused for a moment, collecting his thoughts, and Rathen found himself already regretting it. "You haven't been as closed off since we left the roads," he said slowly. "Even when we encountered the ditchlings, you were less...uneasy than each time we've been in any cities or villages. Why is that?"

Rathen, too, hesitated before speaking. "I said we live an isolated life," he replied finally, though his careful thought remained in his tone, "but that's not necessarily through choice..."

Anthis searched his eyes by the firelight as he paused again, trying to read beneath his vagueness before Rathen could continue. They were hard-edged, as usual, but over the past two weeks, he'd come to see a kindness within them. It wasn't one put on display for anyone to see, in fact more often than not his eyes were bitter, acrid, or perhaps even violent, but even when he was scrutinising a detail or claiming, less than delicately, that faith was a waste of time, it was always there, just beneath the surface. A detail one wouldn't notice without getting to know at least a little of his true nature that lay beneath his bitter husk which, Anthis suspected, could only have been born of something tragic.

Rathen's eyes soon dropped back to the weakening flames that crackled and danced before them, either having decided that he didn't want to continue, or that he needn't bother since Anthis was working it out for himself. But as the historian continued trying to read him, suggestions began forming in his mind, and he found himself suddenly quite uncomfortable about having posed the question at all. And yet, even as those suggestions both grew and shrank by likelihood, he was just as uncomfortable with letting it lie.

"You were banished for something, weren't you?" He asked plainly, though uncertainly, and when Rathen barely reacted, he knew he'd come to the wrong conclusion. Until Rathen nodded.

His eyes widened. It took a long moment for the fact to sink in, but as he continued to analyse his unaffected expression, again his eyes narrowed in doubt. He threw a speculative glance towards Garon, who lay with his back turned to them, and considered him for a moment. This was an official investigation and so his presence was required, but he had noticed more than a few times that Garon kept a closer eye on Rathen than he did on him, and while he had initially taken it as the same distrust most held for mages, now he wasn't so sure. If Rathen *had* been banished, nothing less than an inquisitor could take custody of him. But why would he seek the help of a banished mage rather than turn to the Order? Was this threat of a rebellion *truly* that serious?

He looked back to him steadily. "Why? What did you do?"

The mage's knotted brow tightened further in thought, and though he parted his lips to speak, something held his tongue.

"You were a soldier, you said - sahrot?" He pressed. "Did something go wrong? Did you disobey orders? Because, forgive me, but from what I've seen of you I can't believe for a moment that whatever you would have done was without good reason."

Again, the flash of Rathen's dark eyes froze his blood. They turned upon him so sharply it was as though he'd intentionally said something to wound him, despite the confusion they were met with. He shrank even further as the mage rose to his feet, and a storm engulfed him as he made for his bed roll, snarling beneath his breath even as he blocked out the world and everyone in it. "You know *nothing* about me."

"Rathen, I'm sorry," he said quickly, silently scolding himself for being so invasive, but the mage ignored him. He threw his shirt aside, blinding him as moonlight glinted from a band about his arm, snatched his blanket over himself and lay with his back turned to stare off into the endless black of the forest.

The camp fell still. Anthis's shoulders slumped in defeat, and the voice in his mind kicked off and berated him once again. The man's past was absolutely none of his business, but he just couldn't ignore his own curiosity, and the one time his walls had finally come down, he'd managed to insult him. But how *could* he ignore his curiosity after what he'd seen in Rathen's eyes? He stood by what he'd said: whatever Rathen had done, banishment had been an unfair punishment, either unjust or entirely undeserved. A man truly guilty of treason or insubordination wouldn't be quick to leave their home and protect their country after betraying it once already, and yet here was Rathen, uncomfortable, daunted, and carrying a task he clearly didn't want, all while being pushed on by his own conviction. And though Anthis's imagination still stampeded away from him, he just couldn't ignore the value of the man's spirit. It was too clear in his eyes.

A soft hoot ruffled the stillness, drawing him out his thoughts and back to the cold, surrounding night, and he realised he was the last one up. Out of nowhere, fatigue fell upon him like a mail blanket. With a sigh of defeat, he rose, kicked out the fire and prepared himself for bed, seeing little reason to remain.

He was painfully aware of every sound he made in the enveloping silence, as every step and every rustle seemed to be returned and repeated by the towering trees. Neither Aria nor Garon snored, and Rathen was surely still awake, though both pretended otherwise, so as he loosened his belt and the two blades hidden beneath his shirt, he made sure to keep the two apart and at least avoid the clatter of their hilts.

Stuffing his clothes into the bag he'd set beside his blankets, he silently slipped one dagger down the side, hidden from anyone rifling through. He moved to conceal the second within his clothes, but as its half-foot steel edge caught the moonlight from between breaks in the cloud, a troubled frown descended.

He looked closely at the three cut glass crystals embedded in its arabesque hilt, and though two were clear enough to reveal the steel settings beneath them, the third, sitting just above the tang of the blade, had more than just discoloured. It had turned a deathly black.

His heart jumped and his eyes tore quickly to the second, peering closely into its depths, straining through the cold, weak light, and he gradually noticed the slightest clouding within that one, too, spreading like a pestilence.

A fire sparked in his stomach. It was three days too soon, but now he'd seen it, he was sure he could feel the crystals' corruption spreading within himself as well. It was all in his head, he was sure; two had to turn black before he would feel anything, but evidently the quality of his last contribution hadn't been what he'd thought.

With a deep breath, he steadied himself and put the blade away within the folds of his clothes, pushing the thought aside. It didn't really matter; his luck was on balance. With the military moving off and roads reopening behind them, they'd be in Mokhan in just three more days, and then he could solve his predicament before it became an issue. There were papers enough in his saddle bag, and in a city so big, he was sure to find something.

He sighed wearily as he finally lay down and pulled the blanket over him, making himself as comfortable as he could on the uneven ground, and let his tired mind wander until he slipped into dream.

He had risen cautiously the following morning, still weighted by multiple concerns despite his restful sleep, but, to both his surprise and relief, Rathen had been strangely neutral, as though their altercation hadn't happened. He said not a word about it, offering no explanation for his turn - though Anthis decided that such would be unusual behaviour for him anyway - and Anthis similarly chose not to address it despite his usual curiosity and the overwhelming need to apologise again.

Instead, everyone's attention had turned towards their purpose in Mokhan and the opportunity to finally begin the search for the relic. But while over the following days Rathen had grown restless beneath his urgency to deal with the situation after Kienza had well and truly thrown the door open on it, as they drew closer to the city, Anthis became increasingly irritable. It had started with a few sharply answered questions, then during the second day he'd barely spoken at all as they rode, and by the time they'd stopped to make camp for the night, he'd closed himself off completely. Aria was hurt the most by the change, and while Rathen had initially put it down to impatient excitement, he soon thought he saw a touch of fret in his young brow. Perhaps he was feeling the pressure, concerned he couldn't deliver. He could certainly appreciate that sentiment, but the historian's mood and doubt only served to add more weight to his heart.

On the final night they set camp only an hour or so away from the city, choosing to stop and rest before heading in on the morning when they'd have all the daylight they'd need, and it was a decision Rathen had been grateful for. Despite his priorities, he still wasn't inclined to spend another night in the city if he didn't need to. Anthis had said - back when he was still speaking - that it wouldn't be a matter of finding what he needed within just an hour or so of searching, so they may end up having to find an inn for the night. The idea of such a long search had weakened Rathen's resolve, but instead of giving in to it, he reminded himself that Anthis had been there before. Surely that meant he at least had some idea of where *not* to look.

So, as Garon read a book by firelight and Anthis stormed off into the darkness to 'clear his head', Rathen lay on his bed roll with Aria huddled and snoozing beside him, her doll and toy cans-and-string tangled between them, making the most of his last night of comparative ease. He stared at the familiar stars and absently pondered on the coming events, wondering how he could help the search, as he was quite confident that he would only be in the way and quite probably standing right in front of exactly what was needed. That in turn fed into the wonder at whether he would even understand anything they might find. Would he recognise the significance of a rune if he saw it, or would it just be a marking on a sheet of parchment? He didn't much like the idea of embarrassing himself - assuming they found anything to present such an opportunity.

But didn't let himself entertain that concern for long. He would advise where he could, using the limited knowledge he had, and hope that it was enough. After all, Garon had decided to approach him rather than a scholar, so Rathen's

shortcomings would rest equally upon his shoulders.
   That, at least, helped him sleep.

Chapter 13

Rathen awoke on that final morning to the smell of frying bread and gentle, off-key humming. He'd thought at first, in the slipping grasp of sleep, that it was the song of a rather ambitious bird, but as the familiarity of the tune began to settle, a slow smile crept across his face. It took him a long, sluggish moment to notice anything amiss about it - he'd not yet found the bearings to recall where he was nor even to think to open his eyes - but before his tranquil mind could place it, a lighter voice interrupted and repeated the tune quite correctly.

Memory returned, his brow knotted, and he opened his eyes, quickly shielding his sight from the bright, low sun with a curse. Surely Aria wasn't teaching her goat song to Garon.

No, indeed she wasn't. At that very moment the inquisitor stepped into view with waterskins in his arms, presumably freshly-filled from the nearby stream. Instead it was Anthis who prepared the food that morning, with Aria's own brand of help, and he who was being tutored in the fine art of serenading livestock. He was clearly in much better spirits that morning. Perhaps his impatience had been replaced by excitement now that the wait to reach Mokhan was almost over.

They ate shortly after Rathen rose and, as usual, didn't linger before setting off, but despite the warm, spring light they'd woken to, a thick sheet of cloud rolled in to smother the sky not five minutes later. It wasn't even mid-morning by the time the tall, twisting elven towers appeared over the top of a hill, but one could be forgiven for thinking it was almost evening. But, as miserable as the weather was, it would at least mean fewer eyes to glimpse their arrival.

Aria stared in wonder at the bewitching towers as they descended towards the city, keeping to what cover they could as they made their way towards the back gates and the infernal district beyond them. They dismounted at the edge of a copse of trees and crept to hide behind an outcrop of rock, but as they peered around to assess the guard, they were surprised to find only two figures standing at either side of the ancient, golden framework.

"We need to get rid of them," Garon whispered needlessly, turning to Rathen. "Can you cast something to distract them?"

"Of course," he replied easily, but as he raised his hands to begin forming quick seals, an idea already in mind, Garon grasped his wrist and gave him a wary look.

"Make sure it doesn't *seem* like magic. We don't want to encourage their superstition."

Rathen's lip curled in distaste as his hand was released. "Stupid superstition." His fingers twisted, crossed and intertwined faster than Anthis could follow them, and all but Rathen jumped as a dog suddenly barked from close by.

The animal appeared from around a corner of the wall, heading away from the bustling main city and straight towards the two inattentive guards. Neither of them paid it much heed, even as it stopped right in front of them and continued its fervent barking, casting insistent glances back the way it had come as it did so.

It wasn't that either were particularly dedicated to their job of guarding the empty district - it seemed to be a rather novicial assignment - but rather that they enjoyed the ease of having so little to do and dozing, even so early, against the city's wall. Apparently not even the dog's clear alarm could interfere with that. And so, it was only when it finally charged forwards and grasped one of them by the trouser leg that they reacted.

At first the guard simply tried to shake it off, but as the dog continued tugging, the other spoke up from beside him. What was said, they didn't catch, but after the brief exchange the first guard's shoulders dropped and he reluctantly began to follow the distressed dog away, leaving the other to return to his dozing.

Anthis cursed, but Rathen raised his hand for patience. They watched as the first guard disappeared around the corner, and after the subtlest countdown beneath the mage's breath, a name was called with urgency and the second guard hurried away after him.

"Go, go!" The very moment he stepped out of view the four darted back to their horses and ushered them across the short, open stretch to the ruined gates, through the disintegrated metal and safely out of sight behind the city wall.

They slowed their pace once they were clear, and Rathen spared a confused glance behind them to the warped gate. "Are they really so afraid of this place that they haven't dared to even board this gate up?" He mused aloud. "It's as good as open - anyone could get into the city this way."

"Clearly," Anthis grinned. "But they don't think anyone actually *wants* to come in here. Those two were just there to make sure that the occasional person who turns up with the inclination of doing so *doesn't*, for the sake of their safety." He bobbed his head in concedence. "And to avoid upsetting any ghosts."

"People like you, you mean?"

Anthis's grin widened mischievously. "They had no such luck."

The region was a mess of bent metal and shattered rock, and yet many roads were clear of debris despite being unmaintained, as if the ghosts who were feared to remain had taken up the task themselves. But this was not the site of a city razed in war - Rathen knew well what that looked like. Rather the buildings had crumbled and collapsed on the spot, like a tent whose central pole had been removed. As they looked uneasily about themselves, they found that, in most cases, only a few walls of each building remained standing, the rest forming a tangled heap in the middle of their foundations. There were a few exceptions, with one or two remaining in surprisingly good condition despite seven hundred years of neglect, though they were still far from liveable.

But as they passed quietly through the eerie streets, safe from prying eyes even in the open, Rathen could feel the ancient magic, the aged spells that continued to collapse, the magic that continued to disperse. It felt little like the previous ruins; there the magic was dense and lively, but here it was sparse and lethargic. It was clear that this was nothing more than the magic of broken spells, with nothing unusual or fearful about it - but though the sensation in his veins was slight, it was still difficult to ignore. This was the first time he'd been in such a place for years. Had he still been with the Order in Kulokhar, he would have felt such a thing every single day and wouldn't have noticed it for a moment, but here it served only to remind him how far removed he was from his old life. But the time he *had* spent in the Order was not inconsequential; adjustment came quickly and he soon stopped noticing it.

The atmosphere, however, was harder to ignore. The ruined city seemed to press down on them as they followed Anthis's lead, turning from wide streets to narrow lanes before returning to the main road, and all the while the half-standing buildings watched them as they passed. There was little shadow cast over the roads as few walls stood at their original height, but their presence still dominated the district. There were no people here, no humans, no elves. Instead it was the buildings, the standing memory of a long-lost civilisation, that occupied the area, and it seemed as though they were just as confused by the elves' sudden disappearance. Surely they should have crumbled to dust by now, the spells long fallen, but instead the city appeared to be waiting patiently for them to return and restore its glory, and it frowned menacingly upon anyone who was not of such ancient blood.

Aria shrank back against Rathen. "I don't like this place," she whispered, as though she feared the buildings would hear her, and Rathen squeezed her hand before quietly admitting the same.

He looked over towards Anthis as they stepped back onto the wide road and spoke up. "Where are we heading?"

The young historian pointed towards the towers.

"And what's in there?"

"Knowledge."

Rathen sighed. "Please don't start being vague and mysterious."

"Those towers were the centre of the city," he elaborated eagerly, his previous evasiveness no doubt nothing more than a ploy to evoke intrigue, "both geographically and socially, just as those were that still stand in Kulokhar, Tarun, Stoke and so on. It's where records were kept, high-status meetings were held, items of cultural or local importance were contained - you get the idea. But," his enthusiasm dropped warily, "this place has already been cleared out by treasure hunters. The best we'll get, as I've said, is information."

"And you're sure everything you have points here?" Garon asked from their other side as he peered up at the buildings with a shadow of Rathen's discomfort.

"I am."

"Is it possible the artefact itself would have been kept here?"

Anthis shook his head. "Not likely. Mokhan was too small and insignificant."

"But there would have been mages here that they wanted to take magic from or oppress, wouldn't there?"

"Eh, it's possible," he conceded, "but that fact is neither here nor there if the place has already been cleaned out."

"What about papers?"

"Treasure hunters don't care for papers. If it isn't shiny, it's worthless. What we want will be here."

Rathen sighed to himself doubtfully, but at least Anthis was confident, and he looked down as he felt Aria's eyes peering up at him.

"Is your magic going to disappear if we go in there?" She asked him quietly, and as he told her he'd be fine, he found himself unappreciative of the abstract interest that was mixed in with her concern.

The towers loomed before them, structures that stood as tall as perhaps twenty houses, but it was only as they stepped into the wide, open square at their foot that they could see how ruined they truly were, despite still standing so proudly. From within the populated city these twisting towers would have seemed almost pristine, if irregular, but from so close, the holes in the silver and golden metal walls were saddeningly clear. Aria decided they looked as though they had been eaten by the equivalent of a giant wood worm. In many cases great portions were missing, lying instead in a crumpled heap at the foot of the twin buildings, or leaning against the lengths of silver that spiralled counter-clockwise around the towers which, though equally ruined, were complete enough to create a dizzying effect when stared at for too long.

Rathen turned his eyes to the floor to avoid falling over. Aria should have done the same, but with a gentle pull on her arm to counter-balance her as she began to topple, he was able to keep her on her feet and the others from noticing.

With no one to hide their presence from, they tethered their horses outside of the tower, far enough that they would be safe should another panel decide to fall, took what they needed from the bags - which, for Anthis, seemed to be everything - and warily ascended the steps to slip in through the broken doors.

It was only a little darker inside than out, as daylight flooded in through the decay to illuminate what would once have been the foyer to such an official building. But with the walls, floor and high ceiling ruined and the rest reclaimed by wild plants and the expanding reach of the city's unkempt gardens, little of its sophisticated charm remained. But despite its size and regality, Anthis told them there would have been more guards in there than anyone of status, and they would have served only as a reminder of the building's importance rather than to maintain any kind of order. Their uniforms would have been elegant but imposing, making the guards themselves into decorations, but they would still have been more than capable with their magic. "Our status is determined by wealth and bloodline," he explained as they walked, though no one had actually asked, each torn between looking up and around themselves as well as where they put their feet, "but for the elves, wealth didn't come into it. With their magic, everyone had access to the same things, so instead it was bloodline and magical strength that determined their importance. The kinds of guards that would have stood in here may have been nice to look at, but they weren't given their armour on a whim, they had to earn it, and that training elevated them socially, too."

"Does that mean this place is full of their ghosts?" Aria asked warily, but Anthis cast her a handsome, reassuring smile.

"I expect they're all with their gods. And anyway, I've been here a few times and never met any."

There were scrolls and books strewn everywhere, many torn and broken, and as Rathen turned his eyes up to the collapsed ceiling and the rooms revealed beyond it - and the rooms beyond *those* - he realised that most of them hadn't been stored in the foyer at all. Clearly Anthis hadn't been kidding when he'd said that papers were worthless to treasure hunters, but *surely* they had to be worth something to a historian. How Anthis wasn't picking everything up and trying to find space in his bag and pockets for it all, he really didn't know.

Aside from the weather-beaten tomes, little else had remained in tact. The only furniture to be seen was broken - chairs having fallen beneath broken legs, side tables shattered by collapsed walls - or things that were simply too big to steal, like enormous display cases or a long conference table he spotted in a nearby room that would have seated at least sixteen. Little decoration remained, either, as that had surely been the first to go, but the damage to the walls made it clear that some latecomers had been so desperate as to try to pry the gilding from skirting and crown mouldings.

They stepped carefully over the debris and avoided the tangled mat of roots, keeping close together, never straying from Anthis's lead nor what they felt was the reach of Rathen's magic, and after edging with particular caution around a hole partially concealed beneath a tattered and rotten rug, they reached the end of the hall and the foot of the elaborate, twisting staircase.

Anthis chose his steps prudently. He kept at first to the outside edge, then shuffled over tightly to the right after three, where he remained for another five. The others followed his chaotic path exactly, noting that many ledges were rotten while others were missing altogether, and when the need arose, whoever was in the best position lifted Aria over the gaps, though she still tried to make the stretch by herself. And so it was with much trouble and greater relief that they finally reached the top of the staircase - but no sooner had they done so and Anthis had led them along a short, shattered corridor than he had them climb another. But no one complained. He seemed to know precisely where he was going, passing countless rooms without casting them even a cursory glance, and after twenty long minutes of careful footing, they followed him into a room so small that the four of them almost filled it, and there were far fewer parchments and books within than any but he seemed to have expected.

The young historian shared not a word as he ducked beneath the beam that obscured the second half of the room, dropping his bag down on an upturned wooden box with barely a thought to begin rummaging excitedly through the remaining boxes and shelves, forgetting the others as he fell into his element.

They frowned at him curiously but didn't distract him with questions. He was looking for something quite particular - that much was clear by the fact that he didn't stop to pore over every little thing he found - but it left the others quite uncertain of what to do with themselves.

Rather than stand idle, Garon began looking through the shelves beside him much more carefully. Perhaps he thought that Anthis's haste was foolish, but Rathen doubted that the inquisitor had much of an idea of what he was doing. Rather than make an equal nuisance of himself, Rathen stepped back outside, taking Aria with him. She objected initially, wishing to watch him work, but soon huffed and folded her arms when he explained that there was simply not enough room. No sooner had he turned his head away, however, than she'd charged off into the equally dishevelled room next door, and it seemed that in the very same moment he heard the careless patter of her feet moving away from him, she'd already occupied herself with ancient books.

His heart leapt into his throat. He dashed after her as she made herself comfortable among the papers on the floor, surely the largest book in the room resting open in her lap, but after a very close look around, by nothing less than luck, she seemed to be safe where she was - though he gave her a stern word all the same.

The pages she peered down at were a mixture of words and runes, and though there were no pictures to capture her amazement, she still gasped at the sight of the flourishing lettering, their shapes so elegant she could never have read them. "Did they write this with magic?" She asked him, and though he knew her question had been posed out of disbelief, he found himself unable to answer. But surely the elves had never truly been that pompous.

Aria so amused herself for what seemed like an hour, and whenever she tired of a book, Rathen fetched her a new one rather than have her move around carelessly herself. He had taken to peering over her shoulder in between as there was little else to do, but even that seemed as good to him as doing nothing. He found their contents just as cryptic. He'd been taught a few elven words during his time as a student in the Order, as all mages were, but reading even simple sentences was beyond him. It was only through the occasional and far too elaborate sketches that he was able to glean a vague idea of the subject matter, but accounts of the city's construction or events in local history didn't seem relevant to Anthis's hunt. None of it interested him in the slightest, and time dragged by just as slowly as it would have had he stared at a wall.

The tower was quiet but for the occasional thud from the room next door, always followed by a muttered curse and the sound of paper brushing paper, but never any cries of success nor even a single, encouraging mumble. Rathen's hope dropped even further with every such scuffle, but when a different series of sounds disrupted the stillness, punctuated by hurried footsteps, Rathen was quick to react.

He almost walked right into Anthis as he blustered out of the doorway, who in turn almost elbowed him in the face as he slung his bag over his shoulder, but though he jumped slightly at the sight of the mage, barely a moment later he seemed to have forgotten him.

"It's not in there," he explained mildly before he could be asked, and immediately started further along the corridor without waiting for a word.

Rathen frowned, but he and Aria quickly followed as Garon fell in behind, a look of disappointment creasing the inquisitor's middle-aged brow. "I thought you knew where it was."

"No," he said as he passed blindly by more rooms again, paying little attention to anything more than the ground as he spoke, "but I know where it *isn't*."

"He did say it wouldn't be quick," Aria reminded him, and Rathen sighed as he recalled it. He'd been foolish to hope.

The search continued along the same pattern: without a word to the others, Anthis would enter a room picked seemingly at random, spend up to an hour rifling through books and papers and then move on without offering any update. They hadn't even had the chance to question him as they took a break for lunch, as he chose to eat as he worked instead. Despite the consistent lack of results, Anthis's mood remained buoyant, but that only made the hunt seem even more endless. If the passage of four hours of fruitless searching didn't faze him in the slightest, they could be at this for days. Rathen could only hope there weren't enough rooms in the tower for that to be the case.

Aria continued to enter anywhere the historian had missed when the room he picked was too small, but rather than try to stymie her insatiable curiosity, Rathen attempted to carry out his own futile search to try to hurry the pace. Anthis *could* have missed something, after all. But, as each time before, everything he found appeared to be worthless, and those recounts with a comparative abundance of images served only to worsen his opinion of the elves. It was clear from the attention that had gone into particular details that they placed too much emphasis on insignificant matters, like the aesthetics of the city rather than the running of it, the fact that there were too many humans walking around freely and invoking stricter curfews and punishments for them, or the import of hand-crafted silks being a catastrophic three days late. By comparison, the human mages they so despised were far more noble, both in their time and the present.

Rathen entertained that little sense of smugness.

But try as he might, he found no reference to a 'great magical advancement', nor anything that resembled that description in any of the rooms he searched, and they moved on again and again with no clue as to their progress even when they asked.

Upon leaving the next room, however, Anthis didn't immediately hurry off. Instead he stood quietly in the hallway, a thoughtful frown creasing his face as the others watched him impatiently, though none of them gave their feelings voice through fear of distracting him. After so long, none of them wanted to risk interrupting any train of thought.

Finally, he shook his head. "There's nothing for it," he mumbled to himself, but once again, rather than elaborate, he turned on his heel and marched them back towards the staircase. They were already quite high in the tower, but rather than climb further, they descended three floors and followed him across to a closed door. He stopped and turned to face them, his expression finally shifting from the mask of focus he'd worn since entering the building, but they weren't quite sure that his sudden hesitance was a change for the better.

He opened his mouth to speak, but seemed to change his mind and reached for the door handle instead. "You're not going to like this..."

Despite the pleasant warmth of the early afternoon sun as it spilled across their skin, panic sparked through their cores like struck flint and they each recoiled a swift half-step. But despite the dread that sank their faces, Rathen's lips did momentarily twitch into a grim smile. It seemed strangely fitting that the only door still wholly in tact actually had something to hide.

The collapsed ceiling buried the floor, trapping whatever little the most desperate scavengers had left, while the broken chairs and tables from the floor above stood upon the debris as if placed there intentionally. Even the rug that had accompanied them still seemed to lie where it had originally been unrolled, as though the whole room had simply been displaced to a lower level. But while the wall to the left still stood and the wall to the right was no more broken than any of the others, the rounded wall directly ahead was nowhere at all to be found.

A sudden wind whipped in, tousling their hair and leafing through the water-washed pages of the heavy books that lay open upon the floor, while any loose sheets had long ago been blown away. Every soft surface - torn upholstery, tattered rugs and moth-eaten tapestries - had been stained by the rain and bleached by the sun, and smattered evidence of congregating birds lined the outer edge. But the mess went unnoticed. Instead they found themselves looking from the doorway directly into the tower beyond, its corresponding wall having equally collapsed and, by chance, fallen outwards to land in this room, either caught by the empty space or having been the very cause of the destruction.

Rathen's flaming eyes turned slowly onto Anthis. "Tell me you don't mean what I think you mean."

"I could," he replied carefully, "but then I'd be lying."

"We have to cross that?" Garon asked, daring a tentative step forwards even as the ceiling creaked beneath his feet, and he peered with wide eyes out through the gap and along the bridging sheet of magic-warped metal.

"There's no information in here," Anthis explained, stepping carefully past him and towards the edge, his footsteps their most cautious yet, "so it's most likely across there."

"If it's even here at *all!*" Rathen snapped, and Aria clung onto his hand tightly and pulled back a step, highly reluctant to let him follow the others.

"It *is*," he assured them, "it's just not in *this* tower. Trust me, it's perfectly safe, I've been across this before."

"How many times?"

He hesitated and looked back at Rathen's stern tone. "Once."

The mage shook his head. "By all means," he said, grounding his feet, "*you* go ahead. Aria and I will wait here."

"No." Garon met Rathen's dark eyes steadily as they snapped onto him. "You're coming with us, and that's an order. We need to stay together. It's not safe over here, and it's not safe over there, and if anything happens it could well be your magic that saves us."

"And I might need your help," Anthis added from behind him.

He stared at the two flatly, but though he desperately wanted to remain behind and keep Aria safe, he had known even as he'd said it that it wasn't an option. So, with more than a little reluctance, he stepped after them, squeezing Aria's hand reassuringly and casting her a smile of apology. "Looks like we have no choice."

Her brow remained knotted in objection, but she seemed to have come to the same conclusion. She was quick to follow him.

After a few experimental taps with his boot, Anthis took a deep breath and the first step onto the makeshift bridge. It shifted immediately, and he braced himself against its precariousness. Its concavity removed the fear of slipping off of the edges, but it also removed stability, rocking with every step no matter how small, soft or cautious. The others watched him uncertainly from the edge, but after five paces, Garon took a similar steadying breath and stepped along after him. Rathen tightened his jaw and did the same at the following interval, and Aria kept closer than his shadow, squeezing his hand just as tightly in return.

Every footfall made by one threatened to throw the others off-balance, but rather than split their focus by cursing or over-compensating, they each concentrated on matching their pace with that of whomever was in front. Time slowed as they held their breath. It seemed to take forever to reach the other side, but the moment their feet left the rocking metal and found the comparatively safe flooring of the second tower, as equally ruined as it was, there was a shared sigh of relief. But while the adults were content for the moment to feel a more stable surface beneath their feet, Aria dropped her father's hand and stormed over to Anthis, her eyes burning with a blue-grey fire and round lips pursed furiously. "I," she declared with a venom to match, "did *not* like that."

He hesitated beneath her imposing glare, his expression creasing in guilt, and it twisted further as he saw the fear her anger cloaked. "I'm sorry," he sighed regretfully, "but we're safe now that we're across. I promise." He cast the others similar looks of apology when he noticed they shared her sentiments, but chose not to offer them anything to retort to. Instead he turned around and stepped carefully through this ruined room, assuring them he knew where to go next, and left them to follow begrudgingly in single file.

"I'm not happy with this," Rathen told Garon quietly. "He's said that countless times already, but all he's done is lead us from one mess to another based on nothing but a hunch. What if he's wrong and there's nothing here?"

"Then we'll have wasted time. We have no other choice. This is our best lead - I know that and you know that. All we can do is trust in him." The inquisitor cast his eyes, very briefly, back towards him with a look of assurance that only served to bother the mage. "He's a professional."

Rathen didn't respond. He turned his gaze back to the ground while his unpleasant expression that had grown only deeper that day turned all but black. He knew Garon was right. Or, at least, he hoped he was.

The interior of this tower was little different to the first. It may once have had a different purpose from its twin, but its equal chaos made it impossible to tell, and Anthis didn't offer any such information either. He returned quickly to his silent focus as the search process began anew, and as nothing at all seemed to have changed, Rathen found that the sense of it being all too hopeless similarly returned.

They passed once more from room to room, Aria leading Rathen carefully into others where he similarly continued his own blind and desperate search, and she sat remarkably content with tome after tome in her lap. Perhaps she was trying to help as naively as he was, or perhaps she recognised that there simply was nothing else to do - he'd insisted she left her whittling tools behind, after all. But she dedicated herself to the self-imposed task anyway, whatever it might be, as though Anthis had asked her to do so himself.

But after the fourth hour in the second tower, they had both grown weary of such work, and as Anthis continued filtering through what remained of the elves' records next door, and Garon presumably did the same with far less finesse, Rathen merely stared out through the broken wall at the world beyond, allowing his flagging mind the room to wander while keeping Aria safely away from the gap.

The overcast sky had thickened. By his judgement, the sun would set in two hours, but it would be too dark to continue this and get out safely by the end of one. They would have to leave before then and find an inn for the night, and given what little luck they'd had so far, they would undoubtedly be returning the next day.

He sighed to himself in resignation. But if that's what it took...

If that's what it took. For what? There was nothing here.

"*Ah-hah!*"

Chapter 14

Heads rose at the abrupt cry, but neither otherwise moved, even as their hearts dared a leap in hope. It was only when a giddy chuckle followed a moment later that Rathen and Aria came to life. Forgetting their caution, they hurried out of the room and blustered into the next, where they found Anthis grinning down at the pages of dusty tomes which Garon read over his shoulder. The inquisitor's expert eyes revealed only a trace of his bewilderment.

"What is it?" Rathen asked, and was immediately silenced by the historian's hand even while being flashed his wide grin. Aria bridled impatiently beside him as they watched him turn the page and drink up its contents, then look quickly to another book that lay open on the crowded and broken table before turning back again, curtly closing the second and pushing it aside.

He nodded vigorously to an unspoken question as his eyes continued to absorb the words. "Beyviin Dreyal," he said quickly, flicking back a few pages and tapping at the paper, "Beyviin Dreyal and, directly, 'great magical advancement'." He grinned triumphantly once again. "I've found it."

It took a long moment for Rathen to process the declaration, and Garon seemed to share in his surprise. Even Anthis appeared slightly taken aback, as though he'd had his own silent doubts despite his consistent assurances.

Though he knew he wouldn't understand it, Rathen stepped forwards to look for himself anyway, his scepticism settled and reluctant to pass after eight long hours of searching. But as his foot struck the edge of the table, he froze mid-stride, the great crash that shattered the stale air propelling his heart into his throat.

All eyes widened as the others fell still and silent, and it took a painfully long time for Rathen to understand that the sound had not come from beside him, but above. Gazes turned towards the ceiling, the only movement they dared, breath bated until the tapering string of thuds that followed had drawn to a stop.

They cast slow, wary glances to one another, and only after another long and mercifully silent moment passed did they share a sigh of relief. An unfortunate coincidence, nothing more; a casual shift in the balance above. Rathen fought to suppress the heat in his face that had come with the idea that he had been somehow responsible.

Anthis smiled weakly. "We're okay."

No one was given the chance to agree. Metal creaked mournfully, then, an excruciating scrape as something slid oh so slowly across something else. A thud. Then another. A subsequent tumble of small objects dragging with them things only larger.

Eyes shot back to the ceiling as the clamour amplified. A single impulse passed across them like a breeze and, one by one, they began stepping back towards the door, their footfalls as light as humanly possible to avoid somehow worsening the destruction above them.

Garon gritted his teeth as the cacophony slowly dragged to another unpromising stop. "We have to leave," he whispered, and Anthis managed only a peep of a protest before he turned dark, commanding eyes onto him. "What you've got will have to do. We leave *now*."

Rathen and Aria needed no encouragement, but as Anthis mumbled and reluctantly began gathering his things to follow their tiptoe to safety, another long, loud scrape loosened and hurried his pace.

The rumbling threat seemed to follow them, spreading as they made for the broken hallway and intensifying in their wake. Rathen cursed beneath his breath as he ushered Aria's short strides across the threshold, his thoughts immediately turning to the worst possible outcome - and, as if to punctuate them, just as he turned to see how far behind the others were, he was deafened by a heart-stopping crash and blinded by the dust that billowed out of the room they'd left only a second before.

His grip on Aria's wrist tightened as he wrenched her around to shield her from the dust and debris, and he fought to swallow his heart back down as his wide gaze pierced through the cloud.

A uniformed figure shortly stumbled out, nose and mouth hidden in the crook of his elbow, and Anthis was close behind him, his bag slung over his shoulder, coughing as he went. There was little opportunity to notice the inquisitor's daze; both were on their feet and moving, and as the floor began to shake, that was all that mattered. Anthis rushed ahead of them, gesturing down the hall even as he struggled to catch his breath, and Rathen snatched Garon by his sleeve to lead him along as he struggled to regain his bearings.

Another crash shook the air behind them as the tremors intensified, but no one spared a moment to turn and watch the floor they'd crossed only seconds ago crumble beneath the weight of the ceiling, nor to observe the cracks that formed and chased them as they raced on the historian's heels.

Like dominoes, one collapse triggered another. The ceiling continued to fall behind them, dragged down by momentum, which in turn shattered the decaying floors they and their furniture landed upon, plummeting the weight down to the next. They only just managed to stay ahead of the cascade, Aria keeping pace with the adults' longer strides as though she was carried on a zephyr of panic, and when they reached the ruined spiralling stairs, their pace flared again. They were all too aware of the fact that the ceiling they sought to escape was no longer obstructed by another, and tore their feet free with little care of injury whenever they happened to stomp through a weakness.

They flew down the tower, case by case, floor by floor, and slowly became aware of the growing distance between themselves and the cacophony. It sounded as though it was diminishing, but they didn't dare slow. Only when it seemed to be drawing to a stop did they begin to steady their frantic pace, their hearts hammering and threatening to tear free from their chests.

But before any of them could catch their breath, let alone spare a sigh of relief, another creak of metal invaded the immediate air, carrying on its tail a curious wave of disorientation.

"Stop!" Anthis cried above exasperated curses, needlessly, as everyone had already instinctively grasped what remained of the handrails. They braced and steadied their spinning heads as best they could, but the rocking sensation only increased by the breath. Anthis shortly bit off his own string of profanity and told them to keep moving instead. It was only then the others realised that it was the staircase itself that was moving.

They covered the final two cases in moments. Fighting with every step to remain upright, each of them lost their footing and managed to recover through necessity alone, not one stride ever breaking. Relief surged through them like a tidal wave when they finally thundered into a ransacked hall, a foyer identical to the first, and hope gave their pace one final burst of fire as they barrelled towards and out through the enormous, grand doors.

They spared not a glance to the state of the tower until they were well away from it and already skirting back to the first. Anthis was the first to dare, and as shock immediately faltered his steps as he half-turned in his run, Rathen reluctantly followed his wide gaze.

The tower was leaning at a dreadful angle, as though somehow ripped from its foundations and pushed by a giant, and it was set to strike the other and invoke further destruction if it fell any further. But while its precarious balance was alarming enough, Rathen's blood froze when he found that the first tower was now in motion instead. Countless outer walls were bending and breaking off to strike the street below, dragging whole rooms down with them - but the debris wasn't falling as close to the structure as pieces had in the past. While surrounding buildings had collapsed inwards, this one was falling wide; for the fact that none of them had yet been hit, they could only thank Vastal.

But they were too close to where they'd left the horses to waste time rerouteing. This chaos wouldn't be missed from the city; they had to be away.

Rathen released Aria's hand, trusting her panic to keep her alongside him, and prepared to cast any spell he needed to even as they crossed the square. But as they reached the tethers, they found that only one of the three horses remained, its grey-dappled body lying motionless on the ground, head lost beneath recent debris. There was no trace at all of the other two.

They cursed as the disheartening sight brought them stumbling to a halt, but there was no time to dwell, despite Aria's sorrowful cry - a fact that proved itself before they could even begin to flee on foot.

They spun towards the clamour of voices and watched with growing defeat the crowd that ran towards them from amongst the ruined buildings. Shouts of startlement, questions, then declarations of doom; despite superstition, their nosiness had been unmatched, and given the distance between the towers and the city's edge, the noise must have drawn them all immediately.

But before they could curse at their growing misfortune, more of the building came crashing down above them.

Garon and Rathen each growled in frustration and shouted for the approaching crowd to turn and run for their own safety. But though the inquisitor invoked his authority and Rathen boomed with the unfaded command he carried over a decade ago, nothing could douse the mob's fervour. They continued their advance, civilians and guards alike, even as Rathen heard another silver panel loosen from above.

His eyes pulled upwards, heart leapt into his throat, and he watched it begin its slow plummet towards the crowd. And though he knew what would come of it, he also knew he had no choice.

His fingers wove frantically into a spell and a sudden wind gusted up like a geyser. It struck the metal, sending it wide and hurtling off into the nearby ruins, well clear of any bystanders. And, as he'd expected, not one of those bystanders missed it. But even as their cries of fear and wonder at the calamity shifted into anger, and voices shouted of 'magic' and 'curses', and accusations fell upon the group as heavily as the panel would have upon them, an almighty crash blanketed the district. The four knew, without even a glance, that the second tower had struck.

Heedless, the angry citizens renewed their march, their sights locked on Rathen in particular as all those who were armed drew their swords. Garon bellowed an explanation, but his words, his uniform and the insignia he presented were all equally ignored, along with the countless falling fragments loosened by the shockwave.

Rathen turned his back to them, whole-heartedly cursing their presence, their foolishness, their superstition and the spiteful need he felt rising within himself to protect them all anyway, and caught as much of the debris as he could in a net of magic, disregarding whatever appeared to be flying too wide. But an angered cry close behind him snatched his attention, and he turned to see a flurry of red that asked the question 'what in Vastal's name are you doing?!'

Another fragment buckled from halfway up the tower in his moment of distraction, falling closer down its length than the others had, and it hurtled straight towards him.

But it didn't strike, and Anthis released a sigh of relief before sparing a moment to look inquisitively towards the figure who had not only distracted the mage, but had also run ahead of the advancing city and now stood beside Garon to oppose them all, even meeting the blades of those who tried to slip past and attack him directly.

But Rathen couldn't afford to spare more than that initial glance, even as Anthis stared in wonder. He flung aside the captured wreckage while cries of 'mad mage' and 'rebellion' began to rise above the rest, and a moment later they were all that could be distinguished above the clatter of steel. Rathen shook his head and gritted his teeth, changing his tactics in a brief reprieve in the rain of missiles. "I can't hold it all back," he shouted to Garon over the din even as he began forming another spell, and the inquisitor growled in matching frustration as he held off another raging attacker.

"We have to run," he shouted back. "If we leave, they'll scatter; our presence is only provoking them and they're not listening to me!"

"*Of course* they're not," Rathen replied spitefully, "*magic* is involved!" He released his spell and an unseen barrier assembled over the area, finishing not a moment too soon as another hail of books, furniture and pieces of ceiling slipped from one of the highest rooms.

He didn't wait to see how much it would hold. He snatched Aria and lifted her into his arms, fleeing the ceaseless destruction with Anthis close behind them while Garon brought up the rear. The jeers continued to chase them, but their tone began to shift; there were encouragements to follow and accusations of involvement, and as they looked back they found that every blade that had sought to cut them to pieces had now turned onto their unexpected ally.

Garon cursed and immediately dashed back, certain of what would happen if they left her there under such condemnation, and snatched the woman by her elbow with a command to follow. She was given no chance to agree nor object as he dragged her along, only to growl in anger, then again in defeat. As a number of the attackers began to pursue, crying claims of a mage sympathiser, a distraction while mages slipped in to destroy the city, to sow seeds of chaos, she knew she had no choice.

"They're all insane," she growled once more, and remained alongside them as Garon released his grip to hurry to the lead of the group.

He directed them along a twisting route through the darkening ruins, their sudden and senseless turns hopefully losing their pursuers while avoiding any more, and as they neared the district's broken gate they found that neither guard was present on the other side. Despite their easy job, they'd likely made their way towards the towers. But when they crossed the edge of the city, the inquisitor didn't lead them into the forest like they'd expected him to - as, indeed, would their pursuers. Instead he took a sharp right along the edge of the wall, followed its length for a full running minute before reaching a deep gully, which he jumped into and followed further away from the forest. They ran for an age but took little distance from the city, and its walls were still within sight over the edge of a gorge when he slipped down into a shallow valley and finally drew them to a stop.

Aria grunted as Rathen dropped her to the ground, panting for breath as Anthis similarly doubled over beside him, but she didn't spare a moment to make sure either were all right. She scrambled back up the grassy slope to look out through the evening shadow and back towards the city. She couldn't see anyone approaching, but her sight was too blurred by tears to have noticed even if they were only ten paces away, and though she tried to stifle the little hiccuping squeaks that came with them, they burst out of her relentlessly. She shook with fear - indeed she was terrified - but she tightened her small hands to try to stop that, at least, if only for her dignity in the adults' company. But she just couldn't. She didn't understand what had just happened - the tower had fallen, somehow, and they'd nearly been crushed by it, but then they'd gotten outside and poor Fog had been killed and the other horses had fled, and then people had arrived and her father had saved them from being killed, but then they'd tried to attack them instead, like they weren't even grateful.

She squeezed her eyes shut tight as another whimper rattled from her throat, and she gritted her teeth against it. She just didn't understand.

She jumped at the gentle pressure of a hand on her shoulder, but as she spun around she found the eyes that looked back at her were protective, the pretty lips that asked if she was all right bowed downwards in sympathy, and her face, framed by blood red hair even in the weak light, was creased in sincerity.

For a moment, surprise pushed Aria's fear aside. "It's you!"

Garon turned to Rathen and Anthis as the two fought for their breath. He was barely winded, though Rathen supposed an inquisitor could well be more used to chases than either of them were, if from the other end, and he looked at them both with grave, grey eyes.

"We have a problem," he said in no uncertain tone, his voice low enough that only the two would hear, and Rathen forced himself to stand and regain his pride, even if his chest burned.

"You can say that again," Anthis wheezed from beside him, still doubled over.

"But we got what we needed, didn't we?"

"Mm..."

Rathen blinked at him as the historian bobbed his head uncertainly from side to side, then his widened incredulously, his fingers curled in frustration, and he seemed barely able to restrain himself from strangling him. "*Mm?!*"

"*Yes!* Yes we got what we were looking for, but it wasn't enough to balance out all of this chaos!"

"What *did* we get?"

Garon's eyes turned to him now, and Anthis shrank under their weight, and further still beneath the threat in Rathen's. But rather than answer, with a final, steadying puff, he crouched down beside the bags and began rifling through one of them.

Rathen frowned as he recognised both his own and Aria's among them.

"I took everything that remained from the dead horse while you were deflecting the falling tower and Garon was shouting into deaf ears," he explained without glancing up, as though he felt the need to defend himself. Garon glared at the last remark.

Anthis lifted a book out from his bag and flicked through to the page he'd folded over. "It does mention Beyviin Dreyal," he said as he rose slowly back to his feet, as though the others had been heard the name before that day, "and a great magical advancement..."

The two watched him expectantly. "...But?"

"...But," he continued carefully, "it seems that the 'advancement' referred to here was the ability to create a force of air out of nothing - sort of like what you did to the debris, I suppose, but as simple as it seems to be now, it was evidently a big deal at the time - actually," he amended quickly, avoiding meeting either gaze by burying his nose safely in the book instead, "what it says specifically is that this was the *'greatest development* since *the ability to silence the magic of humans,'* and...it seems that while Beyviin *was* the head of the project, he was only loosely involved. It was his protégé who was actually responsible for the artefact, which Beyviin *also* headed, and that's why I made this connection I suppose."

"So what does that mean?" Rathen asked with great restraint. "That, after all that, we still have nothing?"

"Yes and no."

"*Stop it!*"

"'Yes' in terms of not having what we expected," he said quickly, now truly hiding behind the safety of the old tome, "and 'no' in terms of being given a new lead. I know the name of his protégé, Radekh Sov, it's been stuck in my head since I first read it a few years ago, but I've only come across it twice."

"And why did it stick in your mind?" Garon asked hopefully as Rathen once again appeared ready to throttle him. "What do you know?"

"Oh, uh, because 'Radekh Sov' sounds kind of like 'ahrizov', which is elven for 'yellow'," he explained blandly. "But anyway, as few as his mentions are, I remember him being tied very closely to Bowden, down south."

"Bowden," Rathen reminded him in a low, dangerous voice, "is a bustling city."

"Yes," Anthis nodded, "but *because* of that, the Order has made sure that some areas have been preserved."

"And after all of this, you think we're going to be able to just walk in?"

Anthis shrugged. "It'll take about three weeks to get there on foot in this season, we'll just lie low for a while on the way over and we'll be fine, I'm sure."

Garon shook his head. "It's not that simple, Anthis. Those people back there think *we* caused all that destruction, and they saw Rathen use his magic--"

"I had no choice," the mage declared, and Garon raised his gloved hand to calm him.

"I understand that, but nevertheless, you've revealed yourself as an unmarked mage and that will have not only reinforced the idea of a mage rebellion, but you'll have been seen as part of it. And the rest of us are in no better a position, either. Aside from your distinct appearance, Rathen, I am clearly an inquisitor, and there is a *child* with us." He shook his head and folded his arms across his broad chest, his black uniform dusty with the evidence of their involvement in Mokhan's ruin. "Our description will be easy to pass on and easy to remember, and we can argue that it's a mistake all we like, but with the present situation as it is and the threat of rebellious mages on everyone's mind, *no one* is going to listen. Even the Crown's hands would be tied."

"They view things in black and white," Rathen agreed distastefully, looking past the officer towards Aria where she was being comforted by the woman, "and such a severe incident involving a banished mage can *only* point one way, *especially* now."

Garon followed his gaze. "And now Petra is involved as well."

Anthis frowned. "You know her? Who is she?"

"She...bumped into us when we were looking for you," Rathen replied, then sighed regretfully. "You're right. But we should still lie low and avoid settlements, lessen the sight of ourselves for the time being. We've lost our map, our bed rolls, our horses and most of our food. I can conjure some of what we need, but we'll have to live off of the land for a while - trap animals, gather plants and the like. But we can manage that..."

"I have experience *sleeping* in the rough," Anthis frowned dubiously, "but I've always brought supplies with me..."

Garon, shamefully, agreed, and Rathen's eyebrows rose in surprise. "Well, then I suppose I'll have to manage for all of us. But - Anthis, you might be a renowned historian, but such isn't a profession to encourage remembering a face. If we pass near a settlement, you can go and gather what we can't get by without."

The sound of approaching footsteps snatched their attention, and Petra appeared beside them. Even in the low light her young face was seen to be grave, her eyes severe, and she'd barely come to a stop before she hissed. "What the hell happened back there?!" She turned her steely gaze upon each of them in turn, her voice as low as theirs had been. "What were you doing?!"

"It's classified," Garon replied immediately on impulse, but his response only earned him a fiery glare.

"Classified be damned!" She growled. "*I* was chased out of there just as *you* were, so I'm lumped in with you now whether you like it or not. I demand to know what was going on!"

"No one asked you to get involved," Garon reminded her calmly. "And just what were *you* doing?"

She straightened defiantly. "Returning the favour. And you?"

"We were looking in the ruins," Anthis replied, and as Rathen glanced at him, noticing he'd been a touch quick to offer the information, he found his eyes lit by more fascination than they should have been.

"With a mage, an inquisitor and a child?" She asked doubtfully, folding her arms and either not noticing or just ignoring Anthis's interest. "What was it? A family day out?"

"We're trying to stop the magic."

The small voice immediately caught their attention. All eyes looked past her to fall upon Aria as she stepped almost defiantly towards them, her eyes still red though she'd stopped crying, and her small hands tightened into fists at her sides.

"Sorry?" Petra's tone was suddenly far gentler, though her eyes were no less harsh.

"Aria," Rathen said softly, shaking his head, "hush."

Her small shoulders straightened boldly, and she stared back at her father with only the slightest trace of apology before looking decisively back to Petra. "The magic in the old elven places, it's not supposed to be there, and it's making trouble." She ignored her father's defeated sigh, and the similar pleas of the others. "It's killed people and it's upsetting spirits, and it has to be stopped before it gets worse. It's gotten worse everywhere else already and we can't let it happen here, too. Anthis thinks we can find an arty-fact that can help, and that's why we were there when the tower fell down, we were looking for it."

Rathen stepped forwards and knelt down beside her, wrapping his arms around her to soothe the shakes from her voice, and he couldn't help a small smile twitch across his lips as he suddenly understood why she had been looking through the books of elegant, flourishing writing with such dedication.

"Why did the tower fall down?" Petra asked, looking back to the others.

"Because we interfered."

"It wasn't magic," Rathen added, remaining beside Aria, "it wasn't curses, it was just old and unmaintained. Our presence upset a precarious balance and it collapsed. It would have happened if anyone else had gone in there instead of us."

Petra nodded slowly, her arms folded across her chest, one still concealed beneath a sleeve. "And did you find it?"

"We found what we needed," Anthis replied, and Rathen frowned at how easily she'd been convinced away from blaming magic.

Her eyes snapped onto the historian. "Don't you dare be vague. Did you find it?"

"No, but we found information we need to lead us towards it."

She nodded slowly again, her long, red hair tousled by the wind, and she regarded them each for a long moment. Anthis stared back in cautious interest, Garon looked away to the side with frustration and wounded pride at having been undermined by a child, and Rathen held the little girl close, asking her a quiet question to which she nodded. Petra narrowed her eyes curiously, but didn't give voice to her thoughts. "I have heard of something like this," she said instead, "something unnatural, that mages have supposedly done. Some say it's part of an attack by Skilan, others say our own mages are doing it." She cocked her head. "What's *actually* happening?"

"Why do you doubt the rumours?" Anthis asked with a note of intrigue, heedless to the thought that such a response could lend the rumours credence. "Why aren't you more concerned about the magic?"

She frowned at him slightly. "Why would I be?"

"Because it's magic," he reminded her, frowning back.

"My little sister is a mage. Magic doesn't frighten me like it does other people. I know very well that mages have control over their power."

Rathen frowned to himself as he recalled the unwanted information Kienza had left him with, but he decided it best not to alarm one of the few who didn't immediately jump to blaming mages.

"Now," she said again, "what's happening?"

"We don't know."

"If you don't know, then how can you stop it?"

"We're working on it." Garon appeared to have gotten over his sulk, and he loosed a small pouch from his belt. "Miss, you would be better off leaving before you're seen with us again."

Her arms tightened and her small chin rose. "I can't. I left all of my belongings behind in the inn. I've got nothing but what's on my back, and given the driving off we received, I can't return for it, either. Whoever you all are, I've doubtlessly marred my reputation by getting involved in that little incident."

"All the more reason for you to leave right now," he said, dropping the pouch into her hands, "and forget everything you were just told."

Petra frowned at the weighted purse.

"Head to Pelas. Do yourself a favour and tell anyone there that you were uninvolved, that you chased us off with the rest and that we headed north through the woods."

"Could you not go back and claim innocence?" Anthis suggested as she looked back to the inquisitor in confusion.

"I could," she admitted, pressing the pouch back into Garon's hand, "but I don't want to. My reputation has already been sullied, and from my experience in such matters, it's better to let it lie, go forgotten and pretend I wasn't in the area at all rather than try to deny it or claim it was someone else." She smiled humourlessly. "I might stand out like a sore thumb, but my appearance has proven to be easily copied."

"You would rather circulate the suggestion of an imposter?" Rathen frowned. "Won't that also sully your name?"

"To a far lesser degree. In fact, it could even work in my favour."

"How?"

Her lips half-curved mischievously. "An imposter will always claim to be the original, and if people think I am my own imposter, I'll get more challenges while they try to take advantage of the opportunity and make a name for themselves.

Meanwhile, my own actions will provide the truth, and I'll make more money."

Garon shook his head in familiar disapproval. "Not only are you encouraging violence and gambling, but now also deception."

She laughed drily. "No offence, Inquisitor, but you *also* have an unwanted light shining upon you right now, and I have to wonder just what you intend to do to save your *own* reputation."

He looked at her for a long moment, reading her eyes while the others glanced patiently between them. His lips soon twitched into a smile. "I would claim I wasn't involved, and was nowhere near the area when it happened."

Petra smiled victoriously.

"Steal an official sword and dress in black," Anthis nodded, "no one would know the difference. You're right: easily done."

Garon's brow dropped a fraction. "I'd like to think I was a bit more memorable than that."

"Not when no one looks past the uniform."

"I have no intention of staying for long," she assured them, turning back to the inquisitor. "I have my own matters to attend to, but for now I'd rather disappear, and if you're all doing the same, then it gives you the chance to repay me."

"I thought *you* were the one repaying a favour," Rathen frowned, finally rising back to his feet.

"I was, by trying to stop an attack. I had no idea I was going to incriminate myself by doing so, though."

Garon sighed and drummed his fingers on his folded arms, thinking for a long moment before sighing again and shaking his head. "Fine," he grunted. "So you're staying, for now. But understand this: whenever you should decide to leave, no one is to know anything of who we are or what we're doing."

"Why?"

He didn't react to the plainness of her tone. "Because," he replied precisely, "if it should get to the wrong people, it could easily spell trouble. We want to take care of this as quickly and as quietly as possible without alerting anyone who might try to stop us."

"And why would anyone stop you?"

"To try to use the magic themselves," Aria replied, having made a nearly full recovery after her father's attention, and Petra cast a thoughtful glance over her and the others.

She gave a single nod of understanding as Garon stepped past her to look back over the ledge, and after announcing that there was no one following, he began to lead them through the valley, heading east to find somewhere to set up for the night with their new tag-along firmly in tow.

Chapter 15

Salus roared.

He snatched the mug from the desk, still half-full with a strong brew of tea, and threw it hard at the furthest wall where it shattered and stained the drab, grey paper. He whirled around and kicked the chair, breaking one of its legs though he barely felt the impact, then lashed towards the desk, sweeping away the papers, pens, inkwells and burning candles with equal disregard. He bellowed again as his fury boiled over, the candles extinguishing themselves as though intimidated by his own fire while he turned to tear apart the bookshelf.

Teagan stood silently in the centre of the dimly-lit office, staring unaffected at the wall ahead as the keliceran indulged in his most recent bout of ire. He didn't flinch even as a book flew close past his head. Salus had been fickle in his moods for two days, quick to anger and quick to calm, and yet as tense as a bandit's bowstring throughout. Teagan had predicted his reaction to this news when he'd received it not ten minutes before, and he had been correct: he did not like it.

Salus punched the top of the desk. His rage must have been subsiding, for he didn't mark it, and with a final long and drawn out growl, he leaned on his hands, hanging his head in hot frustration as he finally fell still. For a long while, the office was silent.

His eyes soon turned upon him, calmer though they remained set within a visage of fury. "Find out who he is. Find out what he's doing and who he confers with. I want to know everything."

"Of course, but it will take time. The operative lost him."

Salus shook his head sharply. "Magic concealed him; Elran wouldn't have lost him. He won't be far."

"Then would it not be better to send a mage after him?"

Salus's jaw knotted and his eyes momentarily flashed at the suggestion. "No," he managed calmly, despite his brief darkness, "it's too risky. The last thing we need are more mages gathering in one place." He pushed himself away from the bare desk, absently rubbing his red knuckles as he released a long, deliberating sigh. "We'll leave it to Elran. He knows who to look for. Send another to take his place in Mokhan."

Teagan noted the distraction in his eyes. "What do you think?"

Salus shook his head again, though far more slowly as his lips pursed in thought. "I don't know," he admitted quietly. "It's not like the first movements in other lands. And the Order already denies involvement. Of course."

"So you have doubts?"

He paused. "Purely for the fact that they failed in whatever they were trying to do. But the Order would deny it regardless, and their failure could be down to incompetence, or an alternative strategy to anything they've tried so far."

"Unless 'failure' was the desired result."

His jaw knotted again. "I agree. The Order simply *isn't* incompetent." He snarled and leaned back upon the desk. "Damned magic. Damned mages. They've never sat well with me, even before they all lost their minds the world over and started slaughtering people en mass to get their way. *No one* should have that kind of power."

"This behaviour isn't a new development. Even in Turunda."

"Mm..." Salus murmured doubtfully, to which his lip curled in resentment. "That is true, but I think the case a few years ago was unrelated. Two massacres and then nothing? And why leave it so long to pick it back up?"

"Perhaps their movement was too small at the time; one of them became over-eager."

"We'd have had the chance to find out if the Crown hadn't gotten involved so quickly...but I suppose that matter was never in the Arana's hands." He sighed roughly as he tried to push that matter from his mind, reminding himself instead that the search for the artefact, at least, was progressing. That gave him some hope. It was moving much quicker with Drassa's involvement, and once they recovered it, the mages wouldn't pose a problem anymore. No, then it would simply be the whims of foreign kings.

"What of the meeting with Malson?"

Salus's distant gaze returned and he glanced regretfully at his broken chair. "I've told him that Skilan will be attacking from the north-west, through the mountain pass, trying to get a jump on us." He gestured for Teagan to pass him the less comfortable chair from the other side of the desk. "Jalund may be dense, but General Norkan is wily. I'm not too surprised by his intentions - though I do wonder what he'll do to draw his force back together since we've managed to split them up so efficiently. But if we can prevent him from doing it, they'll be easier to crush and perhaps a few more lives can be spared."

"They're tired," Teagan agreed as Salus dropped into the unfamiliar seat and his lip curled slightly in distaste. "The fragments won't be quick to rejoin - if some of them even arrive at the border at all."

"If the people we have working to incite desertion are successful, their numbers should have dropped by a sixth..."

The lightest frown creased Teagan's brow as Salus's gaze stretched for miles once again, exhibiting another sudden bout of quiet thoughtfulness. He stood silently for a while, waiting for him to shake himself out of it, but wherever his thoughts were, they had him in a tight grasp.

"What is it?"

"Nothing," he replied even before his eyes flicked back to him. "You're dismissed."

The portian inclined his head and duly turned towards the door, showing no reaction to his abruptness. "Good night, Keliceran."

Salus frowned after him as he left. Guilt began to prod him, and he wasn't sure why. Perhaps it was because Teagan was the closest thing he had to a friend, despite past events. But a portian wouldn't take such a tone as offence...

He sighed. He was quite aware that he was being short, but he was tired and just wanted to go to bed. And he would have, had it not been only eight in the evening with things still to take care of, but his mind wouldn't keep quiet enough for him to do so. New thoughts tumbled into focus before he'd finished with the last; new problems presented themselves, old ones he thought he'd handled resurfaced, and potential issues that wouldn't arise for months, if not years, if at *all* continued to plague him out of nowhere. But none of them could be ignored, none were obsolete, especially the latter. Distant threats had a habit of suddenly becoming *present* threats, because, once one got into the habit of brushing them off or tucking them away, they were able to grow while out of sight. It had happened to others, those before him and those over the borders - in fact such disregard had resulted in numerous successes under his own command, so while sealing his victories, he did his best to learn from his enemies' mistakes, lining up countless plans for equally countless situations.

But those were easy, in a sense. He had the room to stand back and view each scenario from afar, the time to assess opponents, predict movements. Present troubles were not so accommodating. Trying to keep three steps ahead without the time to cross-reference their intel as far as they would like made the Arana's actions both in the field and within the offices were crucial. They had no room for failure. They had to take any and every opportunity they could because it was he and his people who were the true front line of Turunda.

But the Crown either didn't seem to see that, or didn't *want* to see it. They hindered their actions by wasting time talking about what had to be done when Salus had already told them. Even now he was cursing the Crown for rejecting his plans - he wondered if there wasn't some way to reword the requests so they might actually *understand* them...but even if he did, could he risk the Crown rejecting them again?

Above all else, he *needed* eyes along the least patrolled regions of the border so he could watch the small advance forces the enemy sent through - but saying *that* would have them in an uproar. *He* knew they couldn't keep Skilan's forces out absolutely, even if the Crown thought the border was iron-clad, just as he knew that a few vanguard weren't as severe as anyone else would think. There was an irritating sense of patriotic pride that blinded every man and woman in the country, and from that stemmed the black and white ideals they shared with the Crown. Any number of enemies crossing the border, be it five or five thousand, would be considered a threat that needed immediate eradication.

But letting in just a few enemy soldiers, a controlled handful, would ultimately work to Turunda's advantage. They could learn precisely where they were entering from and plug those holes in the future, and encampments would provide the opportunity for observation. It was all well and good to know their general had made plans, but with his operatives as low in Skilan's ranks as they presently were, they only had access to so much so soon, and there was little opportunity to uncover any hints while they were marching.

But once they crossed the border, they would be unable to act without giving *something* away - as long as one knew what to look for, and his people certainly did. He had a few on stand by for precisely this; individuals who were encouraged to delay before officially reporting in from tasks in order to cut down on paperwork, allowing them to take care of the necessities he knew the Crown would rather not know about.

Not that he'd ever used them in such a severe situation. It was only ever for small, niggling details, tasks that weren't *worth* keeping the records of. But this was serious, and the Crown and military needed to be kept apprised of such things to prevent accidents or misunderstandings.

But again: could he risk the rejection?

He snarled in exasperation. There were far too may other details clattering together in his sleeplessly addled head that equally needed addressing, and this new development in Mokhan had only complicated it. They'd been watching the Order closely, but there had been no hint at all of this attack. That was partly why he doubted the intent behind it, but at the same time, what else could it be? None of his people planted in other countries had caught any whiff of rebellious activity, even those he'd sent out specifically to look for it, but it had happened none the less.

Hopelessness washed over him at the thought that the rebellion had finally begun, that the accursed mages were moving as silently here as they had everywhere else. How could they ever hope to stop it while their attention was being torn away by war? And what of these strange magical occurrences in the wilderness? What were they? What was the Order up to?!

He growled again, certain he was becoming a beast as his frustration began to boil over. He thundered up from his uncomfortable seat in an attempt to redirect it, but still lashed out at the desk, slamming his foot through a drawer. He snapped off a curse as he pulled it free, then turned and gave the chair another swift kick. This time it didn't break, and he certainly felt the impact. Pain shot through his toes, flashing a white sensation through his mind which only fuelled his anger, but as his foot drew back to kick it again out of spite, a knock came at the door.

"*What?!*" He caught himself with a curse and attempted to bite back his sparking anger. But it was late, and he wasn't expecting anyone else. "Come in!"

He shifted his weight off of his smarting foot as the door opened, but surprise bluntly shoved aside the lingering pain and his acrid mood. "Oh." The brown haired phidipan woman closed the door behind her, her face, empty of expression the last time he'd seen her, marred slightly by caution as she noticed the state of the ransacked office. It could hardly be missed. But she didn't turn that look onto him, even as he made a hasty attempt to straighten up the mess. "I'm sorry," he said, standing his chair back up and scraping together his papers from the floor. He thought he saw a twitch of surprise in her fine eyebrow at his apology, but he was probably mistaken.

"I'm sorry for intruding, Keliceran," she said with a shadow of hesitance as he dropped the muddled reports and stationery back on the desk, "but I thought you'd like to see this report right away."

He frowned curiously, returning the misshapen candle back to its saucer, but as his eyes dropped to her papers, a heavy mixture of hope and dread lurched in his stomach.

The location of an unmarked advance party in the north west. Half a Skee platoon moving ahead of the main body and towards exactly the point of the border he had wanted to reinforce.

His jaw tightened as the question of risk and rejection reverberated, once again, through his mind.

"Thank you..." His tone was distant as he discarded the report on the table and began filtering through the disorganised mess, fishing out a few maps, located only due to their size, and marked a number of their points with hastily scrawled notes. He glanced up as she stood patiently, waiting to be dismissed. "Good work on Moore, by the way."

This time her eyebrows did rise, but his gaze had returned to the paper. "Oh...thank you..."

"He's tightened his security, but it seems it wasn't as necessary as I'd feared."

"It did prove to be a challenge."

"Which, I suppose, is a very good thing." He straightened, then grunted as a wash of heat suddenly swelled in his skull. His fury had abated only to be replaced by a headache, through which his thoughts still tumbled uncontrollably, reigniting his frustration. His hand rose to his forehead as he grumbled beneath his inescapable woes. "How can we protect the country when it seems to want to destroy itself?"

"Keliceran?"

He blinked, remembering himself, but he couldn't seem to stop his tongue. "The mages in the Order are drastically stronger than any the Arana has. How can there be any hope of stopping a rebellious faction if the rest of them won't even acknowledge its existence?"

Her frown lingered, but rather than let her gentle brown eyes fall upon him to assess the intention behind the outburst, she seemed to gauge the weight of the silence instead. "Perhaps the Order is already handling it," she said at last, surely feeling his expectant eyes upon her. "After all, just as the Arana does not reveal all to them, neither will they reveal all to us. And I cannot believe that they would all be involved, or they wouldn't wait for the distraction of war to make their move."

"You think it doesn't warrant concern?" He asked thoughtfully, regarding her a fraction more closely.

"I think it may not warrant *our* concern, Keliceran. It takes magic to fight magic, and given the state of other lands, the Order would not run the risk of ignoring a threat within their own ranks. Perhaps you are piling more work onto your shoulders than you need to; after all, what can the Arana do against magic with the little we have? Would it not be better to turn it towards the war, where we can do more?"

"You speak boldly, Phidipan."

"Forgive me, Keliceran."

A smile twitched across his lips as he watched her cheeks redden, but still she didn't look at him. "No, it's all right. I asked you a question and you answered it. What's your name?"

"Taliel."

He nodded. "Taliel." He wouldn't forget. "Thank you. You're dismissed."

He watched her incline her head, turn away and slip back out through the door. He sank slowly into his seat, thoughtfully, still staring at where she'd stood.

It takes magic to fight magic. Yes, he'd thought of that before, and as he'd said himself, the mages within the Arana were both weaker and far less numerous than those of the Order. In truth, there was little they *could* do against mages - that was part of what made it so infuriating. He refused to accept that he, one of Turunda's highest authorities, could do nothing about it. That was why he'd chased the rumours of the elven-made relic, because if he had such a thing, he could use it to silence the magic of Skilan's mages as well as local rebels - and there were just too many learned men convinced by the stories for him to be able to disregard it.

But he hadn't considered that the rebellion *wouldn't* wait for war to make their move if there were so many involved, as it was that very war that clouded his own mind. But though it was an idea that certainly had merit, he couldn't trust in it absolutely. Mages were revolting and he had no way of knowing just who was among them. It was safer to assume guilty until proven innocent and maintain a scrupulous eye. What if their insurrection reached higher than a few lowly scholars or preservers? What if it reached all the way up to the elders?

No, his present actions stood, whether it was more work than some deemed necessary or not.

But...it was a side he hadn't considered. He felt doubt begin to wriggle into his mind like a worm in an apple as he wondered what else he may have missed...

At that moment, he was startled out of his thoughts by another knock at the door, provoking a growl as his frustration suddenly doubled. He just wanted to go to bed!

"This whole matter would be a foolish one if it were anyone else pursuing it, but he has the means to take it as far as the king himself could!"

"The ability to neutralise magic in the hands of someone so absolutely against its existence is dangerous. He would be able to use it indiscriminately - he could unravel Turunda's magical defences while they're in the midst of *preventing* an attack!"

"But wouldn't that mean he removes magic as a factor *entirely?*"

"Would that not be for the best? Especially after what happened in Mokhan today?"

Malson sighed and shook his head, folding his thin arms over his chest, and he looked across the uneasy faces around him. Though the light was dim in the back room of The Cockatrice, Kulokhar's busiest tavern, the doubt that pooled deep within their hearts was clear to see. And it was not misplaced, whether it be for committing acts they hadn't believed in upon their superior's order, or for standing there at that very moment, whispering with Malson against him. Such were these uncertain times. "It would remove magic as a factor, yes," the king's envoy replied cautiously, "but who knows what protective spells are in play? Only the Order could list them off for certain, and he's not likely to confer with them before using it. *None* of us can truly make an informed decision without first speaking with them."

"Perhaps we should," said the young man, though he didn't sound very convinced by his own words, "perhaps they should know about this."

"And then they will accuse the Arana of treason and the Arana will certainly retaliate in its own way. Things are already too unstable to risk an internal struggle while we try to deal with the war."

The older man opposite him sighed and shook his head in bemusement. "I still don't understand this artefact thing. Wouldn't a spell to stop magic also stop itself?"

"Not if it's properly woven," replied the blonde woman, "and an elven artefact wouldn't be carelessly made."

The dark haired woman beside her turned Malson a steady look, one that suggested she was just as unhappy going along with the search as she was standing against it, but prepared to do whatever was best all the same. "What do we do?"

His deceptively young eyes met her gaze. "Nothing. I don't believe he will succeed. Drassa is an intelligent man, but he gets ahead of himself and makes desperate connections. He's been shunned for it in the past and it's been happening more and more often in recent years. I believe he's growing desperate in his old age to find something to leave as a legacy. But, as long as Salus is focusing on that, his mind won't be straying into areas it shouldn't be."

All eyes turned onto the blonde woman, who nodded regretfully to their unspoken question. "It's still there, and growing fractionally stronger, but fortunately it's also still very subdued. He's unaware of it."

"Let's hope it stays that way."

"I'll be sure to inform you should anything change."

The young man sighed again. "Forgive me, Lord Malson, but this doesn't feel right, speaking against the keliceran like this."

"Are you not uneasy with him in charge?" Asked the blonde. "No keliceran has ever been a portian before."

"He's hardly a portian anymore," he reminded her, "and either way, he gained his position fair and square. If he was able to assassinate the last, then she'd lost her touch. That's how it's worked since the Arana was first established, and though I admit that I wonder at a few of his decisions, I'm not prepared to say he's unfit to lead. He's kept Turunda safe so far - none of us can deny that. Perhaps this is how he'll continue to do so."

A doubtful frown touched Malson's weathered old brow, but he said nothing. "Continue working beneath him as you have been for now. I'll tell the others the same. When and if the time to act comes, you will be notified. I understand how uneasy some of you are, but this is an extraordinary matter that we need to keep up with." He turned and stepped towards the thick curtain behind him and spoke to the man sat on its other side. One who had been stationed in the tavern by the keliceran himself as a standard watchful eye in the city. "We weren't here."

"The same as always," he replied, peering into the bottom of his mug with convincing disappointment. He then rose to his feet to head back towards the bar, opening the way for them to pass through unseen by any others and out into the cool night air, where they each left for different directions.

Malson pulled the drab cloak tighter about his person, better concealing his stately robes as he made his way from the building and out into the centre of the city. He sighed heavily to himself in the quiet streets. He didn't like the way this was going. Salus himself seemed to think that Malson had no idea what he was up to, but he had been working alongside kelicerans for the past forty years and could see quite clearly when reports didn't quite add up. Of course, just what *else* he might be hiding, he couldn't know. The hunt for this relic had only come to his knowledge because it had been handed to him out of concern by Vari, the blonde Aranan mage, something she hadn't done lightly. Then, when others with similar concerns had sought him out, including the operative who appeared to the world as little more than a frequent tavern-goer who sought to drink his troubles away, he had truly begun to question the keliceran's honesty to the Crown.

But despite the distress of this small handful of operatives, phaeacian and phidipan them all, he didn't believe there was anything truly sinister at work. Concerning, yes - as had been said, the thought of Salus wielding such a power with his ideals promoted sleepless nights - but nothing dark or evil. Salus was no such man. Driven, yes; confident in his convictions, certainly. But he would never do anything that would lead the country to ruin. He lived and breathed for Turunda.

And he wouldn't succeed in finding the artefact, anyway, assuming any mage in the Arana was even capable of wielding it on his behalf. From the information these operatives had passed to him as well as Salus, he knew that it took magic to operate, and he doubted any in the Arana were truly strong enough to do so.

His old frown deepened.

So what was this knotted sense of dread in his stomach?

Chapter 16

Rathen grunted sourly as he rubbed the sleep from his eyes. He'd barely rested all night, and it wasn't until the sun began to rise that he had finally, and typically, slipped into dead dreams, and that stiff slumber was interrupted all too soon by cold light piercing his eyelids.

He hauled himself up from his bedroll with resignation and looked with bleary eyes towards the reaching slivers of light. Best guess, he'd been out for little over an hour. What did that make? Three and a quarter total, at best? The thought only made him feel heavier, and he almost indulged the desire to drop back down beneath the blankets and not rise until midday.

He didn't - a decision which only darkened his mood - and more frustrating still was that he knew his restlessness hadn't stemmed from being hunted, but from exhaustion. He hadn't used his magic so much in a single day for years; aside from a general loathing of it, he'd learned quickly in his isolation that if he saw to his chores with spells, he'd end up bored for most of his life. And so this selfless spurt of spell-casting had exhausted him to the point of being unable to rest while the others slept so sickeningly deep.

But, rather than stew, he'd taken it upon himself to keep watch that night, a decision made in part to ease Aria who had initially been just as awake as he, her eyes filled with alarm as she stared into the darkness at the slightest sound. Even the hoot of a distant owl had rattled her.

But as the morning sun crept leisurely higher, trickling into the lengthy gorge they'd followed the night before, unease began to pull at the edges of his mind. Something didn't feel right, and as he looked across the camp, counting the conjured bedrolls, he found his suspicions confirmed. Though all laid out were occupied, including his own, they numbered only four. His eyes flicked quickly to the fifth, which he found neatly rolled and tidied away beside the remaining bags, its blankets folded on top.

Where was Petra?

A flicker of panic forced him to his feet, his mocking fatigue forgotten. Had she changed her mind from following them as far as Bowden? Had she returned to Mokhan to clear her name after all? Was she leading the city right to them?

He flexed his fingers. He could hide the camp if she had. But...Petra also knew what they were doing...

He frowned as he looked closer, noticing amongst the bags a glimmer reflecting from a surface too long to be a buckle. She'd left her weapons behind. After being chased off like that, would she really risk going back, unarmed?

Whatever her intentions, she planned to return.

He noticed a few smaller glints; pursing his lips, he decided in her absence to indulge his curiosity. Stepping closer, he peered down at the worn sheaths and glinting hilts. The sword she carried openly at her hip lay across the pile, its crossguard as ornate as its sheath, but practically shaped. Clearly such a thing was meant to be more than a simple tool, but not so extravagant as to be displayed and collect dust. It was made to be used, and used only by a skilled and respectful hand.

Beside it, and far less embellished, were the two small, matching daggers he recalled had been concealed within her cinch, and beside those the strange coil of weighted rope somehow similarly hidden at the small of her back. It was another moment before he recognised it as a bolas.

He frowned and shook his head in bafflement. How could she carry so much and run with them as fast as she had?

With grace, strength and practice, he supposed. Thinking about it, she'd been just as unaffected by the previous night's escape as Garon had been...

"She's a touch dangerous, isn't she?"

He glanced around towards Anthis who stared over from his own bedroll, eyeing the steel warily as he reached for his clothes.

"More than a touch, I'd wager," he replied, rising, and turned to fetch his own as he felt the chill of the morning against his bare skin.

"Where is she?"

"Here."

Both twisted in fright at the sudden voice, and found Petra emerging from around one of the gorge's bends. Her red hair had deepened from bathing, but she was notably more clothed than they, and both grew quite conscious of that fact beneath her gaze, despite her disinterest. Rathen hurried to his blankets as coolly as he could, earning him a curious glance. "There's a small spring about five minutes that way..." she explained slowly, but as she considered the shameful alarm in their averted eyes, a small smile crept across her face. "You thought I went back to Mokhan."

"No! Absolutely not!" But Anthis had declared all too readily, and she cocked an eyebrow in doubt as she returned to her weapons, her smile only broadening as she turned her back.

As Rathen lashed his shirt about himself, he couldn't help feeling that she wasn't particularly troubled by the situation they were all in.

Their road continued through the gorge, the old, dry river bed reclaimed by various bushes and shrubs, none of which offered much to shield them from sight. But the few that bore flowers at least gave them something to look at, while the countless holes pecked into the stone that towered to their right housed small birds that sang out to their returning partners.

But as pleasant as those songs were, they weren't gladly received. The five followed the route in silence, straining to hear anyone that might be around. They were a good distance from Mokhan, it was true - Garon had led them with a mind to get away and out of sight rather than to reach their destination any sooner, and their pursuers had surely been thrown off early on by his decision to avoid the dense forest - but while each of them doubted they'd been followed this far, no one could help the occasional peek over their shoulder.

"You're making me nervous."

Anthis faltered in his step as Petra glanced back towards him, her eyes wary beneath his pondering gaze.

"Don't take it personally," Rathen spoke up from behind him, "he stares like that at everyone."

"I do?"

"Yes, you do."

He looked away sheepishly following even Aria's fervid assurances. "I'm just curious, that's all."

"About?"

"People and things in general, but in this case, you--uh, who you are, I mean, not..."

Petra sighed and turned her eyes back to the dusty riverbed. "My name is Petra," she replied flatly while Aria giggled at his flushing cheeks, "I'm a duelist, much to your inquisitor's disgust, and I travel around, making my living from fights." Her sharp eyes fell upon the back of Garon's head, and though he made not a sound, his lips were still pursed in disapproval as he stared down at the map Rathen had conjured, marking details as they walked.

Anthis frowned curiously as he watched her watch him, but equally remained silent. She had answered his question, he supposed, as vague a response as it was, but even then she'd been more open than Rathen initially had - not that he'd been willing to share anything since the mysterious Kienza had disappeared.

"What about you?"

When no response came, even Garon glanced back curiously, but his eyes widened in surprise when he found her staring at him just as expectantly. "Me?"

"Sure," she nodded. "Why did you take this case? And what else have you worked on?"

"I didn't take the case, it was given to me," he replied with sudden dispassion, returning his attention to the map as Rathen shook his head. "And as for what else I've worked on, that's classified."

"You said that about this matter, too."

"And it's just as true now as it was then. Circumstances are all that have changed."

"But if past cases are closed, then surely there's no harm in talking about them?"

Garon sent Anthis a dark look for his sudden participation. "The subject matters are sensitive, closed or not."

"Well you don't have to give us any specific details," Petra pressed. "Have you caught any killers over the last few years? Or are there some that have eluded you?"

"The Hall of the White Hammer has extensive resources," Anthis frowned, "surely cases don't go unsolved..."

"Are there? Any killers you've not caught?"

"Classified." Garon drew to a sharp stop and snapped around towards her, his grey eyes narrowing in suspicion as his voice grew as solid as his bearing. "Why all the questions?"

"Just curious..." She looked back at him with wide, innocent eyes, and seemed to shrink a little beneath his gaze.

The inquisitor analysed her for another long moment, unreadable himself, then turned suddenly and continued along through the gorge without another word, his full attention once more upon adjusting the map.

Anthis frowned in disappointment as they followed on. Few ever had the chance to work alongside an inquisitor, but though his curiosity in him was great, he'd been hesitant to quiz him and take advantage of the unique opportunity. Garon was closed off, reserved and official, and that roused more than a small degree of intimidation.

But Petra, a woman whose spirit he could already see great value in, hadn't been so hindered, and though Garon hadn't given in to her questioning, he suspected that his own curiosity would soon be satisfied. He doubted very much that she and her forceful personality would let it lie for long. And she seemed to have a very specific interest - neither a historian nor a mage caught her attention, but this inquisitor apparently did.

He frowned slightly as he pondered her possible reasons, but shrugged it off as he stepped up alongside her. "Don't take it personally," he assured her quietly. "Garon's not a particularly approachable person."

"I noticed. Is he always like this?"

He took a short breath to respond, but was suddenly unable to decide how to answer. But that, it seemed, was answer enough. She nodded slowly, and he chose not to question the thoughts in her eyes as they returned to the back of the inquisitor's head.

"Can I ask you a question?"

Petra looked down to find Aria peering very critically up at her from her father's side, and though the severity of the girl's thoughts were plain upon her face, she was unable to hold back a smile. "Go right ahead."

"Why is your hair that colour? Do you dye it with the blood of your enemies?"

"Aria!" Rathen cried in surprise.

"What?!" She cried back defensively. "A man in a book I read did it!"

"Yes but that was just a *story!*"

Petra, however, simply laughed. It was a surprisingly elegant sound for one so forceful, and Rathen sent her a wondering look. When he caught himself lingering, he forced his eyes away, but noticed in that moment that Anthis and, more surprisingly, Garon had both done the same.

An hour passed before the gorge finally widened, broadening into a grey, rocky landscape that became more troublesome to traverse. But while the loose stones slipped and rattled dangerously beneath their feet, at least the chances of meeting strangers along the way were reduced. In fact they made that evening's camp without having crossed sight nor sound of another person, and the day had passed uneventfully. Rathen had said little, and while Anthis assumed he'd regressed with the addition of a new stranger, he'd been merely trying to stay awake. Anthis, on the other hand, was the only one to offer Petra conversation; he answered her questions of where they'd been and what they'd done, though she often aimed them towards Garon despite his aversion to socialising, and when Anthis had asked her questions about herself, she'd been consistently evasive. He'd taken to analysing what little she *did* say to satisfy his curiosity, and as he sat by the fire that evening and looked across the four peculiar individuals, he found it hard to miss the fact that everyone he seemed to be associating with lately were unnaturally difficult...

*

Having lost his original in Mokhan, Garon had done his best to transfer all notes, routes and details onto this new map instead, and while it had been more than a little toilsome, he was confident that he'd just about succeeded in getting it up to scratch. One didn't get to his position without a memory for detail nor a mind to make use of it, after all.

He looked up and around himself, glancing back along that morning's path, and for the first time in two days, finally pin-pointed their location. But he felt little need to sigh in relief. As inconvenient as their present situation was, it was still only that: an inconvenience. They had to travel south for Anthis to continue his work anyway, and if it was still needed after three weeks, there was someone in Bowden who could repair any damaged reputations and quell unwanted rumours. And while it was a nuisance to be unable to stop and gather information on other magically-affected sites, he suspected there were a few points along this route that they could learn from first-hand instead. In short, it was far from a situation he couldn't handle.

Rathen's passive, thoughtful scowl caught his eye as he began rolling away the parchment. He hadn't asked him about his work on the spell since presenting him with the task, and in that time hadn't noticed even a hint of progress, let alone any sense of impending victory. But he'd been under no illusions that it would be a challenge to achieve, if even possible - and yet, despite being equally aware of that fact, the mage had taken it on anyway. Unfortunately, while Garon sought to do all in his power to help, there was little he could beyond leading him to ruins in the hope that the magic's presence might offer something up, and he had no way of knowing if that was even a possibility. But, as Rathen hadn't said otherwise, he saw no reason to stop, and he trusted that the mage would speak up if he had anything worth sharing.

Petra laughed at something Aria had said, and his eyes narrowed across at her.

He had appreciated her gesture in Mokhan, but it had been unnecessary. He'd been quite capable of holding off the attackers - in fact he was quite confident that, had she not stepped forwards herself, they wouldn't have dared to try. But her involvement had provoked them and landed her waist-deep in their business, creating yet another unanticipated factor in the matter.

His eyes flicked then towards the unexpected little girl who continued speaking animatedly about something or other. He would have blamed Aria for her sticking around, but he had the sense that, if she hadn't told her what they were up to, Anthis probably would have. He looked at the crimson-haired woman every now and then with a little more than just curiosity.

But, for now, all he could do on that matter himself was ensure that she truly understood its weight and kept quiet about it when she finally left them. And he resented that that meant she had to be told more. Not everything, just more.

He turned his head slightly, scanning the area behind them with his peripherals.

And then there was the unshakeable sense that they were being followed.

His thoughts were silenced as his ears pricked at a nearby sound, the slightest rustle, and he drew the group to a quick and silent stop. The rustle came again, followed by a shriek so sudden it made his hairs stand up and skin turn cold.

Anthis's eyes widened. "Harpies," he breathed, sending Aria into a silent panic while Petra turned incredulous eyes upon them.

"*Harpies?!*"

With a curt jerk of his hand, Garon silenced them. His jaw tightened. Harpies. They'd neither seen nor heard anything of them since the incident five days ago, but he hadn't forgotten them, and he doubted that Rathen had, either.

A voice rose, stilling him again, a brief call the others couldn't decipher. It was a name, he realised, but far more importantly, the voice was unmistakeably human.

Rathen sighed quietly in relief. "Hunters."

"We still need to reroute," Garon whispered, glancing off to the left. "There's no knowing where they've come from or where they're going." The voice came again, another missed word, ahead and to the right, beyond the second shale dune thirty feet away. The clattering sound of footsteps over loose stones was carried downwind towards them.

He slipped off to the left and gestured for the others to follow. They picked their way gingerly despite their haste over the barest of ground and the largest of rocks, and slid with gritted teeth to a quick, rough stop beneath one of the many steep overhangs, leaving an betraying cloud of dust behind them. They listened closely, holding their breath as the dust settled, the footsteps drew closer and two voices spoke low. A bird shrieked from overhead, making Aria jolt in fright, but it didn't seem to notice them.

Neither hunter reacted as it swooped down to join them, and though Garon caught mention of footprints in the younger hushed voice, the other was quick to brush them off. Whatever they were hunting, they had no interest in distractions.

They waited silently as the hunters passed, and Garon held them for almost a full minute longer even once their footfalls had moved beyond range. They watched him impatiently, straining their ears in case he'd heard something they hadn't, and only after his brief nod did any of them dare to move. They slunk along behind him, following the overhang in the direction they'd been heading before branching off abruptly eastwards.

"Where are we going?" Anthis whispered frantically as he hurried up beside him, spinning as he went, looking for sign in the stark emptiness of anyone else they might have to hide from now they were back in the open.

Garon didn't slow his pace. "Stonton."

"We're that far east?"

"Indeed we are. Keep your voice down."

They walked with their eyes fixed over their shoulders as he led them across the exposed ravine, and Rathen felt a shadow of panic lurking beneath the shared unease. The capital city was too close. He could almost smell the magic of Kulokhar's Order House.

Ahead, a patch of green stood out from the miserable greyness like a beacon, a cluster of tightly-knit shrubs, taller and fuller than the rest, bursting from a crevice in the wall. All but Garon eyed it curiously, and even as they reached it, his stride didn't break. He stepped through without a moment's pause and disappeared amongst the leaves. Equally eager to disappear, the others hesitated for only a moment, and found as they began shuffling their way past the sharp branches a hidden but climbable drop in the canyon wall, worn in long ago by another, smaller river.

The land around them changed as suddenly as if they'd covered miles in a single step, and they vanished at last back into the embrace of Turunda's forests, breathing a collective sigh of relief as greenery closed the way behind them.

"What's at Stonton?" Petra asked, her pace slowing with theirs. She straightened her back as she realised she'd been stooping in her tension.

Anthis's eyes glittered once again in excitement. "A marvellous sight!" He beamed. "An old elven village built up and around a single pillar of rock, carved into the stone itself."

Boredom dulled her tone. "Oh." But then a frown creased her brow. "Is it...doing what other places are doing?"

"It's affected, yes," Garon replied. "Severely so."

"It is?"

A tingle passed through Rathen's veins, standing his hairs on end as though a chill wind had brushed him alone, and his stomach lurched at the sensation. His eyes widened warily. "It is."

Petra's question disintegrated to a gasp as she and Anthis stepped across the unseen boundary behind him, but the historian only frowned. "It feels no different from the others."

"You're not a mage..." Rathen turned dubious eyes onto Garon. "How is--"

He was answered by a low hum touching the edge of his senses, one even the others slowly became aware of. It grew louder with each delicate step, fiercer, and as it rose sharply into a roar, a terrific force whipped up from nowhere and pummelled them into its current, ushering them into its thundering glory.

"Daddy," Aria called in alarm, covering her face with her sleeve to keep the gale from snatching her breath away, "do something!"

"There's nothing I can!" He hissed as long hair lashed across his face.

"Everyone just keep together! Move on!" They gritted their teeth and pressed through the force at the inquisitor's stoic lead, constantly fighting to maintain their grounding with every step. But the wind only intensified, threatening first to push them backwards, then to blow them away. Rathen kept ahead of Aria to shield her from the worst of it, while Petra's free hand twitched impulsively towards her sword, as though she thought she could cut the suffocating force away. But they were nearing the edge of the forest, where there was less to impede its fury.

"It's only getting worse!" Petra yelled over the roaring in her ears. "Why are we risking this?!"

"Just keep going!"

"You're mad, Garon!"

Even despite his battle against the wind, he managed to shoot her an impatient, irritable look. "You can always turn around and leave!"

A growl vibrated in her throat, but she bit her tongue and continued her struggle alongside the relentless group, and from daring glimpses made between fingers and over sleeves, a cliff face soon appeared beyond the thinning trees.

"We can't get any closer!" Petra insisted again as the wind continued to bully them. "It's not safe! Especially not for Aria!"

But this time it was Rathen who shook his head. "We'll be fine, just keep going!" There was no opportunity to rebuff her surprise. Somehow he found the strength to pick up his pace, gut certainty sparking a fire beneath his feet, and he all but charged into the unnatural wind.

And after just three more difficult steps, the mage stood suddenly upright, his black hair gently tousled rather than whipping around, even as the others continued to fight behind him. And as they crossed another unseen line, they too discovered that the force had subdued without warning, dropping abruptly from gale to breeze.

The silence was deafening, but relief enveloped them as they grasped the opportunity to regain their breath, and only then did they take notice of the enormous stone structure that towered before them, dwarfing the forest into a copse.

It was no cliff. There was no land above nor beyond it but that of the young forest that sprawled out from a ring at its base. This was a singular column of rock, standing at least eighty feet high by half as wide, growing out of place and by itself as if it had been planted there. It was colossal.

But of course it was. A whole village had been carved from it.

Aria wasn't the only one to gasp in surprise as her eyes began to pick out the details. There were various facades cut into the stone, their doorways and windows suggesting individual homes rather than a single, hollowed-out community shelter, and though all bore the same smooth, doming shape, there were countless etchings of runes and symbolic images that set each dwelling apart from the next.

Anthis suddenly blustered through the group, shoving them aside in his excitement and racing off manically towards the rock.

"Slow down," Rathen shouted after him, rubbing his smarting shoulder. "Surely you've been here before."

"Of course I have! But there's never enough time!"

He shook his head at the childish grin he flashed back towards them before scrambling onto the carved, twisting path. "Just be careful."

"I am never anything but!"

With far less enthusiasm, the rest of the group approached the long-abandoned village, their footsteps hastened only to leave the creaking forest behind them. But it was eerily quiet; the wind still raged, spiralling around the tower through the trees like a moat of sheer energy, but the muffled silence within the eye was unsettling.

"So where do we look?" Petra asked, keeping close to Rathen and Garon, both of whom seemed to have a far greater sense of self-preservation than the historian.

"For what?"

"This relic of yours."

"We don't. Not here."

Her dark eyebrows drew together. She glanced towards Rathen, and even to Aria, but both of them displayed the same lack of expectation. "Then," she turned bewildered eyes back to the inquisitor, "why have we stopped?"

Rathen turned away while Garon begrudgingly divulged as little as he could, and looked around at the area. His eyes immediately glazed as he turned his mind inwards, Kienza's guiding words ringing in his skull, and he reached himself out to the magic that undulated around them, drawing that extension to a stop near the foot of the chiselled village.

'...how it feels, how it moves and flows, what form it's sitting in...'

He breathed, exhaling his thoughts away, and let the magic gather around him. Immediately, he identified it as a puddle; too dense to be a cloud, too thin to be a brick. He didn't really know what that meant for him, but it was a result he was comfortable with. At the very least, being half way between the two, perhaps his options for affecting it were broader.

But...one step at a time.

He discovered the slightest of smiles on his lips. Suddenly he had direction: he knew what to look for, and he was making sense of it - meagre, even grasping sense, but sense none the less. The magic sat in puddles, clustering here and there but leaking into one another. It didn't sit as a blanket of fog, nor as defined bits and pieces, but there were areas of concentration and dilution. And it felt familiar.

He *had* felt this in the other ruins.

He straightened himself, feeling a sense of victory for some kind of progress at last, as small a triumph as it was. But his smile quickly faltered as he considered the wind.

Rathen glanced towards the nearby trees. This was the first place he'd been to that had affected the elements, so was as good an opportunity as any to analyse that detail as well.

Again his dark eyes softened as his attention shifted, doing his best not to reach, grasp or strain, and he found the expected concentration of magic within the winds. It was powerful, easily felt from where he currently stood, safely away from the buffeting edge, and its presence didn't seem to reach beyond the field of magnetism. And the gale was certainly not natural. Perhaps it had been, initially, but magic had fuelled it out of control, or perhaps it wasn't wind at all but the chaotic movements of the magic itself. It was a whirling mass of power, whatever the case.

He narrowed his eyes in thought. No. His first guess was right: some degree of it *was* real, magic had simply empowered it.

The idea that raw magic could affect the elements didn't really surprise him. It had long been theorised by the Order's scholars. Magic was very nearly considered a fifth element, so unique was its structure, but as it couldn't exist on its own, unbound or unwoven, they'd never found a way to prove it. But that had always been just as well, because it was also generally agreed that its interaction with other elements would likely be extreme, even hazardous - an idea this unrestrained magic had now proven all by itself.

But why, if the magic was the same, weren't the other sites affected this way?

And where was that phantom tug of peace?

His frown deepened uneasily. Stepping away from the others, he began to wander, peering absently up at the rock while Aria hurried to stay at his side, and broadened the reach of his magic. There was something more here. He could sense it, feel its presence with a certainty, but whatever it was, *wherever* it was, it hung just a hair out of his reach.

It continued to elude him as he circled the base of the village, skittering away just as he was almost upon it. Rathen's skin prickled in irritation, and he stretched himself again in pursuit. He didn't feel Aria's frown boring into him as his pace increased to an erratic jog.

Something was here, he was *sure*...something different...

He stopped suddenly and snapped around. But there was nothing behind him. Only Garon and Petra standing a distance away, safely out of reach of the forest, the first keeping an observant eye on both himself and Anthis while the duelist watched the bending trees.

Aria puffed as she ran to a stop beside him. "What is it?" She panted, though her tone and eyes were equally weighted. "What can you feel?"

He shook his head and looked around feverishly, his shoulders dropping in confusion while his frown deepened. But it wouldn't defeat him. He was too close.

He extended his reach once again.

His heart leapt. A tremor passed through his veins.

He had it.

Victorious adrenaline spiked his blood, but in that instant another jump paralysed his chest. Heat seared into his right arm, shattering his concentration and sending his mind and magic hurtling back to him with the force of a stampede. He hissed, stunned, clutching at his bicep while Aria's severity doubled with alarm.

The metal cuff clamped about his skin burned hot even through his sleeve, and he half expected to see the steel turned red as he snatched the fabric back. But it remained cold to both his sight and Aria's, who continued to stare on in panic.

Then, just as suddenly as it had begun, the burning subsided. A long, slow sigh of relief escaped through Rathen's lips, and he stared down in confusion at the slightest reddening of his skin at the edges of the metal.

Aria reached up and touched it quite gently. "Are you okay?"

"I'm fine," he sighed heavily.

"What happened?"

"I...don't know...I was reaching out to the magic and it started to burn..."

He pulled his sleeve back down and made a show of shrugging it off, forcing all his strength into a smile as he bottled his raging panic. He knew she wasn't convinced by it, but he also knew she wouldn't pursue it.

And indeed she didn't. She dragged her eyes away from him and looked up instead to the towering village, curiosity returning to colour her previously cynical gaze. She pursed her round lips. "Can we go up there?"

"Why?"

She shrugged. "Reminds me of home."

He frowned at her softly. "Do you *want* to go home?" He regretted the question immediately. He knew it wasn't an option.

Fortunately, she grinned. "Nuh-uh! I just haven't seen anything that reminds me so much of home that isn't a forest, and I like to remember what's waiting for us when we get back. It makes it more exciting! Home but *not* home!"

Rathen chuckled and pulled her against him by the shoulder, but as he looked back up at the skyward rock and heard Anthis laughing giddily to himself some way above them, his mind was drawn reluctantly back towards the magic. Aria noticed the change fall over him immediately.

"What did you find?"

Exhausted from her vigil, Petra turned her back decisively to the trees and regarded the pillar instead. She counted the doors, picked out the differences from facade to facade, and as Anthis traced his hand over the rock face, high up along the carved, winding path, she began absently to picture the bustle, ancient residents going about their forgotten days. She pursed her lips in contemplation. "Why would someone think to build a village out of a rock?"

"Off the top of my head," Garon began with indifference, "because temperatures would be more stable, it wouldn't leak nor get blown down in the winds, it's elevated and built at a slight angle so it wouldn't flood in heavy rain, and, if the forest wasn't here at the time, it would have provided a good look out." He shook his head as he continued carefully observing the mage. "Otherwise, you'd have to ask Anthis."

"Mm." She folded her arms and watched the young historian hurry away to another door along the path and then back again, presumably comparing some minuscule detail or other, but he didn't hold her attention for long. Her thoughts shifted, and she regarded Garon from the corner of her eye before her curiosity once again loosened her tongue. "So, what drove you to being an inquisitor?" She asked as casually as she could. "Why do you do what you do?"

"Because," he began with his usual apathy, "someone has to do it, and I am capable."

She nodded slowly, having expected such a practised and evasive answer. "But is there nothing that drives you, personally? No dream as a child? No pivotal event in your life?"

He didn't reply. Instead he walked away from her without even a glance - in fact his eyes hadn't so much as grazed her since they'd reached Stonton. She stared flatly as he passed. "This," she grumbled to herself, "is going to be harder than I thought."

A long groan creaked out of the forest behind her and startled her feet into moving. She hastened after him, but faltered as she cast a wary look back towards the trees. They were swaying with a greater force than they had been only a few minutes ago, and their aged protests had equally risen from a warning to a threat. She looked anxiously towards Garon as the winds began to lift her hair and tug at her sleeve, but he didn't seem to notice it. Even as it began to drag at his jacket, his attention remained in the grasp of something else. Her breath was snatched away before she could discover what.

In an instant, they were under assault. The unseen force beat them both with such power it was as if the trees themselves had lashed out, buffeting them forwards as it twisted furiously towards the village. In seconds it ensnared Rathen and Aria, who braced themselves against the sudden force, then Anthis further up who was almost pushed over. It ripped across them all from one direction to another, changing its course on a whim, and the bellowing trees behind them cracked and snapped as they gave in to its ire.

Finally Garon dug his heels into a reluctant stop, but even as he looked around with harsh, calculating eyes, he still seemed distracted. But Petra had little care any longer as to why. "We're not safe here," he bellowed needlessly over the gale, bracing himself as his eyes began hunting for a solution.

"Oh, *now* you agree!"

He ignored her remark "Rathen! Have you had enough time?"

"Plenty!"

"Wait, we're *leaving?*" Anthis called incredulously from above.

"*Of course* we're leaving!"

"You've been here before!" Rathen snapped as he tightly grasped Aria's hand and attempted to keep her from the full brunt of the shifting wind. "Get down here! *Now!*"

He growled in objection despite the force that howled around him, but obeyed all the same, gathering his books and sorting them quickly but precisely into their higgledy piggledy order, seizing the loose, escaping pages as he went.

Petra cursed as a heavy branch hurtled past her, catching the sound of the crack with barely a second to turn and stumble out of its way. Another quickly followed further down the treeline. "Anthis!" She yelled with increasing panic. "Hurry up!"

Another branch tore free behind them, larger than the last, and it flew on the gale in whichever direction the force twisted as if the limb was little more than a twig, fracturing as it struck the edge of the carven village.

"*Anthis!*"

"I'm coming!" He roared in irritation, slinging his bag over his shoulder, but his words were lost to the sound of more trees being torn apart. He found his feet as boughs and branches spun through the air, flying wide of the rock, and hurried down the twisting path as quickly as he could while the others rushed back towards the forest, seeking the comparative safety of the forest's clutter. Their eyes were everywhere, tracking each piece of debris and trying to predict where they might go, hoping all the while that the wind didn't shift again.

A warning was called, disembodied by the gale, and a limb a foot thick and surely too heavy to be lifted by wind alone ripped free and swept low over head, its bulk barely missing Rathen as he ducked beneath it at the last moment.

He breathed a brief sigh of relief and watched it spin away, but it didn't strike the ground and roll to a stop as he'd expected. Another change in the wind gave it a renewed lift, raising it higher and propelling it straight towards the rock.

Just as Anthis appeared from around the other side.

Panic surged. He dropped Aria's hand and began contorting his fingers while Petra shouted his name in warning over the roaring wind. But there was no hope of him hearing it, nor time to complete Rathen's spell. But still he tried, weaving the signs as quickly as he physically could even as they watched the bough strike.

"*Anthis!*"

Despite the strength of the blow, Anthis barely noticed himself slam into the rock face. Even as he dropped heavily to his knees, he was aware of the pain between his shoulders, the trickle of blood running down the side of his face and the far deeper stinging in his stomach, but it was all disconnected. He felt almost nothing, and his mind had emptied but for one single thought.

Wind whipped, thundering past his ears. He could hear the others calling his name between its roars, but he didn't respond. He reached quickly down to the hem of his shirt, ignoring the blood that soaked into it and the wound that it oozed from.

The knife. He needed to hide the knife.

He felt a distant tug of relief as he pulled the ornate dagger free from his waistband. Its blade was clean and its jewels were clear, and he murmured gratitude beneath his breath at the stroke of luck that this blade, one forbidden from sheathing, hadn't been the one to puncture his skin.

Shaking, in confusion or urgency, he reached immediately for the bag that had dropped from his shoulder and dragged it towards himself, acutely aware of the approaching footsteps, and stuffed the dagger as deep amongst his books and papers as he could. Only once the flap dropped back into place and the blade was safely hidden away did he spare a sigh of relief, and in place of his panic came the belated and stinging rush of pain.

He doubled over, his attention now fiercely upon the gore in his stomach and the far plainer dagger that had been loosened from its sheath by the impact. He pulled it free from himself as shock began to set in, his hands shaking so much he risked making the injury worse, and dropped it carelessly to his right as a shadow drew up on his left.

Rathen knelt quickly beside him, and as Anthis looked up he noticed with increasing dizziness that his usually grim expression was twisted in concern. The mage grasped him roughly by the chin and turned his head to see the wound beside his temple, then back again to look closely into his eyes as if searching for something. Petra shortly arrived beside them, her beautiful face marred in the same way.

"Is he all right?" She asked, her voice, coloured with worry, only just rising above the wind.

Rathen stared at him intently for a moment longer before nodding in reply. "The branch only clipped him," he called back. "He's dazed, but he's okay. Help me get him up, we can't stay out in this."

The two lifted his arms over their shoulders as Garon arrived with Aria in hand. Anthis groaned at the pain of the movement, and he heard Petra curse in shock beside his ear. Panic warmed his blood, but then remembered that his blade was hidden. Whatever she'd gasped at was no longer of any consequence.

Garon rushed ahead to push open the nearest door, the wood rotten but tightly sealed by a matt of vines and moss, and they stumbled inside and out of the reach of the elements, all but dragging Anthis along before wrestling the door closed behind them.

"I thought he was clipped?" Said Petra as they set him on the ground in the small, dark room, a conjured blanket appearing beneath him to ward off the cold of the stone.

"He was," Rathen replied, but as a light flickered into existence at the flexing of his fingers, his eyes locked immediately upon the dark blood that spread over light cotton. "What--"

Petra shoved a knife beneath his nose, one she'd snatched from the weeds as the wind tried to tug it free. He frowned at it in confusion, then she whirled onto Anthis. "Where did you get this?" She demanded as the mage pulled aside his shirt and studied the wound.

"It's mine," he slurred, looking back at her with empty eyes.

"Why do you have it? What could a historian need a *blade* for?"

"Protection," he said just as innocently.

"And a wonderful job it's done." Rathen shook his head and pressed against the bleeding. "The wound is superficial. He'll be fine." His dark eyes rose to meet Anthis's, disapproval stark within them. "Although his intelligence is another matter."

When Aria hurried over with her father's bag, he began dressing the wound with supplies he'd brought in anticipation of whittling injuries, shaking his head throughout with an expression of condemnation one might turn on a child.

If Garon had concern for him, however, he didn't show it. He stood quite still beside the door instead, and Petra noticed the distant look in his eyes.

"What is it?"

His troubled gaze flicked towards them. "We can't stay."

"And for the moment," replied Rathen, "we can't *leave*."

"We're safe in here," Petra assured him, but the inquisitor shook his head, and though he opened his mouth to correct them, his attention was snatched by a sound outside, hidden within the persistent howl of the elements. Whatever words he wished to speak were replaced by a warning - though what that warning was, precisely, none but he knew. His voice was smothered by the shattering of the door and the whipping of the wind as it surged inside, tearing around the billowing figure that stood beyond the threshold, shadowed by the light behind him.

Chapter 17

In an instant Rathen exploded to his feet and stormed towards the door, the wind trying and failing to beat back his every step while the others braced themselves against the gust. But the cloaked figure didn't flinch under his wrath, neither shrinking back nor advancing to meet him, and as Rathen raised his hands to begin shaping a swift spell, so, too, did the shadow.

Garon was close on his heels, either bravely or foolishly heedless to whatever spells the two mages were preparing to cast as he lunged forwards to reach for the figure from around the fractured door, his sword already in hand and more than prepared to use it. But before he could make his intentions known, the inquisitor was suddenly thrust aside, thrown by an phantom force hard enough to remove him from either's line of sight. He crashed into a rotten table, a billow of dust rising around him as the breath was knocked from his lungs, but he pushed himself right back up and began to advance once more.

Petra gritted her teeth as she watched over her shoulder, tightly fastening Anthis's bandage while her fingers itched to take up her sword and join them.

The sunlight began to dim outside, concealed by another wave of cloud, and Rathen no longer had to bar his eyes against the brightness. But as his sight adjusted, hesitation gripped his movements. His signs faltered and a frown pulled at his features as he stared at the figure before him, and he saw a similar reaction quickly befall him in turn.

"*Rathen?!*"

Quick movements from the shadows to his right snatched Rathen's attention as Garon barrelled back towards door, and a new wave of urgency took hold. "Wait!" He yelled, fighting to be heard over the wind as it tried to shove his voice back into his throat, but Garon continued his advance, either not hearing or not heeding.

He grunted and stepped forwards, catching him at the very last moment, just before he could leap upon the man who now stared into the ancient elven home in disbelief. The inquisitor's wide, grey eyes shot towards him and searched his in confusion.

Everyone tensed as the atmosphere froze, even if the wind continued to assault them, and they looked between Rathen and the attacker as they stared at one another in growing confusion.

"Owan," Rathen began carefully as his opponent's hands began to lower in shock, but at the tentative sound of his voice, a new rage fell over him, twisting his increasingly familiar features. The mage's fingers twisted before Rathen could react beyond shoving Garon aside, and released a spell to knock him backwards.

Rathen grunted as he struck the cold, stone ground, and he heard Aria scream nearby. "Stay there," he warned her as he began pushing himself back up, but before he could rise even to his elbows, another unseen force slammed him right back down, pummelling the breath from his chest. Suddenly the mage was upon him, pinning him in place and grasping his collar.

"Owan!" Rathen shouted, pulling at his hands as the mage shook him furiously, but his voice didn't reach him. He sharply warned the others away as Petra and Garon started towards them, their blades drawn.

"*How dare you?!*" The mage bellowed over the top of him, his blue eyes burning as Rathen continued to struggle. "*How dare you?!*"

"Owan, it's me!"

"It *can't* be you! *You're dead!*"

"All due respect, I'm *not!*" His frenzied attacker was relentless. Rathen gave up trying to restrain him and threw him off with strength alone, and the moment the mage landed hard on the floor beside him, he pinned him down instead.

"Who are you?" He demanded, leering up at him, but Rathen could see by the conjured light a haunting realisation enter his eyes even as he spoke, one he was reluctant to accept. "...And how...?"

Rathen sighed as the struggle against him weakened. He rose to his feet and stepped over him. "It's a long story." He offered his hand, ignoring the others' warnings, and after a moment of intense deliberation, the mage took it. Back on his feet, he stared closely at Rathen, and Rathen let him.

The tension over the others tightened as they held their collective breath. The wind still tried to continue the fight, but Owan's shoulders were the first to ease and he shook his head in disbelief. "By Vastal," he breathed as he analysed his face, but though his lips continued to move, nothing passed them. He shortly gave up, and a wide smile spread across his middle-aged features instead. He clasped him on the shoulder as one similarly brightened Rathen's grim visage.

Petra and Garon looked between the two in equal confusion, their blades slowly lowering, while Anthis frowned sluggishly and even Aria looked upon them in surprise, though a grin began creeping across her face.

"Truly, you are the very *last* person I *ever* expected to see!" Owan managed at last, still smiling incredulously, his aggression forgotten. He briefly flexed his fingers, and the door repaired itself and shut the wind away. "What are you doing here? How are you alive?! *What happened to you?!*"

Rathen's lips parted to answer, but he hesitated and his smile weakened as he glanced behind him to the others, each of whom stared back expectantly. Owan followed his gaze and his brow, far less weathered than Rathen's, softened in thought. He turned his eyes back to him, sharper now as they calculated. "Later, then."

Rathen inclined his head gratefully, but as he looked up again, his dark eyes narrowed and grew weighted. "You're here about this magic, aren't you?"

Owan blanched. His eyes flicked past him to the others, none of whom had moved, and breathed a laugh in defeat, dropping his voice against them. "You always were too perceptive."

"I thought the Order wasn't looking into this."

"We're not, officially. That's why I'm here alone."

"I'm sorry," Garon started, finally stepping forwards, "who is this?"

"Owan Mal," he replied with a friendly smile and well-practised bow. "Scholar." His smile weakened into shame as he straightened again. "I'm...sorry for attacking you, Inquisitor. These are uncertain times and I didn't expect anyone else to be here..." he looked to Rathen, "least of all, you. But tell me: why *are* you here?"

"The same reason you are." He spared only the briefest glance towards Garon, but the officer showed no sign of disapproval. While Rathen hadn't lied, he hadn't revealed anything, either. He looked back to Owan and severity returned to his eyes.

Owan's dropped to match. "You felt it, too?"

"So I didn't imagine it."

"Imagine what?"

Rathen looked across them reluctantly as Petra stepped up to join them, his discomfort mounting under the weight of their gazes. "The magic here is acting as though it was part of a spell."

"I thought you said that wasn't possible," Anthis managed slowly from the floor.

"I also said I wasn't a scholar."

"Well, he was right," Owan assured them in his defence, "it shouldn't *be* possible. Spells disintegrate too slowly and in too few particles for fragments of the spell to move around, but that seems to be what has happened. There's a small, single spell chain here that--"

"'Spell chain'?"

Owan blinked at Anthis, and Rathen knew immediately that he'd worked out that there was more to their activity than he'd first assumed. How could one so uninformed about the basic principles of magic provide anything useful against the matter? His eyes flicked towards the presence of the inquisitor, then back to Rathen, but he didn't return the stare. He turned towards answering the question instead. "Spells are made up of small chains of information," Rathen explained, "details needed to create the full incantation. A spell to create a piece of fabric, for example, would consist of several chains, one for weight, one for colour, one for weave, softness, flexibility and so on."

"But what we have here is a *single* chain," Owan continued, turning his suspicion away from him, "a small fragment of a spell which is still trying to do its job without direction or purpose."

"What's the chain?" Anthis asked, but they both shook their heads. "Could it have anything to do with wind, by chance?"

"I can't rightly say," Owan confessed, and it was clear to them all that that fact made him uneasy, "but I don't believe so. All I know for certain is that it's here, and it *shouldn't* be. There is no evidence of any spells having been cast here, let alone anything substantial enough for...all this."

"Magnetism?"

The mage frowned slightly at the young man's suggestion, but what suspicion remained seemed to subside, at least fractionally satisfied that they weren't as uninformed as they'd seemed. "Yes, the chain and the raw magic were both drawn here from somewhere else."

The knot that had returned to Rathen's pale brow deepened. "What about other places?" He asked, turning towards him with a flicker of urgency. "Have you looked anywhere else?"

"I've been to a ruin with stronger magnetism and another with weaker, but I didn't notice any chains in either. They both had an unnatural beauty, but that was all, and no chains seemed to be responsible for it. That I could detect, at least."

He nodded slowly in agreement, noting the absence of peacefulness.

"Could you not just be mistaken about no spells being cast here?" Petra asked, but they both shook their heads again.

"The Order wouldn't miss it. This is a lot of magic, and the accumulation is too sudden to be from an undetected spell - even if it was cast in secret, we would have known about it in very short time." The concern in Owan's tone had worsened and hesitance was creeping in to join it, growing more prominent with every word he spoke. He glanced doubtfully to Rathen, but the look of involved concern in his eyes seemed enough to convince him to continue, if just for his sake. "This magic did come from somewhere else - but it isn't human."

The connection fell into place in Rathen's mind the moment he said it. "No...it's elven. Of course it is. There's a resemblance between the magic here and what remains in M--Kulokhar," he amended quickly.

"It's being drawn to elven ruins," Petra frowned, "why is that a surprise?"

"Elves built on the sites out of faith; they're not responsible for the magnetism pulling it there - but, they're really fragments of an *elven* spell?" Anthis's eyes glittered weakly as he tried rising to his feet, having grown tired of sitting at Aria's level during such a crucial conversation, but the pain in his stomach was still too sharp to fight against for pride alone, and his head, though clearer now, began to swim from the exertion. He sighed and leaned back against the wall. "How is that possible? Shouldn't elven spells have disintegrated *long* ago? Or has the Order recently stopped maintaining one?"

"They should have, and we haven't. That's why I'm here: to find out why and how it's happening."

"So the Order has no idea what's going on," Rathen summarised in defeat, and Owan gave only the slightest of nods, as though afraid to confirm it in front of non-mages.

"Unfortunately, for the moment, this is all we have on the matter."

Rathen released a long and heavy sigh. If the Order had no idea, how was *he* supposed to work anything out? Up until ten minutes ago, he didn't even have this much, and he'd doubted it all even as he'd felt it. But he was grateful, at least, that he'd had the unexpected opportunity to confirm it all before that doubt could stretch its roots.

"What about the raw magic?" He asked suddenly, even while the thought was still forming in his mind.

"What about it?"

"It's interacting with the chain, isn't it? A small, single spell-chain couldn't be this powerful on its own, regardless of what kind of spell it had been a part of."

"No," the mage frowned, "but since I can't work out what the chain itself is, I also can't be certain on that point, either."

Rathen sighed heavily once again. The others watched them uneasily, listening to the words even if it was clear that not all of them understood them. Owan glanced towards them, but as Anthis hissed in a sudden pang of pain and stole back some of their attention, he returned to Rathen and gestured to one side, leading him to the far end of the near-empty and long-abandoned home, provoking a renewed sense of dread.

"What are you doing here?" The mage asked, his voice suddenly low and grave in a manner that Rathen deemed uncharacteristic even despite the passage of time.

"I told you," he replied flatly, but a similar hint of unfamiliarity flickered through his eyes.

"No, you told me *something*. Come on, Rathen, we were friends once. You've been gone for over a decade, we all thought you were dead - no one's seen sight nor sound of you, at any rate - and all of a sudden here you are, in a place like this, alongside an inquisitor to boot." His aged eyes narrowed. "What are you doing?"

"Trying to fix this."

"Why?"

"Because the Order isn't."

"Forgive me, Rathen, but what can *you* do against this?"

He stared at him for a long moment, considering the challenge in his voice and simmering in his eyes. His jaw tightened in indecision, but his tongue moved on its own. "We have a plan."

"You have a plan? You and the others?" He glanced beyond him briefly. "You're the only mage among them."

Rathen's eyes hardened. "We have a plan."

"...And you're not going to tell me what it is."

He shook his head regretfully. "I can't."

Owan stared at him, trying to read his once-familiar eyes, and Rathen found himself trying to read his in turn. What was he thinking? Did he think he didn't trust him? That he thought Owan could be a part of a rebellion? Or was he thinking in kind, that Rathen may be involved instead? Owan's eyes flicked past him towards the others again, and he knew they'd fallen upon the inquisitor. He watched them narrow, and something within them changed when they turned back onto him. "As it stands," he began with a sudden note of detachment, looking away again as though he wasn't speaking to him but merely thinking out loud, "the Order *doesn't* have a plan. Our attention is occupied by the impending war and the Crown won't spare us to look into this matter as we should. Some in the Order think the Crown suspects we're responsible for it and wants to keep us away, while others think they're just worried we're preparing to rebel. But magic is very much our obligation, so we've been forced to work outside of orders just to do our job. We've been restricted to looking at sites within two days of Kulokhar so our absences won't be noticed, but that has also made it easier for a few to have been caught investigating it. Fortunately things aren't so bad that the Order's jurisdiction over its mages has been revoked, so the elders have been allowed to seem to punish them, but even so, it's a difficult situation, and in this time all we've managed to gather is this meagre information and we have little idea what to do with it." He finally looked back to him again. "Whatever plan you have...all I can do is wish you luck."

"You've already done more than that just by confirming my own findings."

The briefest, familiar smile flickered across his face. "That *almost* makes me feel a little bit less useless, and most certainly like I've defied the Crown - not that that's a bad thing," he added distastefully. Rathen frowned in understanding.

"What *is* happening in the Order?"

"Things are...tense, to say the least," he replied with a puff, folding his arms heavily across his chest. "The rumours and reports of mages in other countries are straining people's trust towards us much more than usual...and if I'm honest, I'm not certain that none of our own are guilty..."

Rathen's frown twisted further. "What does that mean?"

"A few mages seem distracted."

"Well, given the martial state of things right now, that's not really surprising..."

Owan's lips slanted in doubt. "I'm not so sure it's that..."

Rathen stared in another futile effort to read him. He'd been easy to work out once, but now he seemed only increasingly closed off. That moment did absolutely nothing to reassure him.

"But," the scholar continued with a sigh, "I can't say anything for certain. It's just conjecture." He cocked an eyebrow. "As for the conjecture about *you*..."

Tedium suddenly fell over the black-haired mage. "What conjecture about me?" He frowned as a smile of fascination tried to grip Owan's lips.

"No one believes what happened to you is as simple as non-magic folk think. Not even the most complex curses or spells could result in such a thing - but as for what it *could* be...no one has been able to work it out..."

"Well, I'm afraid I can't help you, there, either."

Disappointment tripped his hopeful stare, but he smiled apologetically a moment later, and nodded his acceptance even though it was clear he didn't believe him. "Very well. Then at the very least you can tell me where you've been this past decade."

The group watched the two mages as they spoke quietly together, expressions of shock, assurance, relief and incredulity passing between them, but, infuriatingly, none were able to catch their words.

Petra was the first to give up trying. She turned her attention onto Anthis instead and poked his wound through the bandages. He winced and looked back at her with shock in his eyes, but shrank immediately beneath her sharp and disapproving stare. "You are an idiot."

"Why am I an idiot?" He asked, unreasonably hurt, looking past her towards Aria and Garon for defence but found both focused on the distant conversation with similar looks of concentration.

"If you had just moved when we told you to--actually, no, if you hadn't run off in the *first* place you wouldn't have gotten hurt at all."

"Or," he began slowly, "would I have been *killed?*"

Her brow dropped and she turned her attention decisively onto Garon instead. "You, however, endangered us *all*."

His grey eyes flicked towards her, but his attention was fleeting.

She rose back to her feet and approached him. "You knew this place was dangerous but you led us in anyway."

"It was a calculated risk," he replied flatly, his eyes fixed to the mages.

"Anthis got hurt."

"I'm not a babysitter and he's a grown man. He can look after himself."

"How very responsible of you."

The slightest crease formed in his brow and he seemed to flinch at the venomous remark - but it was so brief and so slight that she wasn't sure she hadn't imagined it.

Anthis cocked his head as he, too, observed the mages. "Seems to have been worth the risk, though. Rathen's uncovered a few things which should prove useful for all of us."

"But at what cost?"

"Little, I think. He seems to trust this man and I don't think he does that kind of thing easily."

Garon grunted, but there was a flicker of concedence in his voice.

Almost ten minutes passed before the mages concluded their quiet but animated conversation, and the newcomer didn't hang around. After a simple and suddenly rigid handshake, Owan Mal headed towards the door and stepped back out into the unnatural wind without even a polite nod in the group's direction.

Quizzical eyes fell upon Rathen as he joined them.

"What did you tell him?" Garon asked him critically the moment the door had closed.

"Ultimately, nothing. And as far as either of us are concerned, this encounter never happened. He didn't see me."

"Did you get anything else from him?" Anthis asked as Petra frowned at the precision of Rathen's statement. "Or...from the air in that corner of the room?"

"No. He told us everything he and the others have on the matter. But as little as that is, at least I've got reliable confirmation."

"Can you do anything with it?"

"At this point, I don't know, but I'm sure it'll help in time." He glanced uneasily towards the door as the wind roared against it, attempting to force its way back in. "For now there's nothing more to learn here, and the longer we stay the more certain I am the wind is only going to worsen. We'll end up trapped in here."

Garon cut him off before he could make a single step towards the door, and he was pinned under the inquisitor's careful, scrutinising stare. "Are you sure you can trust him?"

"He was sneaking around," Petra agreed.

"He was not sneaking around."

"Then how did you not notice him? Garon noticed him."

"My attention," he began with growing urgency, "was on the magic itself; I could have sensed his magic if not for the chaos around us. But Owan *can* be trusted. He's...an old school friend." A momentary frown pulled at his brow as he realised how silly the statement sounded, but he shook it away and looked down towards Anthis. "Are you fine to walk?"

The young man forced himself to his feet, biting back a wince as he did so, and Petra quickly lent him her shoulder. "I'll manage."

Collecting the bags, they moved to leave, and Aria frowned thoughtfully up at her father while a small smile played on her lips. But she didn't voice her thoughts as Garon dragged the door back open, instead bracing herself against the incessant wind as they all stepped back into its assault.

They moved doggedly, most of their focus limited to where they put their feet, though Anthis was acutely aware of the danger of flying branches as he limped along beside them. But the turmoil had improved: little was carried through the air but leaves, the weakest limbs having already been torn away, and as they contended with the force, it underwent another abrupt shift and provided them with a tail-wind. The cover of the trees quickly loomed before them and their feet moved faster at the promise of safety.

Until the world fell silent in the wake of a shrill squawk loud enough to rival the gale, and their hearts turned to ice.

"Run!" Garon yelled as Petra turned to search in horror for the source. "Don't look, just *run!*"

"What is it?!"

"Harpies," Rathen growled, though he hadn't spared a glance over his shoulder either.

"*Harpies?!* Did that mage summon them?!"

"Of course not! We have...business with them - just run!"

They barrelled in amongst the trees, but the copse was sparse and young and their soft limbs could never restrain the winged beasts. Suddenly its protection seemed far less certain.

Their assailants darted in behind them, weaving far too easily between the thin trunks as though they rode on gusts rather than their own wings, and they dove upon them at every opportunity, their long, sharp talons reaching out for skin, hair, cloth and bag straps. They were delayed only by Petra's quick thinking; falling to the rear of the group and pulling branches back, she loosed them when they were close enough, whipping them back into place and forcing them to pause or divert to avoid the recoil. But they were persistent. They had no intention of simply chasing them off.

"They're gaining!" Petra warned, and Rathen glanced towards Garon for his decision. But the inquisitor was silent, his brow creased in thought as he led the way. Petra shouted again, this time with greater urgency as she loosened the bolas from the small of her back, but still he didn't respond.

Rathen stole a look over his shoulder. The raptorial figures were barely ten feet away.

Panic and helplessness suddenly swelled his heart and lungs, his chest fit to burst at the inquisitor's indecision. His blood ran only colder as he found the sensation horrifically familiar.

'Oh, sweet Vastal, not now!' He pleaded. *'Not now!'*

"Garon!" He roared as he battled against himself. "Make a decision!" A shriek from directly above them jerked a growl from his throat, and before Garon could finally make the call, Rathen made it for him. His fingers shaped seals and three quick, successive blasts of air burst from the final formation he twisted and aimed towards the harpies. The first felled a tree, crushing the trunk as it met the opposing wind, and a startled caw rose as one collided with it as it dropped into its path, while the second blast missed any chance mark. But the third hit directly, cutting through the feathered waist of one pursuer and sending it crashing into the ground, squawking in pain and alarm. Collective shrieks of fury rose from the rest, and suddenly their chase intensified.

"What the hell are you doing?!" Garon yelled towards him, his grey eyes finally aflame. "You're only making them angrier!"

Rathen didn't respond. His jaw clamped in regret, but he shook it off. Injury wasn't his intention; a show of retaliation, something to encourage them away before it grew worse than even *they* could imagine. It had been a foolish hope, but at least taking action had returned him some control over himself.

'In for a penny,' he decided with resignation, and began forming another series of seals. Fire sprung to life and hung in the air inches from his crossing fingers before arcing up and over the heads of the fleeing group. It torched the trees easily, as though their leaves and branches hadn't seen rainfall for months, and spread over the feathers of the two fastest harpies whose haste carried them straight into the unnatural inferno. The rest managed to reel to a short stop and avoid the same fate, and they shrieked in panic, either for their kin or for the forest's destruction - which, didn't matter. This time it had been enough to divert their attention and hold them at bay, and Rathen breathed slightly easier.

"Keep going," Garon commanded, "run!" They followed his sharp right without question, and within moments the forest darkened and thickened. With barely the room to run half abreast, the harpies could never manoeuvre amongst them, and the canopy veiled the sky so entirely that tracking from above was impossible.

But before their triumph could set in, the ground gave way quite suddenly to a broad and impassable body of water.

Petra growled in frustration as they skidded to a halt, but Rathen considered it tactically. Just as in Mokhan, their pursuers would assume they'd continued in their original direction and sought to hide in the widest, thickest region of the forest, not move towards its most open edge - though, this time their pursuers could take to the sky. It would be little trouble for one of them to break off and check the lake.

They would just have to hope that they were underestimated.

Garon whirled on him as Anthis dropped to the ground, struggling for his breath under the strain of his wound, but once again neither the inquisitor nor the duelist seemed too ruffled by the exertion. At the very least, Garon still had breath enough in his lungs to rage at him.

"If he hadn't taken charge, we'd all still be running," Petra challenged from beside the mage before he could find the breath and mind to make his own defence, tucking her unused bolas away, "assuming Anthis was even able to keep up for much longer. And I didn't see *you* doing anything about it."

"I didn't want to make the matter worse," Garon returned, his voice strangled by his own restraint. "Apparently we've gotten ourselves involved in a *war*, and it is *certainly* better that we get attacked and do nothing about it than give them any *real* reason to pursue us by incriminating ourselves! And we don't want to leave any kind of trail for anything to follow!"

"And that would be just fine if those things weren't actually *trying* to *snatch* us!" Rathen finally shot, his panic only just subsiding and giving way to exasperation.

Petra shook her head and breathed a long, frustrated sigh. "Well, it's done now," she reminded them wearily, looking back the way they'd come. "We can't undo the actions."

"*Is* it done? As far as I can see, we've only given them fuel for the fire!"

"We did more than that - I can still smell chicken."

Garon glowered briefly at Anthis. "They will be hunting us more aggressively now."

Rathen snarled and turned away, looking back through the forest and intently searching the spaces between the trees. "They were hunting us anyway," he reminded them quietly, "and keeping away from settlements as we have been has probably only made it easier. They didn't only just catch up with us, their timing was too precise. They were taking advantage of the wind and Owan's absence, and they would have kept following us whether I'd done anything back there or not."

"Then we could have found the opportunity to set them straight, tell them that we're not involved!"

"When?! When they snatched us in their talons? Dragged us through the air? Tore us to shreds and fed us to their chicks?"

Aria silently shrank back beneath the thought as she continued vigilantly surveying the dark forest.

"They are the hunters, they're not going to show themselves unless they're ready to strike. If they wanted to talk to us, they *would* have."

Garon opened his mouth to respond, but his voice halted behind his tongue as a tell-tale squawk echoed in the distance, stilling the calls of nearby birds and, for a moment, the movement of the now-natural breeze.

Aria finally turned her big eyes away from the forest. "We shouldn't stay here."

Rathen took her hand and pulled her to her feet before starting quickly along the shaded lakeside, and the others shortly followed suit. He growled in irritation, however, when Garon stepped past him to steal the lead without even a sidelong glance. But he didn't truly care. He was still shaken by what had almost befallen them, himself most of all. If the inquisitor truly had to be in charge all the time, then let him. Rathen had no desire at all to re-assume the mantle of leadership, especially if there was someone else more than eager to do it instead. Though whether he could do it *well* was becoming another matter...

Chapter 18

The air remained mercifully still for the rest of the afternoon, and when evening finally began creeping in, they felt just safe enough to stop for the night despite the harpy-haunted forest still looming over the lake. They'd followed the edge of the water into older woods on the far bank, hoping their assailants would assume them long gone by now, and pitched their camp a short distance from the treeline with a disappointingly modest fire. They ate immediately, a few small birds Rathen had gathered and concealed from Aria to avoid upsetting her, then began ignoring each other.

Though they'd managed to lose the harpies, the atmosphere that followed the means had lingered by Garon's doing, and no one felt the desire to endure its weight. Even when he rose and stepped away from the camp without a word, the clouds seemed to remain.

But despite Rathen's near equal fault, he stayed within earshot, his back turned against a tree, and shut the matter out. He allowed himself to get lost in his thoughts, absorbing himself in the day's unlikely events, but despite his findings, their peril and the unreasonably intense panic that he'd only just prevented from taking over his body, he was surprised to find himself dwelling above all else on the encounter that didn't happen.

When he'd entered into the Order's military wing and Owan turned towards more academic pursuits, their friendship, as well as others, had dwindled under the strain of their diverging paths, and in time had devolved into an acquaintanceship. And yet, at the sight of him, Rathen had felt a ridiculous childish glee. He'd enjoyed it for a moment, until it mutated into a sickening reminder of how his life should have proceeded. He should still have been in the Order, leading his regiment against Skilan as the sahrot he was - if not promoted to sahrakh and issuing commands from a more strategic position. In the passage of eleven years, that could have happened.

He should have been in Kulokhar with a true family of his own, and Elle would have been by his side, crying with their should-have-been children that he was leaving to go to war, while he assured them that a man as strong as he, with a family as loving and faithful as his, couldn't possibly fall to defeat, let alone against a force already so exhausted. But they would have cried anyway, and made him promise that he would come back...

But that hadn't happened.

He felt something light roll down his cheek, and grunted to himself as he wiped it away. He could not lose himself to those thoughts, especially not after what had almost happened that afternoon.

With a rough breath, he took a hold of his himself and tightly locked his regret away.

From what Owan had told him, the Order was as good as ignoring the matter after all. If they were moving so few in an attempt to remain undetected, they couldn't hope to solve the matter quickly even if they were utilising minds as intelligent as his. There were too many places affected, and it seemed that not all of them presented the same evidence nor the same strength - and those two factors didn't seem to line up, either. Had the war not been on their doorstep they might have been able to handle it, more effort could have been put into concealing their movements. But as it stood, the magic looked set to grow only worse before the Order could put a stop to it.

Rathen's lips, already downturned, twisted only further. It seemed he'd been unfortunately correct in what he'd said: he really *was* the only mage with the time to see to this.

The weight on his shoulders intensified as though another anvil had been strung to his burden. He found he'd been hoping all along that perhaps they *were* doing something about it, and that his involvement in this merry group of misfits would be both short-lived and pointless. But now he understood, and painfully, that the situation's outcome hung entirely upon his spell and Anthis's artefact.

Still, as his body grew heavy with dread, he forced himself to realise the one thing of comfort that came of the non-encounter: Owan hadn't shrank back from him as he'd imagined his old friends would. While the Order had no answers for his personal predicament, if so light a term could be used, at least they didn't view him - or his memory, he reminded himself - as a monster.

He sat a little taller against the tree, feeling an unusual sense of pride slip in, and allowed himself, for a moment, to indulge it. To feel like more than just a shadow of the man he used to be.

But then he remembered that he *was* just a shadow, one with a terrible secret that had just tried to tear itself to the surface, and the feeling quickly escaped as if in fear of him.

He sighed in defeat and slumped back down again, turning his mind onto the only thing that was presently expected of him. It may not have been as grand and noble as leading soldiers to the defence of Turunda, but he found himself now far more willing to accept the ill-suited task. At least it was better than shovelling Oat's damp straw.

He focused his mind as best he could, blocking all else out. Elven magic, spell chain, interaction with the elements. Despite his wavering concentration, he compared these among other details with everything he could recall from Kienza, trying to line it all up, make some kind of sense of it - work out a solution as soon as possible. But no matter how he tried to rotate the details, it was like trying to press together two conflicting pieces of a jigsaw.

There was still too much missing to make the connections, but just how much? One detail, or ten?

Exasperation began to block his throat. Despite these new details - *significant* details - he was still no closer to working anything out. And they'd been out for so long already, moving from one futile location to another, getting themselves into dangerous situations along the way, and yet they had nothing at all to show for it. No information had been put to real use, neither his nor Anthis's research, and who was to say how long this would take? Or how long they *had?*

Only one thing eased his mind, if fractionally, and that was that no mage could be responsible if the magic was elven. That meant that they weren't unwittingly going up against an organised and likely vengeful movement - but it also meant that there were no plans to discover and upset in order to delay whatever he or Garon had feared may have been happening. Instead, all they could do was continue chasing ideas. Because, in the end, that was all they had been doing.

A small voice cleared beside him, nudging him back to the forest. He looked up expecting to find Aria grinning broadly back down at him, her face lit by the weak fire, but he found her sitting quietly in the roots beside him instead, her head hung, a shadowed frown marring her brow, and her doll clutched in her arms. He hadn't noticed her join him.

"Can I talk to you?" She asked softly while he frowned at her strange temperament, but as she turned her deeply conflicted eyes up at him, his heart dropped and expression softened. She'd probably been sat there trying to work up the courage to speak for a while.

He gave her an encouraging nod.

"I'm frightened." She shuffled closer as he sighed and looped his arm around her shoulders, pulling her close alongside him and kissing the top of her head. "It nearly happened again, didn't it?"

His jaw tightened as he rested his cheek against her fair hair. "You noticed?"

"It's hard to miss when you get that panicked. But that's not why I'm frightened."

"So why are you frightened?"

She only shrugged.

"Do you want to go home?"

Aria shook her head silently and pulled at the grass around her bare feet, her doll still wrapped in her arm. As always, she'd discarded her shoes the moment they'd stopped.

He raised his head and considered her carefully as she scrutinised the ground, and he knew in a moment that she was simply letting him know how she felt. After the events of the last few days alone, it came as no surprise, but she hadn't confessed it easily. He knew well that her trust in him was absolute - perhaps too much so - and admitting her fear must have felt to her like some kind of betrayal. He could see that in her eyes now, too. She was easy to read.

He squeezed her, but didn't address the point, choosing to let her think such a conclusion would never even occur to him. "You have been quiet lately."

"I just feel...useless."

He frowned. "Why ever do you feel useless?"

"Because I'm not doing anything to help."

"But no one *needs* you to, little one." He watched her make a face and understanding snared him. He smiled softly and breathed a laugh, squeezing her once again. "That's the problem, isn't it?"

"Anthis is reading things, Garon is guiding us, you're working on the spell," they both glanced down at the conjured notebook resting in his lap, its open page filled with crossed out words. "Even Petra is helping by protecting us."

"Petra isn't really a part of this group, though," he reminded her. "She's leaving us at Bowden. And we have and will get by just fine without her. It's just for convenience's sake."

"Well, either way, *I'm* not leaving at Bowden," she replied dismissively, and threw down the grass she'd pulled in the beginnings of a sulk. "I feel like a burden."

Rathen turned and embraced her properly. "You," he said softly as he pulled her in, "will *never* be a burden. And have you forgotten about your help with the ditchlings?"

"Arkhamas."

"Arkhamas," he amended obligingly. "If not for you, we would have been in trouble."

She sighed and let go of him. "They wouldn't have done anything to you."

"Whether their abduction and changing of children is rumour or not, they *are* thieves and they *are* known for attacking people, especially in groups *half* that size. Don't underestimate what you did for us."

"Yeah but either way, that was only one time."

He didn't give in to his growing defeat. He considered her instead, his dark eyes masked in a practised way so that she couldn't possibly think he looked condescending, judgemental or dismissive.

She was upset, that much was plain to anyone, but he knew that this was no childish turn. This was important to her - very important. Something had lodged itself in her head, perhaps because she was beginning to understand the importance of their activity, and she'd turned it over and over until it had become something negative, and the ideas it had given her - that she was useless, a burden - had become convincing. She wasn't looking for reassurance, and he knew that to try would only give her negative thoughts deeper root by appearing to brush it aside. She simply needed to be told that the voice in her head was wrong.

A sudden idea hardened his eyes. "What do you want to do?"

"I want to *help!*" She managed to stifle her desperation into a coarse and exasperated whisper.

"I know. But in what capacity do you want to help?"

Suspicion subdued her. She cast him a sidelong glance, narrowing at his curiously level tone, but though she certainly searched for the trick in his eyes, she found nothing but expectation. She frowned and replied carefully. "The same way as you and Anthis: something only *I* can do."

He nodded slowly, folding his arms and looking up through the leaves to the stars above as his lips pursed in thought. "Well," he began tentatively, "things are likely to get difficult again. The harpies aren't going to leave us alone - but I don't know that songs about Oat will subdue them... And you didn't bring your rubber ball, so I don't know that you'll be able to provide many fresh stories to entertain us with..." he sighed and looked down, lifting the piece of half-whittled wood from the ground nearby and turning it over absently. "Your smile certainly brightens my day and, to be honest, can get you anything you want, but I don't think the artefact will appear at the sight of it..." He glanced towards her but suppressed his smile at the suddenly enthusiastic grin that now stretched across her face.

"I know what I can do!"

His brow cocked in doubt. "I don't know that pretending to be Anthis's shadow is going to be all that helpful..."

Aria's cheeks flushed red. "No, that's not what I meant."

"Well," he dropped the wood and thoughtlessly lifted the knife instead, "what then?"

Secrecy fell over her impish face, squinting her eyes as she glanced surreptitiously towards Anthis who snoozed nearby against a tree. "We might not be able to find the arty-fact," she whispered, as though the thought hadn't occurred to anyone but the two of them. "Elf houses are either empty or a complete mess, and they're all broken. That's why you have to come up with a spell."

"Yes..."

"But you said the spell would be too big or something to be cast all in one go by yourself. So, what if *I made* something for you to cast it into, bit by bit, like the elves did?!"

His jaw dropped, his brow rose, and he slapped himself in the forehead for good measure. "Why, Aria!" He beamed. "That is a *genius* idea! So very clever, I must say! Why ever didn't *I* think--wait," his black eyebrows bolted together. "Bit by bit?"

Aria blinked. "Well if they couldn't cast it all in one go, perhaps they did it in pieces, or in chains like you and your friend were talking about."

Rathen's eyes widened as his mind suddenly raced a thousand miles ahead of him. "Why ever didn't I think of that?" He repeated at a mumble. "Well because it's unorthodox...but the elves were better - *much* better - at using magic than us..." His gaze flicked down to Aria, who looked back with narrowed eyes. "You, my dear, are a genius."

"I played along for a while, Daddy, but you're laying it on kind of thick now..."

"No, truly," he beamed, this time whole-heartedly, kissing her firmly on the forehead, "*truly* you are a genius."

She had seen what no one else had.

Assuming, for a moment, that it was real, very little information seemed to have been recovered about this artefact and its spell. But, if it could have been used against other elves, its details would have been closely guarded even in its own time, and having few involved in its creation would certainly help in that regard. And as what *had* been recovered seemed to suggest that they'd never *actually* turned it against their kin, it was possible that there had been no great rush to create it, either.

So perhaps, instead of starting and finishing the spell all at once with the hands of a number of casters, drawing attention to the active creation of a potential weapon, why not just *one* caster who built the spell up subtly over time? The container, if lined with suitable spells, should be able to prevent the destabilisation of the spell before it was completed as well as mark their progress, putting it in the reach of *anyone's* abilities, elf *or* human, as long as they had the patience for such precise and careful construction...

Of course, if this *was* the case, it would mean fewer reliable sources of information, making their hunt for the artefact harder than they expected - but it also meant that, on balance, Rathen's own task was suddenly much more manageable.

Ah, the simplicity of children and adults' ability to over-think.

His eyes dragged back to Aria and found her grinning up at him. He realised he was smiling, too. "It looks like you have a job to do, little one."

"I will make a vessel worthy of your magic, greater than *anything* the elves could ever have crafted." Her eyes burned even as she leapt eagerly to her feet.

"Of that I have no doubt at all." He tore paper out of his notebook and conjured a stick of charcoal at her request, and she immediately sat down beside the fire to begin sketching. Usually she would have dived blade-first into a chunk of wood, but this, it seemed, she was taking quite seriously.

Rathen, meanwhile, rose to his feet and approached Anthis.

The historian woke with a start as he poked him in the shoulder, and recoiled additionally at the sight of him. Rathen's brow dropped, but he otherwise ignored it. "What do you know of the habits of elven casters?"

Petra sat at the riverside, relishing a moment of peace with her feet in the cool water, running her toes over a small, smooth pebble beneath the surface.

She breathed a sigh of contentment as the water lapped around her ankles. The past two days had been hectic, constantly on the move with barely a moment to rest. She was used to not staying in one place for too long - if anything, it was company she was unaccustomed to - but her travels were usually distinctly uneventful and not particularly hurried. Things didn't get interesting until she reached her destination, and even then it usually happened on her own terms. Lately, however, things had been more...exciting than she was used to.

But she had little choice but to endure it. Despite the need to shed the association, she'd decided it wiser to stay - among other reasons, she'd lost her money and her belongings, as few as they were, and that had left her with no means of obtaining food or lodging. Honestly, at least. And while she could seek out challengers, there were little more than villages for days around, and brazen aspirants with a need to prove themselves heroic didn't tend to reside in such places.

But at least she wasn't bored, and she had to admit that she rather enjoyed their company, as unusual as it was. They weren't boring, either.

She sat back with another peaceful sigh, leaning on her elbows, and stared out at the stars as her mind began to wander. But the thoughts that were quickest to reach her made her jaw tighten, and a sense of determination hardened her fists. She smiled slightly. The reaction was just as familiar as the thoughts themselves, those that lingered always just beneath the surface of anything that happened to be more relevant. They were comforting. Almost safe. Her strongest connection to home.

They drove her every breath, kept her anger and despair at bay, gave her a reason to rest well every night and rise with purpose every morning - but she cautiously kept them at arm's length, within reach but not close enough to smother her. That distance allowed details to grow mercifully hazy and easy to ignore. She was well aware of what they wished to show her, she didn't need to turn her mind's eye upon them to remind herself of her purpose, nor her resolve. She had mastered the memories, the thoughts, the feelings, and she used them always to her advantage.

But she would answer their needs, when she was able. When she had the information she required.

She closed her eyes and sighed in comfort once more, hanging her head back, content in her patience. Her long, red hair, damp and scented with rosehips and spice, tickled the back of her bare arm as it brushed across her skin, but a gentle breeze pushed it aside and she stretched her legs out further into the water.

But her relaxation was short-lived.

She sat bolt upright at a gentle splash, and strained her ears through the suspicious silence that followed. It had been far too weak to have been caused by an animal, nor to have been intentional or the result of casual clumsiness. No, it was certainly an accident. Something was out there, and it didn't want to be noticed.

She reached for her sword, but as her hand searched through the grass, a curse snapped past her lips. She'd left it back at camp. She flexed her fists. She'd be fine. With precise movements, Petra slipped her feet from the water and rose from the bank, her ears pricking when the splash came again. It was weaker than the first, but this time she isolated it. It had come from the edge of the lake.

She started towards it, moving with practised swiftness while making barely a sound. She peered around trees before stepping out from behind them, searching for who, or what, was out there before it could spot her first. But she saw nothing. If it was harpies, perhaps one of them had dragged their talons over the water to lure them out before taking to the forest canopy to attack from above. Or maybe, for now, they just wished to know whether or not they were there. And she was playing into their curiosity.

But her careful steps faltered when she discovered the familiar figure kneeling at the lake's edge, and she sighed in relief. Garon spun at the sound, moving even more suddenly and silently than she had with his blade already in his hand, and she bounced in fright.

"Dammit, Garon," she grumbled, forcing her heart to slow, "it's just me."

With a long, irritated sigh, he lowered the weapon and glared at her before crouching back down to the water. "You startled me."

"Well, you startled *me*. I thought you were a harpy."

He didn't bother to respond, and splashed his face instead. The disruption of the lake surface was soft in his caution, and it eased the tension out of her shoulders. He glanced up in annoyance as she stepped out from the trees with an easier sigh and looked across the lake, but he said nothing, choosing to ignore her unwanted presence rather than try to do away with it.

The still water passed in ombre from indigo to black. Like a second sky stretching at her feet, the stars that dazzled above also twinkled below, and the nightlarks danced in the void between them. All that kept the twins from merging and being lost to comprehension was the thin but stoic strip of forest, a silhouette, silent and unwavering, preventing the water from trickling away from the earth.

A soft breeze brushed past her, coaxing gentle ripples across the water, breaking the illusion along with the half-moon's perfect reflection. Petra released an easy breath as the sight corrected itself. "It's beautiful."

"You're unarmed."

She looked down at Garon.

"You thought I was a harpy. What did you plan to do?"

"I would have managed," she replied blandly, folding her arms, but as she turned her eyes back out over the water, her attention was caught by a discolouration on Garon's arm. She frowned, wondering why she'd not spotted it before, then realised that this was the first time she'd seen his bare arms - any part of him, actually, that wasn't his face. He maintained his official status so very rigidly that even removing his gloves and rolling up his sleeves seemed uncharacteristically improper.

She found herself tracing her own scars through her blouse, and her brow furrowed sadly. "How did that happen?" She asked before she could stop the words, but realised that, even had she been able to, she wouldn't have - and she'd spotted an opportunity. "Was it while on a case?"

"Why do you do that?"

She blinked at his abruptness as he whirled around to face her, tugging his sleeves back down and his gloves back on, but she couldn't see his expression for the moon that shone behind him.

"Do what?"

"Ask all the questions," he snapped. "Why do you pry? There are more important things to deal with right now than my identity."

Her eyes narrowed as she considered him. "Actually," she began, taking a thoughtful step forwards, "I'm not so sure about that..."

"What does that mean?"

"You don't socialise. You're completely consumed by your task - believe me, I know what it is to be so focused on something that you forget to live."

"...What does *that* mean?"

"That it's easy to absorb yourself in something you consider important." She stepped casually around to his other side so she might read his reaction. "Personally or truly. And just as easy to forget the world around you in the process. You don't sit and talk with the others - even Rathen is more sociable than you are."

"Why is any of this important?"

She smiled despite his clear frustration. "Now who's asking all the questions?"

His brow dropped and eyes flicked away from her, out towards the water, but she noticed that he made no move to leave.

She pressed on. "I get the feeling you've forgotten how to breathe."

"I know how to breathe."

"All right, fine, but you've certainly forgotten how to exhale involuntarily with an embarrassing wheeze or snort." Her eyebrows rose in surprise as she watched the shadow of a smile tug at his lips, and she knew she hadn't imagined it because he turned his head away to hide it. "Vastal save me - was that a *smile?*"

"Look," he said sternly, turning back towards her as it vanished as suddenly as it had appeared, "you are aware of the situation. You've seen some of it for yourself and you're not blind to the severity of this magic's existence since your sister is a mage. But it's my responsibility to see this through, whatever it entails, however long it might take, and it's such a...an unusual situation that it requires a great deal of consideration. And since we can't just waltz into towns and cities for the moment, I can't gather up-to-date information on this to make our movements a little more straight-forward, so I really can't afford the distraction of 'socialising'."

Petra frowned. "It's been two days since Mokhan. What would you expect to uncover in that time?"

"I never had the chance to gather anything in Mokhan, but that point aside, rumours travel fast."

"Working with rumours? You're starting to sound like Anthis."

"Well they seem to serve him very well."

She looked at him carefully as she considered his words. She noted the relative softness of his eyes compared to their usual ice and authority, and the ever so slight upward, almost pleading pull of his brow. But that wasn't all. Despite his ever-secretive and closed off choice of words, he'd delivered them more personally than usual, and they numbered more than he'd normally deem necessary. It was like a break in the clouds, if one that would surely soon close up again, and she felt the need to take full advantage of it for his sake.

She sighed. "Fine, I understand all of that, I suppose. I may not grasp the *true* weight of the situation, no matter how may times Anthis might try to explain it to me, but I already knew it wasn't as simple as 'mages dunnit' and that has had me concerned, for my sister's sake above all else. But I *also* know that if you blanket yourself in the matter and don't let yourself take off your blinders - or remove your gloves and roll up your sleeves - your life and its opportunities are going to pass you by without you even noticing they were there. And missing them so entirely is worse than realising too late. You'll live as a tool rather than a person - a tool for the country, in your case."

His eyes narrowed thoughtfully. "And in your case?"

She straightened. "Justice."

Garon stared at her for some time, and she matched his gaze perfectly. He found her unwavering resolve personally familiar; he knew with certainty that she wasn't going to say any more, just as she knew that he disapproved of her motivation. But still they stared, reading each other's minds rather than asking the questions.

He nodded slowly after a while. "Thank you, Petra," he began with a smile whose sincerity she couldn't decide upon, "but I'm afraid you're wasting your words, if you're even old enough to understand them yourself. Even if you knew who I was outside of this task, this situation is still too severe and our position against it still too precarious to let my guard down. And though I'm not here to make friends, I doubt the others are particularly keen to socialise with me tonight, either. Now, if you'll excuse me, I'm quite tired and really quite frustrated, and I came out here for some peace. So, if you'll excuse me..."

And with that, he turned and walked away, disappearing into the trees without leaving her time to object.

She stared after him, dropping her arms defeatedly to her sides while her jaw knotted in concern. She recognised his behaviour all too well. She may have been young, not even thirty winters, but she had once been just as closed-hearted. The difference was that she'd been lucky enough to meet someone who set her straight early on, who had given her the opportunity to become aware of what she was doing to herself and where it would invariably lead her. And though she'd decided to continue on as she was, at least she'd been informed, and had since learned to understand what her heart and mind really felt.

Garon may think he meant his words, but no normal person truly sought solitude. Their work may demand it, but their hearts certainly didn't want it. She travelled alone because anyone else would slow her down or try to hold her back, but there was a definite loneliness that only her dedication managed to hold at bay.

There were times when she wanted nothing more than to share a story with someone who would appreciate its irony because of another she'd told them two weeks before, or times when she could leave the gathering of water to someone else while she tended to the occasional wound she'd sustained in a duel.

She was certain after his strange shift, as brief as it was, that the same applied to Garon. And he may well have been just as good at hiding it, but he wasn't allowing himself to indulge in his present opportunity as she was. Inquisitors always worked alone, after all, and perhaps after doing so involuntarily for so long, it had grown to feel more like a rule than a circumstance. He probably wouldn't relax at all until he retired - assuming that rule of 'one' hadn't become so deeply embedded in his heart that he died old and alone.

Slowly, she grew aware of the tension in her brow. With a heavy sigh, she trudged back to her spot along the river, collected her boots and returned to the camp, forcing the matter from her mind. For now.

Chapter 19

The Rigger's Knot was bustling with activity, which would have been strange for a tavern at mid-morning had it not been for the troupe of travelling musicians that had arrived in Roeden only the evening before. As it was, the building was packed from wall to wall, and all attention was rooted upon the impromptu performance. The buoyant music of pipes and strings pleased the ears while the young women who danced among the performers held the eye, and their cheerful melodies flowed out through the windows to wash exuberantly over the town square, where those outside could enjoy it from their market stalls.

And so no one paid any mind to the blonde man with focused, needle-sharp eyes as he stepped in from the sun-bathed streets, nor when he slipped silently into the crowd and wove a haphazard route through them. A waitress was the only one to pay him more than a cursory glance, but his eyes didn't even graze her as she stepped forwards and asked what she could get him. Instead he continued to scour the vast room, straight over her head, and she frowned in insult as he moved on without a word.

He wended his way through the throng, his mind sharp and frantic. His veins tingled. His eyes darted everywhere but he found nothing worth his attention. In fact he saw nothing at all.

His heart thumped, thumped, pounding so hard he would think it could erupt from beneath his ribs if his mind was capable of producing such a thought. As it was, that very thing could happen and he wouldn't notice.

His mind was utterly consumed.

Where is it?

Where is it?!

He turned left, then switched right.

His eyes flicked around chaotically, searching everywhere within reach of every sense he could muster. He could feel it, he was *sure* he could feel it. Beauty, peace...power... He'd searched for so long and now, *finally*, he was almost upon it...

No...no, he wasn't. It wasn't there.

But it must be! It has *to be!*

He spun around.

Where is it?!

His veins burned.

Where is it?!

A white hot pain shot through his head, as if his very brain had caught fire, and his feet fell still in shock. But he was aware of it all for barely a moment. Even as he clutched at his skull and his clothes were fanned by bursts of air that puffed around him from nowhere, like the popping of hundreds of flies, he reached out even further with his every frantic sense. Because it *had* to be there.

Fire sparked into life, weaving and arcing over him in ribbons.

A sudden shriek of panic silenced the music and all eyes crashed upon his hunching form, but still he didn't notice. His own were squeezed tightly shut as a hurricane of confusion ripped his mind apart, and he began, unknowingly, to weep in unsuppressable frustration.

The revellers' cheers had crumbled into shouts and screams, and all around people attempted to escape him - but the tavern was too cramped. A few nearest the door managed to flee, but the whipping flames quickly caught on floorboards and tables, erupting across the wood, its enthusiasm encouraged by the age-old infusion of ale, and the door was quickly blocked by a towering inferno.

Lightning began to crackle about him and bursts of sheer energy joined the chaos, while the flames raged and grew in swells like the breath of a demon.

The man's weeping suddenly lurched into a maddened cackle; hysteria swallowed him. He stood straight, his eyes wild, spread his arms and allowed a sheer light to engulf him.

The sun was warm and comfortable, but while a few merchants had set aside their work to absorb its offering and enjoy the music while the market was quiet, this one of several fishmongers was ever-vigilant. And so the blonde man that hurried towards the tavern in an unnatural haste caught his eye, and his interest spiked when he recognised him as one of Kulokhar's preservers even without the Order cloak that should have been draped over his back.

He shifted his weight uncomfortably as he kept a close peripheral watch, even as he looked up to the sun, appearing to note the time. Then, as a few others had, he left his stall with a weary sigh and made his way across the square towards The Rigger's Knot to sit at a table outside and rub his sore feet.

Sounds of merriment spilled from the window, riding the cheerful tunes, and though he appeared to enjoy the music just as everyone else did, he paid close attention to everything but. And soon, to even his surprise, came panic.

He leapt to his feet as a handful of people burst out from the door, shouting and screaming in fear or for help, and he hurried over through the fleeing bodies. He reached the doorway a moment later, greeted by manic cackling before a sudden explosion blew him backwards. Sharp splinters and flaming panels of wood were sent hurtling with him through the air, and he raised his arms to shield himself from them as he landed hard on the road. One small but sharp piece would have found his head if not for his forearm barring the way.

He paid no attention to the injury. He had to inform the keliceran.

He pushed himself to his feet as the tavern was engulfed by flames and raced away through the gathering crowd of terrified onlookers, his sights set on the nearest moth cellar a few streets away.

The pen flicked sharply back and forth between his fingers, firing spots of ink across parchment, wood and porcelain, blotting notes, staining the desk and discolouring the long-cooled tea. One or two freckled his chin, but he didn't notice them land.

Salus snorted in irritation. Reports couldn't come in fast enough; things were happening and he wasn't hearing about them.

'That only means there's nothing worth reporting,' the irritating voice in his head reminded him for the thousandth time, but, as always, it didn't offer much comfort. Who was to say what wasn't worth reporting? *Every* detail counted, *every* detail mattered. Sitting in his chair, trapped in his damned office, he wished he didn't have to rely on reports, that he didn't have to wait to hear from the messages he'd sent to the other head authorities just to find out why their people were popping up in those recounts. If only he could have his *own* eyes everywhere. Then he'd know everything he needed to know in real time, as and when it happened, and he could act on everything so quickly it wouldn't have a chance to take hold. He could prevent invasions, weed out every spy, even prevent crime...Turunda's safety would be absolute.

As it stood, he felt as though he was just sitting around and waiting for things to happen just so he could reverse them. Worse still, the only reports he *was* getting were regarding the barbaric tribes and their bloodshed, and that matter was beneath his attention. The only real cause for concern was that their raiding parties might target nearby settlements - a few small groups had already begun leaving their territory to attack their enemy tribe directly, and the brutes weren't above striking civilised towns and villages to steal food and supplies on their way, nor killing the residents in their blood lust. But there were guards for that; it didn't concern him.

He puffed a rough sigh while his frown deepened in thought.

Beneath his regret for the impossibility of providing such absolute protection, even against that niggling little matter, he felt something else pull at the fraying edges of his mind. Something which affected a sense and provoked an emotion but neither of which he could identify. Far from the first time in three days he felt an intense, pressing necessity...but whether it was *for* something or to *do* something, he just couldn't tell. And yet, despite being at the mercy of the disembodied sensation, as it certainly felt like it belonged to someone else, the need was so great that it felt as if it had formed within his own heart - a closely cradled desire, and yet so far beyond it.

He grunted longingly and sat back in his seat, dragging his mind away from the analysis as he found himself chasing it in circles yet again, just as a knock came at the door. His eyes focused and flicked towards it. It sounded urgent; he wondered if this wasn't the first time they'd announced themselves, just the first he'd noticed.

"Enter," he called, sitting straight again, and three phidipans promptly stepped inside. Though he'd expected Taliel to be among them, his heart still jumped at the sight of her. "Orders from the Crown," he said, ignoring the reaction as the three lined up before him and stared over his head. "There are soldiers causing trouble in the city, but they can't be openly opposed within the capital, of all places, or it will weaken their position of authority. Given the demand on the guards and the military, we've been asked to step in and put a stop to it instead. They will seem to go unpunished." No one spoke, though he didn't expect comment. "The people should not fear their own military," he continued for the sake of the small voice of doubt a phidipan may have towards such a decision, though they kept it dutifully silenced, "but that fear will keep people out of their way and from hindering their efforts. They can't be allowed to continue their activity, of course, but all those involved seem to be covering for one another and no one knows who the perpetrators are - none of the civilians have caught their names, and their faces are covered by their helmets.

"I need each of you to fall victim. Remember their voices, find a way to encourage them to take off their helmets if you can. Uncover anything that will reveal their identities, then it can be handled quickly and discreetly."

"Understood, Keliceran," the three replied rigidly in unison, and he dismissed them.

"Taliel, a moment," he added, rising to his feet as the two men left ahead of her, and she stopped and turned, her eyes ever averted. "I must apologise for assigning you to this task. Apparently they're a little rough with women."

A frown flickered across her brow, just a twitch of confusion at his concern, and a similar expression then passed over his own. Why *was* he concerned? She could handle herself.

He cleared his throat and forced authority back into his tone. "I have another task for you: I want you to speak with Renan in The Cockatrice. Everyone who comes to Kulokhar passes through there eventually, whether they want to be seen or are looking to hide. I want to know of the most recent arrivals."

"Do you suspect infiltration?"

"I always suspect infiltration, but at least with the war approaching the idea may be justified." He smiled at his own expense, but of course she didn't look back. It quickly faded. "It's just to be on the safe side. Keeping a close and subtle watch is our area, as simple as that work is. Guards can't leave their posts or routes to follow up on a hunch, if they're even able to spare their attention long enough to develop one."

"Understood."

"Thank you. You're dismissed."

He watched her as she turned and walked away, absently noticing the way her cream blouse hugged her waist, then caught himself and forced his gaze back down to the table, reassuming his seat with a shadow of a frown.

Another knock interrupted him before his rear could find it, even before the door had closed, and he looked up at the clearly shaken boy who peered back inside.

"Come in," Salus commanded, his irritation returning as Taliel disappeared from his sight. "What is it? What have you got?"

The young man regained control of himself and hurriedly stepped inside, extending towards him the miniature scroll of paper. He held it gently between thumb and forefinger, barely bowing the shape. He seemed almost afraid of it.

Salus managed to take it without snatching, though the effort was conscious, and set to reading the frantically scrawled abbreviations.

Heat began to rise in his face. The veins on the backs of his hands swelled and his jaw knotted. The phaeacian wasn't looking directly at him, but he was acutely aware of his rising anger.

"Get out." His eyes flashed as a darkness descended, his tone all the more menacing for the control he'd spoken with. The messenger needed no encouragement. "And get me Teagan. *Now!*"

It took an infuriating twenty minutes for his favoured to arrive, by which point Salus had read the report over and over and thoroughly picked it apart, but every possible conclusion he'd come to was increasingly alarming and only further stoked his temper.

He threw the report at Teagan when he stepped in through the door, but of course the younger man took no offence. He merely unrolled the tightly wound and slightly torn paper as if he was used to such treatment.

"Find me a mage!" Salus roared before he could begin reading. "They will *not* destroy this country from under our feet while we try our *damnedest* to hold it together! And we will *not* let the Order have this one, either. Find a means of holding them off - mask the mage's presence somehow, delay their ability to get him back!"

"Will our mages be *able* to contain him?" Teagan asked coolly as he rolled the paper back up. "None of the mages we've incarcerated have made any attempts at breaking themselves out, presumably because they know the Order will come to get them."

"They would be *more* than capable of breaking themselves out," Salus replied sharply, stung by the admission, "and if they start to think that the Order isn't coming for them, they might panic. But if the magic of our *own* is strengthening, we should put it to use!"

"Do you really think we can throw the Order off the trail of one of their own?"

"We have no damned choice but to try." He dropped back into his seat, drumming his fingertips impatiently upon the desk. "There's too much magic and the Order *is* responsible..." He mumbled to himself, then grunted humourlessly. "At times like these I wish *I* had magic. At least then I'd know there was *some* sorcery being put to good use..." His eyes flicked back to Teagan. "Go to Stonton. We've found none there yet, but the area is in chaos so they'll certainly be nearby. It's the best place to start. Leave now."

"Keliceran."

The portian turned on his heel, but a sharp curse was hissed from behind him. "Wait. On second thought, I'm coming with you."

Teagan's voice creased instead of his brow as Salus shoved himself up from his desk. "But you're needed here, and you said yourself it's chaos--"

"I don't care!" He suddenly snapped. "I'm sick to death of these accursed walls. Call the two strongest mages we have available. One will come with us, the other will prepare a cell, and we'll just have to pray to Vastal that it will be enough to contain him." He stormed past him and threw the open door even wider, striking the bookcase behind it and certainly denting the wood. "And Zikhon if She won't answer!"

It took three hours by carriage with the horses barely spared to reach the woods that enveloped the old ruins, in which time Salus had cursed mages again and again in a variety of colourful ways. How much could have been done for the war effort in that time? What else could the agent in Roeden have learned if this hadn't stolen his attention? What had managed to take place in the distraction? Curse time and its restraints! If only they could be in two places at once!

He champed back his frustrations as the three started through the woods on silent feet, following the mage's lead, though they burst back out as a sharp snarl when a clawing wind rose from nowhere and swept them up in its frenzy. He braced himself as Teagan did and looked expectantly towards the mage, but he did nothing against it but throw up an arm, even as unease invaded his harsh face. "What is the Order doing?" They heard him mumble through the roar that began buffeting their ears, then he looked back towards them, his expression dampening. "I can't use magic. If there's a mage here, we risk alerting them to our presence."

Salus nodded his begrudging understanding, for the wind certainly wouldn't let him speak it, and within moments the three had split up. Skulking through the trees and circling towards the centre from different directions, they became shadows even against the wind's onslaught, and only then did Salus find peace. His mind was silenced but for necessity, regressing back to the portian training he'd received at the age of nineteen. His senses were sharp and keenly focused, absorbing everything around him - the scattered branches ripped free by the wind; the single track of recent footprints flattening the grass, made with even pressure as though the wind had not hindered them in the slightest; the snatched scent of seared wood carried on the twisting gale. He noticed and noted every detail.

The stone village rose up ahead of him and the wind relented as he neared the trees' edge. But there was no room in his mind for marvelling.

He searched the area from the shadow of the trees and quickly picked out a figure standing high up on the structure, walking slowly where the wind didn't reach, leisurely, trailing his hand over the stone.

He was lost in thought. Distracted. Careless.

Salus melted back into the forest.

He joined back with the others and they moved around together, following silent instructions and joint instincts honed by years of experience. They stopped within sight of the column and waited. The man would have to come down eventually.

They were quickly rewarded for their patience.

The man was still lost in thought as he followed the twisting path down towards the ground, but they didn't move from their hiding place until he neared the final ring. Then, following Salus's lead, they darted across the grass towards the base of the stone pillar and followed it around in the opposite direction, moving to the left as the man moved clockwise, and drew to a stop to wait again where the stone could still conceal them.

The footfalls on the path just above their heads were consistently lazy, and each could gauge with ease precisely where he was. They tracked him by sound, and as soon as his foot struck the damp remnants of a puddle that filled one of the many weathered dips in the path, they slipped away.

They were perfectly silent. They crept with neither crunch, squelch nor rustle beneath their feet; their breath and movements were precisely controlled. And yet something still stirred their target's attention.

But when he stopped in the grass and turned to look inquiringly behind him, they were already in action. As confused, pale blue-grey eyes fell upon Salus, the others caught him in a pincer. The man was left no moment to react; Teagan restrained him easily while the Aranan mage froze his hands with a spell. There was a technique used by the Order to bind and numb the hands of an enemy mage, but they had not taught it to any within the Arana. Salus had always thought that suspicious.

The man, pale-skinned and dark brown haired, made no struggle as Salus stopped in front of him. He was a mage, the phidipan's decisive and urgent actions had confirmed that, though no cloak draped his back, and he met the keliceran's authoritative gaze with a strange mixture of interest and confusion.

"You," Salus declared, suppressing the ill smile that tried to pull at his lips, "are under arrest."

The man's pale brow knotted further in shock. "Why?" His eyes searched him intensely as if to reveal the answer for himself.

"Suspicion of crimes against the Crown and country." Salus nodded to the others and they began to drive the mage along, back towards the trees, but still he didn't struggle. His bewilderment only deepened, and once he turned away, Salus finally indulged in his triumph, if just for a moment.

The mage was silent throughout the return journey, his gaze fixed for the most part to the floor of the carriage, except for the occasional moments when they shifted instead onto Salus. But he ignored the looks, refusing even to dignify them with a cursory glance or note their certain disdain.

When they arrived at Arana House they bundled him along through the side entrance to conceal him from prying eyes, leading him through a dimly lit passage towards the house's extended cellar.

"I want soldiers stationed around the House," Salus told Teagan quietly as the phidipan mage steered their captive ahead of them.

"That will need to go through Malson."

"I doubt even he will object to this, and the civilians might be unsettled by all the soldiers, but I think they'll see reason."

They soon reached the holding cells, the second mage tasked with suitable preparation standing beside an open chamber. The prisoner looked at it as they drew level, surely feeling the magic that surrounded it, and even Salus thought he could feel its hum. To conceal a mage from the Order, it would have to be that strong.

The prisoner stumbled as the phidipan mage shoved him inside, unable to hide even his own disdain for the Order's actions, and Salus moved up to follow him in and begin the questioning himself before the Order had a chance to circumvent them.

"Keliceran," a voice came from the far end of the line of cells, interrupting his purposeful stride as it bounced off of the cold stone walls, and he found another operative hurrying towards him with another folded parchment in hand.

He growled as his tension grew tighter and extended his hand impatiently. He'd either been sought out or waited for, so it must have been important, but at least this man didn't seem to be quivering. Perhaps the news wasn't that bad.

But whatever it was, it wouldn't be good, either.

He growled once again as he read the missive, then looked up to its runner. "Bring Nolan in here and have him question him," he said with frustration, then looked to the second mage, "and you stay here and watch him. He goes absolutely nowhere." Folding the parchment back up, he turned and stormed away, gesturing for Teagan to follow.

"What is it?" The portian asked with irritating indifference once there was distance enough between themselves and the prisoner.

Salus's blue eyes were sharp with resentment. "Karth has been found."

"He has? Where?"

"In the company of the mage responsible for the first attack." He was confident that Teagan would have blanched at the sickening idea had he not been portian. "The Order is after the artefact after all. Likely to destroy it if it really is the only thing that can stop them, or to deconstruct it and use whatever power is in it for their own means."

"What can we do about that?" Teagan asked, and though Salus was surprised to notice a hint of concern in his voice, he realised after a moment that that concern was his own. But it was warranted. They'd been after Karth's help from the beginning, but the man wouldn't keep still long enough for even the Arana to find him. His routes were chaotic, and without knowing his present research, as he kept his notes with him at all times, they couldn't predict his next movements. Drassa was a highly respected historian, but even as their second choice, a chasm still stood between them.

"We get there first."

"That may be easier said than done."

Salus raised his chin defiantly. "Which is why we're going to see Drassa immediately. Get changed."

Another two hours was wasted on travel and darkness had set in by the time the coach rolled up outside of the historian's home, but Salus's increasing tensions were bitten back again as he and Teagan each reassumed their roles of lord and servant and stepped out into the evening.

"My Lord Baymont!" Drassa cried as he opened the door, immediately dropping into a bow at the sight of their regal faces. "What a surprise! I have not seen you since--"

"I am well aware of the last time we spoke directly, Mister Drassa," he sighed, "I believe I was present." Lord Baymont stepped through the door as Drassa moved aside, his personal assistant and guards duly following in silence. "Mister Vakh has been relaying all of your reports," he continued as he walked into the sitting room, the older man hurrying along to join them, "and that has me concerned."

"Concerned, my lord?"

He absently leafed through the papers that littered the table. "I can only assume you are holding information back."

Drassa's old brow, wrinkled by years of thought, twisted in insult, and he puffed for a moment in a fluster. "With all due respect, my lord, I take my work quite seriously and treat all of my employers with equal courtesy regardless of their social position, and *never once* have I held back any information, so I certainly wouldn't *dare* to withhold anything from someone of your esteem!"

"My esteem? I thought you treated all of your employers equally." Baymont looked up mildly.

Drassa's cheeks flushed. "I *do*, I mean of course that you would be no exception anyway, but even if I *did* prioritise status--"

"Enough." The noble's expression darkened as he waved his blustering away and turned to face him directly. "You told me this would be an easy matter."

"I did say 'easy matter', my lord, but I did not say 'quick'." Despite the weight of Baymont's gaze, Drassa began to calm and a childishly excited smile began to creep across his face. "However, it is a curious stroke of chance that you should arrive when you have."

Salus suppressed the hope that pattered through his chest. "Oh?"

"I believe I am about ready to start reaching out to contacts - collectors, proprietors and the like." The historian ushered him over to another study-cluttered surface and showed him a number of papers and findings, explaining them as he went, but none of the words had much meaning to Salus. He nodded all the same, however, and tried to keep his mind from racing ahead in anticipation.

"You have done all of this from within your home?" He asked, looking around at the other pockets of research scattered throughout the room.

"Of course not," he scoffed. "I've spoken with colleagues from the Fellowship in the city and cross-referenced findings in the library."

He decided not to clarify that that hadn't been what he'd meant.

"Of course," the historian continued a touch more carefully, "regarding the collectors...I can't guarantee what price they will ask, if they're even willing to part with it. Elven collectors can be...anyway, are you certain that no price--"

"I am willing to pay whatever they ask, should they hold what my grandmother sought, as you were told upon our first meeting. That has not changed. How long do you believe this will take?"

"I would guess at a few weeks."

Salus restrained any reaction. "How many?"

"Three? Four?"

"So a month, then?"

"Yes, my L--"

"Three weeks."

"I--"

"And your payment will double."

Distress edged in on the old man, but he didn't argue. "Yes, my lord, I will do my very best."

"Good. As before, continue relaying progress to Mister Vakh, no matter its insignificance. This matter is quite important."

"I remember, of course."

Lord Baymont turned and left with his entourage without so much as a farewell, Salus's mind already turning onto other matters as they abandoned Drassa to return to his work in resignation. But despite the gravity of the painfully long day's events and the desperate glimmer of excitement that concluded it, he yearned only for bed. He'd drifted into wonderful dreams every night lately, but their peaceful effect no longer spilled over into his day. Instead he awoke tense and that tension only grew with every passing hour. He spent his days wishing above all else to sleep, to slip back into the world where his heart lightened, where he could escape the Arana's growing trials and forget his duties and expectations. Where things were easy and peaceful. Where he was able to feel, to breathe.

He sighed to himself as the carriage set off. Teagan cast him a sidelong glance, but he didn't speak, and Salus lost himself in the moon-bathed scenery as it rolled by and let his thoughts wander to wherever and whomever they wished.

Chapter 20

The sky was shrouded by thick, black cloud and a curtain of rain was already falling to the north. But the wind was weak, little more than a breath, and while the threatening downpour was certainly moving in their direction, they would be gone long before it hit. But Rathen had conjured cloaks to ward them against the miserable sight anyway, and they followed the narrow, twisting and hilly road with a little more assurance, meandering alongside thin trees and an even thinner stream.

They'd not passed sign of people for hours, and though the events at Mokhan were a week behind them, they remained ever on their guard. It would still be too easy to be recognised, and seven days were far too short for word of such events and identities to quieten down. Fortunately the nearest settlement was two days' past, a small and poorly stocked village they'd sent Anthis into for supplies, and nothing else stood for miles. They each breathed a little easier; the increasingly unkempt road seemed set to grow only quieter.

Though not silent just yet. Hesitance slowed their strides as cheerful voices rose up ahead, and two stout men dressed in marvellous shades of red, one of whom carried a large, wooden box upon his back, shortly appeared on the path where it curved out from behind the trees.

Rathen pulled up the hood of his grey cloak long before they were near. Petra followed, though only enough to cover her red hair, and moved to his other side to be furthest away when they passed by. The rest simply kept their heads down.

Unfortunately, one of the pair cried an enthusiastic hail and waved his hand at them merrily, and Rathen cursed beneath his breath at the foolish hope that they might have slipped by without interruption. But the route was so quiet, these two probably welcomed the idea of sociality.

"Afternoon," Anthis returned, successfully concealing his similar disappointment as Garon nudged him to the front.

"Lovely day, isn't it?"

They came to a mutual stop as Anthis frowned and looked to the sky.

"Well it's not raining *yet*, is it?" The merchant grinned. His cheer certainly belied his true age. His thick, grey eyebrows rose hopefully. "I don't suppose I could interest you in my wares...?"

Garon grunted quietly, though the subtle encouragement was needless. They were all aware that what the village had been able to offer was meagre.

The historian nodded and smiled amiably, but rather than lower his box of goods, the old man turned around to display what was actually a cabinet upon his back, while the younger, his son perhaps, spread wide its doors and pulled out a drawer which he then similarly unfolded. All five of them peered in curiously to find a vast array of herbs, spices, fruits and seeds, many of which none of them could confidently identify. But despite the variety, there seemed to be little of any real use, which was strange for a trader working the roads.

"Strawberries!" Aria suddenly gasped, her eyes brightening as they locked onto the small, red fruits.

"Yes, some of the best!" The old man declared proudly from behind the cabinet. "My nephew here grows them himself! You won't find sweeter nor more nutritious strawberries in all of the world, I'll tell you that for truth! And a bargain for 'six!'"

Aria's eyebrows rose further in longing, but Anthis was already fishing around in his satchel for coins while the others hid their doubt at the substantial claims.

"Terrible business, aren't they, those mage attacks?" The younger man said as he bagged up the small, plump fruits, but he was quickly silenced by a hiss from his uncle.

"Hush, lad!" He gasped. "Let's not weigh these travellers down with such dark talk!"

"No," Anthis frowned cautiously, "no, it's fine... Mage *attacks*, you say?"

"Certainly. First one tried to bring down the tower in Mokhan, then a few days ago another blew up the tavern in Roeden! Such a lovely place, too, a real shame. Their snugs were the comfiest."

Anthis blanched, and even the others turned to look at the younger merchant in shock. "Blew it up?!"

"Yeah! Strode in, bold as brass, fire and lightning bursting all around him with a wind twirling to keep everyone away from him, then he cackled, declared the Order was going to rid Turunda of non-mages and blew himself up, taking damn near everyone inside with him, and a good number outside, too!" He seemed less concerned by the matter than he did fascinated. "They're taking a page from the book of foreign mages, I think, rising up and trying to take the country for themselves while everyone's looking to the war."

"Nonsense," Petra declared. "The Order is here to protect us, just as the army is."

"Recent events suggest otherwise, miss," he replied apologetically, then looked across them as a whole and exchanged the strawberries for one silver and a particularly battered copper coin. "Where are you headed?"

"Uh, Tamley."

"Mm. Not heard of anything happening around there, nor Bowden or Toakh. But keep your eyes open, aye?"

"We will."

"Vastal watch over you all."

"Thank you, and you."

Anthis dropped the small bag of fruit into Aria's hands as the two closed up their little store front, and the group started away tightly. All eyes shortly fell upon Rathen, and they needn't have voiced what they were thinking.

"That doesn't sound like an attack, to me," he replied quietly after glancing back towards the finely-dressed merchants, noting the distance as a troubled frown marred his hood-shaded brow.

"The facts have certainly been muddied by now," Garon reminded him.

"Even so..."

"But it *sounds* like the attacks elsewhere..." Anthis frowned, but Rathen only shook his head, his doubt unwavering.

Garon looked at the mage levelly. "What are you thinking?"

"Most of it sounds like loss of control."

"Loss of control?"

"I don't know how or why, but it's what I've always thought about the other attacks..." His frown deepened. "Owan said a few were acting strangely," he mumbled to himself, then Kienza's words of mages driven mad returned to haunt him.

"You think he meant this?" Anthis pressed. "That they were losing control of themselves? But how is that possible?"

He shook off the thoughts. "I don't know, but I think it's what it could boil down to. At the very least, Turunda's Order isn't so desperate, nor treated poorly enough to revolt. In that, I'm confident."

"Perhaps not as a whole, but there are bound to be a few idealistic individuals among them."

"And yet," Rathen managed not to snap, "that's just not how this seems."

"There's nothing we can do about it," Garon declared, stepping back into the conversation from the sidelines, where he seemed to spend a lot of time lately. "We have our own matters to take care of."

"Which has me concerned." Anthis's face creased warily as he cast a careful, sidelong glance towards the inquisitor. "Are we to keep heading along this road?"

"Yes."

"We're nearing the Wildlands..."

"We're already in them," Rathen replied with a lightness that belied his words. "I'm not so sure those two traders were what they seemed."

Alarm twisted their necks as the two continued along the road quite merrily, pausing as one pointed up at a tree and the other peered along the gesture at something apparently marvellous.

Garon was the first to dismiss them. "We're two weeks from Bowden. Straying from the road will mean at least two more before we reach it."

"And what of what dwells between there and here?"

"No choice."

Rathen caught Aria's cautious stare, but he also noticed her fascination, though she seemed uncertain that she should indulge it. He offered her a warm smile. "We'll be fine."

"Well, at least we know we won't encounter anyone," Anthis sighed in resignation, but Petra wasn't so reserved.

"Yes, and for good reason! There's a fork ahead of us; we should turn right, head away."

Garon shot her a brief, sharp look. "You're free to take that route if you wish. The rest of us might do better without your noise."

She leered at him, but brushed the insult aside easily enough.

Rathen's lips pursed thoughtfully as he looked away from the two. In the past week it seemed that Garon had become even more rigid and distant than usual, and grew colder still any time the young woman in particular spoke. And yet Petra barely reacted to his moods or sharp tones beyond such a brief, irritated look, and had thinned her interrogation by only a fraction. Something had happened, of that he was sure, and whatever it was, Garon was uncomfortable with it. He wouldn't have bothered to muster more distance to wedge between himself and the rest of them otherwise.

Of course, just what it could have been, Rathen had no idea. Since the harpy attack, he'd been keeping his own wary distance from the others whenever interaction wasn't necessary, and only now was he beginning to feel the tension loosen between his shoulder blades and the accursed shadow recede back into the depths of his heart. Only Aria had kept close to him throughout, but he trusted her instincts - she'd come to no harm from him in their six years together, at least.

"Daddy," she began quietly, a note of curiosity colouring her little voice, "why is everyone afraid of the wild land?"

"Simply because it is wild," he replied. "No one lives nearby so creatures have been given the chance to thrive, and because of that no one *wants* to live nearby, which gives them even more opportunity."

"But that's good, isn't it? This world isn't ours alone, everything should have the room to live."

"Yes," he smiled, "you're right, of course, but it makes venturing into the Wildlands very dangerous for those who have no choice. Even I assumed we'd be taking the longer way around..." He glanced uncertainly towards the back of Garon's head, and noticed the others do the same.

Aria, however, didn't share in the unease as wholly as the rest. She had never been afraid of monsters. Instead, excitement brightened her eyes as an unheard thought occurred to her. "Creatures like what? Kvistdjur?"

Rathen sighed. "You've read too many stories, little one," he smiled wearily. "Keep close to me and don't stray."

For the past two days the land around them had been growing less familiar; there was little sign of cultivation and the forests in the distance were becoming taller and denser. The road they followed was in increasing disarray, and the land it trailed across more rugged. Rocks jutted up in the middle of the route to trip anyone under the slightest of distractions; parts of the trail veered close to the water and had collapsed into the seasonally swollen stream, while others were covered by collapsed overhangs that had toppled from the other side.

But there was beauty to it, a wonderfully natural one. Despite the blackening sky, the light that managed to peek through the briefest breaks in the clouds was golden and turned the parallel stream turquoise, intensifying the verdant grass. Wild animals were plentiful and serene; large herds of deer grazed just beyond the reach of the trees, and countless species of birds were seen and heard all around them. Insects, many wonderful butterflies, danced on the air, and Aria particularly delighted in them.

But Rathen was not eased. The deer's position near the trees was unsettling. They were clustered and none appeared willing to stray more than ten feet from the edge of the forest. They may not have feared people, continuing to feed even as he and the others passed, but they did fear whatever may be in the sky.

He didn't point this out to the others, though he kept a vigilant eye above them.

Over the dragging hours, the path led them deeper into hostile terrain. Trees towered and plunged them into an early dusk, the rippling stream had meandered away and left them instead with the rustling of shrouded beasts, and the path itself vanished beneath the long and tangled grass. Soon all they followed was a trail beaten in by hooves - among other things.

Tensions only continued to rise as true night descended. Sheer blackness surrounded them, and despite all of their unease in the foreboding forest, they had little choice but to light their way by setting alight a fallen branch as a torch. Rathen had been reluctant to conjure any such thing, and the others were quick to agree when they thought on what could easily lurk in the shadows.

Fatigue hounded them, made worse by their skittishness, but stopping for camp was no easy matter. Nowhere felt safe. In time they passed by a small, old house, long abandoned and reclaimed by the forest, and it would have been perfect had they been anywhere else. But instead of sanctuary, the eerie sight of a dead home only encouraged them to stumble onwards. They settled amongst the trees after another tormenting half hour when they were certain it was closer to dawn than to midnight, and here Rathen had no choice but to turn to his magic to sign vigil spells, all the while hoping the magic itself didn't attract the very individuals it would warn them against.

But despite the atmosphere and constant glancing over their shoulders, Aria seemed strangely comfortable that night. Rathen decided that the dense forest simply reminded her of home. She spent her time, as she had the past three nights, hunched over a notebook he'd conjured after she'd gotten through more pages of his own than he had, scribbling, scrawling, rotating and scribbling again. And she jealously guarded her work - even those leaves she tore out with dissatisfaction she threw into the fire.

No one else lost themselves so easily; their knotted muscles tightened all the more with every strange, high-pitched and fortunately distant shriek that emanated through the night.

All but Aria raised their heads at the sound of the first, for she was already asleep, and Anthis's eyes grew wide in particular alarm as he spun around where he sat, only to be quickly stilled, wincing at the motion. "What was that?" He dared to whisper as the forest again fell deathly silent.

"Certainly not a harpy," Petra replied, her hand instinctively coiling around the hilt of her blade, and the eyes of the two shortly fell upon Rathen. But he only stared deep into the surrounding blackness, unblinking, and offered not even a grunt of agreement.

There was little sleep to be had that night.

Resorting to guessing when the sun had risen, they were quick to set off the next morning, choosing to share what little food they had while on the move. There was over a week of aberrant landscape ahead of them, and the sooner they were through it, the better. Though that wasn't easy when it was their own weariness slowing them down.

A stone concealed within the grass caught Petra's foot as she stared sideways off into the darkness, ripping her focus quite abruptly back to the path. She glared down at it and hissed a curse, then sighed in mounting irritation and kicked it aside. She was tense - they all were - but she couldn't stand her attention lingering for much longer on the shadows of things that weren't there.

She looked towards Garon and thought for a moment. "Inquisitor," she began politely, walking closer to him in the hope of some kind of distraction, "does your work take you through these kinds of places often?"

He didn't even turn his head, but she didn't let it his disinterest discourage her.

"No," she answered for him, "I suppose you'd skirt around them if you could - but would a lead in a case ever force you through?"

"No one in their right mind would travel through here," Anthis replied instead. Petra would have been annoyed by his interruption had she thought there was any real chance that Garon would have answered himself. "Even I haven't."

"One wonders if Garon *is* in any 'right mind'."

"No one knows for certain what's out here," the young man continued, breezing past Rathen's mumbled remark, "there are only rumours and snatched sightings, but no one's willing to chance coming in to find out. This whole region is wrapped in mystery."

Petra squinted at him. "You're enjoying this."

"Well you have to admit that there's an element of excitement," he frowned, "but I can't say that having my eyes glued to the space between every tree and my ears cocked at every midge's wing beat is a prerequisite for a good time."

"If nothing is known, what are you afraid of?" Rathen asked from ahead.

"The possibility. And those screams last night weren't exactly dissuasive."

No one was willing to disagree.

Rathen glanced down at Aria, expecting her to ask about the rumours or the screaming, but though the questions did indeed seem to be forming on the tip of her tongue, they remained behind her teeth. It seemed their unease was finally beginning to touch her. He gave her hand a small, reassuring squeeze, and she readily tightened her grip.

Anthis gazed up to the forest canopy and sighed to himself. "What time do you suppose it is?"

Rathen looked at the thick shadows. "Almost midday."

"We've been walking for at least seven hours," he groaned, his face twisting in discomfort as a stitch began to pull at his already aching side. "Can we not stop for a moment?"

Garon shook his head. "We've not moved far enough."

He sighed in frustration, but chose to save his energy for walking rather than arguing.

Petra frowned at him sadly and dropped back a few paces to walk alongside, offering a walking support if he needed it. He smiled gratefully, though it didn't reach his eyes, and it vanished completely as he lost his footing in the distraction. Petra caught him before he could drop too far.

She shook her head. "Garon, we need to stop. Anthis hasn't fully recovered yet."

"I'm *fin--oooww!*"

She shot him an unconvinced look while Rathen stepped up beside the inquisitor. "We're not going to cover much ground in an hour or two," he told him quietly, "not against the reach of this place. We should stop. We all need it."

Garon looked past him doubtfully, along their forward route, and his lips parted to argue. But he said nothing. He sighed in defeat instead. "Not on the path," he said finally for the others to hear. "Who knows what else uses it..." Looking about, he shortly spotted a fragment of light filtering through the trees to the left. "This way - carefully."

They followed eagerly as Anthis breathed a private sigh of relief, stepping in amongst the forest and realising only once they'd left it just how bare and worn in the path truly was. Mere feet away, thick, gnarled roots lay in wait to trip prying wanderers, low branches snatched at clothing, and ditches concealed within the overgrown grass threatened to twist ankles. Only those versed in the Wildlands could traverse it so freely, and not one of the five ranked among them.

But as suddenly as they'd found it, the density fell away, opening the way to a compact and vibrant grove secreted amongst the tangle, whose sheer but simple beauty struck them to a halt. But magic, for once, was not responsible. Perhaps it was merely the rays of the sun that made the grass appear so emerald and the water in the lily pond so richly azure - everything they'd laid eyes upon over the past day and a half had been shrouded in shadow, after all - but it was astounding to behold nevertheless, and the sight settled the erratic beating of their hearts just enough to take a single, calming breath.

Petra helped Anthis over to a near-level rock and took a moment to rest against it herself, while Aria rushed to the water's edge and peered down to its shallow bed, pulling Rathen along with her while Garon, as usual, surveyed the area.

Tiny green fish the size of Aria's own fingernails flicked about beneath the still waters, creating the slightest ripples along the surface as they turned, their scales glistening as they caught the light. Aria gasped softly as she marvelled at them, and settled down on her belly to watch.

Petra smiled at the girl's simple fascination. "Shouldn't we fill the waterskins while we're here?"

"Not from a standing body of water like this."

"It's not a canal..."

"It's not stagnant water I'm concerned about." Rathen looked around from his place close at Aria's side, distrust tainting his dark eyes. The grove, as tiny as it was, was wonderful. Too wonderful. It was wild, it was true, but there seemed to be intention in its appearance - as if something cared for it, nurtured its growth.

His thoughtful gaze fell upon a rock face at the far end of the clearing, and he noticed a shadow to it. A hole.

"Move away from the edge, little one," he said softly, rising with a frown to approach it, pushing his long, black hair back from his face, sticky in the mild but persistent humidity. He didn't stop too close, in part to avoid drawing the others' attention, and peered in from an angle instead. It was narrower than it had seemed from the pond, and reached higher into the rock. The gap was enough that he could have stepped in with Aria upon his shoulders, but certainly not beside her.

He heard footsteps, light and certain.

"Is it ditchlings?" Garon asked quietly, stopping a few paces away with similar concern of drawing interest from the less careful members of the group.

"If it was, they've gone," Rathen replied. "We wouldn't get so close to one of their setts unmolested." He looked at the worn ground that lead into the cave, noting the leaves and mud that had been trekked inside, then the edges of the stone itself and the lack of any decorative markings that ditchlings would have left. It was only when he raised his eyes higher that he spotted a single detail of note: long, thick vines descended from above and reached into the gap as if holding it open, draped in broad leaves with pure white veins, among which peeked funnelled blue flowers.

Rathen's pale face twisted nervously as he turned his gaze back to the bright green grass, the impact of which was still stunning. It should have worn off by now. He noticed Aria still close beside the water's edge. "Aria, *back*, I said!"

She scrambled obediently several paces away.

"What do you think?" Garon asked gravely, observing the scene. "Kvistdjur?"

"Or a näcken. But we'd do well not to chance upon either." He turned towards the others and raised his voice, ensuring as he did so that his alarm was well-hidden. "It's about time we moved on."

"We've been here for less than five minutes," Petra protested as Anthis pushed himself up from beside her with a grumble, knowing that if he didn't do so then, he likely wouldn't at all.

"And we have a very long way to go. The fewer nights we have to spend in here, the better for all of us." He stepped over to Aria and took her little hand, smiling apologetically against her disappointed frown, then started back towards the path at Garon's lead, the others reluctantly in tow.

They trudged on through the afternoon and made only one more brief stop for Anthis's sake, but despite the weariness that crept over them as the early night began to fall, the encroaching darkness only spurred them to keep moving. They covered much ground before their fatigue became too much, already worsened by the previous long night, and stopped to camp amongst the trees just far enough from the path to avoid being spotted by anything that may use it.

Anthis eased himself down against a tree trunk with a long sigh of relief, his concern for the forest's denizens forgotten as he forced his tense muscles to unlock. "Sedentary at last."

"How can you possibly relax in a place like this?" Petra asked him quietly as she continued to watch the forest around them.

"Because," he replied, closing his eyes and taking a deep and careful breath, "I have little choice but to."

Rathen thrust the torch into the ground, choosing not to risk a bright campfire, then began rummaging through the bags. There was plenty of food - bread, cheese, some preserved meat - and it would have been enough to last them until Bowden, with some supplementary foraging along the way. But no one had expected to pass through the Wildlands. Starving was preferable to catching food within these forests, as at least walking on an empty stomach was less likely to invoke the wrath of whatever might guard the creatures one would hunt for supper.

Rathen grunted. They could ration it all easily enough - he just hoped it wouldn't lead to clumsy footing or poor decisions, invoking the wrath of whatever might guard the creatures they *weren't* hunting for supper.

He passed out fractions of the food, and Aria looked down at the torn bread and sliver of meat in her hands with disappointment. "I know, but it'll be enough, little one."

"I suppose we've no choice but to tighten our belts for a while," Petra sighed as she took her share and gave it an equally grim look, but her complaints were silenced as her stomach rumbled and she made an eager start upon the bread.

They finished eating far too quickly and sat restlessly in their efforts to relax, but while it was exhaustion that made it easy for Anthis to settle, Aria again found no trouble absorbing herself in her work, faithfully pulling out her sketchbook and charcoal. She hadn't touched her knife for some time - no one was distraught by that fact - but whenever any tried to take an interest in her change of activity for their own distraction, she became guarded and secretive.

While Rathen checked over what remained of his wound, Anthis watched her work. Her face was pressed close to the pages though she couldn't possibly see by the minimal torchlight, and her tongue poked out a few times in her concentration. He smiled as it happened a third time. "Has she gotten anywhere with her project?" He asked Rathen quietly. Aria hadn't told anyone what she was doing; Anthis only knew the details because he'd guessed correctly while speaking with the mage.

Rathen shook his head. "I have no idea. She won't even let me see it. But she's not torn anything out for two days, so that has to be a good sign..."

"Why is she doing it?"

"Because she wants to help."

Anthis nodded slowly, and turned his eyes back to him as he finished applying a clean bandage. "And what about you? Have you gotten anywhere?"

Rathen looked up at him. "Have *you*?"

"Probably not until Bowden," he conceded.

"If we even find anything useful there." Rathen sighed and dropped the young man's shirt back over the bandage, then glanced behind him across the camp. Petra caught his eye, as she did from time to time, but while her eyes were turned down towards her blade, her focus was certainly fixed upon Garon.

"She's somewhat attached to him," Anthis said very quietly, surely noticing the same thing. "Reckon she'll actually leave at Bowden?"

"She has little reason to stay, so I don't see why not," Rathen replied just as carefully, though there was a doubtful frown upon his face as he said it. Then he turned knowing eyes back onto him. "*You* want her to stay, though."

"Sorry?!"

There was the slightest smile upon the mage's lips, though it was neither unfriendly nor mocking. In fact, it seemed sympathetic. "I've seen how you look at her. Let me save you the time: she isn't interested."

Anthis seemed to bristle for a moment. "In me?"

"In *anyone*. She has other priorities."

"Which are?"

"I have no idea, but they're there, without a doubt. She can do nothing to help us, and she knows it. She might hesitate when the time comes, perhaps, but she won't stay. They'll take precedence, whatever they are."

A frown creased his young face as he puffed his reluctant understanding. "Yeah, you're probably right," he grumbled. "I get the sense that there's a big chunk of her we're not getting..."

"Everyone is entitled to secrets."

"Aren't they just?"

Rathen gave his speculative tone a flat look, but Anthis only smiled. "Sorry."

Silence smothered the camp as a desperate wail rose in the distance. It was quiet and far off, but there was already such an edge to the atmosphere that none of them could possibly miss it.

"It's the same as last night," Petra dared to whisper.

"At least it's further aw--"

Another shriek cut Anthis off, much closer than the first.

The five fell perfectly still; only their eyes shifted in fevered search. Rathen didn't rise from the balls of his feet, Aria didn't stroke her charcoal across the paper, and Petra didn't pull her fingers free from combing through her hair. Every one of them favoured their hearing, straining their ears for any other sound. But the forest was perfectly silent. There was nothing to be heard. Not even the sombre song of a nightlark.

The shriek came again.

"It's getting closer," Petra breathed in a panic.

"But *what* is getting closer?"

Rathen was the first to move, standing and staring hard through the darkness, and as the air shattered from another, still nearer scream, the others hastily followed. Ice formed in their blood at the cold and vengeful howl, one eerily without echo. Anthis hauled himself to his feet with no thought to the sting in his side, and the group tightened up together, Petra and Garon with swords in hand while Rathen flexed his fingers, Aria clinging to his clothes.

Rustling snatched their attention, quick movements beyond the limited range of the torch flame, and they stared off to their left, each picking apart the blackness with bated breath.

The rustling came again, this time from their right, but as they spun towards it, its source changed again.

They'd have gasped in fright as another cry pealed from right on top of them, had that very fright not choked their throats instead.

"Oh sweet Mother Vastal," Petra managed over the beat of her heart in her throat, gripping her sword tightly as they huddled up even closer. Her arms tightened in preparation to strike at whatever might descend upon them, while Garon grounded his feet and Rathen's fingers twitched, a number of spells for a number of circumstances already firmly in mind.

The scattered rustles stopped.

Silence stifled them.

Their heads spun frantically left and right, looking for any eyes that might catch the torchlight, any toothy grins that might glow in menace, any tree-like forms or creeping vines that had not been there before.

Not one of them dared a breath.

The air was torn by another wail, a little further out than the last.

Had another shadow joined?

Another shriek, more distant.

Rathen's shoulders loosened and he lowered his hands a fraction, but still he strained his ears in search, waiting for another, either right upon them or further out again. But there was nothing.

It took a long minute before they dared to loosen their formation, reluctantly following Rathen's lead as he tentatively dropped his hands to his sides, straightened himself and released his long-held breath.

"Whatever that was," Anthis whispered, desperate to break the silence with familiar sounds despite feeling far too tense to condone making any noise, "it knew we were here."

"It probably knew the moment we stepped into the forest"

"We should not have come in here," Petra said with a substantial note of panic rattling in her voice. "We should have skirted around. What's two more weeks compared to our *lives?*"

"Rathen," Anthis whispered, his own tone uncharacteristically heavy, "do you know what it was?"

The mage sighed regretfully. "I don't."

Garon stepped away from them and approached the edge of the light. "Get some rest," he said firmly, sitting down in the grass and facing out into the darkness. "I'll take watch. The going will be easier tomorrow."

Aria seemed willing to trust him as she headed towards her blankets, eager perhaps to see the morning, and though Anthis and Petra cast one another doubtful looks, they followed her lead.

"Wake me if you start dozing off," Rathen said, pausing beside him. "Assuming either of us manage to get any sleep."

The inquisitor nodded as he stepped away, then settled himself for a long night, his sword unsheathed and laid ready upon the ground beside him. He heard more gentle footsteps approach him a moment later, but didn't turn his head.

"Good night," Petra said softly. She didn't pause for a response, and so Garon said nothing.

Though he did glance around at her as the torch was extinguished.

Plunged into blackness, he cleared his mind and looked back out to the forest while the rest of the group settled down to try to sleep. His eyes adjusted quickly, and with practised ease he filtered out the whispered exchange between Rathen and the child as he tucked her in, turning his focus outwards and away from the camp.

He couldn't sense anyone following them anymore, but that persistent feeling that had shadowed him since Mokhan had been replaced with more immediate concerns. He had a good idea, as Rathen did, of what called this forest home, concealed in its boughs, beneath the leaf litter, within its shadows - but just which of them were the most likely threat, he couldn't tell. After all, while he knew which rumours of the Wildlands were credible, they were still little more than that. Those few who *were* brave or stupid enough to study the place never dared to stay long enough for solid findings, and those who presumably were were never seen nor heard from again.

It had been a risk to lead them into the Wildlands, of that he had been fully aware, but who knew just how much time they had to find the artefact?

'Who knows if we'll even make it through to the other side of this accursed place?'

He suppressed the doubtful voice easily enough. Such thoughts would serve no purpose now they were there. And he had faith in his own abilities, as well as Rathen's. And though Petra may not have been part of the plan, he was confident that she could hold her own, too. It was a part of who she was, that was clear for anyone to see - alongside her insatiable curiosity. In that detail, she was worse than Anthis.

The slightest movement in the nearby leaves drew his keen attention, and his hand twitched towards the black hilt of his blade.

But it was nothing. A spider out to hunt.

He watched it scurry across the forest floor and pause just out of the reach of a fragment of moonlight, its silver glow reflected back from its eight orbs. It was small, no larger than his fingernail, but its species was easy to identify by those two oversized, forward-facing eyes, calculating and fiercely intelligent. He watched it closely as it stared back at him, then tracked it as it dashed off deep into the leaf litter to continue its hunt for food, until his own sharp eyes lost it to the darkness.

His back stiffened and purpose sharpened his focus, and as his ears pricked at distant sounds, his hand once more twitched towards his blade.

Chapter 21

It was the tell-tale cacophony of birdsong - hoots, trills and caws that sounded like something being strangled - that announced the arrival of dawn. Fingers of mist trailed through the trees, rolling softly in the breeze channelled beneath the canopy, moving as if in search of something, while distant beasts rustled and rummaged as the scent of the rising sun marked the end of their rule. From the camp, the forest looked alive with ghosts.

They had managed, somehow, to find some kind of rest through the peculiar night, but none wasted any time with slow waking and rose more than ready to leave, regardless of whomever may still have been in a fitful sleep. Rathen had been the first, whom Garon had awoke to find standing vigilantly ahead of him and staring out into the trees, while the inquisitor couldn't recall falling asleep.

"Are you feeling better?" Aria asked Anthis as they set out, noticing sooner than the others did that he walked without the slight sideways hunch he'd been plagued with since Stonton.

"I am," he smiled appreciatively, at which she blushed. "I think a good night's--well, a *night's* sleep, helped. All this walking is hard-going."

Her small nose wrinkled in distaste. "It is. I hate it. I mean, it feels nice, the grass and the mud, but it hurts my legs - they're not as long as all of yours. I wish we still had horses." Her expression collapsed. "Oh, poor Fog!"

Anthis frowned sadly. "I can carry you if you'd like," he offered in an attempt to make her smile, and it worked, though she blushed again and turned away to hide her cheeks.

"Thank you, but I'll manage. I'll only make your clothes dirtier."

He followed her gaze down to her feet and noticed that she wasn't wearing any shoes. He glanced towards Rathen as he spoke quietly with Garon, wondering if he was aware, but he decided not to mention it.

"What's out here?"

Anthis looked back to her in puzzlement. "Pardon?"

"Out here, in the wild lands." She cocked her head, far more thoughtful than concerned. "We're all hearing things at night, but Daddy won't tell me what it is."

"Well that's because he doesn't know."

She narrowed her eyes in great suspicion and turned them upon the back of her father's head. "He knows."

"Well," he said slowly, looking briefly towards the mage in similar distrust, "all *I* know are stories; talk of creatures that never leave the reaches of these forests or venture near populated areas - despite no one ever having seen them, the descriptions are vivid."

"Yes but creatures like *what?*" She groaned impatiently. "That's all anyone keeps saying!"

"Well, like--"

"Kvistdjur?"

"Yes," he smiled curiously at her enthusiasm, "kvistdjur, supposedly, and vakehn, stendjur, creeping vines and moving trees, faces in the water, phan--"

Rathen sharply cleared his throat.

He smiled sheepishly and looked back to the eight year old. "But they're just rumours. Stories, like I said. It's easy to get lost in woods this dense so it's safer to just not go through them at all. Telling people those kinds of things lurk in here keeps them from coming in."

"But it didn't do that for us."

"No," he admitted, "it didn't, but we'll be all right."

"We will - even though they're clearly *not* just stories."

"And just how do you know that?"

She fired him a suddenly flat look. "Because we all heard something screaming last night."

Anthis blinked, his plan foiled. She had only slept through the first night's near-encounter. "Heh... But we *will* be fine."

"What will we do if we *do* meet any?"

"We'll leave them alone, and they'll leave us alone."

"If it's that simple, why are you all so frightened?"

"Because," he began easily despite her sceptical frown and the others' concerned glances, "we're worried we might startle them. No one likes to be made to jump, kvistdjur least of all."

Aria frowned for a moment as she chewed over his reasoning, but appeared quickly satisfied. She nodded and smiled. "My daddy doesn't like that, either."

Rathen suddenly stumbled at the lead, and Aria's smile vanished immediately. But he didn't look back or growl in embarrassment. His attention was fixed among the trees. His pace slowed as he examined them, and Garon shortly faltered beside him and began looking about in similar caution.

"What is it?" Anthis asked quietly as he and Aria hurried behind Petra to join them, but before either could answer, they wavered in their stride just as the first as they crossed the boundary into what seemed to be an entirely new forest.

All around them the sharp and jagged shadows they'd become so accustomed to were replaced by a soft but deep shade, and the towering trees seemed to bend away and ignore them rather than loom overhead and gawk. What had first simply been 'green' was now emerald, pea and pine, and the dew that balanced on the tips of delicate blades of grass shone like tiny, ethereal diamonds. There drifted the gentle babble of water, and accompanied by the rustle of leaves as a breeze passed overhead, shifted the ambience into something comfortable, soothing away their ever-present, underlying agitation. There was room for a single, easy breath before their caution returned.

Anthis's eyes widened as the familiar but troubling beauty settled. "Magic." He looked towards Rathen. "Does that mean there's a ruin nearby?"

"I wouldn't know...but we've yet to find magic without one..."

The young historian peered beyond the others and down along the path, keeping a tight hold on his inappropriate enthusiasm. Ruins in the Wildlands weren't unlikely - the forests hadn't always been so feral - but he knew of none here by name or purpose and the prospect of discovering one, or even just setting foot in one he'd never visited before, filled him with a childish excitement.

But this was no place for that excitement to be allowed to lead him, and the pain in his abdomen had receded enough that he was now just as alert to the prospect of danger as the rest. Anything could be hiding just feet away from them in these enchanting woods - or within the ruin itself.

He kept close to the others and followed the mage's far more certain pace.

Rathen barely noticed Garon step back and concede him the lead, and neither was he aware of how closely the group followed him. His mind was torn only between focusing on the magic, where he wished it to be, and being dragged off by what came with it.

He hadn't realised he still carried such tension between his shoulder blades; it was only now as they slumped and his back eased that it revealed itself, drawn out by the unnatural peace that swirled like a golden mist around his heart. But it and the unreasonable compulsion he felt to succumb to it was stronger than it had been in any other instance, and he had to fight to keep his mind where it mattered.

Aria suddenly gasped from beside him, jolting his attention back to his surroundings, and he stumbled at the sight of the sheer drop just three paces ahead of him, concealed not by what he'd thought were bushes, but by the tops of trees. He cursed beneath his breath as he caught himself, but the landscape's sudden descent hadn't been what had provoked her, nor indeed the others who came to a stop on either side of him and followed her gaze with awe.

His own black eyebrows rose in surprise when his addled mind finally gave him leave to notice the obvious.

From their vantage atop a sylvan cliff, the forest sprawling out below them revealed its endless reach, as if a viridian blanket had been dropped by Vastal to smother the world in life. It rolled for as far as the eye could see, thick and lush, but imprisoning, and obscured all that lived within from the hateful, hunting gazes of the world that may have been beyond - for who could say that this forest had not suddenly engulfed it?

Rathen's heart dropped despite the magic's buoying influence as he realised just how far they had yet to go, and he sensed a similar cloud of dejection fall upon the others.

But Aria didn't sigh wearily as the rest of them did. Instead she squinted out across the canopy, peering at something that caught her eye, then took a small, very careful step forwards, though it made no difference to her perspective. She pointed out over the colossal thicket a moment later. "What's that?"

"What's what?" Rathen asked, gently pulling her back from the edge as he followed her gesture towards a small patch of forest where the trees had thinned. Against the magnitude of the landscape it was easy to miss, but once attention had been drawn, it stuck out like a sore thumb. Nearby, rising from the tangle, were six pillars of sandstone, each perfectly pentagonal and arranged in a wide circle perhaps twenty feet wide. All six arched towards the centre, but while two managed to meet and three others tried, the final had been shattered and stood a few heads lower than the rest.

An irrepressible grin wrapped over Anthis's face. "That would be our ruin."

Rathen dared a step closer, his mind braced expertly against the peace that had initially been dizzying, and peered cautiously over the edge. As far as he could see, there was no downward slope to the cliff in either direction, no narrow trail to follow even should they press their backs to the cliff face, and the path they'd followed simply ended as abruptly as the land dropped. But though that drop was steep, the roots that latticed over its surface looked old and thick enough to hold strong foundations.

Petra sighed with resignation. "We're going down there, aren't we?"

"It looks safe enough, if we're careful."

Aria peered over from beside him. She made a dubious hum. "It's a long way down, Daddy. I've not even climbed a tree this high..."

"Then this will be a new experience for you," he smiled reassuringly. "All part of the adventure, right?"

A grin swept across her face. "Absolutely."

"Good. Wait here - all of you. Anthis, keep Aria close. I'll go first."

Garon appeared about to object, but Rathen gave him no chance to do so as he crouched and reached for the highest roots. The surface was smoother than he'd expected, worn down, and as he peered along the cliff face again it seemed that the path did in fact continue after all, only vertically. With a little more confidence, he tested their strength with a firm shake before pulling himself over the edge, squeezing his breath as he delicately sought his footing on a lower limb. Everyone stepped forwards as he dropped below sight, equally holding their breath with each movement he made, expecting him to slip, while mentally noting precisely which roots held his weight.

He called for them to follow once he'd made it a quarter of the way down - Aria first, then Anthis, Petra, and Garon taking the rear - and before long he'd dropped beneath the highest trees and found the ground beneath, the daunting sight of the endless forest mercifully concealed once more.

He reached up and helped Aria down from the roots, who had scurried after him with surprising agility and now beamed proudly at her accomplishment, then turned to look around the enchanted lower forest as the others continued their descent.

The trees that swallowed the area were just as dense and beautiful as those on the ground above them, and he was finding it increasingly easy to ignore the magic's peaceful lure despite being closer to its source. But no birds sang. No animals rustled. Having spent as much time in forests as he had, that was a detail he found difficult to ignore.

Rathen frowned, but he sensed no illness surrounding it. It was likely that the magic had frightened everything off...

Anthis reached the muddy ground and stared off solidly in the direction of the ruins, edging half a step closer every few seconds while casting impatient glances towards Petra and Garon as they covered the last few feet. Once they'd joined them he remained behind Rathen's lead, if barely by a full pace, but as soon as the very first traces of white stone appeared through the undergrowth, his self-control escaped him.

"Be careful," Rathen warned as the foolish young man surged past him, but Anthis didn't slow, and Aria giggled as he cast them another of his brief, impish grins.

Rathen looked down as the ground hardened beneath his feet. The damp earth and knotted roots had given way to broken sandstone tiles, once surely laid neatly but now shattered and pushed apart by the unstoppable growth of the wilds. Roots wended their way through the seams in a curious geometric pattern, while others were raised and pulled apart by the expanding trunks of trees as they grew into giants over centuries. It was an intriguing sight, Rathen mused romantically, as if trees had been planted within a temple floor so that their own canopy might serve as a roof.

But the woods soon grew sparse, and as the structure they'd seen from above loomed into view, it was immediately evident that this ruin was unlike any of the others. Aside from the fact that the stone used was not local like the rest, the masonry was of an exquisite standard. Details were finer, even besides the fact that they weren't as worn or weathered as they had been elsewhere, and edges and corners were sharper. It was so clearly cut that it could have been carved within the last century. But of course it hadn't, because it was certainly elven.

The elevated pavilion, tall and open to the elements, was laced in vines and roots that encased its base, reached across its flooring and wound up and around the elegant columns, like jewellery wrapped in fine, silver wire, and the light that dappled it between the shadows of leaves made the pale stone appear almost golden.

"It's beautiful," Petra breathed as they stepped out from the trees and onto neater paving, staring up at it, enthralled, while Garon only stiffened and Aria nodded vigorously from her side.

"Even prettier than the others! Is this one elf-made, too?"

"It is," Anthis said from within the pavilion, having already found his way up to peer closely at every minute detail. "Short post-magic. I make it about...nine hundred, nine fifty years old. Maybe just short of a thousand." He stepped back into the centre of the platform and looked straight up to where the two arches met. "They put a little more thought into aesthetics here than they did pre-magic, but it's still reverent. They hadn't fallen to arrogance yet."

"So this still wasn't made by magic?" Rathen asked as he ran his hand over the rough stone.

"No." He turned his studious gaze down to the centre of the floor. "It was made by hand and with a lot of care; magic just polished it up, which is why it's still standing as well as it is. Like I said: they were still reverent enough to put time and effort into these things. It wasn't until they realised just how much magic could do for them that they turned away from honouring the gods with their time and just cast quick spells instead - when they honoured the gods *at all*." He smiled to himself as his eyes grew distant. "It must have been wonderful to see in its prime."

"Broken, crumbled, swallowed in moss and vines...I actually think it looks wonderful as it is." Petra's eyes widened as each gaze fell upon her in surprise. "What? I can't appreciate the beauty in something?"

"No, that's not it at all," Anthis replied quickly. "I agree completely - unless," he glanced down to Rathen, "that's the magic's doing?"

The mage shook his head. "I doubt the magic can take all the credit." But as he looked back to the others, his eyes suddenly hardened and his tone changed to match. "Something might live here. A standing structure like this would offer easy shelter."

"In a place where nature is so valued?"

"This ruin is a part of the wilds now, reclaimed like everything else in its boundaries. Just be vigilant." Then Rathen turned his mind away, leaving that matter to Garon as his focus returned to the magic. The sooner he was done there, the sooner they could be away.

Among the elegant columns and finely carved runes, Anthis easily lost himself in his work, his heart at greater peace than it had been for weeks. Kneeling on the stone flooring, shuffling between the flagstones, he peered raptly at the engravings in the tiles, sketchbook in one hand, pencil in the other, and spared only half an absent glance when Petra and Aria found their way up to the top of the platform a few minutes later. The two paid him equally little attention, circling around the pavilion and looking with less practised eyes at its details, until Aria wandered over to the altar set upon a dais.

"They made a bird bath!" She cried in approval, standing on her tip toes to peer into the basin.

"That's a ceremonial bowl," Anthis corrected distantly, though he didn't rise from his knees. "For wine, flowers and so on. Priests would have addressed a gathering here - small groups of people would have filled this pavilion in some cases, or collected below while the priest stood up here with a few other religious figures."

"Why?"

"For rites and observance one kind or another - mostly to Feira, Vastal's Face of Nature, though this forest probably wasn't this dense or wild back when it was built."

"Rites and observants like what?"

Smiling at her curiosity, he finally looked up. "Worship," he replied, surprised to find her suddenly standing beside him, "offerings, pleas for a good harvest or hunt, or to give thanks for one, rituals--"

"*Rituals?*" Petra repeated from across the floor.

"No, not sacrifices, not bloody sacrifices!" He groaned tiresomely. "*Teas!* Offerings of their harvests! Anointing new priests and priestesses!" He shook his head as he looked back to the tiles. "Not even pre-magic elves were so barbaric. They worshipped their gods with clear consciences; they knew what They wanted, and they gave it to Them."

"How do you know all of this?" Aria asked with a curious tilt to her head.

"I found out a lot of it for myself, and I've read the rest from libraries and other people's findings."

"But how can you find it out for yourself if they're all gone?"

He pointed down at the pictographs he'd been studying, and her gaze dropped to follow. They were difficult to make out, but she soon began to notice people etched among them, then animals and plants, all arranged in lines like words on a page. She followed them towards the centre of the floor where they all collided, and there, set in an even lighter stone, was a depiction of a face - it was certainly a face, though it was made up from carven leaves. Curiously, though the incursion of the forest extended far, it didn't grow across this central image, as though even the Wildlands recognised and respected this face of the goddess.

"These pictures tell me what happened here, events of note, why this site was built upon..."

"Which was?"

He looked up at Petra, surprised by her interest, though she wandered over with disregard - feigned, of course.

He rose and moved to the centre, following the lines until he found the one he sought, and tracked slowly along its length. "'The roots that burrow beneath our feet reach to the depths of the world, where Feira's heart beats, connected to her by wooden veins, all trees, all plants, all bushes; her essence feeds all creature from insects and fungi to the beasts that feed upon them. Sylvan glades, hidden among tangles of Feira's tresses, offer protection for those pure and in need, whatever form they may take'." He looked across at the two. "Though in elven it would have rhymed."

Aria smiled. "I like it. What does it mean?"

"That this Feira protected animals," Petra guessed. "And She is also Vastal?"

"Yes. And it actually says She protects anything and any*one* that seeks refuge in the forests," Anthis added. "Provided they mean it no harm." He cast his eyes over the surrounding woodland. "This is probably one such glade."

"And that's why it was built here?"

He nodded. "Which would *also* explain why the Wildlands are exactly that. This structure is elaborate, even for post-magic elves, and there are probably a few other pavilions hidden in here, too." He moved towards the edge and peered down at Rathen, who wandered around below with distant eyes, though he managed to avoid tripping over any roots even without such attention. "I wonder if there's anything different here..."

Rathen's eyes were still glazed in thought as he cast a glance to the golden light that brushed the stone, then up towards the deep grey, dappled sky. He sighed to himself a moment later as he stopped seeing once more. That was another theory nipped in the bud. He'd thought perhaps that the peace and affected weather were at odds with one another, that they couldn't both exist in one place, but the warm glow that dappled the ruins was not, in fact, natural. He should have realised sooner - for a start, it was light akin to evening despite not even being midday, and secondly, the sun barely had presence enough to cast such a strong glow even had the timing be right. But it had been too inconspicuous, too quiet, too calm for him or anyone else to notice.

He folded his arms, his face relaxing, so distant was his thought.

He could find nothing but puddles of magic, the usual beauty and peace, and, as it turned out, artificial sunlight. There was nothing else, nothing they hadn't already encountered, not even a spell fragment. And he was looking very closely.

He found his fingertips drumming the metal band clasped around his arm, and a frown pulled at his brow.

The last time he'd extended the reach of his magic, it had burned, and he still had no explanation for it. If it had been his magic that had grown hot in his veins, why had nothing else against his skin reacted in such a way? Was it simply because no other metal was in direct contact with him?

Though...it was true that he hadn't touched on his magic so deeply in years. He'd already been riddled by exhaustion from over-use once - though that 'over-use' would have been a typical Wednesday to any other mage.

His frown deepened in self-reproach. Had he really become so weak in his isolation?

A tinkling giggle caught his attention, drawing him out from his thoughts. He followed it up towards the top of the enchanting pavilion and found Aria climbing up a pillar, using the vines as footholds while Anthis waited below, watching her sharply with an expression torn between amusement and panic.

Rathen smiled and looked away. She'd be fine. And though Anthis was both a fool and really quite irresponsible, he found a strange trust in him, especially where Aria was involved. And anyway, he had other matters to think on.

Garon lingered impatiently near the treeline, trying to ignore the hairs that stood up on the back of his neck. The sensation was unfounded, this he knew, even in the Wildlands, and it certainly stemmed from the magic's haunting beauty. It unsettled him here just as much as it had everywhere else, and how Anthis could lose himself in the ruins as easily as he did, or the child play so carelessly, he just couldn't fathom. Perhaps it was youth.

He grunted to himself in what he assumed was indifference.

Petra caught his eye as she wandered over the crumbled stones of a ruined portion of the platform, and she stopped to scrutinise something within the knotted vines. She didn't seem as relaxed as the others. There was a rigidity to her form, tense, as though she was as expectant of trouble as he was, though she was likely just as unsure of what.

She rose a moment later, her eyes still glued to the ground, and called Anthis over to look at whatever it was that had captured her attention. He caught a few words - she asked what it was, and Anthis replied that it was some kind of story; Garon was disinterested as to what. Petra said something about it which he didn't catch, and Anthis smiled at her and nodded.

Garon felt a spark of something in his gut.

He turned his eyes away from them, and it vanished as his attention shifted.

Rathen stepped into view from the far side of the clearing, lost in thought, and Garon couldn't miss his troubled creases. But he couldn't rightly tell if he was simply touched by the same unease that he and Petra were. Being a mage, he probably interpreted it differently, inherently understood the nature of the magic and knew where there was a threat.

He wondered what he was thinking, but trusted if there was anything to share, he would.

With a sigh, he turned his back to the group. All he could do was keep watch and give him time. He didn't wish to linger anywhere, especially in this place, but it was along their path and, he hoped, it could only do good. And while he greatly preferred to find the artefact, this at least gave him some sense of progress - or at least reduced the feeling of standing still.

Rathen wandered around the ruin for some time, and Anthis wasn't about to complain. He seized the opportunity to study this new site with gusto; it was entirely unknown to him, surely seen only by dead historians, so he was making the most of it before he was inevitably called away, which was sure to be right in the middle of the most exciting discovery. But despite his zeal, he hadn't forgotten where he was, and a small part of him actually wanted Garon to give the order to leave.

But all of that hinged on Rathen, and he seemed to be taking more time than usual. He wondered what that could mean, though his mind didn't dally on the thought for long. He was absorbed in sketching out stories and pictographs.

He'd found, as he'd suspected, that it was a secluded site by intention, highly revered - a fact which only sent the butterflies in his stomach into somersaults - and had been used for the most part for small but intense ceremonies to the goddess: consumption of poisonous or hallucinogenic plants, either to prove their worth to Vastal or raise their minds to another plane to speak with Her - he couldn't honestly decipher which - and pledges of their life and efforts to the protection of the wild. Though, just what that meant, he couldn't decide upon either. 'Become one with the wilds' could mean anything where religion and elven contexts were involved.

His eyes drifted towards the sky in his pondering, and he set the time at just past noon. His blonde eyebrows rose. Had they really been there for two hours?

He quickly looked about himself, wondering for a moment if the others hadn't actually set off and left him behind. But no. There was Garon, pacing slowly around the perimeter, staring into the forest, and he spotted Petra on the other side of the clearing doing much the same. Rathen was sat upon a stone bench nearby, the only one of five that circled the pavilion which was still recognisable, and the unfriendly expression upon his face which Anthis had come to realise was one of caution and thought only deepened in his engrossment.

It seemed he still had time.

He assessed again the ruin which had now become quite familiar to him, and folded his arms in consideration. Such hallowed sites weren't usually so bare. It was true that things of value to the present world were used in ancient ceremonies, but they weren't so dearly coveted back then that they needed to be under constant guard, and so countless sacred relics had been uncovered from unassuming sites - scrolls, ceremonial artefacts, even ancient tea leaves. He wondered if there wasn't perhaps a small, concealed storage chamber here, too. If there was, it would surely be untouched - unless of course those that had come before him had cleaned it out before getting themselves killed...but the place seemed intact aside from the obvious rigours of age and the relentless force of nature...

His veins buzzed at the thought.

He turned frantically away from the etchings, his fascination of their stories and teachings forgotten, and hurried towards the broken steps that ran down the back of the structure, skipping over the mess of foliage in barely contained excitement.

The pale stone of the foundation's walls could only be peeked at between the overgrowth, so he forced his pace to slow as he made his way around it, peering carefully between the vines and roots for tell-tale cracks and crevices, where he pushed and pressed any loose-looking stones. None gave way, but he continued along, unconcerned, confident that he would find something. He might miss it the first time around, but so grand a monument simply *couldn't* be without a single one-foot cubby hole.

He'd not gotten far when rustling close by froze his feet, and he spun around to stare into the forest. The trees were still thin, leaving his sight unhindered, but he could see nothing out of place at all. It was true he hadn't been paying very much attention, but he was absolutely sure none of the trees had moved.

The sound came again, followed by the crumbling of small rocks, and he realised that it had come from behind him, within the ruin itself.

His heartbeat jumped before its pace began to hammer, and he looked towards a particularly thick knot of green and brown a short ways along his path. He could see that the stone had given way behind it; while the platform was whole directly above, something had undermined the foundation. It could have been what he'd been looking for, or it could have been weathering - or it could have been hollowed out by something in search of a home.

He swallowed hard. He knew he should call for the others, but he didn't, and stepped tentatively, foolishly towards it instead.

Again came the falling of dust from broken stone and the snap of dried roots, but as he stopped just a single step away from the knot, a small voice uttered a childish curse.

He frowned and leaned inside. "Aria?"

The young girl turned and looked at him from the other side of the tangle with innocence flooding her eyes, but as she recognised Anthis rather than her father, it was replaced by a great, beaming grin. "Good! Help me!"

His frown deepened, but he looked for a way through. She'd wriggled between the roots and found her way into what was a short, descending tunnel, but though it first seemed to have collapsed, in the little spot she'd nestled herself he noticed the stone was far too smooth for it to have been chance.

He squeezed his slender form through the gap as Aria shuffled aside to make room, then clambered over the fallen stones that he guessed had once blocked the way. There was barely enough space for the two of them in there, but he found that there was enough room to stand. Whatever it was, it was made for one.

"What are you doing in here?" He asked her in a whisper, though he wasn't sure why.

"Just help me push!" She was already forcing all of her slight weight against a particular spot on the wall. At first Anthis could see nothing there that was worth her attention. It was only when his eyes had fully adjusted to the narrow shaft's diminished light that he noticed the slight shadows that lay within the face of the stone, a detail he recognised immediately as a carving, though its circular shape was unfamiliar - at least in this setting.

"Oh, Vokaad..."

Immediately, he added his efforts, focusing his strength upon the carving just as Aria did. With his help, the circle of runes began to shift, pressed back into the stone in which it was set. It gave an inch upon the first push, then another upon the second before Aria lost her footing. Anthis caught her before she could even graze her knees, but the heavy sound of stone scraping over stone continued without them, and they both looked up to see the disc pivot sideways in its setting before the distinct sound of released latches came from the other side.

Anthis hurriedly pulled Aria back and shielded her as dust fell from above and the stone around them shook, and he watched as the small, carved wall before them began to sink deeper into the rock before dragging itself heavily to one side.

They stared into the darkness that opened ahead as the movement drew to a slow, rumbling stop, straining their eyes to see beyond what little light reached in.

Anthis was the first to move. He did so cautiously, shaking the dust off of his back as he stepped towards it, holding his hand back to keep Aria where she was despite having been the one to discover it.

"You can't see in there," she reminded him curtly, folding her arms across her chest. "You'll need a torch."

He looked back towards her. Of course she was right.

Footsteps neared outside, and the already meagre shaft of light was shortly blotted out.

"What's happened?" Petra asked as Garon and Rathen arrived in due course behind her, but Anthis simply smiled broadly.

"We've found something."

Chapter 22

A small flame sparked into life, illuminating the tiny alcove from a torch made of a gnarled and broken root. The space grew and shrank in the dancing light, and restless shadows were sent skittering across the tight walls as Rathen peered in towards the black doorway, where the fleeing darkness seemed to gather. Tentatively, he stepped down into the tunnel, cramped already by Anthis and Aria, and stretched his every sense into the blackness.

But Anthis showed no such caution. He rushed ahead and eagerly waved him through after him.

It took only three and a half steps for the flickering light to find the encircling walls. The small, round chamber that had been shrouded in shadow was no more than eight feet across, and Anthis gasped as his eyes drank in the assortment of books, scrolls and oddities that were revealed around them, silent and undisturbed for countless centuries.

"What is it?" Rathen asked a little calmer as he looked around at the not so sinister room, but he received no answer.

"Torch," Anthis commanded instead, clicking his fingers unceremoniously in his excitement, and he peered closely at the back of the stone door as light flooded over it.

His fingers traced the intricate etchings of the rotated disc, perfectly smooth to touch, and chuckled gleefully as the others stepped in to join them. "This wasn't carved by hand," he said, turning wide, childlike eyes towards them for a fleeting moment before they were ripped back to the stone. "It was magic."

"And that's unusual?"

"No," he said giddily, his grin broadening. "Not for this kind of symbol. This," he stepped even closer to the door, all but pressing his nose against it, "*this* is a sign of anarchy."

The four watched him expectantly as he stared enraptured at the carving, but he made no attempt to elaborate.

"Which means?" Rathen asked, finally.

Anthis jumped and looked around at them all in surprise, then grinned once again with eyes as bright as Aria's. "Not all elves were of one mind," he explained quickly, "just like we're not. I believe there was a small faction of rebels working against the rest on a moral level, disagreeing with the direction their culture was taking. To what ends, I don't know, but whatever their intentions or plans were, they didn't succeed. Every elf, *including* the rebels, are gone, and while the most virtuous or radical among them may have carried guilt by extension and believed they were just as deserving of death as the rest of them, I don't think even you, Rathen, will argue when I say that there's no way any elf or number thereof would've had the power to eradicate their *entire* race to the point of leaving no remains at all. Assuming they even sought such an aggressive solution."

"What does all this mean, Anthis?" Garon asked with well-tempered patience.

"It means that this symbol was put here long after this structure was built, *and* abandoned." He turned suddenly away from the stone and stepped towards the table in the centre of the room, upon which stood an array of pots, boxes and cloth wrappings. But it was the small wooden box that drew the eye, standing out for its stark simplicity. He stopped in front of it and looked across the group with sudden severity, though his passion lingered around the edges. "Which also means that not everything in here belongs."

Rathen sighed. "You're being cryptic again."

"I've seen this emblem pop up a few times in the past, only ever in *late* post-magic journals and personal letters when speaking of disgust or despair for their culture - especially alongside mention of the artefact in the context of a weapon. Which means that these discontented elves, or at least one of them, returned here for one reason or another, and hid this very box and its contents. Whatever is in it, it would have to have been important for them to go to these lengths."

"Hiding something in an old storage cellar doesn't exactly take much effort," Petra pointed out. "Or imagination."

Anthis was already shaking his head. "It took thought - spiteful thought. That door wasn't protected by any spells."

"I sensed no traces," Rathen admitted.

"See, to me, that suggests that it's nothing of any value."

"Until you consider that they came to a short post-magic site, long-abandoned in the middle of nowhere even back then, and put this box in the place's storage cellar - in plain sight, you could say. No elf would think to come here, whether they were fervently looking for something or not, especially with no active spells to draw their attention. It would be completely overlooked. By hiding it here, they used their dependence on magic against them."

She sighed dubiously. "This sounds like a whole lot of conjecture..." Her eyes dropped doubtfully to the box upon the table, then back at him in kind, though there was a degree of patience in them. "What do you think it could be?"

"The arty-fact?"

He smiled sadly at the hope in Aria's voice, for he certainly shared it. Unfortunately, experience had taught him better. "I doubt it," he replied regretfully, "but if it's even remotely related, it could be the best lead I've had yet."

"Anthis."

He looked up after Rathen's commanding tone.

"Open it."

All eyes fell to the small and unassuming box. Plain and unadorned, it seemed displaced among the exquisiteness of the surrounding ceremonial relics, and Anthis suddenly found himself quite reluctant to touch it. It was only upon an encouraging but mostly impatient cough from Aria that he finally took a hold of the lid, which he lifted slowly, as though he feared something might leap out to bite him. His hesitance began to creep over the others, and they found themselves just as reluctant to look inside.

But when he set the lid down beside it and they saw nothing inside but parchment, they each shared some small degree of disappointment.

Anthis was the only one to disagree. Delicately, he lifted the first few sheets, crisp and unspoilt after seven hundred years of preservation, and scanned over their elegant, scrawling scripture. The others watched him in silence as he skimmed over one page, then the next, and as he blindly withdrew a book from his own satchel and compared something between the two before returning to the first. Anxiety rose and they watched him even closer, but his eyes were unreadable. He seemed excited, cautious, hopeful, and a touch confused.

"Anthis," Garon said at last, but though the historian shook his head and seemed about to speak, he ended up saying nothing at all, his eyes firmly glued to the parchment. Garon didn't try a second time.

Minutes passed as he sank deeper into words written by a long-dead people, and Rathen's arm soon began to ache. As Aria pushed herself tiresomely away from the table and began to look around at the rest of the chamber, he set the torch in a sconce and obediently followed. Petra followed the young girl's lead, leaving Anthis to his work, and Garon returned to the doorway to keep watch outside until the young man finally found his tongue. "I don't know."

Startled by the broken silence, they turned expectantly but found him still fixed to the pages.

"I need to look through it all properly, but...I think we might have something here..." He continued to compare sheets as the others abandoned their nosings, and glanced over an open journal that had also been within the box.

"What do you *think* you have?"

Anthis finally turned his pensive eyes upon the inquisitor. "Something about the artefact, that much is certain - it's mentioned a few times - but whether it's of any considerable use, I don't know. Like I said, I need to read through it all..."

"But it's useful?" Garon pressed. "Or it could be?"

"It *could* be *quite* useful..."

"But is it *reliable?*" Rathen asked.

He released a long, slow sigh in deliberation. "They're all notes, theories and thoughts about a few different things, but all linked by their overall intent...and this here seems to be a journal of--" He finally noticed the weight of their impatience. "Yes."

"Then why do you seem so uncertain?"

He cast Petra a shaky smile. "Because I don't dare to hope..."

"Gather it up." Garon stepped back towards the doorway and peered outside uneasily. "We've lingered here long enough and we'd do well to be away. Study it when we make camp tonight."

"No, we should stay here."

Garon glowered at his defiant tone. "Your own studies will have to wait, Anthis."

"It's nothing to do with studying these ruins," he assured him, "but with saving time."

"How?"

"Because Bowden may no longer be necessary." He glanced across the curious frowns. "If it works out that we have to turn around and retrace our steps out of here," he crossed his fingers, "then by staying put we can save time; we won't have to back-track as far."

"But if Bowden *is* still on the cards, by staying put we could be *wasting* time," Rathen countered, and all eyes followed his as he looked towards Garon for a decision.

"We stay," he said after a moment, then looked to Anthis who smiled at his easy victory. "You have the rest of the day. If you come to no conclusions that can give us a direction by nightfall, we will continue on to Bowden in the morning."

He nodded his agreement and eagerly set back to reading, the conversation forgotten regardless of further questions.

Rathen sighed heavily and followed Garon as he moved back outside to keep watch. "I don't like this," he said quietly.

"Anthis is right. The odds are high that we'll end up turning around; there's little but Bowden to the east. And if not, then we'll have lost an afternoon. You said yourself that in the scale of this place, it won't make much difference."

"That's not all I mean." He glanced over his shoulder and lowered his voice as Aria and Petra peered at some of the more ornate items. "I'm not happy here."

"Believe me, I can appreciate that," he sighed quietly, "I have an uneasy feeling myself, but Anthis knows what to look for. We'll be back on our way in a few hours and we can set up camp somewhere less conspicuous."

Anthis spent every last moment of that afternoon in the cramped old chamber. No one interrupted him, even as their impatience mounted, leaving him to find the answers, understanding or whatever it was he sought without hindrance in the hope that they could be away before nightfall. But there was no such luck.

"Well?" Petra asked hopefully as Rathen returned to the nook they'd found at the edge of the ruins, safe from sight by a cluster of trees and a fallen statue and bordered now by subtle, watchful spells.

He shook his head. "Nothing." He sat down heavily beside her, dropping his hand away from his upper arm and glancing around to note Garon still standing guard atop the darkened pavilion.

"You don't sound sure..."

"It's the magic," he replied, his nose wrinkling, but he offered Petra and Aria beside her an honest smile. "But I don't think anything lives here. I walked all around and checked near the cliff. There are no dens or warrens, no make-shift beds, no caves. I saw nothing to suggest anything even passes through here. This magic, or maybe the structure itself, probably discourages them."

"But *you said* there might be something living here," Aria reminded him, and she earned herself a flat look.

"Then this must be one of those rare times in which I am wrong."

"At least you admitted it." She grinned impishly as her father shook his head, but a frown warped her brow as she noticed a glint about Petra's neck as she chuckled between them. "What's that?" She asked, leaning over and pulling a necklace free from beneath her blouse.

"Aria," Rathen sighed wearily, "*manners*, you can't just--oh, never mind."

Petra released another elegant laugh, one that continued to contradict her harsh demeanour, though that, too, had begun to give way in recent days to something more approachable. She raised her hand to take back the pendant and show it to the girl herself, moving her fingers deftly through the fabric of her elongated sleeve, and again Rathen wondered at the extent of her scars. "This," she replied, turning back to Aria and opening the silver oval, "is a locket. It has a picture of my father and mother here, and my sister, Celise, here."

"It's beautiful," she smiled with enchantment. "Do you wear it because you're afraid you'll forget what they look like?"

"No," she laughed, "of course not. It's to keep them close to my heart. I don't...I don't see them as often as I'd like."

"Why not?"

"I travel a lot," she replied easily, but Rathen noticed the subtle, evasive tone, and how intensely she stared down at the pictures.

She looked back up a moment later and smiled at the girl, pushing aside the darkness that had befallen her young features, and Rathen chose not to mention it.

"I want one," Aria grinned, though a frown of disappointment quickly slipped into its place. "But I'm always with my daddy. I'm not sure there would be much point..."

"I can always leave you at home when I go to meet traders."

"*No!* You wouldn't dare!"

He smiled teasingly. "I was only offering you a solution."

"Well it isn't worth it."

Petra smiled at their bickering, but her gloom returned as her eyes dragged back down to the small, faded portraits. "You're not with the Order, are you?" She asked suddenly, looking up at the mage.

Rathen's surprise was replaced just as quickly by resentment. "What has Anthis said?"

"Nothing," she smiled softly, "I figured it out for myself. You sound disconnected whenever you mention it, and other mages. How did you get away from them?"

Something besides curiosity had tinged her voice, and as he noticed her touch the illustration of a young woman within her locket, he understood why. He frowned in sympathy.

"I don't like how people view my sister as a monster," she continued before he could answer. "Celise wouldn't hurt a fly."

"Believe me, I can understand your frustration. Mages aren't well-liked *anywhere*. People are ignorant to what we can do and how we work. But honestly, I promise you that mages in Turunda are far better off than they are anywhere else. Here we have freedom, for the most part. More freedom than most will *ever* see."

"*You* do."

Rathen flinched beneath the accusation in her eyes, but his guilt was quick to pass. "Neither of you would wish upon her what I went through for my freedom," he assured her firmly. "If you can even call it that." He folded his arms and turned a thoughtful gaze towards the black sky, the stars entirely hidden behind the swollen clouds, as was any clue of dusk. "But, if I'm honest...I do believe that mages belong with the Order. For their safety as well as everyone else's. If mages were allowed such individual freedom with the power they possess...well, I'm sure the world would be in an even sorrier state than it is. One rotten apple, and all that. The Order is, at the end of the day, a necessary evil." He nodded to himself. "The trouble comes from the cloaks."

She cocked an eyebrow. "The cloaks?"

"They draw attention, isolate the mage in crowds. They make segregation much easier - to some degree I think that's the point. But they're there for...people's safety and peace of mind." He shook his head, and she hadn't missed how unconvinced he sounded of that last, recited statement. "And that won't change. But," he offered another confident smile, "she'll be all right. Dirty looks have never killed anyone, and no one is brave enough to take it any further than that. Lack of understanding might lead to hatred and mistrust of magic, but the mystery also lends mages protection." He cocked his head as curiosity formed a crease in his brow. "What wing is she in? Your sister?"

"Military."

Rathen baulked in surprise. "Really?" He paused as he considered the nature of the woman sitting on the ruined stone tiles before him. "I suppose strength must run in the family... In that case she'll *definitely* be all right." A grin of amusement tugged at the corner of his lips. "'She wouldn't hurt a fly'?"

"Not if it was unarmed."

"What about midges?" Aria asked thoughtfully.

"Oh, they're certainly armed," Petra assured her, and Aria nodded in agreement. She tucked her locket away safely beneath her blouse, but paused in a wash of fear as a low rumble rose very close by. She looked first to Rathen, but he only smiled, and then to Aria, whose little cheeks had flushed red.

"You know, little one, I suppose it *is* about time we eat."

It was meagre, but the warm broth would at least lift a few spirits against the tense and eerie atmosphere, and the very moment Rathen reached for a bowl to begin dividing it up, Anthis stepped out from the chamber as if he was carried by his nose. He stumbled in momentary surprise as he discovered the darkness.

"Well?" Rathen asked as the historian joined them, and Garon stepped to the nearest edge of the pavilion to listen and maintain his watch, but once again, the young man was difficult to read.

"I learned a few things," Anthis began in an unidentifiable tone, "about the artefacts, and about people and places."

"And is any of it of any use to us?"

"Yes..."

"You sound uncertain again," Petra warned him. "Have you found anything useful or not?"

"Well...the artefacts are certainly separate," he began quite carefully, "which renders our initial--"

"Wait - what do you mean 'the artefacts are separate'?"

He turned his increasingly cautious eyes upon the mage and shrank a little beneath the ferocity of his gaze. "Well, context plays a big role in elven language - I've told you this before - and more times than anyone in the Historical Society would like to admit, it was thought that two or three separate things made up a full set when it was really just one item referred to in entirely different ways, other aspects and details ignored whenever they weren't relevant. Elven can be...ehh, challenging to decrypt..."

"All right," Rathen growled, doing his best to restrain his frustration as Aria reached out to calm him, "so what does this mean? In this case, it's reversed? There *are* multiple?"

Anthis hesitated. "...Yes - *but*, it does explain why what we found in Mokhan was considered a 'great magical advancement'. Being able to create a force of air out of nothing was being compared to something certainly on par, but not as grand as we thought. Being able to silence the magic of *humans* was clearly a feat when it was created, but with the way they lorded themselves over them, it probably made the ability to silence their magic seem like a bare essential, even if it was a new advancement. It was quickly taken for granted, just like creating that force. But rather than that comparison being made to an *aspect* of a certain item, it was made to a specific item in its *entirety*."

"So it was your misunderstanding," Garon said flatly from behind them.

Anthis turned red, though the torchlight didn't reveal it. "I'm not the only one that would have done so," he bristled.

"How can you be sure you're right about this? That you're not just misreading context again?"

He raised the sheets of parchment he'd brought out from the chamber with him and snapped them up towards him. "Because this says as much. Clearly and concisely."

"I notice you don't sound surprised by this revelation," Rathen said suspiciously. "I'd almost go as far as to say you already had an idea."

Suddenly, Anthis felt every gaze harden and bore into him from all sides, and his aggravation returned to submissive caution. "Well...I sort of did--but I never had anything to back it up with, it was just a feeling, so I didn't want to mention it. But now I know, and then some, which is why I just *did*."

"*Anthis!*"

"In short," he hurried, "we should go after the weapon, not the magic-removing artefact."

Rathen blinked as his growing exasperation faltered. "That makes no sense."

"It makes *plenty* of sense. The magic remover was made for use against *human* magic; the weapon, against elves. It should have no problem targeting elven magic, which is what we're dealing with. From what you've told me, the human artefact *could* be modified, but there's no telling that it would work as we want it to, while the elven weapon might need no modification at all."

"Could the elven weapon not be used against humans as well?" Garon asked, and Anthis frowned in puzzlement as he looked back around towards him.

"Maybe; human magic did descend from elven - but why would we need it to be?"

"We don't. But my concern is that the magic may not be as simple as Rathen's friend thinks. It's already disembodied, that might change things, and Rathen couldn't tell it was elven--"

"I am--"

"Not a scholar, we know, but even so, mistakes can be made by anyone, and if the artefact was capable of affecting *any* magic rather than exclusively one or the other, would we not be better off?"

Anthis thought for a moment. "You have a point. But honestly, I couldn't tell you for certain." He looked slowly to Rathen.

The mage's irritated frown twisted in thought. "Neither can I, but I'd be willing to hazard a guess. Going by what you've said about elves and context, I'm not so sure the artefact itself would be tailored specifically to people. They would have to distinguish between loyalties and regions that way, so I think it's more likely that it would be aimed at the magic itself, directed by the wielder's intent upon his enemies and away from his own allies, because both allies and enemies can change by circumstance." Rathen sighed meekly as his thoughts progressed. "If - and I *stress* 'if' - this most certainly complex spell can be adjusted, it may not be a big leap. But that's assuming I can make heads or tails of it at all."

"And what would happen to the original spell if you got it wrong?"

"I could remove my interference. Mages can't deconstruct spells, we can only patch over them, so the original spell, breaks and all, remains beneath it - and from what I've gathered, I'm probably going to have to patch it anyway."

"Well, I'd say that's that decided, then," Anthis smiled, feeling somewhat redeemed.

"Do you know where it could be?"

He hesitated once again, and the group's suspicion returned.

"Never mind," Rathen sighed, giving up to save himself a headache. "What else did you find?"

"Well, there were a few different mentions of places and people. The latter I can't glean much from, but the places could be helpful. There's also vague mention of somewhere being referred to as 'ravein'okh', which literally translates to 'place of magic', but nothing by name - though I have a few ideas of where that might be and I assume it to be our best bet. Then there's talk of where the artefacts were originally created, again not by name but that the location was famous for its craft, so again I think I can work it out, but I'm not actually sure that would be worth pursuing."

"Why not?"

"Because why would it still be where it was created? And why would it be hidden there? It's a bit too obvious."

"But it could provide us with some information about the spell itself," Rathen suggested.

"Not about the weapon, it wouldn't. That kind of information would be locked away, and tightly. They'd risk someone else making one and turning it on them if it wasn't."

"I suppose you have a point..."

"What can you tell us for *certain*, Anthis?" Garon asked, his commanding voice easily stealing the helm of the conversation.

"Well, I've not figured out precisely where any of this points - there are three or four options - but one thing I *do* know for certain is that Bowden *isn't* necessary."

"You couldn't have decided that earlier?" Rathen groaned.

"It wouldn't have mattered," he replied regretfully. "I still have no real direction to give you."

"What are these options?" Garon asked.

"They're wide spread," he warned them, but all eyes were surprisingly patient. "Well, there's Tarun, the grandest of all elven cities, if the artefact remained under guard; Sunscale Lake, east in Qenra, where it's believed they were gifted their magic, if it was hidden away; Enhala, the elven cultural capital in Kasire, as an alternative 'place of magic', and finally Lofton down south, once famous for the metalwork that produced the artefacts."

"I thought you said that wasn't worth pursuing."

"Well I've only added that to the list because it will niggle at me otherwise. Make me feel like I've forgotten something. But, don't worry, I'll spend the night cross-referencing and have it narrowed down by morning. Then we can be on our way."

The mage grumbled in discouragement but he chose not to voice it, then looked down to find Aria handing out the bowls of soup he'd neglected. He smiled softly as she took what she offered him, then handed it to Anthis. "Eat. You might as well take a break for now."

"Wait..."

He frowned as Anthis fished about in his pockets and withdrew a piece of metal so ornate that it took he and the others a moment to work out what it was. "A key?"

"There was nothing in that box or in that room that even had a lock on it."

Rathen nodded slowly. "It could be relevant. Keep it with you."

"Believe me, I was going to."

"Good. Now: eat."

Aria started towards the pavilion with another bowl in her hands, but the inquisitor turned away. Aria pouted.

"Are you not eating tonight?" Rathen asked as he watched him return to his attentive spot at the centre.

"Not yet. You go ahead."

Anthis returned to the seclusion of the chamber shortly after he'd finished, already lost in thought before he'd seen the bottom of the bowl, and Petra soon excused herself only to vanish behind the pavilion, sword drawn and rolling her shoulders as she went. Rathen didn't want to ask her what she was doing.

Aria similarly turned into herself and began working in her sketchbook by torchlight, and in the silence, Rathen was left little option but to see to his own matters. But it was far from that simple. With his notebook open upon his knees, he made his notes, thoughts and guesses on the magic, crossed them out, made the same notes with different words and then crossed them out again. He kept at it for some time before finally giving up with a huff and tossing the book aside in frustration.

"Having trouble?" Aria asked from a few feet away, nestled cosily in a nook between the foot of the shattered statue - of Feira, Anthis had needlessly told them - and the roots of a thick tree.

"No."

She raised an eyebrow at his waspish tone, and he sensed her disapproval. He glanced sidelong, certain that she was silently declaring him a liar.

"It's just...difficult to know where to start," he amended.

"What did Kienza tell you?"

"...To stop getting bogged down in specifics."

"*Aside* from that. I'm sure she gave you some kind of instructions. She knows a lot about magic - more, I reckon, than she lets us think she does."

Rathen considered the eight year old. It was one of those curious moments where she sounded older and wiser than she should have, and on this occasion she even appeared to look a few years older given how elegantly she was sat, sketchbook on her folded legs and charcoal held like a fine quill. All accidental, of course, but he couldn't help wondering for a moment what she would grow up to become, and, not for the first time, if she would show any magical talent.

His jaw tightened as defiantly as it had each time that thought had risen before, and he promised himself he wasn't going to give her up to the Order if she did. He could teach her the basics himself, and the rest she was smart enough to pick up on her own.

"Yes," he replied, "she does...and she did."

Aria smiled - a childish one that returned her to her true age, much to Rathen's relief. Sometimes he wondered just how much she'd learned from Kienza. If, for example, it didn't stretch beyond general knowledge, whittling and wrapping Rathen tightly around her little finger. "It's all right, Daddy," she assured him. "It's easy to forget things you've been told, no matter how many times you might hear it."

He narrowed his dark eyes as a smile crept across his face. "You mean like when I tell you not to do something and then you do it anyway?"

"See? It even happens to me!"

He laughed and shook his head, then looked back down to his book of scratched-out notes. Yes, he had to stop over thinking it and just go back to basics. *'Try to affect it as a whole - push it, compact it, expand it.'* That's what Kienza had recommended as a second step. He just had to affect it in some way - *any* way. So far all he'd really done was look at it, and he'd learned as much as he could by that means. Now he had to reach out and touch it.

He straightened where he sat and released his grip from the cuff around his arm, suddenly aware that he was squeezing it in his thoughts, and forced himself to relax and embrace the flow of his own magic.

Immediately the elven magic that surrounded him became sharper and clearer than before, bright to his senses though there was nothing to see. It had been impossible to miss even when he wasn't looking for it, but when he focused himself in such a way, it was as if it had become tangible.

He was about to rush in and try to push it, but he managed to restrain himself before his certain, thoughtless failure and considered it instead. A general force push spell would be useless. Though it may have seemed it to him at that moment, this magic was *not* material and it wouldn't move by sheer force any easier than light shining on the ground. He needed to form a spell specifically to interact with it.

...But how? A spell to interact with disembodied magic just floating around like this? Such a thing had never been tried - no such opportunity had ever arisen! In spite of himself, he wished he was still with the Order. They might have had more details or theories, something he could use rather than being left in the dark with his own limited devices.

Where was Kienza when he needed her?

He frowned and silently chastised himself. He would do this himself. He couldn't keep relying on her every time he had a problem.

He took a deep breath and refocused his mind. *'Don't get bogged down in specifics.'*

What if...the idea of a spell was just a distraction? It seemed an obvious step, even a necessary one, but what if it was just a red herring? What if he just needed to use his own magic, but unshaped? He could extend it as a sixth sense, it was that which enabled him to detect the puddle of magic that existed just a few feet in front of him while non-mages couldn't. Perhaps that's what was required. After all, this was just raw magic, like that which flowed within his veins. Why couldn't something so basic work?

Hope suddenly overtook him and he didn't stop to think on it any further. He extended his magic as easily as he breathed and focused it upon the puddle, channelling his strength into it, assaulting the magic with his own.

Nothing happened right away, but he wasn't discouraged.

He applied more strength to the force, certain his own was washing over the other, but still he could see no change. And still he wasn't discouraged. It was such a simple thing, pure and uncomplicated. It couldn't *not* work. He just needed to focus more strength...

Just a little more...

A piercing pain sent a flash of light through his mind. A curse was torn from his throat, and as fire enveloped his arm, his efforts were shattered.

And just as suddenly as it had begun, it receded, the pain lost as his magic settled.

His jaw tightened and teeth barred in frustration. It hadn't worked. That couldn't be it. He'd looked at the magic, gathered what he could, but as for reaching out and touching it, it was like reaching out and trying to grasp fog. And that damned pain...this was the fourth time it had assaulted him, taunted him, and the second that very day after he'd set up the camp's protective spells. But *why?!*

He sighed though it escaped as a growl, channelling his anger into that single breath as he sat fuming in hopelessness instead.

"What is that cuff?"

Startled first out of his defeatist thoughts, he was surprised again to find Anthis not in the chamber beneath the ruin but sitting beside Aria, who still expertly shielded her drawings from him even as she stared at her father in concern.

His eyes dropped down to his arm as the question registered and he realised he'd been audibly tapping it. He moved his hand away. "It's nothing."

Anthis lingered curiously at his blunt tone, but decided not to press. Instead he returned to trying to get a subtle peek at Aria's work, but she shortly huffed, got up and walked away.

But as Anthis apologised and tried to encourage her to sit back down with promises that he wouldn't try to look again, Rathen's frown softened as the almost-forgotten thoughts the question had dug up floated to the surface. He even found himself feeling guilty at being angered by the cuff's presence. "Actually," he said a moment later, suddenly feeling the need to speak of it as if in way of apologising to little more than a memory, "it was a gift from my mother before she died."

Anthis looked around at him, surprised for his answering while regretting his asking. "Oh, I'm sorry..." He sat back down as his curiosity got the better of him. "So that's why you hide it? Or keep it close?"

"No," he smiled strangely, "it's because I can't get it off. Not that I would if I could, I suppose." His smile weakened. "Maybe."

Anthis frowned. "You can't get it off?"

"No. And there's magic to it."

"Magic? How do you know?"

"Well because I can feel it, for starters," he said, raising his sleeve to peer at it. "Then there's the fact that I've worn it for as long as I can remember - she died when I was three, and it's grown with me since."

"I'm sorry..." But his careful interest was persistent. "So your mother was a mage, too?"

"I presume so," he replied slowly, looking at the smooth metal band that was neither too tight nor too loose; a perfect fit. "My father never spoke of her. But then, he barely spoke at all."

"Difficult childhood?"

"I wouldn't know that, either." He lowered his sleeve as a chill passed over them. "My magic surfaced when I was seven so I was whisked straight off to the Order."

"*Seven?!*" Anthis's voice was only just restrained to a rough whisper, and his eyes were wider than he'd ever seen them, but Rathen saw within them more than incredulity. There was also that same, tiresome conclusion that almost every other mage in Kulokhar had come to, including those who should have known better.

"No," he said wearily, putting it to a quick end, "I am no prodigy. I was just unfortunate enough to have it surface early, that was all. It happens occasionally, and it's exciting at the time, but you quickly suffer for it."

"High expectations?"

"They went beyond 'high'," Rathen replied, his lip curling.

Anthis frowned in thought. "Do you think all these older mages that are popping up could be the same thing? Just a natural phenomenon like yours, but later rather than sooner in life, and a number have just occurred, by coincidence, all at the same time?"

Rathen shrugged as he looked towards Aria, and though she had only moved to the other side of the torch, she didn't appear to be paying any attention to their conversation at all. "I couldn't tell you," he replied, looking back to him, "but when is life that coincidental?"

He nodded slowly in thought, then his musing frown deepened. He edged a little closer to the mage, noting Garon still sat upon the pavilion, and lowered his voice. "What do you make of the attack in Roeden? Truly? Could a mage *really* lose control of their magic?"

"They could."

"H-How?"

His brow creased beneath his black hair, troubled, and he looked down at the notebook he'd tossed aside. He retrieved it and opened the most recent page of futile notes and ideas. "I don't honestly know, but...it has happened before."

Anthis watched him as the page grasped his attention, and he nodded slowly in thought. "I remember there was an incident in Kulokhar when I was younger," he said quietly, glancing towards Aria to make sure she hadn't begun paying attention. "A highly-respected mage killed people in the market. But, the strange thing was, he shouted a warning first, before wrapping himself in some kind of spell and setting upon anyone too slow to get away..."

Rathen nodded. "I am aware of it. I was in Kulokhar at the time."

"Did you know them?"

"Not as well as I thought, it turned out. But if you're asking whether or not I believe his magic went out of control, then yes."

Anthis studied him for a moment. "Does that frighten you?"

Rathen finally pulled his attention away from his notes, and the haunted eyes he turned upon him answered the question themselves. "Yes. It does."

The young man decided not to pursue the matter further as he dragged his eyes away from the lock of his gaze, and Rathen did his best to push away the shadows that had suddenly clouded his mind. "Did, uh, did you find anything else? In there?"

His young face suddenly brightened. "I did, actually! At the very least, I've decided upon a heading."

"Already?" He turned to catch Garon's attention but the inquisitor was already making his way towards them, and Petra shortly from around the side, having certainly noticed him leave.

"Tarun," Anthis declared once they'd all gathered. "As I suspected, that seems to be our best bet."

"What brought you to that conclusion?" Garon asked, though his tone was neutral, searching for facts rather than challenge.

"The mention of a 'place of magic'. I think that the grandest city the elves ever built fits the title nicely, and while I would usually entertain argument that the site of their gifted magic is equally as likely by description, the elves that created the artefact had given up their roots. Such a site would mean nothing to them."

"Then why did they hide this *here?*" Petra asked, confused.

"The elves that hid this here didn't hide the artefact itself, only what they had in regards to it."

"Which included a key."

"Which may not be relevant."

"Anthis," Rathen suddenly warned him, "I promise you that I am coming to understand how much of your work requires making assumptions and asking questions, but your increasingly theoretical attitude isn't particularly helpful."

He laughed nervously. "No, I suppose not. Well, either way, we should make for Tarun in the morning. If we turn around and retrace our steps out of here, we shouldn't encounter anything more than a few more rough nights' sleep. Assuming our luck holds."

"Luck?" Petra scoffed. "Is that what you call this?"

"We'll stay off the roads," Garon said, ignoring her. "We have enough food to last us the road out and we can catch what we cross beyond. It should take three weeks to reach Tarun given the rain in the north, and we should be more than safe by that point to risk a stop in Carenna to resupply."

Petra's ears pricked, but Rathen's brow twisted doubtfully. "I don't think people hearing about what happened in Mokhan is really our greatest concern in a place like that," he sighed dubiously, "but I suppose, if we really have no other choice..." He turned then towards Petra. "What about you?" He asked. "Will you follow us out of here and then take the fork around to Bowden?"

"You forget that I have no money," she reminded them, "and no food. If I can't catch anything in the first few days after I leave you, I'll be in trouble. I'm better off staying with you for the time being and gathering as I go. There's nothing in Bowden that can't wait."

Anthis and Aria shared a small and victorious smile while Garon looked away, grumbling in frustration, and Rathen's suspicious eyes narrowed ever so slightly. But he didn't question her. She was no hindrance to him. "All right."

"For now, we should all get some sleep," Garon suggested, turning back to them while doing an adequate job of suppressing his irritation. "We know what's along the path; the better rested we are, the better time we'll make. And I'll be happy once we're out of this forest and further north." He turned away and started back towards the middle of the pavilion, but this time Rathen followed him, kissing Aria good night and leaving it to Anthis to put her to bed.

"No you don't," he said as he reached the top. "You get some sleep. I'm taking watch tonight."

"Rathen, I'm not--"

"Go," the mage commanded, steering him unceremoniously by the shoulder towards the descending steps. The inquisitor stumbled along the way, and it was not because he was being pushed. "You've not eaten yet, either."

He growled and began, belatedly, to object to his handling, but Rathen only groaned. "Shut up, Garon. I'm not usurping your authority, I'm just giving you some forceful, friendly advice. You're little use to anyone if you're dead on your feet." He gave him an encouraging nod as the officer looked around at him uncertainly, and he shortly sighed in defeat.

"Fine. Just, wake me if--"

"Yes, yes, yes. Good night, Garon."

"Good night, Rathen."

Chapter 23

Malson slammed the report on the cluttered desk top, sending a stack of papers wafting away with the force, and stared Salus fiercely in the eye. "The information your operatives gathered was *false!*" He roared, but Salus did not flinch. "General Moore fortified the north-west as your 'intel' suggested, but Skilan attacked from *dead west*. Not *only* that, but every single one of your people *failed* to pick up on any movement in the *east!* The military cannot have eyes everywhere, *Keliceran*, so it relies on you and your grass roots for exactly this kind of information! And now there are three towns and cities occupied in the east, and another in the west, and we're in no position whatsoever to reclaim them!"

"That intel was *correct*," Salus replied as calmly as he possibly could, his eyes aflame as he held his gaze with equal fury and spoke through barred teeth. "The agents that gathered it have never once made a mistake."

"There's a first time for everything." Malson took a half step back and straightened, his superior air only enraging Salus further. "Regardless," he continued flatly and with a great degree of disapproval, "the Crown wants more operatives out there to help clean this up. The Arana and the Order will be quicker to arrive than the military, so it will be up to the both of you to do what you can while Moore reroutes a division."

Salus's lip tried to curl into a snarl, but he managed to compress it into a twitch. "I'm not happy about having more of the Order involved right now."

"Quite frankly, I'm not inclined to entertain what you are and are not happy about. Just get it done!"

Salus stared at him, biting his tongue so hard he thought blood might bubble from his mouth. "Of course, my lord."

"Good."

And with that, the sour old man turned and left, slamming the door closed behind him.

Salus stared after him, his jaw clenched so tight his teeth hurt. He punched the desk.

War had thundered down on them out of nowhere. Skilan's force had barely even arrived when the attacks and occupations had begun, and a small but persistent voice in his head which just wouldn't shut up wondered if his efforts to scatter the western military hadn't played right into their adversary's hands - or if his focus on the Order's activity hadn't distracted the Arana from this relocation of Skilan's forces.

But that would imply tactics far more clever than they were capable of. No military movements had been seen, and no one within Skilan's ranks or listening from the edges had heard of any such plans.

But they could have had allies; they'd likely forced Kalokh into their service and sent small groups of them through Ivaea and on through the mountains to attack from the east while Doana's back was turned, occupied by their own matters across the sea.

He slammed his knuckles into the desk again, but this time found enough self-control to keep himself from sweeping everything away. It had taken far too long to re-organise everything the last time.

He had to get people out there. The western force was broken; Moore could spare a division, but Malson had been correct in assuming that the Arana could get there quicker. And the Order.

He smiled grimly. Though he had yet to get anything of substance out of the mage in the cells - little more, actually, than close and calculating stares, and Nolan, his top interrogator and head of the breaker division, hadn't personally managed even that - at least they hadn't noticed that one of their mages had been missing for almost two weeks. Which was strange, but Salus was willing to accept it as a blessing. Vastal, it seemed, had heard him this time. It was just a shame that the mage was so determined to stretch that blessing to its limits.

He pushed himself away from his desk and managed a deep, steadying breath, and though that unyielding voice continued to berate him, he found the strength to ignore it and headed purposefully towards the door. There were agents stationed in the east, one even in now-occupied Bowden, and it was imperative that they be given their new orders. He needed to find out just exactly what had happened, and who was responsible.

He covered the corridor, engrossed in thought, and descended the three staircases to the estate's modest foyer, respectfully disregarded by all as he went. Upon reaching the foot of the final and grandest, he swung around and behind it to a small hatch concealed in the floor. It was old and stiff, and took a slight jerk to open to reach the ladder beneath. He followed it down, dropping the hatch back in place above him, then started along a short corridor lit fully by just one torch, until he reached the single heavy, wooden door.

He knocked, and after a few shuffling steps on the other side, it opened onto an old man. He didn't look at Salus directly, having recognised the impatient pattern of his rap, though Salus was sure he knocked no differently to anyone else, and stepped aside to let him in.

"Didn't expect to see you down here, Keliceran," he mummed as Salus slipped through the fine mosquito netting draped just behind the door and into the small, cramped room. Like the corridor, it took only two torches and the occasional daylight that might creep inside to light it, though the high and meagre window was more suited to a prison cell than a workspace. Stranger still were the abundance of fine mesh cages; some stood along the ground, others hung from the stone ceiling, but all were filled with large, fluttering insects, and the smell of ink, parchment and rotten fruit permeated the air. But as cold and unpleasant as the old cellar seemed, the old man was quite happy down here. He had to be, to have been the master lepidopterist for the past twenty years.

"Can I get you a cup of tea?"

"No, thank you, Tom," Salus replied, a small and curious smile touching his lips as it always did at the old man's ability to remain both respectful and familiar at the same time. It came with age, he'd decided, and he'd also noticed that he liked it.

"I just have orders to issue."

"And you're wondering if anything has come in that I haven't passed on." He shook his balding head as he stooped over one long cage that stretched the length of the room, opened the lid and set a plateful of fruit inside it. The fist-sized moths swept towards it immediately. "I always pass on everything as it comes in, Keliceran, you know that."

"I know you do," he replied, "and I thank you."

"Mhm." Tom gestured towards the small, cluttered desk in the far corner. "Everything is in its usual place."

Salus reached it in three steps, and as he leaned over the desk he felt, not for the first time, like a giant. Every sheet of paper was no wider than half an inch and no longer than two, and the quill and inkwell set within reach were also peculiarly small. He'd often wondered if Tom hadn't chosen them as a joke when he'd taken the position, but the quill tip was extremely fine and quite necessary for such small script. Still, he would have found it all amusing had he not been so tired and frustrated.

He found a grip on the half-sized quill and began noting out his orders while the old man muttered behind him to his moths.

Salus shook his head to himself. His day simply couldn't get worse.

Skilan had attacked in the early hours; they'd taken the three most strategic locations in the east and one in the west while their inhabitants were still asleep in their beds, and Turunda was only just beginning to scramble to try to do something about it. He'd received word himself before sunrise, but it had not been obtained primarily by his own people. Instead they'd gained the intel by following a messenger sent to the Crown from the invaded region itself, and that fact had only agitated him, as though there was already a substantial weak link in his supposedly solid chain.

But they had attacked from the east! The *east!* Their eyes - the eyes of *every* authoritative body - had been turned towards the west, and they'd come up from behind them! *And his people should have seen it.*

His teeth grated. It was his accursed fault. He'd underestimated Skilan, he'd assumed they were too bold and arrogant to ally with anyone, and that they would be too fatigued for anything more than simply charging straight in themselves, fuelled only by their recent winnings. Because of that, he had focused the Arana's resources on the Turunda-Skilan border, completely ignoring that of Ivaea and Doana because they were far from present threats. And he'd been watching the Order.

No, that was a decision he stood by. Even now. In fact he'd been in the cell with his captive mage when Malson had summoned him for an ear-bashing, and before that he'd been frantically juggling his people around, trying to balance reassignments in order to regain solid footing without sacrificing too much. And he had managed - just. But it meant he would be blind to a handful of matters for a few days while those reassignments fell into place, and though he deeply resented it, that included the activities of Karth and his mage friend. Elran's skills were needed elsewhere - but another, equally capable operative would be sent to shadow them in his place.

And of course the elven relic was yet another headache. Drassa had been contacting collectors for a week and a half now and, by Salus's reckoning, was getting nowhere. He'd had no word from him since he'd begun, not even a whisper of uncertainty or of false hope, and now that chaos was already beginning to spread through the city and beyond by war's arrival, everything would be that much harder. People would close themselves off, shut their doors, stop socialising, and that would impact Drassa's pursuit - and with the Arana's resources so thinly stretched, their own search for the artefact, as fruitless as it had been, would have to come to an end. He would be putting all of his faith in one man.

One man who was not bound to the Arana. One who didn't even know it existed.

Which was as it should be, of course, but he had little trust for anyone outside of his ranks and less, even, for Tem Drassa in particular. Karth's consistent movements concerned him. Why was Drassa carrying out his research in his living room while Karth was running around in the Wildlands?

Salus dipped into the inkwell with little care, and growled sharply as he flicked little black spots onto the next tiny scroll. His hands were shaking, and his eyes stung in the weak light. When had he last slept? Two nights ago? Three?

He pushed the ruined parchment aside and took up a new strip. It didn't matter. He was thinking straight enough; he didn't need to waste time sleeping. He couldn't afford to, not now everything had come crashing down around him. He had to fix this damned mistake - *his* damned mistake - immediately.

He needed to locate all of Skilan's forces, pick them off and block the stragglers who had yet to find their way into Turunda. He had to identify their allies, keep tabs on them, work out their precise intentions and find out what indentured them to Skilan and break it, because it certainly wouldn't be loyalty. He needed to find out how Skilan had managed to attack from due-west while still appearing to be to the north, because magic alone surely couldn't conceal or suggest such movement, and find out how his own people hadn't caught on. He also needed to uncover just how much of it *was* magic and why none of Turunda's mages had noticed it, the Arana's own included.

Or, rather, his *operatives* needed to. *He* was stuck behind his damned desk.

Lately he felt like a guard dog chained to a stake in the garden, unable to use the powerful legs or long, sharp teeth he'd been chosen for, and so barked wildly instead at anything he thought might have been a threat whether it was a churl or a chimney sweep, because there was nothing he could do about any of it himself.

And it would all take time - something that seemed to be slipping through his fingers faster and faster each day. Nothing would happen soon enough; in the time it took to address the present problems, more would have cropped up in their place. He couldn't just simply *remove* the invaders, block the borders, build a wall a mile high all the way around the country.

But how easy his job would be if he could make even just *one* of those oh so simple ideas a reality. If he could just transport the villains away in the blink of an eye, raise walls or raise the ground - move the country *itself* away and out of danger for good.

Magic could do it. Some of it, at least, he was sure... So why hadn't the Order already done so? Why had no such order ever been given? Had it truly never occurred to anyone?

No, surely, *surely* the idea had come to someone, but it had been shut down or locked away. But why? So the mages could do precisely this? Allow chaos and then take advantage of it for their own means?

Salus felt his heart race and the quill began to jitter in his hand. He set it down and leaned upon the desk as sweat trickled down his temple.

Why would his mind tease him like this? Conjure such childish ideas and hang them in front of him like a carrot on a stick? Was it *trying* to work against him? Even in his dreams, his mind, his imagination, continued to taunt him, creating a sanctuary he was eternally doomed to be torn away from, one in which he could never remain.

He could swear he felt his mind begin to unravel. Perhaps he needed rest...

No. He was fine. He could manage. He didn't need sleep. He didn't *want* sleep.

Another idea sprung to mind, and this one he didn't entertain with any consideration. He lifted his quill, took another scroll and immediately began writing. His lettering was steadier than before, and his mind had fallen quiet, satisfied with this spontaneous decision, and once he was done he was able to write out the remaining orders on other lengths of parchment without distraction. He dusted and dried the ink, rolled them tightly and tied them off in fine, leather thread. He turned towards the old man and announced his completion.

Tom said nothing, merely grunting in response, and turned to the nearest cage to coax out a number of large moths, all of which obediently fluttered out and landed along the length of his arm. Then, with a delicacy that belied his frail and shaking hands, he affixed the scrolls to their flossy thoraxes one by one as he muttered to each their recipients, though not in any tongue Salus recognised.

When the last moth danced away, out through the small, high window, apparently unhindered by the additional weight, Tom gave Salus a single, final nod and returned to tending his swarm, leaving the Keliceran to see himself out.

Half an hour later Salus sat again behind his infernal desk, drumming his fingers and penetrating the wall with a wide-eyed stare, ignoring the urgent papers stacked on either side of him. He felt irritated, frustrated, desperate, helpless - but above all else at that moment, nervous.

What had he been *thinking*, summoning her like that? He'd acted on impulse, sparing no thought nor sense, and though she'd been working within the city anyway, her work was not unimportant. *None* of the Arana's work was unimportant.

...But...hers *could* wait. She was far from the only pair of eyes and ears he had working in Kulokhar. The capital city could never be left to just two or three.

But...*what had he been thinking?!*

A knock came at his door, shattering the silence and jolting him out of his fretting. He stared at it for a moment, his heart skipping a beat, then swallowed it down and called for her to enter in as calm a voice as he could muster. Taliel stepped in readily, dressed in plain, civilian clothes, and closed the door quietly behind her before standing as rigidly in the centre as usual, her eyes fixed on the wall behind him. She seemed in a bad mood - closed off. Or perhaps it was just formality...

Of course it was formality. She was expecting orders directly from the Keliceran himself.

Realising his whole body had turned rigid at her arrival, he forced himself to relax in the additional hope that she might also ease. But, no, she didn't. She was a model subordinate. She wouldn't react to any atmosphere in the Keliceran's presence.

It took him a moment to realise he hadn't said anything yet.

"I'm sorry," the words tumbled out, "I...don't know why I summoned you..."

The slightest flicker of a frown passed over her brow, but it was so fleeting he may have imagined it. "It's all right, Keliceran," she said, of course, with no hint of inconvenience, "I'll return to the trade district."

"Very good." But he felt a wave of disappointment the moment she turned away. "Wait."

What was he doing?

She stopped and turned back, frowning again, though this time it was a little more persistent. "Keliceran?"

He blinked in his own confusion, then, slowly, his shoulders sagged in defeat. He leaned back in his chair and stared thoughtfully at the desk, only to find his mind had vacated him, and when he glanced back up in search of a clue, their eyes locked. His heart jumped as hers flicked away.

"Forgive me."

"No," he frowned, "no, it's all right..."

"Is there something wrong, sir?"

"Well nothing's *right*," he replied drily, but she didn't look back at him.

"What can I do?"

He blinked. "What do you mean?"

"You summoned me, sir," she reminded him carefully, finding the fine line between formality and insubordination, "for one reason or another, which suggests that there's something I can do, even if you've yet to decide what it is."

He nodded slowly, thoughtfully, and sighed in defeat once again. "I suppose...I'd like to talk."

"Talk, sir?"

"Salus."

"Pardon?"

"Never mind." He gestured to the chair on the other side of the desk. "Please, sit down, Taliel - and drop the formalities, if you could. For now...for the moment, I..."

"You need to talk to another person, not a subordinate."

He looked at her in surprise.

"Forgive me once again, Keliceran, but would Teagan not be a preferable choice?"

"He isn't here at the moment, but I'm not sure he would be very helpful anyway..."

"Because he is portian. I understand." Finally, she took the seat, and though she turned her eyes heavily upon him, sending his chest fluttering again, it clearly took her a great deal of effort. She seemed only increasingly uneasy.

"This was a bad idea," he said, suddenly rising from his chair as he fought the returning disappointment that tried to pull his lips downwards.

"You look tired."

He hesitated at the statement, and when he looked back at her he noticed immediately that, though something within her was clearly telling her to break her stare, she didn't. She held his gaze, fighting against all she'd been taught, for his personal sake. He lowered himself back down. "...I suppose I am."

"Are you not resting well?"

"...No, I suppose I'm not." He frowned. "No, I'm definitely not."

"You have a lot on your shoulders," she told him lightly, though not without consideration. "Anyone else would react the same way in your position - or worse."

"Perhaps."

"If it's not too bold, when did you last take a moment for yourself?"

He thought for a moment. It wasn't so much a question of recalling the last time, but rather the first.

She smiled, slightly. "Perhaps a walk through the forest would help to settle your mind. It's helped me in the past."

"Really?"

She nodded.

"Mm...perhaps that isn't such a bad idea..."

She studied him for a moment, and he suddenly felt too uncomfortable beneath her gaze to notice how nervous she was with the action, but something still encouraged her to persist. "It's more than just the war, isn't it?"

He hesitated again.

"I'm sorry," she said quickly, finally looking away, and though he breathed a little easier, he felt something in him lurch at the idea that she'd given up. "That was a bold assumption of me, forgive me."

"I've been having strange dreams."

She looked back at him in astonishment for the statement he'd all but blurted out. "Strange dreams?"

He nodded. "There's...a place I've dreamt of a few times now. A forest, with animals, blue sky, thick trees. But it's somewhere I've never been - somewhere I don't think could ever exist. But it's so...so *normal* at first glance, like it really could stand somewhere within our own borders, but I *know* that it doesn't...and the feeling I get when I'm there...it's so..." he groped for the words. "The place is more than peaceful, more than beautiful. More, somehow, than *perfect*."

"You dreamt it," she replied. "A refuge your own mind created, probably as a ward against your stress. It's likely a sense of belonging and absolute safety that you feel."

"Yes..." his brow creased thoughtfully. "Perhaps that's it...that could well be it..." He looked across at her. "Have you ever experienced a dream like that?"

She took a slow, steady breath. "A few times in the past," she confessed, "when I was young and struggling with things." Her cheeks suddenly flashed red in shame. "It has never affected my work, though, I assure you, Keliceran."

"I know it hasn't," he smiled. "There's no mark on your record."

"But why do you believe these dreams of yours are strange?"

He found himself suddenly reluctant to respond - not so much to enlighten her, but rather to acknowledge the reasons - but as he looked back at Taliel, who watched him patiently from the other side of his desk, her brown eyes focused yet gentle, it suddenly seemed a very small matter.

"I used to wake from the dreams feeling calm, refreshed, focused," he replied slowly, "and it would last for most of the day. I would go to bed wishing for those dreams, and every night that they came I would wish for them even more the next. But about three weeks ago, something changed. I would wake up feeling calm, but as the day dragged on I'd become distracted and frustrated, just...*enduring* the time until I could go to bed again. And I feel this...longing for something, something I can't work out, but I know it isn't for sleep or for the dreams, and now..."

She continued to watch him patiently.

"Now I find myself..."

"Afraid."

"Of course not!" He snapped.

Her cheeks flushed red. "Forgive me," she said quickly, "I do not mean to suggest that you fear sleep, of course, only that you have an anxiety towards to it, and that, perhaps, you have been avoiding it..."

"And how would you know I've been avoiding it?" He demanded.

"I don't, of course, but your office light is on into the smallest hours while those of your home haven't been seen for days."

His harsh blue eyes hardened further and something within him changed - or something dislodged suddenly fell back into place. He sat taller, an air of authority enshrouding him, and all of his patience and humour vanished as though it had never been.

Taliel noticed, but rather than shrink beneath his stern gaze, she turned her eyes away and re-assumed her position as a subordinate. She took the transition quite easily - almost gratefully - and rose from the chair.

The crevice of rank and authority sprawled between them once again.

"Permission to leave, Keliceran?"

"Dismissed."

She obliged immediately, and he watched her leave.

A now familiar wave of defeat washed over him as the door's latch fell back into place, followed by an abrupt strike of regret.

...What had he been thinking?

Chapter 24

The air hummed with energy, as if spirits beyond the black-blue clouds were poised to release a volley of thunderbolts and were merely waiting for the most devastating moment to do so. They were already deploying an assault of needle-sharp rain across miles, and after two days of the relentless deluge, it appeared that their supply was inexhaustible.

Moods were grim as the group moved sluggishly through the dark and early morning - all but Rathen, however, who found himself quiet and ponderous, strangely relaxed even in the downpour and despite a non-existent breakfast. His stomach duly rumbled, but he only half-noticed. It had been protesting for days.

For the past three, they'd been running on fumes. Garon's route - the one he'd claimed they had enough food to see them through, even if Petra remained with them - had taken them through barren land with little to no prey to catch, and it hadn't earned him any friends. They'd rationed drastically, and when their bags had finally come up empty and animals began dotting the fields, they were moving through small farmlands. A detail that seemed to have escaped Garon's planning. In the end, Petra had convinced him that they had little choice but to take one of the beasts, and though they left compensation on the farmer's doorstep, it had left a bad taste in Rathen's mouth.

The city ahead of them would at least end their hunger, but he felt another anxiety begin to creep in to fill the space that solution left behind - one that increased as Carenna's unsavoury skyline finally loomed into limited view through the early afternoon rain, and it crushed the final remnants of his curiously tranquil dreams to dust.

The others shared his unease, albeit for different reasons, but while Anthis seemed worse than the others - short, irritable, distracted and generally bitter - Petra appeared almost completely unconcerned. She continued a few hankering steps ahead of them before she noticed that Garon had drawn the others to a stop just out of view of the main road, and she returned to them with visibly restrained impatience.

"It's been just over a month since Mokhan," the inquisitor announced, ignoring the humourless glares he received, as well as the strained atmosphere that had been growing steadily over the group for the past two and a half weeks. "It's old news by now, so it shouldn't cause us any trouble in the city, but we still shouldn't chance drawing attention to ourselves - you least of all, Rathen. The rain will help to mask our arrival - the streets will be quieter and no one will bat an eyelid at people wearing hoods - but we still ought to avoid the front gates. We--"

"Then we should use the *west* gates."

Garon gave Petra a flat, disapproving and unappreciative stare. "That is the red-lantern district."

"Yes, Garon, I am well aware of that," she replied curtly, "which means that the guards there are distracted. They'll pretty much ignore a handful of travellers, and we'll draw less attention than if we try to enter without using any gates at all."

Rathen nodded reluctantly in agreement. "She has a point, but I can't say I'm happy about it..."

"Just cover Aria's eyes," Anthis snapped, and as Rathen sent him far from the first scowl, the suddenly petulant young man started towards the road without waiting for the others, glower up at the sharp rain.

They stared after him, wondering at his increasingly prickly attitude, but Petra was the quickest to shake it off and follow along behind, even overtaking him as her hold over her apparent urgency was released. Rathen's thoughtful frown shifted onto her instead. She'd been keen to keep moving even after they'd left the reach of the Wildlands, the journey out of which had been welcomingly quick and uneventful, and he'd yet to work out why. But when his empty stomach lurched and a wave of nausea followed it, he abandoned thought in favour of simply putting one foot in front of the other, and suppressed his climbing anxiety.

They trudged through the rain as Garon tried to maintain the lead over Petra, and avoided joining the slick road that rolled straight towards the city, keeping to the shadows of the trees instead.

The height of the old walls were all the rain would allow them to see, but as they drew ever nearer and skirted around towards its western side, the tallest roofs began to poke out from above it, and one wide silhouette soon dominated the city from its centre. It could only be the Crucible. Carenna was a city of rough society - thugs, thieves, gamblers and very much more - but its ancient arena was a magnet to combatants who sought to prove themselves as both clever and capable warriors. Considering that fact, it was no wonder Petra was so eager to reach it...

Rathen, however, only felt his disquiet rise as they left the concealment of the trees, and he bitterly realised that his month-long association (though it felt twice that) with these three people had done nothing to assuage his fears of public areas. And the nature of this city only worsened the hammering of his heart.

Aria squeezed his hand as they followed the far less orderly road towards the western gate, just as she had upon entering each settlement past. He smiled down at her gratefully and tried to appear reassuring, then took a deep breath to steady his own nerves.

He instantly regretted it. A sickening mixture of burning scents hung in the air as they neared the side entrance. Some were perfumes, others incense, and while they'd perhaps have been pleasant individually and in far smaller doses, together they threatened to turn his stomach inside out. Fortunately it was so empty that nothing would have come of it, but it certainly exacerbated his headache.

What the western gate lacked in size and impact, wide enough only for one small wagon while the main could have easily handled three abreast, it made up for in activity. There were more people here than any of them had expected for such narrow streets, but while some wore the rich and elegant cloaks of the upper class and others what seemed little more than tattered blankets, every one of them carried the same shifty, furtive eyes.

And the noise! It was deafening - at least by Rathen's standards. Above the immense din of the rain, there was a cacophony of laughter, shouting, jeering and other such debauched sounds, and the confusion almost overwhelmed his spinning head. Aria squeezed his hand now for her own sake, suffering in much the same way.

Steeling themselves, they walked two abreast through the small gate, moving cautiously while trying to seem at ease, and though the guards did indeed not hassle them, Rathen felt scrutinised even under their half-attentive gaze. Then, not two steps into the city, they were engulfed by bodies.

Scraggly children with starved expressions brushed close by them, managing to keep one sharp eye glued to the guards and the other on everyone else's coin pouches all while still looking hopelessly desperate; good-humoured and over-friendly men called out from the edges of the street to lure travellers, including themselves, into their shops to 'sample' their goods and no doubt pressure a purchase; women, scarcely clothed even in the rain, whispered seductively to any who passed or simply reached languidly out towards them, and every one of them seemed either too weary to notice that Petra was a woman, or were simply unconcerned by it.

Rathen pulled Aria close alongside him.

"Daddy, you're hurting my hand."

"You'll live."

They made their way through the district as quickly as possible, and breathed a collective sigh of relief when they finally stepped out onto broader streets and the assault on their senses waned.

But despite the nature of their welcome and the city's reputation, they didn't stay together.

Anthis was the first to leave, continuing off into the city as the others slowed to a stop without so much as a 'see you later,' let alone an explanation. They stared after him, but none could say they were too sorry to see him go.

Petra was the next, but she at least paid them the courtesy of stating hurriedly that she had something to see to, even if it was vague, and she then turned and walked away with that same purpose in her step, leaving only Garon, Rathen and Aria together.

"Are they coming back?" Aria asked, looking up at them both hopefully.

"Anthis had better be," Garon replied as he watched the historian turn down a nearby street, rummaging feverishly through his bag as he went, then he turned towards the two who remained. "This wouldn't usually be the best place to split up, but given recent events, it might not be a bad idea."

Rathen hesitated.

"But not the three of *us*," Garon clarified, and the mage's doubt faded. The inquisitor looked around at the city, busy despite the weather. "We'll get the supplies, and there's someone I'd like to talk to while we're here."

"Who?"

"A contact. There are a few things I want to check up on. We've been out of touch with the world for a while."

"What a shame."

Garon gave him a flat look then turned and started through the city, leaving the mage and the child to follow obediently behind him.

*

The variety of food available in the market was almost overwhelming, and Aria, led by the growling of her stomach, wanted absolutely everything she saw. Fortunately she was not the one with command over the purse strings, but one wistful old shop keeper was so taken by her smile and enthusiasm that she allowed her a small sweet-bread bun on the condition that she would never lose the sparkle in her eyes.

Once they'd procured the food - and Rathen had silently decided that it *was* enough to see them to Tarun - they moved deeper into the city in search of Garon's contact, leaving not only the bright colours and deceptively pleasant smells of food shops and stalls behind them, but much of the malignant atmosphere.

As they moved towards its heart, Carenna quickly began to change. The roads narrowed, the buildings that lined them were no longer of brick but of chiselled stone, they became more round than square, and at the centre of it all, looming above them even while standing several streets away, was the Crucible itself.

Aria was bowled over by its sheer size and its crown of crumbling peaks. She stared up at its curved and ancient walls, and peered down the length of alleyways to get a clearer view of it whenever the opportunity rose. But she didn't voice her awe, nor her thousands of precise and unanswerable questions. She knew her father was in no mood to entertain them, and she doubted Garon was about to break his habit of all but ignoring her. He had yet to respond to her in any kind of friendly way - though that hadn't stopped her from trying.

But she spared her father a glance anyway, hoping he was enjoying the sight at least a little, but instead found exactly what she'd expected: his head slightly bowed in his hood, his shoulders pulled back tightly, and his sharp eyes darting around to note each individual and every divergence of the roads. Her lips pulled downwards. There was nothing she could say or do that would help, and he seemed worse in this city than he had been in any other.

But she squeezed his hand anyway, tugging his attention towards her, and gave him her best, most reassuring smile. "It will be okay."

He nodded and smiled in return, but, as she'd expected, it was fleeting, and he quickly returned to his rigid and watchful tension.

The city's tone gradually improved to offer some vague idea of safety as they continued through the archaic district. Carenna had grown and sprawled out from around these carven buildings in far more recent centuries, and though its seed was undeniably elven, whether it was pre-magic or short post-magic, they really couldn't know. Even had Anthis been with them he probably wouldn't have been interested in discussing it given his recent turn, and no one would have been inclined to ask. But its lack of ostentatious elegance at least made it clear that it was old even by elven standards, and for that, Aria found herself only further enchanted.

Rathen's anxiety, however, rose with every passing moment despite the air's improvement. He tried to predict where they would be stopping, searching almost desperately as they walked for any kind of authoritative establishment, and he felt he might explode with apprehension as the roads began to widen and fill with people once again. But he followed in silence, biting his tongue, suppressing the leaps of his heart to focus instead on breathing while berating himself for being so foolish - though he wasn't sure if the voice in his head was chastising him for being afraid, or for having left the scowles in the first place.

Finally, Garon brought them to a stop beside another aged building, and Rathen felt a desperate touch of relief at their arrival. But he had little chance to enjoy it. Confusion tumbled in as he noticed that the glass in its elegant, iron-wrought window panes was fogged and clouded, and the scent of damp and rose petals tickled his nose. He frowned up at the elven building, and the crease only deepened as he spotted the comical basin-shaped sign that hung above the door. This was no authoritative establishment.

"A bath house?" He asked sceptically as Garon continued ahead and opened the door. "Your contact is *here?*"

"And you're welcome to take full advantage of the fact," he replied drily. "Otherwise, don't stray."

The heat was the first to hit them, engulfing them before they'd even stepped inside, and the smell was dragged close behind it, damp overpowered by floral fragrances that concentrated in the muggy warmth. Next was the light, but not for its weakness. Even as the door closed behind them, it was far brighter than Rathen had expected. The elves had positioned their windows precisely, making the most of daylight whatever time it might be, and the few burning torches seemed to serve primarily as ambience, casting soft shadows over the delicately carved screens that shuttered the entrance from the old baths beyond.

A middle-aged woman approached as a bell tinkled their arrival, and after a brief exchange, she stepped aside and graciously welcomed them in. Rathen felt her sharp, business gaze turn curious as they passed, but as they stepped behind the screens and out of her lingering sight, he suddenly didn't know quite where to turn his *own* eyes, though he was quick to cover Aria's.

Garon, however, spared little attention to the very naked bathers that occupied the three expansive baths. Instead he scanned purposefully across the humid hall until he spotted one of the towel girls. "You two wait here," he told them firmly, and started away without waiting for response to tread carefully across the wet stone that ran between the lengths of the baths.

Rathen sighed in frustration at his usual abruptness, then glanced around himself, discovered a private seating area nearby, and quickly ushered Aria inside it.

He dropped heavily into one of the chairs and pulled loose his already sticky shirt as Aria clambered up into the seat beside him. She peered discreetly through the shutters until her cheeks flushed red, then spun quickly back around. She turned incredulously bewildered eyes upon him. "Why are they...?" She didn't seem to have the words to finish her sharply whispered question.

Rathen managed a smile. "Well *you* don't have a bath with your clothes on, do you?"

"No - I also don't have a bath with everyone in the forest!" Her eyes widened slowly in realisation. "Is this what people do in cities?"

"Sometimes." He grinned as he watched her confusion deepen. She remained beside him with her gaze fixed firmly on a plant pot after that.

Rathen did his best to settle, allowing the smothering warmth of the bath house to ease his senses. But it could only do so much against a mind so knotted. His attention latched spitefully onto every detail behind him: the splash of water followed by sighs of relaxation, the hiss of fires as they were stoked in steam rooms, and he had to fight his neck not to twist at every playful giggle or delicate patter of footsteps. The calming bath house was doing him little good at all.

Defeated, he sat forwards in the chair to stop his knee from jittering, covered his eyes with the heels of his hands and attempted to draw in his mind. Slowly, finally, peace began to edge in, and soon he was able to ignore the approaching footsteps more easily, as well as the voice that whispered as they stopped on the other side of the screen.

"It's a long way to Toakh," a young woman said quietly as his shoulders finally began to loosen and he found some kind of appreciation for the warmth. "When did you say she left?"

"Two weeks ago," another replied.

"Ohh, then she'll be *fine*. She won't have even arrived yet."

"I'm not worried she'll be trapped in the city," the second replied, and Rathen frowned slightly at the desperate touch to her tone, though he tried to ignore it, "I'm worried she'll have been killed along the way!" She sighed mournfully. "How did this ever happen?"

"Because the military got duped," a third said cynically.

Rathen lowered his hands from his face as one of the women hushed her.

"They did!" She continued. "Skilan are smarter than we've been led to believe."

"Quiet, Ness, you're not helping!"

"I'm just being realistic. They knew we'd think they would come in from the west, so they made a show of it while sending small groups to the *east*. While our boys were moving one way, they were sneaking along through the shadows in the other. There was no one there to protect Toakh, Bowden *or* Ferna, they just walked right in and took over."

"But," the first added hurriedly, "Elaina will be *fine*. She wasn't travelling alone, and for them to have moved unnoticed like that, it can't have been a big force. She's not likely to run into them, especially not on the roads."

"Big force or not, they were *smart*. Apparently only a few are guarding--"

"Mages are going in to fix it."

"Like they're *really* going to help." Rathen could hear the woman's sneer in her voice. "Either way, most of the soldiers who took over have vanished. I reckon they've been concealed by magic and are moving deeper into the country."

"Ness!"

"*What I'm saying*, if you'd stop interrupting me, is that none of those three were their *real* targets, which means they have other intentions, and whatever they are, I doubt they'd risk drawing attention to themselves by attacking travellers. Elaina *will* be fine."

A thoughtful silence hung for a moment before the most concerned among them spoke. "You have a very odd way of comforting people."

Rathen stopped listening as Ness was scolded again.

War had arrived, and they'd almost walked right into it. In fact, had they not stumbled upon the ruin in the Wildlands, they would have reached Bowden just a few days ago. When had it happened? And with Turunda's resources, *how?*

He'd felt the tension in the city as soon as they'd arrived but he'd been too preoccupied to consciously notice it, and even had he, he'd probably have dismissed it and put it down to the city's nature or the weather. But in hindsight, the atmosphere could have been cut with a knife - even in the bath house there was a certain suspense. And there had been no sign of any soldiers on the streets, either. Only guards, and despite the thread of corruption that ran through Carenna's force, they seemed more alert than usual, more keen-eyed and thoughtful.

Rathen's frown deepened in growing concern. The military wasn't to blame, he knew that well enough. Evidently the Arana had been distracted - though he quickly turned his mind away from wondering at what could have been holding their attention. Those were troublesome thoughts he was neither trained nor inclined to entertain.

Suffice it to say that it was surely important.

But, that point aside, this *was* smarter than Skilan ought to be... What were they doing?

He had little time to ponder it. Garon appeared at the edge of the seating area, his expression just as troubled as Rathen's. The mage leaned back in his seat. "I guess your uneasy feeling in the east was justified."

Anthis clutched the parchment beneath the folds of his cloak, concealed from the rain and any prying eyes that might take too much of an interest. He needn't have carried it at all, in truth; he knew its contents well enough, but his apprehension enforced a hampering need for precision. And at least his grip gave him somewhere to channel his anticipation rather than trip himself up over it.

He scanned across the masses through the dim, cloud-choked light, looking from one face to the next, his eyes quick but attentive from within the depths of his hood. He recognised no one, but that didn't matter. These searches were rarely so easy.

He followed the winding roads, the tall, narrow alleys offering momentary relief from the falling rain and the sludge the unkempt district's filth had churned in to. No one paid him any attention as he passed, as he looked just as shifty in his cloak as anyone else around him, and that alone kept him safe. No one knew who he was, nor his intentions, so no one risked attacking him.

Not that his safety was a present concern.

He turned onto a busier road lined with even more watchful caitiffs, and he absorbed their details even as his eyes flicked fervently from face to face. He swallowed hard, forcing his growing anticipation into submission, and tightened his fists as his hands twitched towards his blades. It was too soon, too obvious.

But he was so close.

Impatience threatened to overtake him. The third and final crystal set in the hilt of his dagger had turned jet-black days ago, and he could feel its corruption pumping through his body. He felt sick, shaky and distracted, and he could do nothing to hide his irritability from the others. He woke in sweats throughout the night, he felt watched throughout the day, and there were a thousand voices second-, third- and fourth-guessing everything he did. He suffered waves of energy that only fuelled his restiveness and what he hoped was paranoia, and bouts of fatigue when all he wished to do was sleep or weep. It felt as if an inescapable shadow of himself clung to his back and judged his every action, criticising everything, telling him he was doing everything wrong, and yet offered no suggestions.

Perhaps this was what it felt like to go insane.

There was only one way to stop it.

Rather than slow him, his desperation now focused his mind. He was close. He could feel it. A few more minutes and everything would be all right.

He turned down a south-eastern alley and forced his feet to keep their even pace. He couldn't afford to run, to draw attention to himself. Not now.

The path forked and he took the left. He was close to the western gate; he'd moved in a wide circle, but she was also on the move. And it was raining; it was easy to remain hidden in plain sight with weather like this, so of course she would take advantage of it. But while it worked to her advantage, allowing her to pass unnoticed even mere feet away from guards, it worked to his, too.

She flashed into sight. He was sure it was her. He hadn't seen her face yet, but she moved like the others did: lightly, quickly, and with the shadow of suspicion. But she didn't know he was there. She'd be moving quicker if she did, feeling his pursuit. This was simply a guilty conscience nipping at her heels. Something she was surely used to.

The cloaked figure turned down another alley and he let himself drop behind. There was no need to hurry. He wouldn't lose her now. Her presence stood out like a beacon, so valuable she was, and he tracked her easily through the shadowed lanes. He glimpsed her face twice in that time; young and beautiful, if also a bit plain. She had the look of someone to be trusted, someone to confide in. Essential for a nurse, really, and it was almost a shame that she matched the bounty. But what would anyone see in a serial infanticidal lunatic?

The passes were growing emptier now. Darker in the shadows of the taller buildings and deepening clouds. The rain hammered all around him, the clamour of thundering raindrops intensified by the acoustics. But he couldn't do it there, not in an alley. It was too easy to be spotted, and evidence would be found too quickly.

Vokaad must have heard his silent pleas. The nurse paused and Anthis ducked behind a wall. She hadn't spotted him. She stepped instead into a small alcove, the door of an old, dishevelled house. It was empty, he could tell that much already.

It was perfect; well within his comfort zone.

He counted ten breaths after he heard the latch fall back into place, then followed along, keeping close to the deepest shadows. The door was unlocked - she was that confident. It would have sickened him had he not been so focused. Instead he pushed it open slowly, carefully, just far enough that he could slip in while avoiding the creak he'd noted when she'd opened it herself, and stepped inside with feather-light footsteps. Now, at last, he allowed his hand to reach for the plainer of his two blades.

Petra fought the urge to take a deep breath. The air was sooty in this district, pumped out by the blacksmiths' forges, and the heat was almost stifling. Rain hissed as it struck the fires, and clouds of steam were belched out as red-hot metal was plunged into troughs, making pockets of the street stiflingly worse. How the smiths could handle it day in, day out, even in the thick of summer, she had never been able to comprehend.

But despite the discomfort of the heat and the darkness that crept up in her heart, she couldn't help the smile that tugged her lips. She hadn't been in Carenna for...could it really have been a year? She found it surprisingly good to be back. Despite everything, this was her home, even if her most dominant memory of it bitterly consumed her entire being to that very day.

"Petra?!"

Well...perhaps there was a smidgen more lingering just behind that memory, but that detail only contributed to a spot in her heart that she'd shut away years ago.

And yet she looked up and ahead to the most familiar of the forges and found the man of early thirties operating it. His hair was darker than she remembered, though his angular, grinning face was just as blackened by soot as it should have been, and she smiled in spite of herself.

"Egan!" Her feet rushed across the street before she could stop them, artfully dodging around the buyers who were out despite the weather, and stopped at the edge of the young blacksmith's stall as he headed around to meet her. The next moment was pleasantly awkward. She wanted to reach out to him as he stopped in front of her, and she could see he wished to embrace her the same, but all either of them did was smile.

But Egan's smile, charming as usual, and a touch giddily absent, soon faltered. "What are you doing here?" He asked urgently, his eyes flashing in panic as he tugged her back behind his stall and towards the forge, out of public earshot. "I've heard rumours - tell me they're not true."

"They're not true," she sighed, "and I'd hoped *you* of all people wouldn't believe them."

"I didn't," he assured her quietly, "and no one else does either, thanks in part to my *own* efforts to quell them - but where did they come from? They say you aided the Order's attack in Mokhan!"

"*No one attacked* Mokhan, the stupid old towers just collapsed," she explained wearily, already sweating from the heat of the flames. "They were rickety and unkempt, it was only a matter of time. And a mage *was* involved, but *only* as far as trying to protect everyone who came running to gawk at it. I got involved because everyone else was about ready to kill him, and that same mage had helped *me* in Edam. I was just returning the favour."

Egan's dark eyebrows drew together. "He helped you? Why?"

"Sore loser. The usual story."

He nodded slowly as his brown eyes passed over her, and she suddenly felt heat rise in her face. He looked away a moment later, feeling similarly inhibited, and turned his attention back to his work. For appearances, of course, though whether for her benefit or the rest of the city's, she couldn't tell. She felt her smile return, but it didn't linger.

"Has Celise suffered for it?" She asked softly, finally acknowledging the only concern she'd carried away from the event, but he looked back up at her with unreadable eyes.

"No," he replied after a moment, to her relief, "not that I'm aware - but things aren't exactly easy for mages at the moment, and for *precisely* this kind of thing." He shook his head and sighed gruffly. "How did you ever get wrapped up in this?"

"Because it was the right thing to do. ...But, thank you for dissuading the rumours."

"Like I'm really going to let people speak badly of you."

She smiled gratefully, and it broadened in amusement as he seemed suddenly unwilling to look at her. It was silly to still behave like children around one another, but she found that she quite enjoyed it. And she also found that while a part of her wished to embrace whatever spark still flickered between them, the purpose of justice she'd forced upon herself seemed to have set it out of her reach, as if she'd captured that spark in a jar and preserved it high up on a pedestal, unwilling to let it grow into a fire, nor to fizzle out.

She had the sense that Egan's ideas mirrored her own, and she wasn't sure whether she was grateful for that or not. But she knew at least that he respected her wishes, and for that, she *was* thankful.

Her smile faded. "Have you heard anything?"

His eyes had changed when they fell back upon her. They were grim and regretful. But hers were hard, and she hid her disappointment as he shook his head and looked away again. But she hadn't truly expected him to say otherwise. She'd have been back sooner if she had.

"Not a whisper," he replied, turning back to the blade he was forging, twisting the untamed metal in the firelight, "and believe me, I've been looking and listening, especially in arena season." He looked at her, sidelong. "Have you had any luck?"

"Actually...I may have."

He suddenly lost interest in his work.

"I fell into the company of an inquisitor. He's stiff, won't talk about work, but I figure he or one of his colleagues could know something about it, so I've been trying to soften him up. Not that it's working - but if he knows anything *at all*, it could be a substantial lead."

Egan's eyes narrowed suspiciously, though their hopeful brightness remained for a moment. "There was mention of an inquisitor in the earliest rumours..." He turned squarely towards her, his eyes suddenly incredulous. "Petra, you're not still with them all, are you?!"

"It was the only choice I had! I was lumped in with them before I had the chance to explain myself so I got chased out of Mokhan, too, and since I'd left everything at the inn, all I had left was what was on me at the time." She gestured to herself. The situation hadn't really changed. "It was either follow them or risk going alone and starving, because I had no money and you know my trapping skills aren't exactly exceptional."

An unstoppable smile suddenly pulled across his face. "I find it hard to believe your skills haven't improved in *fifteen years*."

"I just don't have the knack," she confessed. "So I leave it to others and appreciate their abilities at the butcher's counter."

She smiled as he chuckled, but his solemnity was quick to return. "Well, I suppose you could be in worse company...but I do hope something comes of it, that it's not for nothing..."

She could see there was more he wished to say on the matter, but, as always, he left the words unspoken.

"Well," he continued a little lighter, brushing those thoughts aside in an attempt to brighten the atmosphere, "if you're still in need of income..." He smiled at the

enthusiasm that already glittered in her eyes.
"You know where I can find a challenger."
"I know where you can find *two*."

Chapter 25

"It's so..." Aria peered up at the Crucible's lofty, crumbling heights, pursed her lips and considered it for a very long moment. "Big."

"That was the best you could come up with?"

"It's appropriate." She stepped closer to the imposing walls and stared at the carvings that had long ago been etched into the stone. "It's elven, isn't it?"

"Yes," her father replied, "but that's all I can tell you."

"So you don't know what these pictures mean?"

"They're stories." Rathen and Aria looked to Garon in surprise as he continued to survey the city from beside them, his face twisted in its usual authoritative glower. He didn't return their stares. "The Crucible is an arena now, but it used to be a stage for plays and arts. The carvings are the stories that were played out here."

"He's right, actually," said an astounded voice close from their other side, at which Rathen visibly jumped. He turned a scowl, and Anthis smiled apologetically/sheepishly - an action lately quite unexpected of him. Something had clearly changed. The inherent kindness had returned to his eyes, so easy and natural it was as if it had never left...but there was more, some kind of elation. For reasons unknown, it made Rathen deeply uncomfortable.

The historian frowned as he edged a half step away, then shrugged it off, closed his satchel and stepped back from the defaced public notice board of pleas and bounties to smile fondly up at the coliseum. "Pre-magic, originally, but it was used and maintained by hand by short post-magic elves, too. A thousand years ago this would have been a truly magnificent place..." the corners of his mouth pulled suddenly downwards. "I wish I could have seen it as a theatre and watched these stories in motion...not as an arena of bloodshed." He brushed his fingers delicately over the stone, then looked wistfully across the city that sprawled away from it in all directions. "All this history, this passion; a city built by such wholesome people, and now look at it... This place is...a shame."

"That's a mild way of putting it," Rathen mumbled, then glanced off to one side, his attention snatched by more phantom movement. He sighed to himself and tried to suppress his skittish agitation yet again.

"We should leave." He turned towards Garon. "We have what we need and enough to last beyond Tarun. There's no sense in staying." He made his feelings so excruciatingly clear in his eyes that Garon simply couldn't miss them.

"Fair enough," he nodded. "Let's go."

"No, we can't without Petra!" Aria protested as Rathen began to pull her along, having yet to let go of her hand for more than a moment since they'd arrived.

"She isn't coming with us," he replied softly.

"But we haven't even said goodbye!"

"I'm sorry, little one, but she's better off away from us; we only seem to attract trouble, and it's not fair to drag her into it." He offered her a reassuring smile. "It's for the best, I promise."

Aria scrutinised his expression for a very long time, but she remained unconvinced.

"Just where have *you* been, anyway?" Rathen asked, turning towards Anthis as they moved away from the Crucible and back into the city at the inquisitor's lead.

The young man frowned. "You're a very suspicious person, do you know that?"

"That's just his face," Aria assured him, and Anthis chuckled.

"I was securing us some horses, actually. I don't know about the rest of you, but I wouldn't mind my boots lasting a little longer."

"Where did you get the money for those?"

"There it is again. Well I don't shout about it, but I'm not exactly impoverished..."

"Remember, Daddy? He lives all on his own in that great, big house!" Clearly, Aria was still in awe of the fact.

Rathen hushed her as he glanced around at passing groups of people, but he conceded to the point, and silently admitted that he wouldn't mind not having to walk everywhere anymore.

They hadn't gotten far when a ruckus sprung up ahead of them. A crowd had formed, hidden initially by the shadow of the Crucible itself, and as they drew closer along the western road, the cheering and jeering became more fervent. The four moved cautiously and made a point of keeping themselves to themselves as they neared, but it was quickly apparent that the mob was quite engrossed.

Anthis frowned and peered across curiously. "It's a fight." He glanced around, expecting to see guards hurrying towards the scene, but the streets were conspicuously clear of them. "Where are the guards?"

Garon grunted and his pace slowed as he caught a very informative glimpse through the crowd. "Distracted."

"Then should you not intervene...?"

"No."

They frowned as he drew to a stop and followed his gaze back towards the chaos. The onlookers had formed a ring, and at its centre were two figures with swords drawn, dancing nimbly around one another. One of them was Petra.

Rathen and Anthis stumbled and stood with their mouths agape, staring in from the higher path and watching as the young woman faced an adversary of certainly stronger build. They watched her ground her feet as her opponent charged towards her, his blade angled to hasten his approach rather than hinder it, making his skill in combat already quite evident. He held the sword easily, neither choking the hilt nor sliding his grip, and he swung it precisely with no unnecessary vigour.

But by the smile she seemed unable to contain, Petra wasn't deterred. Indeed, she appeared to be willing him to attack.

Moving her sword in a smooth arc, their blades met.

Garon pulled Anthis back as he took a panicked step forwards.

The combatants pushed off from one another and circled for a moment, then, upon an unseen cue, the man flew into a rapid attack. Quick shifts, timely counters and nimble side-steps made it clear that Petra could stand against him, while a single, precise riposte proved she was a match, and the subsequent flurry of short, sharp stabs and slices which pushed him several steps backwards and very much onto the defensive set her out on top.

For the first time since entering Carenna, Rathen forgot his own anxieties. They all did. Instead they watched her intently, holding their breath against every close scrape, then feeling foolish when she easily turned each to her advantage. Even Garon observed with more interest than a figure of the law should have.

But whoever her opponent was, he wasn't blind to her skill. He was taking her seriously - rather than grinning and taunting her, declaring that a woman couldn't do him any harm, he was silent and observant, timing his own attacks and responses accordingly. But it still seemed to the four of them that he was underestimating her - and it also seemed that she was allowing him to.

Perhaps it was the unmissable fact that she was female. She couldn't hide the point - or, rather, she made no attempt to - and instead seemed to use the instinctive male sense of superiority to her advantage. They knew they were about to fight a woman, despite the fact that she was not only clearly armed but also clearly skilled. She made no effort to deceive them. And yet they still fought her willingly, as if they thought she couldn't *truly* stand against a man, reputations aside. In fact, it was probably that very detail that had allowed her to make some kind of a living out of duels.

As he watched her in growing awe, Rathen absently supposed he'd fallen for the same thing by feeling the need to see to her wounds in Edam rather than leave her to them herself.

The expert strikes continued, the clash of steel competing with the hammering rain, and every one of them was met by a parry or a counter-attack by the other. They seemed to read each other with every action - even following a particularly fearsome blow, Petra responded in perfect time, having surely gleaned his intentions by his movements. Not even its strength had surprised her.

But despite their intensity and precision, neither blade found contact with anything but the other. They were evenly matched, and both had an affinity with their blades that Rathen would have considered romantic drivel had someone merely described it to him. They were used not only to block or attack, but to force distance, aid in balance and improve the finesse of the rest of their body's movements. The weight of the sword hindered neither of them; it truly was an extension of their bodies.

And though they both moved fluidly, even as they each slipped on the rain-sodden road at one moment or another, Petra's grace was particularly difficult to miss. She moved and evaded as if she was dancing, as if she weighed nothing and the wind could just carry her away. Disregarding the arsenal she carried, and her apparent prowess with them, she was not unladylike, but it was ironic that she seemed her most feminine when putting those very factors to work.

Petra's footing slipped on the greasy cobblestones again, and Anthis took another hurried step forwards. There was nothing he could do but gasp, of course, but Garon pulled him back anyway, and their concern was quickly proven unwarranted as she artfully recovered, using the momentum of the sudden misstep to evade another quick attack.

Anthis growled as the crowd cheered. "He took advantage of that."

"Of course he did," Garon replied. "What would it do to his pride if he lost to a woman?"

Her opponent was becoming desperate. He came at her harder now, forcing her to parry when she should have counter-attacked, to step away from strikes when she should have parried. Even the enthusiasm had dwindled from her eyes.

Rathen felt his heart hammering, and he sensed the same tension from the others. Even Garon edged a half step forwards and stared with growing intensity.

She was being forced back towards the crowd under the assault, and in her efforts to regain ground, she slipped again. But this time she didn't just drop to one knee; she landed on her rear, her weight on her elbow - but her sword was still in her hand, so the bout was still live.

Anthis cursed, Garon gritted his teeth, and Rathen held Aria back as she tried to hurry forwards to help in some ill-conceived manner.

Her opponent took full advantage. He moved in for a strike, a single blow meant to end the fight while he had the upper hand, and it seemed his desperation had forced aside his reason. These duels were not supposed to be to the death...but sometimes, in the heat of the event, that little courtesy was forgotten.

This time all three of them stepped forwards in a panic as his blade descended, making for the crowd in an attempt to break the fight apart, as it should have been long ago.

But they'd made it only three paces when her opponent suddenly faltered. A kick to his leg had knocked him off balance, and Petra rolled aside the very moment he began to teeter forwards. He used his sword to catch himself, completing his strike to plant its tip in the ground where she had been only a second before, but she shot another sharp kick towards the flat of the blade and knocked it out from beneath him. He lost his grip and his fall resumed.

She sprung immediately back to her feet, her smile having returned from nowhere, and planted a dirty boot on his back to press him the last distance to the ground as the tip of her blade kissed the back of his neck.

The three of them stumbled to a stop. The crowd fell silent.

A long moment dragged by before a single voice erupted into a cheer, and the rest shortly followed. There were ovations, complaints, curses and 'I told you so's - but Petra didn't celebrate. She stepped back off of the man and offered him her hand, and though his cheeks were ruby with embarrassment, he accepted her help, rose to his feet, and graciously inclined his head before reclaiming his sword and limping away.

Only then did she accept the congratulations of the audience.

Rathen folded his arms as they watched her, a small and pleasantly surprised smile playing about his lips. "Well..."

Anthis nodded his full agreement, his eyebrows high in shock.

They watched as Petra turned towards someone in the crowd, a man of similar age who had only smiled at her victory as though he had readily expected it, and threw her arms around his shoulders.

Garon turned away. "Go and get the horses," he said to Anthis who frowned curiously at the sight, "the rest of us will leave through the western gate. We'll meet you outside."

"What about Petra?" Aria insisted again as the young man walked away and the crowd dispersed but for those collecting on their bets. She stared at Garon almost pleadingly, but he barely glanced at her, his expression unreadable. "She'll be fine here."

"But how do you *know?*"

"Because this is her home."

Rathen looked to him in surprise as they resumed along the road, pulling the reluctant young girl along. "How do you know that?"

"Aside from it being my job to know these things," he replied tediously, stepping ahead of them, "I overheard her mention it to Anthis. Now let's move. We've been here too long."

The dirt and grime returned to the city the further they ventured from the Crucible, and the air became just as foul, laden with the myriad of heavy scents that had assaulted them as they'd arrived. But the rain had begun to weaken, and the streets were busier than they had been before.

They kept their heads down, their hoods up, and passed by the pickpockets, whores, drunks and addicts among the increased populace without drawing any attention. Rathen breathed a little easier when they turned a corner and the small, weakly guarded gate elbowed its way into view. They were nearly there.

"Oi!"

A flash of heat filled Rathen's chest, and he knew that the brusque heckle from up ahead was aimed squarely towards them.

"Don't turn," Garon warned quietly, maintaining his pace, "just keep walking."

"Oi! I'm talkin' to you!"

Rathen held Aria's hand tightly and pointedly kept his eyes fixed to the gate as five suitably shifty figures broke away from one of the buildings, losing interest in the young women they'd been harassing who took the opportunity to sneak away.

They blocked the road, forcing the three to stop, and Garon stepped forwards to confront them. They were far flimsier in frame than he, and the inquisitor's naturally powerful bearing made them seem even slighter. But what they lacked in build and physical intimidation, they made up for in numbers and gruesome smiles.

"Step aside please, gentlemen," Garon said with far more civility than the thugs could likely comprehend. "I'm sure you're unaware, but you're in our way."

The man at the centre raised his blonde eyebrows. He was suspiciously cleaner than the others and free of any visible scars, though he carried the same hint of desperation and instability in his eyes. "Oh, I'm *so* sorry," he drawled, turning to his lackeys. "Apparently, we're in the way."

"No need to apologise," Garon said with a far too easy smile, "these things happen."

But the thug stepped in front of him again as he attempted to make his way around them. "They do seem to, don't they," he replied conversationally. "You know, you're a little too well-dressed for this part of town. You wouldn't happen to be lost, would you?"

Garon followed his gaze down to his own boots, for his cloak concealed the rest of his uniform. They were dirty - such here was hardly surprising - but they were certainly in far better shape than that of his adversary, or of anyone else around, for that matter. Some had no shoes at all.

He looked back up and offered his smile once more. "Won them in a card game just now - brand new, too! Luck was with me today."

The man nodded, but his already insincere smile became downright hollow. "I'm afraid it's just run out."

He looked across at the others as they stepped up on either side of their leader, a shared hunger in their eyes. "Oh, come now, gentlemen, there's no need for that. It's all I have! But I'll tell you what," Garon stepped closer, glanced about and lowered his voice, his eyes suddenly revealing the possession of worth-while secrets, "one of the other fellows, he cleaned up pretty well. I didn't get a seat in the game until he left, and the pot was weak by that point, hence the boots - another stroke of luck, that was, if you'll believe me. I'd've lost everything if I'd been in a hand sooner. But this fellow, he cleaned up nicely, like I said - and I know where he went, and I also know he's soused out of his skids by now. He'd already had a skin full when he left, and he was shouting about spending his winnings in the Golden Lily. If I know him, he'll be there for a while..."

The thug analysed the suggestion in Garon's eyes for a long while. Rathen watched them carefully, as did the others, and the rain seemed to fall more heavily during that lengthy minute, as if it couldn't contain itself in the suspense.

Finally, he nodded and clapped him on the shoulder. "Thanks for that piece of advice, mate. It'll do much to help us in our time of need. But it seems there's no rush, so we'll follow it up *after* we've finished with you."

"But we have nothing," Garon assured them.

"You couldn't have joined the game with nothing to stake, yourself, and I'm sure you won more than one man's boots." He drew the dagger that was sheathed at his hip, the others following suit behind him. But his eyes shifted beyond Garon for a moment, and he gave the slightest nod of his head.

Rathen grunted as his knee buckled beneath a sudden kick from behind him, and his descent was hastened by the dazing strike to the side of his head. In that brief moment of broken attention a scream rose from his right, and as the clouds in his vision began to clear, he watched disorientated as Aria was snatched away.

"No..." He scrambled to find his feet despite the dizziness, but he was quickly kicked back down.

Two new figures restrained her, both pressing a blade to her throat. There was sheer terror in her eyes. Rathen's heart tore to shreds and a white-hot fire exploded in its place.

"Do nothing!"

Rathen stared up at Garon in utter disbelief, but though it was only a glance, he didn't miss the intensity of the warning that had been in the inquisitor's eyes.

"*Daddy!*"

"Garon," he growled in a grave warning, but though he thought he'd sounded furious, he hadn't noticed the tremor of panic that had rippled through his voice. "Garon, you had better do something *now*..."

The inquisitor didn't reply. He drew his sword, his previously friendly and urgently helpful demeanour having long crumbled away, and he squared his bearing to his foes.

But as Rathen stared at Aria, trying to smile reassuringly, making her promises that she would be just fine, he pressed his fingertips helplessly into the ground and swallowed his blinding need to form every spell he could think of.

A new scent broke through the tangle that hung in the air, carried towards him by a shift in the breeze, and the instant it passed beneath his nose he noticed the tell-tale darkened veins on the backs of the hands of both of her captors. Their skin looked thin, slightly translucent.

He looked back to the twisted faces of the men, a new but cautious hatred piercing his eyes. These were not only thieves, they were addicts. He could smell the opiac, see the madness in their eyes. These men were more than desperate; they were looking for a fix, and they were prepared to do whatever they had to to fund it.

He glanced around, but once again the guards had been distracted. Or paid off. This *was* the western gate...

"Garon, they--"

"I know." He stared across them all and let his gaze weigh heavily upon each. "Turn around and leave." He spoke clearly, steadily, leaving no room for misunderstanding. "Trust me when I say that this is not a fight you want to have."

The leader stared sharply back at him, but when he glimpsed the ornate hilt of his blade peaking through his cloak, though the white hammer insignia itself was turned away from him, a rage flashed through his eyes. His gruesome, poisonous smile returned. "What luck, what luck indeed!"

"He's an inquisitor, Ren," one of the lackeys who held Aria warned him, one with a clear view of the other end of the sword, the sight of which had drained the blood from his face.

"Yes," the leader replied, "and he thinks he's better than us because of it, *so* high and mighty. But that means he has more coin -" he glanced towards the two who held Aria, "and he has a pesky sense of responsibility."

Aria whimpered as the blades pressed more firmly against her skin, just hard enough to draw a single, crimson beadlet.

Rathen's fire-heart thundered in his chest and sparks began to ignite his blood. He gritted his teeth as his head swam. All he saw was Aria. He didn't notice the sound of footsteps splashing through puddles as Garon darted towards her, or of a sword knocking aside the blows of several daggers as the thugs moved to stop him. He was aware only of her terror, the tears streaming down her cheeks, the sheer desperation in her eyes - it was more than he had ever seen on any face in his lifetime. Not even on men and women who had lay dying on the battlefields.

The edge of his vision grew cloudy, his head thumped and his ability to comprehend his own thoughts was strained. Even had he finally been given permission to cast a spell and draw the attention of every mage in the city, he wouldn't have been able to complete it. The seals were lost to him. Instead he understood only the panic, the fury, the sheer helplessness that invaded and walled in his mind. He could feel himself slipping beneath it. Succumbing. And this time, he had no desire to fight it.

Garon could easily fight off the attackers; they were unorganised, thinking only for their own safety, and a few times they had gotten one of their companions injured in their own attempts to defend themselves. But just as Garon didn't truly intend to inflict injury, neither were they trying to hurt him. They were meant only to occupy him, and though he realised this early on, there was little he could do when the four men continued to throw themselves at him like rabid dogs.

The leader, Ren, had stepped back from the skirmish. It was no wonder he was so much smoother-skinned than the others, if certainly still sickly. He must have made a habit of leaving the dirty work to his lackeys. These men had far less control over their impulses than he seemed to, and were unlikely to stop under injury once the blood haze hit.

But even as Garon pushed them back, he kept his sights on Ren. He watched him stride leisurely towards the child his two new cohorts had taken hostage, and his smile suggested that he was more than prepared to press on her capture to get what he wanted.

Garon cursed as he planted his boot firmly in the chest of one man charging towards him, firing him backwards beneath the crunch of breaking ribs. He wasn't going to give him the chance to use her.

His eyes flicked back towards his assailants. One was down, and the others could be dispatched easily enough. He'd already caused a scene by engaging them so it would make little difference now if he hurt them, and Ren might just lose his nerve if the bulk of his force was taken out.

He turned his sword and prepared to sweep aside the blade of the oncoming attacker and slam him into the nearest wall with his shoulder, but a young voice suddenly shrieked in panic - and it was not a cry of self-concern.

Even the attackers faltered, and as Garon glanced towards Aria he found her staring at her father with an entirely new kind of fright. His eyes flicked towards him as he side-stepped an opportunistic attack, and his own heart lurched as he understood.

Rathen stared back at the two captors, but it was not the primal hatred in his eyes that made his blood run cold - and that of everyone else. It was their colour: they had turned black. Entirely. Even the whites of his eyes were consumed. His skin had also faded to a pure, milky white which only made his eyes more striking. But there was something more about his face that had changed, something that couldn't be placed.

Maybe it was the pure agony that creased every miserable wrinkle and knotted his jaw so tightly his teeth should have shattered, an agony so clear yet so great he was sure none of them could ever have endured it, if even comprehended it.

And yet still he stared at the thugs, that torture embraced and focused into daggers fired by his unwavering jet-black gaze, rather than falling at its mercy and letting himself curl up into a weeping ball.

Everyone within that street fell paralysed beneath the glare: Garon, the thugs, and countless onlookers who hadn't retreated at the start of the fight, no doubt used to such events. Though this, of course, was something new.

His animalistic stare finally became too much for a few, and a handful screamed and fled. Others around them immediately followed, long having learned to respond to the reactions of those around them in this district, and the thugs, the focus of his deathly and unblinking gaze, released Aria and slowly backed away, somehow able to contain their horror in favour of appearing insignificant.

"Rathen, get a hold of yourself," Garon demanded, though he knew already that it was too late, and he pulled Aria close to him as she tentatively backed away from her father.

Guards suddenly appeared from around the corner, lured by the screams and the stampede of fleeing bodies, their blades already drawn. Rathen couldn't have seen them, couldn't even have heard them, and yet he spun around immediately, moving with frighteningly unnatural speed. They came to a stop so abrupt it was as if they'd turned to ice. Three heartbeats later, they turned and fled like the people they were supposed to protect.

The opiac addicts took their opportunity to flee while he was distracted, but the slightest movement immediately snatched the mage's attention. They'd not moved even an inch as he shot back towards them - and he'd changed further in those few seconds - but he gave them not even a moment to begin their get away.

He exploded to his feet and bolted towards them, that same inhuman speed powering his chase and ripping screams from their cowardly throats.

Garon lost all interest in them. He had a new problem on his hands now.

"Rathen, stop!" He bellowed as he moved to give chase, but Aria pulled him back.

"No! We have to hide! *Nothing* will stop him, *nothing at all!*" Tears of desperation blinded her, streaming over her cheeks, and she seemed unaware of the blood that trickled down her neck.

Garon shook her off, though more urgently than unkindly. "*You* hide," he commanded, "*now.*" He broke into a run. "I can't let him rampage!"

Rathen was in close pursuit as the thieves flew around a corner, but the movement of the inquisitor instantly stole his attention away again, and he turned onto him in a flash. He had no focus, no concentration. He didn't seem even to recognise Garon. He was like a rabid animal, mad and senseless, driven only by wild and unmanageable urges.

But the transformation the man had undergone in the space of one minute again turned Garon's heart to ice. The once-average man had become a full head taller, as lean as a lifelong soldier and his shoulders substantially broader as they heaved beneath ragged breath; his clothes were torn and his whole form had become perfectly imposing. His face was gaunter, his cheekbones sharper, and he was barely recognisable as the man that had walked beside him five minutes earlier.

But more alarming were the sharp and jagged finger-length protrusions that pierced through his bone-white skin at his shoulders and beneath his throat, as though spines had erupted from either end of his collar bones. His veins also appeared black at first glance and too easily visible beneath his skin, as though he showed the same signs of opiac use, but they were much darker and too needlessly ornate to be veins. They scrolled like a tattoo or tribal paint, but beneath the skin, as if they had been applied from the inside out or were precise and deep-grey bruising.

But perhaps the most disturbing detail was the cracking. He'd heard it before and had assumed it to be distant thunder, but as Rathen's monstrous form faltered and new skeletal hooks erupted from his elbows and his ribcage seemed to expand, they came again, the sickening cracks of bones shifting, breaking and reshaping.

Garon swallowed hard and tightened his grip on his sword, trying either to shake off the smothering sense of primal fear, or refocus it and put it to some kind of use. He'd been lucky, for a moment; every change that took place stalled him and excruciating torment ripped across his beastly face. But as quickly as it occurred, it passed, and Rathen's black eyes refocused upon him.

He hurtled towards him in a flash.

Garon's blood thawed in an instant at the guttural cry that accompanied it and he braced himself to spring to the side, left little time to consider any defence, let alone an attack. But while he'd intended to shift aside at the last moment, Rathen moved so quickly that he only just made it. That instant confirmed Garon's assumption: there was no way he could stand against this demon.

Rathen pulled himself to a sudden stop a short way behind him, then turned and charged again with another horrific growl, and he jumped aside this time with a little more preparation.

He stopped, turned and charged again, and it was then that Garon truly realised that his attention was *entirely* upon him. Movement around them could snatch it away again, but no one was about to come out of their homes and present themselves as a distraction - had he been able to spare a moment to glance at the windows he'd have seen countless faces staring out in horror. But perhaps movement of his own would help to *keep* that attention, should he be wrong.

The western gate lay behind him, unguarded, and Rathen seemed prepared to chase. He could lure him out of the city, return some kind of safety to the people and reduce the chances of another massacre - if Rathen didn't kill *him* first.

He had no time to think. He gritted his teeth and jumped aside once more, but rather than watch to see what Rathen would do next, he turned towards the gate and ran. "Aria," he shouted, "wherever you are, *stay there!*"

He didn't get far before he heard rapid footsteps pounding over the wet stones behind him, or ragged, uncontrolled breath from a bestial throat, and was forced to break off of his straight path to avoid any impact.

Long claws, fingers encased in bony armour, only just missed his ear as they slashed through the air where his head had been less than a second before, and only managed to clip his hair as he ducked in anticipation of the sweep of the other hand.

He darted to the right, then to the left, somehow managing to avoid the impossibly swift strikes, and he thanked his luck every time.

And then he fell, tripped by a loose stone, of all things, mere feet away from the gate. He could hear Rathen barely a step behind him, but he hadn't the time even to roll away. He tensed, braced himself, and prepared a backwards attack for when he inevitably fell upon him.

But it didn't come.

Another savage howl ripped free in response to a curiously familiar roar of fury, and any questions she surely had she reserved for a more appropriate time.

"The gate!" Garon shouted as he used the opportunity to leap back to his feet, hoping in the process that he might steal his attention back again. "Get him out of the city!"

But this time it was Petra who retained his attention, and though she tried to fight and subdue him, evidently seeing something familiar enough about him not to turn and flee, or strike to kill, she wasn't prepared for his speed. She did all she could to hit and to evade, but anything that landed had painfully little effect, and she seemed to resent the need to retreat. But she did it all the same, and without Garon needing to shout the order a second time.

The inquisitor shoved open the gate while the monster hunted Petra, and they spilled out from the city and into more open land. Now there were places to turn, and with a second body, there was opportunity to confuse him.

Horses bellowed in a panic some distance behind the inquisitor, and suddenly Rathen's focus shifted again.

Some fifty feet or more away, Anthis turned pale and froze, staring in terror as the black and white beast bolted towards him, picking up far too much speed on two legs in such unhindered terrain.

"Anthis, don't move!" Garon shouted over the roars as he and Petra raced behind him. "Keep perfectly still!"

He obliged only because his brain had stalled, but the horses whose reins he clutched bucked and panicked, and there was no way either of the mage's pursuers could catch his attention again. But they tried anyway, running as fast as they possibly could and still failing to keep up.

Anthis stumbled back in horror and raised a defensive hand, though such a gesture could never have done anything in the face of this assailant.

But Rathen suddenly heaved backwards, his momentum abruptly reversed, and Garon jumped to one side to avoid being impaled by the elbow thorns as he landed. Of course, when he did strike the ground, he wasn't even dazed, and leapt back up to charge again as if nothing at all had happened.

Something whipped through the air from behind Garon and struck Rathen at the ankles, and again his frenzied pursuit was stalled as he stumbled back to the ground. This time, however, he couldn't get back up, and his strength surprised Garon again as his advance persisted, dragging himself along towards the panicking animals that Anthis wrestled to keep a hold of, bolas tangled around his feet, but he gave himself no time to marvel.

He noted every jagged spike, bony protrusion and piece of unexplainable skeletal armour, then jumped upon him, pressing down with all of his weight to keep him on the ground. Still he managed to haul himself along, but Petra was quickly behind him, having made the same decision at the same moment, and as she added her weight, Garon finally had the opportunity to subdue him. It was only after he made the very precise strike to the carotid artery and Rathen's struggle weakened that he realised the transformation could have supplied some kind of protection against the act.

Fortunately for all of them, it hadn't, and Rathen soon fell limp.

A rumble sounded in the distance, so sudden that each of them in their heightened responses braced for another attack. The ground beneath them shuddered and screams rose in the city that now stood a surprising distance behind them, its outer walls shaking, loosening bricks that crumbled as the tremor continued. Birds fled from the nearby trees, the horses renewed their panic and stamped their hooves, and wolves howled mournfully from the depths of the forest.

It lasted for almost a minute, and when the ground finally ceased its quaking, a heavy silence hung for miles.

Garon, Petra and Anthis looked at one another with wide, harrowed eyes, and though thousands of questions began to weigh upon two of their tongues, neither found the courage to ask them.

Garon's heart jumped when he realised that Aria wasn't with them, but as he leapt off of Rathen to turn back to the city in search of her, the first who dared to move, he spotted her small form walking close to the broken wall, peering cautiously towards them.

He paid no attention to the immense relief he felt at the sight of her safety as he hurried over towards her, and she rushed to him in a flood of similar desperation. She grasped his hand immediately, as tightly as she would have her father's, but her eyes were fixed on his motionless body as she was led cautiously towards him, ignoring the dust that still rose from a portion of the walls behind.

Petra stepped back as they arrived, her own confusion brushed aside in concern as she watched the child stop silently beside him. The empathy in her brow twisted deeper as Aria stared with little more than a mere touch of worry in her eyes. There was no grief, no confusion, though she surely couldn't comprehend what she was looking upon. *None* of them did.

Petra was quick to retrieve the doll from the child's bag and slip it into her empty hand.

Garon frowned more critically as he stopped beside her. Rathen hadn't moved. The inquisitor's blow should only have subdued him for a moment, giving his mind the opportunity to clear and allow Rathen to reassert himself. But the transformation, as brief as it was, must have come at a greater price than he'd first guessed - but then, the last time this had happened, he had very nearly died...

He knelt down beside him and brushed his long, black hair from his face. He grunted in satisfaction. Rathen was beginning to revert. He looked a little more like himself again; his bone structure had returned, the sub-dermal pattern had vanished, and the colour no one had ever noticed was returning to his face.

But there was a lot of blood. It leaked from countless visible wounds, his skin more torn than broken, and it seeped into his tattered clothing. His shoulders, elbows and fingers had suffered the most at first glance, the eruption of sharp bones through his flesh leaving frightful holes as they receded, but when Garon considered the reshaping the rest of his body had undergone, he suspected that what he couldn't see was far worse.

Suddenly, he found himself at a loss for what to do.

"What just happened?" Anthis finally managed, the words tumbling out to shatter the steel silence, and yet spoken with a mild tone, his confusion that extensive.

But before Garon could organise his troubled thoughts to even consider giving an answer, be it the truth or not, the light around them suddenly dimmed, the thundering rain above them ceased, and the soft, muddy ground beneath his knees turned to gnarled roots. Their surroundings had shifted, and they were quite suddenly back in the familiar, concealing terrain of Turunda's forests.

"Oh, Rathen," a disappointed voice mumbled from beside the inquisitor, and as he blinked, he found a dark-haired woman rolling Rathen very gently onto his back, tutting quietly to herself and shaking her head, her storm of forest brown curls bouncing. "What have you done?"

Chapter 26

"It's not his fault, Kienza," Aria whimpered from beside the sudden woman, her small voice studded with regret. "It's because I got captured."

"Whatever do you mean by that?" She frowned softly, but before the remorseful young girl could stutter a reply, a firm hand grasped Kienza's shoulder and attempted to tear her away from Rathen's side.

"*Don't touch him!*"

"And just how am I supposed to help him if I don't?" She returned mildly, all too easily shaking off Petra's sharp grip as she continued to brush his hair aside. Her plump lips pulled downwards for a moment as she stroked a fingertip over his torn cheek.

Petra's eyes blazed wrathfully as she moved to snatch for her again, but she choked to an abrupt stop when she noticed the glistening crimson that masked most of Rathen's disturbingly peaceful face. Anthis pulled her back to keep her from interfering, having recovered from the wave of nausea that had hit him after their sudden relocation. He'd fully expected her to resist, but she threw her arms around his shoulders instead and buried her face in his neck, shaking as she wept, her rage crumbling into an equally powerful grief.

But he was too distracted to notice her contact. He held her absently as he stared back and forth between Garon and Kienza, neither of whom looked as troubled as they should have by what had just occurred. "*What happened?*" He implored them desperately once again, his eyes wide with shock, utter lack of comprehension, and a fear that would have been more suitable on the face of a child.

"Yes, Mister Inquisitor," Kienza said with suspicion as she tore Rathen's shirt open, revealing the extent of the blood that covered his torso, "what *did* happen?"

He sighed and folded his arms, but his usual superiority was nowhere to be found. Instead he explained, in the best terms he could, of their encounter with the thugs, Aria's capture, and Rathen's subsequent reaction.

Kienza sighed, searching his skin with careful precision as she gauged the severity of his wounds. As Garon had expected, these were far worse. His chest was riddled with uncountable rips, like an aged sack that had been routinely over-stuffed throughout its lifetime. Petra blanched again when she saw them. "I see."

"I don't!" Anthis proclaimed. "How did this happen to him?!" Against possibility, his eyes widened even further, a thought striking him as hard as a herd of stampeding cattle. "His magic...he said he thought the mages were losing control of their magic - did *he* just lose control?!"

Kienza shook her head and stopped probing his skin. She flattened her palm and passed it slowly over his lacerated chest. "No mage has ever lost control of their magic to an extent like this. This is something else entirely."

Anthis stared at her closely. "...You know what it is, though, don't you?" His eyes flicked towards Garon, and there was an immense distrust within them. "Both of you."

Rathen's flesh began to knit itself back together beneath the passing of Kienza's hand, and she looked up at last, giving the young man a small, sad smile. "You know a little more than you let on yourself, Mister Karth," she said gently. "It sounds familiar, doesn't it?"

The blood slowly drained from his face. "The mage in Kulokhar... That was...?"

"Rathen," she nodded mournfully, "yes."

"What mage in Kulokhar?" Petra asked. She stood on her own now, though she hugged herself and her voice still shook.

"Eleven years ago, a mage within the ranks of the Order went on a senseless rampage." Kienza spoke with curious disconnection, her voice lilting as if she was recounting a revered but over-told story. "He killed sixteen people in the market of the capital city in broad daylight. Even now, no one knows why or how it happened; it was completely out of character. He was a respected sahrot, one of the highest ranking mages present on the battlefield, in command of a full regiment. But that day - a day outside of war, and no different to any other of its kind - something within him...changed. His body mutated physically and chemically to become something like what you all just saw. He lost total control of his mind and turned by all rights into a beast: unstoppable, inescapable, unreasonable and frightfully strong. He attacked and killed everyone who caught his eye that day, no matter who they were. Men, women, children..."

With a delicate touch, she unlaced Rathen's trousers and turned to the wounds along his legs and hips while the others averted their eyes. "It only lasted a few minutes," she continued, "and it ended as abruptly as it had begun, stopped only by his loss of consciousness. But he had no memory of what he'd done when he awoke. He was exhausted, and the change had put such a strain on his body that it almost killed him. It took him a week of bed rest and constant tending to recover - and his injuries then were far less severe than these."

"What does that mean?"

She didn't look up. "That Rathen's transformations are worse now than they were then.

"But that, of course, wasn't the end of the matter," she sighed wearily, "and neither was the end as straight forward as it should have been. It was a terribly political situation; it occurred in public and involved a figure of significant authority. The people needed justice, but the Crown needed to save face. They couldn't come down as hard as the populace wanted them to or it would raise questions about the competence of everyone else under their command, and it would reinforce the fact that they'd been taken by surprise by one of their own. So instead, they allowed the suggestion of a conspiracy, the idea that the Crown had been aware that something like this *could* happen. Of course, that also allowed the implication that they were already taking steps to remedy it when this instance occurred. It was so brief, after all, that no one could tell whether or not those measures had been hurriedly put into effect to quell it."

"The decision caused a lot of trouble for all branches of authority," Garon agreed, "but we all recovered more easily from that than if it had been handled hastily."

"Like I said: they needed to save face. But they *also* didn't want to upset the Order in case it was something *every* mage was capable of. The Crown needed the Order on their side."

"Is it *not* something any mage could do?"

Kienza pulled her eyes away from the repair of his inside hip at Petra's hopeful tone, and she gave her a brief but penetrating look. "No," she replied a moment later.

"You said it was 'something else entirely'," Anthis reminded her. "So it wasn't magic?"

"It wasn't a *spell*, if that's what you mean."

"Then *could* he have lost control of his magic?" He pressed. "The magic *alone?*"

"No."

"...Then..." The young man's brow knotted tighter at her flat and unhelpful responses. "I don't understand."

"I am confident that this would never have happened to him if it weren't for that fifth chamber in his heart," she stated categorically, gently tapping his fully repaired chest, "but I don't believe that it's related to the magic itself. And as for *why* it's happened, I can't say. But the trigger seems to be extreme tension resulting, usually, from feeling that he's completely out of control of a situation."

"Who are you?"

Kienza smiled softly and looked back to Petra following not the simple question, but the cautious hope with which she'd delivered it. She also noted the affection and knew immediately that this deeply troubled woman considered Rathen a friend. That broadened her smile. "I am his..."

"Girlfriend," Aria finished.

"It's a little more complicated than that," she grinned almost as childishly, "but I suppose it's the simplest way of putting it."

"And you're a mage...but I didn't think mages could heal wounds..."

"They can't."

Petra frowned, and both Anthis and Garon displayed a trace of the same uneasiness towards her as they had upon their first meeting. But when they didn't press this contradiction and Kienza turned her attention onto redressing Rathen and mending his clothes as easily as she had his body, Petra decided it best not to pursue.

They were silent as she worked. Aria and Garon stood nearby, watching the mysterious woman weave her impossible magic, while Petra and Anthis mulled over the words and their implications while trying to ignore the voice in their heads that screamed for them to flee his company.

Kienza soon grunted in satisfaction. "He'll be better in the morning, but it's just as well you've leased some horses. He won't be able to walk very far for the next day or two."

Suddenly remembering the beasts, Anthis spun around and looked towards the tree he'd hastily tangled their reins around. He hesitated as he counted them. "There are four..."

"Well you *did* pay for four..."

"Actually, I returned that last one."

She blinked. "...Oh well, no harm done." She conjured a blanket and spread it over Rathen's body.

"Wait, in the *morning?* I thought he'd need at least a week of bed rest..."

"Oh, I wasn't the one tending him back then," she smiled. "We didn't meet until his banishment. Since then he's had *much* quicker recoveries, which is just as well given how these transformations have progressed..."

"You say it like it's happened more than twice..."

"What I just recounted to you was, itself, the *second* incident." She paused to stroke Rathen's cheek again once she'd finished tucking the blanket around him. "There were no witnesses to the first, and only three victims."

Anthis eyed her warily. "How many times *has* this happened?"

She stopped to think for a moment and began counting on her fingers, which was already enough to tell them that they didn't want the answer. "Well, there were the two in Kulokhar, then three while he was in my care, and...six thereafter?"

Aria shook her head. "Seven."

"Seven," Kienza corrected.

All eyes crashed onto the eight year old girl, and though the same question formed on everyone's lips, their tongues were too horrified to ask it.

Kienza turned away from them in dismissal and gave Aria a warm and affectionate smile, asking her quietly if she was all right. She nodded and smiled sadly, squeezing her doll as she told her she'd hidden just like he always told her to - he could never find her when she hid - and accepted the long and tight embrace her mother-figure offered, as well as the whispered words that no one else managed to catch.

Kienza then rose to her feet and turned towards the others. "You may as well make yourselves comfortable here. You won't be going any further today with Rathen as he is - assuming, of course," she added carefully, casting a gentle and sympathetic gaze over Petra and Anthis, though it was one that suggested she already knew their intentions, "that you're staying with him."

They looked to one another, but neither could read their own minds, let alone each other's.

"Where are we?" Garon asked, finally looking about himself and noticing the dryness to the air. He, of course, would stay.

"I've teleported you somewhere safe," she replied, stepping purposefully towards him. "You won't be troubled here." She looked at him critically, and suddenly he felt the need to take a step back from her, desperate not to fall under her fiercely studious gaze again. "Take off your shirt." She smiled in amusement at the uncensored shock that passed over his face, then pointed towards his chest. He looked down and found a long rip through his shirt, its edges stiffened by dried blood, and a broad cut across his skin beneath it that he surely should have noticed sooner. His eyes widened in a second wave of alarm. "You did a fine job keeping away from him, Inquisitor. Truly commendable. In fact, I'm surprised you've come out of it so cleanly."

He recalled the first of Rathen's charges. He thought he'd managed to jump aside just in time, but it looked like he'd been slower than he'd thought. It must have been the spike on his elbow.

But then she twirled her finger, and as he turned around he found another cut across his lower back, one he'd likely gained while baiting him. This one, however, he could feel, and the young clotting had broken back open as he'd twisted to see it, causing it to bleed once again.

"Both superficial," she assured him. "Now, like I said: shirt off."

Petra and Anthis turned away as he obliged with severe resentment, though Petra was a touch slower, and they began to do as they'd been instructed. But as they left to gather firewood for the approaching evening, both cast a glance over their shoulder towards the unconscious mage, whose daughter sat devotedly beside him, holding and stroking his hand, and felt their ferocious misgivings pressing in. Neither were quick to return to camp.

Almost two hours had passed when the darkness beneath the forest canopy began to deepen, the sun's descent masked behind the boughs, and the air had stilled with the fading light. The tension was finally beginning to wane, and spirits were eased by the comforting light of the fire and the smell of the food cooking over it.

But Rathen still hadn't stirred.

Each of them sent uneasy stares from the fire a short distance away as Kienza sat quietly and patiently beside him, but no one voiced their questions or variety of concerns, to her or to each other. It was only once dusk had truly set in that she rose to her feet, startling everyone after being motionless for so long, and gave them the update they silently craved.

He was fine - or 'out of the woods', which they excused - merely sleeping, which he would do for the most part until dawn. The others were doubtful that it could be that simple, a response which this time the sorceress excused, but she was confident enough in her diagnosis to leave him untended, and Aria seemed equally as trusting.

"What if something happens?" Petra had asked worriedly as the two left for a walk in the woods not five minutes later, but Kienza had smiled and assured her that if anything happened and she was needed, she would know.

Petra was sceptical, but she had seen her magic and knew already that this woman was capable of things she shouldn't have been, and saw little choice but to accept her response - especially since she was already walking away while delivering it.

But despite her foreboding in his presence, she found herself equally uncomfortable with leaving Rathen be, so she remained diligently beside him in the healer's absence, keeping watch for either another transformation or any sign of discomfort. But after a short while of listening closely to his soft, rhythmic breathing and staring intently at the peace in his face, she soon fell deep into her own heavy thoughts.

Garon, meanwhile, had stayed by the fire to tend the meagre meal, though it was one undeniably more luxurious than what they'd recently become accustomed to. But as he turned the thinly-salted fish on their sticks, he heard footsteps approach from behind. He lowered the hand that had been absently tracing where the cut had been across his chest and braced himself for the accusation. He'd been waiting for it for an hour, and he was surprised it had taken so long.

"You knew about this," Anthis declared with the expected condemnation as he came to a stop beside him, but he didn't sit, and Garon didn't rise.

"Of course I did," he replied flatly.

"Do you not think it was a bit irresponsible not to say anything to me about it when you recruited me?"

"You would never have agreed. Besides, Rathen was never to leave my side."

"And what good it did, too."

Garon brushed off the sarcasm. "I had already spoken to Rathen about this when I recruited *him*. It was his leading concern, in fact, and his overriding condition was that, if the need arose, I did whatever I had to to prevent a repeat of Kulokhar. Fortunately, I didn't have to."

"And what would that be, pray tell?"

Garon finally looked away from the flames and turned steady eyes up to the historian. There was nothing in them but cold duty. "Kill him."

Anthis stared back at him for a long moment, a thousand thoughts racing through his eyes. Eventually, he sighed and sat down on the spot, his silence persisting. Garon turned the fish again.

"...Forgive me, Garon," he said at last with a more considerate tone, "but I don't see how you *could* have killed that--*him*. I don't see how *anyone* could."

"You don't need to worry about that detail. Suffice it to say, if I couldn't have subdued him, I already had a number of other options planned out. As I will if it happens again."

Anthis buried his face in his hands, exasperation completely overcoming him, and he released a long, hot breath into his palms.

"What will you do?"

He dropped his hands as his eyes shifted back towards the inquisitor, and though he opened his mouth to speak, he began chewing his lip instead. "I..." He sighed in defeat. "I don't have much of a choice but to stay. This goes beyond a simple research commission...things were already too complicated, I can't run away just because of this..." He laughed suddenly and shook his head. "'Just because of this'..."

"I assure you: I can handle him."

His eyes flicked back to him again, and he analysed the officer for another long moment. "Well, you'll have to, won't you? Because *I* can't, and Aria...oh, Vastal, watch over her..." He became lost in thought again, and Garon didn't interrupt. "Yes," Anthis finally grunted, his attempt to sound decisive somewhat unconvincing, "I'm staying. Vastal watch over *me*."

Garon nodded and offered a brief but genuinely grateful smile.

The slightest groan behind them gripped their attention and they twisted around in their seats, but they didn't rise or move towards it - Kienza had been quite precise when she'd told them all not to crowd him. They turned back to the fire and listened silently instead.

"Did I kill anyone?"

Half way between human and monster, the meek voice was rough, as if his throat had been shredded, and it startled Petra out of her ponderings. She looked down and found Rathen's eyes half-open. He wasn't looking at her; he didn't seem to be looking at anything, but bleary though they were, there was a definite expression within them. Guilt, dread and immense self-hatred were hard to miss. Unlike in Kienza's story, it seemed he had since come to learn what he was capable of, and it clearly sickened him.

She looked quickly back into the dark forest, but there was no sign of Kienza or Aria. Would the woman know he'd stirred? It would have been better if one of them had been at his side when he'd woken - or perhaps one of the others. Anyone, really, but her. Of everyone, she'd known him for the shortest time - what comfort could she offer at a time like this? She was the worst possible choice...

But she had something she needed to say, and she thought him the best to hear it.

"No," she replied softly, "and Aria is fine. Garon and I stopped you."

His eyebrows twitched, a weak expression of surprise, and he dragged his eyes towards her. They opened a little wider after a long moment, only then recognising her. "You're still here..."

She breathed a laugh. "Yes, I am, even after you all tried to leave without me."

His eyebrows twitched again, and his lips followed suit, curving into a mildly sheepish smile. "We...meant nothing by it."

Petra reached over for a waterskin. "Here." She lifted his head and encouraged him to drink in manageable sips, but whatever had happened to him must have made him thirsty, as he all but drained the skin. Gently, she lay him back down and took a deep breath. "I am out for revenge," she stated clearly, well aware that, in the still of the night, the others could also hear her, "and you should know that, if I get the information I need, I *will* act on it."

Rathen blinked slowly. "Okay...why are you telling me this?" His voice, at least, had cleared a little. Now he sounded as if he'd just woken from a long and deep sleep.

"Because it seemed like an appropriate time to confess a personal issue that may well cause us trouble. And because my problems seem relatively simple now, compared to yours."

"'Us trouble'?" He blinked slowly again. "You're staying with us?"

"We've already established that this situation is not the workings of the Order, and it has them concerned, which means it's serious. I'm worried about what it could mean for my sister, be it the way it reflects on the Order or if this loss of control is related to it. If you all think you can fix it, then you need all the help you can get, and with the state of things - you must have heard about the war while we were in Carenna - another sword arm couldn't hurt. And," she added carefully, "after seeing all of that, I cannot, in good conscience, leave you with the others. And I don't think you want me to. You need someone who can beat you down, if the need arises."

He managed a smile, but it was not one of mockery - at least, as far as she could tell. "Beat me down?"

"If the need arises."

"I don't think you could."

"I'm the reason we caught you."

Surprised tugged at his black eyebrows again, but it shortly passed. "Then you must have gotten lucky."

"You're underestimating me."

"And you're underestimating this curse. But..." he managed another painful smile. "Thank you." He turned his head towards her, the first movement beyond his face which he'd made by himself. "So - revenge?"

She hesitated.

"Oh, come on. You can't say a thing like that and then clam up..."

She sighed, smiling in grim defeat. The others were still listening - she could feel their attention as if they were staring, but as she glanced over her shoulder towards them, both seemed enraptured by the fire. "Someone very dear to me was murdered," she said without lowering her voice, pretending she hadn't noticed. She supposed they needed to hear it, too. "You don't need the details, all you need to know is that I will avenge them as soon as I'm presented with an opportunity, even if it means walking right into trouble. I don't expect any of you to follow me into it, or to change your own plans to fit around mine, but if I am in your company when that opportunity appears, it will take personal precedence."

Rathen stared up at her, and the two by the fire equally absorbed her confession, but not one of them spoke.

Rathen nodded, a laborious action in his present state, but he committed himself to it. "Thank you," he whispered. "I...appreciate you sharing this...and for..."

"Not running away?" She smiled. "I didn't really know quite what was going on - I didn't even know it was *you*. I just acted on impulse to help Garon. And then I was swept up with the rest of you and dumped in this forest."

Rathen's eyes widened and he tried to raise his head. "Kienza, where is she?"

"Here."

Petra looked up in time to see Aria burst through the trees with the sorceress only a few paces behind her. The girl skidded across the knotted ground and stumbled to a stop beside him, and grinned broadly, her face hovering very close to his. He chuckled, then coughed, and she threw her arms around him as best she could where he lay while Kienza looked on in affection.

Petra rose to her feet. "He seems fine."

"I would expect no less," she smiled, but as she looked up at Petra, there was a deep sympathy in her piercing dark eyes. Somehow, she knew what she'd shared.

But Petra found that she wasn't troubled. She smiled back, her heart strangely lighter, then turned away and left the three together. She glanced down at Garon and Anthis as she passed them, heading off into the forest herself in search of a stream or river, but neither looked back at her. Not until she'd looked away. Then they watched her until she disappeared amongst the trees.

"What are you doing here?" Rathen asked feebly as Aria lay down in the dirt beside him and wriggled her way beneath the blanket.

"Well, initially, because I have something you all need to hear - but now isn't the time. It can wait."

"And secondly?"

"Because I sensed what was happening to you just as I was about to make my way over."

"'Make my way'," he smiled slowly. "Teleporting isn't really 'making your way' anywhere."

"No," she agreed, "it's more like 'being', but 'be my way over' doesn't really sound right, does it?"

"No, I suppose not..." He released a deep breath and closed his eyes as she settled down on the ground beside him, her perfectly curved form visible to him even in the darkness. He was sure it was a spell of some kind, a constant enchantment either over herself or just over him, but he'd never been able to find it. "I'm tired," he mumbled.

"I know," she whispered. "So rest."

"Mm. I hope I have a dream as peaceful as I did last night."

"Peaceful dream?" Kienza asked.

"Mhm... It was...strange..."

She watched him expectantly, a troubled wrinkle in her otherwise perfectly smooth brow, but he slipped back into a long, unbreakable sleep.

Chapter 27

It had been four days since the occupations. The Arana had arrived in the east on the second, and the Order on the third. The west had been reached far sooner since most of the Arana's focus had been on the impending war.

Reports claimed Rokhar was half-razed and held by soldiers and a handful of mages; a typical occupation that would take manpower to overcome. But besieging was always a pointless endeavour that cost more than it delivered, and downright ridiculous when their own towns and cities were the prizes. Rokhar was important, of course it was, as were the lives of the surviving citizens trapped within it, but it was far better to focus Turunda's own divided resources on rounding up the remaining fragments of Skilan's force - as well as the small approaching companies from Kalokh that had been pressed into their servitude. Putting the majority under pressure would force the rest to abandon their early trophies if they hoped to come out on top.

The same could also have been applied to the three locations in the east, if not for one particularly painful detail: every one of them had been protected by spells alone.

Not a soul had remained to fortify them, instead the populace had been locked inside and abandoned by the attackers who left as suddenly as they'd arrived. That was unusual in itself, but was not what had had Salus sitting in his office all afternoon berating himself - once Malson had had his turn, of course. In fact, handing over the latest information his people had uncovered of Skilan's intentions - to lure Turunda's military into a valley where they could attack from the slopes - he'd found himself overcome with the desire to simply withhold it in case he was wrong again. He didn't, because he'd had it triple-checked first, and though it had been met with scepticism on the liaison's part, he'd accepted it all the same.

No, what made him wish the earth might open up beneath him was the revelation that those three settlements had been attacked from the east, *by* the east. Despite their woes with Voent, Doana had come out of nowhere and set upon Turunda with no obvious motive. They'd arrived in inconceivably small forces, no larger than platoons, twenty men at most to each, and had taken the three most significant eastern settlements at the same time. And then they'd just vanished. All before dawn.

According to those who'd managed to send a messenger to the capital before the arcane lock-downs, the assailants hadn't worn armour, nor even Doana's colours, and they'd not spilled a single drop of blood. Salus had to trust them on the first of those counts, but the last he knew to be untrue. Two bodies had been discovered by reassigned operatives, one just outside of Toakh, the other Ferna.

They'd been his local observers.

It couldn't be misunderstood. But not only had his long-term plants been discovered by a newly-arrived invading force, they had been discovered *quickly*.

Someone had to have known, which meant that Doana - simple, small and sinless Doana - had operatives of their own, and they were already in Turunda.

Salus mulled this over for the seventeenth time as he stared down at the bed sheets through the pitch black of night, his head in his hands and slumped body slick with sweat. He'd braved going to bed that night - though only after falling asleep at his desk - but he'd woken with a start from that wretched dream again. He had no idea how long he'd slept, and had no desire to find out. He decided to believe that it was hours rather than minutes if just so he wouldn't have to try again.

So he sat in the dark instead, his mind spinning, spiralling into thoughts and feelings he couldn't understand. He could have subdued them - he'd been trained as a portian as soon as he'd been old enough - but something weary and perhaps a little bit masochistic stopped him from trying, and a small, tormented part of him wanted to see where they would lead.

But they had no organisation; unfinished thoughts looped chaotically into another, and any time he thought he had a grasp on some kind of comprehension, it squirmed away from him.

All he could identify was the longing, though its object still eluded him. But the sensation had grown in recent weeks, becoming a spectre that followed him all day, every day, standing just over his shoulder and whispering in his ear in a language he couldn't understand. It was dragging away his sanity, he was sure, but though he looked - and he looked *hard* - he could see no other signs of madness.

Desperation lodged in his throat and he wished, wished with all his being, that he could do something, *anything*, to stop every threat absolutely, to eradicate every enemy with a single thought or sweep of his arm, that they would fall as easily as the pieces on the palace's war room map. Then...*then* he might just get some peace.

Something dropped from his chin and he heard it hit the sheets. He lowered his hand and brushed his stubble. Was that a tear? Or sweat?

The bed springs creaked as he jumped, startled by a knock at the door.

He felt dread make a knot of his intestines. Teagan was on shift. A knock at his home this early in the morning - it could not be good.

For a moment, he considered feigning sleep and ignoring it, but he knew it would only eat him alive if he did and he needn't give his mind any additional fuel to torment him.

Defeated, he threw the damp sheets aside and rose to his feet to make his way blindly through his dour home, stumbling as he went, and opened the front door to find his favoured standing outside, waiting patiently. In hindsight, if he *had* chosen to ignore it, he would probably have continued to knock and wait.

"Teagan," he nodded, standing to one side to let him in, silently resentful of the usual portian lack of emotion that kept his face unreadable and Salus unable to predict the news.

"You weren't sleeping."

He sighed as he closed the door behind him. "Would I have answered if I was?" He turned and led him into what passed for a sitting area, sparsely furnished but for a sideboard, sofa, table and fireplace, and the occasional plant which the private cleaner took care of - he assumed, at least. He'd never watered it, and it hadn't died yet.

He didn't think to light a candle, but Teagan's eyesight was as good as his own, so he sat and gestured for him to do the same. He didn't, of course.

"Teagan," he said flatly, "it's too early for this. Please, just stop."

The slightly younger man's eyes shifted onto him at last, and in that moment the formality dropped. But he still didn't smile. All it really meant was that he might call him by his name in place of 'Keliceran', and that he would direct upon him his indecipherable and highly perceptive gaze. But after such conditioning, that was the best Salus could ask for.

Teagan finally took a seat. "I won't keep you. The eastern settlements have been reclaimed."

Salus's eyebrows rose.

"According to our mages, the spells protecting them were simply-constructed and the Order easily dismantled them. They were meant only to delay."

His eyebrows fell again. "And the occupations meant only to distract. So Doana has other plans..." His eyes turned grave in the darkness. "They had help. A small force, no colours or armour; they'd have been easily missed with our own attention so..." He shook his head and breathed. "But they *would* have been noticed entering each settlement, and they *would* have been stopped."

"A guard, then?"

"It's possible. But it was the early hours of the morning, the guards could well have been drowsy, easily distracted. It could have been a chimney sweep."

"We already have people on it."

"Find out if anyone is missing, and if no one is, look for someone who seems suspiciously unrattled by the whole situation - or unusually put out. They'd have been locked in, too."

"We already have people on it," Teagan repeated. "What of your suggestions to Lord Malson?"

Salus's brow flattened and he grunted back into his seat. "Turned down again, every one of them." He shook his head. "We have no allies of our own, we have to see this through ourselves, and while Skilan and even Kalokh can be predicted and handled, Doana is a wild card. *No one* could have expected them..." *'and now Turunda could be in trouble.'* He silenced that voice immediately. "It's as if the Crown isn't willing to do what it must, make the decisions Turunda *needs* of it."

Teagan studied him with his sharp gaze. "Then...perhaps you should just issue the orders yourself, if you believe them to be the best course of action. Have them done and face the music when it comes. You've done it before - your mage, for example."

"Yes, but not after being explicitly told 'no'..." He chewed the inside of his cheek for a long moment. "But," he continued slowly, "I will. I am responsible for the safety of the country in far many more ways than the king or the general, and as long as the country *is* safe, I'll take whatever punishment my 'insubordination' is issued."

"Then you have new orders?" Teagan straightened expectantly, and Salus's eyes hardened.

"Hunt Doana down and stop them. Send our best trackers. They'll be moving in small, scattered groups, and they'll be adept at avoiding detection. They were able to get close enough to kill the watch guards along the mountains before they could raise the alarm. And lift from them any and all information possible, by any means necessary." His tone had steeled upon that final point, becoming almost spiteful. "We need to find out not only what they plan and why, but what they know about *us*."

"The bodies."

Salus nodded.

"It will be done."

But Teagan rose too quickly.

Salus's eyes grew speculative as he watched him move in the darkness. "This could have waited. What did you really come here to tell me?"

The portian hesitated as he turned towards the door.

"Oh, the irony." Salus smiled briefly. "You needn't protect me, you know."

Teagan sighed and his shoulders slumped - both were only slight, but it was more than would ever usually be seen of this or any other portian. He turned back to Salus, reached into a pocket and removed a miniature scroll.

His jaw tightened at the sight of it. It seemed his office was filling with more of these moth-delivered 'urgent's than standard reports, and he was growing quite weary of them. But he didn't voice it. He lit a nearby candle and held out his hand.

Teagan remained at his side as he dropped it into his palm, braced for what would surely follow, but Salus ignored him as his eyes adjusted quickly to the dim, unsteady light and rolled across the abbreviations. He stared down at it for a long while, and a slight frown began pulling at Teagan's brow as he waited for some kind of reaction. But Salus wore no expression at all, revealed not even a hint of his thoughts. He only stared in silence, his eyes roving over the words again and again. He'd become erratic as of late, but at that moment, it seemed to Teagan that that unpredictability had become distinctly predictable. He would usually have shouted or thrown things, if not both, but here he simply sat in a disconcerting silence with the parchment held loosely in his fingers.

Perhaps he'd burst something.

Finally, Salus blinked. "How...?" He spoke too calmly, but as Teagan waited for him to elaborate, he began reading over the report once again. He shook his head after two more attempts, lowered the parchment and scratched his stubbled chin.

"More information is being gathered," Teagan offered, as if the silence was beginning to disturb him. "It should be on your desk within the next hour."

He nodded and rose lightly to his feet. "Then, I suppose I'd better get dressed."

No sooner had the office door closed behind them than Salus erupted into a white-hot fury. Teagan found himself almost relieved as he shouted and kicked things, his eyes blazing wildly. A delayed reaction, no doubt; the contents of the report must have finally registered and he'd been bubbling over as they walked through the early dawn light towards the main building. Not that he truly understood its extent, of course, but he was portian. Such a reaction was beyond his own ability, let alone comprehension.

"*But he is dead!*" He bellowed, certainly audible several rooms over. "*Dead and banished! A decade ago!*"

"It seems--"

"The Order hid him," he decided fervently. "They hid him all the way back then *precisely* for this. That's why he's out there with Karth right now, helping him look for the artefact! If everyone thought he was dead, no one - not us nor *anyone* else - would notice him missing from the Order while all this is going on!"

"That's--"

"*How could anyone even work alongside him?!*"

A knock came at the door.

"*What?!*"

The arrival didn't hesitate. The door opened, the operative stepped inside, and silently extended a wrapped bundle of parchment without her gaze once brushing him.

Teagan noted Salus's abrupt reaction. His mouth closed despite having been gripped by a snarl, his back straightened and his contorted brow relaxed. His cheeks may even have turned the slightest shade pinker, he wasn't sure.

"Taliel, thank you," he said, catching himself immediately and returning at least to a brusque formality, and took the folder she offered. He didn't dismiss her as he untied the catch and leafed through the papers, and his scowl shortly returned with its original severity. "Sahrot Rathen Koraaz; banished, presumed dead; no body recovered." He shook his head in disgust. "Either this is a major cover-up, or the archivists are idiots." He frowned as he read on. "Married; wife deceased. How and when?"

"One of his victims," she replied.

Salus grunted. "I suppose that's what they call poetic justice." He turned over to a list of those victims and his revulsion intensified. "Three of them were children under five. How can he live with himself?" He flicked through the final few sheets then dropped it onto his desk with more force than he'd intended, and turned his eyes upon his subordinates. "How is the Order? What are they doing?"

"They're quiet," Teagan replied.

Taliel nodded. "They're not reacting."

"Then this attack was part of their plan - which also suggests that your theory of few being involved in this uprising is incorrect. There would be some kind of surprise otherwise." His gaze shifted off of Taliel and onto the wall behind her, his eyes becoming sharp, precise, though still a touch wild. The office was smothered under a heavy silence as he thought. "We won't approach them," he decided. "The Order wants the artefact, though for what purpose, we don't yet know. Perhaps to prevent it from being used against them, or to use its magic themselves. Either way, they have Karth on their side and they're surely making more progress with him than we are with Drassa. We'll let them continue and they can lead us right to it. I suspect Drassa's leading us in circles anyway."

"What makes you say that?"

"Aside from the distinctly opposite techniques he and Karth are using in their search, there's the likelihood that the Order has had this lined up for a long time. They had Koraaz on the sidelines and got to Karth before we could. It's just as likely that they reached out for the second most logical choice, knowing we would turn to him eventually, and paid him off to delay us."

"What do we do about him if that is the case?" Teagan asked mildly.

"He has to deliver us some kind of information, but he's no doubt holding back and giving it to us as slowly as he can without raising too much suspicion. But that means he can still be useful, so if we let him continue to believe he's leading us along, the Order will believe it, too. They'll ignore us while we continue to track Karth and Koraaz. But..." His expression became puzzled. "But why did he attack Carenna? He's only drawn attention to himself..."

"That could well have been the point," Taliel supplied. "With the war, we're already stretched thin. Perhaps they wanted to distract us with yet something else."

"Baiting us to use up more resources trying to stop him rather than chasing the artefact, or to keep us from realising they're after it too." Salus nodded firmly. "In fact the artefact could well take care of him more easily than we can... Perhaps we *should* ignore him."

"Keliceran?" Teagan frowned in surprise.

He raised his hand to reassure him. "Not *truly* ignore him. Hower has already caught up with them, he'll--"

"I'm afraid you're mistaken, Keliceran."

Salus frowned at Teagan, who looked back vaguely confused himself.

"Once they left the city gates, they seem to have vanished. There were no footprints to follow - it did state as much in the report..."

Salus closed his eyes and tried to breathe away his boiling frustration. It didn't work. His jaw knotted and he spoke through his teeth. "It did. You're right." He sighed again, then stopped in thought. "Observing Karth is already a standing order. Add Koraaz to that - now we know who the mage is, he'll be difficult to mistake. Hower is an expert tracker, but if he doesn't manage to find them himself first, someone else *will*. We don't need to devote more than that."

"If we ignore him, won't the Order think it suspicious?"

"Not if I say the right things to Malson. It'll get back to the Order one way or another." His lip curled. "You can count on that."

Another knock came at the door. It was still early - too early for Salus to reasonably occupy the office, but in recent weeks it seemed that no one particularly thought of that. Unless his office door was *always* under assault at dawn and only recently had he been in to notice it.

He called to enter and a messenger stepped in, a phaeacian who carried himself notably weaker than Taliel - though in fairness she carried herself with almost the grace and focus of a portian. In fact, she could well be due for a promotion soon.

The idea of ridding her of emotions sent a curious note of distress through him. He decided to push the thought aside for now.

"Keliceran, your presence is requested in the cells," he announced rigidly.

"At this hour? Why? What does Nolan want?"

"It regards the mage; he didn't otherwise specify."

Salus hung his head. "Thank you. Dismissed." The young man managed to turn and leave without making his relief too obvious. "I feel like I'm being pulled in a thousand directions," he mumbled, already feeling the impending pressures of the day, then turned to the others and spoke up. "I've got some questions for our guest that might just rattle something out of him. This early in the morning, a single reaction could be enough." He pushed himself away from the edge of the desk and straight towards the door, but hesitated just behind Taliel. "You're dismissed, phidipan."

She didn't seem to notice his softened tone as she inclined her head and turned to leave ahead of them, but Teagan did. As always, however, he said nothing, and followed the Keliceran out.

"Has he still said nothing?"

"Not a peep," Salus replied as they moved down the hallways. "We don't even have his name. Perhaps that's what this is about, perhaps Nolan has finally broken him."

"I'm surprised it's taken this long. Nolan is brutal."

"I wouldn't be too impressed. He probably placed himself under some kind of spell - stilled his own tongue so he couldn't talk, or numbed his body so he had no dying need to give in."

"He doesn't believe Nolan would truly kill him."

"Well I certainly wouldn't *authorise* it unless he was about to blow this place sky-high, but Nolan has had three 'accidents' in the last two years by pushing prisoners too far."

"Or so he claims."

He nodded, though the slightest smile touched his lips. "Or so he claims. Still, the uncertainty among his team in such circumstances could only help. Prisoners pick up on that."

"The intelligent ones."

"I think this mage probably falls into that category."

Salus's pace increased impatiently once they reached the tunnels, and when he all but ran into the steel-barred cellar with Teagan close behind him, keeping up with little trouble and no lapse at all in composure, Nolan was inside waiting for them. He was a young man, a phidipan, and fiercely dedicated to his work, but there was a disconcerting glint to his eye that suggested the presence of a severe violent streak. Brutal though he could be, however, especially with stubborn prisoners, he seemed able to keep a curiously tight control over it and himself. And he had a true talent for reading people - he seemed to know precisely how to work his assignments to present the most efficient results. He was the lead breaker for a reason.

But this mage, it seemed, was another matter, and at that moment the interrogator looked far from impressed.

"Has he said anything?" Salus asked as he reached him and the two Aranan mages who stood on either side of the locked alcove.

"In a manner of speaking," he replied flatly.

"You're in a humorous mood."

"The pun was not intended, Keliceran." Nolan gestured a leather-wrapped hand towards the cell. "He wants to speak to you."

Salus's brow knotted as he peered through the steel bars towards the mage. He could still feel the hum of the spells that coursed through them, as, no doubt, could their prisoner.

The mage stood at the centre of the small, stone cage. His face was taut, very much the countenance of a man who generally said little, though there was a degree of expectation in his focused and equally pale blue-grey eyes. His dark hair was still neatly tied back and braided in places, and the plain clothes they'd given him when they'd confiscated his rich robes were still quite clean. Somehow the dust and grime of the place hadn't touched him. Salus found that that irritated him, but his aggravation was satisfied by the sight of bruises across his sharp cheekbones.

Salus nodded to one of the guards, and the cell door creaked open. Teagan was about to protest - he heard him inhale - but he silenced him with a gesture and stepped slowly inside. "Close the gate."

He fixed the mage with imposing supremacy as the steel clattered shut behind him, the same look that made almost everyone who stood before him shift uncomfortably. But this mage, like one or two of the others, didn't seem at all affected. Instead, he gave Salus a close and studious stare in return, the same dauntless look he'd given him on every other occasion he'd come in to speak to him himself - even on the ride back to Arana House following his arrest. It revealed a great deal of intelligence, so sharp and analytical that it could have belonged to an Aranan operative. The fact that the Order had people like this unsettled him.

"You need my help."

The words took a moment for Salus's mind to process. He'd first been distracted by the slightest lilt to his voice, an unidentifiable accent that set him on edge. He'd never heard it before, but the only thing this man had ever said in his presence was 'why'. Then he'd noticed his inflection. Accent or not, the gravity with which he'd spoken couldn't be missed, nor the fact that he'd delivered the statement as news rather than a shared truth.

Salus's fair eyebrows twitched. "Why?" He asked, his voice carefully unaffected.

"If you have to ask, you must need it all the more." The mage continued to stare, unmoving until his strange eyes narrowed a fraction. "You can't feel it, can you?"

"Feel what?"

"The magic."

Salus glanced around at the bars. "Yes, I can," he replied, turning back. "I ordered it put there to keep you detained."

"I don't mean these rudimentary spells," the mage scoffed. "I mean that which is swelling in your heart, mingling with your blood."

"What are you talking about?" His voice had yet to break its careful mask of indifference.

The mage seemed to smile dangerously, but his bruising prevented it from truly taking hold. "Your veins burned, didn't they? When? How long before you captured me? A week?"

Salus straightened. He could see what he was doing, and he wasn't about to let his questioning become waylaid by this nonsense. The mage finally felt like speaking and he *would* get from him what he needed. "Are you with Turunda's Order?"

"That is irrelevant," he replied, brushing the question aside with his increasingly irritating arrogance. "I have no intention of turning you over to them for training. I can do that myself."

"How did the Order hide Rathen Koraaz? And why?"

"I haven't a clue - you seem to be missing what's important here--"

"Is Anthis Karth working for the Order?"

"I don't even know who he is!" The mage's composure fractured and he took a sudden and exasperated step towards him, but motion outside quickly caught his attention. His eyes snapped towards the two mages whose hands had raised in preparation, and he halted his advance. "Salus," he said brazenly, "I've felt your magic growing every day since you've shut me down here, and if it continues to do so, and remains untamed, there will be trouble for *everyone*."

"Enough!" Salus's mask shattered, and his bellow reverberated ferociously through the stone chamber. "I will *not* fall for the Order's tricks. Answer my questions or you will lose your fingers - then at least I won't have to worry about the Order taking you back. You won't be much use to them if you can't cast any spells."

The mage narrowed his eyes with a flash of abandon and stepped towards him again, but this time he ignored the mages outside as they began forming and releasing their spells. Not one made it through the bars.

Quicker than Salus could think to stop him, the prisoner contorted his fingers and pressed his palm firmly against Salus's chest.

Heat spread. His eyes tore wide open, and a choked gasp escaped his throat. He couldn't move. If he did, the mage would surely rip his heart out. He was certain he had a hold of it; he could feel his fingers wrap around it, feel him squeeze it - and yet, somehow, it didn't hurt. But even had he been inclined to try to escape, his body was in shock. It wouldn't had responded.

The mage withdrew after only a moment, but he didn't notice the cool wave of relief. He was gripped instead by the glowing image that vacated his chest, following the mage's palm.

"Why aren't the suppression spells working?" He heard Teagan demand in his usual authoritative, dispassionate voice, but he sounded distant. Salus didn't turn to check. He stared, stunned by the blue light. It was a heart - beating, pumping more luminescence out through the arteries to vanish in the air. Was it *his* heart?

He became acutely aware of his pulse, the thump of his blood throughout his body.

The mage drew his finger across the image and cut it neatly in half. He had expected pain, or to experience another curious sensation at the least, but there was nothing at all.

The image rose, floating away from his palm to hang in the air between them, and the mage looked back to him, ignoring his pallor. "Your heart has five chambers, Salus. Look closely." The smallest chamber, nestled at the centre of the cross-section, began to glow brighter than the rest. "The magic forms here, and enters the blood as it leaves the ventricle and pumps into the aorta." He pressed his hand then to his own chest and pulled out a similar image, though this heart seemed a touch broader. When he cut it open, the fifth chamber was equally enlarged. He looked at him imploringly. "Our hearts are the same."

Salus finally found his feet to take himself a hurried step backwards, and his expression had turned from alarm to rage. "The Order truly *is* desperate to keep us distracted," he snarled.

The mage's hand dropped, and the two lucent projections vanished. "You won't believe me, will you?"

Salus had already turned curtly on his heel and made for the cell door, which opened in time with his stride. He raised his hand as Teagan started towards him. "I'm fine." He turned to Nolan, his lips pulled into a bitter snarl. "He's all yours. Make him talk."

"Of course, Keliceran."

"By *any* means."

The young man smiled. "Of *course*, Keliceran."

He stepped ominously into the cell at his superior's passing, but Salus didn't turn to see the mage's reaction.

A growl rumbled free from the depths of his throat as he stormed through the cellar with Teagan close behind him, his jaw knotting, eyes a blue inferno. "He knows a great deal," he spat once they'd stepped back into the tunnels. "I could see it in his eyes. He's undoubtedly involved."

"What was he talking about?"

"Who knows?" He shook his head and folded his arms tightly across his chest, feeling for the reassuring thump of his heart. "But he must truly take us for fools. Untrained magic is harmless - *useless*, even. Everyone knows that. He's only trying to distract us with this nonsense..." His eyebrows drew even tighter together. "But why, when Koraaz has already struck?"

"He likely doesn't know," Teagan suggested easily. "He's been in here for almost three weeks."

"True...though I can't help but notice that he hasn't made any hint towards regaining his freedom...and what concerns me all the more is that he *could* have broken himself out. Those spells *were* in place around the cell, even while we were in there just now, but he was still able to conjure that...heart..."

"How do you *know* the spells were still in place? He could have broken them. Order mages are far more proficient than our own, and generally stronger."

"No, they were still in place, I could feel them." He shook his head again and puffed a long sigh. "Perhaps the Order *does* know he's missing and this is just another part of their plan..." He grunted. "We're not going to fall for it, but if the Order is going to let him stay, we will be obliging hosts. We'll break him yet - he might just have to witness more brutal treatment first...which means we need another prisoner to make an example of."

"The city's notice board is covered in bounty posters. It would take no more than an hour for a phidipan to track one of the criminals down."

"It's not standard practise, but they certainly wouldn't be missed...and we'd be doing the city an extra favour..." He nodded his approval. "Get it done."

"Of course - but may I make a suggestion?"

Salus turned to him expectantly.

"Evidently, the Order wishes to distract you with the notion that you possess magic. They cannot prove it to you, and without training, you wouldn't be able to cast a spell anyway - and it's worth remembering that not all can truly grasp that training. They may well be relying on your unyielding sense of responsibility above anything else, trusting that it will lead you to embrace the suggestion that you have magic with the intention of using it to protect the country. Then they will waste your time trying to teach you to wield it when there's nothing there to wield. Eventually they will 'give up' on you, or you on them; the matter will be closed, and they will be further ahead of us."

"That's awfully deceptive for the Order - in fact it sounds like something *we* would do..." A brief twitch of a smile brushed his lips. "I'm glad I have you on hand, Teagan. But what was your point?"

"Perhaps you should go along with it."

He frowned, bemused. "Why?"

"Because the mage will stay more willingly if he is fulfilling his own task, and he'll open up a little to encourage you to trust him, which will make it easier for you to get information out of him directly. And, as we already know it's a trick, we can watch them while they're satisfied that they have us running in circles. They won't be looking for us over their shoulders anymore."

"Work out what they're doing, get a step ahead of them." He nodded again and took a steadying breath. Control was finding its way slowly back into his hands.

Now he just had to work out how to quash the invaders swarming into Turunda from both sides.

The Cockatrice was quiet, though that wasn't necessarily unusual for so early in the morning. But despite being less than three hours past dawn, Renan had already been there for two, sitting in his usual corner on the upper half-floor and drowning his perpetual sorrows in an equally bottomless mug. There were a few other vagabonds and drunks doing the same on the main floor below, but the city's most popular tavern was silent.

Though that was in part due to a subtle spell that curved through Renan's table and shrouded himself and the curtained-off room behind him, concealing from everyone else the heated discussion that was taking place beyond it.

He looked up as the usual dark-haired woman arrived, giving her a quizzical frown for her tardiness, but she smiled apologetically and slipped in through the curtain behind him. His attention seemed to fall back into his mug.

"Did he believe him?"

The blonde mage shook her head. "He got angry and stormed off. He believes the Order is trying to trick him."

"Perhaps they are - but this *is* a grave concern." Malson sighed and folded his arms over his fine robes. "The idea has been planted in his mind and we have no way of knowing whether or not he will heed it. He may not believe the mage at the moment, but that could change, and it's not a chance we can risk taking." He cast his sharp old eyes across the thirteen gathered, giving each of them a severe look. "We need to prepare for the worst. Move things into place.

"I will put word out to my contacts - I have many fingers in many pies, and the ear of countless authorities. Though many seem to be taking action on their own these days, I can rely on a few to turn a blind eye where we need them to. And while our own search is already in motion, it seems there's now a greater urgency. Initially we needed only to keep the elven relic away from him, but now--"

"Now we may have to use it against him," a troubled-looking middle-aged man finished.

Malson nodded. "We need to improve our resources. Should he succeed in awakening and wielding his magic, he won't be rational in its use. In the mean time, we need to do all we can to stop this from getting any further; try to ensure he doesn't believe the mage, and discourage him from pursuing it should we fail."

"Keeping him occupied is a good start," the man suggested. "Give him no chance to think about it. He's dedicated to his work - we can use that to our advantage."

"I can do that easily enough myself." Malson looked to the mage. "Vari, is there anything you or the other mages can do?"

She sighed reluctantly, invoking doubtful discomfort in a number of those around her. "We can't affect his magic, if that's what you mean. He's the one who has been unknowingly suppressing it, and he is the one who will awaken it. No one else can do it for him - which at least means that this mage can't, either. But what we *can* do is talk, try to push the idea out of his mind before it can take root."

"Could you convince him that the mage is lying?"

She nodded slowly. "He might be more likely to believe that if it came from another magic-user," she replied carefully, "but I'm not sure how effective it would be without some kind of proof. I think he'd respond better to the idea of a threat or a violent deception."

Malson's serious frown became intrigued. "Such as?"

"Suggesting that the process of learning to wield his magic would involve making himself vulnerable to the mage, giving him the opportunity to do something to him. He's a prisoner - it wouldn't be much trouble to imagine a motive."

"Salus is already mistrusting and paranoid. He'd certainly be receptive to that..." He nodded. "See to it."

"Of course."

"What if we remove the mage as a factor *completely?*" A young man asked. "Stop him, somehow - talk to him, threaten him. Even kill him if we have to."

"He's under constant guard, we'd never manage to reach him, especially not with only Oliver among the cell guards. Plus the breakers enjoy their job too much. As I understand it, they're in and out all the time. It's not an option. And killing him might be going a bit far at this point.

"Otherwise, we need to try to delay Salus, divert his attention. The rest of you will continue to work beneath him, follow his orders, but create complications. Keep intercepting his every communique, and start delivering reports more slowly - keep him in the dark, and..." he waved his hand lightly, "*embellish* them a little. Use the war as an excuse. He's expecting it to get in the way, but if it interferes enough, he'll put more focus onto it and distract *himself.*"

"What if all this fails?"

All eyes turned onto another young man, and he looked back with the same doubt and discomfort he always wore in these meetings. He was phaeacian, and he was undeniably torn between his loyalties. Malson didn't truly trust him and often watched his wording in his presence, but he knew that the young man only wanted what was best for Turunda. He just didn't seem very sure of where to find it.

"If it fails," the old man replied patiently, the same question ringing at the back of his own mind as well, no doubt, as in others', "we should begin to consider a way to approach the Order. Should it get that far and we fail in our search, they may well be the only ones that can repair the situation. But acting upon that is a last resort. It would cast great mistrust over all mages in the Arana and no doubt result in their removal. And the Arana needs mages."

"Would you really risk getting the Order involved given everything else that's going on?" He pressed with increasing concern.

"You're referring to the incident in Carenna."

"If by 'incident' you mean the return of a *monster*, yes."

Malson cast a reassuring gaze across each of them. Most apparently carried the same concern. "I don't believe that Rathen Koraaz is a real threat."

"I can't fathom how you can possibly say that. He is a concern for *all* of us, not just the Arana. The country is in chaos, and a man like that on the loose could easily complicate *all* efforts against the war!"

"His movements are that of *one* man, Jora," the old man said firmly, "*not* the Order, nor any rebellion. This incident, as alarming as it is, is nothing more than an irregularity. And Salus will no doubt be taking action against it himself. It needn't occupy *our* attention, so put it out of your minds. We are too few, and Salus is a far more real and organised threat - do you disagree?"

The phaeacian straightened, but his eyes weakened in submission. "I don't. You're right. I apologise, my lord."

"It's all right. I understand your concerns. It feels like we're trying to protect the country from its own people, doesn't it?" He smiled reassuringly. "But we *will* succeed, on all fronts." He looked across them all again with the same focused certainty. "It's early, but time is not on our side. I'm sure you all have work to do, and we don't want to arouse suspicion. You're all dismissed."

The thirteen turned and left the dark little room, managing to avoid the notice of anyone in the tavern despite their number. But the late arrival had hesitated, lost in troubled thought as the others brushed by her, and when she finally turned to follow, the Crown's liaison was suddenly standing in front of her, smiling sympathetically.

"You seem troubled, Taliel."

She mustered a weak smile. "Things are getting a bit complicated..."

"There are a few balls up in the air at the moment," he agreed, then turned his head curiously. "But it's more than that, isn't it? What is it you know?"

She frowned only gently, but even the very few and slight creases upon her face made her concern abundantly clear. She didn't speak for a long moment. "I think Salus is attracted to me."

The old man's grey eyebrows rose so high they might have flown off of his forehead, and an equally unexpected smile spread wide across his wrinkled face. He didn't seem amused, however, but genuinely pleased. "He listened."

Her frown deepened in confusion. "Sir?"

Malson shook his head and considered her for a moment, then lowered his voice to a guiding tone. "Salus was a child agent, and a prodigy. He was taken in as a phaeacian at age eight and became a phidipan at age sixteen. He was one of the few operatives to ever have been promoted at the earliest opportunity. His conditioning took incredibly well and he was promoted once again after further conditioning at nineteen. He was denied a childhood, denied an adolescence - which means that there are many, many feelings he has never, ever known, and can't hope to understand.

"Since his conditioning reversed and he took the mantle of Keliceran, he's been faced with the resurfacing of emotions, but they have only ever been negative and he's struggled to know how to handle them. Even now, after eight years, he is still vulnerable to them, and, lately, he's been increasingly and unnaturally temperamental. He knows only anger, suspicion and frustration. But having the chance to explore these brighter feelings might...introduce him to another side of humanity. It could help to settle him - maybe even finally get him to clear his head, see sense and *just stop* what he's doing. Love - even just infatuation - is, after all, *essential* to life."

She looked at him uncomfortably. "You want me to encourage him."

"I don't expect you to reciprocate any feelings, only to let him continue admiring you. It could do more good than you know. It could even provide us with a solution."

Taliel chewed the inside of her cheek before nodding, albeit reluctantly. "All right."

"How did this come about, anyway?" He asked with a more childish curiosity that would usually have been seen on the face of the rich and bored.

"I don't know," she admitted, just as curious herself. "He summoned me one afternoon, insisted that I drop formalities and said that he wanted to talk."

Malson frowned. "Talk? What about?"

"His dreams."

"His dreams?"

"He's been having trouble sleeping, and he's felt tense, stressed - not that that's very surprising."

"No, it isn't," he replied, chewing his lip thoughtfully. "And he summoned you specifically? You didn't just happen to be the next one to step into his office?"

"No, he summoned me, specifically, by moth. And there's been more: looks, strange comments - he apologised for assigning me to investigate some soldiers in the city because he said they were 'a bit rough with women'."

Malson breathed a brief chuckle. "How strange...how curious indeed. Well, it seems you have yourself an admirer, Taliel, whether you want one or not, and it couldn't have been more convenient."

"I suppose..." Then, she straightened formally and gave him a steady, obedient stare. "I'll see it done and do all in my power to make this work in our favour."

"I have no doubt that you will." He placed his hand on her shoulder and gave it a gentle squeeze, and his eyes softened sympathetically again. "And I'm sorry."

She smiled appreciatively, then turned and left the dark room. He shortly followed her out and found Renan still sitting in his usual chair, though he turned him an astonished glance. Malson simply shrugged as his own surprise returned.

Chapter 28

It was mid-morning, one bright and musical with the onset of spring - but, while the rest of the camp had been up and appreciating it for some time already, Rathen's eyes had only recently opened. He'd slept soundly even as the rousing sunlight crept in between the trees to streak his face, and though the others were restless, no one had wished to wake him - in part because Kienza had stood guard over him all night. Even now, she remained close to his side as they loaded the newly-acquired horses with the equally new blankets and bedrolls, watching him with the same soft smile she'd worn all night as Aria helped him into his shirt. The others had identified the nature of her vigilance early on, one of affection rather than concern, and respectfully kept their distance.

Except Anthis.

He chose to use her defence as an excuse to keep away while maintaining a very close watch from the corner of his eye. But far from signs of a monster, all he'd observed that morning was how startlingly different Rathen was in Kienza's presence. Upon first meeting him he'd been cold, closed off to any kind of interaction and extremely uncomfortable in almost every setting - though the reason for his social anxiety was now quite screamingly apparent. But once he'd adjusted to Anthis's company...well, he was still cold and disinterested, but from time to time a human being flashed through that exterior, and those flashes grew into a warm and welcoming flame when he interacted with Aria.

But when Kienza was added into the equation, his unapproachable shell disintegrated and that welcoming flame became a steadily burning hearth fire. He smiled, he laughed, he loved, his unwavering melancholy forgotten. It was as if he was a normal person, part of an ordinary family - though, considering the three individuals, that was probably stretching the term 'ordinary' to its limits...

Anthis quickly diverted his gaze as Kienza turned around, stepping away from Rathen for the first time in twelve hours to wander quietly off into the forest. He made a show of moving to the other side of his horse and fiddling with his bags, lifting his gaze back over only once she was gone to watch Rathen stare thoughtfully after her. His expression was similarly ordinary, one of someone absently pondering the unquestionable affection of their lover.

The sight unsettled Anthis all the more. How could anyone look past his monstrous revelation so *easily?!* Garon seemed to accept it as little more than an inconvenience, while Petra...of *all* people, Petra should have had the hardest time even just *tolerating* him after the nature of her confession last night, but instead it seemed to have created some twisted sort of bond between them! It utterly boggled his mind!

As if hearing her name in his thoughts, Petra suddenly appeared on the other side of the horse, perfectly blocking his view. His eyes slowly dragged up to her, and her steady, critical stare coaxed a wave of guilt. She *must* have been reading his thoughts. Or perhaps it was his face. He became aware of the knot in his brow and the unbridled mistrusting curl of his lip and forced them both to loosen.

"It's not something he's in control of," she told him pointedly, confirming his suspicions as she moved around beside him, her hands resting disapprovingly on her hips. "And *especially* not proud of. It's just a part of who he is - most people carry a dark shadow through their life, his is just darker than most."

"Well, *I* don't like it," he replied, trying to ignore the childishly stubborn note that had slipped out with it. "He could easily have *killed* us without a moment's notice, and he kept that to himself. I thought I was getting to know him, but that...he's been deceiving us all along."

"Secrets will do that." She sighed wearily, then cast him a sidelong glance. "*I* trust him. And I trust Garon's judgement. Perhaps you should just talk to him about it. I doubt avoiding him is going to help *either* of you. Or me. I can only just handle the atmosphere *Garon* creates." Her eyes trailed off towards the inquisitor as he stared ever-watchfully into the forest.

Anthis noticed her gaze soften as she considered him and felt a small spark of jealousy. "I can't do that," he said, shrugging it off.

"Why not?"

"Because it's so...personal..."

She looked back and flashed him a beautiful, crooked smile. "I'll bet that's never stopped you before."

He gave her a flat look and was about to respond in protest, along with a few other reasons that needn't truly have been mentioned, but he spotted Aria wandering about and decided to swallow them back. He smiled as she lifted a long stick from the ground, looked subtly towards Petra, then held it to her hip as if it was sheathed at her side. He pretended not to notice as she then ran off in search of something to fix it in place with.

He looked thoughtfully back towards Petra as she adjusted the straps of his bags, but his next words were forgotten in a brief wave of panic and he quickly took over, shooing her aside and assuring her he could do it himself. "You were quite impressive in Carenna," he said, partly in an attempt to distract her from his abruptness. "That duel..."

"Thank you," she smiled modestly.

"Though there were a few close scrapes..."

"I wouldn't say that."

"He was going to *kill* you!"

She returned his incredulous stare with a sly and self-assured smile. "I could see what he was doing; I was in complete control. He was getting desperate, taking advantage of every opening, and he was getting clumsy in the process. The moment he stopped thinking and stopped concealing his movements, he'd lost. I needed only to make the final move."

"...What does that mean? You slipped on purpose?"

"I put myself into a compromised position knowing full well that he'd leap on it."

"Which he did, blade-first, and nearly killed you."

"I knew what he was going to do, Anthis, you don't have to sound so concerned.

I've been doing this for six years, not to mention training with swords since I was a little girl."

"Well, it shows," he sighed, and a touch of bewilderment descended upon him as he shook his head. "And people fight you voluntarily. Are they mad?"

She grinned proudly. "Some even seek me out."

"But why do you do it? It seems *unreasonably* dangerous..."

"It makes good coin."

He paused in interest. "How much?"

"That one fight, two hundred and thirty five crowns. And I usually win."

His surprise faltered. "Usually?"

"I can't always, can I? Sometimes I have to throw it to keep other people thinking *they* could win. And other times I just have a bad day, get a bad read on opponents, get unlucky - sometimes they cheat. The list goes on."

"Cheating shouldn't be allowed," Aria injected as she passed them, heading back to her father with her stick-sword now securely fastened to her waist by a few knotted branchlings.

Petra both frowned and smiled at her in bemusement. "It isn't."

"And neither are the duels," Garon equally added from the edge of the camp.

"I didn't see you stepping in to stop it, Inquisitor," Anthis poked as Petra sighed in irritation.

"I didn't want to draw any attention to us."

Anthis rolled his eyes despite his amusement, then pardoned himself and hurried towards Kienza as she returned to camp from the opposite direction she'd left.

"Excuse me," he started politely as he fell in beside her, then stumbled as she smiled in return - another beautiful smile. She chuckled, quite aware of his reaction, but she didn't pause her stride to chat.

"Is, uh," he continued uncertainly, dropping his voice lower, "is the...*all that*...likely to happen again?" He watched her closely, hoping she might answer favourably, but she simply shrugged as easily as if he'd asked her where his left boot was.

"Who knows. It could. The longest he's gone between bouts is two years, and the shortest...a few hours."

Anthis faltered to a stop as she walked on ahead to rejoin Rathen, and he turned a doubtful gaze upon the pale mage once again.

"Well," Garon began in declaration as he turned back towards the camp, "thank you for your help once again, ma'am, but we had better be off."

Kienza turned and her eyes slighted at him thoughtfully. "Time is of the essence, is it?" She asked him mildly.

"There's no sense leaving a problem be if it can be corrected, is there?" He replied in kind.

She nodded slowly as he held her gaze, though her eyes didn't soften right away. "I suppose not. Well," suddenly a fifth horse, one unnecessarily white and with unnecessarily long tusks, appeared beside her. "Let's be off then."

"You're coming with us?" Anthis asked as she hoisted herself easily up into its side saddle, unsure if he was pleased by the idea or simply relieved.

"For the moment. I can't leave Rathen so soon."

"I'm fine," the mage protested as Aria hurriedly led their own horse over and handed him the reins, "you don't need--"

"Oh *do* shut up, Rathen. Even *you* know that isn't true."

Aria giggled as a small breeze lifted her from the ground and set her down in the front of the saddle, and a box appeared beside the horse before Rathen could begin to struggle himself. He sent her an unappreciative look, but they both knew he was grateful that at least *some* of his dignity had been spared.

"And anyway," she continued as the others climbed into their own saddles without such help, "apparently we're in a rush, and there's something you all need to know."

"Which would be?"

Her lips parted, but then she turned towards Garon and smiled quite politely, waving her hand in the forward direction. "After you, Inquisitor."

He looked at her suspiciously, but took the lead all the same.

"The earthquake outside Carenna."

"What earthquake?"

"You wouldn't remember it, dearest, you were quite suddenly incapacitated at the time. It was a minor tremor, but the ground has been rent, and magic was to blame." A troubled shadow fell over their brows, but she continued, disconnected, as if reading from someone else's notes. "The site was unremarkable, and there were no apparent magical effects on the surrounding elements, until now."

"Is it linked at all to...Rathen's...?" Petra let it hang, and Kienza turned her a quick and bemused frown.

"No, of course not. That was just an unfortunate coincidence. But it does mean that this 'loose magic' is becoming more abundant and concentrated. We knew this already, of course, but the pressure of so much magic is finally reaching breaking point and becoming a serious threat to Turunda. Chasms in the north are growing wider, deeper, longer, and a few are starting to join up. Voiland has very recently been split into three pieces and one of those divides is creeping south through Ivaea and straight towards us. I expect it'll join up with the one that just formed outside of Carenna, given time."

The atmosphere had grown surprisingly thick in the space of less than a minute.

"Where was it?"

She cast Anthis a regretful look. "Halen."

He blanched. "That's not a ruin, that's a *village*."

"Was," she corrected with even greater regret, but as the atmosphere thickened further, a shared guilt adding its weight, she frowned at them all in disapproval. "This was far from the first settlement to be destroyed by this magic," she reminded them firmly.

"And you *don't* think time is of the essence?"

"Isn't it a bit bigoted to only discover a sense of urgency when it's your *own* people being affected, Inquisitor?" She sighed. "It's been going on for *months* beyond these borders. And anyway, you won't succeed in stopping this before more lives are lost - you still have to find the artefact, figure out how it works, work out how to use it for your intended purpose and then *do* so, quite likely one place at a time. I'm sorry to break it to you so bluntly, but it's a truth you need to hear if you're going to continue along this quest of yours." She brushed a passing glance over each of them, noting the varying degrees of guilt they openly carried. Even Petra, which she felt was curious, but evidently the young woman had formed enough of a bond with the others to share in their stake. "You can't put the weight of the matter on your own shoulders. This magic is not your fault. Your responsibility to try to do something about it is self-imposed, and while incredibly noble, that doesn't mean that you have to take responsibility for every single aspect of it. If you were to find a stranger wounded in the street and you rushed him straight to a medic, would it be your fault if he died before you got him there?"

No one answered.

She sighed wearily. "Taking it upon yourselves to try to fix this matter is already more than *anyone* could ask of you all," she said softly, "but you *can't* blame yourselves for what happens to others along the way. It'll only slow you down. So you had all better get your heads around the fact that it's only going to get worse from here on out so it doesn't trip you up. And perhaps you should try to avoid settlements - distancing yourself from people will improve your concentration. And given recent events..."

"It may not be a bad idea," Garon agreed.

Kienza looked over them again. She saw Anthis sigh doubtfully, but he didn't protest though it was clear he wished to, while Petra and Garon shared each other's resolve. It was Rathen who seemed the most troubled, but the greatest expectations were hanging from his coat. She smiled sadly and rode closer beside him. He returned her smile, his eyes softening, and the two began sharing quiet words.

Anthis watched them as subtly as he could, but soon felt Petra's eyes boring into him and turned his gaze away again. But he frowned when it fell upon a dead tree standing among countless living, its boughs bare while its grey trunk was split down its length by a force only nature could conjure. "How are we here already?!" He all but cried in astonishment.

"What point would there be in just teleporting you ten minutes away from where you were?"

Petra frowned as the trees began to thin and a glinting mixture of onyx, silver and gold began to take shape ahead. "Where are we?"

"Tarun..." His eyes narrowed, but he smiled, suspecting already that she would give him a vague answer to his next question: "How did you know where we were going?"

True to form, the sorceress simply shrugged. "Lucky guess."

Tarun, the grandest of all the elven cities ever constructed by hand or by magic, rolled out before of them as even the trees bowed away in awe. Majestic, enchanting, even by the standards of the imperious elves of its time; it stole the heart of all whose sight it graced, inspiring any number of songs, poems and romantic comparisons.

Exquisite buildings of gold, silver and ebon caught and reflected the sunlight, filling the city with softly twinkling stars in the winter and fireflies in the summer, while their shapely structures, some towering and twisting, others slanting and flowing, created an intriguing skyline that seemed from afar to blend into the clouds themselves.

The finest public gardens blossomed amongst them, filled with countless lattice-trunked trees and many flowering and fruiting plants of abnormal beauty, attracting equally unlikely birds. Benches were concealed within the lush foliage, offering privacy for those who pretended to want it, while in the open, statues of pure silver men and women rose from equally elaborate fountains, their enviously perfect forms populating the gardens and certainly changing position to frolic with one another when no one was looking.

But the miniature paradises and urban marvels did not vie for superiority over one another; they were in perfect harmony, melding into one another, stitched together by the small streams that meandered through the city like veins beneath glass walkways. They connected every district, be it gold and silver or green and blue, to the perfectly oval lake that stood at its heart and the great tower that rose and twisted from its glittering surface.

Truly, it would have been the pinnacle of beauty in its time - but now, the city was even less than a shadow of its former glory; miserable and eerie, the bright and beautiful morning light was reflected back from the city's tangled bones not as stars or fireflies, but as blinding shards of shattered glass.

The group followed the fractured road, silent but for the clop of the horses' shoes, and looked ahead and around themselves at the time-worn ruin.

The twisting structures were falling apart. Their decay was far worse than even Mokhan's neglected towers, and that detail alone revealed to those with the mind to comprehend it just how much magic had been woven into their construction. Without the spells, there was nothing to hold them together but wishful thinking and crossed fingers. And it would be far worse inside. The city was a veritable death trap.

The gardens, too, were overgrown, more tangled than the Wildlands, no doubt also tended and cultivated by magic. The streams were either dried up or clogged with algae, and the glass was certainly no longer clear - in many places it was shattered, and they each held their breath every time the horses crossed over one, expecting a crack, a sudden downward jolt and an equine cry of pain - and the enchants that would have accentuated and intensified every once-spectacular detail had unravelled and long since vanished.

The statues were also defaced, but rather than a result of the rigours of time, they had been the victims of human hands. While most chose to leave what they considered the imprisonment of the cities when their elven masters vanished, others turned to anarchy and destroyed whatever they could, seizing their chance to claim the world as their own before the elves' throne had even grown cold.

"Daddy," Aria whispered from the front of the saddle as she looked around them with an uneasy wrinkle in her brow.

He nodded, wearing much the same expression. "I know, little one." He encouraged the grey horse, which Aria had named Fog The Second, to drop back alongside Anthis. "Where do we need to go?"

"To the archival tower at the centre of the city," he replied quietly. He seemed to have steeled himself against the haunting sight of these ruins. In fact he barely looked about himself at all, as if he didn't wish to see it.

Rathen, however, found himself unable to keep his eyes from roving, and they soon fell upon precisely what Anthis must have sought to avoid. He quickly covered Aria's eyes before she could notice the skeleton half-concealed beneath a broken ebon spire. "Are you sure?" He asked with greater urgency.

"Quite. I've been here countless times. I know where to look."

Garon allowed him the lead, and after half an hour of silence and imaginary blinders, they couldn't reach the tower soon enough. Unfortunately, when they drew up to the building, which seemed so tattered and stripped by the elements that it might just teeter over in the slightest breeze, the door was entirely hidden by a great jumble of wall, floor and jagged metals.

"Can you move it?" Petra asked hopefully, looking between Rathen and Kienza, but neither looked optimistic.

"The city has crumbled in the absence of magic," Kienza explained. "Suddenly reintroducing it to interfere with this mangled mess could destabilise it further."

"Then how are we going to get in?"

"Through the crypts."

Increasingly reluctant gazes shifted heavily towards Anthis, who had raised the suggestion with just as little enthusiasm. He nodded towards one of the rounded stone mounds that rose from the edge of the dried up lake, the single architectural detail that linked these long post-magic elves to their pre-magic ancestors. "They were carved from stone by human hands. They're the most solid structures here."

"And they'll lead us into the tower?"

"The tower was the most secure area of the city; it housed a lot that the elves considered important, and social status was included in that. Higher statuses demanded guarding even in death, so the highest in the social hierarchy were buried beneath it - along with the valuables and secrets they decided to take with them."

"Secrets?" Rathen repeated carefully. "Do you think...?"

"It's extremely unlikely," he replied, "but not impossible." He slipped out of his saddle and Kienza was close behind him. The others followed their lead. "We should keep our eyes open for that sign of anarchy, too. I'd say that was even *less* likely, but if we found it in the Wildlands, of all places, I don't see why it couldn't be here, too."

They followed him uneasily towards the nearest of the projecting half-domes and down the few short steps to its recessed door. It was elaborately carved, but its weathering suggested that it, too, had been cut by hand - so rather than swinging on its hinges while magic crumbled around it, it was heavy and stiff and took the addition of Garon's weight to shove it open. But whether spells had once locked it or guards had stood in place, whatever deterrent had once protected the dead within had left them just as exposed as the decrepit city above them.

The thought disquieted the group as they peered dubiously into the silent darkness. The daylight reached barely three feet beyond the threshold, and it revealed nothing but the short stream of dust that fell through a weakness just above the doorway.

Suddenly not even Anthis was keen to continue, but as Kienza lowered Rathen's hand and conjured a light herself, he steeled his nerves and stepped inside. The others shared wary glances before following him into the constricting tunnel.

The air quickly became cold and dank, thickened by an unearthly density and tinged with a scent that could only be described as 'historic'. Their footsteps, quiet and careful, were muffled rather than intensified by the stone, as if the crypt had been designed with silence as a priority, and the passage seemed never-ending under the short, flickering reach of the flame in Kienza's palm.

The atmosphere was intensely oppressive, and though the tunnel broadened suddenly into an alcove-studded chamber, none were inclined to breathe easily. Here the air became even heavier, weighted now by an ominous presence as if they'd just walked uninvited into a stranger's home. And it seemed, in a way, that they had.

The caskets that should have lined the walls were strewn instead across the floor. Some were in one piece, though their lids were tossed aside or set skewed on top, while others were shattered, corners crushed or side panels completely torn away.

Kienza manipulated her flame. It grew enough to illuminate the small chamber from wall to wall, but the shadows that shrouded the contents of the once-elaborate coffins deepened to midnight-black. It only further drew the eye, though not one of them had any desire to look upon the dead.

"This isn't broken magic," Petra whispered in disgust as she closed her eyes rather than succumb to the pull.

Anthis shook his head in agreement. "Thieves. Treasure hunters and historians alike." He picked up his pace and the others did the same, flinching at the sound of crumbling rock and the shift of dust disturbed by their presence. They readily averted their eyes from the bones that had spilled out from one of the final caskets.

The atmosphere released them as they entered the tunnel at the far end, but its clawed grip returned with a vengeance as tiptoed around a corner and into another chamber in an identical state.

"Why are they here?" Aria asked, her voice the lightest whisper yet coloured by a strange, sober interest.

"This is where they were buried," Rathen replied softly.

"They don't look buried to me..."

"Grave robbers." Rathen noticed a number of much smaller nooks set between the coffin recesses. A few were occupied by urns, some incomplete, their lids missing, while others were simply broken, but there were certainly more piles of ashes in here than jars. He jolted in fright when he felt the gentle brush of dust on his shoulder, and reminded himself silently and desperately that it was surely only stone.

"'High social status', eh?" Petra repeated doubtfully.

"Among elves," Anthis reminded her. "And to have been laid to rest here, yes. Leaders, nobles, 'artists'..."

"And the urns?"

"They would have only just qualified."

As they moved through into another tunnel, Aria dragged her thoughtful eyes away from the crypt behind them and tugged on Rathen's arm, her hand already firmly in his. "Will I be put in a place like this when I die?" She asked with that same curious tone, and the question didn't strike anyone particularly well.

But Rathen considered her, then mirrored her tone. "Would you want that?"

She looked back towards the chamber as it returned to abyssal darkness. "Mm...no. It's too dark and cold. I'd rather be outside with flowers and animals." Then she considered him. "Would *you* want to be down here?"

"No," he smiled. "I agree with you on all counts."

"Then why did the elves want to be down here?" She asked Anthis, twisting to face him as she walked. "Or were they forced to?"

"No, they strived for it, actually. They didn't want to be buried in the ground, they wanted to stay pristine, untouched, and with as many of their valuables as possible." He said the last with a carefully subdued tone, and his eyes flicked towards the shifting shadows cast by Kienza's slender fingers as she carried her flame, which, he noted, was surprisingly bright for something so small.

"But it's so *miserable* down here..."

He smiled sadly. "They didn't *always* want this. Before their magic, they wanted what you do. They were laid bare in the ground, no box, no headstone, no clothing but a simple veil of spider silk and leaves. Their bodies were simply returned to the earth that bore them while their spirits passed on into Vastal's care."

"So what changed?" Rathen asked.

"Need you ask?"

"I suppose not. Magic - they got arrogant and decided they should be preserved, not covered in dirt and worms."

"Exactly."

"Who knew power could corrupt?" Rathen mumbled drily.

The firelight was reflected back from something ahead of them, and their pace slowed cautiously as they approached the glint.

"Water," Anthis surmised, and sure enough, the old stone floor disappeared beneath several inches of standing water. He strode in without hesitation and Kienza was close behind him, leaving the others lingering uncertainly at the edge. With a resigned sigh, Rathen lifted Aria onto his shoulders and shortly followed along, and Garon and Petra reluctantly followed suit, wading their way onwards into another burial chamber. "Of course 'corrupt' in this case is an understatement," Anthis continued thoughtlessly. "They used to be so pure."

"So you've said." Rathen tried to ignore the bones that lay just beneath the surface, but his sight was caught by a skull that broke the water and stared back at him with empty eye sockets.

"The magic changed them at their very roots. In fact, I struggle to fathom how such a drastic change could have taken hold of so dedicated a people. In the space of just three hundred years they completely forgot all of Vastal's faces. They knew Vastal and Zikhon by those two names alone, as Life and Death, Good and Evil, Light and Dark. Feira, Nara, Doru; Nature, Hands, Mind - They were all forgotten."

Dark clumps floated past them in the water. They seemed at first to be some kind of grey moss, but Petra tightened her jaw when she realised they were clumps of ash.

Anthis didn't seem to notice as he continued to deliver his history lesson. "*We* learned of the gods' identities through the elves' fear - their carousal was, in part, because they feared death. They lived extravagantly rather than fully, leaving menial tasks to 'lesser beings' - humans - while they lived in indulgence. Because we were never exposed to their faith when it was at its richest, Vastal's many names and faces never appeared in our own religious texts. They're forgotten to history, even by the clerics.

"And just as their devotion to the gods faded when they chose to no longer honour Them, taking life for granted while ignoring or hiding from death, so, too, did they lose what made them worthy of the gods' attention."

Rathen gave up and closed his eyes - fortunately Kienza noticed and guided him along by the elbow - but he couldn't help his musing, even despite their surroundings. "Perhaps your theory that Zikhon got to the elves is more justified than you think."

"Meaning?"

"That Vastal *let* Him destroy them."

He looked back at him critically. "Do you believe that Vastal would truly do that?"

Rathen shrugged, though he hadn't missed his irritatingly pious tone. "Maybe. If they were so corrupted by the magic She apparently gave them and, as you say, 'lost what made them worthy of the gods' attention', then perhaps She decided that their time had come."

"That's a tidy view," Kienza mumbled.

"*Please* stop talking."

All eyes turned onto Petra and they found her looking far more deeply unsettled than her squeaked plea had suggested. Even in the orange light she appeared as white as a sheet, and her usually thoughtful hazel eyes were wide enough that they might fall out of her head.

They looked away shamefully. "Sorry..."

The group continued through and out of the freezing flood water in a tense and jittery silence, their eyes snatched by the flitting shadows as they followed the passages until, at last, they reached another heavy-looking door. But this one, unlike the first, could only have been engraved by magic, and it had presumably been locked in the same manner. It opened far too easily.

They surged eagerly out of the oppressive crypts and into the tower's cellar, and though it was just as old, dark and derelict, the air at least felt fresher - and they didn't feel dogged by vengeful spectres.

They pulled the door shut quite firmly behind them and released a collective sigh of relief.

"Where to now?" Petra asked, her colour returning as Anthis started across the cobwebbed chamber to the door at the far end, and she cast a paranoid glance towards the crypt that lay sealed behind them as she and the others followed close on his heels.

"Right to the top. That's how this building was organised."

"Right at the top so people won't want to walk that far," Aria reasoned. "I bet it's also on the highest shelf."

"It would also have been protected by spells, I suspect."

"This place has never been maintained, they should be long gone."

"As is half of the tower!" Petra turned her desperate eyes onto the two mages. "Is it safe?"

Kienza offered her an easy smile. "It is now."

Garon narrowed his eyes, though he chose to spare himself and quickly ignored the fact that she had just done something with magic *without* weaving signs. "I thought you said reintroducing magic would destabilise it."

"If I were to use it to remove a tangle of debris," she replied innocently, "yes. I could dislodge something. But freezing everything *exactly* where it is is harmless."

Rathen nodded his approval from beside her, but Garon's suspicion barely decreased. Petra, however, accepted it, and became troubled instead by another detail. "What if what we need is buried under what's collapsed?"

"It isn't," Anthis assured her. "I've been here before it fell, they were nothing more than study rooms. The secure storage was aligned to the eastern half of the tower."

"It collapsed recently, then?"

"Yep - and not my fault."

"But how do you *know* it will be up there?" The red-haired woman pressed. "And, while we're at it, what is 'it'? This artefact, or more paper?"

"Honestly?"

"No, *don't* ask him that..." Rathen groaned, and decided not to try to read Anthis's unfavourable expression. Instead, he stepped through the door and into the darkened tower, encouraging the others to follow and climb carefully over the debris-littered floor behind him. He found it little different from Mokhan; there was just as much mess and uncertain footing.

Again the historian was yielded the lead, and he moved though the crumbling building with the confidence and surety of a weekly visitor. He knew precisely where he was going; he warned them in passing when they approached an unstable floor or a step which was primed to splinter, he skirted around the edge of holes and climbed quite specifically over broken stairways, avoiding the obvious but surely precarious lengths of wood and metal that bridged what remained.

With every floor they climbed the tower looked more and more likely to collapse, but nothing moved as they added their weight to the clutter or brushed close by teetering floor boards displaced from the level above. There was no domino-esque chain reaction, not even a puff of dust. None of them had realised how literally Kienza's spell had taken hold until they passed a collection of panels suspended in the air, frozen mid-fall. Even Rathen, who was familiar with how far her mysterious and impossible magic could go, found himself surprised, and looked at her sidelong in his usual wondering when they discovered two grinning ditchlings, stalled in their climb to the top of a cabinet. But, as ever, his curiosity didn't manage to creep onto his tongue.

At one moment in their ascent, Anthis made a curious point of directing their attention out of an obscured window which offered a very limited view over the ruined city. The Pavise Mountains, which were suddenly surprisingly nearby, could just about be glimpsed if they craned their necks far enough, but otherwise it was far from spectacular and certainly not worthy of being pointed out. The informative little speech he gave as they continued to climb past it seemed equally strained. Rathen discovered why when he looked away in boredom and his eyes fell upon the pair of legs crushed beneath a collapsed ceiling, its dusty garments and rotting ankles indicative of a disturbingly recent death.

Eventually, Anthis drew them to a halt outside of one of the many identical doors, though this one seemed in better condition than the rest, and he turned immediately towards the two casters. They looked at the door, then back to him.

Kienza blinked. "Go on, then," she said expectantly, and after he gave her a brief, fleeting frown of confusion, he reached out to its handle and pushed it open.

The spell that had prevented him from entering every time before had vanished.

He turned and furrowed his brow again, wondering whether she'd removed it with no gesture at all, or if it had finally broken down. He supposed it didn't matter, and led them inside.

Finally, there were things to see. The room was large, semi-circular and cluttered with all kinds of scrolls and various ornaments that could have been anything from the very artefact they sought to an over-dressed spice jar. But where there would once have been meticulous organisation, now was only chaos. The room was in the same disarray as the rest of the building.

Anthis stepped with more caution than he had through the rest of the tower. "There are a few rooms from here onwards I've been unable to get into, I'd guess because of lingering spells," he said as the others spread out with equally tentative steps. "Those are where we should look - and be careful."

"We'll be fine," Rathen assured him. "Kienza's spell has everything held in place."

"Nothing will move unless you touch it or pick it up directly," she promised them, then began wandering quite carelessly through the room, stepping over the unmoving wreckage with perfect grace and surety while she looked about with a curious twinkle in her eye. Aria chased after her with Rathen obediently close behind, and though the others weren't quite as prepared to accept her assurances, they soon began to indulge their own curiosities.

Something half-hidden behind a fallen bookcase caught Aria's eye as Kienza stopped and lifted a scroll from a damp yet dusty table, and she began a struggle to push it upright and out of the way. It moved immediately when the sorceress glanced at it, and Aria immediately crouched down to peer at the exposed painting that must have been as tall as she was.

It was a portrait of a man - or perhaps a woman in men's clothing. The face was too elegant to tell for certain. His hair was long and black, though it distinctly glowed blue where the light had hit the model, and the white skin was similarly tinted silver. The clothing he wore was of black and gold and patterned with a scrolling and twisting design that reminded her of the city itself, and it was clearly unreasonably expensive, while thin, black-edged golden gloves covered his hands. But his eyes held her attention longer than any other detail, piercing and far too lightly coloured for his complexion.

She narrowed her own as she stared at him, then a thought occurred to her. "Is this an elf?" She spun on the balls of her feet to look at Anthis who already seemed to be lost in a box of parchments. He spared only a brief glance and a nod.

She looked back to it in greater consideration, then noticed the elaborate edge of another picture frame behind it. She stood and pulled the first out of the way to find another beneath it, and another beneath that. At first they all seemed to be of the same feminine man with blue hair and silver skin, just in different clothing, but a beauty spot on the chin of the second and a smaller, finer nose on the third encouraged a closer look. It was on that final painting of a woman with highly-dressed hair that she noticed the sharp and elongated ears.

She smiled to herself in satisfaction, then her eyes dropped to a small plaque set into the bottom of the frame. Her eyes widened in surprise. "Koraaz!"

Rathen looked up in confused expectation.

"An elven house," Anthis said blandly. "Your ancestors were most likely in service to them - mine were to House Karth, though they, like all the others, would have been referred to as 'of House Karth' rather than just 'Karth'..."

"Humans in elven servitude didn't have surnames?"

Anthis merely shook his head, mumbled what sounded like 'none of them did', and continued to sink deeper into his reading.

Kienza peered down at Aria as she released a soft little sigh beside her, and found her looking across the rest of the group with a lopsided purse of her lips. She knew the look. She felt like a useless child. Kienza's eyes turned then upon Anthis.

"Aria," he said suddenly, glancing up very briefly from the scrolls he held open in each hand, "we'll need your help."

Kienza smiled in satisfaction and turned back to her own reading while Aria grinned in hope. "How?"

"Your usual way," he smiled charmingly, and as his attention returned once more to the parchments, where he thought it had been all along, she began striding around the room with immense purpose, looking far too closely at everything insignificant before trying to push, pull or twist it.

Rathen smiled as she all but hung off of a wall sconce, and Kienza stepped over beside him. "You can help, too, you know."

"I have absolutely no idea what to look for."

"Magic," she replied, noticing how ready his response had been, "obviously. If the artefact itself is here, it could well be protected by more spells, just like this room was."

He considered her carefully. "And will you be doing the same?"

"Of course."

His eyes narrowed further. "Why do I get the feeling that you already know whether it's here or not, and that you're not going to tell us either way?"

"Why, Rathen!" She gasped. "You *wound* me."

His brow flattened.

"Anyway, hop to it."

He sighed in irritation but didn't press the matter. He should have known better than to ask in the first place; the woman was a beautiful but unshatterable bottle of secrets - and he had a growing suspicion that a few new and quite relevant secrets had found their way into her care since their previous meeting.

But he decided to ignore the fact that she was certainly withholding important information and turned his focus onto the room instead, searching among the lingering traces of spells for something that might once have been, or still be, concealing something.

It wasn't long before a fine but sturdy wisp hooked his attention.

Chapter 29

Rathen followed the presence of the small and subtle spell, trailing it to its source like a loose thread. He lifted away the mound of fallen plaster, ignoring the lack of cloudy residue that should have billowed out with its movement, and tossed aside the ruined painting of another blue-haired elf to discover the dusty old box beneath. It was small, little bigger than his own splayed hand, but decorated to such an extent that it could have rivalled a number of buildings in the city.

"What is it?" Garon asked, stepping carefully to his side. Anthis followed, but his eagerness was restrained by another caution that imposed itself in Rathen's presence.

The mage turned the box over in his hands. "I don't know, but it's locked as tightly as the palace doors."

Anthis hurriedly withdrew the old elven key from the bag that never seemed to leave his side, and a small intrigue creased Kienza's brow at the sight of it.

"There's no lock," Petra pointed out.

"No, it's magic." He glanced to Kienza, but she looked back at him with the same expectation as everyone else. Clearly, this spell was his to break.

His eyes dropped back to the gold-filigree lid and he extended his magic towards it, investigating the enshrouding spell. To have lasted this long it had to have been cast by a powerful elf, and that encouraged his heart to skip a beat in hope, but the contrasting simplicity of its construction also made him hesitate - although he was quick to remind himself that the ruin in the Wildlands had been hidden by no spell at all and yet had contained their best finds yet.

Whatever the case, this counter-spell would be little trouble.

He shifted the box into his left hand and began a simple contortion with his right, but the moment he released it and the seal popped free, that familiar but mercifully brief heat encircled his arm.

He gritted his teeth as he fought to suppress any obvious reactions, but Kienza had been watching him closely and noticed immediately the resentful gleam in his eye. She snatched the box and shoved it into the hands of the hungry-eyed historian before steadying him against a sudden wave of dizziness.

"I'm sorry, my love," she sighed softly, "you're still too weak for magic, it seems." Giving his shoulders an affectionate squeeze, she turned her attention after the others onto the increasingly ominous box.

They waited for an agonisingly long moment for Anthis to open it, hesitant despite his enthusiasm, as though he desperately didn't want to feel the bitter pang of disappointment, but the steadily mounting weight of the air soon made his hands move on their own.

The lid flew open, and he blinked at its contents.

The others felt their hearts stop.

Petra sidled closer alongside him and a frown knitted her brow. "Is that..."

Kienza nodded. "Tea leaves."

"...But..." Anthis shook his head, his expression having slipped away to leave his face blank in his lack of comprehension, "the spell was still active..."

"A number of them are," Rathen sighed, "that's how the place is still standing at all."

Petra grunted in disappointment. "I suppose this says something about the elves' priorities."

Their luck continued along such lines for hours. They left the first room and entered another that had remained magically sealed despite the centuries, then another after that, and another after that. Rathen had searched them all for magic, but any time he'd discovered anything and Kienza had unlocked them in his place, there was nothing inside but more disappointing trivialities. Aria similarly pulled on candelabras, tilted pictures, pushed walls and pulled cabinets, but her search for hidden rooms and compartments came up just as empty.

Rathen had hoped that Kienza might encourage them to stay a little longer despite this, having perhaps found something herself but preferring them to find it on their own - she often only helped him as far as getting him started before leaving him to make it the rest of his way by himself. But she hadn't once spoken up and her absent, childlike interest in the contents of every room hadn't wavered. She read scrolls, studied pictures, opened drawers and peered behind cabinets as if she was merely window-shopping.

It wasn't until the top and final room of the tower, where everyone shared a distinct sense of hopelessness, that Anthis decided to divulge that he'd actually found something after all. But that restraint was only testament to how feeble the discoveries were if the excitable young man couldn't muster even a premature gasp of hope when he'd found them - three floors ago.

"It's not much," he admitted mildly as he continued to pore over the dusty journal he'd brought up with him, though his eyes seemed to be under some kind of magnetic influence as he fought to keep them from wandering onto a number of the irrelevant parchments he'd found in that same room, "but it's the only mention I've found in here."

His dismissive attitude wasn't shared by the others. That honour fell to Rathen's incredulous stare. "They wanted to use it against the *gods?!*"

"Well, they certainly thought about it. Lots of 'what if's and 'if we could just's and so on." He grunted thoughtfully. "It was the pinnacle of their arrogance, really..."

"It doesn't sound like it's of any use to us."

Anthis nodded in agreement with the inquisitor, though he still didn't look up. In fact, his eyes finally gave in to the pull of the papers. "It's nothing more than symbolism really, albeit from a pivotal point in the collapse of their culture. If they'd succeeded in creating something capable of removing or blocking the magic of a god, be it an artefact or just the spell itself, it would have secured their superiority over Vastal and Zikhon, the bestowers of their own magic. Theorising may not be the same as doing, but, in this case, it's enough. They were bold enough to think about it, and think thoroughly. With just these words they completely cut their ties from the gods and made their magic their own..."

"Really?" Rathen frowned sceptically. "It was that easy? Just some words on paper?"

"When you're dealing with things as intangible as gods and beliefs, words become extremely powerful. With 'just some words on paper' they had forsaken their ancestors and their history. But Garon is right: it's of no use to us. This line of thought was probably a divergence from the creation of the artefact we're after, but it won't help us *find* it.

"Otherwise," he continued, dragging his eyes back to the parchment he held in the same hand as the journal, "all I've found are repeats of what I've found before, most notably that the artefact against the elves and the suppressant against humans were separate items, but there's still no confirmation on anything else. The only thing we know for sure is where the *weapon* was made, and, now, both of their names."

"So we can stop calling it 'the artefact' now?" Petra sighed in relief. "Thank goodness. It sounds pretentious. And cumbersome."

"I doubt you'll like this any better. Itakh which means 'Balancer', and Zikrahlehveyn, which means 'Preserver of Eternity'. But, fortunately for us, even the elves who named it found it too foreboding and shortened it to Zi'veyn instead, which means 'Eternal Magic'. Which sort of makes the weapon seem less imposing, to my mind, but then again I don't possess magic, so..."

Everyone stared back at him, blinking absently as they tried to process the jumble of syllables he'd spoken so easily despite the riddle of exotic nuances, while Kienza simply smiled and shook her head, her forest-brown curls bouncing. "Oh, Anthis." Her voice was tinged with a note of genuine pity. "No."

He looked towards her quizzically.

"'Preserve' in this case doesn't refer to the item," she explained quite simply, "but its intention, and even then it's a...matter of perspective. And as for 'eternity', that doesn't refer to time."

The renowned young historian lowered his hand and poured his attention onto her, his eyes both sceptical and intrigued.

"Zikrahlehveyn," she declared, speaking the word as easily and presumably as flawlessly as Anthis had. "'Zi' of *zii*, not *zin*. 'Eternal', not 'forever'. Unstoppable, inescapable, unending. *Zii* carries the full weight of the word; it is academic, while *zin* is more suited to a child's exaggeration. And it's 'leh' of *lehiin*, not *lehzan*. 'Preserve', not 'protect'. To disallow change or diversity."

Anthis's brow had gradually become tightly furrowed and, when she'd finished, his eyes dropped quickly back to the parchment. He seemed to read the word over and over and over again, mumbling to himself and bobbing his head from side to side in consideration. When he looked back up, his eyebrows had risen surprisingly high. "It is. 'Eternal Preservation' - their superiority... You're right."

"What does that change?" Rathen frowned in confusion as he struggled to keep up.

"Nothing for your task," Kienza assured them as Anthis's gaze dropped back down again.

"Right." He squeezed his eyes shut tight and tried to shake the new yet useless information away. "And zik--zika--"

"Zikrahlehveyn," Anthis supplied. "Zi'veyn."

"Yes. That one. That's the one we're after?"

"Yes."

"And this is *all* you've discovered?"

"It is." He looked up again as he felt their expectation bearing down on him, and he finally lowered the ancient texts and squared himself towards them. "This place has been scoured and picked clean over seven hundred years," he reminded them. "In fact, elven anarchists could have taken everything themselves and scattered it across the continent. What we have right here is the best we're going to get."

"What about hidden passages?" Petra asked.

"None," Kienza replied.

"How can you be *sure?*"

"Because Aria has been unable to find any," she said, glancing down at the young girl who looked both disappointed in her lack of success, as well as to blame for it. "And I can't either. Anthis is right: there's nothing else here. You were lucky to have found *this* much."

"And I didn't say this place *would* yield anything," Anthis quickly added.

A careful menace filled Rathen's eyes, and the young man inched back as he took a step towards him. "It was at the top of your list."

"Which means we have two more places to try."

"You're still not counting where it was made."

"I don't think we're that desperate yet..."

"I am inclined to differ..."

"Enough."

The two stopped, their attention snatched away from one another by Garon's official tone. "Magically frozen or not, we're risking our lives by staying here unnecessarily. We need to leave. Anthis, what is your next best guess?"

He smiled doubtfully. "...You're not going to like it."

Garon stared at him patiently.

"The elves' cultural capital - Enhala."

"That's in Kasire!" Petra protested. "A *desert* stands between there and here!"

"And that desert is *tribal territory*," Rathen added just as hotly.

"We can edge around it--"

"No," Garon shook his head. "We shouldn't." All eyes fell on him in disbelief. "Ivaea and Kasire are brokering a treaty so the fighting over there is at a stand-still, and with Skilan's campaign against us having only just begun, we're safer cutting *through* tribal territory. We can avoid Skilan's military movements - they won't want to pass through that terrain, nor encounter the tribes."

"For very good reason!"

Garon sighed. "The wind and earth tribes in that region haven't yet gone to war with one another, and while the situation is still tense, neither side will attack travellers in case they are somehow affiliated with the other. And we are too few to be considered a threat to either."

"You give them far more credit than they deserve," Rathen growled warily.

"That may be, but my point still stands."

All eyes remained in doubt upon the inquisitor, but as Kienza silently nodded her agreement from beside him, Rathen's shoulders sagged in defeat. He found that small gesture immensely more convincing than Garon's misplaced confidence. He grunted and folded his arms. "I never thought I'd have to cut through *tribal* territory as a means of safe travel..."

"Fortunately," Anthis chirped, "assuming we travel as the crow flies, there's a ruin along the way that could be of use to us, if it's one of these magnetic places. It's where the elves used to praise Feira, but given its location, only the most devoted could participate in the ceremonies."

"Vastal's face of...nature?" Aria looked at him hopefully, and she beamed as she received a nod of surprise and approval from the young man.

But Rathen's incredulity had returned tenfold. "I'm not so sure that's 'fortunate'!" He blustered. "*You're* suggesting we enter tribal territory, and *you*, Anthis, are suggesting we *linger* there! Both of you seem to have forgotten what the tribes are like - shall I remind you?" No one answered, though Aria turned eyes of fascination up towards him. "*Barbarians,* at the *best* of times, but the majority of them are made to look *civilised* compared to the isolated groups! The ones high in the mountains, on the edge of volcanoes, in the *very desert* you want us to trek through! And they have no idea what 'civilised' means! They've been cut off from most of their *own* people for *centuries*. At least the tribes along the east are close enough to us to have grown to the point of understanding trade, but the rest have had no such example! *And they are cannibals!*"

"You sound afraid."

"*Of course I'm afraid!*"

"As am I," Petra admitted with considerably more control, and she turned grave eyes between the historian and inquisitor. "What makes either of you think they won't attack us?"

"Nothing more than wishful thinking," Rathen replied tartly.

"They will help you," Kienza began calmly, "because the site Anthis has mentioned is in fact *sorely* affected, and it's sacred to them. If you tell them what you're doing, they may be more inclined to listen. And either way, you won't be able to get near it without their consent anyway. If you try, you'll be putting yourselves in even *greater* danger."

Rathen scrutinised her for a long moment, his eyes deep and calculating. "Is this your way of telling us that it's the right course of action?"

"Why ever would I be telling you that?"

His gaze didn't break. "Is it?"

"Well I think it could certainly help you, so we'll go with 'yes'."

Rathen squeezed his eyes shut tightly as a thousand thoughts - mostly doubts - hurtled through his mind, but he knew despite them, though he wished otherwise, that Kienza was quite often right. About everything.

And if Garon wished to go that way, he had no choice but to follow.

Again his shoulders dropped in defeat, and he opened his eyes. The inquisitor didn't appear troubled - his thoughts were hidden, as usual - and the unreasonable brightness in Anthis's eyes only increased his cynicism. It was likely that the historian was thinking only about furthering his personal research than any of their safety. Only Petra seemed to share in his trepidation, but even she looked as if she could push it aside if she really had to.

Rathen sighed in his greatest resignation. "Vastal, save us all." He turned to

Kienza. "This--"

"Shh..."

He frowned at her sharp interruption, but he knew better than to ask. Her dark, piercing eyes had become troubled, and though her gaze was intense, it wasn't focused upon anything nearby.

They glanced warily at one another, straining their ears for whatever had grasped her attention so completely. But they didn't have to wait long to find out. A shrill avian screech pierced the air, so loud and so close it would surely bring the tower down itself, and it turned their blood to ice.

"I thought we lost them!" Anthis yelled, alarm tightening his grip about the parchments, but as he and the others covered their ears, Garon braced himself, drew his sword and prepared for the impending attack, turning to face the largest hole in the wall as plaster crumbled around it.

Petra quickly freed her own blade, but as Rathen followed, raising his hands to ready a spell, Kienza whispered an apology and his world suddenly went dark.

She caught him as he slumped on the spot, lowering his limp body carefully to the ground even as huge, feathered forms began diving in through the shattered wall. Garon swung his blade in the tight space with undeniable skill, but he may as well have been swatting at flies. The harpies avoided his every attack as if he wasn't even there, and Petra's just the same, and yet still they had the opportunity to snatch their sharp and gleaming black talons out towards them with every sweeping pass.

"Against the walls!" Garon shouted while their assailants darted back outside for another sudden strike, and as Kienza turned her attention to the harpies' point of entrance, the rest of the group was quick to obey - except for Aria.

Garon cursed as the child hesitated between running to her father's side or joining the others at the nearest wall, and that brief, single moment had left her exposed. A deep-beige harpy suddenly burst in through another crack on the far side of the room, and its sights were set keenly upon her. She spun around immediately, and though she scrambled to her feet rather than freezing in fright, she was still too late. It would catch her all too easily. But no sooner had she chosen the direction furthest from the beast than Garon barrelled in beside her, shoving her unceremoniously out of the harpy's path and grasping it by its scaled foot.

With a quick, backwards shift of his weight he sought to drag it off-track, but its wings were too powerful. With little more than an irritated squawk, it turned abruptly, wrenching his arm in the process, and made for a hole any would have guessed too narrow even for this creature's lean form. It was not, but fortunately Garon was much too broad to follow.

Before he could even release his grip, the beast was gone, and he grunted in pain as he slammed into the wall after it, his shoulder twisting in its socket as his catch freed itself with another rough jerk.

More harpies dove in from all around them - one even ripped more of the decaying wall away as easily as meat from a carcass - and they continued to sweep through the air and snatch at them before diving out to try again from another direction. Petra continued her attempts to slice and stab at them as they passed, but as always, they remained just out of reach of her blade.

It seemed to each of them that they were finally at the mercy of their relentless pursuers. And so the room fell into a brief, stunned silence as one of them flew directly into a wall.

It could have simply been poor judgement in the chaos of the moment, but another shortly did the same, and then a displaced gale suddenly pummelled them all, snatching their questions away.

Kienza had given up trying to block the holes. Her gale couldn't have been walked through, let alone flown against, and she easily blew them back outside, emptying the room of harpies without causing them injury - for the most part - as Petra and Garon had sought to do.

But no sooner had the final tail feathers vanished from sight than the door burst open, and they jointly assumed that they'd taken to using the stairs instead - but what stormed in on joyful war cries were not avian giants, but small, pale-skinned, big-eyed children, their slender bodies caked in mud and leaves with slingshots and sharpened sticks in their hands.

The harpies darted back in after circling around outside, but their attention was now fixed exclusively upon the ditchlings. Their yellow eyes glinted with hatred as they rushed upon them, reaching with their talons to rip rather than snatch, but the small and wily ditchlings were able to confuse their attackers by wending and weaving around one another, avoid their reach by scrambling over and under the wreckages, and yet still manage to successfully strike them with their crude weapons in the process.

It took a moment for their surprise at these new arrivals to pass as they darted around them like armed mice, bellowing and piping nonsensical noises while waving about their spears, but Kienza appeared to have adjusted almost immediately.

The ditchlings quickly fell victim to the force of her gale, knocking them all away from the harpies and sending some tumbling back down a small mountain of plaster and ceiling. But they weren't troubled, if they even noticed, and with childlike determination, they got back up and charged in again. So she knocked them back a second time while equally holding the harpies at bay. But with her attention being pulled in so many directions, and Petra and Garon's attempts to take advantage of the distraction only contributing to the confusion, she simply couldn't keep track of everything. Two harpies managed to free themselves from the spiralling wind to dive upon the wild children, ripping cries of pain from their victims as their talons pierced their painted shoulders. The others roared in anger as their comrades were lifted into the air and dragged towards the holes, though they kicked, screamed and jabbed with their spears as they went, refusing to be carried off without a fight.

Kienza growled in frustration as the matter began moving out of her control. With a far less elegant spell, she tore the three captive ditchlings back from their grasp, doing their shoulders a little more damage in the process, then turned her piercing emerald eyes onto the harpies and shrieked as if she was one of them.

The room was stunned to stillness. Garon, Petra, Anthis and Aria stared at her in shock; the seven ditchlings covered their ears and grinned wickedly towards the harpies; the harpies themselves stalled mid-flight and peered down at her in both astonishment and some kind of comprehension before wheeling about and fleeing through the countless breaches.

Garon spun around and peered through the nearest gap, watching them fly away in their confusion. Not one of them cast even a momentary glance behind them.

"Thanks, beautiful," one of the ditchlings puffed as the startled daze lingered over the four, "but we weren't the ones what needed saving."

"Neither were we," Kienza replied sternly, her hands on her shapely hips.

"That much is obvious."

"Now," another ditchling added.

The seven childlike warriors then looked towards Aria. She still clung to her father's side, but she seemed unconcerned even as everyone else finally became aware of his unconscious condition. The ditchlings, however, ignored it just as she did, and stepped towards her with familiar smiles, their oversized silver-green eyes glinting joyfully.

She smiled back, though she didn't display the same recognition.

"Nug says 'hi'," said one of the girls as she had her turn of hugging her. She had various twigs tied into her hair - woven, Aria noticed, into plaits.

Aria's smile brightened. "You know Nug?"

"Never met 'im." She shook her head with a vaguely baffled frown, and Aria returned her confusion.

Kienza knelt at Rathen's side and gently patted his cheek. He grunted and twitched, his relaxed expression slowly knotting as if his sleep had been both voluntary and comfortable, and when his eyes finally opened, it took him a moment to recall his settings. He had to look twice at the seven big-eyed faces that peered down at him from behind Aria.

"What happened to him?" Petra asked, stepping over with the others as Kienza rose to her feet and helped Rathen to his.

"After what happened yesterday, all this could have triggered a relapse." She smiled at him apologetically, but he returned it with a very flat look. "I thought it better to remove it as a possibility." She turned towards the red-haired duelist as she noticed her clutching at her chest, and shooed her hand away to see to the long gash that extended from her breast to her shoulder. Evidently she'd narrowly avoided being snatched herself, but with an easy pass of the sorceress's hand, the blood cleared and the skin resealed itself.

Petra's eyebrows rose in surprise as she pulled at her blouse and looked closer at her skin, but just as with the others' the previous night, it was entirely clear and unmarked.

"Is everyone else all right?" She asked, moving then towards the injured ditchlings who lined up quite readily before her, presenting their wounds with pride. Everyone else stayed where they were.

"What did you say to them?" Aria asked, watching with her usual curiosity as her magic healed their bony shoulders.

"I told them to leave or I'd curse their forests."

"Can you do that?" Anthis asked with a note of concern.

She smiled at him, baffled. "No, of course not. ...Well...actually, I suppose I could. As far as appearances go. And isn't that all a curse really is?"

"Where did you all come from, anyway?" Aria then asked their rescuers.

"And why?" Garon added.

The seven exchanged amused glances. "There's all kinds of ways in here that ain't the front door," a particularly muddy one replied. "Just have to know where they are. And as for why, we had summit to give you. We saw you when you got to the city."

"Why didn't you give it to us then?"

"Had to write it down, didn't we?"

They rolled their eyes, as if it should have been obvious, then one of them stepped forwards from the group. She extended her skinny, mud-crusted arm towards Anthis and offered him a few sheets of parchment. He took them carefully, surprised initially that they could write at all, then that they'd done so on paper rather than leaves. But as soon as he looked down he discovered they'd simply torn out pages of an elven book and scrawled over them in charcoal. And it was almost illegible.

"What is it?" He frowned.

"Stuff about magic."

"You could sound more grateful, y'know," the twig-haired girl scowled. "We're tryin' to help."

"We're smaller and faster than you are," another declared quite proudly, "we can get into smaller, higher and more per-carious places than you - and we know 'bout places you don't. So we been in and we got this for you."

"Say 'thank you', Mister Karth."

Bewildered, he glanced towards Kienza, then back to the ditchlings. "Yes, thank you, of course...but *where*--"

"It's all on that, Mister Karf," the girl told him, tapping the back of the parchments, "but don't ask us about it. We don't get it, but we know what you're after."

Anthis's doubt only increased, but he, and the others, hid it well enough.

"But this don't come for free - not now, anyway. We wanna know summit ourselfs." The muddy boy's tone had become serious - it reminded Rathen of how much Aria could age in a single moment when a difficult subject weighed on her mind. "It ain't just the harpies what are after us now, you big 'uns have started attacking us, too. And not just when we try to steal yer pies."

"What do you mean?" Garon asked warily.

"People, hoomans like you, coming into our forests and trapping us, killing us, dragging us away. We wanna know why."

Everyone exchanged confused glances.

"We don't know anything about that," the inquisitor replied.

All seven pairs of far-too-sharp eyes narrowed at him in scrutiny.

"All right," the boy said, finally, "we didn't think you knew. Otherwise you wouldn't be doing what you're doing."

"Which is?"

"Not attackin' us." Then the ditchlings turned around together and made for the door. "Good luck with everything," they threw back, "oh, and make sure you don't forget to un-magic the others. Would be a shame if they missed dinner forever." And then they hurried away, leaving the others blinking after them.

Anthis looked back down to the parchments. "I guess our progress is important to ditchlings outside of Wrenroot, too. They must have spread the word..." He chuckled grimly. "No pressure, then."

"What is it?" Rathen asked, peering over towards them.

Anthis squinted at it. "I...can't tell. I need time to pick it apart...but, from what I can make out, it *is* about magic - the intricacies of elven casting; practice, structure of spells, things like that." His eyebrows rose. "This could actually be really, really useful..."

"It could help us to understand the artefact."

"Or to recreate the spell."

Rathen managed not to shoot Garon his instinctively doubtful look. Instead he glanced towards Anthis and found him looking hesitantly back at him.

"I will need help understanding it..."

Rathen's jaw knotted at his dubious tone. He knew it had nothing to do with the parchments. "I'll do what I can," he replied as neutrally as he could.

"What about the harpies?" Petra asked as she peered out through the broken wall, fully expecting them to return while they were distracted. "They'll be back."

"They will," Garon agreed. "We've been tracked all along. They're obsessive in their pursuit. We should leave." Petra, Rathen and Aria were close behind him as he made for the door, while Anthis tried desperately to stuff as many books and papers into his satchel as he could. Kienza had to turn him around and usher him along herself.

"We covered three days' travel in an instant," Petra reminded him as they moved along the short, tattered corridor towards the stairs. "How could they track us through that? And how can we get them to leave us alone?"

"Harpies are masters of the winds," Kienza replied from the back. "Three days' distance in a second isn't enough to shake them - it's also possible one saw or heard us last night."

"And didn't attack?"

"They don't attack alone. And as for leaving you be...I hesitate to ask, but have any of you tried talking to them?"

Garon grunted. "If I'd been given the chance."

"You were given the chance," Rathen reminded him sharply, "and you ran with the rest of us."

"The harpies think you've sided with the ditchlings--"

"Arkhamas."

Kienza smiled obligingly at Aria. "Arkhamas. And just as the Arkhamas thought you were responsible for the magic, so, too, may the harpies. The difference is that the Arkhamas gave you the chance to explain. That doesn't necessarily mean they're any smarter than the harpies, just that one of them had the idea *not* to attack right away and shared that thought with the others. But, of course, at that point none of you had expressed any form of alignment in their conflict to provoke them."

"That doesn't explain why they're so focused on us, though."

"Well, the magic *is* a concern - for us, for them, and for everything in between - and if they think you're responsible they might want to displace you first, take you somewhere you won't have an advantage, and *then* question you about it. You wouldn't quiz someone you considered a threat on the spot where you found them, would you? They could have anything up their sleeves!"

"So we should just *let* them carry us off?"

"Goodness, no, anything could happen. This is a war, if one of talons and slingshots. But I suspect you will get your opportunity to speak."

"We will?" Petra asked sceptically.

"Of course." Kienza grinned. "They're obsessive in their pursuit, remember?"

Chapter 30

After racing through the tower and crypts as quickly and carefully as they could, their pace hastened by the threat of returning harpies, they continued off into the forest until darkness had firmly set in. They made camp amongst the densest trees they could find, but already so far north, Turunda's forests were beginning to thin and the air was growing drier - but before too long they wouldn't have any cover at all and far more to avoid being seen by, so they tried to make the best of it and stifled their concerns while they could.

That evening, Anthis was bent firmly over his books while the others ate, scribbling across numerous pages. His expression was twisted in unbreakable thought, and he periodically returned to some of those scribbles, crossed them out and rewrote them elsewhere, only to cross most of those out once more, ponder for a while, sigh and turn to Kienza in defeat - to which she would reply that he'd had it right the first time. Clearly, her correction of his earlier translation had thrown him through a loop.

"Well," the sorceress began once the last of them had finished eating, a dubious note of finality to her voice that not one of them had missed, "thank you for dinner, and for the exciting day out. I wish you the greatest luck in your search - I'm sure you'll find something more substantial soon."

"You're leaving?" Anthis asked with barely concealed alarm, sparing a moment from his work to protest as she rose to her feet and dusted off her long, bark-coloured skirt.

She smiled apologetically, "I only remained because I needed to make sure Rathen was all right. He is, so now I have my own matters to attend to."

"Which are?"

Rathen shook his head to himself at the inquisitor's brusque question, and looked up to find Kienza giving him the disapprovingly raised eyebrow he'd expected. Surprisingly, however, she answered - which meant that it would either be only part of the truth, or that it would be needlessly complicated in order to put him off of asking her again in the future. She was always so very secretive.

"The magic is expanding in range, circumferentially, which suggests that it isn't just appearing on its own but rather spreading out from a single point and accumulating at these ruins, drawn by the magnetism and then spilling over onto the next. I've been following the magic backwards, ruin by ruin, broken spell chain by broken spell chain, to find the centre and, hopefully, its source, because - if I am correct, and I'm certain that I am - this flow of magic will need to be halted before the rest of it is removed or it will just collect all over again."

"How do you intend to halt it?" Garon asked as the others slowly processed the information.

"I don't," she replied simply. "I'm hoping the Zikrahlehveyn can do it. But, as there's no sense in waiting for you to find it first and dragging the whole matter out, I'm tackling it from that end while you continue your hunt. And," she turned towards Aria, "aside from that, Oat needs feeding.

"But first..." She turned then towards Rathen, who looked back at her with bereaved disappointment. It was a gaze she received every time she left him, but following such an episode, it was always coloured by a pleading desperation that pulled at her heart more than she could let him know. She smiled sadly and her tone softened. "I'd like a word with you."

He nodded with resignation, making his usual decision not to beg her to stay, and rose to his feet. He glanced down to Aria, who worked as vigilantly in her own sketchbook as Anthis still did over his notes, then to Garon and Petra. "Could you--"

"Of course," Petra smiled, and shuffled a fraction closer to the girl, making a point as she did so to turn away so she wouldn't appear to be trying to look at her drawings.

Rathen nodded his thanks and turned to catch up to Kienza as she wandered off into the trees.

Darkness enveloped them. The reach of the campfire's glow was weak, but it was a small flame, its heat undesired in the warmer northern air, and Rathen pondered as they walked over the uneven terrain the fact that it could get so warm so suddenly just by moving a few days north.

"Tell me," Kienza began in her soft, beautiful but knowing voice, catching his willing attention, "how long has your cuff been causing you pain?"

He blinked at her in surprise and quickly mulled over how to answer, but when her dark eyes fell upon him, he sighed and looked away in defeat. There was no point even trying to lie. "Since Stonton. I probed the magic there, deeper than I have before, and then it just happened."

"And it's been happening since?"

"Not that often, at first, but now it feels like every time I try to cast a spell it starts to heat up." His lip curled as he considered how rotten his fortunes had recently become.

"What does it feel like? Tight?"

He looked back at her, frowning lightly at her curiosity, for it was that more than it was concern, and he found her peering back at him in a thoughtful consideration remarkably akin to Aria's. For once she seemed genuinely uninformed about something, rather than just playfully ignorant.

And in that case, he would answer her as best he could.

"Like fire," he replied, failing immediately. "Like the metal is suddenly red-hot, searing my skin and burning my veins...like..." he growled in exasperation. "Like *fire*. As if someone had truly set my arm aflame... I can't do better than that."

She nodded in understanding. "That's all right."

"You couldn't get it off, could you?"

She gave him a sad, crooked smile. He'd asked only partly in jest; he already knew the answer. "No, I'm sorry..." He nodded, but she noticed that his disappointment was more pronounced than usual.

"So," he said, brushing it off as best he could, "this magic. You've been analysing it closer than I have, I'd wager - I don't suppose you have any other ideas about how to stop it?"

"Beyond what I've already told you, no. ...How *has* that been going, anyway?"

He didn't need to look at her to know her forest green eyes were shining with their usual acuity. He sighed wearily. "I've identified the accumulation, and there were a few small chains in Stonton which eradicated any doubts that the magic *can* be shaped, but when I tried to affect it in the Wildlands, my cuff burned again."

She looked at him steadily even as she navigated a drop in the earth, despite it being perfectly concealed in the darkness. "You know that you could well not find this artefact, don't you? In all this time searching, how much luck have you truly had with it?"

His jaw knotted. "Only what we found in the Wildlands."

"And that's it." Her tone was stern. He didn't like it. "Anthis Karth is leading your search, he knows well what he's doing so it was inevitable that you'd find *something*, but even leading experts have been proven wrong in their fields in the past. You can't neglect your own task based on a single, feeble stroke of luck."

"I'm not neglecting it," he objected.

"You're afraid to try again, though, aren't you?" Her gaze didn't waver, and Rathen shifted beneath it even as she smiled. "Next time, push through the pain. It won't kill you."

"Isn't that what pain is supposed to prevent?"

"Fundamentally, yes, but it's also an automatic response that can be overcome in many cases. This is one such case. Don't fear it."

He sighed in exasperation. "Can't you just *help* me? You know more than you let on, you *always* do. You can keep your millions of secrets, just give me one piece of *advice!*"

She pursed her lips as she reached for his hand. "Have you not asked the others?"

"How could *they* help?"

She giggled, a wonderful sound that made him smile despite his woes. "You're so dependant on me - it's quite sweet, really."

His smile vanished and he looked back at her humourlessly. Perhaps a different, more direct approach would work. "How would I create a spell to interact with magic?" He asked as plainly as he could.

"How do you usually do it?"

He blinked at her in confusion. "What?"

"Well you interact with magic every time you form a spell, don't you?"

"Yes, *my* magic, formed in *my* heart, flowing through *my* veins. Not floating around crumbled stone..."

She waved her free hand lazily. "And yet..."

"No," he assured her, wondering if she'd finally lost her senses. "That's not possible."

"No, I suppose it isn't."

"Then why *suggest* it?"

She smiled. "To open your mind."

Rathen felt his stomach lurch. Their surroundings became a fraction lighter, the unnoticed song of insects was replaced by an oppressive silence, and the unmistakable quiver of magic permeated the air.

He turned her another flat look. "Would a warning kill you?" But she only smiled impishly. He surveyed their new surroundings as his heart settled under the familiar, unnatural tranquillity, and he found the small, modest houses, exposed by the slightest sliver of the moon, curiously beautiful even in their desolation.

He stepped slowly into the abandoned village, rocks crunching into the shattered road beneath his feet, and stopped cautiously at the edge of a black chasm that had opened in the ground, splitting the village and swallowing the buildings unfortunate enough to have stood along its fault. He knelt at its edge and swished his hand through the abyssal space. "Halen."

"Halen."

He looked around at the destruction. This village couldn't be salvaged. It wasn't a case of draining a flood or rebuilding after a fire. Halen was finished, little more now than a black mark on a map.

He spotted a stone archway across the fragmented square. He'd visited enough ruins lately to know on sight that it was elven, but though it stood in a better state than the surrounding village, the centre of its arc had split and the two pieces now leaned into one another, its limbs standing on opposing sides of the crevice's narrowest point. The fact that it still stood at all left a bitter taste in Rathen's mouth.

He looked about again and rose silently to his feet, weighed down by a great sympathy for the survivors and an even greater regret for the loss of the rest.

Kienza stepped up quietly beside him. "Affect it," she said softly. "Just let go, and affect it."

At this sobering sight, Rathen was in no mood to argue. Despite how she'd lectured them that morning, he did feel very much to blame. He had to ensure they made some kind of progress.

He recalled his earlier reasoning to use his magic alone rather than a spell, and he was still convinced that it was the best course of action. The magic wasn't tangible, it was similar to that in his own veins and couldn't be affected by any conventional spell. To his mind, extending this sixth, arcane sense had potential if he focused its pressure enough - and if he was wrong, Kienza would surely speak up.

He took a deep breath, closed his eyes, and emptied his mind to touch the surrounding magic.

"Now push it," her voice brushed past his ear.

He isolated a puddle, its existence sharpened by his increased awareness, and breathed again. His own power washed out and over it just as it had the first time he'd tried, extending like a second sense of touch to grasp the ethereal. But his effort sent not even a ripple across it. He sharpened his focus and tried harder, supplying more of his magic to strengthen his intent from a wave into a surge, but still it only slipped over the top like a swollen stream over a pebble.

Heat shortly gripped his arm, and the slight knot of effort in his brow tightened in anxiety.

"Push through it."

He gritted his teeth as it began to burn, but he did as she told him. He turned his mind as far from the heat as he could and pressed his focus into his task, but its searing was persistent. As his concentration began to waver once again, so too did Kienza's soft and luring voice brush past his ear, and his determination renewed. Every part of him suddenly resonated the same thought: if he wouldn't be beaten by his curse, his illness, his loss of control, *whatever* his transformation was the result of, he *certainly* wouldn't be beaten by this.

But as he continued to fruitlessly drown the puddle with that resolve, a small voice spoke up in the back of his mind. Perhaps it would take more than just brute magical strength to achieve this; maybe the simple reaction required finesse - but how could he focus his magic without shaping it into a spell? Kienza hadn't spoken a word against his actions yet, so he had to at least have that detail correct.

'How would I create a spell to interact with magic?'

'How do you usually do it?'

The fire around his arm threatened to storm back into his mind as his concentration lapsed, but the sudden idea that had opened the gate to it equally allowed him to push it aside.

How *did* he usually do it?

He ceased his assault over the magic and drew his mind back in, focusing his attention on his own as it moved through his veins, regaining control over himself and his senses. The burning ceased in the process - she'd been right, he hadn't died even after pushing through it - and his mind began to clear.

Then, a moment later, he reached back out. But this time, rather than throwing his magic upon it like an over-eager child, he first sought out the edges of the puddle as precisely as he could. They were cloudy, but they were there, and once he had them, he pressed his magical consciousness against them alone rather than smothering the puddle as a whole. Then he began to steadily increase its strength, but instead of forcing it all out at once and pushing harder and harder, he held it back and slowly built up the pressure behind the point of contact. His focus remained rigidly along the puddle's edge, but he spared enough attention to note its size and shape and adjusted his own to match so that it couldn't slip back over the top.

His cuff began heating up again, but his careful optimism made it easier to ignore.

Slowly, carefully and with the utmost control, he continued to increase the pressure until that, too, matched that of the puddle, and then, with a deep, steady and hopeful breath, he dared to exceed it.

It was only a fraction, a raindrop in a bucket, but it was enough. Without a doubt, it moved.

And as it did, he discovered something more within it.

His eyes opened in shock, but of course there was nothing to see. Only Kienza nodding beside him, a satisfied smile upon her perfect face and her arms folded confidently across her ample chest. She hadn't doubted him for a moment, but he couldn't help feeling stunned by his own success, and he mumbled to himself in awe. How could he have missed this?

"What did you find?" She asked him, though she surely already knew.

"Spell chains," he replied, still stunned. "*All* of it. And they're weaving into things, affecting the place as if the spells were cast directly upon it...but they're so *small*, like a single word, a single intention...too small to notice until it moves... It's like--"

"Like a thin film over a pond," she nodded. "Not even your friends in the Order would have noticed this. But what do these 'words' say?"

He turned towards her and couldn't help his victory from forming a smile. "Beauty, for the most part. Which explains why every site was so..." His eyebrow twitched in puzzlement as a thought hit him. He'd found no chain of 'peace', and yet it was certainly here... He glanced back towards Kienza to see if she was still looking at him in expectation, but she'd become distracted by a firefly, a somehow fitting visitor to this tragic site.

"You knew all of this," he said softly, smiling while she held her finger out for the furry insect to land upon. "Why do you insist on holding back?"

"Because it keeps you interested," she smiled slyly. "And because you need to take every step yourself if you're going to put a spell together."

His eyes narrowed in suspicion, but his smile remained. "You're very adamant that I'm going to need to do so. *Will* we find the artefact?"

"Who knows? But you'll still need to understand this magic if you do. You won't be able to use the artefact against it otherwise."

"You're holding something back again."

She dropped her hand as the insect flew off, and she gave him another roguish smile. "I'll tell you what," she began, her hips swaying as she walked languidly towards him, "if you stop asking, I won't hold back for the rest of the night." He frowned at the contradiction, but the thought slipped from his mind as she stopped just inches away from him, her piercing eyes grasping and holding his gaze as if they'd cast a spell upon him. "Do with that what you will."

He didn't need a moment to think about it. Her stare had captured him - he was more at her mercy than the tiny, vulnerable firefly would ever have been.

He leaned in and kissed her, and he knew the moment his lips met hers that their surroundings had changed once again. But as she pressed herself against him, he didn't give that much thought either. Instead he lay her down on the blankets that were always spread out over the grass beside the lake that seemed unmarked on any map and ran his hands over her perfect body. He kissed her neck and felt her pulse quicken, pressed himself against her as her warm, deep breath passed his ear, and felt his own heart jump as she trailed her hand down his spine, her touch humming with magic. He smiled and moved down to her collar bone, and for the first time since he'd set out from the scowles almost two months ago, he felt every tension release, every concern slip away, and he felt the closest to happy as he'd been in as long as he could remember.

Chapter 31

"Kienza didn't come back to say goodbye last night," Aria pouted as they ate their breakfast around the doused campfire. She pushed the porridge around in the bowl and her lower lip extended even further. "I wanted to show her something."

Rathen shuffled guiltily. In truth, he couldn't remember returning, himself. The last he'd known he'd been drifting off beneath the stars with her in his arms, and the next he was back under his blankets and Aria was shaking him awake from the best night's sleep he'd had in weeks. He wasn't even sure how much of the night had actually happened - his only certainty was that he *had* dreamt the visit to the familiar, peaceful forest, lit by the golden morning sun, and just as every time before, a mild tranquillity lingered over him through breakfast, turning him calmer and more contemplative - though his thoughts on that particular morning were still with Kienza.

"What did you want to show her?" Petra asked, who Aria had informed him had looked after her well and taught her how to wield a stick-sword, though she added that she'd been made to promise not to tell him about that, so he'd been sworn to secrecy in turn.

The little girl pursed her lips as if that, too, was a great secret. "My drawings," she said eventually, and Rathen looked up with a flash of hurt in his eyes.

"Why does she get to see them and not me?"

"Because I need her help," she replied stiffly, then turned back to her porridge, refusing to speak any more of it.

Rathen grumbled and shook his head, then glanced across to the edge of the camp where Garon stood in silence. He was about to look away again and ask Anthis if he'd made any progress with the ditchling's notes he had yet to tear himself away from, but a small, quick movement renewed his attention.

A sparrow flew from Garon's hands.

"Word from the Hall?" Rathen asked, recognising the body's subtle yet trademark messenger as the inquisitor started back over, folding the small piece of parchment it had carried. Petra looked up sharply.

"Yes, but nothing relevant to us. A long-term case has just been closed. We're under standing orders to look out for certain things whether it's our case or not, and when such a matter is closed, so is that line of observation."

"What was the case?"

He cast Petra his usual disapproving glance. "Classified."

"Of course it is."

"Did you finish planning our route?" Anthis asked as they began tidying up and Aria hurriedly licked her bowl clean.

"It's more or less as the crow flies, but if we're going to this ruin you've suggested, we're going to need to speak to the wind tribe first which means taking a detour north-west. Otherwise, there's little between here and the other side of the desert we'll have to avoid."

"What about food?" Rathen asked warily.

"Anthis picked up plenty from Oak Knoll last night. We'll have to ration, but we should have enough to last us for three weeks. That should get us through the desert."

"Uh-huh. And water?"

All eyes shifted onto the inquisitor.

"There's a river at the edge of the mountains, the last reliable source along our way. If you can conjure containers when we reach it, we can carry a great deal of water with us - but that will have to be rationed, too."

"What about from here, though?" Anthis pressed as Aria took the collected bowls from his hands, distracted in his urgency. "Are we heading straight north?"

"I understand your concerns, but the bandits in this forest have already been removed."

"Bandits?" Petra frowned. "So close to the border?"

"Borders don't come into it," the young man replied, his face strangely aged in worry. "Of all the elven cities still standing, Tarun is the most impressive, which makes it an obvious target for both theft and research. Historians and looters visit from all across the continent, and any who come down from the north have to pass through *this* forest to get back home. Bandits lie in wait near the northernmost edge, just far enough from the ruins for travellers to drop their guard and get comfortable with their prizes."

"They let them do the hard work and rob them on the way out." Petra nodded. "Clever." She looked towards Garon as she kicked apart the firewood, ensuring nothing was left smouldering. "But they're gone, you say?"

"Arrested quite recently. I overheard it in Carenna."

"Well, I'm relieved to hear that," Anthis sighed. "I've had a couple of run-ins with them myself."

"*You* have? How did you manage to get out of that?"

"Well I carry a knife for a reason," he retorted unappreciatively, "but they weren't idiots. They were the type to hold you up and strike a bargain rather than out-right attack you - it usually involved handing everything over for your life, but they generally didn't waste their time on anything that couldn't turn a quick profit. Parchment and research didn't interest them so I usually left with everything, scrolls and myself, in tact."

"But if they let people go, then people could tell on them," Aria pointed out. "*That's* not very clever."

"Which is presumably exactly how they got caught." Garon straightened. "We'll be fine. Let's head out. We should reach the edge of the forest just after midday and the mountains by nightfall."

Aria frowned and looked up searchingly through the roof of leaves.

The horses had been stabled with Anthis's errands in the village. They weren't made for deserts, and their fleeting lease had been made pointless thanks to Kienza's interference, so, despite the aches that still raked through Rathen's body, they set out on foot with their bags and bed rolls slung heavily over their backs. But such convenience had robbed them of their chance to adjust to the changing landscape, which was already dry and thinning, and left their minds burdened by thoughts of heat and featureless landscapes they were simply not prepared for, and the savage people they were expected not only to encounter but to reason with. There was little enthusiasm as they trudged through the forest; not one of them looked forward to finding its edge.

Though when an unforeseen delay arrived to oblige their hesitation, none of them welcomed that, either.

They'd been marching for not twenty minutes when the slightest rustle drew Petra's attention. She slowed and frowned, looking through the soft shade and narrow, generously-spaced tree trunks that lined the edge of the path, scanning the ground and the rocks for whatever small creature lurked among them. But she found nothing. She grunted to herself. It must have been the wind - even if it was barely a whisper.

Her eyes returned to the vaguely beaten track, but the brief scrape and rustle rose again from the other side, and instinct compelled her to reach for her sword.

In that instant, the forest around them erupted into life; bushes and rocks leapt from their positions, sprouting arms, legs and daggers, and launched themselves upon the group with a shrill, blood-curdling cry.

For a heartbeat, shock paralysed them, but in that stunned half-second all eyes thundered as one upon the inquisitor, each bearing the same dismay and betrayed trust as the last.

Petra's sword arm moved by itself, whipping around and blocking with the flat of her own the blade that sought to pierce her, and the sharp, ringing contact snapped them all back to attention. Garon braced his sword and deflected similar blows, having drawn it as readily as she, while Rathen raised his hands in preparation and Anthis pulled Aria close.

Bandits - with an alarming skill for disguise. The clouds of dust that followed their ambush immediately betrayed their methods. Covering themselves in the sand of ground-down stones along with cloaks made of grass and thorns, they'd balled themselves up and waited just paces from the faintly worn trail, becoming part of the landscape. It had taken preparation, which meant they'd known they were coming, and as soon as they'd had them surrounded, they'd pounced, shrieking to make the most of the element of surprise.

And it was clear that they were not about to propose a trade. They were vicious, their eyes brimming with the intent to kill. These bandits had no intentions of ending up like the previous gang.

They fell upon them ferociously, but Rathen immediately buffeted them away, ignoring the anticipated burn around his arm as he released his spell, embracing the confidence of the previous night's success. But the path was tight, no doubt the very reason the bandits had chosen it, and it would be all too easy to catch the others in his attacks - in fact, though he didn't notice at the time, he clipped Petra in his second flurry, but she'd been quick and graceful enough to regain her balance against it. A substantial magical attack was out of the question.

And yet, somehow, despite the cramped conditions, both duelist and inquisitor were still able to swing their swords and hit only their intended targets. For a moment it even seemed that the two could take on the six attackers between them, but an audible pop and yelp of surprise quickly smothered that idea.

With his attention focused on wearing down the two that sought to shatter his defence, Garon was attacked from behind by one of three newcomers, reinforcements who had almost certainly been waiting for their comrades to spring the trap before adding to the chaos themselves. Petra only just managed to slip in between him and his original adversaries as his sword arm was snatched and wrenched behind him, and with a swift backwards kick she disengaged Garon's new assailant, leaving him clear for Rathen to handle.

Then, as abruptly as they'd appeared, they scattered, their aggression muted by panic and instinct when the mage opted to throw searing fire instead of wind, and the brief but intense attack subsided - making way for another.

Even before the sound of their frenzied, fleeing steps had faded, Rathen whirled upon the inquisitor, his eyes blazing in rage while Petra and Anthis stared with a more sober but equally grave condemnation. He closed the distance between them in a flash. "*You said they were gone!*"

Garon raised his chin defiantly, maintaining his ground, his eyes void of vulnerability even as he clutched at his arm. His usual superiority reigned. "How was I supposed to know that others would be so quick to move into their place?"

"You should have seen the signs!" Anthis cried desperately, stepping up behind the mage as Aria looked worriedly from one to the next. "You're usually so vigilant - what's *happened?*"

But an acidic curl took Rathen's lip. "Nothing," he said, calmly, thoughtfully. "This isn't the first time he's led us into trouble. If memory serves me...this is the *fifth*." His narrowed gaze had become lanced by a deep, branching suspicion, and it pressed even heavier upon the inquisitor. "The ditchlings were the first." His tone was dangerous. "He was supposed to be leading us away from their territory, but instead we walked straight into it. He didn't see the signs all that well then, either."

"No one was hurt," Garon stated.

"No, you're right. We just got embroiled in their war instead." His tone grew darker. "Then there was Stonton - where someone *did* get hurt. You knew how severe the situation was and you still took us there. Then you led us into the Wildlands, then mapped a damned poor route to Carenna, and now you've led us straight into bandits you *confidently* told us were no longer here." His eyes were a near-black inferno. "Are you actually *trying* to get us all killed?"

"Rathen, stop," Petra urged, but though she had intended to defend, her doubtful tone did little to convince even herself. Rathen paid it little attention anyway.

"Answer me this," he continued instead, "how long have you actually been an inquisitor?"

The words dropped like lead. From nowhere, a slow and heavy wonder began unfolding in Petra and Anthis's eyes, their gazes gripping the inquisitor like a vice, tighter and tighter, until a reluctant but rapidly swelling mistrust began to take over. Garon looked from one face to the next as his jaw tightened. He couldn't afford to hesitate. "Almost two years."

"So you're a *novice*, really." Rathen smiled acridly, while disbelief knocked the doubtful expressions clean off the others. "That's the only reason your superior indulged you at all, isn't it? To be *rid* of you." Something else flashed suddenly through his eyes, a momentary panic that sharpened into another piercing rage. "*Do* you have the Crown's agreement for me to be out here?!"

"What difference does it make?" He growled, still mystifyingly superior. "You're needed."

"*What difference?!*"

"He's right, Rathen," Anthis said with bitter resentment as Petra stepped closer, prepared to separate them if the need arose. "Permission or not, you...you *are* needed. The Order isn't working on this matter, *we* are. Besides, out in Ivaea's desert and beyond, in the middle of *nowhere, who's going to know?!*"

Rathen didn't seem to hear him, nor notice his increasingly irate tone. He stared at Garon with such intensity, his eyes so wide and jaw so tightly knotted that it seemed he might truly attack him. Garon must have also realised this, and yet still he challenged him, steadily holding his gaze. The air sizzled, vibrating with rage - but no one could move to intervene. That same air paralysed them again, shoving their hearts up into their throats. They'd seen Rathen's impossible fury once, and there was nothing to stop it from unleashing itself again - and if it didn't, he still had the power within his own blood to both easily and willingly burn him to a crisp.

His mad, white-hot gaze shifted abruptly onto Anthis, and the young man immediately blanched, flinched and gasped beneath it. "The ruin," he said tersely. "You've been there before?"

"N-no."

"Then you don't know the way to the tribe, either." Rathen snatched the map that was rolled and tied at Garon's hip, then turned and stormed away. Aria was obediently close behind him, though it was clear she didn't truly understand what had happened.

"What about the route Garon planned?" Petra asked as she followed with less certainty, lingering between them and the officer.

"I am not following *any more of his routes!*" He roared so sharply they faltered in their steps. "We'll all wind up in the middle of *another* conflict, or *dead!*"

She looked back towards Garon, but whatever doubts were passing through her mind, she seemed unable to disagree with them. She shortly turned and hurried to catch up with the others, leaving him behind.

The breath Garon had been holding finally escaped in a ragged puff. He hadn't expected Rathen's rage to be so suffocating - he had little idea how he'd managed not to visibly quaver under such a bestial gaze. But he was acutely aware of the fact that he'd gotten off lightly. Every one of them had looked at him in loathing, utterly deceived, and it was fair that they should feel that way. He had misled them all, and Rathen more than most. But it had been necessary. The mage wouldn't have worked with him if he'd known the truth.

He forced his feet to move. This time, he made no attempt to reclaim the lead.

Rathen's pace thundered across the hard, dry ground. His jaw was still tight, and his perpetual misery lines had grown even deeper in his scowl. He was furious. He was a *fool*. He'd trusted a stranger and stepped out of his home on the basis of words alone. There had been no official documentation - he'd seen the uniform, the emblem on his sword, and apparently that had been enough. And he felt exposed. He was a risk to everyone around him, but he'd assumed, *foolishly assumed*, that preparations would have been made if the Crown had temporarily suspended his sentence, that other people might be safe! How naive could he be?! What kind of preparations could possibly have been made?!

Light footsteps pattered up alongside him, but he didn't look around.

"His shoulder's dislocated."

He gritted his teeth. "I know."

"Will you help him?"

He could feel the persistence of Petra's gaze. His jaw knotted and unknotted in thought. "Yes." He turned immediately, eradicating the few feet the inquisitor had left between himself and them as he followed. Garon hesitated as he approached, faltering as he braced himself for what he must have assumed was a delayed attack. And, in a way, it was.

Roughly, Rathen grasped the arm he protected, and with a single movement both expertly and brutally wrenched it back into place, dragging from him no more than a grunt of discomfort, then conjured a bag of ice and shoved into his other hand before turning and retaking the lead, a dark and spiteful shadow following his every step.

Petra, Anthis and Aria watched him silently as he overtook them, then glanced back towards the inquisitor as he held the ice to his shoulder and fashioned a sling out of his jacket. None of them spoke a word.

Suddenly, the desert didn't seem quite so daunting anymore.

It was just short of midday when they stepped out of the forest, a full hour earlier than expected, and left the last of the towering shade behind them all too soon. Where the trees abruptly thinned, the air became still and starkly warmer, and the western Pavise Mountains were revealed across the now bare and grassy surroundings. But if anyone marvelled at the snow-capped colossals, they did so silently. Even Aria, who had never seen such a sight in her life, didn't voice more than a solitary peep of awe.

The landscape was otherwise flat, studded with small rocks but carpeted in lush grass which thrived in the unbroken reach of the sun. But while it was verdant around them now, they glimpsed an ochre shadow in the distance, tufts of near-yellow grass sprouting from the ground like a moth-eaten rug. Without the impeding trees they could finally see far more than ten feet ahead of them, but there didn't seem to be much to look at. In fact, the single positivity of the naked landscape was that nothing and no one could sneak up on them - assuming they chose to disregard the fact that it also left them nowhere to hide, themselves. Which they didn't, and that left them feeling even more jittery.

The mountains, too, became quickly disheartening, so massive and unmoving that even after two hours in their shadow it felt to the group that they'd not covered more than five minutes of ground.

The only reasonable landmark seemed to be the river Garon had mentioned, and even that was a disappointment. It was slight, far narrower than its banks, but the stream that rolled down from the mountains, looped out briefly over the land before meandering off into the lower lying reaches of rock behind them was the last source of water for miles. And as they looked off towards the thinning grass ahead of them, they dreaded to think how long it might be before they would next see any flowing freely.

They'd stopped as planned, and Rathen had conjured four corked and strapped jugs just small enough to carry without being over-burdened, and in so doing had found some glimmer of relief to ease his shoulders. He was certain that his cuff had burned less with this spell than the last, and he had thought the same before; either the oddity was passing or he was truly overcoming it. Which, didn't matter. Either was a relief. If they were heading into the desert, he couldn't afford to be afraid of using his magic.

Petra considered the jugs as they lowered them into the gentle current. "Can you not just conjure water?" She'd asked, the first words spoken for goodness only knew how long.

"Yes," he had replied with a bite that surprised even himself, "but it wouldn't be real so it wouldn't be of any use if you drank it. Not enough substance for your body to use. It would be the same as having nothing - you could bathe in it, though."

"So we can have a nice cool bath if it gets too hot," Aria grinned. She'd decided long ago to simply shed the atmosphere and stare at the mountains instead. "Good!"

Despite the pain in his shoulder, Garon carried his jug on his back without complaint just as the others did, and they continued along their way. None of them knew how long they'd been walking; the only sign of the passage of time came with the eventual dimming of the light, but with nothing to obscure the sun above the horizon, not even a single cloud in the perpetually blue sky, the evening stretched on for far longer than should have been possible.

And so there was a great relief when Rathen finally called a stop for the night. The spot he'd chosen seemed like any other, dotted with dry shrubs, rocks and tufts of grass, devoid of breeze and just as dry and warm as the rest. But Garon didn't voice any objections - not that the others would have listened to them - so they made themselves as comfortable as they could while he made himself useful. Mindful of his swelling shoulder, he built the fire and cooked the food while no one gave him more than a passing thanks, and once everyone had eaten, they went their separate ways, desperate to finally escape the stifling mood. Garon turned to his usual solemn duty of keeping watch, and no one could tell in their secret glances whether he seemed guilty or sulky - though neither was anyone inclined to bother finding out.

Things were little better the following morning, but at least no one was afraid to speak over breakfast. Garon kept to himself, avoided conversation and returned to his spot at the edge of camp as soon as he could to keep watch or assess the weather. That was little different from usual, but everyone else was acutely aware of it even while pointedly ignoring him. Only Aria seemed to have a problem with his treatment, but she made no attempt to act upon it, certain she was misunderstanding something.

"Here," Anthis said, pointing to the map Rathen held open to him. The mage didn't miss that he'd flinched when he'd addressed him. It had become a habit over the past two days, as had inching away from him if he got too close and only sitting down when there was someone else between them - in this case, Petra. But Rathen didn't point it out. The atmosphere was so heavy already, what was a little more weight?"

He frowned down at the point he'd indicated and nodded. "That's a strong magnetic site. Kienza said the ruin was sorely affected - now I'm not surprised."

"Do we have any idea how to approach the tribes about it?" Petra asked warily. "Whoever this Kienza is, she seems to think they'll want our help. But if it's that sacred to them...well..."

"The ditchlings--"

"*Arkhamas.*" Aria sighed wearily. "For goodness sake, Daddy."

"*Arkhamas*, Arkhamas." He shook his head just as tiresomely. "The *Arkhamas* thought I was responsible for what was happening in their woods, and the harpies likely do, too. The tribes will probably be equally untrusting and turn us away."

"Assuming the exchange is a *civilised* one. We'll need to find a way to approach them and let them know of our intentions right away, leave no chance at all for misunderstanding. I don't know about the rest of you, but I rather like my limbs un-chewed."

Aria nodded in agreement while Petra frowned uneasily. "Can I ask a question?"

They looked up at her expectantly.

"Why are we even bothering with this? There are bound to be loads of other places we can try that we *don't* need permission to see. Halen, for example."

"I've already been into Halen." Rathen ignored the confused looks. "I've got everything I can from there, so while I'd like to agree with you, I think it's best we stick to the plan. Kienza seems to think this is a good idea, and I learned long ago to listen to her."

"But you forget so much of what she says," Aria reminded him.

"Not when it's important."

"Well *that* just isn't true..."

Petra and Anthis smiled to themselves as Rathen pursed his lips unappreciatively. "Anyway..." He looked back to the others while Aria grinned innocently, leapt to her feet and wandered off towards the edge of camp. "If the site is sacred, convincing them that we mean no harm probably won't be that simple. We'll need payment of some kind, or a bargaining chip."

"Money?"

"They have no need for money."

"Supplies, then. We don't have much, but we must have *something* they want...or," Petra glanced towards Garon as he stared back along their tracks, "be able to get it."

"We could end up insulting them if we offer them supplies," Anthis replied, then his eyes suddenly lit up. "What if we gathered something for them instead? As a gift? Caught something, an animal - brought them food."

"But they're *cannibals*."

"Surely not *exclusively*...and...well, if so, perhaps they might like to try something different..."

Rathen frowned. "Anthis, look around you." The young man did so. "What do you expect to find in a barren expanse like this?"

"Well they must eat *something*..."

Petra nodded slowly for his benefit. "Each other."

Rathen rolled the map back up and rose to his feet. "Well, we'd better give it some thought. We've only got a couple of days before we reach them and we don't have the supplies to dawdle. If--"

"*Daddy!*"

He spun around at Aria's panicked cry and the others leapt immediately to their feet, but though they stared with keen eyes, no one could see what had alarmed her. She was probably twenty feet away, standing amongst patches of grass no different to the rest, and she was staring at something on the ground another distance away. Whatever it was, she clearly had no wish to approach it.

Anthis cursed. "Aria, don't move!" He glanced to Rathen and dropped his voice low. "It's probably a snake."

He started towards her immediately.

"Wait, see if you can catch it! It might be edible!"

Rathen ignored him. Straining his every sense, he tried to pinpoint the snake's location as quickly as he could to get Aria safely away from it - but as he neared her and finally spotted what she had fixed so anxiously upon, he frowned.

Snakes didn't have feet.

His jaw tightened under his sudden misgivings, and though he felt a clawing reluctance to continue, unwilling to prove his twisted new assumptions correct, he couldn't seem to stop himself. "Stay here," he said quietly as he stepped past her, giving her shoulder a firm squeeze as his caution shifted, his mind turned now towards sparing her a particular sight rather than keeping her safe.

The bare feet, as he'd expected, were human, tanned and dirty, as were the legs revealed by the shrubs that shrank away as he neared, and a few steps later his eyes fell upon precisely what he'd wished to save her from.

He stopped short, deflated by a regretful sigh as he looked down upon the body of a young woman lying sprawled on the desolate ground, scarcely clad in thin, rough hides, her skin bruised and bloodied. She'd been attacked by something, and from her position, he guessed she'd been at least unconscious when she'd dropped. But even aside from the blood that trickled from a number of blade-wounds, she made for a startling sight. There was a subtle but definite metallic sheen to her bronze skin, her long and perfectly straight hair was bone-white, and streaks of black, white and light grey paints had been brushed across her young body.

But there was another detail that struck him just as quickly, and it was one that revealed to him in no uncertain terms that this tribal girl was not in fact dead.

Compelled, he knelt quickly beside her and began to investigate her wounds. There were more than there had first seemed, but they were not deep enough to kill her. He heard Petra stop behind him and curse at the sight. "Bandages," he demanded without looking around.

"Are you mad?!"

"*Now!*"

She stalled, doubtful of the wisdom of helping someone who would very likely turn around and attack them as soon as she was able, but after he sent her a brief but pressing glance, she turned and dashed back towards the bags, her face still twisted in disapproval.

"What's happened to her?" Aria asked quietly as she came to a wary stop beside him, Anthis closely in tow. Despite the immense caution and discomfort the others shared, Aria peered down at the bronze young woman with enchantment in her eyes.

"She's been attacked," he replied as he busied himself with identifying the worst of the wounds. "By those bandits, quite probably."

"Why?"

"Because, she's tribal."

Aria's eyes shot in a panic towards him, but barely a moment later they returned to the young woman more thoughtfully, and he knew without looking that she was in the process of deciding quite firmly that she wasn't a threat. But even as Petra brought him his first-aid bag and he began to clean the wounds, Rathen himself wasn't so sure. "Or it could have been self-defence."

"Self defence?" Anthis scoffed. "From *her?*"

Rathen spared him only a glance, but the gravity in his eyes in that moment knocked the young man's cynicism. "She is a mage."

Chapter 32

Rathen tended to all of the tribal's wounds, staunching the bleeding and cleaning away any potential infections. Then a fevered debate had ensued, one in which even Garon participated. None of them - except Garon - felt right abandoning the painted girl in the stark and dry grassland, even if her home was close by, but more importantly, no one was at all comfortable with the idea of keeping her in their company. As a mage, she had the potential to release the same destructive power from her fingertips as Rathen could, even if she was surely no older than seventeen, and given the savagery of the tribes as a whole, let alone the remote groups, there was no telling how she might react when she regained consciousness. Combined, the two points almost promised disaster.

They argued for almost an hour, during which most of them had changed sides at least three times, and one had stormed off. Then insults started to fly. It was only after Aria had ordered them with embarrassing maturity to behave like grown ups that they finally and reluctantly came to an agreement, and it was also, shamefully, her suggestion that they might be looked upon favourably if they tended her wounds and returned her safely to her people that decided it. The tribal was coming with them.

Laid in a small, conjured litter lined with blankets, the five shared the task of dragging her along, a job Aria set to eagerly even if she struggled, while one remained at the back to keep an eye on her should she begin to wake.

Tensions cooled, and swapping turns proved to be the most eventful points of the day. The terrain didn't change and they encountered no one along their way, hostile or otherwise, and though they spotted buzzards circling nearer to the mountains, there was no clue to their quarry.

It was mid-afternoon when Anthis took his turn to pull the litter, sending wary glances behind him while Aria kept watch - another important task she relished in. She walked alongside it, staring in scrutinous fascination at the young woman while asking questions that none of them could answer - why she was painted, why her skin was metal, why she wasn't really wearing clothes, and so on - and so she was the first to notice when the girl's eyelids flickered open.

She gasped in excitement, then roughly whispered "she's awake," giving a last-minute thought to trying not to startle her - though she'd startled everyone else with her initial response - but as the young woman's frost-blue eyes turned drowsily upon her, they still flashed with alarm.

She was awake in an instant, her eyes darting frantically about herself as the litter clattered to a stop, and before anyone had the chance to react, she launched herself up to flee or to attack. Fortunately, she didn't make it off of the pallet.

Doubling over, her breath snatched and body stunned, she dropped back down with a hiss.

"Don't try to move," Rathen said slowly and clearly as he knelt beside the litter, his expression softening to become as friendly as possible - a look none but Aria had ever received from him, and Petra a trace in Edam. But though the girl shuffled away to the edge of the cart despite his effort, her eyes coloured in panic and hand pressed tightly to her side, she made no new attempt to try to escape.

Gently, he took her free hand, a gesture the others thought both brave and strangely affectionate, though it was nothing more than a preventative measure. She flinched at his touch, but she didn't struggle. Clearly she understood her position, and she must have felt the magic within him as he had in her. Her eyes remained wary, but he saw a distinct intelligence within them which seemed to read him deeply. Or perhaps it was just the depth of their icy colour.

"You were attacked," he continued slowly, "but not by us. I've cleaned and tied your wounds, so you will be all right."

She continued to stare.

His brow twitched doubtfully. "Do you understand what I'm saying?"

Still she said nothing.

He sighed, but had expected as much. With his free hand concealed from her sight, he flexed his fingers into a binding spell. Her eyes dropped immediately to her own hands in alarm, but when she looked back up at him, there was a hateful recognition in her suddenly hard gaze.

"Sorry," he said with a less concerned tone as he rose back to his feet, "but it's for our safety. We're taking you back to your tribe, so just stay put - and speak up if we start heading the wrong way. None of us want to get lost." He turned around and reassumed the head of the group, the fretful eyes of the others trailing him all the way. "Let's go."

"What if she tries to cast a spell?" Petra asked in a hushed but frantic voice as she hurried up next to him.

"Well she's welcome to try, but I've numbed and bound her hands. She won't be casting a thing until I remove it - which I won't do until I'm sure she understands that we mean her no harm."

"Taking away her only means of defence may not have been the best way to do that..."

He cast her a doubtful glance. "You would rather I left it in tact?" He looked back to their flat and desolate heading and sighed glumly to himself. "Looks like this is going to be harder than we thought."

The grass had become even sparser over the course of the afternoon, and still not a cloud graced the sky. But even more disconcerting were the growing traces of sand beneath their boots and the fact that they'd almost reached the horizon. By the time they made camp that eternal evening, the drop in the land beyond was surely little more than an hour away, and there was no doubt that once they reached the crest, the desert would be sprawling out ahead of them. They could already feel its heat, the air warmer and drier with the passing of the mountains. No one dared a look to find out for certain.

But though their feet hurt and their minds were humming with boredom, no one was comfortable with stopping for the night. Even as they ate they sent doubtful, frequent glances towards their new travelling companion, and she had yet to make a peep.

"All she's done all day is watch us," Petra noted quietly as Rathen headed over to check her wounds. "She probably sees us as her captors - maybe even the reason she's hurt."

"She's not tried to run off yet, though," Anthis reminded her, watching the girl thoughtfully as he tore away a piece of bread.

"Because Rathen cast a spell over her hands. She's probably waiting for him to break it." She sighed heavily, feeling the eyes drilling into her back, and she couldn't help glancing around for the seventeenth time in five minutes. The girl looked away as she did so, shifting her sharp attention onto Rathen instead as he knelt beside her, announced his intentions and began unwinding her bandages. She watched him very closely, but there was more thought to her eyes than there had been earlier, as if her own mistrust was being very slowly replaced by curiosity for the fact that they had yet to mistreat her. Or perhaps she was simply plotting something.

Petra turned away and sighed again, shaking her head as she raised her waterskin to her lips. "I don't like this at all. I won't be getting any sleep tonight."

"She's one girl, since the harpies, someone's always on watch. She won't have the chance to cause us any trouble. *My* concern, however, is that we won't manage to smooth things over before we run into her tribe. I don't think it'll help matters if it looks like we've taken her prisoner..."

"I don't want to run into them at *all*. She might be 'one girl', but they *won't* be."

"I'm sure you can defend yourself if things turn sour."

"Against an opponent with a familiar weapon on fair ground, yes, but tribes use poisons. One scratch and we'll be foaming at the mouth, having fits and turning blue! And then they will *eat* us."

Anthis nodded with as much composure as he could muster while the colour drained from his face, and his eyes dragged back towards the girl as he considered how unfortunately accurate her apparent overreaction was. "I hadn't thought of that..."

"She's not dangerous."

Both looked down at Aria, who they had forgotten was sat between them, picking the crumbs of bread from her skirt, but just as Anthis was about to ask how she could be so sure, a new voice rose behind them, one guarded but coloured by a musical tone that immediately snatched their attention.

Rathen's eyebrows rose as he looked away from the tribal's lacerated skin to her hard and expectant expression. "You can..." He brushed it off and answered her question instead. "I helped you because it was the right thing to do."

"You seek something in return. A reward of some kind." Her eyes were as sharp as a harpy's, and only enhanced by their sweep of black paint.

He frowned, guilty, and resumed redressing the wounds. "You're only partly right. We seek no reward, just help." He glanced back up when she didn't respond, aware of her steady gaze, but it didn't trouble him as much as it seemed to the others. "My name is Rathen. That's Anthis, Aria, Petra, and over there is Garon."

She peered over as they stared back, but shortly disregarded them and fixed her thoughtful gaze back onto him. She paused for a long moment, chewing over a thought, then seemed to end her silent debate. "Eyila."

He hesitated. "Ay-la?"

"Ay-*yee*-luh."

"Ay-*yee*-luh."

She nodded, and he thought he saw the slightest, briefest whisper of a smile. He was quite probably mistaken, but he nodded and smiled in return anyway, much more openly. "Nice to meet you, Eyila." He then finished tying off the bandages and left to find her something to eat, hoping as he did so that it wouldn't harm their supplies to the point of running out before the far edge of the desert. It was a matter of pride that he didn't repeat any of Garon's mistakes.

But when he returned not five minutes later, her steely, unreadable attention was no longer nailed upon the group as it had been throughout every second of the day, but on the sun which was just about to disappear beyond the near horizon. He noticed the yearning desperation in her eyes, but said nothing about it. Instead, he knelt back beside her, set the bread in her lap, and took her immobile hands in his. "Don't do anything." He warned her in the most friendly way he could while still implying that he could, and *would*, stop her by any means he had to if she disobeyed.

But his words and threat slipped by; she only glanced at him, her eyes golden in the sunset, gave a fleeting and distracted nod, then looked back into the depths of the fiery indigo sky.

He frowned and followed her gaze, searching fiercely through the encroaching twilight with his every sense in case she was aware of something - or some*one* - that he was not. But he found nothing. Nothing and no one. Uneasily, he released the spell.

Whatever her concern, she eagerly accepted the offer of food. She snatched the meat and ate it more ravenously than he'd expected for not knowing what it was, and she displayed far fewer manners than even Aria did when they were at home. He tried to quell the turning of his stomach at the thought of the young woman tearing into human flesh with the same vigour, and he knew the others were thinking exactly the same thing as they watched, haunted, from the camp.

"I must ask you for something," she said after a few mouthfuls, her gaze not once breaking from the horizon.

"What would that be?" He managed to suppress a heave.

"I need to feel the wind."

He blinked, certain he'd misheard but too wary of insulting a tribal to risk asking her to repeat it.

She looked back at him when he took too long to answer. "I cannot meditate if I can't feel the wind," she explained patiently. "I need to sit over there. There are no plateaus here, but a weak current flows that way. It is the only suitable place."

"Meditate..." he nodded, pretending to understand. "And you just need to sit over there?" He looked to where she had indicated but it seemed no different to anywhere else, and try as he might, he saw not even a blade of grass twitch in the dusk light. Suspicion edged in.

"You do not trust me," she informed him plainly, even resentfully, "just as I do not trust you. But I am your prisoner, so I must ask permission. Will you permit me?"

He regarded her carefully and saw the burning desire in her eyes. It was a need too great for her claims, but his doubt tore him equally in two directions, and there was only one option he could choose if he wanted to win her trust. His jaw soon tightened in decision, though he second-guessed it immediately. "Finish eating. Once I've bound your hands again, you can go over there."

She nodded her acceptance. "Thank you."

The others watched in confusion as the young woman rose to her feet and Rathen escorted her fifteen paces or so away from where she had been, only to stop, sit back down in the rough grass and stare out at the sky. They looked at him quizzically as he rejoined them.

"She's meditating." As their bewilderment only deepened, Rathen simply shrugged, then looked purposefully towards Anthis. "Watch her. I've bound her hands again, she can't cast a thing, but she could still try to run and get one of her own to counter it. And we need her."

Anthis nodded his understanding and left to see to it, taking his many papers with him. Again, Rathen didn't miss the haste and abruptness with which he'd done so, even if there had been no reason for him to linger. He sighed to himself, but pushed it away before finally sitting down to eat.

For a long while, the only sound was that of Aria's knife sliding expertly through soft wood. She'd begun to whittle for the first time in weeks, returning to work upon what Rathen was increasingly convinced was a ghostly woman, and her dexterity with the blade continued to astound and alarm everyone else as they watched. But between cringing glances, their attention was persistently occupied by the presence behind them. Vigilant even while purposely facing away, their ears strained to hear anything or anyone that might be approaching in the creeping darkness, or for any sign of deception on her own part.

Finally, a whisper broke the silence, and from Petra's indecision to voice it, it was clear that the question was burning her mind. "What do you think?"

Rathen needed no elaboration. "I don't know," he confessed very quietly. "I can't get a read on her. She doesn't trust us, but she said that much herself, and I can't say I'm willing to turn my back to her." His tone became grave. "She has an understanding of her magic - to what extent, I don't know, but I'm quite certain she knows how to wield it..."

Petra stared towards her from the corner of her eye. "I can't believe there are mages among them."

"I knew it wasn't impossible - they're human, too - but I admit I'm still surprised. There can't be many..."

"Enough to teach each other, it seems."

"Though I'd wager most go uninstructed."

"Do you think she knows anything about the ruin?"

He frowned and chewed the inside of his cheek. "Maybe...but it might not help us if the tribes have the *wrong* understanding of magic."

"What do you mean?"

"That they might view it theologically rather than biologically," Anthis replied in a barely audible whisper, having stopped ten feet from his charge, half way between her and them and well within earshot. "That it's gifted by their gods to a chosen few, or that it's dependant on the moon they were born under. Or, perhaps, that it's a curse, some kind of black mark on their soul."

"If they mistrust magic like everyone else does, it could have been her *own* people who attacked her..." It wasn't clear if Petra's concern was for the girl or for their delivering of her.

But Rathen was already shaking his head. "I've already told her we're taking her back. If it was a problem, she would have said something." His lips pursed in thought. "What are the odds they *revere* magic?"

"About as likely as our being welcomed," Anthis mumbled, and he began wandering around, pacing in thought as he managed somehow to split his attention between them, the tribal and the torn, scribbled papers in his hands. Despite his distraction, the girl hadn't once even twitched under his guard. "It doesn't really matter if they understand magic the way we do," he mused. "The elves built their temples and monuments on sites of magnetism by chance. There was something about each place that drew them and, they believed, put them in close touch with the gods; it was only *after* their construction that magic became a part of their lives. Even if these people consider their magic theologically, there's a reason they revere the site, too, and it could well be similar to the elves. So *whatever* they believe, truth or not, it could be of help to us." He waved his papers imploringly. "It may not seem relevant, but perhaps a simplified outlook could be just what we need to get a better understanding of this rogue magic - and Kienza said we won't be able to use the Zi'veyn against it without it."

Rathen frowned to himself as Kienza's musical but matter-of-fact voice swept through his mind. "'Don't get bogged down in specifics'..."

"And," Anthis added, "making the effort to understand their culture rather than reject it could also help relations..."

"Assuming we're given the opportunity for such a civilised exchange."

"We're going to have to try. We won't get to the ruin without it."

"If you are speaking of Ut'hala, you would do well to keep away."

The young woman's voice was no less surprising than the first time they'd heard it, still melodic despite the additional abruptness that accompanied her defence. They spun around, startled, and found her on her feet, her blue eyes hard and full of warning as they stared steadily from one face to the next.

"Ut'hala," Anthis repeated slowly, grasping the word's subtleties as easily as had it been common tongue. "Is that what you call it?"

"It is an ancient shrine in the Singing Sands," she replied with little care for his interest. "It was built before my people, but whoever by, they no longer go there. It is the only structure not shaped by the winds where Aya'u will hear us."

"Aya'u." Anthis took a step towards her, his curiosity in his academic state of mind getting the better of him, but rather than back away, she raised her chin and met his gaze squarely. Her eyes were not cruel, nor were they angry. In fact, they seemed to him to bear only concern. He stopped after a second step so as not to upset her. "Aya'u is your god?"

"Aya'u is the Goddess of Wind. She rules the sands, and She is our charge."

"*Your* charge?" Anthis frowned, his intrigue only growing. "You look after your goddess?"

Rather than answer, her eyes flicked onto the others, dismissing both him and his prying. "You cannot go."

"We understand that it's important to you," Rathen assured her, and he was pleased for the fact that it was true, "but we still have to go. We're prepared to bargain with your leaders for permission - we won't harm anything in the vicinity, no animals, no stones."

"It is not harm I fear you will bring, but harm you will *receive*. Ut'hala is unsafe - dangerous. Not even the priestesses have been near it for an entire moon..."

Now Rathen took a careful step towards her, and she watched him just as closely as she had Anthis. "Why has it not been safe? What's happening there?"

She seemed reluctant to answer at first, as though she saw the sudden focus in his eyes as something to be wary of, that his interest was borne of ill will. But her eyes revealed another deep consideration, one that weighed many factors very quickly, and she shortly made a decision. "No wind blows," she replied finally, though her instinctive hesitance remained, "and the sands are drowned, flooded by rains that never fell."

"What does that mean?" Petra frowned. "The water just appeared there? In the middle of the *desert?*"

"We have no understanding of it, either," she admitted, "but there is more besides - a beauty, an unsettling one, unnatural." Suspicion pulled at her brow as the group sent each other brief and unsurprised glances, and accusation suddenly tainted her voice. "What is it you know?" She demanded, taking a sharp step closer herself this time, and if she had intended it to be menacing, she'd succeeded. Each of them shifted back, their guards immediately rising; Petra's hand twitched towards the hilt of the sword she'd made a point of keeping beside her that night, and Garon, too, reached to draw his own from further back where he kept watch. But she paid them no mind, as if physical weapons were of no concern to her.

Only Rathen's defence remained constant, for he knew her hands were still useless.

"We know that this same thing - or something similar - is happening all over Turunda, Ivaea, and other countries besides," he replied calmly as her eyes burned into him. "It isn't our doing - we're trying to *stop* it. But part of our plan involves visiting various sites and seeing how they're affected so we can develop an understanding of it first."

The ferocity of her eyes barely softened as they continued to sear him, their blue colour now blistering ice, but the crease in her painted brow did ease a little, and she considered him more carefully. "It is magic. You know this, don't you?"

He nodded, surprised but pleased for the fact that the tribes at least recognised this much. And hopeful. "We've seen it in a number of other places, but we need to see it in Uth--in the desert. Your desert."

She stared at him for a long moment, and he felt hope rising further at her ever-thoughtful gaze. Then she nodded to herself in conclusion. "You should turn around."

Confusion shattered his brow. "What?"

"I can make my own way back from here, but you shouldn't waste your time. If other places are in such turmoil, you haven't time to lose."

"No."

She stared at his abrupt and stubborn response, as did everyone else.

"Sorry," he continued unapologetically, "but we've got little choice. We have to get there."

"Well you can't," she said with much the same tone.

"I would prefer to hear that from your leaders."

"What makes you think I am not one of them?"

"You wouldn't be out here on your own if you were, lying in your own blood."

Her eyes sharpened. "This is why you helped me. You *do* want something."

"Like I said: you were only *partly* right." He walked towards her again, but this time he didn't stop after one or two steps. He drew up right in front of her, folded his arms across his chest and loomed with the grim authority one often used over a child, using his own well-aged obstinacy to cancel hers out. "We *are* going to the desert wind tribe for permission to visit this ruin, and for you to be out here, I would guess you belong to that very tribe. In which case I would ask you to help us convince your elders in payment for saving your life. You are free to leave us alone and make your own way instead, if you wish, and feign unfamiliarity when we arrive, but arrive we *will*, and ask we will. This is important - for the sanctity of your shine as well as the safety of your people, never mind the world beyond."

Once again, she met his gaze levelly, and all other eyes flicked carefully between the two.

"How close are you to being able to fix it, if that is truly your goal?"

He let no trace of doubt nor hesitance cross his face. "I don't know," he replied honestly. "We could be months away, or weeks - or the very detail we need could be within the ruin you so jealously guard. Until we get there, none of us will know for certain - but I would prefer to explain all of this to--"

"To my chief." She sighed heavily and looked across the wary, expectant faces of the others. Her own expression changed now - it was still just as reserved, but there was a new kind of thoughtfulness, one that revealed she fully understood the weight of what they were trying to do. But there was also a responsibility, an obligation to her tribe and one that could sway her decision in either direction: she could take the group at their word and hope they could restore her people's sacred shrine, or lead strangers to her home and risk harm to her loved ones. Because Rathen realised as he watched her internal deliberation that what little they knew of the tribes probably mirrored what little the tribes knew of his own culture.

Then her thoughts were concealed. She closed her eyes, took a deep breath, and let a soft, brief but sudden breeze tousle her long, white hair. She opened her eyes the moment it passed. "I will lead you to my people in the morning. If we leave at dawn, we will reach them in two days."

"And you will ensure us a safe arrival?" Petra added nervously, but the girl only gave them an unreadable frown.

"Of course..."

Chapter 33

Small, grey clouds dotted the sky, encouraging a game of hide and seek between the mid-spring sun and the underlying land. A light breeze, neither too warm nor too cool, rolled over the mottled hills and tousled the trees' boughs like a grandparent would a child's hair, the sound of competing birdsong drifting upon it from the forests to the west, laced with the scents of distant rain and the churned earth of ploughed fields.

In short, it was an unremarkable day.

And yet, despite such ordinariness, the surrounding atmosphere was tense and watchful. The endless armoured bodies stood out painfully from the rich, green landscape, if not for their numbers then certainly for the way their steel caught the sunlight and lit them up like beacons - a fact of which all were acutely aware. The watch's attention sharpened in their exposure, rendering each as alert and hawk-eyed as if they felt dogs were ever an inch from nipping at their rears. A steel ring formed around the camp, their eyes cast out to the furthest reaches and their swords close at hand, sheathed readily at their hips or strapped across their backs, while the soldiers within shot watchful glances over their shoulders while tending their weapons, armour and rumbling stomachs.

But their shared concern was for more than being a conspicuous feature in the landscape.

Skilan's forces were still inexplicably scattered and it was difficult to know where small battalions might pop up, or what they might do when they did. It was true that Turunda's forces were more collected and organised, and that they were on familiar ground, but Skilan seemed to be applying unorthodox tactics and equally had two allies at their disposal, of which Doana was quite an unexpected addition.

They were doing all they could against the situation, but after yesterday's loss, their confidence had been knocked. It was the result of not the first, but the *second* questionable decision by their superiors, and even General Moore had been unable to contain his frustration in front of his subordinates.

But the whispers of discontent beneath the air were weak. Unconventional Skilan may presently be, but Turunda still had the upper hand. And more fortunately still, General Moore's soldiers weren't the only ones standing vigil across Turunda.

Among this very division stood other men and women, equally armoured if curiously unarmed at first glance, absorbed in the same outward concentration. Some were grouped in small, uniformed ranks, weaving their fingers into the same movements at the same time, casting spells in perfect unison with a certain if subtle result, while others stood alone and as still as rock, their eyes distant and focused intently on something unseen. With their magic, the Order's martial wing were the only ones capable of confronting enemy casters - either to stop them or to occupy them, whichever present tactics required - and protecting the military itself from magical assault while they saw to the rest. But, with a few simple spells, they were also capable of detecting anyone or anything's approach far more quickly than soldiers' eyes and ears alone.

Privately, more than a few war mages found it ironic that so many soldiers breathed easier when martially-trained casters were around, but soldiers were far more wisened to the necessities of war than ordinary people, most of whom blindly feared even the Order's tame scholarly wing.

Thoughtful and observant, Sivaan Rosh had pondered it many times himself, and he found it even more curious and yet quite unsurprising that he worked better with General Moore than he did a number of the Order's own elders.

That day, however...

"You're distracted, Damien."

The grandly armoured mage turned his head sharply towards his military counterpart, startled out of his obsessive thoughts. He blinked at him for a moment. "Yes. Sorry."

The general shook his head with brief amusement and looked across the camp from beside him. "Heed your lieutenants' advice, my friend. Whatever weighs on your mind needn't consume your whole being. And it shouldn't, especially not now. Your mages need your leadership, and we need their skills."

"I know."

Moore's stern brow knitted more tightly as he considered his strangely distant colleague. Damien had never been the type to keep things to himself if they were relevant, but neither was he the type to let *irrelevant* things distract him. He was a professional with forty five years of service under his belt, and an open book when it mattered.

It was possible that he was simply troubled by Skilan's unexpectedly advanced tactics - but while they were certainly shocking and had caught even himself off guard, the sivaan should have adjusted by now. Or perhaps there was something arcane at work that he was still trying to solve - but again, that wasn't something Damien Rosh would keep secret from him, not in a time of war, and neither would he withhold it until he had an understanding of it. They were fighting the same enemies; everything was shared as soon as it was learned, whether they could make heads or tails of it or not. Every detail mattered.

His eyes narrowed. No, it was neither of those things, and nor was it anything personal. It had manifested only in the past few days and his home had been long behind him by then...

Then perhaps - just *perhaps* - his age was finally catching up to him, turning him into a bitter and brooding old man. It claimed most soldiers in time, those who lived long enough to see such age, and in the sivaan's case it had certainly taken long enough...

Moore grunted quietly to himself in conclusion. That had to be it. "If--"

The mage-general abruptly walked away. "Sorry," he threw back as an afterthought, "I've really got to..." But he didn't finish.

The general said nothing as he watched the sivaan hurry away. He'd never been a rude or haughty mage so something must have grasped his urgent attention, but

Moore didn't want to cause a commotion among the already tense ranks by hurrying after him to find out.

And he was presently too alarmed himself to even think to.

He watched him closely, tracking him through the maze of bodies.

He hadn't missed the flash of distress in the old man's eyes.

The subtlest trace of magic had been sitting just at the edge of Rosh's senses for days, dragging away more and more of his attention with every rising of the sun, as if his mind had been chained to an old and stubborn work horse. He'd fought against it with all his strength, but it had grown so very curious, compelling - almost seductive - over the past week that it simply wouldn't be ignored. He felt his dedication slipping, increasingly unable to resist its pull, but each time he'd found himself giving in he discovered he could see it a little more clearly. Before long, he'd become unwilling to even *try* to brush it aside.

The enrapturing sensation was unfamiliar, and yet, somehow, he knew it as well as the presence of an old friend. But try as he might, he couldn't identify the magic's source, even as it grew steadily stronger with their march across the western reaches. He'd thought at first that it was following him, approaching from behind and preparing to overtake him, and that had prompted him to keep the Order marching long into the night to try to rid himself of the harassment. Now, however, it was different. He'd spent so much time consumed by it while lying rigidly awake on his cot that he'd realised it wasn't following him at all. It was luring him, as if he was an animal being led into a trap.

He'd decided upon that striking recognition that he would find it himself, first. To lure him, it would have to lie in wait, which meant that *he* could hunt *it* down instead. He would find it, he would silence it, and he would claim it. That was his duty. That was his compulsion.

And now, at last, it was close. When they'd drawn to a stop that afternoon he'd felt as if they were right on top of it - he was *certain* they were right on top of it. And he had to find it before it understood what he was doing and escaped.

He'd searched and searched from where he'd stood as the camp continued its cautious activities around him, the sensation, the presence, the lure entirely engulfing him and giving him nowhere at all to turn. And then, finally, he'd found something: a trace, a tendril snaking out towards him from a kaleidoscope of magic which he followed with the sheerest focus, grasping it almost with his bare hands to make sure it couldn't suddenly flit away.

With every step, he could feel it coaxing him. It wanted him to find it. But his guard was keen; he wasn't walking towards it - whatever or whoever it was - blindly. It wouldn't get the better of him. It wouldn't.

He would find it.

The tendril wended through the camp and he followed its every twist and turn, stepping unknowingly passed the soldiers who moved respectfully out of his way, mage and man alike.

A dull throb reverberated through his head to settle behind his brow. It was a familiar pain, the same headache he'd had for weeks that simply wouldn't budge, but it had grown more intense in his recent agitation and now it all but fogged his mind.

A sudden desperation flooded his being as his addled mind lost track of the magic, and the tendril disappeared into the myriad of energy like a breath puffed in a fog. He stumbled to a stop, ignoring those he'd startled.

He couldn't afford to lose it.

But where was it?!

There!

It snaked back out, curling towards him like a ghost's finger. His attention was hooked, his frustration forgotten, and he followed it willingly, ignoring everyone and everything around him.

But again it slipped away!

His exasperation returned, boiling his blood, burning his veins, and his pace hurried as he sought it out once more. It was right here, *right here*, and he wasn't going to let it get away from him! He needed to find it!

Innumerable eyes followed him in his chaotic search, most confused by his indecisive movements, some concerned by the torment in his brow, but one or two others were moving around on an identical hunt through the camp of two thousand, feverishly certain they could sense the same thing. But if that was the case, they didn't appear to be working together. He paid them no attention and they similarly ignored him, each focused intently on their own individual missions which led them all in opposing directions.

It didn't matter. He didn't care. All he wanted was to find the magic, that above everything. Above rest, above food, above breath.

But where was it? Where *was* it?!

Where had it gone?!

There was a charge in the air. The hairs on the back of one soldier's neck stood up, but as he looked around at the calm and quiet camp, he assumed it to be little more than wartime tensions. He dismissed it and returned his attention to his rations, but his hesitance returned when he noticed the movement of a handful of others across the way, each raising their heads and glancing around with the same wary expectation he had.

He frowned and looked about again, more attentively this time, and almost immediately a small flash caught the corner of his sight. It would have seemed nothing more than the glint of armour to any other eye, but having spent half of his life in the ranks, the soldier knew better. The armour was as steel as his own, but its details of royal purple set the woman apart from the military as a war mage, and it wasn't the glance of sunlight across her breastplate that had shimmered, but a spark of magic.

His heart shuddered. The Order had found something, and from the distant but concentrated look upon her face - an expression all soldiers had become unerringly familiar with over the years - it could only be magic.

He dropped his bread and hollered an alarm, and all around him the camp sprung to life. Mages raised their hands and immediately set to forming protective barriers while the soldiers drew their weapons, and as more sparks rose and crackled around the woman, others caught his eye, scattered across the commotion. Some were even bursting around Sivaan Rosh, who stood not far behind him.

The lack of organisation disturbed the soldier, but whatever the mages had detected, it had to be severe to provoke such a response from the mage-general himself. If that was how it was to be handled, then so be it. Magic was the Order's domain.

He, like all the other soldiers around him, locked his attention onto trying to locate the attackers, as a magical assault was almost always a distraction, and when cries of alarm rose shortly from his left, his sharpened focus was snatched towards it. They had to be over there.

But the cries continued for a fraction too long. They were not those of startled warning, they were entirely involuntary, torn free from their throats by panic.

His heart skipped a beat as his mind was assaulted by a sluggish lack of comprehension, and in that moment the unmistakable orange glow and crackle of fire burst into life from the corner of his eye.

The cries grew louder as the fire burned brighter, shocking his attention back to him, and as he spun towards it and passed an assessing glance over the rest of the glinting bodies, he noted that the magical chaos was very much focused within the force rather than anywhere outside it.

He gritted his teeth. The enemy mages had gotten in amongst them, and they'd surely brought soldiers with them, concealed beneath their magic for an internal strike - but how had they managed without the *Order* noticing?

He shook his questions away and gripped his sword readily, only then noticing the absence of clashing blades. The air was filled only with the sputter of arcane fire. And his comrades were fleeing; he caught snatches of terror on their faces as they scrambled over one another to escape an indiscernible threat.

More bawling rose suddenly from close behind him and he whirled around to seek them, but a doubt had begun to snake into his mind, echoes of recent rumours picked up from towns and cities, and he found that he didn't need to have turned to know what was happening. It was all falling dreadfully into place.

He was blinded immediately by powerful sparks and popping flashes, momentarily dazed by their brilliance, and as he wrestled back his bearings he found himself watching the dance of countless elements as they coiled and arced wildly around Sivaan Rosh, whose head was buried in his hands all the while, his knuckles bone-white, and his voice, he was sure, racked by sobs.

The soldier stared in turmoil even while fully understanding. He was only partially aware of the voice that barked orders close by, and the movements of several other war mages as they responded, promptly contorting their fingers in the mage-general's direction.

Then, time seemed to stand still. He heard the sobs of the respected old man and sivaan of twenty years twist into mad and tortured chuckles. He watched the fire flare like a fallen candle spreading over a drunk's old coat. He felt the charge of lightning as it ruptured, threatening to set the grass alight.

And he could think to do nothing at all.

Yells erupted around him, light flashed from behind, and as he stood dazed in his sheer, maddening confusion, Sivaan Rosh straightened, wept and laughed, and let the chaotic magic that had circled around him like a shield of elements draw in to sear him.

The soldier had only a moment to stare in horror.

The magic exploded and engulfed him in a heartbeat, and the last thing he knew was betrayal.

Salus was careful about keeping the disdain from his face, but his fury was so white-hot that he couldn't prevent it from injecting acid into his eyes. So instead he simply tried not to watch the inordinately superior envoy too closely, his teeth clenched tightly behind his lips, and he forced his fists to relax on the desk top.

Lord Malson didn't seem to notice any of this, however, and neither did he make any attempt to hide his own ire. "Are you *trying* to sabotage the country?!" The old man bellowed, his surprisingly powerful voice filling every corner of the room and giving him even greater dominance than his position usually granted him. But Salus didn't flinch, despite the choice of words clawing right through him. "Because this is the *second* time you've supplied incredibly false intel! Anyone would think you were working *with* Skilan!"

"The intel was not false," he replied so calmly he surprised himself.

The old man laughed bitterly, but his venomous smile quickly gave way to a spiteful stare. "Your report stated that they were moving southwards with the intention of luring us into the valleys and attacking from the slopes. Instead, General Moore had his forces move south to skirt the valleys and ambush them from behind while their numbers were still thinned by the effort to take that vantage point." He slammed his open palm on the surface of the desk. "*But they were not there!*"

Salus turned defensive eyes upon him.

"They'd moved as if they'd *intended* to lure us through the valleys, but instead they turned sharp-east, made for more favourable land and *took a whole province!*"

Salus's lip twitched into a snarl as he spoke through his teeth. "The intel *was not false*."

"Then they must have known you were spying and fed your people lies, but that *still* throws the Arana's capabilities into doubt!" He sighed roughly and shook his head, looking upon Salus now with desperation. "Please, *tell me:* what are we supposed to do if we have no reliable eyes in Skilan's force? *Can* we win this if we're blind?"

"It is only Skilan--"

"Yes, only Skilan, except they suddenly seem to have become quite adept! Unless your people simply compromised *themselves!*"

Silence dropped, and it was as loud as a church bell.

Malson sighed and ran his hand through his thinning hair. "Fix this, Salus," he implored him, "*please*. We're all relying heavily on the Arana."

"I'm well aware of that," he replied, his bite softened by the desperation in the old man's voice. "But we are not blind, and we *will* succeed. There is no other option - I won't settle for anything else, and neither, I suspect, will the General, High Inquisitor, High Magister, King Thunan or any member of his council."

Malson nodded slowly, then breathed a brief, humourless laugh. "I wish I had your optimism." He straightened and reassumed his composure, which apparently included insolence, then cast a suitably disapproving look over Salus. "Do *not* let this happen again."

Salus merely stared at him as he turned to leave the office without another word.

Of course he had no intention of letting it happen again - as if it had been his intention *at all*. But how it had happened to begin with required deep investigation, and that would be yet another drain on resources. He begrudged the fact that it had to be done at all, and those at fault would *certainly* know how he felt about it.

"Portian," the Crown's liaison nodded as he stepped out through the door, and Teagan inclined his head respectfully as he moved into view.

"My lord."

Even in Salus's acrid mood, he noticed the slight look of foreboding creasing Teagan's face. He never seemed to wear anything but, these days. "You were supposed to rescue me," he reminded him as the door closed.

"I'm sorry, I was waylaid."

Salus waved it off. "It's all right, it wasn't that bad." He held out his hand for the report he'd brought with him. "What is it?"

Teagan didn't reply, and despite the heightened trace of hesitance in his bearing, he handed it over and waited patiently while the keliceran read.

He grunted mildly once he'd finished. "I thought as much." Truly, it hadn't told him anything new, only confirmed his suspicions - though he *was* more than a touch troubled by the fact that the woman who had aided Skilan's takeover of Rokhar hadn't been a new arrival in the city, but had actually lived there for six years after moving from Kalokh. That was, at least, what she'd claimed upon arrival, but a simple investigation had revealed she was in fact a Skee. And Salus suspected that the two additional settlements seized by the west that past night had fallen to the same tactics. "At least she's been apprehended." He discarded the report and leaned back in his seat, finally allowing himself to release a long, tense breath. "Now we just need to find these most recent two, those who helped Doana, and whoever is feeding us false information - to name just a few."

"We have people working on all details," Teagan assured him, "though Doana looks to be a more slippery matter. We're making slow progress with finding their collaborators, and while we have found and eradicated one of their small groups, the rest of their forces seem to have fallen off the map."

"Find them."

"It is underway."

Salus grumbled and shook his head. "It looks like splitting up Skilan's forces wasn't a good idea. They're too hard to keep track of - if anything, it's worked to *their* advantage..." He could feel Teagan's eyes drilling into him, and when he looked up from his distant, thoughtful stare, he found him, to his surprise, watching him carefully. He was reading his thoughts, and he knew well that there was no point trying to hide them. "I'm not convinced."

"That they're working together?"

His doubts must have been well-founded. "Doana seemed more precise in their attack; they chose particular targets, took them quietly, then disappeared shortly afterwards, leaving us running around in a panic and trying to look both ways at once. But Skilan chose a pointless target which they're still trying to hold on to, and their campaign felt...louder, clumsier. And the two last night have the same feel to it."

"I have considered the same thing. But it could be a collaboration of tactics. If the desired goal was to simply confuse us and divide our forces, I would say that they have certainly succeeded."

He nodded slowly, chewing the inside of his cheek. "Mm. Well, whether they're working together or not, all of our settlements are under threat. They *must* be reinforced. We have no way of knowing where they might try to strike next - not if we can't use new arrivals as a hint."

"I doubt the Crown will be in favour of using more man power to fortify every single town and village."

"Oh, of *course* not," Salus drawled. "That would be *too* safe. They've already rejected trade route restrictions, curfews, lock-downs - even *now* they seem dead set against using the evacuation plans *they* drew up *themselves!* It's as if the king doesn't want to upset his people or inconvenience them in the *slightest*, even if it's for their own protection."

"Other measures *are* in place--"

"And those measures clearly aren't *enough!*"

Teagan closed his mouth.

"And the Hall of the White Hammer *still* won't respond to my communiques - they won't even confirm that one of their own is out there alongside Karth and Koraaz, let alone what he's actually involved with!" He snarled as he shoved himself restlessly to his feet, then stormed towards the window to look absently out over the opulent, stately houses that surrounded the Arana's grounds - buildings in which the severest matter would only ever be the loss of personal wealth. "And we're all expected to work together. It's just another hurdle we have to overcome to do our *own* job. An elaborate joke." His eyes narrowed as his mind continued bitterly along ahead of him, tracking a nobleman who strode pompously down his garden path, making a spectacle of himself as he climbed into his ornate carriage. His needless entourage bowed and shuddered in his presence, playing their own part in the show.

His lip curled. 'Nobles'. By blood, not by action - the faux nobility *he* wore under their sight was more credible.

Then, a thought suddenly presented itself, and though it left a foul taste in his mouth, it equally offered him a glass of water with which to wash it away.

Perhaps, by asking permission from indecisive politicians, he *was* sabotaging the country - and perhaps both he and it would be better off if he just took the necessary steps himself. Teagan had already suggested such a thing and he thought he had taken it into consideration, but it seemed that he was *still* trying to play by the Crown's ill-conceived rules and getting nowhere absolutely with it...

'As long as the country is safe, I'll take whatever punishment my 'insubordination' is issued.'

His eyes trailed off deeper into his thoughts, then, a moment later, returned decisively to the room.

He turned away from the window and looked towards Teagan, who was staring patiently at the wall. "What about the tribes?"

"Most of them have taken to attacking one another now," he replied. "Their barbarism was restrained while they focused on trying to protect their boundaries, but now it seems that they've finally decided to go onto the offensive and outright slaughter one another instead. Remove the threat rather than try to hold it at bay."

"My, how clever of them," Salus replied drily. "Well, that's fine. They're more than welcome to kill each other off."

"But," Teagan continued, making him hesitate as he sank back into his seat, "the more distant, isolated tribes still haven't raised a hand against one another."

'If only the same could be said for more civilised matters.' "Never mind them for now. What about Drassa?"

Teagan thought for a moment. "'It depends on your idea of progress'."

Salus hung his head. "I suppose he also said that 'every failed contact gives the rest of the list more hope'?"

"He did."

A growl rumbled free as he shoved himself back out of his chair, anger flashing in his eyes. "Meanwhile *Karth* is going all over the place like a dog following a scent - and at this rate he's going to get to it first! What is it he knows?! And why hasn't Hower gotten me *anything on them yet?!*"

"He's only just caught up to them, Keliceran, and they've--"

"*That's not good enough!*" Teagan's gaze remained fixed to the wall as Salus turned his desperate, blazing eyes upon him. "We need to stop them *before* they can get the artefact! It *can't* fall into the Order's hands! I don't need to remind you that the mages have been acting out - there've been two more attacks in towns scattered across the country making the chaos of this damned war even worse, and if they get this old relic, *who knows what they could do with it?!*"

Teagan didn't react while he whirled away again, snapping back towards the window where he snarled at the sight of yet more pompous noblemen and women, walking about in clouds of their own misjudged self-importance. He dragged his gaze away from it. He had no patience for the thought that people like these numbered among those he was trying so very hard to protect.

He took a long, deep breath, though it served only to aggravate rather than soothe, and when he spoke again, the bite in his otherwise restrained tone had worsened. "Karth needs to be stopped, him and his entire bloody band of misfits. We have the means, the resources, to do it any way we must, whether an inquisitor is with them or not! The Hall is adept, but the Arana more so! We *need* to put an end to their work, an end to *them* - completely foil the Order's plan!"

"If we foil the Order's plan, they'll look immediately towards the Arana," Teagan reminded him calmly. "Would it not be better to stick to our original intentions? To let the Order think they've got the upper hand while we continue to work in the shadows?"

"And just let them continue their search and hand everything over to the Order?!"

"Karth has the information we want," he proceeded sedately, "and Drassa doesn't. In my opinion, as it is my duty to give it, we should let Drassa continue his task but otherwise disregard him, and try to retrieve Karth's notes instead. Get what we need from him directly, but discreetly. The Order won't catch on quickly, especially if they think Drassa and this mage of ours have us fooled."

Salus opened his mouth to respond, and from the look in his eye it was going to be neither thoughtful nor quiet, but a knock at the door snatched his irritable attention and he snapped at that instead. Teagan didn't miss the fact that his abrupt fury just as suddenly evaporated when the phidipan woman, Taliel, walked in. Just as it always did.

The keliceran straightened and turned his eyes back onto the portian. They, too, had changed, their hysteria replaced instead by resignation. "Fine," he said flatly and with considerable self-control. "Working with someone outside of the Arana never sat right with me anyway. Get Karth's notes and sever ties with Drassa - let him continue his work to avoid questions, but leave him alone. And pull Vakh out. There's no point wasting any more resources." He then turned to the woman and his stern expression weakened a touch further. "Yes, Taliel?"

But she didn't speak. Instead she extended a report, which he read with the same sufferance he had the last Teagan had borne.

Again the portian watched him as his eyes trailed the words, then looked towards Taliel who seemed braced for an outburst. He returned to Salus with the same expectations. He could guess what the report had said.

But he simply folded it back over, handed it to Teagan, then crossed his arms over his chest and frowned, lost in deep, silent thought.

His brow crinkled as he took it, and Taliel braved a glance from the wall to the keliceran in her confusion. He would have mirrored her concern a moment later if he could have, but he did take a second to wonder if it was the fact that *she* had been the one to deliver the report or just another manifestation of Salus's unpredictability that prevented him from reacting to this, of all news.

He set the parchment down on the desk beside them. "I'll get word to Hower," he promised. "We'll have Karth's notes as soon as possible."

Salus nodded and allowed Teagan to excuse himself, leaving him alone in the office with Taliel, but he said nothing to her as he continued to stare off for a thousand miles. She dared another brief but direct look, and though she noted the deeply troubled crease to his brow, there was little else to suggest how he was taking it. He seemed thoughtful. Or perhaps he was just tired and it hadn't sunk in yet.

Her eyes flicked away and she began to shift uncomfortably under the weighty silence.

"You're *sure* this is correct?" He asked eventually, his gaze remaining locked somewhere far beyond her, but his frown deepened a moment later as he answered his question himself. "Yes, of course you're sure..."

She watched him carefully while her eyes stayed fixed to the wall, a vague shadow of her concern edging in. "What can we do about this?"

Burying his face in his hands, he sighed deeply into his palms. He looked tired when he eventually dropped them, and she thought she spotted a taint of desperation or defeat in his eyes. If it had been there, it died very quickly. "The Order has made a direct assault on the military," he stated, certainly for nothing other than organising his thoughts, "the only force under the Crown's command that could reasonably oppose them. And the perpetrators weren't nameless, faceless individuals, they were officers..." he shook his head, his expression now openly perplexed. "*Officers*. Seventeen lives lost at the hands of our *own*...and for *Sivaan Rosh* to have led it..." He stared off into his disturbed thoughts again.

Taliel let him. She watched him with great calculation.

But he returned quite shortly this time and seemed to have suddenly collected himself. Perhaps he'd reached a silent decision, or re-evaluated the facts or simply set aside his alarm through necessity. "There is nothing we can do to keep it quiet.

It's already public, the people just haven't heard about it yet, but I dare say they will *very* soon and alongside word of the Order's *next* attack. But whatever it is *they* expect to gain from a rebellion, we can expect to see violence on par with that over the borders: random and senseless attacks, destructive suicides. We *can* plan against it, to a degree...but with people from so high in the Order's ranks involved, *none* of them can be trusted. We have to watch them all..."

He sighed heavily and turned towards the window once again, but this time he cast his eyes into the city, towards the obtrusive elven tower the Order called home. He became aware of the knot in his jaw. They needed the artefact *now*. "If we thought we had a mess on our hands before," he mumbled bitterly to himself, "things are going to be downright impossible to work through now. But if there was any question in people's minds about the loyalty of the Order and the mages roaming our streets, they've been unequivocally satisfied."

"There will be unrest," Taliel agreed.

"More than unrest, there will be *chaos*. No one out there is going to feel safe, and in Kulokhar *least* of all..." He growled in defeat. Magic. What good had it ever done anyone? The Order was only really needed in defence against other magic-users, but if they were going to present that very threat to Turunda *themselves*, they were an even bigger risk to the country's safety.

No one with magic could be trusted, not *one* of them. They all carried power's corruption in their veins, they all viewed themselves as better than the rest - they were granted high social standing out of nothing more than fear. They were no more deserving of respect or consideration than the noblemen that graced Salus's view from his office window. None of them truly had the best interest of the country at heart - just because their magic had surfaced didn't mean they *had* to learn how to wield it. Nothing would have happened to it or to them if it had been left alone, it would have been no different to having the ability to paint or to sing but never doing so. It was vanity; they'd discovered their power, leapt upon it and let it carry them as high as it could. None of them had taken it on responsibly with the thought of safeguarding the country or its people.

No one.

No one...

"Forgive me," Taliel began softly, startling him out of his spiralling thoughts, "with the greatest respect, Keliceran...have you been sleeping well lately?"

He frowned as he turned towards her, pulling himself quickly back together. "Sleeping? Yes? Why?" His heart jumped as he found her looking directly at him, but though she quickly averted her gaze, there was a very real concern within her eyes.

"You...seem..."

"I'm fine," he assured her, his tone softening as the smallest smile tugged at his lips. "I appreciate your concern, Taliel." And, much to his surprise, he truly did. It sent a very welcome warmth through his whole body and eased his mind better than any deep breath ever could have - but though he would have liked very much to have lingered in her company and enjoyed it a little while longer, his mind was now consumed by another and far more ravenous thought, and he found himself already making for the door behind her. "I'm fine. I can manage...I can do it..."

He fled the office in a hurry, closing the door behind himself, his urgency having already pushed aside any thought of the phidipan woman, and all but ran towards the staircase.

Word had spread of his increasingly temperamental moods and so no one delayed in stepping swiftly out of his path, but he wouldn't have noticed if they had. His mind was deafened by waves of questions and countless warnings, but he found himself clinging tightly to the faintest whisper of the desperate hope which they tried to smother. He was well aware of how foolish he was to indulge it - in fact, if it continued to lead him, he knew he could be bounding eagerly into the biggest mistake of his career. But he just couldn't silence it, and neither could he deny the desire that lurked, ever-present, in the depths of his heart as it lurched to the surface in its wake.

He was more uncertain in that moment than he had been about anything in his life, but he continued to put one foot in front of the other, as if his feet were more convinced than his head, and soon his unstoppable steps were echoing through the stone cells, the sound rushing off eagerly ahead of him.

"Keliceran," Nolan said respectfully as he stepped hurriedly out from one of the occupied cells, leaving the sound of weeping behind him, and he inclined his head as his superior approached though he was clearly confused by his arrival. "What can I do for you?"

"Open it."

He followed the advancing keliceran's gesture two cells down behind him and grunted in understanding. He nodded to one of the mages standing guard outside it, who duly obeyed, and the cell door clattered opened in time with Salus's stride.

The dark haired man sitting in the shadows raised his head as Salus passed the cell's iron threshold. His shocking, pale blue-grey eyes were sharp and expectant. He had known he was coming and, the keliceran suspected, he also knew why. He didn't like that.

Salus drew to a stop, maintaining a few paces' distance, and stared rigidly back at him. It was a gaze that asserted his dominance in any situation, one only the Crown's liaison seemed to have any resistance to - but this mage did not quake beneath it. He met his gaze levelly, brazenly. As if he had no idea what 'keliceran' meant.

Salus chose, however, to brush his spiking irritation aside. He crouched down in front of him, maintaining his oppressive air while the mage merely watched him, waiting for him to begin.

"You are going to help me."

The mage's eyebrows barely twitched. "What brought about this change?" He asked far too mildly in that strange, lilting accent of his, his arrogance increasing now he knew for certain that he had something his captor wanted.

"I have had enough of leaving things in everyone else's hands. If there is some way that I can put an end to everything trying to tear this country apart with my *own* two hands, I will grasp it with all my strength. If I possess magic, as you say, then you will teach me how to wield it."

The mage scrutinised him for a long while, but Salus's steady gaze didn't waver. "And if I don't?"

"I will kill you."

This didn't provoke a reaction either, but Salus knew the mage could see clearly in his eyes that he had meant it. He'd still offered them no information, and he was beginning to doubt that he would, and with the Order's recent activity, he wasn't inclined to release him even if the king himself demanded it. One fewer mage in the world would help everyone sleep a little better.

But he felt a sudden pinch of anger as the briefest doubt slipped into the prisoner's eyes, a delayed response, as though he had weighed the likelihood that Salus could manage it and decided out of favour. But Salus locked down his reaction, just as he also concealed his intentions of delivering the same fate if he didn't see results within two weeks. The mage could well be wasting his time, and he was disinclined to sacrifice much if he was.

But he *had* to find out for certain.

The mage straightened himself where he sat, a decision made in his eyes. "Denek." He rose to his feet. "Not 'him', 'prisoner' or 'mage'. And I want better accommodation - a cell with a window, at least."

"Denek. Good." Then he stood, turned, and walked away, exiting the cell and leaving him standing in confusion.

Chapter 34

Despite misgivings, the lead had been turned over to the tribal girl. They were left little choice in a place so alien, so barren and featureless - but, regardless, they didn't trust her guidance lightly. Following her route through the sands and ever sparser parched grass, they remained cautious and watchful, their eyes keen in search of anyone or anything that might be expertly concealed, waiting only for her signal to pounce.

It was true that she had done nothing to personally invoke such wariness - in fact she'd been downright polite, as far as savage tribals went, and had even chosen a path that was washed from time to time in cool mountain breeze for their benefit. But it was an ingrained mistrust that had no intention of relenting, and it rose again when she informed them that that path meant it would take a little longer to reach her people. But, suspicious or not, no one objected. They had yet to truly set foot in the desert, and the longer they could put that off, the better.

But there was another concern: an earthen tribe lived in the nearby mountains, whose roots they were skirting just as they were the desert, and they were acutely aware of the tribulations that had grown between the tribes. Eyila assured them that conflict hadn't reached her people - the Ikaheka, they called themselves - and that they were still working to keep it that way, but that did little to assuage their fears or lower their ever-heightening guard. Surely lies and deception weren't limited to inquisitors.

And, of course, that grudge was still there. Despite their tensions, they still had the energy to maintain resentment towards Garon, and Garon equally maintained his distance. For the past two nights he ate quickly and immediately left to stand watch, his duty unfailing, and he set his bed roll apart from the others, though no one was sure that he slept in it. But despite his expulsion, he showed no hint of loneliness. In fact, he seemed to welcome the seclusion.

Aria had expressed dismay at their treatment towards him, and though Rathen had tried to rationalise it, he failed quite astoundingly to convince her. But even he couldn't privately deny that they were being childish. He wondered what that said about Aria, and felt another swell of pride for her intelligence and consideration, as well as an equal touch of shame for his own lack thereof.

But he was still disinclined to adjust his behaviour, and ate that evening with his back turned to the inquisitor, who stood as still as stone a distance behind them, while Aria removed herself from the atmosphere with her whittling and Anthis kept a careful watch of the tribal girl as she meditated nearby, sat upon a boulder, having found what was surely the only consistent, if pointlessly weak, breeze around.

Petra, however, sat staring over Rathen's shoulder, her features hardened thoughtfully, and startled everyone when she finally rose to her feet and headed without apology towards the exiled inquisitor.

Rathen and Anthis exchanged quick, curious glances and watched her as subtly as they could.

Her footsteps were just as light and graceful as they always were, and though they made not a sound over the thin sand, she was certain he was aware of her approach. But he didn't turn, nor even glance her way as she stopped beside him, and he took the waterskin she offered just as indifferently. "Much to see?" She asked lightly, but he merely grunted.

"Sand. Grass."

"Lots of nothing, then."

He nodded, skilfully unstoppering the skin with his free hand, and took a conservative sip. "Thank you."

"And you."

"Me?" He frowned in confusion, finally acknowledging her with a look.

"For being vigilant. Even if you have just been trying to escape from us..."

He grunted again and turned away, his brow flattening in his usual disinterest. "I have a duty to your safety."

"Even so, thank you."

Silence descended, as it so often did when Garon was around. "How's your shoulder?" She asked in a casual bid to break it.

"Fine." Evidently, Garon was content with the atmosphere as it was.

She sighed in defeat, but rather than give in and walk away, leaving him alone again, she got right to the point. "Look, I can't speak for the others because they're just as stubborn as you are, but, all this...*I'm* sorry for how we all reacted. It's just that--"

"It's all right. I understand. There's no need to apologise."

Petra frowned as she processed his tone. The usual bite to his voice had softened, albeit only by a fraction, but she noticed that he hadn't yet tried to shoo her away. Sympathy pulled at the middle of her brow. Clearly, he wanted someone to talk to - or perhaps he truly *was* untroubled, just tired. The warmth certainly made her feel drowsy. But at the same time, she couldn't believe that he wasn't in some way regretful for having misled them, even if he wouldn't admit it.

"What will you do now?" She asked softly.

"What do you mean?"

"Well, your secret's out. No one's looking at you with the same respect anymore; your leadership's shot."

A defensive frown creased his face. "I may not be the officer you all thought I was," he growled, "but that doesn't mean that this *task* is obsolete. My superior *did* give me this mission, and I intend to see it through..."

She frowned again. "But?"

He stared at her in that same defence for a moment, but the hint of doubt she thought she'd heard in his voice abruptly won out, replacing his challenge with shame. He looked quite unfamiliar wearing it, as mild as it was, and the sight tugged at the corners of her lips. "'Duty to your safety'." He shook his head and looked back out over the empty land. "I've already disgraced that sentiment, and my honour. I *have* led you all into danger - them, you, Aria. Rathen is right to take the lead. He at least has experience. Whereas I've been fooling myself all along..."

"How have you been fooling yourself? Aside from...well, a *few* slip-ups, you've been keeping us on track and we *are* making progress."

He shook his head more aggressively. "This is too important for *any* slip-ups."

"But *why* is it so important?" She implored him, stepping around to force herself into his gaze. "To *you*, I mean."

His eyes fell onto her heavily, reluctantly at first, then fired by what looked like desperation. "It's not important to *me*, it's important to *everyone*. The stakes are so high, and yet we're the *only* ones trying to handle it. Everything is riding on us. And where have we gotten? Nowhere."

"*Yet.*"

"Well, that had better change soon. I can't let any more people die because of this magic."

"You heard Kienza - it's going to get worse before it gets better, and we need to accept that rather than let it drag us down."

"That's easy for *you* to say," he suddenly snapped, "you don't have a stake in this - you shouldn't even be out here *with* us."

Her hazel eyes flashed in insult, encouraged by the abrupt shift in his, and she stepped around and squared up to him. She may have been shorter than him, far more slender and with a surprisingly gentle temperament more often than not, but there was a definite menace to her bearing when she wanted it. "I know you don't want me out here, Garon," she told him in a low and dangerous voice. "I've understood that from the moment I joined you. You've made it *excessively* clear. But *don't* say that I don't have a stake in this. My sister is a mage, and Rathen won't admit it, but when I spoke to him about this I saw a flash of something in his eyes. He thinks these mages are losing control because of this accursed magic, and that means that my sister could be at risk. And I *can't* lose her, too. If there's *anything* I can do to protect her - or Rathen, or Aria if she possesses magic like her father, or perhaps even my *own* future children - then I will do it. And you *absolutely* won't be able to drive me away. Not now."

"Oh?" He challenged. "And what about this noble pursuit of yours? The revenge you said takes precedence over everything?"

She took a threatening step closer but his stare didn't waver, his veil of superiority falling back into place to render him unreadable once more. "That still stands. But, by the looks of things, it doesn't seem like the opportunity is going to present itself any time soon." He glanced around at the desert in concedence, but when he looked back, she was already walking away. "Get some rest tonight," she told him brusquely, her tone belying her lingering concern. "You look awful."

"To protect people."

Surprise faltered her steps, and she turned back towards him in puzzlement. "Sorry?"

"You asked me once why I do what I do," he reminded her. "It's to protect people. That's the only reason I've ever had."

Even in the late-dusk light, she couldn't miss the distinct honesty that glinted in his eyes as his veil blew briefly to one side. A soft smile, unbidden, began pulling at her lips. With a single nod of approval, she turned around and continued away, wishing him a good night. She knew he wasn't going to say any more - that alone had been a gesture of some kind - so she left him to his watch as he frowned to himself in similar confusion.

Anthis watched the two converse from a distance, frowning as he pondered. "Is it my imagination--"

"She's definitely attracted to him," Rathen replied quietly, having moved so that he could watch them himself from the corner of his eye, and Aria clapped softly in her excitement from beside him.

"But...*why?*" He asked in growing bewilderment. "What is there to be attracted to?"

"You're really asking the wrong person." He turned his head away as Petra started back towards the camp, and Anthis turned casually as if he'd been wandering around on the spot. Aria, meanwhile, beamed openly. Petra frowned curiously as she reached them, but the young girl was often grinning for no obvious reason so she didn't question it as she sat back down, the soft smile of her own remaining firmly in place.

"We should discuss tomorrow," Eyila's distinct voice rose from behind them. They'd grown fractionally used to it so it didn't startle them as much anymore, though she still made Anthis jump, who had been in a leisurely rotation as she had risen to her feet.

"What do you mean?" Rathen asked as they followed her up and Garon approached from the edge.

"We will reach my people in the morning, so it's time you knew what to expect." Nervous and wary glances rippled through them before falling onto her, which she returned with disconcerting mildness. "When we enter the village you must all keep your hands at your backs, fingers laced, so you cannot reach for your weapons - except for you two."

Rathen and Petra frowned at one another.

"You will keep your hands clasped in front of you instead, where they can be seen."

"Why?" Aria asked in a mild strop, as if she'd rather have been grouped with them.

"Because she has weapons at her back, and he is a mage.

"While we're in the village, do not try to take anything, do not touch anything; do not stare, do not speak to anyone unless they speak directly to you. Everyone around you is to be respected. When you meet the chief, the men will raise their left fist to their head and touch their second knuckles to their brow in greeting, and the women will raise their open right hand to their foreheads and sweep it forwards and down, like this." She proceeded to demonstrate, her numbed hands still able to at least perform that simple movement. "The sweep should be quick enough that you feel a slight breeze across your brow. Try it."

It took a few attempts but Petra soon grasped it, and Eyila settled for Aria's slightly more aggressive gesture, one which seemed as if she was trying to rip something off of her face. Rathen stifled his chuckle out of respect for her efforts.

"If he agrees to a meeting," she continued, "you will kneel throughout with your hands on your knees - even if he gets up and starts wandering around, which he is prone to doing, you are to remain where you are, facing his seat. While he is within your sight during the meeting, you will always look him in the eye as a show of attention, and you must not interrupt him. When the meeting is finished you will place your hands on the ground in front of you and bow low where you are until he has left or permits you to rise."

"So he may not even agree to see us *at all?*" Anthis pressed.

"Just as any leader, he has the choice. If he deems you a threat, not only will he deny the meeting, but he could have you killed on the spot."

Anthis's eyes widened.

Eyila suddenly grinned. She had proven on a handful of occasions to have a strange sense of humour, and it seemed that it was showing again. They hoped.

"You may not take anything you are offered, except for food," she continued, though none were inclined to oblige even then, "and you may not try to barter or bargain."

Rathen blinked as he, like the others, tried to ensure that everything she'd said was stored in an easily-retrievable part of their memory. "Is that everything?" He asked in feign mildness, to which she nodded. "All right. Then how about what we can expect from everyone else?"

"They will stare, some will hide, and our hunters will surround you."

"I suppose that's to be expected..."

"But if you do all I said and remain beside me, you won't be harmed." Her eyes flashed with a strange brightness. "Stray, however..." She smiled again, and a few managed a nervous chuckle. "I also suggest that you get straight to the point if he does grant you a meeting."

"Impatient?"

"Not at all, but he isn't going to want you in the village for any longer than you need to be. Neither will I, nor anyone else. The sooner you've said what you need to, the sooner you can leave."

"What's the likeliness that he'll grant us permission to visit...Ut'hala?" Rathen asked, silently proud of himself for remembering the name, though the tribal girl seemed to grimace ever so slightly at his pronunciation though he'd thought it had been perfect.

She took a moment to think. "I don't know. It depends how convincing your argument is. So, like I said: you'd best get straight to the point. Otherwise, I think that's all you need to know."

"You *think?*"

Eyila looked back at him flatly. "It's not often that I have to lead outsiders into my home; I'm doing my best to remember every niggling little detail for *your* sake. I could just leave you all right now - I know this desert like the back of my hand, I could be back home before the sky is black. So," her eyes darkened, "I suggest you be grateful that it's not in my nature to be selfish."

"We *are* grateful," Rathen swiftly assured her, "I'm sorry. Thank you for your help - without it, I don't think we'd have much hope of even *finding* your village." He glanced back over the landscape again, wondering not for the first time just how Garon had intended them to find it with no landmarks of any kind, and was silently grateful for the fact that he himself hadn't been given the chance to fail, either.

She folded her arms across her scantly covered chest, her white eyebrows twitching. "Yes, well, apology accepted." Then she turned away without another word and wandered back towards the boulder she had previously been perched upon, leaving Garon to return quickly to his self-imposed watch while the others tried desperately to recall every detail she'd given them.

The air was warmer the following morning, the welcome chill of the night chased away by a heat that was more than simply unseasonal by Turundan standards, and served as an abrupt reminder of their surroundings even before they left the distracting comfort of sleep. Though spring was slowly giving way to summer, it seemed that by travelling north, they were meeting it head-on sooner than any of them would have liked.

"It's quite cool, actually," Eyila had said as they ate their breakfast, having overheard the group's complaint. "The heat won't truly set in until a moon from now."

"It gets *worse?*"

"Unbearably so in the summer - but we have ways of dealing with it."

She seemed disinclined to elaborate, but truly it was none of their business, even if Anthis's curiosity was so great it was almost tangible. But he had shown uncharacteristic restraint around the tribal girl, almost certainly through fear as manners had never held him back before, and it was more than a mild concern of Rathen's that it would become too much for him in the village, that he'd forget what they were told and both stare openly and try to touch things in his fascination, regardless of warnings or threats. He would have to keep an eye on him - and place upon his hands the spell that still bound Eyila's if he truly had no self-restraint.

Despite the promise of reaching the village that morning, there were no signs of habitation to corroborate it, and the shared but unspoken doubt that they were being led into an ambush despite the girl's helpfulness became only more prevalent in their minds.

And so, when they crested a small dune and found themselves surrounded by a group of bronze men, garbed in animal skins and armed with spears and bows, no one was particularly surprised.

"Put your blades away," Eyila snapped before Petra or Garon had the chance to fully draw them, and stepped hurriedly towards the most painted of their sudden adversaries. The young man's brow, streaked black with some kind of chalk, was momentarily warped in relief as he recognised her, but his hostility was quick to reassert itself and much stronger than it had been. He snatched Eyila by the arm and dragged her behind him, pointing his feathered spear closer to Rathen's face in the process.

He raised his hands in preparation, but as Eyila loosed a few sharp words in a strangely adjusted form of Ivaean, one or two Rathen could just about follow, both he and her kinsman came to an uneasy stop. The tribal's blue eyes, a deeper shade than Eyila's but no less shocking, turned to her in doubt as those of his comrades followed, but she met his stare levelly.

Slowly and unwillingly, he lowered his spear, and Rathen duly lowered his hands. The tribal then turned to the girl and exchanged less heated though equally exotic words, while Rathen and his companions watched carefully, listening for anything familiar or a hint of what was likely to happen next.

All eyes suddenly fell upon them, and Eyila quietly returned. The slight tension that knotted her bare shoulders only put them further on edge.

"Let's go," was all she said, and they were given no choice but to follow as four of the eight men fell in around and behind them, forming an armed escort. These must have been the hunters.

Her pace slowed and she dropped back alongside Rathen. "You had best free my hands before we arrive," she said with a tone of warning, and despite the apprehensions rising in his gut, he held himself taller to reassure the others and gave a subtle nod. He really had no other choice - but he could at least prepare a shielding spell should things turn out as badly as he expected.

Aria walked close alongside him, grasping his hand tighter, but when he glanced down he found her peering up at the armed man beside her, a furrow of curiosity upon her young brow. He quickly tugged her hand when he realised she was staring, and she discovered her mistake in that same instant. She looked away frantically, her wide eyes snapping back to their heading.

They walked on in a cloud of tension and it soon felt as though an hour had passed. Their legs ached from climbing the growing dunes, though they'd lost count of just how many, and as the day dragged on the heat only increased. When Aria dared to reach for a waterskin, their entire entourage had readied their weapons. She suddenly decided she wasn't thirsty after that.

And so it was with a twisted relief that they finally looked upon the cluster of dark shapes that rose in the distance below this tallest dune, breaking the monotonous landscape and offering a change to proceedings, be it for better or for worse.

Eyila dropped back alongside Rathen again, and following a single glance, he released the bindings from her hands. There was a greater confidence in her step as she retook the lead. From then onwards he kept an even closer watch on her, despite his doubt that she'd try anything still so far from her village. If there was to be an assault, it would be within her people's reach.

He spared a glance around at the others, catching their escorts' watchful attention as he did so. But he didn't need to give his companions any kind of hint. Both Petra and Garon had the same quickness to their eyes, and even Anthis was paying very close attention. If they couldn't grasp their own weapons, they at least knew to get behind him and within the protection of any spell he might cast.

"Hands," she said as they neared the bottom of that final sandy hill, and they duly obeyed her previous instructions. But even with Garon's single free hand at his back and Petra's at her front, their weapons were no more than a quick reach away, and Rathen could just as easily form seals no matter where his hands were. It was only courtesy that restrained them.

Aside from a simple framed structure that contained a strange display of five carved and painted clay cylinders, there was nothing to mark the boundary of the village; it seemed to start where the first square, sun-baked building rose, constructed from a mixture of stones and clay with a thatched door, roof and shutters. Someone stepped out from it, though they were too far off to tell if it was a man or a woman, and after standing and staring for a moment, turned and hurried off deeper into the village, shouting something ahead of them.

The group took a collective uneasy breath, but remained otherwise silent.

More villagers quickly appeared in the distance, bronze figures clad in yet more animal skins scattered amongst the mismatched dwellings to watch the approaching party, prompting yet another wave of alarm. It seemed as if the entire tribe had turned out...

Their minds rung with Eyila's words and warnings, each of them certain they were missing one point or another and frantically searching the recesses of their memory to retrieve them, if just to avoid provoking anyone through an accidental insult. Rathen and Garon were the only two to settle for simply being mindful of their manners and focusing instead on noting any potential threat.

They had soon drawn close enough to see the paint across their skin, then the myriad of patterns they created, and then, eventually, the dizzying variety of shades of blue that coloured their gripping eyes. The scent of surprisingly familiar spices drifted towards them on a light breeze, jostling steel pipes in its passage and creating a wonderful, tinkling music, and in its wake a small cloud of red and another of orange billowed up briefly from within the depths of the village.

But their guard was not lowered, the two's eyes still flicking about in search, and after just a few more paces, they were among them.

The tribe stepped back and watched them pass just as warily as the group walked, their pace slowing in hesitation as they made the effort to turn their eyes to the ground and use their peripherals instead, and they refrained from looking up even as whispers rippled through the crowd.

It was only at the sound of hurried footfalls that they finally raised their heads, their hearts suddenly hammering as the four enclosing men drew to a sudden stop, and Eyila cast them all a grave look and commanded them to wait where they were and keep their hands where they could be seen. They did so without question, though Rathen's fingers twitched in preparation, his senses sharpening. The others took a shuffling step closer to him.

The crowd parted and another man stepped forwards. White paint coated his forehead, concentrated at the edges of his hairline and sweeping inwards to fade at the centre above his nose. Vertical black lines had been painted along his jaw, with one reaching up on either side to stop just beneath his eyes, which were almost as pale as Eyila's and steeped in worry. His chest was just as broad and defined as the hunters', and though he, too, wore skins, a collection of lengths of leather were tied about both of his biceps, coloured in reds, oranges, browns and deep greens, with feathers woven into them. No one else, Rathen was quick to notice, wore anything like it.

The worry in the older man's eyes was replaced by a well of relief as they fell upon Eyila, and he grasped her firmly by the shoulders as she stopped in front of him. But his eyes changed again, touched by concern and confusion as he spotted the bandages that poked out from beneath her own skins. She said something too quietly for the others to catch, and though they eased a fraction, they were quick to flick past her and onto her company. Their fleeting note of understanding was extinguished by a flash of rage.

His voice, even in its fire, was as rich and musical as Eyila's, and though he spoke in that same modified Ivaean, Rathen caught just enough to follow.

*

"Why did you bring them here?" He growled, taking little care to subdue his words in the presence of ignorant foreigners. "What are you *thinking*, Eyila?!"

"They can help us," she told him quickly, "they can restore Ut'hala."

"Ridiculous. A pretence! They're cityfolk, they help *no one*."

"They helped *me*." She indicated her injuries, but the curl of his lip only worsened.

"Only because they felt they stood something to gain - getting *here*, for starters."

"They only want to talk to you--"

"You mean pretend to barter before robbing us blind!" He stormed past her and looked over the five of them, scowling deeper as he searched each face, though he faltered briefly in confusion as he looked upon the child. He regained himself easily enough and turned back to Eyila. "Even at nineteen, you are still too *naive!*"

"Or perhaps I am just not as cynical as you, *Chief*."

His eyes darkened as hers flashed in anger, and the rest of the village watched in silence. "You are dangerously close to impertinence."

"Have you really become so pig-headed that you would turn away aid?" She demanded, her tone unchanged. "Don't our people have troubles enough without us stubbornly making them worse?"

"Yes, troubles *enough*." He could feel the weight of the village's stares, though most were unsurprised by the clash, and lowered his voice for her ears alone. "And *they* may have just brought more along with them. The cityfolk are embroiled in far more advanced conflicts than we are - ours may run deeper, but we can still talk our way to peace. But they are destructive, you *know* this, and if they've trailed their war in behind them, we *will* be dragged into it." He looked at her now imploringly. "Against them, we haven't got a chance."

"They are five," she sighed, "and one of them is a *child*. Why would any danger follow them? Let alone out here?"

"Why indeed? And why are they here at *all?*"

Rathen's eyes flicked away as the village chief turned towards them, suppressing the disappointment that had come from his eavesdropping, then stood straight and raised his left fist to his forehead, touching his second knuckles to his brow. Garon was already in the process of doing the same, fortunate that his sword arm, which was supposed to be free during the salute as a symbol of protection towards the chief, was the one that had been immobilised, and Anthis clumsily followed their lead. Petra made the sweeping motion with surprising grace and Aria managed with more finesse than Rathen had expected - but she *had* spent most of the past evening practising.

The chief, however, didn't appear impressed by what amounted to little more than basic manners. "What is it you want from Ut'hala?" He asked them sharply, accusingly. "There is nothing there, no treasures for you to take."

"We don't want to take anything," Rathen replied as respectfully and earnestly as he could as the man came to a broiling stop in front of him, older up close than his bearing would suggest, "we--"

"Then you expect something from us in return for restoring it - assuming you are not at fault in the first place."

"I've told you before, the magic doesn't feel like that," Eyila reminded him none too carefully, joining him in front of Rathen, though she stood beside neither. "They are not responsible."

His eyes burned. "Then what makes you believe they can *fix* it?"

"We've been studying other locations under similar effects," Rathen replied, thinking quickly to simplify the matter without holding anything back, "and researching all we can. We think we have a way to fix it, but we need to study more sites - the worse they're affected, the better." So far, the tribe seemed more angry than hostile, and though he'd adopted a manner both submissive and reasonable, he was more than prepared to loose a spell in a heart beat if he had to. But at least they were speaking directly with the chief.

But now the feathered and painted man narrowed his eyes in intense suspicion. "How is it you know of Ut'hala? And of how 'badly affected' it is?"

Rathen opened his mouth to reply, but it seemed that someone had rattled Anthis's cage. "It's only elven ruins that have been affected," he blurted, "and it's no secret that there's one out here. As for the rest, we were t--"

"We were guessing, initially," Rathen quickly interjected, "but Eyila overheard us talking about it and confirmed our suspicions."

"And you would have come out here, to this desert, on a hunch?"

Rathen couldn't tell how this discussion was going. "Actually, we were passing through anyway to get to Enhala. The desert's safer than easier terrain."

The chief grunted and took a step to one side, casting a deeply speculative glance over the others. "Yes...your conflicts." His eyes flicked back to Rathen. "I hope you've not trailed them in here with you." Rathen didn't miss the grave weight to his eyes.

Then the chief walked away. "Well, you cannot go. It isn't safe, and even should it be, we do not *want* you there. The shrine is sacred; only priestesses of Aya'u may step foot there and those they consider worthy - but in your case," he cast them a feigned apologetic look, "I don't think we need to trouble a priestess to discover that such an invitation cannot be extended to you."

Rathen thought for a long moment, locking with the chief's gaze as he decided how best to respond without insulting anyone, but before he could begin to come to any conclusion, another lilting voice rose from the edge of the crowd.

"I think we should let a priestess decide that for herself, Chief."

The crowd parted to make way for this new figure, a woman adorned in the lightest coloured skins and a soft mantle of feathers which beautifully complimented her bronze complexion. She carried herself with a surprising elegance, and all around seemed to look upon her with as much reverence as they did their chief, if not perhaps more.

Rathen's eyes flicked back towards him, and he decided on the latter when he noticed the restraint with which the chief responded.

"You cannot seriously believe them..."

"I do not," she replied plainly, "but I also cannot seriously disregard the possibility that they might be able to help us." She stood even taller, more imposing, and even Rathen found himself feeling smaller in her presence. "I think we should hear what they have to say."

All eyes turned expectantly onto the chief.

He stared back at the priestess, fire still raging in his eyes, but there was a thoughtfulness there as he weighed her words and, likely, the significance of the fact that she was willing to step forwards and encourage the welcoming of these quite possibly dangerous people. He looked briefly back towards them, his dark lips tightening as his gaze fell upon Aria, and his tense shoulders finally dropped in defeat.

But he said nothing, merely gestured, and the four hunters encouraged them to follow him through the haphazardly constructed village, stopping only once they reached a building far larger and longer than the rest. He then beckoned Eyila, and after a brief, quiet exchange, she gave him Rathen, Anthis and Garon's names, pointing each of them out in turn, then returned to them as he disappeared inside.

"You three go in," she told the men, "and remember what I told you: kneel, hands on your knees, don't turn your head, and get to the point." She looked then towards Petra and Aria. "You two will come with me."

"Why?" Aria asked, her voice edged in panic as her grip on her father's hand tightened, but Petra smiled softly and offered her her own.

"It's all right," she said gently, "you can stay with me."

Aria clung to him a desperate moment longer, but both she and Rathen knew that Petra was perfectly capable of keeping her safe. If they had to be split up, this was the second best outcome.

With an encouraging smile, Rathen gave her hand to Petra with the promise that he wouldn't be long, then followed the chief inside with the others, accompanied by only two of the four hunters. Once the door had closed, Eyila turned and led Petra and Aria away, followed by the remaining guards as well as the village's suspicious eyes and whispers.

Petra raised her chin in defiance under the scrutinous stares, but she didn't let her own gaze brush across any of them. "They seem more untrusting of *us* than we are of them," she mumbled to herself.

"They are afraid of you."

She looked sheepishly towards the sharp-eared girl, but couldn't help frowning in disbelief. "Afraid of *us?*"

"Cityfolk are greedy," she replied lightly. "Everything has a price, and if we do not accept whatever you deem something worth, if we're even willing to part with it at all, you will take it. Sometimes even kill us for it."

Petra frowned. "Sounds like not even a desert will deter bandits."

"It is not 'bandits', it is you people." Despite her words, she hadn't delivered them with venom. Instead she seemed merely to be stating a simple fact. "You have no sentimentality, no sense of accomplishment unless the result is money. Your spirits are corrupt. You pay no attention to one another, only to others' belongings."

Petra wished she could have protested, especially when she looked around and found the two hunter-guards with looks of equal conviction on their faces, but she just couldn't avoid the painful truth in that last statement. "And you fear us because of that?"

Eyila's eyebrows rose as she looked towards her. "I'm surprised you make no effort to deny it."

"I wouldn't want to lie. It's a fair description of some 'cityfolk' - a lot, in fact - but," her eyes were ardent, "*not* the five of us. We're each driven by passion.

Different passions, but passion never the less. Every one of us."

The tribal girl considered her words, her eyes slighting in thought, and she soon nodded. "I have noticed that much," she admitted. "Which is why I have spoken out for you. But please understand, it isn't theft we fear, nor you personally. It's the corruption. Tribes who live nearer to your cities have weaker connections to the gods, and that is only in part because of the weak locations they have chosen to call home. They've also been influenced. They think more of personal gain and wealth than they used to - than they *should*. But we are left alone out here, and for that we have purer, happier lives, and a stronger link to Aya'u, just as the earth tribes in the mountains do Degon, the fire tribes at the fire-mountain do Shiya, and the water nomads do Uq'ua."

Petra nodded, absorbing as much as she could in case it became useful later on. "Do you not trade at all, then?" She asked thoughtfully. "How do you get food? Clothing?"

Eyila frowned in bewilderment. "We do trade, sometimes - a few of your kind meet a few of mine. You do have things we want, after all, like salt, just as we have what you want - though they are more frivolous things; crafts and a few spices. But we don't enter your land to do it, and neither do we allow them into ours. We meet at the borders on an agreed day of the month, and only trade what we can easily spare for what we need. Though we usually just trap or make it."

"Trap?" Petra's eyes widened dubiously.

"Do you like living like this?"

Startled by the outburst, both Petra and Eyila looked down at Aria in surprise. But she was too busy spinning around in increasing amazement to notice, and she was looking too quickly from one thing to the next for it to be called staring.

"Of course," Eyila smiled. "It's freedom."

Aria managed to spare a nod. "I understand."

The tribal girl frowned sceptically. "How could you?"

"I live in a forest," she replied, flashing her a big, beaming smile. "Before Mister Garon came to my house, the only people I'd ever seen were people selling spices and meat and fish. It was quiet, and safe - well, except for the wolves - but I could climb trees all day long, play in the stones, the river, and have all kinds of fun!"

"You'd never seen anyone else?" Petra frowned in concern. "Don't you have any friends?"

"Of course!" She grinned. "I have my daddy, and now I have all of you! I have *loads* of friends!"

She couldn't help smiling at her enthusiasm, but she was quite unsure what to make of it. Eyila, however, was smiling broadly, and Petra could see an affection plain in her eyes that she had felt within herself not so long ago. It was something Aria was able to summon from deep within people without even trying - and while Garon may fight it, she was convinced that it was there within him, too.

"I knew there was something different about you..."

"Of course," Aria smiled. "I'm smaller, for starters."

Chapter 35

The ground within the chieftain's longhouse was littered with yet more animal skins, though these were far bigger than any others they'd seen and many had been stained with additional patterns besides the animals' own, likely to befit the prestige of the place. Unfortunately, that intention was offset by the hides' musty aroma, an odour that made their heads swim as they knelt, unmoving, upon them.

Just as Eyila had warned, in the half hour that had passed the chief had indeed strode all around the room while Rathen had carefully explained their motives, mindful not to turn his head or add to his dizziness. The chief had proceeded to interrupt with plenty of difficult questions, but Anthis answered those too technical for Rathen to tackle, and quickly enough that no one seemed to notice the mage's failing. Garon, however, had barely spoken a word. He hadn't needed to, but it did seem to reinforce the creeping suggestion that the officer was little more than a free pass to bend or break a few rules in the cities, as he contributed little else.

Now, however, the room was silent, and no one moved. The trio's legs were growing numb and invoking a desperate need to shift and fidget, though they didn't dare indulge it, especially when a dropped pin would have sounded like the cacophony of Aria in a kitchen full of pans.

The chief sat quite still in his own seat, little more than a collection of pillows though certainly far more comfortable than the near-bare ground, and his distant, wide-eyed stare made clear how perfectly torn he was between his thoughts. He was flanked by two elder tribesmen who, like Garon, had yet to say a word, and merely stared at them from beneath masks of wrinkles, while the priestess looked calm and contemplative.

They waited for an agonisingly long while for the chief to finish chewing over their words. He eventually opened his mouth to speak, but shortly closed it again.

The priestess suffered no such indecision. "I permit it," she announced, startling the room for various reasons, and the chief looked back at her in disbelief. She elegantly turned her head away from him. "I don't need to explain myself to you, Chief. This is a matter of safety for more than our tribe alone, and as it is Aya'u's shrine that they wish to see, it falls to *me* to make the final decision."

"You *believe* them?" He asked dubiously, his tongue slipping from Turundan to their own dialect in his surprise.

"You do not?" She asked in kind. "You have sat there in silence for five minutes, unable to make a decision, and I can guarantee it isn't because you don't know what would be for the best. You can see as well as I can that the facts are very simple: Ut'hala is in need of something we cannot provide, and these people clearly have a better idea of what is happening than we do, or Eyila, and may just be able to supply it. And if what they say of the broken lands is true and we turn them away, it won't remain a matter of simply keeping away from Ut'hala for much longer. The danger will come to *us*." She turned herself towards him and pressed her steady gaze. "You can fight my decision if you like, but you will not win, if just because your heart won't be in it. Don't be pig-headed."

The chief's eyes narrowed distastefully, then he sighed and shook his head. "When did my authority shrink to that of a child?"

He raised his head and looked over the three Turundans, returning to their language as they stared cautiously back at him. "You will not go alone," he informed them, ensuring that this decision, at least, would be his own. "By the rules of our tribe, a priestess will go with you; she will lead you and make sure you don't mistreat the shrine. When you return, you will share your findings with us, directly. And you will not leave until three hours after dusk. It is spring, but the deeper you go into the desert, the hotter it gets."

Rathen's relief faltered. "We'd rather get there as soon as possible..." he said, taking great care not to appear ungrateful.

The chief smiled, and Rathen didn't miss the barely concealed condescension. "You will cover far more ground by leaving later than you will by rushing out there now. It will be midday soon."

"What are we to do in the meantime?"

This time he hesitated in his response, and still appeared to be debating it even as it left his lips. "Stay here." Uneasy looks were exchanged on both sides, and he sighed in similar dissatisfaction. "There's little other choice. You will stay under guard at the edge of the village. You will not interact with anyone, and you will be informed when it's time to leave." His light blue eyes were severe. "Agreed?"

A small knot formed in Rathen's jaw. "Agreed." He felt Anthis and Garon's gazes shift onto the back of his head, but if they objected, they kept it to themselves. There really was no other choice.

The chief rose to his feet and the three of them placed their palms on the ground and bowed forwards, waiting for permission to rise again, just as they'd been told to, after which the two hunters fell immediately back in around them and escorted them out after their leader.

The sun was piercingly bright, and the heat-cancelling effects of the buildings became apparent as they stepped out into the almost-midday warmth. They fell instantly under the scrutiny of the rest of the tribe, but in the half hour since their arrival, they seemed to have adjusted, their eyes changing from almost violently mistrustful to a resigned but subtle watchfulness.

Petra and Aria were very quick to rejoin them with Eyila closely in tow, and no time was wasted in leading them to their allocated area. It was only partially shaded, but it was enough, and it was quiet aside from a small, roofed area nearby, occupied by an older woman and four young girls about Aria's age. Aria watched them very closely as they enacted a dance composed of strange, jerking movements. In startling unison, they half-crouched while rising onto their toes and bent their arms at crooked angles, somehow still moving them fluidly, while their heads twitched to a shared rhythm and their wide eyes looked here and there as if indicating something to one another. It seemed at first as if they were panicked by something, perhaps intensely uncomfortable about their positions, but given their disciplined synchronisation, it could only have been part of the choreography. Eyila had told them that they represented birds, while the dancers that represented the wind were working on their costumes elsewhere, all in aid of a festival set to take place in the next few weeks. Apparently the dance told the story of the wind goddess's gift of wings to the eagles, but each of them doubted they would be able to follow the tale even if they saw the whole performance several times over.

"Well we couldn't have expected to be allowed to wander off to a sacred site on our own," Petra said once their meeting had been recounted. "We wouldn't let one of them into one of our temples, would we?"

"I suppose not," Anthis sighed, "but I was looking forward to getting away from these people." His eyes flicked about uneasily, observing the nearby hunters, and though intrigue marked his face as they fell again upon the strangely hypnotic movements of the children, his frown of mistrust only deepened. He looked back to the others. "It could be an elaborate trap."

"I don't think they would go through these lengths for the five of us," Petra shook her head. "And anyway, it's this or nothing, right? We need to get out there."

"I know, but--"

Anthis was cut short by a sharp but subtle gesture from Rathen, and he turned in alarm to see the tribal girl stepping around the corner with five clay bowls balanced in her arms, which she duly passed around. They each looked dubiously at the meat that lay within, never mind the purple vegetables.

"What--uh...what is it?" Anthis asked as politely as he could.

"Oryx," Eyila smiled.

"Oryx?"

"What else would it be?"

"That wasn't...well, that wasn't *entirely* what I meant..."

"Thank you," Rathen said, if just to silence him, "but you don't need to feed us."

"Didn't I tell you to accept food?"

"Yes, but--"

"Then accept it." She smiled strangely, but none could decide if she looked suspicious or pitying. "It isn't poisoned."

Poison wasn't the foremost of their concerns.

Rathen looked down at the meat as its pleasantly spiced aroma tickled his nose, then steeled himself and raised a chunk to his mouth. The others watched him in disbelief, but as he chewed, nodded and swallowed, the others saw little choice but to follow his lead. It didn't taste bad, but none of them had any idea what - or *who* - 'oryx' was.

"Good," she said, satisfied, then turned and walked away. No one chose to voice the fact that she wasn't eating - nor anyone else within their sight.

Eyila hurried through the village towards the chieftain's longhouse, darting smoothly around neighbours as she went, too concerned with carrying their oversized jars of coloured dusts, enormous drums and musical pipes to notice her. But when she made it to the far side of the village where the edifice stood grandly at the head of the central clearing, its walls adorned with flowing emblems painted with desert clays while the oldest and most exquisite of the village's wind chimes tinkled in the breeze, the white pennant that should have been hung over the front of the door wasn't there. The chief wasn't in.

She turned quickly on her heel and made for the small wind shrine at the most eastern point of the village, assuming that perhaps he was speaking to the handful of priestesses about the matter, but when she rounded the corner and the oh so familiar stack of carven wind-scoured rocks fell into view, she found that he wasn't there, either.

Despite how small the village was, it took her almost twenty minutes to track him down, and when she finally did stumble across him, he was just stepping out from the healer's hut of all places with an equally puzzled look on his face.

"There you are," she sighed as he announced the same, and she hurried out of another jug-carrier's way to meet him, offering him a sheepish but grateful smile as she stopped at the edge of the sandy path. "I'm sorry for my earlier rudeness, but thank you for listening to them."

"I didn't seem to have much choice," he grumbled. "And I'm *still* not at all happy about this," he added pointedly, "but Kahii seems to have the same loud and ill-founded trust that you do."

"Well, if it's any consolation, I will keep a very close eye on them."

His demeanour suddenly shifted and Eyila felt herself shrink in his presence, her buoyancy melting away. He straightened, growing taller, and his usually relaxed authority became apparent by simply breathing the air around him. She felt the need to stand taller, herself, if just to be taken more seriously, because she knew what was coming, had certainly expected it, and was more than prepared to fight it.

His eyes were hard as he looked down his nose at her. "*You* are going nowhere. Anai will be guiding them."

"But they are *my* responsibility--"

"*No.*"

She tightened her jaw at his low and sharp tone and managed not to flinch, but she was unable to look back at him as he squared himself towards her.

"*Your* responsibility is to tend to our people," he reminded her, sternly rather than angrily. "You are our *healer*, Eyila; whether you like it or not, you were born with rare gifts, and with Liaha watching from the Winds, there is no one else who can do what you do." His frustration was clear in his eyes, edged with beseechment. "You *cannot* go to Ut'hala. Not while it is in such turmoil."

"I cannot leave this to someone else," she declared just as firmly, "not even Anai, as capable a priestess as she is. I will be going in her place."

Exasperation leaked in and freckled his tone. "You would endanger yourself to help *them?*"

"No, I would endanger myself to help *us*."

"You are not a priestess, Eyila, your duty is not to Aya'u or Her shrine!"

A great anger flashed across her face, but she managed to bite it back and smother its heat. "And no priestess could go in my place." She turned towards him now, her eyes as hard as his, and she ignored the curious looks of passers by as they wondered what new drama was unfolding. "Those people are the only ones who have presented any kind of solution to this issue, and if anything happens to them out there, that hope is *gone*. By going with them and keeping them safe we have the best chance of restoring Ut'hala and appeasing Aya'u, and with my magic, I might just be able to help them as *more* than just a salve dispenser."

His disapproving stare didn't waver.

"And they've come to develop some kind of trust towards me. It would be best if that was put to use."

He stared at her for another long while, but soon sighed and shook his head. "No, Eyila--"

"Uncle," she pressed, "you know as well as I do that my skills are not often needed, I'm here 'just in case' - when was the last time I treated more than cuts and scrapes?!"

"That may be true," he conceded, his tone unchanging as he stubbornly folded his arms, "but now you've gone and said that, something *will* happen and you won't be here to help. What about Uyu'una?"

"That's still almost three weeks away. It'll take a week to reach Ut'hala and a week to get back; I'll return in time for the festival - but my skills shouldn't be needed then, either." She cocked her head and offered him a reassuring smile, but it was clear by the stern crease in his forehead and the depth of his smooth, white eyebrows that it was doing nothing at all to sway him. She sighed and let it slip away. "By sending Anai, or *anyone* else, you're putting them in direct danger from both Ut'hala's state *and* these people. But I can defend myself just as well as any of the hunters, and I don't need a weapon to do it."

He grasped her still bandaged arm. "Then how did *this* happen?"

She hesitated as her eyes dropped down to it. "I don't know."

"What do you mean you 'don't know'?"

"I mean I didn't see who or what attacked me - I didn't see them, I didn't hear them, I didn't smell them. I didn't even know I *was* attacked until I woke up from it."

"Mhm," he nodded vigorously, his eyes ablaze. "One of your new friends possesses magic. What if it was them? Hm? What if he masked himself so he could sneak up on you, attack you, then pretend to come to your rescue to get you to bring him here?"

She was already shaking her own head, though far more calmly than he had. "I would have sensed it," she assured him confidently. "Magic can't be concealed like that. I'd have sensed the spell, or I'd have sensed him - do they really seem so malevolent to you?"

"It's my job to be suspicious of newcomers."

"And yet Kahii is willing to trust them enough to agree to sending one of her acolytes with them."

He said nothing.

"You know I'm right. Don't be--"

"If you call me pig-headed again, I swear I will lock you in this hut."

She smiled broadly, her eyes brightening. "Did that work the last time?"

He sighed wearily. "I hate magic." He looked at her now with new eyes, more considerate, more reasonable, and finally the stubborn wall began to collapse. He gestured towards the healer's quarters. "Get in there and see to yourself, then prepare as many long-lived salves, medicines and anti-venoms as you can, the ones we're most likely to need. If you're really going to leave us for two weeks, the least you can do is give us the means to treat ourselves."

A grin stole across her face, her blue eyes gleaming, and she reached out and embraced him tightly. He closed his painted arms around her with another defeated sigh, but smiled at her enthusiasm. She was certainly his sister's daughter.

*

The sun had shifted eastwards, and while it cast deep and welcome shadows over the group's secluded little spot, none of them were particularly sure how far away dusk was in this land of forever-sun - and they were doubly unsettled by the fact that they were unable to see what the tribespeople were up to in the meantime. They spent the afternoon largely in silence and absorbed in their own activities.

Anthis was, as always, buried in the ditchlings' notes, which he had taken to rewriting in his notebook in a legible form, but while he could clearly see it was all related to elven magic, little of it was any help. Mostly it was talk of outlandish feats, and though he wasn't quick to dismiss them as tales, he could certainly see a trend in the ditchlings' interests as well as the fact that they were all given very vague instructions on what to look for.

Rathen meanwhile tried to further the theory of his own task, but with opportunities to feel the magic and test any of his ideas few and far between, he found himself still only writing in circles. He was growing increasingly frustrated with the constant blockades and hoped more and more that Ut'hala would provide some kind of light, that he would find something there to give his task a clearer direction, maybe even a base to build the spell up from. Otherwise, any hope he had of succeeding was fading fast - if it was possible to lose what he didn't have in the first place.

And while Aria's activities were usually of the utmost importance, now she only doodled. Fearful of revealing her knife around these people, she'd returned to her own sketchbook as well, and seemed from Rathen's angle to be drawing some kind of...well it was either a tree or a person. He favoured the latter.

Petra and Garon kept watch for the duration.

And yet it still came as a surprise when the chief appeared from around the corner, Eyila, the priestess and a few other tribesmen in tow, approaching on silent feet. The sand, it seemed, would take a great deal of getting used to.

They dropped what they were doing and rose to their feet, offering the chief the same customary greeting as when they had first met, and this time it seemed to be more favourably received.

"It's time to leave," he informed them. "Ut'hala is a week away and your path will take you deep into the desert. You would do well to travel morning and evening, and wrap up well at night. Midday is hotter than your kind are used to in the south, and the nights are colder." He indicated Eyila, who, they noticed, had an animal skin pack slung over her shoulders, and a length of rope adorned with a variety of leaves, pouches and phials draped across her torso. "Eyila will be joining you. She may be able to offer you help and advice towards the situation - and, if your intentions turn out to be false, she will protect the site." He took a step towards them as his eyes became grave, and as respectfully submissive as the group tried to be, they suddenly felt the need to physically stoop beneath his gaze. "If you attempt to harm her, or further defile the shrine, you will suffer both her wrath and Aya'u's. Do not take *either* of them lightly."

They nodded their fervent understanding, and Rathen was the first to reclaim his composure. "You have our thanks, Chieftain," he said humbly, "but rest assured that we *have* told you the truth."

His heavy gaze still seemed unconvinced, but the priestess who stepped up beside him remained a pleasant contrast, enlightened and reasonable. She offered them a radiant smile, and Rathen found himself feeling strangely lighter for it.

"I wish you the best of luck out there. Ut'hala is of great importance to our people - not just the Ikaheka, but to *all* tribes of the wind. If you can restore its balance, we will be in your debt." She received a subtle glare of disapproval from the chief, but if she was aware of it - she didn't seem the type to miss very much - she did a fine job of ignoring it. Instead, she raised her hands and made a wide, sweeping gesture, similar to the customary female greeting to the chief except that this one encompassed the whole group, and the waft of air that the movement cast across them was stronger and cooler than should have been possible. "Oluya toakan Aya'u tse," she said on the lightest whisper, then lowered her hands and smiled over them once again. "Go forth with Aya'u's blessing."

They inclined their heads gratefully, wondering at the curiously empowering sensation that had fallen upon them when the alien words had been uttered, only to flee as suddenly as it had arrived.

"Saya'a lo toa," Eyila replied just as softly, but though her expression reflected their own calm, there was a new yet tightly restrained enthusiasm in her eyes, one which Rathen found himself already familiar with - it was a glint that often appeared in Anthis's eyes right before he delved into a box of dusty scrolls. His caution rose as he wondered if hers would be just as innocent.

But as she stepped forwards to join them, the chief caught her arm and pulled her back for a few quiet words. Rathen only managed to catch 'be careful' from the exchange, and after she'd nodded and offered a smile to reassure the reluctance in his eyes, she returned her attention to Rathen and the others and moved to align with them.

"Good luck," he called as she led them away, then lowered his voice with a sigh. "You'll need it."

Anthis cast a glance over his shoulder while Eyila spun the five clay cylinders they'd passed on their way in, whispering under her breath, and loosed a careful sigh of relief as they resumed at last, and the village dropped away behind them. "Well," he said quietly, "that went well - assuming that this isn't some elaborate deception."

"It isn't," Rathen replied, and though his voice too was almost a whisper, and his eyes were still glued to Eyila as she walked on ahead of them, he wasn't watching her with as much suspicion anymore. Their time in the village, as brief as it was, had made him wonder if they weren't perhaps a little bit wrong about the tribes - or *this* tribe, at least. They didn't grunt or howl in communication, they lived in well-constructed buildings, if a little small, and more than just courteous to one another, they had at least a few complicated customs and gestures of respect to both their superiors and their faith.

Of course, none of that meant they weren't prone to barbaric responses, as four hours was hardly enough time to get to know a culture, so, for now at least, they would have to remain vigilant in her company.

"And you're sure?" Anthis asked, hopefully rather than sceptically, and Petra nodded from beside him just as Rathen did.

"It isn't."

The historian blinked at her. "...Well, good." His eyes travelled to the white haired girl and he pursed his lips thoughtfully. "They're not really what I expected."

"What *did* you expect?" Aria asked none too quietly, and though the tribal girl didn't turn her head in curiosity, Anthis preferred not to voice the truth. So he replied hurriedly, and louder, for Eyila's benefit.

"Well I thought there would be less of them. They must be very good hunters and gatherers to survive out here. I mean," he gestured animatedly around himself. "I'm quite sure I'd starve."

"You just have to know where to look." Eyila glanced around at them with neither a smile nor a frown, though there was still that excited glimmer in her eyes. "If you know the land, you'll know where to find animals. There are ibex on the lower reaches of the mountains and out among the plateaus, and oryx wander the sands in between, and plants grow around the springs they drink from."

"Springs?" Petra frowned. "So there *is* water out here?"

She cast her the bemused frown they were all becoming quite familiar with. "Of course. But, as with the animals, you just have to know where to find it." She pointed eastwards, seemingly towards nothing. "There's a spring that way."

"Are there any along our path?"

She sent them a wry smile. "There is water, yes."

She turned her attention back towards their heading, leaving the others to share uneasy glances. Some of them may have had their misgivings about the tribespeople thrown into question, but their apprehensions about the desert that lay before them were rooted and growing, and the nature of her apparently simple answer only made it worse.

An anxious silence descended.

"So you're a priestess?" Anthis asked in an attempt to break it, but he spoke with a nervous haste rather than interest which earned him four subtle frowns.

This time Eyila didn't turn. "No," she replied shortly. "I'm not."

"...Oh... B-but the chief said--"

"He decided you'd be safer if I came with you instead. And I might be of more help."

Rathen nodded to himself in satisfaction. He'd kept his protests about a guide silent in the chieftain's presence, and had decided that if anyone *had* to accompany them out there, he'd have preferred it to be the mage. Even if she was a risk, he could at least counter-spell her, and it was entirely possible that she could tell them something that could help his understanding of the magic. They were a simple people, and while it was likely that they had romantic ideas about magic, he hoped that one of them who possessed it would be able to bridge those ideas to the facts and offer a whole new viewpoint.

But he would still watch her closely, especially with that twinkle in her eye and the sudden contrasting note of venom in her voice, but more so for the fact that magically binding her hands was no longer an option, not now that diplomacy had come into play. They would have to trust her, and trust her *fully*.

A task made harder for the fact that her bandages had disappeared and any trace of her wounds along with them - a detail no one else seemed yet to have noticed.

*

They travelled on in silence as the day drew to an end, and though it had still been warm when they'd set out, by the time dusk melted into night there was a definite chill in the air, one that somehow hadn't been present even near the snow-capped mountains, and yet existed instead out on the stifling sands where they hadn't seen so much as a stubby little knot of dry grass for an hour. It intensified with the darkness, and despite the compulsion to stop and pitch camp, the tribal girl kept them moving.

"If we stop and sleep too soon, we'll rise too soon, and then we'll want to stop and sleep too soon again, and we'll end up travelling in the middle of the day," Eyila had said when Aria began falling behind, though not without apology, but soon called a halt if just out of pity for the little girl.

They raised tents, courtesy of Kienza, to keep away the chill and to protect them from the desert creatures they were told came out during the cooler nights, and, as absurd as it certainly seemed, lit a much-needed camp fire.

"We will set out again just before sunrise," she informed them as they settled around it to eat, grateful to finally sit down and rest their feet after the five-hour challenge of walking over deep and unstable sands.

"Aren't you going to eat anything?" Rathen asked as she turned and stepped away from them, having had no trouble at all, herself.

"Not yet. I have to meditate."

Petra frowned after her. "You really don't need to be so tense around us," she said gently, "we're not going to hurt you..."

But Eyila only chuckled and turned them a pitying smile. "That is not its purpose."

"Then what is?"

Her eyes shifted onto Rathen, who looked back with an equal measure of interest and suspicion. The others, she noticed, looked much the same, if to varying degrees, while Garon appeared still wholly distrusting - though he had yet to truly speak a word to her since she'd come into their company.

Her smile slipped and a strange note of regret touched her eyes. She forced her smile back into place. "It is just something I need to do." And with that, she turned and walked away to ascend a nearby dune where she predictably sat, straightened her back, and let the breeze she'd found against the odds tousle her long white hair.

"I wonder what she's up to," Anthis muttered, staring towards her as he raised his bread to his mouth, and Rathen's eyes narrowed as his own thoughts deepened.

"She said Aya'u was the goddess of the wind, right?"

"Mhm."

He nodded slowly as his thoughts fell into order, then decisively looked away. "Leave her to it. It's none of our business, and the last thing we need is to be led out here and abandoned in an ocean of sand because we've insulted some tribal custom." His attention then fell onto the notebook in his lap, though he made sure she was still within his sight, and Aria shortly followed his example and began scribbling secretively into her own, having come across an idea for her previous and highly important task. She'd been yawning for over an hour, though, so he doubted she'd get very far with it, and sure enough, within ten minutes she'd fallen asleep against him with it still open in her hands.

He smiled warmly, shaking his head to himself, and turned to draw her blanket out of their tent with a brief, single-handed spell, draped it over her body and tucked it gently around her as her breath slowed and deepened. He removed her book, closing it without giving its contents even a cursory glance and set it down beside her, then watched her sleep for a moment, letting her breathing calm his own heart, and the burning around his arm soon passed.

It now happened without fail every time he cast a spell, and he could no longer tell if the sensation was dulling or if he was simply getting used to it - but he was at least prepared for it, if he could be grateful for anything. But while the bouts were becoming manageable, their cause still eluded him, and his stifled concern was made worse by the knowledge that even Kienza seemed stumped.

But he had proven to himself that he *could* work through it, and at this point, that was all that mattered.

His eyes dropped back onto his own hopeless scrawlings, most of which were still being crossed out, and as that tiresome futility bubbled up in his stomach yet again, he released a long and weary sigh.

Aria giggled softly in her sleep, somehow dragging the image of the sundered village to the surface of his memory, and he reminded himself then that resigning himself to failure was not an option. Saving the people of Turunda - and *beyond,* it seemed - was a smothering thought. But at the very least, he could do it for her.

Garon stared out across the sands beneath the star-littered sky, his eyes glued towards the south and straining against the darkness to make out anything lurking within it. His skin prickled, hair stood on end, but absorbed in such fretful thoughts, he was hardly aware of the surrounding chill.

His ear twitched at the soft footsteps approaching from behind. Petra. It would be no one else; he needn't turn to confirm it. His eyes remained locked on the blackness beyond.

"Here," she said softly as she came to a stop beside him, and he saw without taking the time to look that she offered him a blanket.

"Thank you," he replied, taking it and sweeping it over his shoulders. He felt immediately warmer, but his comfort didn't last long as he felt the intensity of her eyes drilling into him.

"What is it?" She asked, her soft voice tinted with caution as her gaze shifted away to follow his off into the night.

But he shook his head, his own wary frown deepening. "Nothing..."

She looked back to him gravely and prepared to inform him that she wasn't as stupid as he seemed to think, but the way his eyes had narrowed, edged with an apprehension which was unsettlingly uncharacteristic, stopped her before she could begin.

His shoulders tightened beneath the welcome blanket. "I just have a bad feeling..."

Chapter 36

The country was in chaos; every authoritative body already had their work cut out for them trying to maintain the peace, but when a city full of people felt the same sudden and boiling outrage towards a single, smaller collective, the situation required an exasperatingly delicate hand. Everyone seemed to feed off of one another; every tavern, market, *every* public area was charged with enmity and mistrust, and Vastal save any mage that should be spotted nearby, as that delicate hand only just managed to hold back the masses. There was strength in numbers, and that apparently meant that even the common folk could stand against magic if there were enough of them. Jeers filled the air around any preserver or scholarly mage who passed through the streets, their heads bowed in stealth despite their screamingly obvious cloaks, and while no one had yet attempted any physical assault, only the martial mages seemed to invoke any kind of restraint from the verbal attacks.

But while the Hall of the White Hammer was busy trying to prevent a civilian revolt for the citizens' own sakes, and the guards were patrolling the streets in greater numbers to keep an eye on both sides - though they were sorely ill-equipped to do anything should a mage decide to respond - the Arana were now spreading their own numbers even thinner by keeping a close watch on the Order itself in a bid to uncover their plans.

It was preposterous that the country should have to be protected from itself, and yet, despite the war raging around them, it seemed as if the Order had caused greater damage and unrest than Skilan had.

But that didn't mean that the matter of the war was any simpler.

They still had no idea how Skilan was foiling their plans. Their spies assured them that they hadn't been compromised, and Salus and Teagan had both been inclined to believe them, but the evidence suggested otherwise and it was too late to uproot and replace them. The operatives had no choice but to turn their attention towards discovering who was watching them, stage an incident to discredit them and reclaim the trust of Skilan's superiors for their own as quickly as possible. Until then, no word they received regarding Skilan's plans and movements could be truly trusted.

As for Doana, the Arana had managed to track down and eradicate one of their infiltration units and were finally closing in on a second, but it was decidedly unlikely that there had been only three to begin with. They'd proven themselves intelligent, leaving no possibility that they'd reveal their full numbers so easily - in fact, the only thing their initial occupations proved for certain was that there were *at least* three groups, and the rest, like the remaining known platoons, were adept at concealment. There hadn't been a trace of them.

It had been a long and painstaking effort to weed out the first group, and the second were following by the same means, but the more time that passed the more wide-spread they could become, and moving in such small numbers meant that they could cover great distances quicker than a larger, more conspicuous force. And just as they'd somehow been able to identify the Arana's grass roots in each of the three settlements, never mind eliminate them, they were surely quite prepared for such a pursuit.

Despite that, however, the Arana had taken out one group and were hot on the heels of the second. They *were* getting results. Though, as for uncovering how they'd come by their intel, they'd not had much luck.

All of this had to be balanced with the usual tasks and observations to make sure nothing else could slip by them - a job made more difficult by yet another distraction - and so it had fallen to Teagan to man the office that night and read over the incoming reports before filing them away with more logic than Salus ever seemed to. He'd tried to introduce more organisation in the past, but Salus had assured him that everything had its place. Fortunately he knew well how his mind worked, so it didn't take him long to find himself at home in the chaos.

He also filtered through the outstanding orders and commands and began assigning whoever was available and most suited for each, from merely adding to the observational tasks of watchers to dispatching hunters and assassins to remove troublesome individuals or manipulate a situation.

Truly, this job was more monotonous than it was taxing. Even when he moved on to the orders responding to tribal activity and the conflicts of non-humans that seemed to be moving closer to settled regions, he barely reacted beyond a weary sigh. He simply continued to filter out the appropriate operatives without giving the matters any thought. After all, it wasn't his place to analyse orders. His was to advise, not to second-guess and certainly not to alter them, even if some might think them perhaps unnecessarily aggressive. Salus was Keliceran, and the keliceran certainly knew better than himself. Teagan may have been his second, but only Salus saw every single report and balanced every single detail in every decision he made.

He disregarded his meagre ponderings. These tasks weren't strenuous, either; a mixture of phidipans and phaeacians would do - which was just as well, because most portian operatives were out taking care of higher and delicate priorities already.

Teagan was unaware of the slight and doubtful frown that marred his face as he set aside his choices.

Satisfied that those matters were checked off of the list, he dutifully moved on to the next just as a knock came at the door.

His frown became dubious. He knew that pattern, the pressure, the quick, sharp strikes from two second knuckles.

His usual mask of indifference slipped easily into place as he rose to his feet and called to enter, and Malson shortly stepped inside with a question nestled amongst the lines of frustration on his face. His sharp eyes flicked about briefly, but Teagan's position behind the desk was enough to answer it. "Portian," he said quickly, looking back to him as the younger man calmly and respectfully bowed his head, though he was too impatient to acknowledge the gesture, "it's been three days. Have you identified any of the offending mages yet?"

"Nothing yet."

"Well are you close?"

"Yes." In truth, he hadn't a clue, but no other answer would have been acceptable.

The old man, lively despite his frail appearance, sighed gruffly as the fire in his eyes swelled. "The people are in an uproar, on the verge of *riots* - the Order can protect themselves and their building, but people *are* going to get hurt if anyone steps over the line." He stared firmly at the keliceran's favoured. "I'm sure I don't need to stress this point."

"No, my lord, you certainly don't."

"Then where is Salus?" His eyes narrowed as Teagan hesitated, though his void expression revealed no true cause for suspicion. "Never mind," he said with a softer though no less impatient tone. "Just make certain that this remains a priority. We *can't* be at war with our own people, *especially* not now."

"Rest assured that we are taking care of it."

Malson's eyes narrowed again, the hint of unwarranted scepticism returning under Teagan's unreadable countenance. He didn't voice it. "Good. Then I expect to see results very soon." He turned and strode away, vanishing back into the hallway. "And it had better be reliable."

Teagan's jaw tightened as he moved around to close the door behind him. Of all possible times for the Crown's liaison to turn up. Salus's absence, even in an unplanned visit, would not reflect well upon him or the Arana. People didn't trust what they couldn't see, and if Salus wasn't where he 'should' have been, Malson was sure to think that he wasn't doing anything useful or necessary with his time. Of course, due to the very nature of the matter, Teagan couldn't defend his superior by correcting the ill-founded assumption and neither could he go off and fetch him. *'No interruptions'*, Salus had demanded before vanishing down into the cells. It had been Teagan's own suggestion to indulge the mage in the hope that they might uncover the Order's intentions, but given how things were suddenly unfolding, he found himself hoping dearly that *something* good would come of it, *anything*, and fast.

Denek released a weary sigh as he shook his head in futility, while Salus stared back silently in growing frustration and more than a little mistrust, though he worked to hide that last detail. They stood together in the mage's cell - which had been begrudgingly upgraded to one with a narrow slit for a window - as he preferred to keep him down in the cellar even during such meetings, despite the fact that no one was completely sure if the dampening spells placed over his holding were having any effect against his abilities. But beyond the danger of his magic, he also had no desire to allow him any further into the Arana's house, as neither could anyone guess what his true intentions were, nor how deep they might run.

But at that moment, Salus's concerns weren't so broad. He was finding it difficult restraining himself in the mage's presence, and if his brusque attitude continued, he was either going to turn around and storm off, or find out just how far into his face he could push his nose with his fist.

"It's astounding that you've been able to function as a human being at all," the dark haired mage mumbled to himself, giving Salus a clearer idea of just which choice he'd be likely to make, then raised his head and turned his striking eyes back upon him. Their thoughtfulness stalled Salus's tightening fists. "You've been suppressing your magic for a very long time," he stated matter-of-factly, as if he knew so well, "and if you were once anything like those you surround yourself with," his eyes shifted briefly onto the unaffected guards outside, "then it would have happened while you suppressed your emotions. You would never have even known it was there."

'Isn't that convenient?' He thought to himself, then turned his cynicism to better use. "Why did no mage ever sense it?" He asked instead, being careful not to sound too suspicious, nor too surprised. "Mages usually sense these things, that's how people find out they have magic, isn't it?"

"I suppose you were just that good at suppressing it." Salus found himself unconvinced by the ease with which he'd said it. "And," Denek added, glancing about his cell and then out through the narrow 'window', "because I doubt you were ever near enough for any to have a chance to sense it while it was masked so well." His sharp eyes flicked back to him. "But now that magic is growing and clawing its way to the surface, and it's too strong for you to keep shoving it back down."

"But what difference does that make? If I don't know how to wield it then it can't cause a problem."

Denek raised a slender finger and an unpleasant smile curved his lips. "That is where you are wrong."

He felt his blood suddenly run cold, and everyone within earshot stiffened.

"Your magic is *too* strong, my dear Keliceran, and it could most *certainly* manifest itself. There is a reason that those with weak magic are not trained: because their magic is too weak to *be* trained. There's little to go wrong with people like that. Yours, however, *should* have been trained, but the...workings of this organisation denied it, intentionally or not." The brief curl of his lip faded, and his eyes, which Salus noticed bore a constant but subtle slyness, brightened in amazement. "It's just as well that you've done such a remarkable job of suppressing it for so long."

"Why?" He asked carefully, now trying to restrain an added note of alarm all while chiding himself for believing him so easily when it could just as likely be a trick. "What could happen?"

His pale eyes hardened, and Salus knew immediately that, disregarding everything else he had said, his following words were the unembellished truth. "It could consume you and obliterate every one and every thing within a two-day radius."

He blanched while Denek sighed and shook his head with inappropriate lightness. "This isn't working," he declared wearily, for far from the first time. "You need to *let* yourself grasp the magic."

"Yes, you've said that before, but *how?*"

"By not pushing it down."

His brow flattened. "You've said that before, too." He fought to rein in his cynicism, but after well over an hour of such vague and useless suggestions, he was only growing more and more certain that the mage was leading him on.

And yet...

Despite the words themselves, he could see that there was *some* kind of logic to their intent, and though he didn't really understand it, some small, remote part of him certainly seemed to. There was a a deep, primal shadow of his being that lurched forward at his every attempt to 'grasp the magic' and urged him on in some archaic tongue. And as cryptic as it all was, it only encouraged his pursuit.

"I suppose you've been doing it for so long you probably don't know how to stop," Denek continued thoughtfully. "Your emotions seem erratic enough that you're probably still pushing them down, albeit unknowingly, and really quite haphazardly..." His eyes narrowed curiously. "Whatever happened to break your control?"

"That," Salus began in a steely tone, "is not relevant."

Pale blue eyes stared at him for another long moment. "No, I suppose it isn't." He then straightened and returned his attention to the matter at hand. "I have an idea. Do you have any relaxation techniques--no, no, sorry, of course you don't."

Salus didn't appreciate the surety with which he corrected himself, and hated all the more that he was once again unable to prove his instant assumptions wrong.

"All right, try this: sit down on the floor and cross your legs."

Salus frowned as the mage did so himself, but he soon followed, for what could the mage do to him while sitting that he couldn't while standing?

"Straighten your back, but don't over-arch it, and rest your hands in your lap. Release your elbows down under your shoulders, and your shoulders down your back."

"...What?"

"Just do it." His voice had taken on a curiously dreamlike softness as he followed his own instructions. "Now close your eyes and relax your face."

He did so, despite his misgivings about losing sight of the man, but there were guards outside and his reactions weren't so dulled by that damned office that he'd miss any call of alarm.

"...I said relax your face."

"I have."

"You're scowling. Relax your face."

He forced the tightness he discovered across his brow and the knot in his chin to release, and his face suddenly felt quite heavy.

He heard Denek sigh. "That will have to do. Now drop your feet into the ground beneath you and let the crown of your head float."

"What?"

"Relax your face."

"This is hopeless!"

"No," Denek replied still quite softly, "but it *is* the hardest step - for you, at least. Grasp this and the rest will come far more easily."

Salus cast him another immensely sceptical look, but that primal hunger deep within him roared out once more, louder, and again he heeded it, unable to resist its power. He did his best to regain his position following the repeated instructions, and struggled just as much the second time.

"Now breathe deeply into your diaphragm, but don't force it. Let it happen naturally."

He took a single, slow inhalation, his stomach rising with the movement and falling as he released it. He inhaled again, feeling the stretch of his abdomen once more, then exhaled to contract it. Then inhaled again, and exhaled again.

"You're forcing it."

"I'm not forcing it," he said through his teeth, focusing on the length and depth of his next inhale and the subsequent extension of his stomach.

"You're thinking about it - that's not letting it happen naturally. Just try to relax, then you'll be able to release whatever lock you've got your magic sealed beneath. It's already weakened; it won't take much to reach it, you just have to *find* it."

Salus took another deep breath and tried to block out the irritating mage, but, mercifully, he fell silent, and in the absence of that arrogant voice he found his breath more easily. His body grew lighter with every inhalation and he shortly settled into the pattern, taking notice of each breath without paying any too much attention. But despite the calm that had begun to settle upon him, he soon began to feel a curious tremor creeping up beneath his ribs, one that invoked a sense of apprehension, an excitement mixed with panic and a longing desperation that stalled his mind as it sought a means to locate what supposedly dwelled within him.

But he wasn't about to let himself stumble over it. His mind was the clearest and most determined he had ever consciously known it, and the voice, the presence that lurked deep within him, was coming to life in response. And it felt stronger, almost irrepressible. Hypnotic.

'Let yourself grasp it.'

He handed the lead over to the primal instinct.

Immediately his hunt surged forwards, and he was dragged along with it like a carriage by a maddened horse, and hope lurched in his heart with the sudden momentum. His consciousness hurtled through a foggy haze, one permeated by a distant familiarity which he couldn't place. But he gave it no thought, allowing himself to be guided by whatever part of him knew this place best, and he moved steadily deeper and deeper into the haze. Flashes began shooting by, non-images he thought for a moment that he recognised, but before he could get any kind of grasp on them, they were gone. They were sparse at first and easily forgotten once they were behind him, but they gradually began to multiply, whizzing by faster and more frequently, and every one of them drew closer than the last. There were soon so many that he began to catch snatches of comprehension; the first seemed to be something akin to amusement, the next he thought to be mild fascination. They were strange, curious sensations, but though he knew without a doubt that they belonged to him, there was something interlaced within them that made them unwelcome. Something dark and forbidden urged him to turn away as quickly as he could, but the moment his attention mercifully shifted, he was assaulted by more. A trickle of panic began to run through his spine as the sensations turned darker in nature, when loneliness, fret and fear began to leak into the subconscious landscape and quickly swell to dominate it.

He suddenly pulled back as his eyes tore open, fleeing the cryptic turmoil and returning to his tense and rigid body to find the world around him cold, dark and still, yet curiously safe. But even before he recovered his bearings, he found the mage looking quietly back at him through the shadows. His eyes were knowing, as if he could see into Salus's mind and observe exactly what he was thinking and feeling. His body seized up tighter at the thought.

But then Denek nodded. It was a slight twitch but certainly intentional, and Salus knew from that alone that, somehow, he *could* see into his mind, and that he had been doing everything right.

He straightened where he sat, an air of confidence suddenly gathering around him. No one had said that this would be easy, and if a tangled swamp of what could only be his eternally stifled emotions would create the scenery of his hunt, so be it. As soon as he found his quarry, he could regain control. He *would* regain control.

Spurred on, he took another deep breath, closed his eyes and returned deep within himself, refusing to be beaten by the shade he had suppressed for so long. He lent more trust to his instincts and found the place easier than the first time, then he continued to wade through the dark mess all while doing his utmost to squeeze his eyes shut tight and stick his fingers in his ears against the emotional assault. The joy, the terror, the passion, the hate - they were not relevant, neither wanted nor needed. What he sought was among them, but he needn't look too close. It would be different. This he was certain of; like a pebble among sand, it might be buried but he would know it when he found it.

His instinct continued to force its way through the converging sentiments and he followed resolutely behind it, giving nothing that tried to elbow its way into his sight any kind of attention. He took not even a moment to register the auras. He ignored the wisps of delight, the shadows of ever-present loneliness, the heart-skipping yet compelling mist of love, the beckoning fingers of sheer terror that sent a cold sweat over his skin from even the slightest glimpse.

He stumbled in his distraction and his own momentum faltered, throwing him right back into being dragged along while his oh so brief control collapsed around him. In an instant he was swarmed by the non-images, as if they'd just been waiting for his paper walls to crumple, the coalescing emotions that took on ever more ethereal shapes and sought to overwhelm him to gain the attention they'd been refused for so long. His heart suddenly ached so much with denied love that he felt it would explode, his jaw tightened with such jealousy that it threatened to crack his teeth, his sides squeezed against laughing out with the purest of joy, all while a dark fear and unsilenceable inadequacy wriggled their way into his skin.

His world was permeated with voices, some soft, some screaming, but all together forming a garble of words so distorted they could have been another language, while images and faces began flashing past at speed. But as brief as they were, he recognised them all, and behind each trailed a myriad of precise yet incohesive ideas which further added to the chaos as he tried in spite of himself to make sense of them.

Fear, insult, passion and fury pierced through his chest.

'You're not supposed to lead the Arana.'

Taliel's face, Teagan's, one of someone he barely remembered and yet knew without a doubt was his sister.

'You lack the compassion needed to make the right decisions.'

A figure dropped lightly out from the trees, narrow hips swayed from left to right, candles flickered tiresomely on an old and worn down desk top.

'You would lead this country to ruin.'

The sound of a neck snapping, softly spoken words of advice, the flutter of a moth's wings heralding new orders.

He felt himself shake uncontrollably, his inner voice screaming as either rage, confusion, affection or desperation racked through his bones. Sweat ran all over him, soaking his clothes and drenching his skin. His hair stood up as a chill swept along his spine. He felt his mind begin to unhinge as the internal campaign against him swelled.

But as he lost himself to his panic, some other part of his mind abruptly took over, launching him through a nearby cloud and knocking him off-track for only a single moment. It then handed the lead back over to his primal instinct and suddenly he was chasing after it on his own feet again with a heart of the strongest steel, his resolve returned and strengthened by the cluster of determination he'd been driven through, and he allowed it to enshroud him.

He quickly noticed that his surroundings had become distant and muffled from within the armour; the voices had been silenced, the faces had vanished and his sight was set pointedly on his heading. And then, only a moment later, like the vaguest torchlight in the night, he saw it.

Victory pummelled him.

Lured by certainty and familiarity, like a promise of absolute safety, he rushed carelessly towards it as his excitement built up in his chest. He felt hope flutter in his throat, his desperation grow, injected by longing, by desire. His ordeal and everything around him was forgotten.

Until his imagined footing slipped yet again in his haste.

His concentration shattered; his walls fell and the awaiting fog swarmed over him with a vengeance. The light was lost.

Salus ripped his eyes open, sweating, panting, while terror lay just beneath his surface like a pack of wolves in the shadows. He was haggard, exhausted, physically and emotionally. He had seen it and it had escaped him.

But to his surprise, he was not resentful of his failure, nor even disappointed. Because he'd seen what he'd needed to. It was there.

Magic lay within him.

A smile spread over his lips as he absorbed that simple, impossible fact, and in his elation he didn't notice Denek looking back at him in relief and satisfaction, nor the contrasting fact that his eyes expressed little pleasure for his near triumph.

Chapter 37

No one really knew for certain if they had risen at dawn or at some obscure hour in the middle of the night. It was still dark, and aside from their campfire, which still felt wrong in the desert, the only light came from the thin sliver of the dusty, orange moon and its company of stars. If the sun *had* begun its western ascent, the evidence was concealed by the distant yet still imposing mountains behind them.

In fact, their uncertainty of the time was so frustrating that, when their attention wasn't snatched by the shadows of small, barely-seen creatures going about their night time forage, it was the topic of choice over breakfast. But that meagre meal did little to encourage them into wakefulness, either, consisting of only a tough piece of bread and some kind of soft, white cheese the tribal girl had brought along. None were too sure of that, either, but though they ate it dubiously, at least they were confident that it wasn't of human origin. But just as Eyila shared no hint as to its source, neither was she contributing to the discussion. She merely sat and listened to the debate with a small and knowing smile of amusement.

They wasted little time once they'd finished eating. There was nowhere to bathe, no animals to see to and no routes that needed planning, so they tidied away their camp, slung everything over their shoulders with quiet grumbles and headed out behind Eyila's lead.

Anthis watched her as they began their trudge through the sand, his expression the same conflicting mixture of caution, open curiosity and unwavering unease he'd worn since they'd found her. This time, however, his attention was pointedly fixed upon the sash of leaves, phials and pouches she'd draped over her scarcely clad torso.

"What do you suppose she wears that for?" He wondered aloud as he walked alongside Petra, who was still rubbing the sleep from her eyes.

"Because it gets hot out here, I'd think..."

"What--no, not...not *that*," he pulled his eyes back to the sash. "All the...foliage."

"Maybe she thinks it's pretty. There's not much out here that's green..." She pursed her lips in thought. "It makes me kind of happy to look at, if I'm honest."

"I suppose..."

"You could always just go and ask her yourself, you know, she doesn't bite."

"I know," he replied defensively, "I just...don't think it's my place to go nosing around into another culture."

Petra blinked at him.

"Why do you carry all those plants?"

Anthis stumbled, his eyes widening in panic as the little voice chirped loudly up ahead of them. Aria had skipped up beside the white-haired girl, though her hand was still firmly entrenched in her father's, and she peered up at her with interest plain in her sparkling eyes, so certain that she was being both helpful and discreet.

Eyila glanced back towards Anthis, prompting his cheeks to burn, before smiling warmly down at the little girl. "They're my ingredients," she replied loudly enough for both to hear. "I use them to make medicines and salves."

Aria pursed her heart-shaped lips. "Whyyy?"

"Because I need them to heal people," she chuckled.

"But my daddy doesn't carry anything like that."

Her eyes flashed in astonishment as she spun towards the mage. "Your father is a *healer?*"

"N-no," he stammered, startled by her enthusiasm, "but I know my way around a bandage..."

Her eyes shifted beyond him towards Garon's sling and her surprise promptly faded, while Rathen similarly noted again her lack of wounds and wondered what kind of salve, if any, could heal cuts so quickly and absolutely. His eyes narrowed the slightest in suspicion, but he kept his thoughts to himself.

"Of course," she chuckled self-deprecatingly, realising her mistake, then turned back to their heading as Aria moved back beside her father, still eyeing the verdant braid in enchantment.

But a sudden curse grunted from the back of the group startled them to a halt, and they spun just in time to see Garon's knee heavily strike the sand, and the bag and jug he'd been carrying land beside him with a muffled thump.

The inquisitor growled in frustration as he steadied himself on his hands, his face darkened by a scowl of self-reproach under the absently tired gazes of the others, and he immediately moved to push himself back to his feet.

"Let me help," Petra said, suddenly beside him, but as she took a firm yet careful hold of his free arm, he quickly shook her off.

"I'm fine."

She frowned doubtfully at his waspishness but took a step back anyway, leaving him to rise the rest of the way against the shifting of the sand on his own. Truthfully, she'd expected such a reaction. Even had he needed it, she knew he wasn't about to accept help.

"The water," Anthis warned, and through the darkness they noticed the deeper shadow creeping over the ground as the already sparse water leaked from the conjured jug and into the thirsty sand. Petra immediately shoved the stopper back into its place with the heel of her foot while Garon loosed another rueful curse.

Rathen didn't look at the inquisitor, despite the fact that the fire burning in his eyes was certainly directed towards him. "How much was lost?"

"Not much," Petra replied, lifting it back up and ignoring the curt manner in which Garon reclaimed it. "It didn't break, the cork just came loose."

Eyila, however, didn't seem to share in their concern. "I respect your vigilance," she said as courteously as she could, "but you really don't need to carry all of that with you..."

"We're in a *desert...*"

But Eyila only smiled, and once Garon had slung his burden back over one shoulder, she turned and continued to lead them along their featureless path, the brooding inquisitor remaining at the rear and continuing to struggle in silence.

Not a word passed them as they trudged along through the sand, each taking their own time to wake and settle into the hourless day, but once they'd collected as many of their bearings as they could, that silence began to press, and Rathen soon found himself breathing as tightly and quietly as he could to avoid shattering it.

"Your people," he said at last to Eyila, the words all but bursting from him as he decided to chase the imposing atmosphere away and voice at least one of the thoughts that had been swirling through his mind, "they don't seem to fear you for your magic."

She cast him a bemused look. "Of course not. Why ever would they?"

"Well, because it makes you...different..."

"And that is a crime?"

His eyebrow twitched in jealousy. "It seems to be."

A small chuckle slipped past her lips as they curved into a pitying smile, then her gaze swept out across the sands as the sun finally climbed over the distant mountain peaks and cast its rich, golden rays over the landscape, turning the desert still in its wake. "Magic can be used for awful things," she mused, "but it can be used for good things, too." She looked back to him with surprising wisdom in her young eyes, but whatever romance had been hinted in her voice was nowhere to be seen within them. Instead they bore a hardness, one grown from an unwelcome reality that Rathen found himself strangely unable to appreciate. "Very few of my people possess magic. One in every six generations may be born with it, and as our villages are so small, it's considered a...gift that we should cultivate and master."

Rathen didn't miss how unconvinced she sounded of that last detail. "But you don't."

Her head snapped towards him. "I never said that."

"No," he replied politely, urging away the confused frown that tried to pull at his brow, "you didn't. I apologise."

Slowly, she turned away again. "I use my magic to serve my people. They don't resent me or my abilities, and neither have they any other."

"Do many other tribes have mages, then?" Petra asked, walking closer.

"Like I said, we are rare in such small communities, but most tribes do have one mage. If a village is without, a village fortunate enough to have two may trade one to the other regardless of their fealty."

"Wait, they *sell* you?" Anthis couldn't help chiming in from further back.

"Not 'sell' as you cityfolk know it," she replied wearily, as though she had expected such a conclusion but was still disappointed to see it arise. "We are not possessions, but we *are* valuable. The exchange is always suitable."

"So does that mean you're...?"

"No. The Ikaheka are my own people, as was Liaha, the mage who came before me and was my teacher."

"And what happened to her? Was she traded?"

"No." Her young lips pulled downwards. "She died six moons ago. She's on the Winds now..."

As her gaze shifted mournfully beyond the horizon, all eyes fell disapprovingly onto Anthis who clearly regretted asking the question. No one pushed the subject further. Suffice it to say that she was her tribe's only mage and that she was respected rather than feared. Whatever lay beyond that, though it stoked Rathen's curiosity, was none of their business.

But Aria was disinclined to leave her be, and he couldn't tell if it was because she sought to shake away her sadness or if it was because of her own fascination. She spent much of her time staring at the young woman, considering her clothes, her hair, her skin, her paint, as well as the curiosities she carried. She'd already began emulating Petra, carrying a 'sword' at her side which was a branch she had honed into a frighteningly sharp edge, and he wondered how long it would be before she started *intentionally* smearing mud onto her face.

But he saw little true harm in it - as long as she didn't grow up to be a duelist or decide to live in harsh desert lands and turn to cannibalism.

"Why are you with us?" She asked quite bluntly, though her voice was musical with interest.

Eyila turned another warm smile towards the little girl, a fond expression that Rathen had seen countless times on the faces of the others. "Because I want to fix the shrine. *All* of my people do, we just don't have the means - but we believe that *you* might, and I'm the best person to provide you with guidance while protecting the interests of my people."

Aria blinked. "We don't want to hurt your people's interests..."

"She means she's going to make sure we don't damage the ruins," Rathen whispered.

Aria nodded as her eyes widened in understanding, but another frown soon touched her young face. "We aren't going to break the ruin - but actually, a lot of broken places I've been to are really pretty." She cocked her head. "Is this place pretty?"

Eyila smiled wistfully back into the distance. "It was beautiful."

The desert was soon awash in morning light, but spirits remained low. The illumination only accentuated the idea that they'd covered no distance at all, and the heat that came with it was surely impossible. Spring may have been early that year, but it couldn't be beyond mid-morning and yet the warmth was more suited to a late afternoon in the depths of summer. The path across the edge of Turunda that carried them towards the tribe had been protected by the air that swept down from the snowcapped peaks, but that previous afternoon they had turned away from the sands' borders to head north-east, directly towards the burning centre, and no one could truly believe that ten or twelve hours of travel could have carried them into so hostile a land. Thirst and flinty tempers gripped them, but the water remained on ration despite Eyila's assurances and the sand they trekked over shifted relentlessly beneath their feet, making the going even tougher.

And each of them knew it was only going to get worse as the days dragged on.

"What I wouldn't give for a wind," Anthis muttered grimly to himself as he drew his near-empty waterskin from his hip. "A breeze, a lick, even just a *whisper*..."

"Are you *sure* this heat isn't magic-related?" Petra asked Rathen once again, but he only nodded the same tired response.

Frustrations mounted further when Eyila shortly drew them to a stop.

"What are we doing?" Garon growled as Eyila shrugged off her pack. He seemed not to have even tried to fight back the bite in his voice.

"It will be midday before long," she informed them. "We should stop and rest now through the heat, and then continue when the sun begins to set."

"That seems like a serious waste of time."

But Rathen and Aria had already followed her lead, and Petra behind them. Garon's jaw tightened in irritation, but he didn't argue. He was actually silently grateful to finally loosen his shoulder. His left was still swollen and sore and its movement was heavily limited, but now his right was stiff and aching from carrying the full weight of his share of the supplies - though that had at least lessened in light of his injury.

So, with a firm glower of disapproval, he lowered his burden as the others set up tents for shade and Aria scuttled about with food for the first bite they'd had in hours, after which they all fled for what little protection they had from the assaulting sun.

"You should all try to sleep," Eyila advised, settling down on a woven blanket herself, but she received only startled stares.

"But it's *daytime*," Aria reminded her.

"I know, but we only had five hours of sleep."

"This is how it's going to be, is it?" Rathen asked aridly as he ushered Aria to her bedroll despite her protests and attempts to wriggle out from under his grip. "Six hours on, six hours off?"

"You'll get used to it."

Petra followed Garon as he strode away from their apparent camp, though she could tell he was feigning the energy in his purposeful steps, and he began to pitch his own tent away from the others', as had become the norm.

"You must be as hot and tired as the rest of us," she said quietly as she stopped beside him, "why don't you rest this time around?"

He didn't look up at her. "And then who will watch for harpies and marauding tribals?" He asked flatly.

"I will."

"No." He made a short, sharp gesture back to where her own canvasses had been raised. "Just go away."

Her eyes narrowed, but she turned and did as he'd asked. She was growing quite tired of his temper, but the further shortening of his patience and no doubt her own could easily have been down to the heat, and that equally put her in no mood to argue with him. Stubborn though he may be, if sleep was going to find him, he wouldn't be able to fight it off forever - and at the rate he seemed to avoid it, it would certainly impose itself soon. That would just have to do.

As Petra passed and disappeared into her tent, Eyila peered out from her own to the lonely pitch beyond, frowning thoughtfully at the foolishly black-clad man who sat in front of it, staring out across the sands they had just traversed.

Though she barely knew him, she doubted very much that he would welcome her consideration, but as it was the grim-faced mage who seemed to lead the group, she equally doubted that her efforts would alarm anyone.

She cocked her head. That probably wasn't *entirely* true, but it was clear at least that they welcomed magic more than other cityfolk did. Of course, whether they would welcome her help or not didn't really matter at all. Given the land that lay ahead of them, she would have no choice but to step in at some point, and it would be far better for all of them if it was sooner rather than later...

She turned her eyes down to the shadow her tent cast and nodded to herself, then slipped back inside and tied the doorway shut.

The hours dragged by, and though they'd all genuinely given their best efforts to try to fall asleep, few managed more than a handful of scattered and sweat-drenched bouts. But they all stayed put, knowing it was surely hotter outside than it was within, and tried to go about their own studies and research in the mean time. But once again, the heat made that nigh impossible.

It was only Garon who had managed a stretch longer than half an hour despite sitting slumped against his tent's support, and when he opened his eyes, roused by a tingling sensation in his shoulder, the first he noticed was a red-haired female standing several feet ahead of him, looking vigilantly out over the bright, golden sands.

It took him a long moment as he stared at her to get his thoughts in order, and as the fog of sleep began to clear and purpose returned to his mind, he muttered a sudden curse at his slip of concentration and moved to push himself frantically back to his feet and shoo Petra away.

"Stay there."

The firm yet lilting voice beside his ear startled him before he could even shift his weight. His head snapped to the left where Eyila knelt beside him, her hands hovering over his injured and prickling shoulder, and Rathen stood peering over hers, his face twisted in both interest and confusion - a detail which only startled him further.

Garon tore himself away from her certain but intangible grip and jumped to his feet, his eyes wide in feverish if lethargic panic as he clutched and shielded his arm. "What are you doing?!"

She sighed tediously and followed him up. "Healing you." But, rather than wait for any questions, she simply turned and walked away, and the manner Rathen's intrigued eyes followed her suggested that he couldn't answer them in her place.

His gaze then shifted onto Garon as he tentatively rolled his shoulder with a bewildered look on his face, his thoughts clearly moving faster than he could keep up with, and though Rathen opened his mouth to speak, he quickly changed his mind. The mage turned and walked away, redirecting his ponderings onto what he had just witnessed.

"Thank you."

Eyila looked around as Petra hurried up beside her, and though she found the same lack of comprehension in her eyes as she had in Rathen's, there was also more than a touch of gratitude. She smiled to herself, but didn't voice her assumptions as she glanced back towards the inquisitor. "You're welcome," she replied instead.

"If you don't mind me asking...why didn't you do that sooner?"

"Because you trusted me as little as I trusted you," she replied bluntly, "so why would I risk healing someone who could attack me or my people? And would my help have even been welcome?"

Petra bobbed her head in concedence. "Fair enough - so does this mean that that's changed?"

She pursed her dark lips. "I don't know - but other circumstances *have*. Even a mild injury out here puts too much strain on the body and he was already slowing us down. Not to mention that it's inhumane to withhold help if it can be provided, and as a healer, it's my *job* to help people where I can."

"Well, thank you."

"You've said that," she grinned. They stepped back into the camp where Anthis and Aria were sat, peering into books, but Eyila missed the young man's ever-curious eyes flick away as hers passed over him. "It's time to move," she announced, making for her own tent which she began to disassemble. "Pack up and we'll set out. We'll stop again in six hours. It'll be cooler and darker then - you should find it easier to sleep."

"Thank goodness," Aria sighed dramatically, "because that was just *impossible*. I was sweating so much I kept waking up thinking I was in the *bath!*"

Anthis chuckled as he rose to see to his own.

Rathen shortly joined them and helped Aria with the task, despite her insistence that she could do it herself, but regardless of her comical struggles, he was unable to shed the crease of puzzlement from his brow.

"Rathen," Petra whispered, sidling up to him a moment later with a similar if slightly more astounded expression, "did you know she could do that?"

"No, of course not. I didn't think *anyone* could do that - except Kienza." His pensive frown deepened. "But Eyila wove signs...I've never seen them before, but given the separation between us and them, I suppose that's not surprising..."

"Well, *however* she did it, after everything we've been through lately, *I* certainly welcome such a skill."

"The village healer...if *all* their mages can do that, it's no wonder they're respected..."

Petra considered him. "You're suspicious."

His eyebrows rose. "Not at all. I'm just curious. The elves could heal, it's said, but no mage I've ever heard of has been able to do it..." his gaze shifted back towards the tribal as he began rolling up the canvas, and the creases swiftly returned to his brow. "I just wonder how this skill came to *them*..."

The afternoon was spent struggling through the grainy ocean, lumbering beneath the vast, cloudless sky with no mark of progress and nothing to break the horizon but distant dunes rising like sea swells and the shimmer of heat to complete the illusion. But none were fooled - not even Aria, despite her ongoing awe at the sight of such colossal emptiness, though her reluctance to suggest that it *could* be real was almost certainly brought about by the fact that no one else acknowledged it at all.

Anthis escaped the doldrums by burying himself in his work, and while Rathen dearly wished he could have done the same, he knew he wouldn't manage without tripping. He couldn't fathom how Anthis could juggle several loose papers and a notebook while managing to write and walk all at the same time, and the group were subjected to his little grunts of thought and indecision until the light finally began to fade.

But, once again, they didn't stop to rest until night had well and truly set in, and though the temperature had taken another surprising turn, the afternoon's heat had exhausted them all and eradicated any desire for social interaction. Each kept firmly to themselves.

Except Garon, who watched Eyila surreptitiously while she meditated nearby, absently yet tentatively rolling his shoulder in its socket. He grunted quietly as he narrowed his eyes across at her, his tent finally standing straight.

He was grateful for her help, though he begrudged admitting it even to himself, and he couldn't deny that her abilities were remarkable. He would have doubted it was even possible had he not seen Rathen's curious lady friend achieve the same thing, and despite this girl's boorish culture, he also couldn't deny that it would be useful where they were heading. After all, little had gone smoothly for them so far...

His pondering frown hardened in irritation. Of course none of that changed the fact that they'd picked up yet *another* unwanted tag-along. Cultural respect or not, hers was not company they needed or wanted. What could she offer them but misinformed ideas warped by her feeble culture? She would be nothing more than a distraction, an oddity to drag both Anthis and Rathen's attention.

He would have to watch them, and if the need arose, step in to refocus their tasks. The potential threat to Turunda was too great to let a young, scantily-clad misfit lead its only hope astray, and they had to remember that.

His eyes fell then upon Petra, drawn by the moonlight dancing over her blade as she practised some kind of shadow play a safe distance from the camp, perhaps to maintain her agility, or perhaps just to loosen her tensions.

She, at least, had proven useful. He doubted he could have stopped Rathen's rampage if not for her, and she could certainly protect herself. She wasn't hapless luggage - though she was relentlessly intrusive. First it was just nosy questions about his work, but now she imposed herself into his space. It had come as no surprise at all that she had been the one to take up his watch when he'd fallen asleep.

But at least someone...

At least someone was keeping watch.

He watched her blade catch the light of the stars and the sliver of the moon as she made her quick strikes at the unseen opponent, her long red hair sweeping out around her as she turned in a tidy, well-balanced pirouette, and the sand kicked up about her feet as she pivoted into a fade. Her movements were fluid and precise, executed with great care but little conscious attention, and were almost silent but for perfectly synchronised breath and the falling of disturbed sand.

Such a high level of swordsmanship had to be taught, studied and practised, but she was so young that at least some of it had to be natural. Given who she was, however, that wasn't entirely surprising. No, she hadn't said anything to lead him to such a conclusion, not even indirectly, but he had pieced it together easily enough.

She spun perfectly again, leading her rotation by blade point, and for a moment her skin seemed silver, glittering as moonlight reflected from her sweat.

Garon pulled his eyes away and turned his back to her, shrugging his wandering thoughts away and replacing them instead with vigilance as he looked firmly back over the dark sands and blackened sky.

And in that moment, as if waiting for his attention to return, the small shape he'd been waiting for fluttered towards him, visible through the night only for its movement and the light shining back from its eyes. He was sure he was imagining it, but that same vigilance encouraged him to extend his hand anyway, and as soon as it was near enough, it alighted on his fingers.

He was not pleased to feel its tangible weight. Dread filled his stomach as he removed the white-ribbon message from its back, but though he suppressed it just as swiftly and unrolled the paper before it could creep back up and stay his hand, he quickly discovered that the sensation had been well-founded - not that anyone would have guessed anything was amiss by his eternally-stoic expression.

He thought initially that he'd been delivered what he'd expected, but as he neared the end of the message, it was the extra and quite unanticipated information which truly froze his heart beat - above all else, that the Order had finally thrown Turunda into chaos.

His mind turned the statement over countless times, wondering to what extent, by what means, to what end and whether Rathen had been right at all when he'd scoffed at the idea of an uprising. The message had been painfully vague in every sense. But though his imagination was spiralling into ever worsening scenarios, he knew there was nothing he could do about it. Turunda and the Order were behind them and his superiors knew that well enough; this was not an order but a warning, as this development would no doubt hinder most of the Hall's activities as well as that of the other authorities. Fortunately, however, his own would be unaffected - at least for the time being. That counted *one* detail in their favour.

As he regained control over his thoughts, his mind quickly filed everything into order and his reeling guts settled, he took up his waterskin and poured a small puddle into his palm to refresh his parched messenger, whose frantic and exhausted heartbeat he could feel against his skin. He wondered for a moment how a creature so small and fragile could have made it so far into the desert by itself, but wings, even ones so small, could travel farther and faster than feet.

He sighed to himself at the new weight he felt upon his shoulders and the sudden and unwelcome increase of urgency to recover the artefact. But the fact that the whole report would have to be shared with the others burdened him with another anxiety, one that grew with the knowledge that he couldn't do so yet. It would do nothing but provide another distraction, and they were laden with enough of those already. He would have to pick his moment.

He hoped this 'Ut'hala' would provide it.

As he sighed deeply once again and looked out over the sand, extending endlessly in all directions, he absently envied the ability to fly.

Garon got very little sleep that night.

Chapter 38

Ridiculous sleeping patterns rendered the passing of days a pointless, phantom occurrence. The sun presumably continued to rise and set at the time and frequency it should have, but without the certainty of its dictation, time spiralled away, stretching the already taut and brittle moods under the confusion.

There was no escape from the sweltering heat, nor from one another, and no such thing as privacy beyond the reaches of their tents - which seemed to get smaller and more claustrophobic with every pitch - or fleeing over the top of the now plentiful and towering dunes. And nothing to redirect or ease their tensions that was not staring across those smothering sands or at the equally consuming pages of old notebooks. Garon had been sour to begin with and yet somehow he'd managed to grow worse. Anthis also snapped from time to time, and though he was clearly growing frustrated with his books, he only dug himself deeper into them, too stubborn to admit defeat over some minor translation, which only frustrated him more. Petra, on the other hand, bit her tongue rather than take her irritation out on the others, but it was clear even through the thick darkness that she channelled it into her swordplay instead, which she'd taken to doing almost every night now. Aria simply grew sulky under the bleak spirits.

And so it was curious that, aside from Eyila, who was surely used to such a setting and its trials, Rathen didn't share in the atmosphere. Instead he walked with little complaint and turned his mind within himself to pick apart the vague but certain sense of yearning that hung in the background. If he was to describe it, he would call it a very, very slight discomfort - a niggling...*impulse*. But one he couldn't decipher. Nothing and no one seemed to be connected to it and nothing seemed to have prompted it, and yet it was quite persistent, and stranger still was that, over the past few days, it had put him into a quiet and pondering mood rather than any kind of distressed. In the end, the only conclusion he could draw was that it was a result of the familiar and forested dreams of somewhere that felt like home. He'd had them each of the last three nights and they seemed to have eased his journey. Their images remained fresh in his mind far longer than usual, providing him with a welcome change of scenery whenever he closed his eyes, even if there truly were no dense trees to break the brutal stare of the sun.

But as pleasant as it almost was, it was doing nothing to help his concentration. He couldn't escape the pressure of his task but new ideas still evaded him, so the sooner they reached the ruin and he could attempt to affect its magic, the better. Just like everyone else, he was hoping this 'severely affected' site would provide them with some kind of breakthrough, and he didn't care if it was one that would advance his own task or render it redundant. As long as it was *something*.

"How much further?" Aria grumbled, her sun-freckled face marred by an extensive pout as she dragged her feet and kicked up the sand in an effort to further express her boredom.

Eyila smiled towards her apologetically - somehow she was able to tolerate their setting as well as the mood, and had yet to respond to Aria with anything less than a smile. "We're over half way there," she promised. "Three more days."

"*Three?!*" Aria groaned and her footsteps became even heavier - as did everyone else's.

An hour later, at the top of a particularly large and disagreeable mountain of sand, Aria's footsteps faltered completely. Rathen stopped as she released a short gasp and turned to pick her up from the sands, but he found that she hadn't fallen. He frowned down at her, perplexed as she stood quite still, her legs stationary even in mid-stride. "Little one?" But his confusion as she squinted off into the distance ahead of them turned to concern, and his eyes raced after her gaze as a flicker of panic sent a heat through his stomach.

It took him a long moment to actively notice the small, dark shapes that formed a line along the mid-morning horizon. They were too far away to identify, and though they didn't appear to be human, that did little to ease his mind. He knew what wandered the vast desert.

"What are they?" Anthis asked warily as he and the others stopped beside them, having pulled his nose out from his papers to peer at the distraction and certainly the first thing to see in four days, but his voice was edged in the whisper of irritation that had lately become habit.

"Oryx - what else?" She stopped and took a moment to survey the disparate land, then nodded to herself. "Two and a half days."

"Those are oryx?" Petra asked with some relief. "They look like goats."

"How can you possibly see them from here?"

"Goats don't have five horns."

"And how can you count their horns?!" Rathen shielded his eyes from the sun and squinted even harder.

"You're just old, Daddy!" Aria giggled at his flat look, then grasped his hand and dragged him along as Eyila returned to pace and he grumbled bitterly beneath his breath.

Petra frowned sideways at Anthis as he returned immediately to his work. She couldn't help marvelling at how he could follow the slippery descent all while filtering through loose parchments, some scribbled, some elegantly scrawled, and flick through the leaves of his notebook at the same time without once losing his original page, all while presumably making notes from the myriad of sources, connecting them with thoughts and ideas that would be beyond her and likely everyone else.

"Are you getting anywhere?" She asked curiously at last. "You've been working on that for a week - at least I *think* it's been a week..."

"Hm? Oh, yes. Uh..." he barely dragged his mind away. "Yes and no," he managed eventually. "Mostly it's just things the ditchlings thought were relevant. Pretty much *anything* they found related to magic, so a lot of it is just...rubbish..."

Petra clicked her fingers to regain his attention. "It can't all be rubbish or you wouldn't be spending so much time on it."

"Well it's better than looking at all *this*, isn't it?!" Petra turned him a flat, unimpressed stare and he looked away sheepishly. "Sorry." He didn't sound like he meant it. "I suppose you're right - I *hope* you're right. There *has* to be something useful in here. It's just a matter of sifting through and making sense of it all."

"What *have* you made sense of so far?"

"Not much. It's mostly just a list of frivolous achievements - floating cities, control over weather, reshaping the land and so on - and while it's almost certainly true, I don't see how it helps us."

"All true?" Aria repeated excitedly. "A floating city? *Really?*"

Despite his mood, Anthis couldn't help smiling at her enthusiasm, and he wondered for a moment at just where his own had gone. Of course, when his footing slipped and something sharp beneath his shirt poked into his skin, he was grimly reminded. His smile faded. "Yes," he sighed, "quite possibly, though whatever spell kept the city up has certainly broken down. If there was currently a city floating in the sky, we would know about it."

"That we would." Petra's eyes shifted curiously onto Rathen. "What about you?"

He glanced around at her and smiled humourlessly. "Don't ask."

When they made their routine stop to avoid the midday heat, Petra watched Garon pitch his usual distance. He'd made no attempt to smooth things over during the last week, and neither had anyone but herself made any effort to forgive him, or at the very least to move past it. She supposed she understood on the grounds that they were in no situation that called for an authority figure - had they been in one of Turunda's cities, the matter would have been straightened out immediately. As it was, however, everyone was given far too great an opportunity to brood.

It was about time it was brought to an end, and as no one else was inclined, it seemed that the efforts fell to her.

She turned and headed purposefully towards Rathen as he set up his tent.

"Why are you asking me?" He frowned. "He's the one keeping to himself."

"Because we're not making him feel welcome."

"He's not a child..."

"You know what I mean. We're not exactly making ourselves approachable."

Rathen sighed and thought for a moment as he pulled the canvas tighter despite the unstable foundation of pegs and poles, then he shook his head. "He's not the type," he decided. "He's keeping to himself because he wants to, and if that should change, he'll impose himself upon us whether we want him around or not. But as it stands, he has nothing to contribute right now. It's all on me and Anthis. Frankly I think we're better off without him dictating the lead right now - and," he added mildly, "a little bruising to his pride could do him some good."

She frowned at him doubtfully, but found herself unable to argue.

"Anyway," he turned back to his wobbly tent, "it's hardly up to *me* what the rest of you do. Go make him feel 'welcome' if you're worried about it."

The air stalled around her as she looked hesitantly back towards the inquisitor.

"I'm sure it will be more appreciated coming from you," he added quietly.

Petra finally stepped away, having not heard his remark, and as he glanced around to watch her collect Garon's share of the food and deliver it to him, he immediately felt a pinch of regret. He didn't hear the words, but he didn't really need to. It went as expected: Petra had said something as she handed him the bowl of bread and cheese, but whatever polite greeting she had offered, he'd brushed her off and shooed her away, probably with little more than grunted thanks, if he'd even looked at her.

Rathen shook his head and turned back to his tent as Petra returned to camp, her shoulders slumped and lips pursed in irritation, and pretended he hadn't noticed.

As Eyila had promised, they were all gradually growing used to the unnatural pattern of the day, and midday sleep was becoming easier. That day, however, Aria had no intention of drifting off.

She lay still on her blanket, breathing softly and calmly as though she was in a peaceful sleep while her father lay beside her. She listened carefully to his breath, noting how slow and deep it gradually became, and she paid close attention to his movements, his fidgeting giving way to stillness with the occasional jolt. And once she'd counted to one hundred, or there abouts, and he hadn't moved, she very slowly rose to her hands and knees, untied the tent and crawled outside, careful to keep any shafts of blistering sunlight from falling over him.

Tying it shut behind her, she glanced about and grinned to herself in victory. There was no one outside. They were all shut away in their tents, and rightly so - it may not have been much, but the shade inside did make a difference, even if sleep was impossible.

Keeping as quiet as she could, Aria shuffled through the hot sand towards one tent in particular, though more specifically to the bags dumped outside of it. The jug full of delicious water was hidden in the tent's shadow, kept as cool as it could be, and what additional supplies he'd been lumbered with set beside it. But these were not what she was interested in. She crawled instead towards the worn leather satchel which was always slung over Anthis's shoulder, fit to burst with all kinds of exciting books and scrolls, all of which she knew were filled with pictures and stories of the fabled elves. Though her lips were dry and her stomach lurched eagerly at the thought of water, her attention was riveted upon the bag.

She paused as she reached it, straining to listen carefully into the tent, but she heard nothing but soft, restful breathing.

She grinned again and turned immediately towards the satchel. The countless old buckles keeping its contents from spilling out posed little hindrance for her quick fingers, and she was inside in a moment, pulling out papers and leather books in a bleak rainbow of dark colours. She stopped and glanced over each, but it was quickly apparent that none were what she sought, so she dumped them on the ground and continued her urgent rummage.

A shadow fell over her.

She gasped sharply and spun around on her knees, expecting to find either her father or Anthis looking down at her in anger.

But instead it was Petra who frowned down at her, her arms folded across her chest and her eyebrow cocked disapprovingly.

Aria hung her head in shame. "Damn."

"What are you doing, Aria? You should be asleep."

"It's *impossible* in this heat," she grumbled. "And I wanted to see the Arkhamas' notes and read about the floating city, but it's not here." She looked back up at her pleadingly. "I know it was wrong, but *please, please* don't tell anyone."

Petra breathed a laugh of pity and crouched down beside her. "I won't," she promised with a smile. "But we've better get this tidied up before anyone notices."

Aria nodded vigorously and set to gathering up her mess, and though Petra was certain as she tucked it all away that there was a system to the chaos of Anthis's bags, she doubted she could work it out. He would know someone had been in there.

But that concern was pushed aside when she took the next handful of loose pages and recognised the portraits printed upon them.

"Uh oh," Aria gasped, and in that same instant the tent beside them flung open and Anthis came blustering outside, his eyes wide in a panic which swelled when he saw the papers in Petra's hands.

"Anthis," she began as he froze, looking up inquisitively as she turned the parchments towards him, and while Aria's freckled cheeks had turned red with guilt, Anthis's had drained of colour, "why do you have bounty posters in your bag?"

"Bounty posters? You mean 'wanted' posters? Of criminals?" Aria looked to him with more curiosity than Petra, who instead now regarded him with confusion.

"Because," he replied quickly, though his eyes were still wide, "I like to know who to steer clear of. I mean, I find all kinds of relics in ruins, and if I'm approached by a collector, I'd like to know if he's a conman as soon as possible."

Her puzzlement deepened as she began to look through them. "But this one is a *murderer*."

"Also a very good detail to know."

"*Arenaria!*"

The girl froze at the sound of her father's furious voice.

"Arenaria, *what* are you doing out here?"

She turned and smiled up at him sheepishly, tucking her hands behind her back and looking as strikingly innocent as she could.

"No," he said impatiently as she opened her mouth to make an excuse or present a distraction, but as he stopped and towered over her, he noticed Anthis's panicked expression, then Petra's suspicion, and his own disapproval gave way to equal puzzlement. "What's going on?"

Petra showed him the posters. "It appears our dear renowned historian here is also a bounty hunter."

"What?!" Anthis scoffed a little too readily. "*Nonsense!* I was just telling Petra that I like to know who to avoid in case--"

"Not *one* of these bounties are for conmen!"

"Is no one trying to sleep?" Eyila asked as she joined them, and even Garon began an approach, though he stopped a short distance away.

"Why would he have bounty posters?" Rathen asked, turning the same uncertain suspicion onto him as she had.

"What's a bounty hunter?" Eyila asked.

"Someone who hunts down criminals and brings them in for a promised reward. Dead or alive, unless specified." Rathen raised an eyebrow. "Which I notice none of these are." He looked back to the young man. "Anthis, what do you do with these?"

All eyes upon him were expectant and dubious, and, he noticed, Aria in particular seemed afraid of his answer. He breathed a laugh and smiled nervously. "I already told you."

"Don't take us for fools, Anthis," Petra growled. "We have more respect for you than that, so show us the same in return. *Do* you collect on these bounties?"

He looked again from one face to the next, then hung his head in defeat. 'Bounty hunter' was far from the worst conclusion they could draw. "Yes."

"Why?" Rathen asked.

"And *how?!*" Petra added incredulously.

He looked at her unappreciatively. "I'm not as useless with a blade as you all seem to think."

"Perhaps you're better at wielding it than carrying it," Rathen remarked drily. "But why *do* it?" He shook his head, but Anthis had the impression that his disapproval stemmed more from concern than the idea that he was a fool. Something about that made him uncomfortable. "Voluntarily going up against people like this is *dangerous*. That's *why* there are bounties! Because the guard can't handle it and the Hall is too busy! Why would you take that on *yourself?*"

"Because I have to pay for my work *somehow*," he snarled indignantly, standing taller in a suddenly flaming defence. "The lodging, the supplies - I only get paid for my work upon stage completion, and if I've got a bad lead, that can take a *very* long time. What am I meant to do in the mean time?"

"But you're rich!" Aria declared, and her young face was so twisted in disappointment that Anthis felt another abrupt surge of guilt. "We've seen your house! And you don't even live in it!"

"You're going to get yourself *killed* by doing this, Anthis."

"Rathen's right - I've seen most of these bounties, some are *years* old--"

"*I don't need your concern!*"

The desert fell silent.

His jaw tightened, and though he lowered his voice, its sharpened edge remained. "I have been doing this for *eight years*, and I'm still here. I know what I'm doing, and what's more is that I *need* to do it, so I don't need *any* of you to tell me I'm going to get killed! I *know* the risks - I don't pick up every poster I see then choose a target, any target, and charge in blade-first!" He looked from one concerned and doubtful face to the next, then sighed in increasing fault. "I'm sorry," he said with a softer growl, and looked especially at Aria who appeared slightly heart-broken. "I *do* appreciate your concern, but I honestly don't need it. Though I suppose Stonton hasn't helped my position..."

"It has not," Petra replied firmly. "You're clumsy, and I've been tempted countless times to take that knife away from you."

"Then why haven't you?"

She looked at him levelly. "I suppose I'd like to think that you wouldn't carry it if you didn't actually know how to wield it."

"Well, I do," he assured her, "but magical wind can do funny things to people."

"Stab them in the stomach, you mean?"

"Exactly."

Noticing he'd fallen quiet, Petra and Anthis looked expectantly towards Rathen, but instead of staring back with his usual and strangely paternal disapproval, they found both he and Eyila looking warily beyond the camp and towards the top of a nearby dune instead. Following their gaze, they watched as a dark form stumbled along its crest. Garon, too, had noticed it and even drawn his blade, though he hadn't moved to approach it.

"What is that?" Petra asked, shielding her eyes from the light. "A *person?*"

Eyila suddenly darted forwards.

"Wait," Rathen called after her, "can't you feel--"

"Of *course* I can feel it," she snapped back, "and something's wrong!" She was racing along the foot of the dune when the solitary wanderer toppled from its edge and tumbled down its slope, carried faster by the avalanche of sand his disturbance had caused. He had no hope at all of regaining his footing.

Rathen cursed and hurried along behind her, and the others quickly followed.

"What is she doing?" Garon growled, suddenly alongside him, but the mage's concern stilled his response. The Inquisitor soon cursed just as Rathen had when he made out the stranger's attire, and though his footsteps faltered for a moment, some new urgency imposed itself and propelled him forwards.

Eyila swept to a stop beside the collapsed figure and they could hear her frantically asking him if he was all right, but though he said something in response, his voice was too quiet, the man too weak for them to catch it. Despite exhaustion, he continued to drag himself along through the sand.

"Get away from him!" Garon bellowed, but the tribal girl paid him no attention and tore her shoulder free when he tried to pull her back. Rathen similarly ignored him, but he at least slowed to approach the final few steps with caution.

"He's a mage," Petra warned, seeing his inappropriate black cloak, and the stories from the wandering traders-who-weren't rose unbidden in each of their minds while Eyila continued to ask him questions.

Something unsettling cast a shadow in Rathen's mind.

He turned and grasped Aria's shoulders as she arrived, her eyes wide in curiosity as she tried to peer around him, but he turned her about and looked gravely to the duelist. "Take her," he said softly, "over there, just in case."

Aria looked up and pursed her lips to protest.

"No 'but's," he told his daughter just as she formed the word, and ushered her towards Petra who took her hand and lead her back a safe distance.

His attention returned to the mage, whom Eyila was managing to restrain. "What's she saying?"

She shook her head in confusion. "'Where is it?'" She turned her troubled eyes up towards him and found him looking back with the same unspoken concern, though neither of them were sure where those concerns lead.

Anthis looked critically at the woman - for it appeared she was - and saw her white, dry lips, gaunt cheeks and wild eyes. "She's dehydrated," he surmised. "And quite probably hallucinating." He took out his waterskin and handed it to the tribal. She duly unstoppered it and gently poured its meagre contents into the mage's mouth, but she was shaking her head all the while. He looked between the two doubtful casters. "What is it?" He frowned. "What can you two sense?"

"This isn't dehydration," Rathen replied as the mage cried out in exasperation and shook Eyila off, spitting the water back out, and he stepped forwards to restrain her himself. "Not exclusively, anyway."

"Is it magic?" The young man's heart jumped as a thought landed as heavily upon him as a two tonne boulder. "It's magic, isn't it?" His face drained. "She's losing control - we need to get *away* from her!"

"No," Rathen growled, "we can--"

"*Where is it?!*" The frail young woman, worn down and aged by the desert, mustered the energy from nowhere to throw off even Rathen's grip and stagger to her feet. "*Tell me where it is!*"

Garon readied his sword while the others took a wary step back. "Put that down," Rathen snapped, then turned back to the frantic mage, raising his hands and splaying his fingers to show the absence of weapon or spell. "Calm down," he said slowly, "and tell us what you're looking for."

"It's out here," she replied shakily, "I can feel it, I *know* it's here - I'm getting closer all the time, closer and closer and closer...and..."

"To what?" Eyila asked just as carefully.

"But I keep *losing it!*" She spun around, her severely sun-burned face twisting in sudden desperation, and her eyes when they grazed them were distant. She was looking for nothing tangible. And that only sharpened the dread building in Rathen's gut. "Where is it? Where *is it?!*" She spun again before stumbling in a random direction, certainly not the one she'd been heading in but one she seemed compelled beyond any reasoning to follow. She pushed Rathen off as he reached out for her again.

"Enough!" Eyila cried, and with far rougher handling, she threw the woman back down to the sands, doing away with concern for her frailty.

"Get back, Eyila!"

"Garon, put that damned sword down!" Rathen hissed. He did his best not to upset the mage any further, who now sat crying hysterically though she seemed physically incapable of producing tears, but the inquisitor's sudden aggression towards her inexplicably insulted him.

"She is dangerous," he replied coldly. "And I think you *both* know that better than I do."

Rathen knotted his jaw, unable to argue though he certainly wanted to, but as he opened his mouth to explain that he was not helping the situation, something dark and urgent jolted through his mind, snatching his attention away. "Get back!" He cried instead, even as he shoved Garon and Anthis away while Eyila had already reacted, and little bursts of light began popping in the air.

The crying-cackling mage leapt once again to her feet. The sparks were focused around her.

Garon immediately prepared to jump back ahead of them with his sword in hand, and even Anthis reached for his sheathed knife in his panic, but Rathen and Eyila only stared and watched, paralysed in shock.

The woman's mad eyes were blind to the world around her. Whatever she saw, only she could say, and again something ensnared her attention and compelled her to chase it. No one called her to stop, even as she stumbled chaotically through the sand, threatening to break or twist her ankles, and lights continued to flash and crackle around her. Her laughter grew louder and more desperate the further she fled, unwavering even as she tripped and crawled a few paces before pushing herself clumsily back to her feet to continue, unfazed.

Anthis gasped as fire flared around her, but still neither mage tried to stop her, and neither could they pull their eyes away nor slow their rampant heart beats.

She scrambled up a dune, battling against the cascading sand to make her way to the top. But she didn't reach the peak.

In that final moment, Rathen and Eyila found the strength and compulsion to look away, while the rest bore witness to the violent eruption of fire, lightning and something indescribable which muffled a deadly scream of relief.

Then the desert fell silent once again.

Garon, Anthis and Petra, who had remained behind and shielded Aria from the sight, found themselves unable to do anything but stare wide-eyed in disturbed disbelief through the blinding strength of the flash. Rathen stared at a spot on the ground instead, and Eyila did much the same, though she shook and hiccuped in the meantime as tears of shock streamed down her bronze cheeks.

They were still and silent for what felt like an age before Aria's tentative voice rose from behind them all, though she made no attempt to peer around Petra's hand.

"I don't know what happened," her father replied, but it took him another long moment to finally turn his head back towards the crest of the dune to gain some kind of answer for himself.

His blood froze in an instant, and a heat of nausea to rival that of the desert weighed like lead in his stomach.

The dune in question had been shorn in two, and a dark form rested in its scar, half-covered in sand.

He swallowed hard and forced his feet to move despite his gut screaming for him to turn around and walk away. He didn't want to know what had happened, and he certainly didn't want to see the result. But at the same time, he *needed* to. This was something, he feared, he needed to understand.

He paused beside Eyila and gently squeezed her bare shoulder, and as she dragged her heavy gaze from the ground to look up at him, he saw that same sentiment. He continued on, and with a deep breath, she turned and followed.

The body was smouldering as he approached, charred and blackened by the spontaneous explosion, but the longer he looked at it, searching for details despite his better judgement, he noticed that it and the surrounding sand wasn't just black, but a sickeningly deep red. His stomach turned as he realised just what he was looking at, and he balled up his fists to stop his hands from shaking.

Eyila made not a sound as she stopped beside him and observed the same thing, and he had to commend her strength. All the more so when she knelt down beside the corpse and looked even closer than he.

Anthis, however, released a short string of curses when he and Garon arrived behind her, the latter still tightly gripping his sword, and all three of them tightened up and cringed as Eyila reached towards a charred arm and gently spread the skin with her thumb and forefinger. She nodded to herself. "The veins," she began quietly, having regained regular breathing though a few tears still fell, "they've ruptured."

"The veins?" Garon frowned, daring to look a little closer.

"And the arteries. And when her skin burned, it weakened and split." She moved over and clinically pressed her finger tips across the chest before stopping and nodding again. "The heart, too. There's a greater concentration of blood over it."

"What does that mean?" Anthis asked impatiently, but as he glanced towards Rathen, he found that his usually grim countenance had drained of all colour.

Anthis similarly paled. "Is this what happened to the others? The ones you said lost control?"

Words evaded him, but he managed to shake his head in uncertainty.

Rathen was terrified. He had felt something within the mage, an instability, a tremor in her magic. It was minor, something any other mage would have been hard pushed to notice, but his isolation from other casters had apparently made him more sensitive to such details - he had felt every change in Eyila's magic since she'd joined them and knew when she was preparing to cast a spell even before she formed the signs. And so this woman's trouble had stuck out like a sore thumb even before he'd laid eyes on her. Her magic had jumped and spiked chaotically, but not once had she cast a spell. Not even at the end. And he doubted she could have had she wanted to.

His eyes dragged towards Eyila, who he suspected was attuned in the same way. She had noticed the mage in the same moment he had, and she had been aware that something wasn't right. But he doubted she was making as much sense of it as he was, and even then he felt as if he was clutching a handful of straws.

Garon was suddenly in front of him, his dull, grey eyes urgent. "Is this related to the magic?" He asked bluntly, and at that moment, Rathen could think of no other explanation.

He nodded, then amended: "I don't know, not for certain..."

"Are *you* at risk of this?" Anthis asked, and Rathen didn't miss the note of accusation in his voice.

"I don't *know*," he snarled back at him.

"Then we're all at risk in your damned company!"

"That may well be true," Garon agreed carefully, silencing Rathen before he could spit a defence, "but we need him with us." He sheathed his sword and looked between the two of them, noting not for the first time the charge that coursed between them. He sighed and straightened, then looked down to the tribal girl as she rose to her feet. "Do you make anything of it?"

"Something disturbed her magic," she replied with a final deep, steadying breath. "Traders from Ivaea have told us of events like this, but it is well known that Ivaea does not hold its mages highly. We assumed they were just stories driven by hatred - that their mistrust of mages was reaching new heights and they wanted everyone else to agree with them, or that the mages had had enough of being treated so poorly and were fighting back."

"You listen to news outside your tribe?"

She frowned at Anthis in confusion and his eyes shifted nervously away. "Of course we do. Your conflicts affect us. We don't live on our own little island, safe from the actions of others." She looked back to Garon. "But the stories never sat right with me." The body shortly dragged her attention back, and she observed it quietly for a moment. "And you think this is related to what's happening to Ut'hala?"

"It could be," Rathen replied, having equally steadied himself, "but to what end, I don't know..." He turned and looked back towards Petra. She had turned Aria's back to them, and though she was embracing her, she stared over towards them all the while.

Rathen started towards her. "Let's go. We've got three days of ground to cover."

The others slowly followed, though Anthis glanced doubtfully back towards the body left lying in the heat of the desert sun. He watched with interest for a moment as Eyila made a series of quick gestures that didn't appear to be spells, and muttered a few alien words beneath her breath. Then she, too, turned and followed, leaving the body where it was. She seemed to have no qualms about it, and though he wondered then what her people did with their dead in the desert, he kept it to himself.

Rathen thanked Petra and took Aria by the hand, and though both were filled with questions, they didn't voice them, either. They returned to their camp and disassembled it before continuing through the desert under a deeply troubled silence.

Chapter 39

Salus sat on the cold, stone ground, his feet falling into the floor, the crown of his head floating, and his face as relaxed as he could coax it. These preliminary steps were tedious and seemed to cause him more tension than calm, but Denek wouldn't even begin to help him if he didn't play to his ridiculous rituals, so he humoured him and focused instead on the end result.

Though that end result seemed leagues out of his grasp.

He was more rigid than usual that afternoon and felt little hope for any kind of success. For several hours over the past three days he had been in Denek's irritating company, and despite the promising start on that very first attempt, there had since been no progress at all. And that wasn't in his head. Even the mage was expressing exasperation, and that didn't help him attain the peaceful state the mage insisted was necessary in order to reach the lost and tangled place his magic dwelled.

But that state presently felt just as distant.

He wasn't sure whether he was relieved or not when he heard Teagan's voice from the other side of the prison bars, but he answered it eagerly, eliciting a sigh of frustration from his impatient tutor when he rose to his feet, thanked him mildly for his time and left through the clattering door, which was then locked swiftly behind him.

"You're finished?" Teagan asked as Salus indicated for him to walk.

"For now," he sighed. "What is it?" He was handed a report, and growled through barred teeth as he read. "Doana." He almost tore the parchment as he folded it.

"They've moved deeper into Turunda and they've spread out."

"And these two are probably just the *start* of a second assault." Salus's lip curled. "If we'd affected their numbers at all, they wouldn't have acted until reinforcements had arrived."

"Assuming they *know* we've destroyed some of their units..."

His expression worsened. "They know." He handed the parchment back as they left the cellar and started through the short, dark tunnels. "Send two phidipans and a portian to Bridgend. Have them take it back by any means."

"Moore will be dispatching platoons--"

"It will take too long." His brusque tone rang in the rounded acoustics. "Bridgend is wrapped up in magic and we can't risk *any* mages getting to it, Doanan or not, or it could end up shattered like Halen. Never mind what else they might have planned to have targeted the town in the first place."

Teagan studied him through the torchlight as they walked. Salus glanced expectantly, feeling the weight of his eyes. "Moore will still dispatch. Should you not speak with Malson first?"

The keliceran scoffed. "It will take too long," he repeated. "Get it done."

The portian nodded obediently. "And what of Emberton?"

"Leave that to the military."

Now Teagan frowned. "Surely Emberton is a priority? Their smiths arm the military, the Hall, the guards..."

"Yes, and that also means that Moore will consider it a priority, too." Salus folded his arms, straightened and lifted his chin a fraction. Teagan knew that to mean he was done with the subject, but he found it curious that he'd responded as calmly as he had. "What of the Order?"

"They're hiding in their House. There's been no unusual activity reported."

"That means nothing where magic is concerned. Keep watching them."

"Of course."

Salus stopped him as they reached the old wooden door at the end of the passage and looked at him severely. "What of Karth and Koraaz?"

Teagan shook his head. "No change. They're moving steadily deeper into the desert."

Salus barred his teeth. "What are they on to...?" His wandering eyes flicked back to him. "How far behind is Hower?"

"He's been on them for days." He noted Salus's expression loosen the slightest in hope. "He's not uncovered anything of use, but he's keeping them in his sights. But the inquisitor is vigilant."

"Is he aware of Hower?"

"Hower doesn't believe so, he's just being careful. They've left a mess in their wake; caused trouble in a number of places, drawn attention to themselves and even provoked harpies into tracking them. Though they seem to have retreated since they crossed into the desert. That, coupled with passing through tribal land, it makes sense that he'd be watchful."

"Mhm." Salus looked thoughtful. "And the tribal girl is still with them?"

"She is. She seems to be leading them somewhere - a ruin in the desert most likely, but the rest of her tribe would know for certain. One of their own leaving with a group of outsiders would be known to all of them; none would be unaware of the details."

"They wouldn't, would they..." Salus pondered on that for a moment, then shook his head. "If Hower's on their tail, there's no need to approach them. Stick with the original plans."

"Salus."

The use of his name without ten minutes of nagging surprised him, and he noticed in that same moment the very slight crease in his favoured's brow.

"Are you certain about this?"

He almost smiled. "Teagan, if I didn't know any better, I'd say you were having doubts."

"It's just as well you know better, then. I merely wonder if there isn't another way to handle this - one more subtle."

"More subtle, perhaps, but not as effective." He turned away, finished with the matter, and opened the door. The light that poured in from the house foyer was blinding despite the doorway standing out of sight in a dark corner, but even with such seclusion, all within the vicinity were aware of its silent opening, even if none looked towards it.

The two stepped out into the open, but though Teagan paid just as little attention to everyone else, he noticed Salus look about thoughtfully as if searching for someone. "Where is Taliel?" He asked with a little too much nonchalance.

"In Mokhan."

His head snapped around, and something flashed briefly through his eyes. "Mokhan?"

"Was it wrong of me to send her?"

Salus stared at him as his wide eyes revealed a slow train of thought. "No," he said at last. "No, not at all. She's capable, and the mages aren't moving... They wouldn't strike Mokhan again, there would be little purpose to it. And the watch there has been raised. They're too vigilant for that to happen again..."

Teagan studied him again. "What is it?"

"Nothing at all, Teagan, I'm fine," he replied tiresomely, waving his concern away, then started purposefully towards the staircase and, ultimately, his accursed office. "Now come; let's sort out this most latest catastrophe."

The portian frowned after him for his increasing distraction, but his obedience was silent while Salus led the way, and the keliceran quickly lost himself in thought.

That Hower had found them was a relief. Ties had been cut with Drassa following Teagan's advice, and while Anthis had remained their best option all along, he was now their *only* option, even if he was working with the Order. But if they managed to get a hold of his notes, they would finally be on level ground with the infernal mages, and if Hower continued to trail him, they would get ahead before he could report any of his findings back to his employers. And if Salus's own magic insisted on keeping out of his reach, then for the time being he would have to consider this a minor victory instead. That Hower had managed to find them *at all* after they'd apparently disappeared outside of Carenna was a mix of good fortune and skill in itself, and though he loathed luck as an ally, for it could rarely be counted upon, if it decided in its fickle nature to work with him, he would accept its fleeting help. Warily.

Of course, while all this was going on, he had no intention of letting his magic hang just out of his reach like a carrot on a stick. He was no donkey. The magic - *his* magic - was there, and he *would* grasp it. He just had to work out how to break the stick.

He may have been swamped only with frustration and unreachable expectations in that dank, dark place, sitting, floating and falling into the stone, but when he was away from the intolerable man's instruction he found himself simply desperate to get back to it.

Even at that moment his mind was bent fervently in that direction, and he'd been gone for just five minutes and hadn't even reached his office yet.

He understood Teagan's concern over the time he was dedicating to it, especially when the visits yielded no results at all, but he knew with a certainty deep within himself that it was no trick on the mage's part - no spell could feel that real - and he simply *needed* to take a hold of it. He'd been assaulted with seductive thoughts of what he could achieve since the mage had first mentioned it, even though he'd thought it a trick at the time, a means to distract him, and though he knew he was getting ahead of himself as those same thoughts coaxed him even now, he also knew that his magic was the key to Turunda's safety.

He was the key.

If he could just grasp it...

Chapter 40

Grains of sand struck the skin as sharply as tiny blades of steel upon the assaulting wind, hammering with the weight of dry hail five times its size to sting the eyes and choke the throat of anyone it engulfed. Braced arms could only do so much against its smothering onslaught, for it whipped around from the left the moment they protected their right, waiting to slip in with every desperate inhale and the briefest peek of the eye. Smothering, golden clouds of dust billowed overhead in place of thick blue-grey cumulonimbus, and the desert seemed even drier in the sadistic mimicry.

Over the howling of the lacerating gale, Eyila's musical and incredulous voice rose, muffled by her arm whose bare skin already bore a number of shallow cuts. "This is ridiculous!" She yelled, though it was clear her disbelief was aimed just as much at herself as the situation. "We should be waiting this out! Why do you insist on moving through this?!"

"It will take too long!" Garon yelled back through his dusty black sleeve. Rathen's words had rung true sooner than he'd expected, for that afternoon the inquisitor had quite suddenly snatched the reins and demanded in his usual manner that they brave the sandstorm that had surged in from nowhere. He'd been so adamant that Eyila had been given little choice but to lead them through for fear that he might charge in on his own. "We're an hour away from the ruin, you said!"

"Yes - unless we get turned around in this!" It seemed almost a certainty, each weaving around as they walked, trying to escape the assault of the besieging sands.

But though Rathen had little experience under such harsh conditions, he couldn't help the feeling that something wasn't right - and it extended beyond the apparent sentience of each grain as they navigated their way into his mouth, even when he was sure he had it tightly shut. "This isn't natural, is it?" He dared.

"Not entirely." Eyila seemed not to suffer the same problem, and neither was her skin drenched with sweat and covered in clinging sand. "The wind that carries it is, but the heat that caused it isn't."

"This is magic?" Petra managed, but as Rathen tried to respond, he received another mouthful of sand for his trouble. He growled in mounting resentment and finally contorted his fingers while simultaneously shielding his face, and an instant later the flurry ceased its offence. His relief was fleeting, however, as fire gripped his arm, stronger and hotter than it ever had been before, and the spell began to crumble as his stomach lurched in shock.

He grasped at its ends and hastily repaired it as everyone paused and peered warily about themselves, watching the sandstorm continue to rage though it now pummelled the unseen barrier rather than their bodies. But while relief passed over them like a welcome breath of cool breeze, Eyila stared back in horror. "What are you doing?!"

"Would you rather just keep ploughing through it?"

He was surprised to find that her expression suggested she actually might, but as she bit her lip, she made no attempt to step out of its reach and back into the onslaught. She seemed to settle instead for a quick series of gestures and mutterings - somehow he caught 'Aya'u' over the muffled roar of the wind - but she cast no spell.

"You remembered your magic, then," Anthis said drily from behind him, his voice immediately grating. "Couldn't have done that sooner?"

"Careful. With this much gratitude I might get distracted and forget how many the shield is supposed to protect."

"I think 'protection' is something you forgot about a long time ago."

His lip curled venomously, but it twitched into a smile when he heard the foul young man suddenly grunt, cough and splutter.

"Stop it," Garon and Petra commanded even as the shield reconstructed and Anthis was again safe from the sandstorm, but though they both sneered, neither he nor Rathen responded, turning their attention pointedly away from each other once more.

It was an eerie sensation to move through the sandstorm in a bubble, hearing the howl of the wind but feeling neither it nor its burden. It was as if they weren't even there. Petra found it unbearably haunting. "Do these happen often?" She asked in a bid to distract herself, but as Eyila's eyes continued their nervous search of the surrounding cloud, her agitation only intensified.

"Late summer, usually... Two or three a year, but they rarely reach our village..." She looked back to her a moment later, attempting to shake away her bother. "But there have been three out here already in the past month alone." Her gaze was pulled away again. "If we're going to keep moving through this, we should hurry up..."

"At least the sand is blocking out the sun..."

Aria coughed for the eighteenth time and sighed finally in annoyance. "Daddy, I have sand in my mouth."

"We all do, little one, we all do."

They continued untouched for half an hour until the sandstorm ended as abruptly as it had began, spitting them back out into the calm of the baking desert, and it was only as they cast a curious look behind them that they realised just how fast the colossal, thundering wall of sand had been moving. But though Rathen's spell dropped in its unstoppable passing, the disconnection from their surroundings lingered.

But that alien stillness held none of their attention for long. While Rathen frowned to himself at the familiar sensation of disembodied elven magic, the others gawped off into the distance.

"*Clouds!*" Aria cried in disbelief, snapping his eyes towards the incredible sight of three small, slight, puffy wisps floating in the vast and otherwise empty blue sky.

"Clouds?"

Eyila simply smiled. "Ut'hala."

Aria was given no chance to ask her excited questions. Instead her words were loosed as an abrupt and panicked scream, her feet sucked suddenly into the hungry depths of the sand, and though Rathen reached out in an instant to grasp her hand and pull her free, he was already sinking himself.

"What is this?!" Petra cried as she attempted to scramble away, though each shift of her weight only took her deeper. "Quick sand?!"

"No..." Rathen spared a single moment to watch the desert drain away along a near-straight line, running like an hourglass into its own depths, and even in his panic he recognised the strength of the magic behind it. Realisation threw him into horror.

But before he could form any kind of signs to save them, a sudden breeze gathered. It was only just strong enough to tousle hair, and yet it encircled and plucked them all as easily from their fate as if they had been paper dolls.

Rathen twisted around in swelling confusion even before his feet touched the ground a short yet secure distance away, but no one else seemed to have noticed the oddity. But then, of course they wouldn't. They *expected* magic to be their saviour. Only Rathen was aware that their deliverance lacked any such arcane presence.

His eyes flicked towards Eyila, but she seemed only relieved. "What did you do?" He stepped towards her as she stiffened. "That wasn't magic," he declared suspiciously. "What was it?"

She straightened as she turned her head to meet his probing gaze, standing taller and raising her chin almost defiantly. "A prayer."

"A *prayer?*"

"To Aya'u," she clarified tartly. "Fortunately She didn't seem to be insulted by your barrier against Her winds and answered my call for help."

"That was really the hand of a god?" Despite his recent brusqueness and short, sparky temper, Anthis voiced his scepticism with a little more tact, and perhaps even with the slightest hint of belief.

But she ignored him, remaining braced for Rathen's response instead. She had quickly learned of his bitter position towards any kind of faith, though the subject hadn't truly come up; the lines etched into his face revealed his intolerance as clearly as a sign around his neck. "We don't use magic like you people do," she informed him before he could challenge her. "We don't know how to do the things you do, only to heal or as a basic form of defence."

"But all mages can summon the power of a god?"

She pursed her lips at his virulent scepticism. He wouldn't believe her if she lied, but she doubted he'd believe her if she told the truth. "It isn't magic. Magic plays no part in it - it is faith. And it's also enough to say that it's as beyond *your* understanding as your skills are to me."

Rathen, who had felt no trace of magic from her before, during or after the wind had formed, found himself unable to disagree, and as his tongue had escaped and left him unable to present even the weakest of ripostes, Eyila turned away in dismissal.

She cast a look of desperate concern towards the still-falling sand, but as there was nothing she nor anyone else could do about the twenty five foot crack that had formed in the rock deep beneath the desert, she looked back to the clouds and took the lead once more, her steps determined, if far less certain.

The presence of magic grew clearer the closer they approached, and after a sandstorm and a chasm, there was no debate in Rathen's mind as to whether this site was more powerful than the others. But there was no sign yet of the 'rains that never fell'.

Until they crested the tallest dune.

Nestled between the smaller slopes, a golden-azure lake a quarter-mile across glistened in the sands, its surface still and more inviting than any water should ever have been. Its edges were dotted by small, green sproutlings that had already taken advantage of its unnatural presence, and towering over them, lapping at the water, were a countless variety of animals, all of whom shared the desert's neutral, sun-scorched palette.

Suddenly aware of the parched dryness of their mouths, they stared dumbstruck at the absurd sight, and not even Rathen could decide if magic was responsible for its entrancing beauty or not. But, he forcibly reminded himself, more important than its impossible allure was where the water had come from. Had it been a meagre puddle emphasised like the winds in Stonton, drawn up from deep underground? Or had it been conjured out of thin air? And had these animals been invoked along with it, or had they wandered the sands until stumbling upon this haven?

Dragging him from his considerations, Eyila breathed a sigh torn between tranquillity and heartbreak, and began to descend the dune.

But Anthis cursed as he followed, finally recognising what he and the others had taken to be large rocks protruding through the surface. "The ruin - it's beneath the water, isn't it?"

Eyila nodded silently.

Animals watched them closely as they approached the lake's edge, most unakin to any beasts they'd ever seen, the large eyes of predators and prey alike tracking them warily and unblinking, waiting for the slightest sign of danger. But none would dare move from their spot to flee for safety until that sign came. The water was just too precious.

"It's bigger than I thought," Anthis mused as they stopped. "Grander than that in the Wildlands, for certain." A smile brushed his face for the first time in days. "And we're the first beyond the tribes to see it for two centuries."

"Aside from those who should *not* have," Eyila added drily. She considered the lake and the angled stone pillars that broke its surface while keeping one wary eye on the beasts. "Before the ground opened or the water came, Ut'hala was already swallowed by the sand, but when the ground cracked ten moons ago and drained some of it away, it revealed new reaches. No priestess entered them before the water came two weeks later. We have no idea what lies within it."

The peak of the structure was wind-scoured and sand-worn, and though to the others what little could be seen looked identical to the shrine of Feira in the Wildlands, Anthis's keen eye picked out the subtle differences. Though the visible pillars arched at the same angle and curved inwards to meet at the centre, there were a few opposing hooks that reached out and downwards in reverse half way along the outer-face of two, and broken evidence of the same on three of the others. There was also another break in the water some fifteen feet to the left, the slightest dome that could be mistaken for a water swell had the rest of the lake not been so flat.

"What do we do?" Petra asked dubiously, as though she already knew the answer. "Swim?"

"No," Rathen replied. "I can feel the magic clearly from here."

"No, we have to go in!"

All eyes fell impatiently upon Anthis, Rathen's more so than the others. "We're not endangering ourselves just so you can satisfy your need to be the first to set foot in it," he growled. "This isn't some delightful afternoon jaunt along the coast where we'll 'ooh' and 'ahh' and be home in time for dinner."

Anthis's lip barely twitched, but that slight, meagre movement revealed for a moment a deep fount of contempt. "This is the most sacred site we've visited," he spat, "and according to *your* girlfriend, *sorely* affected by magic. I would think, with what little success *you've* had, that you'd take every chance you were given to get closer to it."

Dark flames erupted in his eyes. "'*Little success'?!* I *pushed* that magic, which--"

"Oh, *well done*, you've *pushed* it. Do you intend to round it all up and tear a hole in Turunda?"

"*You--*"

Rathen lunged for him, but Petra dove between them before his hands could wrap around his throat and shoved them sharply apart. She looked between them in utter bafflement. "What is *wrong* with you two?!"

Rathen's acrid, unblinking eyes didn't graze her, staring needles into Anthis instead, and it took some time before he whirled away with a snarl to stare, seething, back over the water.

"Anyway," Anthis continued fractionally calmer, his eyes still burning into the back of the mage's head, "that's not all. Remember what we found in the Wildlands - what if more is hiding in here? Can we really take that risk?"

Petra looked out across the water. "Can we really take *that* risk? Anthis, it's flooded. Anything in there is already lost."

"Actually," Eyila said quite timidly, "bubbles have been seen rising from the depths around the dome. There are certainly air pockets within it..."

He gave Eyila a grateful nod and looked imploringly to the others. "We *can't* afford to write it off. If anything, the very *state* of this place is proof enough of that."

They shared uncertain glances, but no one was inclined to say otherwise. They had no way of knowing - but then, neither did he.

But as Petra sighed, shrugged off her luggage and began purposefully unbuckling her weapons, Garon strode straight past her and waded into the water without a second thought.

"What the hell are you doing?!" She cried while the others watched him continue waist-deep and beyond in disbelief.

"Finding out." And with a deep breath, the inquisitor dove, vanishing beneath the glittering surface.

"*Wait!*" But of course he didn't hear her. She looked incredulously towards Rathen, expecting him to do something, but instead he simply removed his own burdens and sat in the sand under the gazes of them and countless wild animals', many of whom had finally scattered following the clash. His expression revealed no intention of going to his rescue, though there did appear to be a begrudging respect.

Flustered, Petra turned to Eyila instead, and though the concern on her young face seemed to stretch beyond her responsibility for their safety in this dangerous place - she *had* said 'dangerous' - she made no attempt to change the situation, either.

Aria meanwhile stepped closer to her father, her eyes alight with wonder as she stared at the remaining beasts, their bodies knotted and ready to flee though their furry lips lingered always mere inches from the water. "Are they going to hurt us?" She asked quietly, but even though her father shook his head and she seemed to have made up her own mind even as she asked it, Petra turned her attention onto that more immediate threat. Even the docile, stripe-necked oryx, each with those five immense, black horns, could do them serious harm if they felt threatened. Her body tensed in preparation just as much as the beasts'.

Almost a full minute passed before Garon returned to the surface, half way between the edge and the arches, but he didn't pause even to assure them he was all right or that he'd even found anything before taking another deep breath and disappearing once again. And so they continued to wait.

Thirty seconds later he surfaced again, a little further to the right, and repeated the silent dive. Another thirty seconds passed, but this time he didn't reappear. Then a full minute, and still the lake surface remained still but for expanding ripples from the beasts' thirsty tongues. Two minutes; four minutes and nothing.

"I'm going in," Petra decided, having already removed her weapons, and made towards the water. Anthis turned quickly to stop her but she easily evaded his reach, until movement far to the left halted her instead, and startled a few more creatures into fleeing. She sighed in relief as the black figure - the only one among them to have barely thinned his clothing in the heat - swam back towards them.

"I found a way in," Garon said as he dragged himself from the water, darkening the sand. "The ruin is split in two and tilted, dropping into a chasm, but there are more than just air pockets."

"But is it worth the trouble?"

He looked calculatingly towards Anthis for a long moment before turning to Rathen and nodding. "It could be. Can you do anything about breathing?"

"I can make an air bubble with barriers, enough to last five minutes."

"That will be more than enough." The inquisitor turned back to the water and strode easily back in. "Do it and let's go."

Rathen frowned after him, unconvinced, but did as he was told. He was in no mood to argue, and though it irked him dearly to agree with Anthis, the irritating young man had a point: while he doubted that going in would make any difference at all from studying the magic where he currently stood, there *could* be something in there to narrow their search.

With a few quick gestures, soft flashes revealed the formation of otherwise invisible spheres around their mouths and noses, and a larger formed to encompass the few jugs and bags on the ground. Then he followed the inquisitor into the lake, keeping Aria close. Eyila followed readily, as did their luggage, and though Anthis and Petra didn't hesitate, neither dared to dive without taking and holding a very deep breath.

Though that needless breath threatened to vacate their lungs immediately. The water was warm, but its depth was beyond astounding, descending at least twice its width and stretching on into blackness - and the further out they swam, the faster their uneasy pace became, as the unearthly feeling of being watched by something colossal, hiding just out of sight, crept ever higher along their spines.

Mercifully, the ruins themselves were close to the surface, but just as the lake was deceptively deep, so too were the ruins expansive. This was far more than a mere shrine or pavilion; there were arches, pillars and platforms rising everywhere, and in its prime would surely have been a sight to behold. But at that moment, with his attention fixed on the vast stone dome ahead of them, Rathen only hoped that its walls were still strong enough to withstand the weight of the water.

Garon dove deeper, leading them to an opening in the rock, a crack along its lower wall rather than any kind of doorway, and despite the thick, ominous blackness that skulked inside, they kicked through and after him with the greatest of haste. But they did not swim blind for long; a new light that didn't appear to be that of the sun struck weak shafts through the murkiness ahead, and the moment they were amongst them, Garon swam directly upwards and broke through the surface.

With gasps and grunts of relief, they hauled themselves out behind him onto the fractured, sloping ground, clawing their way over the flagstones to the slightly more level flooring beyond it. The stones were faceted, dressed in worn mosaic detail which was barely discernible in the small fragments of light, though none but Anthis and Aria tried to pay them any attention. The others simply used them as finger holds before they sought their feet and tried to ring out their sodden clothes.

Rather than resort to a spell, Rathen decided to enjoy the dampness, grateful for the first truly cooling relief he'd experienced since stepping into the desert, and looked around himself instead, conjuring a small light to aid what little floated within. And he quickly discovered, as his bounced back from thousands of glinting details, that the light piercing the water *was* of the sun. Rays trickling in through the broken ceiling were caught and reflected by tiny silver shards laid regularly into the encircling walls, mirrors surely once whole, and sent it dancing around the decaying room. And room it was; its ceiling was rounded but far from whole, merely one edge of the great dome, and the break in the wall ten paces to his right was black enough to hint at another expanse beyond, one *without* a crack in its roof.

Chests, tables, bookcases and chairs, most of which were broken, were scattered about the immediate chamber where the ground was still mostly level, while any that had been standing in the sundered corner they'd entered from were drowned, stained and shattered, their contents - parchments, mostly - floating face-down in the water. There were more carvings lining the walls, but these, like those in the floor, were visible only for their shadows, and their once-sharp details were indecipherable.

But the magic - the force that assaulted Rathen's senses more invasively than the scent of musty tomes, the chill of the water and the echo of every footstep and gasp of surprise - was so strong it crept into his very bones. The unnatural tranquillity of the place, the eerie beauty of the silver lights and their glittering reflections on the water, it was stronger and more alluring than he would ever have thought possible, even from a conscious spell.

Concerned wrinkled his face, and behind him, Eyila wore the same disturbed expression.

"What is this place?" Petra asked, looking around herself in awe. "More storage?"

"Storage, praise, ritual," Anthis replied quietly as he soaked up the room with wide, childlike eyes. "Though given its location, it was probably only used by the most devoted to Feira..." He turned around, looking all over the walls and floor with a single sweeping, hungry gaze. "Beautiful..." Excitement gripped him. He darted towards the bags that had floated through the water behind them, snatched his satchel and raced off without another word to begin staring closely at carvings and rummaging through boxes. The others watched him in surprise, his abrupt enthusiasm only emphasising how out of sorts he had recently been. And though it had escalated through the desert, Rathen was acutely aware of just when it had began.

But he forcibly ignored it and pushed aside his own fault and bitterness in favour of the task at hand. Opportunities to experiment with the loose magic were few and far between, and the very foundations of the spell he was expected to construct were beyond him. He *had* to get something from this place; with such a strong concentration of magic, all made up of spell chains which were so obvious now he knew to look for them, he simply couldn't let himself leave here clueless.

He felt Garon's eyes upon him.

"I've interacted with it," he said, answering the inquisitor's unspoken question, "now I have to affect it. So far, I have pushed it - which," he added quickly, glancing sharply towards the historian, though he was paying no attention whatsoever, "is no small feat - but in terms of this spell, it's little better than stirring water in a bucket. I made it move, but I didn't change it in any way."

"So you need to 'change' water, in a sense?"

He nodded.

"Mix something in it," Aria chirped with a thoughtful frown. "That's the easiest way to change water. You don't need to make a fire and wait for it to boil, or wait for it to freeze."

Rathen nodded again. "But you can't heat up magic, nor mix tea leaves into it. There's nothing quite like magic, and so the only thing that I *can* mix into it is more magic."

"*Your* magic." Garon looked at him steadily. "And doing that, changing the magic, will help to create the spell?"

Rathen's black eyebrows slowly knitted together, acutely aware of the expectations that weighted the end of his voice. "It will," he replied carefully. "Recreating the Zi'veyn has just been a distraction; I realised last night that if I have to make this spell from scratch, I can disregard a lot of what the elves *may* have tied into it. I can ignore speculation of affecting the heart or biochemistry and put circumventing it out of my mind; instead I can just shape a spell to affect the magic directly. Unfortunately that's also left me with the hardest target: elven magic, which I don't fully understand, and *loose* magic at that, with no kind of container to manipulate. A heart I could block, chemicals I could separate, but uncontained magic...there are no round about ways of dealing with it. It's direct or nothing. So," he looked around, as if searching for some visible sign of the magic, "if I can affect the magic, change it somehow, then that *will* help me put this spell together, even if all I have to do is contain it..."

Petra frowned warily. "You don't sound too sure."

"I'm not," he smiled meekly. "But it's the best I can offer right now. And if this magic *is* responsible for mages losing control, or for late awakenings, then the magic itself has done that, somehow, spell chains or not. So surely that means it can go both ways..."

"You sound uncertain again."

He offered the inquisitor the same smile before wandering off into the chamber under his conjured ghostly light, but it was quickly pushed aside by the usual dubious yet resigned expression these ruins seemed to evoke. No one tried to stop him. Instead Aria simply skipped along behind him, staring all around herself in amazement as she went; Petra and Garon wandered around with their eyes open for anything that might have made its home there, and Eyila watched every single one of them very, very closely. But despite her people's expectations, she refused to simply stand still and play guard, so, with a few whispered words of promise to Aya'u, she indulged her own desire to see this precious shrine while keeping the others in her sight. And it was only *partly* in the hope that she could block out the haunting feeling that had been forming over the past few days, pushing its way ever further into the forefront of her mind the closer they had come to sacred Ut'hala.

For nearing an hour, Rathen wandered with eyes unseeing as he probed the magic and attempted over and over again the few ideas he'd come up with since his previous night's realisation. But, as far as anyone observing him could see, he was making no progress at all.

Petra and Garon had lit torches and split up to cover all five rooms of the dome - four around the edges and one at the centre - but they found no signs of creatures having sought refuge. There were floods, and one room was still quite full of sand, but they hid nothing malicious.

Eyila, meanwhile, traced the edges of the stories in the stone, some familiar to her, some not, all while tracking the mage and the historian the closest of all from between the two rooms they wandered. She smiled to herself in curiosity as she observed their concentration. Rathen's spirit appeared to have left his body and was miles away in that same room, while Anthis was a stark contrast, enthusiastically present as he hurried this way and that, mumbling to himself and chuckling every now and then in excitement. Aria, too, seemed to be drawn to his energy, and had left her father's side to scamper around the room with him, asking him questions all the while which he seemed more than keen to answer, and he was clearly pleased for her company. Eyila had never seen him so lively...

"Amazing," Anthis breathed to himself in his wonder. "All these pictographs..."

"But it's *not* the same as the place in the wild lands?"

"No--well, yes *and* no." His eyes were fixed rigidly to the stones he paced alongside as Aria trailed around after him. "This *is* a shrine to Feira built by pre-magic elves, but the devoted here were something else, as I thought." Aria jumped aside to save her toes as he took a sudden half-step back and made a quick note in his book. "But the stories here," he continued onwards, "are more intellectual; they've not been honeyed or simplified, they tell straight and clear the importance of Feira's nature - what it does for them and what they would lose without it."

The child thought hard for a moment as he made another quick sketch. "Like water in the rivers? That if we didn't have them, or if we let them get really dirty, we wouldn't have anything to drink?"

"Yes, though that's only a very small part of it. This, for example," he pointed to etchings a few feet to the left. "The balance animals bring to the world. The smallest insects eat the fungi that would smother and kill the plants. These plants are food for larger animals, animals that eat the fruits and carry the seeds to spread the forests. Those animals in turn are food for larger creatures who stop them from getting too numerous and over-grazing. And when the larger creatures die, their bodies feed the earth - the forests, the insects and the fungi - refuelling the cycle."

"People eat animals - where do *we* fit in?"

"We are among those larger creatures." Anthis and Aria spun around, surprised to find Eyila suddenly standing beside them and peering thoughtfully up at the walls. "As long as we don't take more than we need."

"We do, though," he sighed regretfully, noticing something she was looking at and making another quick sketch. "The fat and wealthy eat more than their share, and plenty of that goes to waste. And the use of crypts and coffins mean we don't give our bodies back to the earth, either..."

"What did the elves do with their dead?" She asked, her eyes just as transfixed to the carvings.

"Initially, buried them straight in the earth, wrapped in a thin shroud for modesty. Once the spirit vacated it, there was no need to protect it. By burying them directly in the ground, their bodies were returned to nature."

Eyila nodded. "The earthen tribes do the same, but the rest of us return our bodies to nature in other ways. We believe that our existence contributes wholly to nature. We live and tend to the worlds' gardens, be they of grass or sand, and when we die our bodies feed the earth and its creatures while our spirits ride the Winds to protect it from above until they reach the Frozen Gates."

"The Frozen Gates?" Anthis frowned, sparing her a glance in his growing interest.

"The Winds die at high-north and low-south, and there the spirits are ferried into the next plane. Just as spirits are born where the Winds are, at the centre of the seas."

"So the wind carries life *and* death?" Aria pondered.

"Of course," she smiled. "The wind carries seeds, clouds and rain, it moves the seasons, guides animals - but it can also bring famine. An unfavourable shift can mean death or starvation for both man and beast..." her voice hung as she took a curious pause, and Anthis looked towards her again in the hope that she would continue. "Aya'u is both delicacy and fury."

"Aya'u," he mumbled to himself thoughtfully as he took several steps back from the wall and looked about the chamber as a whole. "What significance does this place have for your people? It was built by the elves for Feira, not for Aya'u."

"But Aya'u has claimed this place all the same," she replied with an impish smile. "The deserts are Her domain, as are the stillest seas and the highest mountains. But we hear Her - the *priestesses* hear Her - clearest in this shrine. Perhaps it is the reason the elves built here. Aya'u is not Feira, She is younger than the old gods, but She is surely born of her, as Shiya, Degon and Uq'ua are."

"The other tribes' gods?" Anthis considered her for a moment. "You don't speak of them with any distaste."

She frowned. "Why would I? Because other tribes are at war? It is true that many have begun to feel that their gods are above the others, that their element is the most important, but not all of us are so blind. There are still a few who realise that all the elements are intertwined - heat, for example, makes water lighten and rise as mist to become clouds, which the wind then push towards where the water is needed. The clouds release their rain to the earth, encouraging it to grow the plants the animals eat, and the earth collects into lakes what the plants and animals don't drink so that it can rise as mist and clouds once more." She sighed and shook her head. "Too many have forgotten this. And for people as ancient as the elves to have appreciated it, I can only wonder how much longer it will be valued before it is finally overlooked by all. Rain won't cease to fall, just as the winds won't cease to blow...but what will happen when no one holds a respect for the natural forces of the world anymore?"

She looked decisively towards Anthis, who stared openly at her in fascination. "Aya'u does not make the winds blow," she said firmly, "but She embodies its spirit and it *will* move to Her desires. Our priestesses care for Her, we encourage Her, and we ensure that there is always *someone* who will recognise Her importance. Hopefully, through our actions, the rest of the world will never have to discover the answer to that question."

She looked back up across the walls with a grave edge to her eyes. "This place needs to be restored." And with that she turned and walked away.

Anthis said nothing after her. He wouldn't have even had she remained. He'd frozen up and felt his cheeks burning in embarrassment, and his eyes quickly flicked away from her in an attempt to collect himself. Though as he turned away as nonchalantly as he could, he found Aria peering up at him with a very pensive look upon her young, sun-kissed face.

"You've been acting very strange lately," she told him slowly after a moment, then wandered off after Eyila, leaving him feeling even smaller.

"Have you made any progress?"

Startled, Rathen spun around to find the tribal girl suddenly beside him and Aria skipping along behind her. There was a severe look upon her face and he felt the weight of her demands press upon his shoulders, along with those of everyone else.

He sighed hesitantly. "I've been retracing my steps," he informed her. "I've tried a few things here that I have elsewhere and it's all worked; there's nothing different to this magic but its concentration. Unfortunately," he hesitated again, knowing Garon was listening closely despite standing several paces away, his back turned to him while Petra paced nearby, "it's been almost two weeks since I last had the opportunity to try this, so it's taken a bit of time just to...get back where I was...and I'm not really sure where to go from here..."

"Mix your magic into it," she reminded him. "You can, can't you?"

"Well, somehow, probably," he replied quickly, feeling the pressure of her gaze, "but I don't honestly have any idea *how*..."

She stared at him for a long moment, and he shifted under her scrutiny.

"My understanding of your culture is limited," she said suddenly, startling him again, "but from what I've been told of your mages, you see your magic as a tool - as something you own, something no other has a right to."

"Well, in the sense that no one else can *use* my magic, I suppose they *don't* have any 'right' to it - but as for it being a tool..." he considered his next words carefully, but she took his lingering silence as completion.

"It's not how you use it," she said, "but how you *regard* it. You were taught the facts, weren't you? That magic is born within you, it moves in your blood and your will is what directs it and shapes it to do what you want."

He nodded.

"And do you see the pattern?"

He blinked.

"*'You'*."

"...I don't understand."

"You've not been taught to feel magic, respect it, or understand its nature, only how to *use* it. Instead you see the magic as a part of you and immediately place yourself above or in front of it when you begin to cast a spell. You force it to do what you want it to, you've never regarded the magic *alone*."

He blinked again. "I still don't understand."

She sighed wearily, but its shortness revealed she'd expected such a response. She spoke slowly. "Magic is not a gift that many are granted, so for those among my people whom it inhabits, it cannot be considered a part of us. And so we learn to understand it instead, like observing an animal before a hunt, and we work *with* it rather than forcing it to do what we want. It's true that you get results with your magic through manipulation, but it's also true that I can do things you cannot, even though my magic is no different from yours except in how I regard it." She saw the change in his eyes, a thoughtfulness that had descended in place of confusion while he chewed over her words and the events they summoned from his memory. She stepped around in front of him and levelled her eyes with his. "You need to remove yourself from your mind and regard your magic's own existence. Feel its structure, its power, and tap into it on a more basic level. Work *with* it, don't force it. That's how my people are taught to use our magic without ever going to your schools, and how we're able to heal: our magic works *with* the body of the person we are trying to help, rather than trying to coerce the magic to forcibly repair the body itself. The two of us perceive our magic differently, but that perception is *everything*."

"The magic floating around here isn't in anyone," Aria pointed out with a similarly thoughtful frown. "It's on its own...and you said you think the magic is affecting *people*, not people affecting the magic..."

The wrinkles in his brow deepened as he descended further into his wonderings. "Are you saying," he began slowly, "that I and all of *my* predecessors have *misunderstood* magic?"

"To a degree," she nodded, "that is what I'm saying, yes. You can use it, you just don't understand how it works. And this 'floating magic' is little different from what is in your veins. If you can look at your own magic as its own being then you can see the magic around you in that way, too. You'll drop the barriers you've put up around what's 'yours' and what's not and it will be easier for you to combine them."

The earnest glint in her eyes steadied his tongue before he could try to dispute the idea. She *was* capable of things he wasn't, things that no other mage he knew of was - aside from Kienza, but she was a category all of her own.

But if that meant that she was right...

The idea struck him unpleasantly. He had no real love for the Order, nor for his own magic, but the idea that they - that *he* - had been wrong about something they'd always been so certain about made him want to close his eyes, stick his fingers in his ears and babble at the top of his lungs if just so he wouldn't have to consider the possibility.

But he was an adult. So he would just have to prove *her* wrong instead.

"How," he began cynically, "would I do that? Regard my magic on its own?"

"By simply regarding it on its own."

His brow flattened.

"All right, try this." She pressed her bronze hand against his chest and ignored his flinching reaction. "Breathe deeply a few times, but not too slowly. In and out." He frowned in growing doubt as she concentrated herself on his heartbeat, but did as she'd told him, breathing neither too slowly nor quickly, and became aware as he did so of just how difficult it was to maintain a normal rhythm. But he continued, taking one deep breath after the next, counting to three as he inhaled and again as he released it. "I'm getting light-headed."

"Good. Keep going, don't stop." He continued with less confidence, and when she spoke again, her voice had softened. "Your heart," she said quietly, soothingly. "Feel it beat. It doesn't do so to keep you alive, not out of fear of you nor any kind of desire or respect. It simply does it. You cannot stop your heart beat like you can your breath, you cannot reverse the blood flow. You have no control over it at all."

His dark eyebrows twitched uncertainly, but he said nothing as the truth of the words seeped into his dizzy mind and he closed his eyes against the rotating room.

"And yet, it pumps the blood around your body constantly, without your effort, your thought, or your direction. You grew the heart, but you have no mastery over it. Everything it does, it does on its own. And the magic that forms within it doesn't form at the heart's instruction, either. It forms there because it can, because there is room in there for it, and it joins your blood without your direction. Whether you want it to or not."

He felt his heart jump - he hadn't told it to do so, nor to speed up, nor slow down. Suddenly, he found himself wondering if this organ was truly his own. The idea sparked a madness within him.

"The magic moves freely into your blood," she continued hauntingly. "It courses through your veins; it joins your will to manifest your desires. It does not need to be ordered; it *wants* to be put to use. Can you feel it swimming in your veins? Filling your body? Your arms, your legs, your chest, your head. It moves as it pleases. It is its own entity."

His head grew dizzier.

"Good - feel it within you, feel its colour. Feel it reach your skin, that within and that which surrounds you."

He swallowed hard and shifted his weight to catch himself before he could fall.

"Envision the water in the bucket. Let your own magic keep moving, don't restrain it. Let it flow - *encourage* it to flow, and keep the water in your mind. That water, the water that you swished, can be changed just as it can be pushed. Guide your magic into it."

His dizzy mind cleared and one single thought presented itself at its centre. *'Blue'*. His fingers moved.

His heart did not lurch. His cuff did not burn. There was no sensation at all. And yet he knew what had happened. His eyes flashed open. Eyila was already following his gaze, and Aria, Garon and Petra joined her. Anthis did so, too, as he peered through the ruined doorway, jealousy still burning in his eyes as they flicked away from the sight of her hand upon the mage's chest.

An insignificant tendril of indigo, vibrant against the dark water and visible only for the conjured light, spread like ink through the pool that swallowed the edge of the chamber. All stared at it, wide-eyed, shocked at first, then sceptical. Only Rathen seemed truly dumbfounded.

Eyila dropped her hand as he made towards the water and peered closely at the colouration. Water wasn't really blue, he knew that, but even in his forties the childish idea was still immediate. But now this water *was* blue.

"A spell?" Petra asked warily, taking a step closer towards it, but Eyila shook her head. She was the only one among them who seemed confident in the result, smiling with satisfaction.

Rathen was hesitant to respond, himself. He crouched beside the water to flood the spell chains with his own magic using his usual technique, and there he identified them as he had when he'd begun. Except the blue water. Those chains, that small collection, the ones he had envisioned in a bucket, had changed. They were longer, though only slightly; one detail, a single link, had attached itself to the ends: blue.

And the change was seamless. It had not patched, it had not overlayed nor cancelled out. It had joined.

His magic had laced itself into the disembodied and ancient elven chain.

A giddy laugh slipped past his lips and his smile widened uncontrollably. Suddenly, anything seemed possible.

Chapter 41

Anthis had taken another of his quiet and moody turns since her father had succeeded in affecting the magic, and as *he* was absorbed in trying to understand just exactly what he'd done, Aria was left to amuse herself. With a small conjured light carried needlessly in an equally conjured jam jar, she pottered about in a room Anthis had already scoured, peering through the darkness with big, measuring eyes. He'd pushed and pulled everything in search of hidden compartments, but he'd also become easily distracted by the place itself with every few paces and she was certain he'd missed something. He'd been adamant at the edge of the lake that something important could be in here, and while he might be oddly content to give up so easily and stare at rocks and soggy books, she was *not*.

She decided that perhaps he didn't know how to find such hidden places. She'd been the one to find the secret room in the tangled forest, after all; maybe he just didn't know where to start.

In that case, she would rise to the challenge.

There were no recessed doorways or arches carved into the stonework - nothing as obvious as that - so instead she focused on anything that looked a little *too* much at home. The magic elves hadn't created the hidey hole they'd left their box in, so why would they have done that here?

Unfortunately, the chamber was so dark and its contents so damp and strewn about that she couldn't tell just exactly what belonged where, so looking for anything suspiciously inconspicuous proved hopeless, as immensely clever an idea as it had been.

And so it was that she wandered about with a light and flitting gaze that soon barely even tried to see through the darkness, puffing to herself in boredom yet still resigned to her self-imposed task. After all, she couldn't begin work on her own arty-fact until she'd spoken to Kienza, so she had to find some *other* way to help in the mean time.

She yawned as a chill passed over her. She had no idea what the time was, but as she'd been up since before dawn and given no rest as Garon had decided they should push on through that amazing and terrifying storm, she knew her weariness was not uncalled for. Of course, there was nowhere comfortable to indulge it.

She sighed again, and heard a small pop as she did so. She smiled to herself, assuming it to have been the movement of her own lips, but when it came again and her lips were most certainly closed, she stopped in her stride and frowned.

Silence.

She shrugged and decided she must have imagined it - but it came again just as she raised her foot to continue her roving.

Her head snapped quickly to the left. The light from her lantern caught the slightest ring spreading across the water surface, close to the wall, and she watched it intently until another bubble rose from the depths, popped softly and sent out another glittering ripple.

She pursed her lips suspiciously and crouched low beside the flood, but she could see nothing through the reflection of her lantern, and without the light, she wouldn't see anything at all. But perhaps...perhaps it wasn't so obvious. Obvious would be easy, and if something was hidden, finding it wasn't *supposed* to be easy. And if her attention was drawn below, then maybe...

She rose back to her feet, lifted her lantern high above her head to brighten as much of the wall as she could, and began walking backwards, eyes fixed firmly to the heights of the stone. She jumped and cursed clumsily as she bumped into one of the narrow decorative pillars, managing at least to stifle a startled scream if not the goosebumps prickling her skin, and muttered in embarrassment beneath her breath as she stepped around it, sparing it only a brief and vengeful glance before looking back to the wall. Those bubbles had to have come from *somewhere*...

But if there was a hidden doorway, she couldn't see it; her light was not the sun. She moved around to the right and raised the lantern higher, and though the shadows lurched and shifted and seemed to transport her into a whole other room, there was nothing new to see. So she moved instead to the left, closer to the edge of the water, and sent the colossal shadow of the meagre pillar sweeping across the chamber.

A flash of something familiar made her freeze.

Eyes widening in a daring flood of hope, Aria took a slow, half-step back to the right and passed her light through its previous path as precisely as she could - and a broad, victorious smile crept across her face.

"Anthis!" She hollered with a grin, and he appeared almost immediately in the cracked doorway, damp scrolls in his hands and a frown of concern shading his alarmed eyes. Her father was instantly beside him and wearing very much the same expression, but she didn't bother to reassure them. She merely pointed instead to the pillar.

"What is it?" Anthis frowned, stepping in more calmly while Rathen hurried around him, but she rolled her eyes haughtily as she watched him peer about on his approach, trying to see it from completely the wrong position.

"You have to stand *right here*," she drawled, pointing down to her feet. Her father had stopped behind her, but when his eyes suddenly widened and he took a few steps forwards, Anthis hurried the final distance to take her spot as she moved aside. Then he, too, grinned in triumph.

"What is it?" Eyila asked cautiously from the break in the wall.

"Anarchy..." He moved forwards as Rathen had to perfect the alignment, then chuckled giddily to himself and took a careless step to the left, breaking the order of the familiar, circular sign.

It was too expansive to mistake, and yet shallow and fragmented enough to hide. Nestled among the noisy etchings of leaves and vines, the central piece marked six feet down the length of the pillar, while the larger, encasing ends graced the wall fifteen feet behind it. To discover the image, one had to stand at just the right distance and just the right angle from an insignificant spot in the room, and broaden their attention far beyond the myriad of distracting details - in short, they had to know it was there. "I *told* you there could be something here!"

"You didn't find it, though," Rathen remarked drily, but the excitable young man ignored him. He dashed towards the wall, splashing into the water, and stopped half a foot deep and perfectly between the crest's outer edges. He immediately began pushing at the bricks, throwing his weight against them one stone at a time, deaf to Eyila's outrage, and before too long, one of them began to give way. Rathen hurried forwards and lent his own strength, and between them they managed to push open a door that had been seamlessly hidden in the low light - concealed once again by masonry, not by magic.

The way was barely wide enough when Anthis rushed inside, and Rathen stifled a snicker when his splashing footsteps were silenced by an abrupt bang, chased quickly by a yelp. In his defence, the historian hadn't given him the chance to conjure a light, which he proceeded to do as he stepped inside after him, and Aria and the others followed close behind. The flooded room was immediately cramped.

Petra grunted as Garon's abrupt weight shoved her back against the door frame, who in turn had been pushed by whomever was in front of him. "This room is even smaller than the last one," she complained, but as more weight pinned the edge of the stone deeper between her shoulder blades, she growled and wriggled her way back out of the door. Garon, too, saw little other option.

Everything inside was either damp or damaged - tomes, relics, cloths of some kind, perhaps tapestries or robes - and it was plain that the entire dome had none too long ago been submerged deeper than it presently stood. But that didn't seem to spoil Anthis's enthusiasm. He giggled to himself as he stood over the familiar box nestled amongst the far more elaborate texts and relics, but this time he had no patience for awe. He raised the lid after only the briefest hesitation, bracing himself for the treasures within. Rathen and Aria watched with bated breath while the others peered in hopefully from behind, and Eyila, her tongue stilled by intrigue, observed with far more caution, a slight furrow in her painted brow at the importance the old chest apparently held.

The lid fell back and an expectant silence emerged. All eyes turned to Anthis as he stared inside, but his face, they noticed, was suddenly devoid of all expression. Each of them felt their hope diminish.

They jumped when he finally moved; his hands lunged into the box quicker than he could stop them and began rifling through its contents, and though, to their relief, a smile returned to his face, he seemed careful not to inspire too much promise. The collection of scrolls and books were little different to anything they'd found before, but as he leafed through pages and skimmed over scrawling elven script, his smile began to broaden, and all gazes shifted, heavy and hopeful, back to the unadorned box.

"What is it?" Aria asked, standing on her tiptoes to peer over the edge.

"Journals!" He beamed. "Journals, diaries, workbooks..." He chuckled dizzily again.

"Is that good?"

"It's *always* good, but in this case it could be *very* good..." Though they waited, Anthis offered no more, losing himself in his reading. They knew better than to bother trying to regain his attention. Reluctantly, they filed out of the compact room instead, but no sooner had the last of them done so than Anthis burst out behind them, raced out of the chamber and on into the next. They frowned after him, and he returned a moment later with his satchel and notebook open in his hands, then disappeared back inside.

"What's wrong with him?" Eyila asked as his frantically muttering voice drifted out through the door.

Petra looked back at her dismally. "What's *right?*"

An hour later, and under Petra's supervision, Aria was practising with her stick sword while her father continued his work. The hopeful gleam in his eye had diminished since his initial victory, and he appeared to be struggling again. There were two new streaks of blue in the water, but he'd accomplished little else, and Eyila seemed unable to give him any new advice - or at least none that he could grasp.

"Elves, humans, and one more mention against the gods," Anthis's voice echoed out from the room a little too loudly for him to be talking to himself. "And it doesn't *seem* to be theoretical... And this 'ravein'okh' has come up again, the 'place of magic', but this one's just as vague as the last time..."

"But the artefacts?" Garon asked, making his way over.

"Hmm? Oh, yes. The first two are absolutely certain: one for the humans, one for the elves. As for the gods, I can't tell." He appeared in the doorway and presented a leather bound journal whose pages went from water stained to utterly ruined. "I can't make out any more to it." He sighed mournfully at the illegible pages. "What a waste."

"What have you *actually* found?" Rathen asked him more directly, and though the young man's lip curled, Rathen was unsure whether he had in fact sneered.

"I've barely broken the surface, but - and I hesitate to say it," though he didn't hesitate to grin, "it looks like we've hit the jackpot."

"Elaborate."

"These papers aren't just speculation on the artefact or vague references - I admit they *do* provide an awful lot of opinions, but they're also filled to the *brim* with technical notes and details..." He seemed fit to burst with his excitement, and tapped frantically at the paper as if his words alone couldn't possibly relay the importance of what he'd found. Nevertheless, he certainly had their attention. "*This is--*" he quickly put everything down and presented the ruined book alone, "this one, this is the journal of one 'Drekath'. He talks a lot about the Zikrahlehveyn as a grave weapon against elven kind, alongside disapproval and speculations for its purpose - conspiracy theories, perhaps, but it looks like this guy *was* in the know. Everything I've read so far has been backed up by details that only someone connected could know."

"If he was 'connected', why was he guessing?"

"Because it seems he was kept *just* enough in the dark - but it says that the qu'ulas - the king - hired someone to create the weapon as a show of power over the other elven lords in order to keep himself at the top, as far as I can see. But Drekath here seems to believe that the qu'ulas had the intention of actually *using* it rather than just throwing it around as a threat. And I'm sure all of this was more than just discontent - I think he was close to the qu'ulas himself, because he speaks of the weapon regretfully, as if he had the opportunity to step in and stop its creation somehow, or destroy it or run off with it once it was finished, but something stayed his hand - some greater obligation, or perhaps a precarious one."

"Fascinating," Garon said impatiently. "And how does this help us?"

"It doesn't really, but *this* might." He flicked forwards a number of pages then showed his frowning audience a few smudged and stained illustrations.

None of them were sure what they were looking at. It seemed at first glance to be an arrangement of triangles and thorns, but the longer they looked, the slightly more sense it made. Eventually they deciphered a rendering of an upside-down pyramid with barbs protruding midway along each of the four edges, hooking downwards towards a jagged-cut tip, while its broad top surface was crowned with larger, double-ended thorns arching into the centre, pointing towards what appeared, perhaps, to be a lotus flower. The drawings were precise - no doubt marked by magic - and depicted its unsurprising gold and black colouring perfectly. It even shimmered in the light.

"Now," Anthis beamed, "we know what it looks like."

"That's the 'zikanilvain'?" Aria gasped. "It's beautiful..." But she didn't smile. In fact she seemed disappointed, but as her task had been to create a vessel for the spell her father was to make, she almost certainly felt that her efforts were beyond 'inadequate'.

"Very nice," Garon said blandly, far less impressed, "but do we know where it *is?*"

"At this point, no, but *these*," he swapped the journal for a series of smaller notebooks, "are even *better.*"

"Better than the Zi'veyn's location?" Petra asked, but the persistence of enthusiasm in Anthis's eyes calmed her scepticism.

"Yes. These are research and creation notes - research and creation of the Zi'veyn *itself.*"

All of a sudden, they shared his enthusiasm.

"The spell--"

"Yes," he grinned, even towards Rathen, "the spell included."

But despite this promising turn, Petra couldn't help a dubious frown. "Anthis, those papers are the most ruined thing you've brought out of there...how much of it can you actually read?"

And now Anthis's slipped, and every expectant gaze grew irritated. "Enough," he replied, straightening under their scrutiny. "Honestly, we *will* get something from this. And if Drekath *was* close to the qu'ulas, this journal might just hold the artefact's resting place. I just need to read through it. It wouldn't have been left here if it didn't contain *something* important..." He watched the exchange of doubtful looks and stared back at them all imploringly. "*Trust* me, please. Give it a chance. None of you expected to find *anything* here, and it's the best lead we've ever had."

Reluctantly, Garon sighed in concedence. "It is, isn't it?" He managed to keep his hand from rising to the scroll of paper concealed in his breast pocket.

He puffed again and considered the historian, then the others, one by one. He paused for a moment to think, then his eyes fell finally upon Eyila. "We'll stay here tonight. It will be cooler than the desert. In the morning we'll start back towards the tribe and return our guide, but in the mean time, Anthis, you read as much as you can and find us a new direction. Otherwise we stick to the plan of heading to Enhala. You've got a week."

Anthis nodded vigorously. "Yes, good, I can do that. I can do that."

"You seem in a hurry to leave," Eyila observed. "Does that mean you have what you need? That you can restore this place?"

"We're a step closer."

"We're more than 'a step closer'," Anthis assured her ardently, overriding Garon's tact, but he shrank when he caught his disapproving stare.

Garon dismissed him and turned to Rathen. "Are you done here?"

The mage's face twisted uncertainly. "I think so..." he looked quickly to Eyila, "though if we're staying the night, I'd like to work on this magic a little more - if you wouldn't mind helping me?"

The tribal girl smiled, earning him another subtle yet malicious sneer from Anthis. "I'd be happy to. *But*," she looked more firmly towards Garon, "if you intend for us to spend the night here, you must all show Ut'hala respect. This place does not belong to you, and neither does it belong to me. Aya'u inherited it from the elven gods, and it in turn fell into my people's care - I expect you to treat it as you would your own place of worship."

Aria frowned up at her father. "How is that?"

"Like you do the garden," he replied quietly, and as a keen understanding dawned, Aria turned back to Eyila and gave her the sincerest smile of promise.

Anthis quickly vanished back into the small, flooded room, and though it couldn't have been later than four in the afternoon, the perpetual darkness encouraged the laying of their bed rolls. Aria took to hers an hour later despite food being heated over a careful flame.

Petra kept an eye on her as she tended it, but in the stillness, her gaze was repeatedly snatched by the inquisitor as he paced monotonously along the water's edge. She ignored him for the most part, but when he caught her attention for the sixteenth time, she grumbled, rose to her feet and made her way towards him. Her footfalls were quiet, but she knew he was aware of her. He was always aware.

"If you keep this up you'll need new boots in about twenty minutes."

He paused and frowned around at her as she gave him an impish smile, but he didn't spare her long. He didn't even roll his eyes as he looked away.

Her smile softened thoughtfully, and she cocked her head as she considered him. "Why don't you sit down? There's nothing to keep watch from in here - as relentless as the harpies are, none of them are going to *swim* to get to us, and I doubt any tribes would, either." She leaned around in an attempt to catch his eye. "We're safe here, believe it or not. The safest we've been for a while..."

"Unless something chooses this night to take refuge here."

She smiled laboriously. "What are the odds of that?"

"It doesn't matter what the odds are, it's a possibility."

She studied him for another long moment, ignoring the usual flatness of his responses, and a thought slowly drew her dark eyebrows together. "Garon, you know, if this is about everything before, we don't truly blame--"

"This isn't about anything but *safety*."

Her tongue was stilled by the sharp gaze he suddenly turned upon her.

"This place is *riddled* with magic. Who knows what could be drawn here? Not one of us is familiar with this ruin - but if *you're* tired of keeping watch, then stop. No one asked you to do it - no one even asked you to *be* here."

A flame sparked to life in her eyes, burning back into him with the strength of his own. "What is the *matter* with you?!" She snapped, keeping her voice to a low hiss despite the fact that the chamber was so quiet even the slightest whisper could be clearly heard. "Why are you always so dead set on being alone? On being the 'strong man' who protects everyone at his own expense? What good are you to *anyone* when you refuse to rest?!" He looked away from her in disregard, but that only stoked her rage and she took a frustrated step closer. "As you yourself said: not one of us is familiar with this place. So what are you going to do if something *does* happen and you're too exhausted to see it before it's upon us? Too weak, even, to act?! You are a *fool*, Garon! Do you know that?"

"And what rest do *you* get?" He snapped back with far less care of being overheard. "You're standing over my shoulder every time I look around!"

"Because I'm watching over *you!*" Her lips abruptly pursed and smouldering eyes closed, as if another mind had taken over, and her shoulders slumped in defeat. "Forget it." She turned away, waving her hand in dismissal. "Watch the shadows by yourself. Just be sure you stay awake *all night long* so you can raise the alarm if a fish comes too close to the surface."

"What's all the shouting for?" Aria yawned, sitting up among her blankets and silencing Garon's retort, and Petra smiled apologetically as she returned to the little girl's side, offering her quiet words of reassurance.

Rathen glared across at him as the inquisitor folded his arms and turned his back to her, and Eyila looked between the two with a sad frown. Neither of them missed the fact that he'd turned so absolutely that he couldn't look back around even if he'd wanted to, though whether because he was angry or simply stubborn, not even Rathen could tell.

"Odd pairing," Eyila mused. Rathen couldn't help a smile.

A few hours later, Petra, too, had taken to her bed roll. Eyila followed once she'd finished meditating, though she couldn't possibly have found even a lick of wind in the drowned ruin, leaving only Rathen, Garon and Anthis awake. The former had retired from his work on the magic and sat with his notebook in the firelight, scribbling manically before his thoughts could escape him, while Anthis sat on the furthest side of the fire and ate his portion of the food which had long grown cold, three books and a scroll laid open around him.

As the others slept soundly, Garon chose that rare moment to address an urgent matter with the only two he had ever intended to be a part of his expedition.

They were both so engrossed that they didn't notice him step into the weak firelight, and jumped when he spoke, though they were given no chance to curse in surprise. The severity of concern in his eyes was impossible to miss. Even his superiority had diminished in its shadow. "We need to talk."

The two exchanged worried glances as he turned and walked away, set their books down despite their pressing desire to continue their work, and followed silently, trying to ignore the dubious air they felt themselves stepping into.

He led them to the edge of the fire's reach - just far enough, Rathen noticed, that they wouldn't wake the others if they spoke in only slightly hushed tones - and when he turned back towards them, his ominous expression had grown worse. Anthis stalled when it turned directly upon him.

"How much have we found here?" He asked abruptly. "No promises, no underestimates - your best assessment."

His green eyes widened. "I really can't say just yet - certainly a lot, our best discovery yet, but how far it will carry us, I don't know..."

"Try."

He swallowed. "Based on what I've read, the fact that this information has clearly been *intentionally* scattered, and what could realistically be contained in the work books of this single cache under those circumstances, I think there's a fair possibility that we could find the Zi'veyn itself sooner rather than later - perhaps just two or three more stops, if the information hasn't been encrypted prior to being hidden. Failing that, there's also a fair possibility that it could contain something to help Rathen's work. I was going to start translating the creation notes and research once we set out."

"'Fair'," Garon repeated, but Anthis seemed disinclined to pin his name to any further guessing. He nodded slowly. "Well, it looks like all of this will be put to more use than we thought. The Order has acted."

"...Acted?" Anthis frowned.

"I received word from my superior a few days ago. The military wing has been on the march with the army, but a week ago a number of martial mages attacked the soldiers from within."

"*What?!*" Anthis barely managed to choke his outburst into a strained whisper.

"Could they not have been infiltrators?" Rathen asked urgently. "Skilan's mages?"

"If so then there's an even greater issue at hand. Sivaan Rosh himself was involved."

Rathen's expression dropped as his pallor whitened. "No. No. Absolutely not. Sivaan Rosh--"

"I know what you're going to say, Rathen, and I'm inclined to believe you. There's no evidence as yet that the Order is truly rebelling beyond these chaotic attacks. But now that one has occurred within the military and taken out a number of soldiers en route to a large-scale confrontation, intentional or not, it has turned Turunda upside down. To everyone out there, it looks very much like betrayal."

"Whatever it is, it's related to this magic," Rathen declared desperately, "it *has* to be! We all saw that mage out there, it's nothing natural and nothing intentional! We *need* to find this thing!"

"Yes, we do," Garon agreed calmly, "and urgently, but not just because of this meddling magic."

The mage looked back at him with almost painful caution as he searched his face for meaning, but Anthis was quicker to catch on.

"You want to use it on the Order."

"I have no intention of doing any such thing," the inquisitor replied before Rathen could unleash his response. "Even if this *was* an uprising, not all mages are involved, and if the Order is disarmed then all of Turunda will be left at risk of magical attack - and that is far harder to defend against by normal means than standard warfare. Unfortunately, not all are prepared to consider that detail." He looked at them both steadily. "What do you know of the Arana?"

Anthis's dubious expression broke into a smile. "The Arana?" He scoffed. "Ghosts?" But beneath the weight of Garon's stare, his laugh weakened very quickly and his smile promptly vanished. His eyes flicked to Rathen, and his suddenly severe expression created only greater foreboding. "I thought--"

"They're no urban myth. Now listen carefully because this is serious. The Arana is a faction of uniquely skilled individuals, many of whom have learned to suppress their minds and emotions so that they can complete their tasks without hesitation, and can seamlessly switch identities to suit whatever situation they're in. They have no families, no identity of their own, and they are untraceable by all but by their own - your 'ghosts'. These operatives are responsible for infiltration, intelligence-gathering, interference, assassination - anything the Crown needs done that it would rather wasn't known to the public, and while many stories you've heard are no doubt false, their nature is *not*.

"But they only act in the country's interest. They receive their orders from the Crown after deliberation between the king and his highest advisors, including the military general and sivaan, and only when no other course of action can be taken are those orders handed to a liaison for delivery."

Anthis merely stared at him.

"The liaison has a lot of power and it's true that there is room there for corruption, but the present has held the position for nearly forty years and isn't considered compromised. He isn't who we have to worry about, but the leader of the Arana itself - their 'keliceran'."

"Salus."

Anthis's stunned expression hadn't changed, but Garon's eyebrows twitched upwards in surprise.

"I have my sources," Rathen explained grimly.

"Don't you just. Then you'll also know what he's like."

"Vaguely: devoted."

"'Devoted' is certainly a polite way of putting it. 'Obsessive' would be another." They both wished they hadn't noticed the unsettled shadow in Garon's eyes. "He will do *anything* he can to protect the country; nothing is 'too far'. And with the recent activity of mages over the borders, even prior to anything occurring within Turunda, it seems he has been hunting for the Zi'veyn in order to use it against the Order before they could become a threat. Few trust magic as it is - imagine what a man prepared to go to these lengths must think of it. We need to get to it first."

"You make it sound like he's just going to happen upon it," Anthis observed carefully.

"The keliceran has access to a diverse variety of 'resources' and the means to 'encourage' them to co-operate. The Arana could get ahead of us with the right help in no time."

But Rathen shook his head as another doubt, one apparently more rational, settled upon him. "King Thunan wouldn't approve this kind of thing."

"No, he wouldn't. Unfortunately, we have reason to suspect that he's acting on his own. The liaison himself has suspicions, and there are a few Aranan agents on his side who feel the same. They raised the matter to him, and he to us."

"So what's being done about him?" Anthis asked.

Garon hesitated. "Nothing. He's wily, tactful and unpredictable, but the country is too unstable for a key authority to be turned upside down. And the Arana is too valuable to stall its operations."

"Even if it's being led by a man like that?!"

"You don't know the half of it." Rathen's eyes darkened. "Garon's leaving out one big detail: Salus was a portian."

"A...sorry, a what?"

"A portian," Garon began reluctantly, having clearly wished to keep some details under wraps, "is the highest rank of working operative. Their emotions are entirely suppressed; they feel nothing, they think nothing. All that matters to them are their orders, completing their missions. By any means."

Anthis looked slowly back to the inquisitor. "Should someone like that be *allowed* to lead?"

"No," he confessed. "He took the position by killing the previous keliceran. That's generally how the position gets passed along, but it's always pre-determined. The individual is agreed upon between the current keliceran and the Crown's liaison to ensure the reins are handed to someone suitable."

"So the keliceran *sacrifices* himself?"

"When they're no longer able to do their job, yes. They know too much to be turned loose and after a life in such service, they wouldn't be able to function as a normal person. The one who takes their place is approached by the liaison directly with a mission of assassination under claims that the Crown wants the current leader removed due to compromisation. They don't generally learn the truth until years later, assuming they give it any thought at all. But it's usually a middle-rank who takes the job, a phidipan, capable of shutting feelings away enough to give their subordinates the difficult orders, but still able to feel compassion and a desire to protect their country."

"All right...but Salus *wasn't* selected...so the previous kel-keliceran? The previous one was still--"

"Yes," Rathen said darkly, finishing Anthis's struggling. "She was still suited to the job." His eyes shifted sharply back onto Garon, his arms folded tightly across his chest and a note of accusation to his voice, though not even Rathen was sure who it was aimed at. "All this - it's on us, too, isn't it?"

He nodded regretfully, and he clearly felt the pressure of this new weight as much as they did. "He can't be touched, and the liaison wants to keep any of this from getting back to the keliceran and provoking him into doing something rash, which is why the Arana isn't being utilised for this despite being far more suited. Something caused his conditioning to break before he took the position, presumably some kind of trauma. As a result, he's unpredictable, and though he has a genuine desire to protect Turunda, he lacks the balance brought by being able to feel and fear as clearly as the rest of us. That's why he's not averse to taking severe action on his own prerogative.

"As such, yes: we are more or less on our own. There won't be much help from the Hall from here on out, either."

"You mean there was before?"

Garon ignored the mage's dry remark. "It would be best to assume that, given his resources and skills, the keliceran knows everything that we do, if not more. We can say, however, that his one handicap is that Anthis has been with *us* rather than *him*."

"What do you mean?" He frowned worriedly. "*Me?*"

"Information suggests that you were a recruitment target of theirs." Anthis's eyes widened. "Fortunately, I got to you first. But you are a leading expert and surely their first choice, just as you were mine. That's all that has given us the advantage. Otherwise, Salus's resources far out-match ours, and they include mages. Despite his feelings for them, he understands the value of having them on his side. Which means time is truly of the essence - whatever we do to obtain this artefact, we must do it quickly."

Garon's eyes flicked beyond them towards the fire, and he straightened cautiously as they followed.

"It seems to me," Petra said quietly as she approached on soft, silent feet, "that we're doing the same thing we always were, just with greater urgency." She came to a stop beside them, the weak light revealing her little concern. "It's just that now we know someone else is on our tail. If we keep our sights fixed on what we're doing, we *will* get there first, and then we can keep it out of their hands and render the matter obsolete. After all, we don't have to divide our attention between this search and waylaying ghosts, do we?"

"You're over-simplifying it," Garon snapped. "If he gets a single lead ahead of us he could very well reach it first, and if he uses it against the Order, Turunda will be vulnerable against attack! Skilan is marching all over us right now, and there are mages among *them*. They wouldn't hesitate to take advantage of the situation!"

"Wouldn't the artefact also affect *them?*"

"Possibly," Rathen replied, "but we have little idea what the spell within it actually does, by detail, nor how far its range is. And if it *did* only affect the Order and not invading mages, any spell I fashion in its place *certainly* won't be able to rebalance the field." He sighed and rubbed his temples, feeling the tensions that had finally fallen away when he'd turned the water blue return in force. "Elven or not, it simply couldn't nullify the magic of every mage in existence - if it did it would have left the elves who used it powerless, too - and if other countries learned that we were magically defenceless, we would become a very large and far too tempting target. The world is a mess right now. We wouldn't *need* to provoke an attack."

"Not to mention what would happen to the mages themselves once powerless," Garon added. "A man that frightened wouldn't take their magic and leave it at that. He'd incarcerate them for life, at best, but with the idea that the Order *has* rebelled, he'd put them to death, and then there would be *no* magic when we needed it."

Petra nodded slowly. "And yet, after all that..." She smiled earnestly. "What has actually changed?"

Garon hung his head and shook it in defeat while Rathen turned away, his face twisted in disagreement and increasingly painful thought.

Anthis, however, spoke up. "To be honest, she's right." Neither reacted. "We've not gained anything useful from this and neither have we been hindered in any way. And, regardless of what resources the Arana has, *we've* got all this in here. So unless we're being followed and we've led someone straight to it - and I'd be surprised if even a *ghost* could have followed us through that sand storm - we've still got the upper hand."

"Now *you're* over-simplifying it."

While Anthis rolled his eyes and turned to reply to Petra, Garon watched Rathen wander a few steps away. Whether he was looking to escape the conversation or just lost in thought, Garon moved after him anyway. But he suspected he knew what was on his mind, and it was another matter he'd been keen to address for quite some time.

But he said nothing as he stopped beside him, their backs to the fire, and neither did Rathen look at him. The inquisitor waited patiently.

"They don't understand," the mage said at last, quietly, gravely, confirming in his tone Garon's assumptions, "but to continue with this...we will be going up against a *very* serious force..."

"All the more reason we need you with us."

Rathen sent him a brief but calculating sideways glance, but again neither spoke for a while. The doubts about his involvement in this expedition had quietened over the past month after all he'd seen, heard and felt of this magic, silenced by the necessity of his role, but all of a sudden he found himself facing them once again, and they had multiplied at least tenfold. The inquisitor must have known this; he'd read his thoughts down to the letter.

If he'd known before he'd set out that the Arana would be involved in this, he would have shrouded his house in any number of spells so that, should the inquisitor come knocking a second time, as indeed he had, he wouldn't have been able to find him.

But now...now he was already neck-deep...

Aria giggled in her sleep, and though he jolted to look around towards her, his fear, he discovered, had paralysed him against even that.

"It's too extreme," he said before he realised he'd spoken, his tongue apparently still loose. "Too dangerous."

"Rathen--"

"I need to keep Aria safe. I have responsibilities."

"Yes, you do, as a former--"

"As a *father!*" His head snapped towards him, and he only just managed to rein his voice into a choked snarl. Garon, however, did not flinch. He simply stared right back at him.

"What about Elle?"

Rathen's expression dropped as if he'd been physically struck and dazed.

"I told you," he said quietly, "I know everything I need to know about you. I wouldn't have risked coming to you otherwise. And now, it seems, I am coming to you again." Garon took a half-step closer. "We still need to remove this magic, which means we will still need to use the Zi'veyn ourselves. You said yourself the spell would have deteriorated, it will need patching, and you are the *only* one who can be trusted to do it, soldier or not. Now that the populace are retaliating against the Order, there may well be some mages who have had enough and decide to stand their ground, and then a *genuine* rebellion *will* ravage the country. We cannot take the artefact to them in your place. If a discontented scholar gets his hands on it he could potentially work out how to use its raw power for other means, and then it truly *will* become a weapon." His measured eyes pierced Rathen's, though the mage's had become glazed and distant. "The original task is still there, Rathen, and very much still a priority. You said it yourself: this all has something to do with the magic."

Silence swirled around them while he waited for a response. Petra and Anthis's voices grew sharp and clear as they continued speaking behind them, and the weak campfire crackled with the power of a pyre.

"Nothing's changed," Rathen mumbled to himself at last, then his eyes finally flicked back to the inquisitor. "I would draw attention to you all. After Carenna--"

"I was aware of that possibility when I first came to you. It's worth the risk."

"Not for Aria."

"I would think, if there was a favourable answer to this question, that it wouldn't need asking in the first place. But something tells me it isn't so simple." He looked briefly back towards the slumbering child. "We need you, Rathen. That fact is absolute. So I ask you, and answer truthfully: *is* there no one who can watch her?"

Rathen followed his gaze and watched the blanket rise and fall with Aria's gentle breathing, while the deeply troubled crease returned to his misery-lined face.

"Could Kienza not do it?"

Undesired, names and faces rolled slowly through his mind, all belonging to people he had counted on, once upon a time. But they were not approachable now.

Garon's eyes were fixed, unblinking. Rathen seemed to shake his head, but it could have been a twitch. He was certainly lost in thought.

He eventually parted his lips, inhaled to speak, but something stilled his tongue. "There..." His voice was quiet, almost inaudible in his reluctance, indecisive about even finishing his sentence. Garon knew what that meant. He turned himself to face him, the firelight blinding his right eye. "There...might be someone..."

Kienza. She only ever appeared when she wanted to - not when she needed something, just when she wanted to - and though he always sensed that she knew when he needed *her*, he wasn't convinced that this was one of those times. He trusted her absolutely, in general as well as a guardian, but what she did in her own time was unpredictable. If it were just for a few days he wouldn't have worried, but this could be...

Rathen became aware of the downward pull of his lips. He forced his face to relax.

This could be a long time. She needed somewhere stable...somewhere he knew was safe and unchanging.

"Who?"

Rathen didn't hear the question. His mind was still spinning indecisively. Above all else, he desperately didn't want to let her out of his sight, let her leave his side. She was all he had, and himself the same to her. She was all that was certain and constant in his world.

But...

'These very scowles could close up and swallow your curious little home with you still in it!'

The knot in his brow pulled upwards a little further, and the conflicting voices of various responsibilities roared ever louder in his mind.

*

Garon watched him for a long while. Regret had softened his features into the visage of another man - one, he suspected, few had seen in a decade - but as his expression took on a slightly firmer edge, he stepped around in front of him expectantly. "Where do we need to go?"

Rathen's eyes focused back upon him. "Nowhere. We continue as we are. Kienza will find us."

Garon searched his eyes, but the mixture of uncertainty, discomfort and resignation within them wasn't hard to spot. He looked away respectfully, belated though the sentiment was, and gave a single nod of acceptance before turning back to the others, putting an end to the matter. "If we're still to head to Enhala," he began louder, catching their attention as he made towards the bags and withdrew a map, "we should go by sea."

"By *sea?*" Petra frowned. "But Enhala is why we were heading through the desert in the first place!"

"Yes, and that was fine until the peace talks between Kasire and Ivaea fell apart. According to my most recent missive, the two countries are at war once again, but this time it's fuelled further by insult to both Crowns. It's not safe." He unrolled the map as they gathered around. Rathen took his time to join them.

The inquisitor pointed to the western edge of the desert, bordering the sea, a narrow bay edged to the north and south by mountains. "Once we've returned Eyila we can sail out from here and bypass the Kasire-Ivaea border, as well as the worst of the fighting. Enhala is to the western edge of the country so we can cover most of the distance by boat and keep out of their affairs, but once we land, we will still be in a serious war zone."

"You make it sound so very simple." Bewildered eyes landed upon Petra, who looked down at the map hopelessly. She tapped the parchment at open water, a little further westward from the proposed travel route. "Ships never make it through these waters," she stated. "*Never.* Huge storms force sailors to abandon course or wreck; sometimes they sail into a never-ending fog, get turned around inside and are so grateful to be out that they don't dare try the route again, and if the weather is with them, the rest simply sail in a straight line by sight and compass and still manage to get turned around, and wind up back where they started. Attempting the journey again always results in the same thing."

"Maritime superstition," Garon said impatiently.

"Sounds more like the talk of drunken sailors and inadequate captains." Anthis observed.

"It's the same thing."

"But how do *you* know this?"

"Coastal towns," she shrugged. "Restless sailors keen for a fight. I make good money in places like that. But too many sailors have said the same thing: any who try to sail the Roquna never make it through. Most no longer even try."

"So what you're saying is that it's quiet and rarely travelled?"

"Yes - and for good reason."

The words sounded unfortunately familiar, and all looked slowly towards Garon, seeing the signs of yet another poor decision they would surely only just survive by the skin of their teeth. And yet, despite that probability, not one of them spoke against it. It seemed it was either 'try to sail an unsailable sea' or 'walk willingly into a battle ground', and every one of them knew which they preferred.

"Is it possible that it's just a natural phenomenon?" Anthis asked in the hope of settling his own mind against the concern. "Perhaps their compasses are reacting to something nearby and making them change course without realising it? Across featureless or foggy seas, I'd imagine it's quite difficult to notice a slight degree's turn..."

She raised her finger. "There is one problem with that idea: the stars never changed."

"Well...that's--"

"That's our route." Garon rolled the map back up and returned it to his bag. "So unless Anthis can find us a new destination by the time we return to the tribe, you'll have to accept it. Now, get some rest, all of you. We head out come morning, and this is a good opportunity to catch up on sleep."

"For some of us," Petra mumbled, but she didn't linger. She turned back to her bed roll, and though Garon sent her his usual flat stare, she didn't care to look back for it.

Anthis shifted uncomfortably under the atmosphere, and after hastily wishing everyone a good night - Garon didn't reply, of course, and Rathen seemed too distracted by his mysterious thoughts to have heard him - he equally retired to his blankets, his mind too addled with revelations to even attempt returning to work. Rathen, silently, did the same.

Garon looked over them as they settled, then to his own blankets. He dismissed them as he stifled a creeping yawn to the best of his ability, and turned instead to look all around the central chamber, noting all possible exits and entrances. He didn't notice himself linger in Petra's direction. He then began to wander as the others drifted off to sleep, but after four more yawns managed to momentarily incapacitate him, he grumbled to himself and sent the sleeping Petra a reproachful look. Only once he was sure everyone was deep in dreams did he turn begrudgingly to his blankets.

Chapter 42

Salus could still hear Denek's voice reverberating through his skull. *'Don't arch your back. Breathe naturally. Relax your face.'* It was enough to drive him insane, and the mage's relentless obsession with his breathing and posture was beginning to revive his doubts. If it weren't for the indisputable proof he'd been handed in that very first session, he'd have given up by now and turned him back over to Nolan to extract every piece of information he could. Teagan had already suggested he do as much. In fact, he was quite pushy about it - he'd mentioned it twice in the last four days. But he couldn't understand. He hadn't felt what Salus had, and there were no words he could find to sufficiently explain it. So he'd given up trying.

But his patience was beginning to slip. He'd made no further progress in the week since he'd first come face to face with his magic, and he was starting to dread going down into those cells every day, knowing each time he did that he was sacrificing time that could have been spent making a real and immediate difference to Turunda's security. But he forcibly reminded himself, as he bit his tongue very hard at each of the mage's dry remarks, that this would yield better and greater results than anything within his present capabilities.

Eventually.

But despite that promise, he'd had to postpone that day's session. His mind would collapse under the weight of his tension if he tried to put himself through those trials again, and there was too much else to do to be able to spare the time.

First of all, Doana and Skilan were both doing far too well on Turundan soil. His people had uncovered all the individuals who had helped them gain ground in the initial occupations, and that very day had exposed one of their most recent collaborators. The fact that every one of them had been of foreign blood didn't truly surprised Salus, but he was deeply concerned that many had been residents of Turunda for several *years* prior to this event. Just how long had they been lying in wait?! And worse still, Skilan had taken two more minor posts in their usual, destructive way, while Doana, far more surgical, had yet again eliminated the local agents in their two most recent marks, which they had abandoned in form before anyone could chase them off, leaving no clue of their intentions and vanishing back into the wilderness.

Salus slammed his fist on the desk. Turunda's damned forests - it was as if the land *itself* was working against them now!

He had no intention of wasting any more time. He already had people investigating anyone not of Turundan blood in the latest discarded town - pattern decreed that it couldn't be anyone else - and he still had people inside Skilan's trophies doing the same. If his suspicions were proven correct, and he was certain they would be, he was prepared to have all foreigners in other key locations watched, too. Grass root operatives already had their eyes open for anything out of the ordinary, this would be no further trouble, especially if it prevented any more assaults.

But a twisting in his gut told him it wouldn't be soon enough. An uneasy shadow stood behind him, making him shift in his chair. Doana was certain to attack again. He could feel it coming. And he knew there was nothing he could do about it.

As for other troublesome matters, information from within Skilan's army was minimal, but he still had little idea if anything reported from that front could yet be taken seriously, and with such little word and so little reliability, it felt very much that they were under their invaders' mercy. And he did not like it.

And then there was Doana, and his increasing certainty that they were not working with Skilan at all...

A sharp pain pierced his temple, provoking a groan as he leaned over the paper-strewn desk and pressed the heel of his hand against his head. He muttered a foul curse. All day he'd been plagued with headaches - mercifully, they were becoming less severe than they had been in the morning - and his concentration was non-existent; it took him four times longer than usual to read through basic reports, he was getting distracted, and his body ached. It was all down to his rotten night's sleep. It had to be.

And to think he'd been braving it. The dreams had still been mockingly peaceful, but in recent days he'd had the resolve to face them, carrying the hope that his efforts would bring them to reality in time and that he needed only be patient. That past night, however, had been something else entirely. His sleep had been riddled with nightmares and phantom whispers, shouts and laughter, flashes of dark images and frightful white faces, and one larger and more brutal than the rest, looming high above them and emitting an air of eerie silence that screamed louder than all else. He'd woken from it countless times but always his eyelids closed again, compelled by the power of fatigue, and he found himself repeatedly back from where he'd just escaped.

He'd never been so relieved in his life than when daylight finally poured through his open curtains and chased the night's trials away, but his mind, it seemed, had gone with them. He'd been more alert after staying awake for three days straight than he was after that ordeal.

He jumped when a knock came at his door, rattled back out of his helplessly tumbling thoughts, and snapped his permission in embarrassment despite no one having been there to see it. Teagan stepped inside wearing his usual unreadable expression, but Salus knew he bore only bad news. "Get to it," he said without greeting.

"Doana has taken Pelas."

He couldn't help a bitter laugh. "Of course they have." He slumped back in his seat, still rubbing his throbbing skull as the pain took its leisurely time to recede. "And they removed Neriss too, I presume?"

"She's dead, yes."

He nodded slowly. Teagan must have been aware of the dark atmosphere in the room, but he didn't flinch when Salus thumped his fist on the table and erupted out of his chair.

"*What do we have to do to root these damned insects out?!*"

"We are working on it, Keliceran."

"Working on it, working on it." Salus kicked the chair and began pacing furiously around the room. "But we're not *getting* anywhere, are we? All our efforts, our resources, our skills, and what have we got to show for it? Everything's come crashing down on us - it feels like we're trying to claw our way out of an avalanche when it's still falling from all sides!"

"It isn't that bad--"

"*Isn't that bad?!*" He whirled and covered the distance between them in a flash, faster than Teagan had expected. "There are *residents* of Turunda plotting against us! Some of them of them even of *native* blood! Even the beasts that plague our forests seem set on our downfall! Casting their distractions everywhere they can, sending guards scurrying after their shadows - if not for them there would have been more vigilance in the cities! But at least they're easy to crush..."

Teagan watched him steadily as he returned to his pacing, losing himself in his frantic thoughts, when a small voice spoke up in his own mind. His eyebrows twitched into a frown as the familiar tone lured him in. "Are we sure," he began carefully, "that that is necessary?"

"That what is necessary?" Salus asked impatiently.

"Killing the non-humans. It seems unreasonable. Could they not simply be driven off?"

"Driven off?!" He snapped around towards him again, his eyes flashing incredulously. "Ditchlings, kvistdjur, harpies - unnatural, all of them; no matter how far we might 'drive them off', they'll *always* find their way back! There's nothing we *can* do but cull their numbers!" Salus's eyes narrowed suddenly as he stared at him. The portian's gaze was level, glassy - as unreadable as ever. But there was a knot, the slightest knot, dimpling his forehead. "You doubt."

"I only wonder if there is not an easier way to handle them." His disconnection was irritating. "And other matters - your decisions have become increasingly antagonistic lately."

Salus chuckled scathingly. His tone became dangerous. "*Antagonistic?* I am trying to *defend* our country. That's all I've *ever* tried to do. I've given *everything* to that goal - my entire *life* has been spent in Turunda's service! And if my decisions to that end make me seem 'antagonistic', then *so be it!*" He squared himself towards him, his face mere inches from Teagan's as his eyes blackened. "Do not question my decisions, Teagan" he growled through wolf-like teeth, "or you will discover how antagonistic I can be. *I* am leading the Arana, *I* am the one who has to balance every matter and work out the quickest and most effective means of repairing it. The Crown does *nothing* but pass on problems, *I* am the one who has to handle them, and I'm expected to do so while they bind my hands. I might be 'antagonistic', but my decisions *will* get us results - and unless I'm mistaken, it was *your* suggestion that I take matters into my own hands in the first place. So until you kill me and take my place, they will *remain* my decisions, and you will have no place to cast aspersions towards them. Do you understand?"

Teagan didn't blink. The knot had vanished and his expression was smooth and attentive once again, but while Salus didn't see the speck of dismay that had come to rest in his hazel eyes, Teagan was all too aware of the changes that had fallen over his superior. His skin, already pale from stress, had become a shade whiter, and his features seemed to have sharpened into the visage of another man - if any man could ever look so fierce. But above all else was the air of certain danger he emitted. Teagan remained still and silent but for a nod of understanding, truly believing, for a moment, at the edge of his instinct and beyond his reason, that his life was at serious risk.

Salus nodded his acceptance. "Good." And then, as suddenly as he had seen it, Salus appeared to be himself again. The keliceran turned away and strode towards the window. He was certainly still seething, but the room felt a great deal lighter and Teagan quietly released the breath he'd found himself holding.

He watched him carefully as he stared out over the city, his mind already far from the office, and after a long moment, he dared a step towards him. "Salus...are you all right?"

"Fine."

His response had been too quick, but though he continued to watch him analytically, another voice, well-trained and reasonable, spoke up in his mind. A portian could not empathise, he reminded himself, could not understand the emotional reasoning behind any decision, be it to kill or to show mercy. Once, as a phidipan, he had been able to grasp such complexities, but now they were far beyond him. What seemed antagonistic or aggressive could simply be a decision charged by urgency. Teagan didn't have all the facts, nor the capability to weigh them. It was neither his place nor his purpose to try.

But it was ironic that it was only thanks to him that Salus was able to.

He straightened and muted the strange stirrings. Both Salus and himself wanted only the best for Turunda, and they had both given so very much for it. But Salus had quite possibly given more.

Two second knuckles rapped against the door behind them, but despite Salus's mood, he didn't even growl. He pushed himself away from the window and sat heavily back behind his desk, another abrupt change dropping over him, and called for the Crown's liaison to enter.

To both of their surprise, however, the old man stepped in with his tail between his legs. Even Salus's eyebrows rose at his timid manner as he closed the door behind himself, and though he turned and stood tall in his ever haughty air, it was clear he was not looking forward to delivering whatever it was he had been tasked to. And that only hiked Salus's interest.

"Afternoon, Lord Malson," he said mildly, tracking him with sharp eyes. "I wasn't expecting you to come in today. Can I help you with something?"

"Actually, I came to inform you of the Crown's most recent decision."

"Oh?" Salus's eyes flicked briefly towards Teagan who had moved to wait quietly beside the door, observing with similar attention. "Regarding?"

"You know damn well what," he snapped.

"It would be foolish to presume."

Malson straightened in resignation, disregarding the keliceran's feigned ignorance as he had Malson's abruptness. "In light of these most recent attacks," he began with such sufferance that it sounded almost rehearsed, "the king has decreed that Mokhan, Adin and Whitemouth are to be evacuated and surrounding areas put under guard, while security in Kulokhar itself will be increased four-fold. You are to put your planted agents on high alert and reinforce their numbers where you can, and have any others you can spare accompany the evacuees and ensure their journey's safety."

Salus muzzled another sardonic laugh and bit his tongue against the derisive remark that so nearly loosed itself. "And where are they being evacuated to?" He asked instead.

"Anywhere able to take them in. Villages are smaller and poorer, but their people are more accommodating, and there is room in the cities, even if they are less tolerant of the disruption."

"This will severely impede the Arana's work," he warned him. "And the Hall's."

Malson frowned. "It's not like you to express concern over other authorities."

"We're all working to the same ends," he replied easily, but rose to his feet as a serious atmosphere descended. "I will spare everyone I can to keep the people safe. You have my word."

"I would expect nothing less." Salus noticed something shift in the old man's eyes as he glanced towards Teagan. "There is something else I would speak with you about..."

The keliceran dismissed the portian with a brief nod of his head, and as the door closed behind him and the latch fell in place - the only sound to suggest his exit - the liaison's eyes became suspicious. "You've been unavailable lately."

"There is a war on..."

"And you are still expected to answer to the Crown." Whatever endurance or timidity he'd entered with had been quite suddenly replaced with that irritating supremacy. "And yet twice I have arrived this week to find *him* in your office and you nowhere to be seen."

"There is much to handle," Salus replied coolly, "and my subordinates are not unlimited in number. I cannot expect all my orders to be carried out in a timely manner if I stay locked in here."

"You have been taking them on yourself?"

"As if I had the time. Suffice it to say, I've been doing what I can from within the Arana's grounds."

Salus watched the curiosity and speculation grow within the old man's youthful eyes and met it levelly.

"It would be best," Malson continued eventually, without breaking his stare, "if you remained reachable."

"I am always reachable - sometimes it may simply require a messenger."

The old man's eyes continued to bore into him for another long moment, but whatever he sought from his expression, he didn't seem to find it if the tightening of his jaw and brief flare of his nostrils were any indication. He broke his gaze and turned away in barely concealed irritation. "I assume you have nothing to share on the Order?" He asked as he walked towards the window, though looked back in surprised as he caught the small folder Salus tossed towards him.

"Little of significance."

His brow furrowed as he skimmed the first page, but quickly dropped in disappointment. "Quite. And what about *your* mages? Any strange goings on?"

"My mages have nothing to do with the Order."

"I am aware. I was speaking more broadly - any strengthening of power? Or new talent?"

Salus's faultless expression didn't waver. "You are aware that the Arana is a small group. I'm not sure it's statistically possible for any new mages to surface among so few..."

"You may be right, but it needs to be asked. The whole matter is concerning. That people could suddenly develop magic past their prime..." He shook his head, and his voice took on a more thoughtful tone. "Word around the court is that the Order has something to do with it, that it's related to all the strange, arcane goings on in Loggerhead and the like. I don't believe it for a moment, myself, but we are severely lacking in any kind of evidence for a sound explanation."

"Well, I'm afraid I can't help you there," he sighed regretfully. "Only the mages understand magic, and I doubt the Order would admit to doing such a thing. The only efficient course of action open to us is to focus our efforts on the mages themselves and stop them from unravelling the country, in any way we can."

"You are keeping them under watch, then?"

Salus leapt quickly from his encroaching ponderings and dulled the sudden sharpness of his eyes. "Only the preservers when they dare leave their fortress. Not even the Arana can get into the Order's grounds."

"Mm...it is a problem, but it's one that I and other envoys are working on. The Crown wants to station guards in there."

Salus baulked. "*Guards?*"

"That was my own reaction," he smiled briefly. "They wouldn't be sufficient. Not even members of the Hall would be capable. It would take nothing less than a mage to hide among them..." Malson's sidelong glance wasn't missed. "Can you spare any?"

Salus's fair eyebrows rose in surprise - some of it genuine. "Lord Malson, this doesn't sound like an official request."

"No request, just a question."

"...I see. Well - speaking broadly, of course - it would depend on the situation. But I would think, should the skills of my mages be required for one matter or another, I could probably reassign a few."

Malson nodded slowly. "And would it take long?"

"Not at all."

He nodded again. "Very good." Then he patted the folder under his arm and made lightly towards the door. "Well, that was all I wished to share. Good afternoon, Keliceran."

"Good afternoon, my lord..."

The door closed, the latch clicked back into place, and Salus's neutral expression dropped into a frown as he regarded Malson's empty space with suspicion.

Had that been discontent? He could certainly understand if it was, and it was about time someone else started to recognise the Crown's incompetence...but he was more than simply surprised to find *Malson* of all people expressing the sentiment. In fact, it unsettled him. Perhaps because his loyalty was only the most recent of the world's constants to be eradicated.

But he was familiar enough with the old man's mannerisms to know he wasn't mistaken. He may not have given any orders himself, but they were certainly implied.

So it was just as well that he'd had Aranan mages stationed in the Order's wall for almost two years; it was a note on an ever-growing list that he didn't need to address, *and* it meant that, should they somehow slip up and get caught now, the repercussions would be lesser than they could have been.

But as minor as this phantom order was, Malson's discontent just didn't sit right with him...

He pushed himself heavily to his feet, lost in thought, and soon found himself staring back out over Turunda's capital city and the tall, spiralling, gold-silver-onyx towers at its centre.

His arms dropped to his sides, eyes closed, and took a slow, deep breath. He released it just as steadily and took another as he felt his heart and mind slow. When he opened his eyes again, a sorrowful clarity had befallen him.

The country was a mess. Years ago, he would have been out there tidying it up with his own two hands. He would have acted on orders, it was true, and he may now have had the entire Arana under his control, but it felt as if his hands were eternally bound. In that office, he could issue orders, but he couldn't see to them himself, he couldn't guarantee they were carried out quickly or efficiently with no unreasonable mistakes.

And his magic...it was still out of his reach, and it seemed so set on remaining as such that he couldn't consider that a reliable tool, either. The only thing he could rely on were his own actions, his own capabilities.

But he couldn't use them.

He breathed a mournful curse as he flexed his fingers, but pushed it away with another deep inhale and focused on its release in an attempt at peace.

He had no time to change that; there was too much to do and he had too many responsibilities. Until he had the power to handle them all at once, day dreaming would do little good. He could only do so much.

Only do so much...

A knock came at the door, startling him out of his contemplation and ripping a sharp snarl from his throat. "What?" He snapped, and in stepped an unaffected, plain-faced portian, ready to receive new orders.

He grunted and dropped back behind his desk. For now, he had little choice but to maintain his trust in his subordinates. They were far from incapable, after all, portians above all others.

But there had to be *something* more *he* could do...

...Was there really anything keeping him locked in that place?

The answer struck him as he rifled through his paperwork in search of the intel this operative would need for a fully informed mission.

Intel. He couldn't risk being away from the office, away from Arana House, if something vital came in - the location of Doana's strike forces, perhaps even a breakthrough on their motive, or immediate movements of the Order.

Or Karth's notes...

His eyes slighted in thought as ease set in towards his entrapment, and after a swift briefing, allowed his gaze to wander back out of the window as the portian left on silent feet, ignoring the pain that hammered at the sides of his head yet again.

Chapter 43

Over recent days, the pattern of light thump-grunt-scuff had become almost as constant as the sky. It replayed itself every few minutes and was faithfully echoed four times, along with the occasional embellishment which couldn't be repeated in good company. But participation in the enforced ritual was half-hearted. Their feet stumbled and struggled across the hostile ground, over which no step was certain for the rocks and buried scrub which harboured the threat of twisted ankles - a threat that remained even as they doubled back, retracing their very particular steps in the face of sudden and impassable outcrops.

Yet not one of them entertained the desire to trade the treacherous ground for the soft, fluid and ever-shifting surface of the desert.

Eyila had altered their route four days ago after spotting what she claimed were signs of kentauri movement - 'ithili', she'd said, and failed to elaborate - and though it looked to the others as nothing more than oryx tracks, while they remained in that barren land, so too were they at the mercy of her expertise. So they'd followed her onto the dusty, rocky escarpment and its far less direct trade route, while the solid terrain grasped every opportunity to trip them up. But though the going was a fresh kind of difficult, the path trailed close to the mountains whose cooler air returned to their days a more familiar structure, and provided landmarks enough to assure them they were actually making progress.

Not that Anthis or Rathen paid them much heed. While the others slogged along, casting wary looks over their shoulders for figures slinking along the horizon, the two experts desperately redirected their attention.

The historian had become unbearably hostile since leaving the elven ruin. He turned within himself every chance he got, perhaps to spare the others or perhaps to spare himself, but though he was surrounded by an air of animosity even then, it seemed to diminish a little when his nose was buried in his books. Lately - mercifully - it had been nowhere but, and, just as in the dunes, he still managed to stumble over hidden rocks only as frequently as the rest, even while paying a fraction of the attention.

As for Rathen, he absorbed himself in the historian's promised translations, and when his fatigued mind began to wander, he could manage only a mournful smile as Aria enthusiastically presented her innumerable questions about the desert horsemen they sought to avoid. He hadn't yet summoned the courage to share with her a certain recent decision, and he found himself foolishly hoping that, if he didn't give the matter voice, it would eventually just go away and he could keep her beside him. But their arrival at the Ikaheka's village was imminent - late the coming morning, Eyila had said, and in time for the 'Uyu'una' festival or some such - and he felt only increasingly suffocated by procrastination and the desperate, fevered wish for more time against the impending parting.

All of which he kept as tightly behind his lips as he did Aria close to his side.

While the two lost themselves in their distractions, the rest of the company stared with what interest they could muster at the sparse, ruined villages dotted along their path. Built for the nearby running of mountain meltwater and later abandoned as the winds shifted and streams ran dry, they now rose silently from the sand like the petrified reach of a tormented corpse. And yet, despite their eerie, empty presence, they'd spent a reluctant night within one that had loomed out of the darkness just as drowsiness began to set in. Eyila assured them many times that they *weren't*, in fact, haunted, but few managed to get any sleep.

Though Aria had at least found something to take her mind off of it. She'd noticed Anthis watching Eyila more than usual that night, but unlike the other occasions, this time there had been such a thing as privacy. More times than she could count, she'd found him looking up and across to where Eyila had left the walls to meditate in the sands outside. Every day she seemed of even more interest to him than his work, and Aria felt the point vital enough to raise.

"Daddy," she'd said quietly, sliding up to him as he worked, her eyes lingering contemplatively on the historian, "have you noticed that Anthis isn't acting the same around Eyila as he did around Kienza, or around Petra?" She cocked her head. "He stares at her in the same funny way, without a doubt, but it's...different."

"Oh?" He didn't look up. "In what way?"

"Well, she takes his attention away from what he's doing no matter *where* she is, but Petra only does it when she's next to him. And he looks like he wants to say lots to her, but *actually* says almost nothing, which is weird. The only time that changed was in the water ruins and he was looking at the big story wall, but that didn't last..."

He cast her a subtle glance. "What do you make of it?" He looked up a moment later when she didn't reply, and found her smiling sadly. He breathed a laugh and embraced her. "Little one, listen to me: when you like someone, and I mean *really* like them, make sure you tell them. People can't read minds. ...Actually, on second thoughts, tell me first."

"Why?"

"Because your happiness is the most important thing in the world to me."

She looked up at him and smiled happily, still squeezing his waist. "And you want to know if someone makes me happy?"

"...Sure. That's it."

That evening, however, Eyila, who had been moving across the dusty, jagged rocks with a certain careful urgency for the past half hour, suddenly adjusted their route to avoid the most recent village to emerge from the growing darkness, and worse still ordered Rathen to extinguish his conjured lights.

"Why?" He asked with a dubious waver as the world around them blackened into the moonlit glow of distant, snow-capped peaks.

"Thieta," she replied simply.

"Bandits?" Rathen frowned, surprised. "Out here?"

"This road is just busy enough to sustain them."

Garon immediately dismissed their concern as they moved from the stone to tread back through the sand. "We continue until we find cover." He turned, then, to Anthis. "We reach the tribe tomorrow. Have you uncovered anything useful?"

The young man looked back to him from the derelict village with eyes as hard and cold as ice. Garon didn't react to their darkness. "The artefact against the gods," he began, clearly mindful of his tone which could, apparently, have been even sharper, "is often mentioned close to the Zi'veyn. And it doesn't *seem* theoretical anymore."

"Anthis, we want the *Zi'vey*--"

"I am aware of that, thank you. If you'd let me finish, I would've gone on to say that twice I've read that it's hidden 'where the gods will never find it'. Which 'it' that refers to, I don't know, but I'd be willing to bet that they were both kept together. Neither a weapon against elven kind nor against the gods would be left within easy reach of just *anyone*, and if something has been hidden where gods can't find it, elves certainly couldn't find it either."

"Will you by chance then go on to say where such a place might be?"

Against possibility, Anthis's glare blackened. "The 'place of magic'," he managed not to spit, "is mentioned again. It seems its existence was known to few, its location to even less, and even those who were so privileged couldn't freely come or go from it."

"A refuge for the very highest status, then?" Petra suggested.

"Or a securely restricted area. Context."

"That's not all that helpful, Anthis."

"*I'm trying!*"

Garon raised his chin as the historian growled a colourful curse, but though the inquisitor said nothing to it, a musical voice dared to rise from the lead. "You're doing fine, Anthis."

Everyone looked up, surprised, to find Eyila smiling around at him. Heat rushed immediately to his cheeks as a childish discomfort leapt upon his back, and it seemed he'd suddenly lost his tongue. Aria narrowed her eyes in intrigue.

But Eyila didn't seem to notice. She nodded encouragement. "Go on."

"Yes, *do* go on."

The petulance flooded back into his eyes as they flicked towards the inquisitor. "This," Anthis snapped, though not as sharply, brandishing the notebook he'd been forced to stop reading at the disappearance of the cold, blue-white light, "is the richest cache of information *anyone* has ever found, and the first substantial mention of this 'place of magic'. It's no coincidence that all of these topics have been grouped together - whoever scattered it all still preserved the information itself; they didn't want it *or* the artefacts to be lost. It's all connected. The Zi'veyn *has* to be there."

"But where *is* 'there'?"

"Is it possible," Rathen mused slowly, ignoring the leaded atmosphere, "that that's where the elves have also gone?"

Anthis looked back at him flatly. "What?"

"Well they all vanished, didn't they? They couldn't have actually been eradicated by Zikhon, so what if that's where they've all gone? Upped and teleported away, leaving no direct mention of the place or event so no one could find them? If that's the case, and we *do* happen to find it, we could be waltzing uninvited into the home of immensely powerful mages..."

Anthis turned his head away in what appeared to be absolute dismissal.

"That does sound quite outlandish, Rathen," Petra agreed.

"The elves were the definition of 'outlandish'..."

They looked back at the young man's suddenly pondering tone.

"They achieved great things with their magic, after all... They didn't even physically touch anything in the end - except each other - and any handmade goods were created by humans under verbal instruction... In fact, that's how we were able to stand on our own when the elves vanished, because we'd been taught how to do things with our hands that they refused to without magic..."

"But they could do just about *anything* with magic, couldn't they?" Aria asked carefully, encouraged by the glimpse of Anthis's usual self, "things we can't even with our hands *or* with magic?"

"Mm...certainly things we'd consider impossible..."

Rathen stifled a hopeless sigh.

"It doesn't sound like this helps us at all," Garon remarked flatly.

"Then you're wrong. What a surprise." His foul air returned just as suddenly, and many shoulders instinctively tensed under its presence as he looked sharply back towards the inquisitor. "The elves were perfectly made for magic, and magic for them. That's why they were so good at it. They didn't have the same limits human mages do."

"I don't see the help."

"It's simple: don't think like a human, think like an elf."

A perplexed silence fell.

"Well in that case this 'place of magic' could be *literally* anywhere. So why, of all places, would it be Enhala?"

"It isn't," Anthis snarled resentfully, "but the cultural capital could give us more clues - information overlooked by everyone else because they hadn't any idea what to do with it. The ravein'okh was undoubtedly held in high regard by those who knew about it, and the words they've used in its context suggest a cultural wonder, even if most of those who knew of it were never allowed to see it for themselves..." He nodded decisively. "There *must* be something in Enhala, if it's anywhere - a deep, dark archive somewhere, or a single document. It would be there. It *has* to be there..."

No one dared to question the thread of hope he clung to for fear it might unravel their own, even as one single concern echoed clearly in each of their minds: what if they uncovered the location but it took elven magic to actually *get* there? After all, by Anthis's own words, the elves had been capable of things even human mages considered impossible...

Not even Garon was willing to pursue his desperation. Instead, he turned to Rathen. "And you?"

For once, the mage didn't fear the question, though he spoke carefully. "From Anthis's notes, it looks like the spell *did* touch magic directly; it was more advanced than simply affecting the heart or biochemistry, and with the loose grasp I'm getting over their perception of magic, I'm beginning to get an idea on how they could *theoretically* have managed it. Unfortunately, any information regarding the spell's actual construction or structure, even ideas or early thoughts, is vague at best. Worse still, the translations aren't complete--"

"Not every one of those damned words can *be* translated."

"I'm not talking about the spell chains," Rathen snapped, managing to restrain the imaginative insult that still threatened to break through his teeth. "I undoubtedly have a better grasp on those words than you do, anyway. No, what I *meant* was that there are portions of the text *missing* - ruined, if even among the papers to begin with. And while what I do have does help, it doesn't go as far as I'd hoped it would."

"What more is it you need?" Garon asked.

"Detail," he sighed, "and if not technical, then the frame of mind of the spell's creator. If I can understand what drove him to create the spell in the first place, I should be able to work out his approach and get a starting point."

Petra frowned. "I thought you *weren't* trying to copy the spell..."

"I'm not, but at this stage, I'll take every bit of help I can get. By all rights, it's still an impossible task."

"You still sound hopeless - you affected that magic, Rathen," she reminded him, "even if you still can't work out how, you *did* do it. And you can work this spell out, too."

He smiled uneasily, and fortunately didn't notice Anthis's most recent sarcastic remark.

"But in any case, the Zi'veyn was created as a show of power, right? Then it was to discourage something - an impending attack, since it's been called a 'weapon'. If the elves were so snotty as to refuse to do anything with their own hands, I doubt they'd have been keen to risk getting even just a little bit dirty in a conflict. And, as I understand it, magic was all they had in the end, so the threat of something that could remove their magic and render them helpless would be a pretty good deterrent. And they'd know that, should it be used, they'd be a simple matter to kill, too. One who relies upon a single weapon is defeated long before disarmed."

"There was no trace of any war," Anthis informed her with a restrained tone of frustration, "active or impending. But you're not wrong about them not wanting to get involved in such a messy business. Long post-magic conflicts between elves rarely went beyond passive aggressive comments, and whenever they did, whomever had been responsible for beginning it - on the opposing side, of course - was assassinated."

"By elves?"

"*Obviously*," he drawled. "And they were rewarded for it. It took great magic to complete such a task unnoticed and even greater magic to defend against it. By becoming an imperial assassin, an individual's skill was acknowledged at the highest level.

"But regardless," he said dismissively, "the Zi'veyn was only *sold* as a show of power. Someone came up with the idea and offered it to the qu'ulas for one reason or another. Probably as an excuse to make it without drawing undue attention to himself. I'd imagine it would be difficult to hide that kind of work from people who can sense magic."

"But why would someone want to make such a thing if they weren't at risk of anything?"

"Ulterior motive, perhaps?" Garon suggested. "Maybe he wanted to use it himself and claim dominion over everyone else."

"But *why?*" Rathen stressed. "That's a villainous plan, certainly, but it's not a drive. Anyone can daydream about something like that, but I need to know what encouraged him to make it a reality where others shrugged it off. Then I can work out from what angle he targeted the magic."

Petra thought for a moment. "The elves were indulgent. We know this. So they probably weren't above spite. Perhaps he suffered a personal loss, or the threat of one - loss of life or maybe something more material like status or wealth. And maybe, in that case, he wanted to maintain his superiority in a more obvious, iconic way. With a power like that, even kings would be at his mercy..."

"If he *was* making it to use himself," Rathen frowned thoughtfully, "why would he stop there? That kind of person would want to humiliate kings, not just overthrow them... If the spell was created to interact directly with the magic, it's possible that he could have found a way to turn their magic against them, put it to use in their veins rather than just holding it still - heat the blood and relive the sensation of magic's awakening, maybe intensify it and burn them from the inside--"

"Vokaad, save me," Anthis growled quietly from ahead. He raised his voice and called back drily, once again without the honour of even a glance through the darkness. "You realise how much trouble *you're* having with the spell, don't you? The elves were indulgent, they were whimsical, *ergo* they wouldn't have put the time or concentration into building a spell like that if they were distracted by spite or delusions of grandeur. Immediate satisfaction, that's all they'd have wanted, and the time and trouble such a spell would have taken was beyond their patience." He shook his head. "It's *far* more complicated than that."

Increasingly weary glances were exchanged behind the irritating historian.

"In short," Rathen summarised as his lip curled in disdain, "I'm not getting very far - *yet*. I've not finished reading through it." He nodded assuringly at the inquisitor as he received a measuring look. "Just give me time."

Garon exhaled sharply as he turned away, and dropped his voice so low that not even Petra, who until a few days ago paid him such close attention, would hear his pessimistic remark.

Half an hour later, with the decrepit, bandit-infested village long out of sight, they pitched their tents among a tall, dusty outcrop of spire-like rocks. Starlight was shut away as equally as their cooking fire, and as shadows flickered fervently across the tightly standing stones, they each sought to escape those pressing walls in their usual desperate activities. Eyila meditated, seated so precariously at the top of the tallest and narrowest spire that it was a wonder she dared to close her eyes, while Garon patrolled at the foot and Petra set about making food with Aria, who comically over-sighed every few minutes to try to catch the attention of her father. Rathen, oblivious to the localised wind, continued to study the translations Anthis had given him with an expression twisted in thought. Anthis was the only one absent from the group, but that was no surprise. Every night he made a hasty retreat into his tent the very second it was standing up straight, regardless of food or the growling of his belly, and as sure as the moon hung in the sky, he was inside poring over his own research.

Except he wasn't.

Just as the stone concealed the stars and the cooking fire, so too it concealed his exit.

After traversing a desert for over a week, a rocky escarpment had no shortage of landmarks, and so it wasn't difficult to retrace their steps, even while his mind raced ahead in excitement and his hand twitched eagerly and constantly towards the untucked hem of his shirt. But it was far too soon to draw, and he wasn't going to let anticipation get the better of him. He was too experienced to succumb to that.

He tightened his fists and focused instead on light, ghostly footsteps. He knew his target; he knew the precise distance and what level of skill it would take to achieve his goal. But while he never moved without a plan, this time he'd formed them for even the least likely course of events. This was far from his first hunt, but in such terrain, he was out of his element, and further gone than he had ever let himself get before. He'd managed through necessity to conceal it from the others, but this, he had no doubt, was what the first man to sputter the syllables had experienced.

He pushed it from his mind and moved on silently through the black and silver desert, but where before his company had swung wide to avoid the broken walls, through which he now saw several scattered, orange glows, he remained close to the dark and ragged edge of the landscape and made directly for it.

His hands were shaking, but his footing was sure, and though his eyes remained fixed on the moon-bathed village, he was so acutely aware of the three gems in his dagger's hilt that he may as well have been staring at it. But he couldn't. He hardly dared to look, and when he did find the fleeting courage to pull it from his waistband, hoping against hope that their state had improved without him in the last three minutes, he found instead that, even in the obscuring glare of the watchful moon, they remained darker than an endless abyss and filled him with a far greater terror.

That terrible sight only steeled his resolve. Even had his fear been for what lay ahead of him rather than the implications of what he clutched in his hand, he had no choice but to continue, or lose his mind completely.

Suddenly the village stood right before him. His steps didn't falter; his focus sharpened, fret for the dagger and his own state forgotten in favour of success.

Taking a moment to listen, he slipped silently through a narrow break in the outer wall and melded immediately into the nearest shadow, pressing himself against the stone of a ruined home before sweeping across it to keep to the edge of the village. He made a circuit along the wall, following the near-tangible traces he sensed of individual presences, and peered between buildings both towards and away from any light to mark the inhabitants visually as he went. There were no more than twenty - a large number for such a company, even despite the size of their residence. The trade route must indeed have provided well. Most of them were loitering within the light of three campfires, but the few who wandered on patrol were barely attentive, scuffing their feet as they went. Their confidence in their fortress wouldn't be the sole cause of their undoing, but it would certainly contribute.

He smiled to himself as he soaked up the sensations. He was spoilt for choice; every presence he felt held the same great value - so he resolved to choose the nearest. Focusing himself in on the presence of the approaching scout, he withdrew the plainest of the two daggers from its sheath, ignoring as he did so the phantom twinge through the parallel scar across his abdomen, drawing it so silently it was as if the blade held its breath with him in anticipation. Then he paused for just a moment, half a heartbeat, before flickering forwards through the darkness like a spectre, quite unaware of the increasingly wolfish smile that broke his face. There followed only the slightest snitch and grunt as its edge flashed true across the throat of his target.

Anthis's palm was already clamped firmly over the dusty man's mouth, stifling any exclamation that would alert those standing only ten feet away, laughing, eating and drinking in their ignorance. He knew they could find him quickly, they knew the village, its dead ends and the areas half-attentively patrolled, and he had no intention whatsoever of being interrupted.

A swift kick to the back of the knee sent the bandit to the ground, and though panic and confusion gleamed in his eyes more brightly than the sun, Anthis did not see it. His desperate mind had focused almost to the point of oblivion; his single concern was the blood that poured from the man's neck - not so shallow a cut that he could fight back, but not so deep that he'd bleed out too soon. He knew exactly how long he'd live with an injury of that practised depth and precision, and he equally knew how long he had to act. Necessity forced his excruciating impatience away.

He removed his hand from the man's face. He wouldn't shout for help now, nor would he kick and scream. He was more than familiar with the onset of shock. It never varied; he could predict it to a second, and once it set in, his victory and the loathsome individual's demise were secure.

Anthis smothered his ardour, tore the dying rogue's left sleeve from cuff to elbow and discarded the bloodied dagger on the ground. His own left arm was already bare, having rolled up his sleeve in anticipation before crossing the wall, and excitement threw his heart back into his throat as he frantically pulled the second dagger, jewelled and naked, free from his belt.

The wonderful moment had finally come - but his hands still didn't shake. Even as the bandit reached out in a final weak and pitiful attempt to swat him away, gargling dismally in place of a shout for help or declaration of innocence, Anthis easily caught his wrist and drew the keen edge of the blade slowly and clinically along the inside of his forearm. It made no difference that the night obscured the guiding blue-green line of the median antebrachial vein, he could have followed it just as precisely blindfolded as in full daylight.

As blood began to bead and trickle and the man looked on in silent, slipping terror, ancient words began to form on Anthis's lips, loosed without thought, drawn out by routine. "Dozhuuk aus vulan," he murmured as he worked open the vein, "iinkravahz suruustin." Slowly, he reached the elbow. A moment before the crook, he stopped and turned the dagger's point towards himself. "Dovat aus sekhisiin Vokaad." The man finally fell still under the blanket of shock while Anthis punctured his own scarred skin, tracing along the same line with total disconnection. "Dokreyt," he did not even bar his teeth, as though the limb he cut with his abyssally jewelled dagger was not his own, as though the blood that mixed with the stranger's had not come from his veins, "aus kreyakhan lehzanzi Vokaadu."

He stopped again just before the crook, and the instant the steel left his flesh, the dying man released his final breath and a curious elation numbed Anthis's senses as suddenly as if he'd been kicked by a horse.

Tremors rattled through his fingers, dropping the blade as his head began to swim. Heat rushed through his legs, his chest, his arms, but it was a familiar and welcome warmth, and though it drained him completely of his bearings, as it always did, he smiled a dizzy, lustful smile, and shuddered in his bliss as his desperation melted away.

But all too soon, a shout snapped him back to the darkness.

A viciously spiteful sneer marred his face as he spun in the direction of the approaching presence. This equally valuable soul was sure to raise the alarm if it saw him, and that would obliterate the joy of this easy kill. He'd barely had the chance to relish it as it was.

His snarl worsened as his malice increased, and that, joined with the white-hot power that pumped through his body, forced him into action.

He snatched up his daggers and vanished into the black as the next bandit walked around the corner, and he dispatched her just as quickly and easily as the first. But the sensation from claiming this soul was only a fraction of the first. He was already sated; this was nothing more than vengeful indulgence.

But Vokaad was still receiving the offerings, and though He was paying a pittance for them in return, they would be put to use. And that, Anthis was forced to remind himself, was what mattered.

And so, when a third followed the second around a corner, searching for her as well as the first, he seized the opportunity and claimed his life, too.

As he lost his balance in this most recent rush and staggered against the wall, he half-realised through his bliss-fogged mind just what he had gotten himself into. More would follow. By killing the woman out of spite rather than vanishing into the night as he'd planned, he had grasped the attention of the whole encampment. Within moments the presences he could feel spread throughout the area would converge on him, following the voices calling out for their delayed comrades, then the shouts of alarm. He could evade them, he could still escape; Vokaad had given him the means to sense a valuable soul, and that in turn meant that he could map the area of threats and make a retreat...

But...the world would not lament the loss of these individuals.

His grip on both hilts tightened in decision. This contemptible band would fall.

He melted into the shadows as two more thugs arrived at the location, but rather than strike, he moved off towards the two furthest and opened their veins instead. The alarm was raised as the second fell and the gang converged on the first two bodies. He tracked around, picking off the outermost, seen and heard by none.

But with every arm incised, every rite incanted, and every re-opening of his own vein as it sought to knit itself back together, he became slower. His focus clouded, he stumbled in dizziness, his gifted sense blunted in the confusion and he had to stifle his elated laughter after every reap. He'd never taken more than two lives in any single situation. He'd never needed to. And now, some small and distant part of him wished that was still the case.

But he could handle it. Even as the bandits smartened up and gathered around one fire rather than spreading out and chasing shadows, he could handle it.

He crouched behind a broken well just beyond the light's reach, raised his hand, baring his palm towards them, and managed to concentrate his mind enough to shape an intention at its centre. A dull thump expanded through the air to stun the gathering, and in that moment, he charged. He slit their throats one after the other, removing each of them as a threat. But it was far from perfect. Two he had cut too deep, and though he tried to claim their souls first, they bled out before he could finish even the second line. He'd lost another in the time he'd wasted on them, but the final six still lay on the ground, grasping at their severed throats.

Now he could enjoy it. Now he could lose himself in the sensation of every reward Vokaad bestowed upon him: the power, the strength, the fervour. He laughed a most elated laugh, there was no more need to stifle it, and in his joy he cackled, chuckled and sighed without care. Nothing mattered. He was surrounded by corpses and blood flowed freely from his own body, but nothing mattered. Not the blood pouring from his open vein - the gifted magic was closing it back up already - nor the blood that leaked from his side.

His laughter only lightened as he looked down at the dark fluid that coated his hand, glistening in the fire light, and he had the capacity only to distantly wonder when it had happened, as well as what the impact was he'd just felt behind him, and at the sudden difficulty he found in breathing.

Fortunately, comprehension of the string of Ivaean curses spat into his ear came much quicker, and his startled mind cleared fast enough to react.

As the wire around his throat tightened and began to choke his breath away, he raised his hand and showed her his bloody palm. She began to say something, perhaps a jibe, perhaps genuine concern from a sudden change of heart, but whatever it was, it was cut short as she was thrown back and off of him by another bassy thump.

Freed, he intended to leap up and finish her, but instead his body stalled and doubled over in its effort to reclaim his breath, leaving him only distantly aware of the pain across his neck if not the blood the wire had drawn when it snapped. But there was no time to waste - even as he hacked and retched, he knew that. Vokaad's gift would protect him. He would have to trust in it.

His throat scored and his breath ragged, he grasped his dagger and shoved himself back to his feet only to be slammed right back down. The woman shrieked as she savaged him, but though the shrill sound was an undoubtedly effective stun, his mind was still too fogged for it to reach him. He managed, somehow, to throw her off of him, and though she was upon him again immediately with a knife in each hand, he had turned over and could finally return every blow his unearthly magic deflected. He didn't try to daze her and claim her soul for Vokaad, though it was, no doubt, the most valuable of all he had been presented with that night. He was too tired, and he had done enough. As it was, he doubted he'd make it back to the camp. He wouldn't die, that was certain - his kind were paid in magic for a reason - but finding his way back in the dark with his focus so shattered was quite impossible.

But if he didn't...

No, he had to get back.

He had to get back, get inside his tent, and pretend he hadn't left. Otherwise they would come looking for him, and with such a still air, his tracks would remain. Eyila couldn't miss them. And then they'd find him, and then they'd know...

He shoved the limp and lifeless body off of himself and clutched at the stab wound above his hip. The blood was still running heavily. He'd never suffered such an injury in tribute before, and he wondered, as he tore strips from the dead woman's clothing to staunch it as best he could, if the magic would be enough this time.

But he had to trust. He had to have faith.

He tied off the final binding, and after quickly wrapping his already healing forearm, collected his daggers and rose carefully to his feet. He hissed with the movement, but he wasn't sure if it actually hurt. It should have, he knew that much, but...did it?

He laughed. It didn't matter.

He staggered against a wall and tried to shake away the haze. He had to get back, *that's* what mattered, and he needed to focus. Just for the moment.

He looked about himself slowly and finally made for the south - then stopped after three stumbling steps and turned to his right. He managed a few paces further before deciding south was correct after all - assuming, of course, that south was south.

He shook his head again and decided to disregard direction. Get out, that's what he had to do first. Get to the walls, leave the village, and then follow the rocky outcrops. As long as the village remained on his right while he followed the small cliffs, he would be going the right way...

Chapter 44

Aya'u's soft caress came as ribbons brushing over bare, bronze skin; all that was simple, eternal and pure conveyed in a brief, single contact that slowed the heart and set the soul at ease. The scent of the mountains was carried on its tail - crisp air, wooded slopes, the musk of rutting deer - and transported the mind away for miles in an instant, as if the spirit and wind were one.

Eyila sighed softly, lost in the peace and freedom her goddess always granted her when she gave herself to the elements, and a soft, contented smile graced her lips.

What a wonder the past two weeks had been. Given leave from the village at last for more than simply gathering herbs, she'd enjoyed the company of some *highly* unusual people and, above all else, had finally been free to meditate openly. For two years she'd been forced to hide it, to sneak out and offer reverence after dark while appearing to bend to the chief's forbiddance and focus on her healing. So it was a refreshing change to feel Aya'u's loving touch without the fear of being caught - a return to what should have been the norm.

She knew she would sorely miss it when she returned, so she was glad she'd taken advantage of the opportunity, even if not to the extent she'd have liked. Her company had been good enough not to interrupt her when she settled into the paths of the strongest air currents, but their very presence remained a hindrance. It was for their modesty rather than her own that she settled for the bare essentials, keeping covered the areas of her body they might take offence to while freeing all else to the elements.

But Aya'u seemed to understand. There was no decrease in Her affection.

She sighed again as her heart floated in serenity, but she soon noticed a tightness above her eyes, then the small crease that had formed in her white-painted brow. A very slight change had also befallen the breeze - one impossible by nature alone. Her focus dragged reluctantly back to her surroundings.

She opened her eyes to the starlight and followed the air's new northward course. Her sight adjusted quickly, and in the same short instant that she spotted the dark form moving irregularly through the sand in the near distance, another sensation grazed her, one she'd last felt only in Rathen's company. But Rathen, she knew - could feel just as clearly - was down in the camp behind her.

He confirmed that himself a moment later as he spoke her name, as well as justifying her caution with the warning tone in his voice. He had sensed the same thing.

Hurriedly, she pulled on her animal skins and descended the pinnacle with both skill and urgency. Rathen was already moving out from between the rocks, cautioning Aria to stay back where she was, but Petra's voice rose from beyond before either of them could reach the sands. But what she said made no sense to either of them.

"Anthis?" Eyila repeated, and all eyes turned quizzically towards the tent they'd all supposed occupied. Aria, who had obediently remained near the fire, tentatively pulled aside the canvas which, it seemed, had barely even been tied. She looked back at them both with wide eyes. It was empty.

The two mages fled, shouting even before they broke into the open for Petra to keep away. It couldn't truly be Anthis - an arcane trick, though by whom or why was anyone's guess. But whatever it was, their shouts were too late. She had already reached the shuffling, limping figure by the time they'd stormed free of the camp.

"He's hurt," she called, and the alarm in her voice made the matter seem even less likely. How could Anthis have disappeared with no one noticing, become infused with magic and seriously injured, all during what couldn't be more than two hours in the lifeless desert?

Garon raced up alongside them as they covered the last distance, his hand already gripping the hilt of his sword. Both mages were equally prepared to loose spells, covering between their natures both defence and attack - but while Petra remained so close beside the mystery figure, not one of them could act. And when the clean, crisp moonlight finally caught the face of her burden, none were sure they should.

"Anthis?" Rathen's bewilderment doubled as the young man was lowered to the ground at Eyila's arrival, who skidded to a stop and immediately set to unwinding the makeshift bandage about his waist. But there was no mistake. On any part. This was Anthis, without a doubt, and there was a definite if diminishing sense of magic radiating from him. "Eyila--"

"Yes," she replied shortly, "I know, but I can't begin to guess how." She spared him only a single glance, quizzical and disturbed, but he could only shake his head in clear and unsettled confusion.

Petra muttered in a panic, ignoring the others' cryptic concerns as he slumped limp in her arms. Whatever energy he'd found to drag himself through the desert in such a state had evaporated at the sight of his rescue. Now he could barely hold his head up. She growled his name again, fighting the urge to shake him to his senses, but though he managed sluggishly to look back at her, somehow he could only smile. Relief, it seemed, had addled him.

Eyila cursed beneath her breath as she peeled away the last of the cloth. The conjured light revealed a gash that sank deep into his side, darkened and made more gruesome by the blood that surrounded it, dried, congealed, and in one corner still leaking. It took Rathen and Eyila each a long moment to understand what they were seeing; Petra and Garon got there a little sooner. It had been a stab wound initially, but the blade had been dragged and twisted to increase its severity. This was no accident. Eyila then spotted the bandage around his arm.

"Dammit, Anthis!" Petra cursed in exasperation as the tribal girl began to unwind that one, too, though it wasn't particularly sodden. "What have you done?! Where did you go?!"

He mumbled something, a single sound that could have been involuntary, but repeated twice before managing to finish: "Bandits..."

"Bandits?" She stared back out over the sands, following his tracks. "The village... They must know we're here; they're seeking us out--" she looked back to him in bafflement. "But what were you doing out there on your own?!"

Rathen watched in silence as the fabric unravelled from his arm.

"Walk," he struggled.

"You should have told us if you were sodding off to clear your head again," she snapped, clearly about ready to add to his injuries out of her own worry. "You're such a *fool,* Anthis!"

"At least you got away." Eyila began to shape her unfamiliar signs over his bloodied hip, but despite Rathen's interest in her magic, he wasn't watching. He looked instead from the wound on his arm, one which seemed far too recent to be so far healed, to the absence and stupidity in his expression. And he was acutely aware of the moment the arcane taint finally dissipated.

He reeled back a step as realisation hammered its way into his skull. "My god..." His eyes widened in horror, and though all others looked towards him searchingly, Anthis's dreary eyes stared back in dreadful understanding. He made no attempt at all to deny the silent conclusion, even as Rathen searched them desperately for any other explanation. "Eyila, stop. Get away from him."

"What? Why?"

"Just *move!*" He contorted his fingers faster than anyone thought possible and several shafts of light flashed through the air, piercing Anthis's shivering torso to impale him on the spot.

"*What are you doing?!*" She bellowed as Petra jumped back in shock, leaving the wounded young man to drop from her knee to the ground with an agonized cry. But Rathen didn't respond. He stormed forwards and grasped the now paralysed arm, closely inspecting the cut's position.

His dark eyes flashed. Unadulterated fury filled him, the greatest he'd felt in a decade. They turned thunderously onto Anthis's hazy green. "Sulyax Dizan," he spat. "Is that what this is?!"

Petra froze, and neither did Garon attempt to move forwards and pull the mage off of him. Eyila looked critically between them, but her tongue remained just as still.

"I know this cut," he growled, leaning menacingly close, "I've seen it before. Tell me right now that I am mistaken."

Anthis didn't reply.

Eyila's frown deepened. "S-sulyak..what? What is that?"

"Sulyax Dizan. It's a myth--"

"It's no myth." Garon's certainty caught Petra's voice before she could continue to deny it. "The Sulyax Dizan is a cult; a group of people who take the lives of others in the belief that they're protecting the world from the Apocalypse." He stared at Anthis, his expression unreadable. "They kill by opening a vein, mixing their blood with their own and reciting some kind of ritual incantation - then they're rewarded in magic."

"It's a *story,*" Petra stressed.

"No," Rathen growled, having not once removed his dagger-like gaze. "Eyila and I *definitely* felt magic, even before you saw him."

"And I've seen the evidence for myself," Garon added. "One of my earliest tasks was to track down and arrest a cultist in Adin. I saw their 'gift' for myself, at close range." All eyes followed his back to the renowned historian. None of them missed the fact that he hadn't yet tried to refute the accusation.

With a curse, Rathen violently cast the limp arm aside, eliciting another grunt of pain, and searched him just as roughly. It didn't take him long to find two daggers stuffed into his boot. He snarled in satisfaction and threw them out of his reach while Petra stared in disbelief. "You went looking for the bandits, didn't you?" He didn't reply; Rathen barely managed to restrain himself from punching him. Then he wondered why he bothered. His fist met Anthis's cheekbone with a pleasing thump. "What happened? You tried to take them all on at once?"

"They couldn't have gotten the jump on him," Garon assured him.

"No, because you can *sense* them all, can't you?" He sneered. "*No one* can sneak up on you, not truly..."

"Only if I'm...looking for them," Anthis rasped. Evidently the punch had shaken free some of his bearings, though his eyes were still disgustingly lascivious. "But she...I hadn't...I was distracted... I could sense her, but I'd...written her off, just...like the others..."

Petra turned her back as a small hiccup tumbled out. Eyila saw her shake, though in shock or rage, she wasn't sure. She, herself, was simply confused - if also a little curious.

Anthis burst into a chest-ripping choke, but his body, still paralysed by Rathen's glowing rods, barely moved. "The magic," he eventually managed, "it's so we can get...get away afterwards...survive... But it doesn't last...depends on...the quality of--" he retched again. "Higher quality souls--"

"Means a longer high."

"High?"

Rathen glanced towards Eyila. "*Look* at him."

She did so, and what interest there had been was slowly swept aside by disgust.

"That's what all this has been," Petra mumbled, raising her voice as she turned back around, her usually thoughtful hazel eyes now blazing with a frightening fire. "Not the desert. You've been so venomous all this time because you needed a *fix*. All this time...oh, Vastal save us, and every time before..."

"And it's been t-torment--"

"*Oh, I'm so sorry to hear that!*" She stormed forwards in a cloud of fury, but an invisible force suddenly blocked her path. She glared down at Rathen, who stared a severe warning to keep back.

"I'm sorry." They struggled to believe him while bliss still lingered around his eyes. "I usually have...chance to deal with it when I'm...alone...it never gets this bad...not normally. I f-factor bounties into my routes--" he howled in pain after another cough ravaged his limp body. "I was desperate!"

"'Desperate'. So if our route hadn't chanced upon those poor bastards, it could have been any *one* of--"

"*No.*" His rattling voice broke in his attempt at a firm tone. "Never. Absolutely n-not."

Rathen stared viciously back at him. "Why?"

"Des-despite what you're all thinking...I have more in-integrity than th-that. Why else is my bag stuffed...with bounty papers? People like them - killing, r-raping for sport, their souls...are the most valuable. They live free lives, by their own rules - fear no one. Their souls...the best that can be offered and the...worst the w-world has to live with."

"How very noble of you," Petra sneered, but a thoughtful shadow suddenly fell over Rathen's grim face.

"But...children live freely, don't they?" He asked lightly. *Too* lightly. All tongues stilled at his musing tone. "Children live by their own rules; they're not concerned with right or wrong, what has to be done, nor the rigours of life and survival. They live happily. Ignorantly." He cocked his head dangerously. "Or am I wrong?" Suddenly Anthis didn't seem to want to provide a half-spluttered defence. "And wandering traders, too. People who go wherever they wish, trading goods so they can buy food and keep travelling, see the world, do what they love rather than being tied down to one place. Not like city merchants, worn down by the same day-in day-out monotony, nor the peasants who live in disease and misery, nor even the rich who live their lives dictated by the worry of what people might think of them, or falling from grace and losing everything. No - not the people who live on a tightrope."

Against possibility, the leaded air pressed down even heavier. Rathen's eyes remained fixed menacingly, murderously, on Anthis, while the others looked evaluatingly from one face to the next.

Rathen lived in the wilds. He was banished, but he was exempt from the law and the Order as long as he kept away from it; Petra travelled and made money doing what she loved simply so she could keep doing it; Eyila, too, lived a free and simple life as far as the others were concerned - and Aria, a happy, intelligent child who had grown up knowing nothing but freedom, and who marvelled constantly at the world around her. It seemed that Garon was the only one not at risk, but as he kept himself locked up so tightly, no one could really be sure.

"'Torment'," Petra repeated, looking slowly back to the rogue. "*Us*. That's what you meant. It's been torment travelling with *us*..."

Rathen suddenly rose and turned dangerously towards the inquisitor. "You knew about my problems. Did you know about this?"

"Of course he didn't--"

Rathen whirled back around. "*You!* Don't you *dare* speak!"

"*Me?!*" Anthis finally erupted, despite his agony. "*Every single one* of us has darkness in our past! And that *you*--"

Rathen delivered his face another swift punch, and this time he was rewarded with a crunch. He'd been a little disappointed that the first was so gently received. "*I*," he said slowly, so there could be no misunderstanding, "am a monster. But *you* do all of this *willingly*." He returned to Garon with a single, purposeful gesture towards the old village, then looked towards Petra as he started away. "Stay here. Aria will sneak out - keep her with you, and away from him."

"You're going back out there. What about Eyila? Could she--"

"They're all already dead. She can't help them. Him," he added, casting back a disdainful look, "she can. Should she want to." He headed north with Garon dutifully at his side, and though he'd known that anger filled Petra's eyes, stepping past her, he saw the true depth of the hurt and betrayal. It was deeper, even, than his own. He offered her an apologetic smile. "Try not to beat him to death," he said softly. "Garon probably thinks we still need him."

She didn't smile, but he hadn't expected her to. His own was short-lived.

Neither said a word as they trekked through the sand. Rathen couldn't speak for Garon, but truthfully, he felt completely dazed, addled and dumbstruck. How a man could hide such a secret so well terrified him. It was true what he'd said - Rathen certainly had darkness in his past, as did Aria, and Petra, and though hers he couldn't guess the full extent of, he was confident it was just as unwilling. But this... Part of him was still convinced it was a misunderstanding, or a magical trick. After all, how could Anthis Karth, of all people in the world, be a murderous madman? It was ludicrous. Nothing more.

But there was another part of him that couldn't deny what he'd felt, seen and heard, and though he desperately didn't want to reach the village for fear of what he'd find, he needed to know for certain one way or the other. But...though he wished not to admit it, he also knew he was driven by more than just personal curiosity. There was a sense of responsibility cemented deep within him that wouldn't be silenced, and he cursed his military past for being unable to ignore it. So he walked beside the inquisitor from the Hall of the White Hammer, carrying the weight of law and containment he'd been unable to shed in eleven years, alongside his own need to view the evidence and judge him for himself.

There was no challenge in following Anthis's tracks, deep and clumsy as they were, and they soon arrived at the roadside ruin. The fires still burned, casting a comforting glow against the walls of ancient buildings in a manner that almost leant hope that they had misjudged the extent of his activities. But that hope was shattered the moment they stepped inside. They found two bodies almost immediately, both with throats slit and arms torn, and as they moved from the edge of the village towards the nearest of the fires, they found nine more corpses lying in the flickering light, each with the same inflictions. The ninth, however, was riddled with cuts - a mess of slashes and stab wounds - which revealed her to be the one who had fought back. From the butchering she'd been dealt, it seemed that Anthis had gotten off disappointingly lightly.

They searched the rest of the village in an increasingly defeated and sickened silence, finding close to twenty bodies. There was no trace of anyone having survived and fled. Rathen wasn't sure what was worse - that it was true he'd massacred the entire village and claimed the souls, it seemed, of all but one, or that such a cheerful man had executed so many so tidily...

The bodies were gathered and set upon the fire, where Rathen encouraged its flames to grow and engulf them. They left before the stench of burning flesh could sting their nostrils.

"You're sure we still need him?" Rathen asked, breaking the dense silence.

"We still need him."

He sighed uneasily. *'Perhaps sending Aria away is for the best after all...'*

Eyila was kneeling beside Anthis when they returned, clearly uncomfortable though focused intently upon his injuries, just as Rathen had expected her to be. His jaw knotted, but he had no right to stop her. She was an intelligent girl, but she seemed to have that same pesky need to help people which ailed all healers, as well as the inability to silence it even when common sense dictated they should.

And he did resent her helping him.

Petra was standing nearby, her furious eyes flicking watchfully between Anthis and Eyila, and the two arrivals. Her sword was drawn in one hand, the point of her blade angled in such a way that it was clear she was ready to pounce at a moment's notice to defend Eyila, despite him still being clearly immobilised, or should the mood simply strike her. Aria's wrist was held tightly in her other, and though her big, blue-grey eyes flickered in relief at her father's return, caution, confusion and disappointment were quick to dull them.

That only worsened Rathen's mood.

He removed the paralysis only once Eyila was finished, after which everyone kept their distance. He was more than prepared to form spells to lock Anthis in his tent, but Garon warned him away from that idea, so instead, he cast spells over his own to keep Anthis out while evading Aria's questions about the night's events with games. He hadn't the heart to tell her. The look in her eyes and slightly higher pitch to her rushed voice revealed she already had ideas, and while he felt no love for the murderous, deceitful man, he found himself curiously disinclined to rob her of a friend. With words, at least. He would make sure she never went near him again.

The camp was silent. Tense and silent. All tents were occupied - Anthis's had been checked - but whether anyone slept was another matter. Garon had stood watch into the small hours, as he often did, but now sought a brief reprieve by the dying fire to chase away the encroaching cold. He was practised enough at operating under little rest - he'd learned even before rising to Inquisitor that work often called for it - and had later been trained, brutally, to withstand it when he had to at the cost of his focus. Fortunately it wasn't his task to think at the moment - he had two other minds for that. He had only to watch.

He knelt beside the flames. They had withered, but they provided enough heat, and so it was no wonder that he didn't immediately notice the lithe figure sitting upon the lowest of the spires. He jolted inwardly when he finally did, several seconds after kneeling, and immediately reached for his sword.

"Put that away," Petra sighed wearily.

He slipped it the few inches back into its sheath and lowered himself back down, composed once again, and returned his gaze diffidently to the fire. "Why aren't you asleep?"

"Good one."

"When did you get up?"

"I gave up trying about...twenty minutes ago, maybe." She cocked her head just enough that the firelight caught her rich eyes. He glanced up, watching her peer upon him like a cat atop a wall. He thought the comparison was fitting. "What's it to you?"

"Nothing." He looked away impartially again, and she, too, dismissed him in turn. He glanced back briefly and frowned to himself. She'd been indifferent towards him since the flooded ruins just over a week ago. She hadn't attempted to talk to him even briefly while he kept an evening watch, and when their voices happened to cross in group conversation - not that there had been much of that going around lately - she acknowledged him politely. Too politely. He found that it was beginning to bother him.

"I can't believe you won't arrest him," she said suddenly, breaking the all too familiar silence. "Or get rid of him." He watched her lip curl in the firelight. "How can you stomach him?"

He took a stick from the fire and began poking at the embers. "My thoughts towards him aren't relevant."

"Don't you care that he's *murdering* people for *personal gain?!*"

"His victims have prices on their heads, wanted dead or alive. If he didn't kill them, either someone else would have, or they would have continued their crimes."

"So he'd have us believe..." She breathed a humourless laugh. "It's funny. I thought I had more to fear from a mage than a historian."

"Appearances can be deceiving."

She grunted flatly. "Can't they just?"

He watched her look up at the stars and saw her lips curve downwards through the darkness. "You're quite angry."

"Sod off."

"You were fond of Anthis."

She frowned down at him. "What does that mean?"

"You were close. Often talking together, laughing and joking. He really gravitated to you when Rathen's secret came out."

"Well, we were friends...I suppose, yeah, we were."

"But it was more than that, though, wasn't it?"

She blinked, but when he failed to continue, a bitter smile spread across her face. "Wow," she chuckled. "You...truly are..." She shook her head and rose to her knees, then clambered down the rock with such agility she could well have been a cat after all. But rather than join him to continue the conversation, or at least finish the thought, she moved on past him towards her tent instead.

"Where are you going?"

She didn't reply.

"Petra," he hurried after her, and was surprised when she hesitated and turned to spare him a moment. He dropped his voice to avoid waking the others. "I'm sorry if I've insulted you," he said honestly, if unsure how, or why it mattered, "and I'm sorry for this, too, but I need you to tell me how your father was killed."

She didn't ask how he had known. She didn't even flinch. She simply stared at him, reading his eyes, and he did his best to conceal his assumptions. He had little idea if he'd succeeded or not as she took a stern half-step towards him, and her voice dropped to a bitter tone. "Butchered in an alley," she told him venomously. "Stabbed repeatedly. A mugging gone wrong; he had nothing to steal." She didn't wait for a response before turning away and vanishing silently between the canvasses.

He stared after her, the small, ever-present knot in his brow tightening as he wondered why she had told him the truth rather than keeping her secrets, as she had been frequently inclined to do. But he soon shook it off, as well as the lingering confusion. He'd been distracted long enough. He had to get back to the watch.

It was half way between midnight and morning, but the desert had been awake for hours. As soon as darkness set in, small, dog-like creatures with oversized ears and silver eyes began yipping as they bounced playfully through the scrub; smooth-skinned lizards moved like fish through the sand in hunt of insects, silent themselves but for the running of dislodged grains, and every few minutes there came the distant bleat of what could only be giant goats closer to the mountains. But such, it seemed, was the norm, and they were all the more lively for the welcome, cooler air. But whether it had been the same nightly scenario for the past two and a half weeks or not, it was no easier to filter out. The sounds of a city - drunken shouts and laughter, the clatter of hooves and wooden wheels over uneven stone roads, the ringing of blacksmith hammers as they worked into the night - were deafening, but familiar enough to ignore. But the sounds of a wild place were undefinable and snatched even Garon's trained attention away from time to time.

But he sat motionless in the darkness and calmed his senses to hear above and beneath it, just as he had every other night.

The light extended no further than a foot beyond the kindling. Nothing within the confines of the camp moved but weak shadows as they danced indecisively across the surrounding ring of canvas, barely distinguishable against the smothering darkness. All was silent but for a soft snore from within one of the tents, and an occasional giggle rippling from another.

The bags were heaped to one side, a corner of the minuscule fortress safe from scavenging creatures, while the jugs they'd carried had long been discarded in favour of the desert-lander's knowledge.

Only one bag stood apart from the collection: the historian's satchel. Filled with ancient books and scrolls and priceless research, it was never far from his side. It was a wonder he didn't keep it in the tent with him while he slept - a wonder, but also a stroke of luck.

Shadows flickered with a brief intensity, but the camp's stillness was unbroken. Even as embers scattered from the dying fire, dislodged by a phantom movement to rest against the tent where the satchel had stood but a moment before.

Chapter 45

"*Fire!*" Garon boomed, staggering through the wave of heat concealed by the glowing stone as he charged into the camp. But his warning had been needless; Petra and Anthis were already trying to smother the four-foot flames. But even as Garon set to helping them heap sand and empty water skins upon it, they could never work faster than the fire could spread.

Eyila burst out of her animal hide tent not a moment after the shout, and Rathen and Aria from theirs an instant later. Even as Aria fled the stones to safety at her father's unheard instruction, the flames immediately died at the banished mage's appearance and plunged them into darkness.

A relieved silence held for a long moment, until Rathen turned accusingly towards Anthis. "What just bloody happened?!"

The young man looked back at him in shock. Despite having surely been asleep until a moment ago, there was a definite light in his eyes, and he no longer stood with a sideways hunch. Evidently, Eyila hadn't allowed him to suffer.

"What makes you think it had anything to do with me?!"

"It was your tent!"

"*Why would I set fire to my own tent?!*"

"Why indeed, but it's a shame it didn't burn you with it."

"That's enough, Rathen!" Garon yelled, but Anthis didn't seem to have caught the last remark. Something else had stolen over his mind, and he darted instead towards the smoking remains of his magically drowned tent and began searching frantically through the tatters. He muttered hysterically beneath his breath, but no one caught a word.

"Is everyone else all right?" Garon asked, looking across the others, and all nodded, if slightly shaken. He stopped at Petra. "What happened?"

"I don't know." Her voice was tainted by a definite degree of mistrust, though she didn't glance towards the frenzied young man. "I was awake, trying to sleep, and when I heard someone shout in a panic, I came outside and found *him* standing there with a stupid look on his face. I started trying to put it out, then he joined in. I don't know how it started."

"But you don't think it was an accident," Rathen summarised.

Garon shook his head. "From the look of it, it started from the outside. Anthis didn't do it. And why would he?" He glanced down towards him as his muttering became more frantic, flinging ash, sand and burned and blackened fabric out behind him. He looked back to Rathen and Petra, both of whom followed his gaze with clear contempt. "Be sensible. He hasn't suddenly lost his mind."

"And you're so sure he had it to begin with?!" Rathen burst, but though he inhaled to deliver more, something other than the officer's steel gaze stilled his tongue just as abruptly as it had been loosened. The inquisitor didn't fail to notice the degree of alarm suddenly present in his shaken eyes, and it sparked unease in the pit of his own stomach.

A horrendous curse erupted from the ground beside them before he could broach it.

"Where is it?!"

"Where's what?" Petra snapped accidentally, preferring to ignore him despite the spectacle he was making, digging like a dog possessed, but she'd been caught just as startled as the rest of them.

"*My bag!* My books, my notes--*dammit, where is it?! It was here!*" Everyone looked towards the ruin in silence while he continued desperately to dig, but he was soon wrenched away by the shoulders.

"Was that everything?" Garon tried to catch his gaze, but Anthis could only stare helplessly towards the wreck. He shook him with little care. "Was *everything* in there?"

Slowly, blank eyes turned upon him. "No..." he pointed towards the three books discarded on the ground, half buried beneath the scuffed sand, and all were immediately familiar: two he'd been pondering over for the past few days, and the other, of course, his own notebook which was often as good as glued in his hands.

Garon exhaled a deep sigh and hung his head in relief, releasing the historian from the tight grip of his fingertips which alarm had encouraged to dig only deeper into his shoulders. But despite the most prevalent books surviving, Anthis didn't share in it. Tears had sprung into his eyes as he dropped heavily to his hands and knees, and he stared still and silent, as if paralysed again, at the spot where his most treasured belongings were always placed.

He was utterly broken.

Rathen was quick to stop Aria, who had reappeared at the edge of the camp, from taking even a single comforting step towards him. He felt her eyes burn into the back of his head with confusion as he barred her way, but he didn't look around. His own were distant and haunted.

Garon circled the quietly, innocently glowing fire and retrieved the three books, Anthis's own somehow just as worn as the two of seven hundred years, and flicked briefly through them. He understood little of it, but he knew what he was looking at. He nodded to himself and his usually rigid shoulders visibly eased. "Get some sleep," he told them all, then turned and dragged the quite unwilling historian back to his feet and drove the books firmly into his shaking hands. "We'll be fine with what we have, won't we, Anthis? Anthis?" He received a single nod, which had clearly taken effort, but his green eyes were still lost to a distant place. Garon accepted it, then looked expectantly towards the others until they began to disperse.

"Rathen," he added a little more quietly after ushering the defeated young man to his own tent instead. "Could you cast some defences around the camp?"

"Why?" He asked - or shrieked? Garon noticed he hadn't moved, and that his dark eyes were growing wider. "You said the fire--"

"No, it's not that." He eyed him carefully, and as he began to comprehend the severity of the alarm that lined his face and the intensity of the knot in his jaw, the unease began to creep back up into his stomach. "Rathen--"

"Aria, hide."

She didn't question the command issued through tightly barred teeth, nor why he now trembled. She didn't need to. Dread sparked in her eyes as she obeyed, turning and scurrying away, snatching her doll as she passed, moving quicker than had a harpy's talons been grasping at her back. She was woefully aware of what was coming.

The girl's haste was all the confirmation Garon needed. He drew his sword in one hand with a quick, sharp movement, grasped the mage's collar with the other, and dragged him as fast as he could from the camp.

Rathen's hand lashed up and grasped his wrist, clutching it tighter than should have been humanly possible, but he didn't try to free himself. He followed willingly despite his feet trying to carry him the opposite direction, despite the gasps and grunts of pain which became increasingly guttural with every stumbling step, and despite the paralysing fear which gave way to the beast and denied him the strength to fight it back.

His grunts soon became wails, and Garon suppressed the sickness in his gut at the terrible cracking they began to punctuate. The camp was still too near, the others would surely hear his unintelligible cries. He hurried his pace. He could handle Rathen himself now he knew what to expect, and it was his duty to protect everyone from his rampage. His duty alone.

His grip around his sword tightened as fingernails began to dig into his skin, and he braced himself against the burning that followed as they finally punctured through. He continued to drag him along, but the resistance grew, and before much longer he knew he would be thrown aside as Rathen's increasingly unnatural strength outmatched his.

He cast a glance behind him to note the distance of the camp, but his sight was stolen in an instant. Locked by jet-black eyes, distinctly malevolent and made darker by the paper-white skin of the monstrous form, which in turn was made whiter by the surrounding darkness and light of the slivered moon. Bony thorns had already erupted from his clavicles and broadened shoulders, piercing his shirt which had torn across his chest by the widening of his ribs, revealing those twisting, scrolling black veins beneath.

Garon's heart stopped as the gaunt, sharp face loomed over him, sharp teeth bared in a malicious grin, and the heat of primal fear surged through his whole body, unreasonable and unsuppressable. This man was no longer human.

The grip on his wrist tightened abruptly, but with a quick and jagged twist, Garon managed to free himself before his bones could be crushed, and he jumped back just quickly enough to avoid the beast's own aberrantly quick response. He spent the next few moments doing his best to avoid the advance and slashing of bone-armoured claws all while looking for an opening, but while this beast had been distracted by anything that had even twitched in Carenna, out here there was nothing to catch the quick, deathless eyes.

Until a nearby bleat snatched his attention instead. Garon didn't waste any time in gratitude. He lunged blade-first towards his waist, the only point of Rathen's body that appeared to be unarmoured by reshaped bone, and his steel duly caught, tearing fabric and skin. Blood seeped out, so dark it could have been black itself, and soaked quickly into the shredded shirt. But despite his own agility, Garon had no time to even draw back his sword before the beast was upon him again, claws slashing above guttural howls.

Once again he was forced onto the defensive, ducking and diving in tight movements, pushed to the limit of his capabilities. His sword didn't weigh him down, but it prevented the short, sharp jabs he would have preferred. With Rathen so close so fast, he hadn't the room to swing it.

Suddenly, Rathen hesitated, and Garon grasped the opportunity immediately, lunging out again to worsen the wound in the hope of slowing him down.

But the beast had only paused to gather his energy. Before steel could make even grazing contact, Rathen burst forwards at frightening speed, his sharp, armoured shoulder angled directly towards him.

Somehow, Garon managed to avoid the worst of the blow as he spun off to one side, planning to strike his flank instead. But though he was only clipped, the power behind the attack was astounding, altering his rotation and casting him off to the ground.

Garon barely had time to curse. The beast leapt upon him as he tried to stagger back up from his knee, and instead dropped and rolled to the side before Rathen's increased weight could pin him down.

He dashed through the sand for distance, fighting his way over the loose terrain. He had to strike him, to subdue him, give his mind a chance to clear. Last time a strike to the carotid artery had sufficed - but only once Petra had tripped him up.

He glanced back, hoping the sand might do that job for him, but his feet, larger, clawed, and having obliterated his boots, were covering the ground like snow shoes, and anything concealed beneath, he surely crushed.

But of course he wasn't so lucky. Something caught his own foot and sent him flat on the sand, just like the last time, and he cursed himself for not paying attention. He pushed forwards and lumbered back to his feet, but just as he was quick to take advantage of any opening, so was his mindless opponent. Talons raked him, flipping him onto his back and shoving him back down into the thin desert floor. Sharp rocks pressed through the sand into his spine and shoulders as claws swiped across his forearms, raised to protect his face, and it was only then that he found he'd lost his sword, thrown from his hand as he was to the ground. He glimpsed it between blows, ignoring the burning agony of every slash, but it was too far out of reach and he had no hope of throwing Rathen off of him to snatch it.

He pushed aside the useless sense of hopelessness he felt creeping up inside him. His unarmed training was vast, but Rathen was much heavier than any opponent he'd ever faced, and stronger, faster, and with limbs longer still. Garon had been trained to fight against people, not monsters.

But he knew he could work it to his advantage.

He squirmed beneath him and soon managed to raise his knee and drive it straight up into his crotch. It had little of the usual effect, but his purpose was to knock Rathen forwards and pull himself down. It worked flawlessly. He toppled, and Garon dragged himself out from beneath him in the same instant, between his legs. He didn't waste time fetching his sword. He turned and leapt upon his back, avoiding as best he could the sharp protrusions along his spine, and raised his hand to strike its edge against the beast's neck.

Rathen roared in fury, stunning Garon for half a second, but that hesitation was enough. The beast rose and threw himself backwards against the ground, caring none for the rocks which broke the surface where the jagged escarpment peaked, his own skeleton more than sturdy enough to withstand any damage he might inflict upon himself.

Garon's, however, was not.

The world suddenly stood still. He stared past the half-foot thorn rising from Rathen's shoulder to the stars twinkling beyond. He was aware of the pain that racked all through his torso, but distantly, as if only vividly imagined. And perhaps it was. Perhaps the howl of victory that drummed in his ears was just as distant as it seemed, perhaps it belonged to kentauri, or tribes, or those pesky harpies. Did harpies howl? No, they screeched. But he could hear screeching. Or shrieking. A brutal, high-pitched cry, whatever it was, one of anger. And it was growing nearer.

Steel flashed past his face, and the world began to move again - slowly, but it was moving; time, sound, his own rapid heartbeat, and he found the metallic taste of blood on his tongue.

The howl came again, returned with another fitful yell, and suddenly the weight was dragged off of him.

He breathed, gasped, and from his own lips he thought he heard a cry. But of course he did. At that moment, he knew nothing but agony, an agony that had intensified when the world had began moving again, and he resented it.

Silence fell - how long ago, he wasn't sure - and a face appeared, a beautiful face framed in red. For a moment his racing, hammering heart soothed, even as the expression it bore twisted into panic. "Pe..." But despite his eloquent reassurance, she muttered 'no, no, no' over and over before turning her fine profile to shout something into the distance. And then another face appeared even before she'd finished, a dirty but pretty face, if a little too young to strike a chord, but one, he felt, that could become beautiful in time. But this one's expression was more severe, and there was a terror in her pale blue eyes alongside a dutiful determination.

He spared her little attention. His eyes shifted sluggishly back onto Petra, and a moment later, everything was black.

Chapter 46

A soft, comfortable warmth enveloped his body; opening his heavy eyelids was a challenge he found himself disinclined to overcome. So he lay peacefully as his mind wandered in a hazy dream, unsure and unconcerned with what was memory and what was fantasy, and it was quite some time before he realised that the voices speaking softly in the distance were not imagined, but beside him. He didn't try very hard to make out the words, but both, one more melodious than the other, were equally tinted with the metallic note of concern.

They fell suddenly silent, and he realised he'd mumbled in a half-dream.

"Garon?"

He managed with effort to pull one eye open to the torch-lit darkness, but upon seeing Petra's shadowed face twisted in barely subdued alarm, memory struck him like a lightning bolt.

His eyes flashed open as he shoved himself up onto his elbow, and he stared down at himself, fully prepared for the sight of deep, bloody punctures from his collarbone to his pelvis.

He blinked in confusion when he found only bare skin, without even a concealing bandage. He touched his chest in doubt, feeling frantically for the wounds he was certain he'd sustained, the ones he was sure should have killed him. But there was nothing there.

He looked back to Petra, confusion further creasing his weary face, then towards Eyila who sat sullenly beside her. At the sight of the tribal healer, realisation slowly set in. He sighed deeply in relief and fell back onto his blanket.

But the atmosphere, he noticed, was suffocating. He turned his gaze - serious, as usual; his former colour returning - back onto the pair, and tried to calculate the situation. Another unease soon began to creep into his gut and he found himself unable to voice the forming question.

"Garon," Eyila began, clearly steeling her voice against whatever pressed upon her, "raise your left hand."

He frowned, but did as she asked, and though he found both his elbow and shoulder were stiff and plagued by a dull pain, he managed easily enough.

"Flex your wrist." There was no change to her tone as, again, he did as he was asked. But he didn't miss the brief flash of something in her eyes, even if it was gone too quickly to identify. His heart jumped when he followed her gaze and found that he had barely managed to bend his hand half way. Suddenly, he understood that look in her eyes, and he reflected it back at her in growing apprehension.

"Make a fist."

He obeyed as quickly as he could, his heart thundering, not daring to hesitate, to let fear set in and prolong his panic. But it gripped him, cold, clammy and unrelenting, as only his ring and smallest finger moved.

The silence was deafening. Eyila stared at his half-closed hand in shame; Petra stared in dismay. Garon stared for miles beyond the edge of his cramped tent.

Eyila took a breath, about to speak, but it took her a moment longer to truly find the courage. "I can't find the damage," she said at last, her tone professionally disconnected despite the tears she tried to keep from falling from her black-painted eyes. "I've never had to treat anything like this, and I can't find any swelling or tearing. With cuts it's easier, it's obvious, but nerves--"

"It's all right."

She bit her lip as the first tear dropped, her shame growing in the face of Garon's passivity. She watched him stare at his hand and try, once again, to form a fist. And once again, only two fingers responded.

Petra shook her head in lingering disbelief. "It will heal on its own, won't it?" She asked softly, searching for comfort, perhaps on his behalf, perhaps for herself. But again Eyila hesitated.

"I don't know how severe it is... It might - but even if it does, it will take months--"

"It's all right," he said again, far too softly as he raised his right hand and successfully contracted it into a fist. His heart was racing. It was surely about to burst through his ribs, and he hoped that it would rather than continue to pump the rush of helplessness and anger through his veins. All he could think about was the unrelenting responsibility to protect his people. It pressed upon him in every waking moment, forced upon him by his own choice of profession and the brutal training to heed its commands, to do whatever he had to in response to any threat. And he resented that that training extended far beyond combat, tracking and maintaining a level of authority. He resented that it had been equally academic, because he could make an educated guess at what had happened to him, and he knew that being given answers to pointless questions wouldn't change the situation. Because, hatefully, he was also fully aware of the risks in every situation.

Feeling the contempt tighten in his jaw, he forced himself to loosen and take a deep breath. Because he was also fully aware that there was nothing to do at that point but accept his circumstance. The task at hand was too severe for personal distractions.

He rolled his right shoulder and clenched his fist. His sword arm was unaffected, and while there was a chance his left could heal - though his education gave him little room for hope on that front - he would have to change his fighting style in the mean time. Fortunately his training had covered that, too, as not even a broken arm was an acceptable excuse for missing an opportunity to complete a mission, and how different was this, really?

He nodded to himself as his blood cooled. But he didn't look back up. "How's Rathen?"

Eyila didn't respond; she hiccuped instead.

"He's fine," Petra replied in her place. "Eyila's healed him and she's confident that he'll be all right, but sore for a while. Like...last time..."

He nodded his understanding, wondering absently if Kienza had come to his rescue again. He considered Petra from the corner of his eye, but a thought turned his gaze towards the tribal. He saw the same haunting in her eyes that he'd noticed outside, what felt like only minutes ago. She shortly excused herself, her voice catching on her tears. "Did you explain it to her?" He asked once the canvas fell back in place, but Petra laughed humourlessly.

"As best a thing like that can be. You realise *I* don't understand it, and it terrifies me just the same." Despite the distress that shook her voice, her eyes had darkened in disapproval the moment they'd been left alone, a formidable shadow that provided him a strange comfort in its familiarity, even as it rendered him suddenly unable to meet her gaze. He knew what was coming, and also knew that his present situation wouldn't earn him the soft side of her tongue. "You are a *fool*, Garon."

He sighed tiresomely, turning his head away and dropping his arm over his chest, even as he continued trying to flex his fingers. "So you've said."

"Don't you *dare* give me that tone. Broken ribs, punctured lungs, one shoulder dislocated, the other broken, shattered vertebrae - you have *nerve damage*, Garon, in fact it's a wonder you're still alive!"

"I don't want to talk about this."

"What if this doesn't heal?" The edge of her shaken voice sharpened. "What then?"

"I said I don't want to talk about it."

"You could have been *killed*."

"So could you."

She clenched her fists at his unfaltering passive aggression and he knew she wanted to lash out. He braced himself. But she sighed, rose to a crouch and made for the doorway instead. He panicked. "Wait."

She stopped but didn't look back. "What is it?"

He didn't speak. He didn't know. Or, rather, he *did*, but he couldn't comprehend it.

She didn't give him much chance before continuing on her way.

"Why did you come out?" He blurted, pushing himself back up onto his elbow as she paused again. "Why did you risk yourself?"

"Because you were about to be...shredded."

He watched her linger beside the canvas, still not looking even half way around towards him. "Petra," he said firmly, "will you come back over here?"

She hesitated, but shortly complied, if with attitude, kneeling back beside him with an irritated huff and staring up at the canvas.

"What is it?"

"Whatever do you mean?"

"That. You've not been your usual...direct self lately..."

"Have I not?" She asked mildly.

"No." He maintained his calculating stare, but came up with nothing, and not for the first time. "I *have* done something, haven't I?"

"Does it matter?"

'Yes.' He lay back down. "No, I suppose it doesn't."

She shook her head, snapping off a growl of annoyance as she rose back to her haunches, and moved towards the exit even quicker than before. He managed to restrain a similar snarl as an immense frustration fell over him in that same instant. His concern, he failed to notice, had left his as-good-as-broken arm.

A flash of red suddenly filled his sight, a soft warmth pressed against his lips, and the not unpleasant mixture of spices, rose hip and sweat tickled his nose.

Then, just as suddenly, Petra was gone, casting behind her an insult as she escaped the confines of the tent, leaving him, once again, in the throes of confusion.

The red scent lingered.

Chapter 47

Shapeless wisps of faces and voices snaked outwards of the surrounding fog, radiating a tumultuous cacophony of primordial consciousness whose every tendril tried to snatch and drag him off course, to mindlessly crush him under its clumsy pressure and devour his unstable focus.

But Salus was faster. He'd been exposed to the coiling limbs' corruption often enough to learn their movements, to be able to predict and avoid them, for they ultimately belonged to him. So he continued to barrel his way through the murk of disembodied presences, all of which he'd known at some point in his life, but now laced with that same dangerous forbiddance no matter how inviting or repulsive they may once have been, until finally the familiar, tenuous glow broke through the dark, swirling cloud ahead.

He reached out too quickly. His anticipation got the better of him. His focus broke, his defences tumbled, and the fog consumed him.

Salus didn't open his eyes. He didn't even growl in frustration. He simply drew another deep breath, released his tightened muscles, and delved into his self once again. He ignored the sweat that trickled down his neck from his matted hair, and the prickling of his skin in barely subdued terror. To unleash the magic that lurked within him, he knew he had to brave the dense, incomprehensible morass of pointless thoughts and emotions which lay over it.

"Take a break," a voice suggested from beyond his tightly closed eyes, its tone not particularly concerned, though neither was it unkind.

"No," Salus replied tiredly. "I can do this."

"You're exhausted."

"I'm fine."

"You're rocking."

He sighed and at last opened his eyes, deciding, perhaps, that he could use a break after all. "I've not been sleeping that well, that's all."

"Ah," Denek nodded slowly. "Work keeping you up, is it?"

"No." Despite the irritating, intentionally imprecise comment, Salus looked up and considered him for a moment. He pursed his lips in thought, torn by sudden indecision, but he knew there was no real harm in asking. He was already painfully aware that he compromised his dominance every time he submitted himself to the mage's guidance - what was making himself look fractionally weaker if it meant he could finally put a distraction to rest?

"I've been having...dreams."

"That generally happens when you sleep."

"No, *bad* dreams, every night this week." Denek seemed about to speak, no doubt another sarcastic remark, but the hardness in Salus's own eyes stilled him.

Good. For once, he was taking him seriously. "No matter what happens in the dream," he continued quietly, lowering his voice against the guards outside, "no matter where I am - in a city, a forest, or anywhere in between - there are always...voices whispering, or shouting or laughing, even when there's absolutely no one around. And they're always distant but...inescapable. No matter how far I go, nor how much other noise there might be, I can always hear them." Salus paused, but Denek, to his surprise, still didn't speak. He merely observed him with his pale and irritating eyes, neither thoughtful nor absent. Salus wondered at that moment if it was wise divulging this to a man he couldn't read, but he reminded himself that he was still his prisoner and couldn't use this information against him even had it been of any value. And he needed to know if, somehow, this was related to his magic. He'd heard many times that mages suffered pain when their magic awoke, but he hadn't experienced such a thing. It was possible that he had naturally suppressed it as he did everything else, and it was manifesting in his sleep while his guard was down instead. "There are faces, sometimes, too," he continued, deciding that he needed to know, one way or the other. "White ones, strange and fierce. Monstrous, even - but there's one which is so much worse than the rest, bigger and always hanging above them, with black eyes and dead, drawn-in cheeks. It feels smothering...it's..." He caught himself as the familiar terror he felt every time he woke from the image began to coil around his throat, heightened by his recent exposure to all he tried to discard. But Denek's expression, tending, it seemed, towards boredom, still hadn't changed.

Salus's jaw knotted. "It means nothing, doesn't it?"

"Just sounds like nightmares to me," he finally replied, and his tone was, indeed, bored. "Perhaps too much skulduggery before bed. Or not enough fresh air." He glanced up to his tiny window. "I know I could do with a little more."

"I certainly feel like I'm trapped indoors..."

Denek cocked a finely shaped eyebrow as his gaze shifted back onto him. "You're awfully open today. Or perhaps just too tired to maintain hostility."

"Shut up."

"Oops, perhaps not."

Salus took a deep breath, straightened himself, closed his eyes and relaxed once more into his position. He didn't notice the breeze that wafted briefly through the window grating, prickling his sweat-slicked skin, because that day, that very day, he vowed that he would succeed. He had tried and failed all too often, some days by a hair's breadth, others by further than he cared to remember - but that day, it would happen. He could feel it. Call it fate, call it determination. It didn't matter. By one means or another, he *would* achieve it.

His mind hurtled back through the tangle of unrecognisable emotions, each only fractionally different from the last, yet all somehow unique and unmistakable at the same time. They pulled at him from all directions, but he braced himself against them, well-practised in such defence. Ignoring them, he'd learned, was futile; by pushing them away, he equally pushed away his goal. But he didn't have to embrace them and succumb to the weakness they invoked to reach it, he had only to acknowledge they were there. The days he'd faced them had brought him the closest to success.

So he struggled onwards, noting briefly as he passed the wisps of pride, of fury, of attraction, of remorse, and in time found himself back at the point of opportunity. The emotions he was never supposed to feel continued desperately to try to steal his attention, to throw upon him the extent of them he had denied himself. But despite their frenzy, he refused to give in. The light ahead of him grew. He kept a tight rein on himself, turning a corner of his mind onto his heartbeat, grounding himself in his body as it thumped harder and harder in his chest against the exertion and excitement, and forced himself to ride his momentum rather than try to rush ahead of it.

The light didn't move. Though continuously obscured by the elements of his own suppressed consciousness, it remained where it was, calm and still, unaffected by the hysteria around him as though oblivious to its dim neighbours, deaf and blind to its surroundings.

His heart hammered so much it hurt; he wanted to reach out to it, to push everything else out of the way and grasp the magic as soon as possible - but that had always enraged the rest. So he remained patient, exercising the quality that seemed to have escaped him in the face of war, and did his best to maintain his control, to disallow any change in his focus or excitement. It was, some distant part of him mused, like a mission in itself. And he would need absolute control in this final moment, just this final moment.

The clouds parted. He almost stumbled. Somehow, he managed not to, and made the final dash towards the light. He reached out. And he grasped it.

Scorching heat surged through his body on contact, flooding his veins with fire and snapping Salus back to the darkness of the cell. He staggered and stumbled to his feet in a panic, hissing in pain as he grasped at his forearms - but as suddenly as it began, it receded.

He slowed and frowned down at his arms, pulling away his sleeves to find no trace at all of any burning on his skin. He looked across towards the mage, still panting in exhaustion as his confusion formed a question on his tongue, but hesitated as he found Denek staring back at him with intensity.

"Light." He raised his hands and twisted his fingers in slow, precise movements, which Salus immediately repeated to the best of his ability. Then stared completely dumbfounded at the small, glowing orb that sparked into life before him, no larger than a sugar cube. "Should it be that small?" Was all he found himself able to say through the dense silence, to which the mage, whose own expression hadn't changed from that first unreadable intensity, guided him through another, briefer series of motions. The ball quadrupled in volume.

Salus stumbled back in shock as he stared, his wide eyes flicking between the light and his own fingers, but as he sought for a rational, a *possible* explanation, only one thought, one *fact*, looped through his mind, so simple and yet utterly impossible for him to comprehend.

He had conjured that light. *Him. He* had conjured that light with his own two hands...

The air was thick; no one spoke even beyond the cell, the guards concentrated instead on not craning their necks to stare inside despite their desperate fascination. Denek observed him silently with his unreadable eyes, watching as a smile of elation, of victory, of power, curved Salus's lips.

The cellar remained that way for some minutes until footsteps began at the far end, sounding as loud in the silent void as the hooves of several galloping horses. Whoever it was quickly noticed the weighted atmosphere, slowing and softening their steps accordingly without losing urgency, and came to a stop outside.

"Keliceran?" He dared to speak, his voice as loud as a scream despite whispering, and yet Salus didn't seem to have heard him. But the phidipan was patient, and when Salus spun around a long moment later, he didn't flinch. Instead it was his superior's immense grin that caused curiosity to flash briefly over his young face. It vanished quickly, and he raised and displayed a tattered old bag.

Salus's own grin dropped at the sight of it, stunned again by disbelief.

He didn't even grace the mage with a thank you or farewell before darting out through the gate and snatching it from his hand, grinning manically once again as he dashed away.

Denek frowned after him as he disappeared around the corner, ignoring the subordinates who locked his cage back up and the mages who sealed it. The floating orb extinguished at his will, and again his thoughts didn't enter his eyes.

Salus all but ran through the corridors, weaving skilfully past the phaeacians while the phidipan and portian agents stepped easily out of his path themselves. Not one looked at him directly, and the higher ranks barely acknowledged him at all, but he was fully aware of the stupid smile on his face as he clutched the bag, and the elation in his chest which made him feel light enough to float off of the ground - and suddenly, he felt it was very much within the realms of possibility that he *could*.

"Going somewhere?"

The voice would usually have provoked a curl of his lip, a grunt or groan of dread and certainly a silently bellowed curse, but this time, Salus's smile didn't even loosen. "Only to my office," he replied with none of the usual resentment, "as always."

Lord Malson narrowed his eyes speculatively as he fell in step beside him, and the keliceran slowed his pace for his benefit as they made their way to the top floor. "You're awfully chipper," he said once they'd stepped inside.

"Well," he put the bag quite carefully onto the table and pushed it to one side while the liaison took his usual seat, "things are looking up."

"Oh really?"

"Oh yes."

His eyes narrowed again at the broadening smile. "Despite Doana and Skilan both striking several more of our cities?"

"Exactly *because* of it!" Salus dropped into his chair and saw the shock wash over his old face. He smiled reassuringly. "I won't bore you with the details, my lord, but we've acted on a hunch and it's paid off. We should be able to prevent any further occupations of our settlements. But did you truly expect anything less? What is the Arana here for if not to move in the shadows and look for things others don't care to see?"

"...Well, I suppose so..."

Salus didn't miss his suddenly reluctant, thoughtful tone. He studied him for a moment, then straightened and allowed his smile to vanish, eradicated by the reassertion of professionalism. To look at the keliceran then, it would seem it had just been a passing amusement. "What do you have for me?"

Malson took a deep, hesitant breath. "Something I don't care to see." His gaze levelled, any suspicion and curiosity erased in its severity, but it still took him a moment longer to find the courage to speak. "There is a spy in the military."

'I told you my people weren't compromised.' He kept that thought to himself, and asked calmly instead: "What makes you so sure?"

"Skilan's responses to Moore's movements are too precise, as if they knew *exactly* what he planned to do as soon as he planned to do it."

"They could be nothing more than calculated manoeuvres. They could have made plans to provoke a certain response, then acted on the most likely outcome - though, that *would* be a bit too advanced for Skilan, even after what they've recently displayed. What else?"

"There is unreasonable discontent among the ranks. Some doubt is to be expected following such strategic blows, of course, but not to this level."

"What level?"

"Desertion, soldiers striking out in groups without orders to try to help the situation, in-fighting, suspicion."

Salus looked at him carefully. "And you're sure you and your colleagues aren't succumbing to the same paranoia?"

Malson met his gaze quite steadily. "We are not."

He nodded slowly. "Well I quite agree with you," he admitted, "but the army is spread over the entire country and there are more than just a handful of soldiers in its ranks. If you expect the Arana--"

"Start with Brigadier General Rackson."

Salus blinked. "Lord Malson, I appreciate the enthusiasm, but I'm afraid there's no room for you in the Arana, our ranks are full."

"I'm glad you're still in a jovial mood," he growled, sitting forwards in his seat, his eyes blazing, "but this is no laughing matter. Not at all."

"And I am not laughing," he replied coolly. "But you understand that all of my people are already spread thin, don't you? An operation like this would need to be seen to quickly and with minimal disturbance, which means it would take more than just one agent, each no less than portian."

"And *you* understand that this is an order from the Crown, don't you?" The old man countered with a snap of impatience. "You are *obligated* to address this!"

"I didn't say that I wouldn't, I'm merely making you aware of the Arana's situation - a situation no doubt shared by all the other authorities. But of course," he smiled, almost pleasantly, "I will address this, as a priority. You have my word."

Once again, Malson surveyed him with suspicion, but before he could finally challenge the matter, a knock came at the door. He tutted shortly in defeat and nodded his permission before Salus called entry, at which Teagan stepped inside, immediately inclined his head to both, then stood patiently to one side with his eyes fixed, as the keliceran's subordinates always did, on the wall behind the desk with unnatural detachment.

"I trust that you will," Malson finally said as he rose to his feet. "And one final thing before I leave: the evacuations--"

"Are going smoothly, my lord, you needn't worry. All on schedule and true to plan."

"Right... Good. Well, in that case, I will leave you to your work. I'm sure you're quite busy." He turned to the door, nodding at Teagan as he passed, then disappeared outside in what almost seemed like a hurry. But Salus didn't notice. Before the door had even closed he was dragging the satchel eagerly back towards him.

"Orders, si-- Is that--"

"Yes, it certainly is." He grinned childishly as his fingers nimbly dealt with the old, stiff buckles. "Our advantage." He quickly spilled the contents over the desk, a jumble of ink-stained and water-marked parchments, and books so old and worn their binding surely threatened to give out upon opening. Some coverings were so dusty that he doubted even a vigorous rub would remove the thick coats.

Teagan stepped forwards and peered down at the collection, his purpose forgotten, but any curiosity was invisible. His face was, as ever, devoid of expression. "What do you intend to do with them?"

"Catch up on what they know. With any luck, Karth's findings and his own notes will put us on level ground, and with our resources, we can get ahead of them quickly enough."

Teagan watched him flick through the books, the excitement in his eyes never once waning, even as he was faced with illegible scripts. "You can't read that."

"It's not a problem. There's bound to be *someone* in the Arana who can decipher this. The point is that we *have* it."

"Even if the texts can be translated, Karth's notes aren't likely to be straightforward. Drassa had his own shorthand; Karth certainly will, too."

Salus cursed as his enthusiasm crumpled. "I hadn't thought of that. And I *refuse* to take this to Drassa. We can't risk the Order getting a hold of it." He pointed off vaguely towards one of the many ledger-lined shelves in the room. "Get me the--"

"There's no need for operatives' profiles," Teagan assured him. "I can recommend someone right now who should be suited to the task: Lucinda Grey; phaeacian. She has an academic background, specialised in history and reads elven, if she doesn't speak it. She could handle this."

He eyed him reluctantly. "Can she be recalled?"

"She isn't in the field. She's on leave; eight months pregnant. But she has been putting in requests for work since war came our way. She doesn't want to sit idle."

Salus's eyebrows rose as zeal gripped him again. "Perfect," he beamed, "call her in."

"Right away. But, in the mean time, I presume there are other orders besides, especially after Malson's unscheduled visit?"

Ah. Of course. Work. He forced himself back down into his seat, curbing his racing mind and dragging his eyes off of the treasure trove before him, deliberately angling himself away from it. "Yes. Orders." A familiar gravity returned to his eyes. "Doana and Skilan. Every attack they've made on our settlements has either been with the help of foreigners or no help at all. This time around we picked out the most likely conspirators, and in the places that were hit, we were right on all counts. Every one of them was of foreign blood and had lived in this country for anywhere between months to years. We even managed to foil two attacks before they could happen. So, now we know how to spot who's helping them, we have to take the next step."

"You want to watch all foreigners within Turunda's borders."

"I do..." his eyes became distant, thoughtful. "And...Malson."

"Malson?"

"He's been behaving peculiarly for some time," he mused, "and now he's come to me about a spy in the military."

"I don't make the connection, sir."

"It's just curious. He flicks between the composure of an old professional to an over-zealous guard recruit with ideas above his station a little too often these days..."

"Are you referring to his own request for us to infiltrate the Order?"

"Not exclusively, though it is a fine example." He tapped his chin in thought. "We've already been watching the discontent within the ranks, but Malson seems to think Brigadier General Rackson is responsible. I want a handful of those already planted in the military to look around it, make it their priority - Reich, Jaq and...Hayla. But otherwise, I want to keep an eye on Malson, too - and the rest of the Crown's liaisons. It doesn't hurt to look a little closer to home. Especially when he seems to have an idea from afar when those we have watching from within the ranks haven't seen enough to build such confident accusations..."

"Very well. Consider both taken care of - though I feel I should remind you that the strain of watching every foreigner is going to compromise other standing orders our watchers are under."

Salus waved his hand dismissively. "This is a priority. It's precisely this kind of thing they're watching for in the first place, isn't it?"

"It is, but at the same time, we are not the only ones keeping an eye on foreigners. Word has already spread to other towns and cities of a few individuals who have helped Skilan, and people are beginning to suspect anyone from across the borders of treachery. It will make observation more difficult. Our targets will behave in a suspicious manner simply because they're uncomfortable."

"It will be fine. If they're innocent, they have nothing to worry about, do they?"

Teagan blinked at his calm response. Usually he would have been rewarded for his persistent realism with an scathing comment, or, lately, the rough side of Salus's tongue before he went into a seething if thoughtful silence. The centre of his brow almost imperceptibly knotted as he noticed in his peripherals the sixth appearance of the smallest of smiles, one that seemed to be tugging relentlessly at Salus's lips though he smothered it at every attempt it made. Understanding abruptly dawned as he noticed a flash of what could only have been victory in his eyes as he looked down at his empty hand.

His heart jumped in a curious sensation he'd not felt for years, too long ago to identify. "You did it..."

Salus's eyes shot back towards him and the smile he restrained was finally unleashed. But he said nothing. He raised his hand instead, moving his fingers slowly in the patterns Denek had showed him, and the portian took a stunned step backwards as a ball of light appeared and swelled in the air between them.

They both stared at it in silence.

"What else?" Teagan eventually asked, though his tone was tame and flattened Salus's pride more than a little, and his words struck even deeper.

"Nothing," he replied resentfully, "this is all he showed me. But the point is that

I did it, Teagan. I have *magic!* And I can *use* it! And with more help, more guidance, I could *finally* make a *real* difference in this country!"

He frowned slightly. "You're making an enormous difference already. You are Keliceran, you command all of the Arana's ranks. What could you alone do with magic that would be so much greater than that?"

His lip curled at his lack of enthusiasm, and he slammed his hand down atop the gathered books. "I could wield this relic *myself.*"

"Even if you possess magic, you don't have the understanding you would surely need to operate something like that on your own."

"What is *wrong* with you, Teagan?" He hissed "Why are you trying to poke holes in this? Why aren't you pleased? This is *good* for us - *all* of us! Now we don't have to rely on the magic of others to see this thing through!"

Teagan watched him, measuring his eyes, and he easily recognised pride, desperation, and the immense desire to protect Turunda and its people by any means necessary - the same things he always saw in him, even throughout his recently foul moods. But each quality had been intensified by the possibility that he'd found the means to truly and personally achieve it, and though the thought set a strange discomfort deep within his gut, he also found he understood it, and appreciated it. With the rate the world around them was crumbling - the distrust citizens were showing towards each other, the disorder in the military, the betrayal of the Order - it was understandable that Salus, a deeply driven man who had reclaimed his emotions and sense of self after being a portian for almost ten years, would grasp such a gift and yearn with all his being to use it to that same purpose.

He straightened and shifted his gaze back onto the wall. "I apologise, Keliceran. Though I feel I should also point out that Denek won't teach you anything useful."

"What do you mean?"

"He is of the Order. He may have taught you how to unlock your magic, but he's not going to teach you how to use it. Forming a light is harmless, and he's going to want to keep you that way."

Again, Salus cursed.

"May I make a suggestion? Continue seeing Denek - he'll grow suspicious if you suddenly disappear, and we don't know what he's truly capable of. And keep pressuring him to teach you more spells, as he'll expect that, too. He won't oblige, but you can learn more about wielding and controlling your magic from him. Then, in the mean time, seek tuition from one of *our* mages. They will be keen to help you - and, after all, the nature of their work has lead them to develop spells that even the Order has not."

Salus nodded vigorously as he absorbed the idea. "Yes...yes, you're right. On all counts..." He sat back in his seat and grunted wearily, burying his face in his hands. "I'm such a fool. How could I think that foul mage would teach me how to truly wield it? Of *course* he would want to keep me harmless. He said right from the beginning that it was for the sake of everyone else that I learn to control it. I just...assumed 'control' meant 'use'." He uttered a curse. Then another. Then turned his eyes heavily onto his favoured. "Thank you, Teagan." He sat forwards, a dangerous flame of determination sparking and flickering in his eyes. "Now get me a mage."

Chapter 48

The morning's trek had been unbearable, to say the least. Though from first light the sky had been freckled with soft, white clouds, the land slowly began levelling out and a stronger breeze swept in from the nearby mountains, the atmospheric bubble that consumed them was almost crushingly unsurvivable. No one spoke; no one exchanged glances. They actively ignored one another, keeping their distance as if feigning disassociation, lone travellers coincidentally journeying in the same direction at the same time and place in the middle of absolutely nowhere.

Garon was the only one not to participate. He maintained a vigilant watch all around them, certain that last night's fire hadn't been an accident, and kept the rest of them under his eye all the while, ready to intervene should someone finally snap and try to start something.

Eyila remained at the lead. She set a purposeful pace, keen to cover the last stretch of open ground and finally reach the village, eager to end their association. No one could say she was being unreasonable. After two weeks, two of her charges were revealed to be far from what they'd seemed - not even 'cityfolk' would expect to be in the company of a cultist or a monster, and a tribal girl with little contact with civilisation, unaware of its gossip or the extent of its corruption, could never have prepared herself against it.

But she had insisted on coming along without deigning to learn a thing about them first. Whether they would have shared such secrets upon questioning or not, it was her own foolish mistake not to try.

Matching her pace, Rathen limped at the rear, wincing in pain from time to time while Aria helped him along, her young face aged in concern. Kienza's care must have been so complete that she'd never seen him in such a state, and while Eyila's healing skills were just as surprising as the sorceress's, they were far outmatched. She'd done what she could, but he was still left to suffer from his bone-shifting transformation. And it was for that second bout that he secluded himself, burying his attention in the translations in the hope that it would be enough to prevent it from happening again, and kept his face twisted in forced concentration when pain wasn't controlling it to discourage anyone from approaching him.

But Garon could see the shameful depth to the lines around his eyes, especially when the mage dared a glance back towards him. Rathen was fully aware that he'd injured him - how could he not have? - but not of the extent. Garon had made it quite clear to both Petra and Eyila that they weren't to tell him a thing, certain that it would be the final mark before the mage finally withdrew his tenuous services. Rathen had surely asked, but however they'd answered, he was clearly unconvinced that it had been the full truth. So he looked around briefly from time to time, trying not to catch his eye while searching silently for the damage himself. Fortunately he was too ashamed to ask directly, and his left hand was an easy matter for Garon to hide.

Anthis, however, strode along near the front, just as oblivious to his company and surroundings as usual, his nose glued in his few remaining books. He'd confirmed when Garon had asked at breakfast - the tensest meal any of them could ever recall having, and more or less the only verbal exchange in the duration - that the most important pieces from the ruin had been left unscathed, safely inside his tent for reading, presumably when he'd wrapped up his other 'activities'. But while that was a relief for all of them to hear, he'd still spent *every* moment that morning juggling the texts, notebooks and pencils trying to scribble down anything he could remember from what he'd lost, relevant to their task or not.

"He'll never get it all," Petra had spitefully remarked, but Garon wasn't so sure. Anthis was, after all, *very* passionate about his subject. So passionate, in fact, that he'd been so broken by his loss that he'd been entirely unaware of the night's subsequent drama, even as it happened. His intense concentration to reverse that loss masked any hint of disgrace, though Garon silently suspected that, unlike Rathen, he felt none at all.

But regardless, very little sympathy had been spared for him in turn, particularly on Petra's part, who watched him like a hawk as she marched along behind, more comfortable turning her back to Rathen than to the once harmless academic.

Above everyone else, Garon found his eyes drifting onto her the most, and his thoughts always turned in the same direction.

Nothing had been said about the kiss.

She had barely spoken to him at all that day, and the fact that he was unsure if he hadn't simply dreamt it irritated him. But he found himself unable to step forwards and raise the subject to find out, and that irritated him even more.

But above both of those frustrations was the distraction. He should have been more than capable of ignoring such a triviality. He was a professional; there was no room in his life for such useless levity - so why was his mind filled with circling thoughts of such little substance every time he discovered his eyes on her? It was as if his brain was stammering, getting stuck on the same senseless meanderings rather than focusing on what was important.

He rotated his left shoulder and flexed his arm and fingers.

Perhaps he'd hit his head. Perhaps he *had* imagined it, and she hadn't said anything because there was nothing *to* say. Dreams had their way of embedding themselves in the mind like a tick, and contrary to popular belief, more often than not, they meant absolutely nothing at all. They were just the chaotic roamings allowed by a dormant mental state, when reasoning was abandoned because there was no need for it, because nothing that happened in a dream could truly affect its author.

He straightened, a little more self-assured, and pushed it aside for the eighteenth time to survey their surroundings instead.

His gaze shifted sharply back onto her as she moved around Anthis, casting him a glare, to fall in beside Eyila.

The tribal girl smiled.

"That was convincing." Petra sighed and shook her head sadly. "I told you not to feel guilty, didn't I? Garon is an inquisitor. He's a stronger man than *either* of us can imagine. He's driven, and he's intelligent - he'll adapt, he won't complain; he'll accept the situation and make do." But the girl's pale blue eyes, their colour made more shocking for the unbroken streak of black painted across them, only deepened in doubt. Petra sighed again. "You did your *best*, Eyila."

"But it wasn't *enough*."

"You did more than *anyone* could have done for him. None of our medics could have repaired half of what you did. You saved his life - and he realises that."

"He can barely use his arm."

"He will work *around* that." Petra smiled reassuringly, her eyes intense, hoping that the weight of their promise would convince the girl to believe her. But Eyila's fret still didn't diminish. Petra shortly sighed again and looked towards their heading. "I expect you'll be pleased to get home. You'll probably never leave the village again."

The girl breathed a laugh. "Perhaps not for a little while."

"Look, let me apologise for all--"

"You have nothing to apologise for. I..." she looked up and smiled, but this time there was a glimmer of honesty mingling with her regret. "I did enjoy this. It's more excitement than I've ever had in my life. More than enough to last...well, 'a little while'." But that glimmer fled as she returned her hardened gaze forwards. "But I didn't come out here to make friends or take the first steps towards bridging our people. I came out here because I want, more than anything, for Ut'hala to be restored. And I think - I *hope* - that I have helped towards that end."

"I'm sure you have. Anthis has learned a lot from the ruins, and Rathen from you. In fact, you've helped us more than any of us thought you could. We owe you--"

"Return and restore Ut'hala, and we will call it even." She smiled impishly, and Petra laughed.

"Deal."

The group walked on, leaving the road and stepping back out onto the sands, climbing the gentle dunes which were each just high enough to conceal the forward landscape from the top of the last. When smooth stones started dotting the slopes, marked with the same dyes and clays that Eyila used to paint her skin, they knew they were getting close.

But when Petra turned to observe the relief of familiarity on her face, she found instead a deep unease.

Her stride slowed beside her. "What is it?"

Eyila shook her head, her straight, white hair flicking with the sharp movement, but her wide eyes remained fixed to the hidden horizon. "It's..."

She didn't finish. A light breeze sent a sudden dread flashing across her face, and she bolted forwards, darting through the sand at a frantic speed, leaving the rest of them behind. Petra raced after her in a heartbeat, following as close as she could while Garon's voice rose from the rear, ordering the others to hurry after them. She struggled with every footfall while the tribal covered the ground with ease, but she pushed on harder to make up the increasing distance yawning between them, panicked by the girl's abruptness. But just as she crested the final dune, tracking through the sands Eyila had sent cascading behind her, she caught a chilling scent on the breeze. A scent that caused the same dread to freeze her in place.

Until a heart-stopping wail pierced the air.

Petra surged forwards, leaving the others just cresting the dune. She skidded down the sand with her heart in her throat, one hand wrapped tightly around her sword's hilt, the other on its sheath. But she didn't draw. Though she clung to a desperate hope, the depths of her gut told her there was no need.

The tribal village stood ahead, across a flat expanse of sand marred only by Eyila's footsteps. But even from this distance Petra could feel the eerie stillness left by the startled birds, and she soon saw the edges of the destruction flattened beneath it. But it wasn't until she levelled with the first sun-baked mudhouse that her frantic pace finally faltered, and she was forced to catch herself against a clay window frame to stay on her feet.

She could hear Eyila sobbing. It was a terrible, heart-wrenching sound for such a melodious voice to make. She knew she should call out, say something, offer some kind of comfort, but she found that her own voice had caught in her throat, and her legs had turned so rigid she felt she was no longer connected to them.

Three paces away, a bronze body lay in the sand, perfectly motionless, hidden from the rest of the village by the shadow of her own home. Her white hair covered her face, and though her animal skins were torn at the seams and left only partially concealing her modesty, the dark blood that had dried over her arms, legs and chest, and spattered across the ground beside her to form black clumps in the sand, drew the eye away. Uncountable lacerations criss crossed her body, freeing the blood from her veins to the thirsty land and scorching sun. These were wounds that could only have been inflicted with deep hatred, but it was impossible to tell from the dried up pools just who had delivered her such a fate, nor indeed when.

But it had certainly been too soon. What clear skin could be seen was smooth, and still seemed to shimmer slightly even in the shade. She was young - younger, perhaps, than herself. Too young for such a brutal death.

Petra didn't notice the ache in her jaw from the strength behind her clamped teeth. Her eyes roved over the body, the blood, the wounds, flicking from one to the next as rage bubbled inside of her. She wanted to turn away, to close her eyes and hide from the sight and the memories they conjured within her, but a greater part of her forced her to keep looking, to stare, and to remember.

A jug lay broken beside the body, one similar to those they'd seen next to a makeshift well a few days ago. She must have been on her way out to collect when the assault had happened. So she had been defenceless. There was nothing in the black, mottled sand to suggest she'd fought back, and the fragments of the pot were too close together for it to have been used as a weapon either for or against her.

But as she spotted the jug, so too did she notice another glimmer of bronze skin, just visible from around the corner of the hut. Though she begged her legs not to, especially while Eyila's nearby cries became more dreadful, they carried her one step forwards, and her rage burned anew.

She was only vaguely aware of the arrival of Garon and the others, of their immediate curses and of Rathen telling Aria, very firmly, to 'stay right here'. He would have been very well to tell himself the same thing, as when he stepped up alongside Petra and set eyes upon the child who lay just as bloodied and motionless at the building's door, he choked a peculiar sound in place of a strangled curse and staggered against the stone just as she had.

From that single step, the village had become painfully unobscured. As far within its boundaries as the four of them could see, the sand and walls were flecked with sun-baked blood. Some of the small, square buildings were damaged, their walls brought down, thatched doors torn and painted markings defaced, and every wind chime that had been hung outside had been thrown and trampled into the ground without exception. Bowls, large and small, lay upturned beside their pedestals, their coloured, powdered contents spilled cross the sand. A gentle wind whipped up and billowed what the sand didn't weigh down, sending soft plumes of neutral colours up and across the countless corpses that littered the village grounds.

Garon took the first solemn step forwards. Petra's legs moved on their own again, leaving the others to stare in the same sickened shock that had paralysed her.

Looking around, it was difficult to tell what was blood and what was paint, but the wounds themselves were all too clear. Each body had been brutalised in the same way as the first, and the only people who seemed to have been armed were the hunters. But the deeper they moved, the denser the litter of corpses, and the worse those inflictions became. Deep holes had been gouged where the skin was bared, and in many cases the holes equated to bare ribs and such gore that Petra had to fight herself not to retch. The stench didn't help.

"Scavengers," Garon grunted without stopping for a closer look. Petra was surprised to find that his face seemed a shade whiter, but she expected her own far outmatched it. She wasn't prepared to confirm his assumption.

She turned her eyes away, keeping her gaze now no lower than the horizon. Her heart lurched when she realised that Eyila's plaintive cries had fallen silent.

Ignoring Garon's order, she hurried off again, choosing a path through the bodies as carefully as she could without looking, heading in the direction she'd last heard the girl's broken voice. She slowed only when the village widened around a corner, opening up before the chieftain's longhouse. Where the body count became even higher. She stumbled to another horrified stop, and all she found herself able to think was that she'd had no idea the tribe was made up of so many.

Had been made up of so many.

She swallowed hard and forced herself onwards, scanning over every one of them without daring to linger for too long, but it was difficult to pick out any identities among the tangle of bronze and white. It was frighteningly silent, but just as she was about to attempt to call out, unsure if her voice would actually respond to the demand, the briefest motion caught her eye.

While other bodies lay, one sat upright, just as still as the rest but for the sideways slump as she slipped off of her heels.

Petra made clumsily straight for her, cursing in relief, but the girl didn't respond to her shout. She skidded to her knees beside her and stared up into her eyes from beneath, unsure with a rattling heart if she hadn't died of shock, but the blink and slight rise and fall of her hunched shoulders as she breathed eradicated the thought. But she didn't look up. She didn't even notice she was there.

But of course she didn't. Her eyes stared into a world Petra could only imagine, even as her absent gaze rested heavily upon the mutilated bodies. But as Petra foolishly followed the line of her eyes, that world suddenly became quite clear.

It was easy to recognise the respected woman who had spoken out for them when they'd first arrived, even with her throat cut, blood smeared across her face and her light-coloured skins and feather mantle stained crimson. Even in death, there was an air of elegance about her, one they had once thought inappropriate for a tribal barbarian, and her face seemed more peaceful than the others', as though she knew with absolute certainty that death would take her to no dark place.

The girl who lay beside her, however, though she wore the same ceremonial garb save the mantle, didn't appear quite as accepting. A small knot remained in her young brow, and Petra knew she couldn't have been older than Eyila. Perhaps they'd been friends. Perhaps they'd been family.

The body that lay directly in front of her didn't draw the eye for any reason other than the concentration of wounds he had sustained, but Petra's eyes passed over him anyway. Over the white triangle painted upon his forehead, fading above the bridge of his nose. Over the black lines that reached up from his jaw to his eyes. Over the remains of several lengths of coloured leather tied about his torn biceps.

Petra's blood ran cold, and Eyila's breath caught for a moment in a haggard wheeze.

Footsteps slowed behind them and a single shadow fell, followed shortly by two more. Whispered curses came after a similar pause.

"I'm sorry." They were the only words Petra could find to say, and she deeply resented having done so. She knew how useless such a statement was. But she couldn't simply say nothing... She frowned as she noticed something in Eyila's bloodied hands, several strings of feathers, every one of them bent, their barbs split and torn. They had been, she recalled, tied among the chief's leather.

"Who did this?"

The sound of Anthis's voice immediately boiled Petra's blood, but as she turned where she knelt, acid ready on her tongue, Rathen had already whirled on him.

"Did you do this?!" He demanded, spitting his own venom while Garon snatched his hand away before he could grasp Anthis by the collar.

"He didn't."

They turned back towards Eyila, surprised by the strength in her voice. She raised the feathers in her hands and finally lifted her eyes. They were hard. Furious. Heartbroken. The running streams of black paint made her appear only more vengeful. "It was another tribe."

Garon nodded slowly. "It was a religious strike, wasn't it?"

They frowned at him in puzzlement while Anthis took the opportunity to put distance between himself and Rathen, but he couldn't keep his own eyes from staring in horror at the violence that surrounded them.

"The leather," Rathen said thoughtfully, forgetting him as he looked back between what remained of the strips and the feathers. "The strips were the mark of the chieftain...and the feathers, birds...the wind..." His shoulders dropped in woeful understanding. "But who did it?"

Eyila turned and pointed towards the building behind her, staring at it with the same vengeful eyes. The longhouse. The very building in which they'd met with the chief under tribal ritual and courtesies had suffered the worst of the architectural assault. But beyond the broken walls, door and shutters, the torn hides and shattered effigies, were the paintings. Where the white emblems had depicted fluid winds, now were what appeared to be images of brown, tangled trees.

"Earth. From the mountains." Despite the knife-sharp edge to her voice, she lowered the chieftain's head from her lap with the utmost care, taking a moment to brush aside the matted hair that had slipped over his face from his ruined braid, and gently removed a pendant from around his neck. She whispered as she clutched it - only Petra caught the words, but she didn't know the tongue - then rose silently to her feet and approached the foot of the longhouse's steps. She lifted something from the sand, a wind chime of the grandest design, with intricately carven wooden tubes, magnificent feathers and dyed and braided animal hairs.

They watched her in silence as she stared down at it, and as a mournful wind blew, softly enough to offer its own unintrusive comfort, the tubes rattled a hollow canticle.

Then she turned. "You should leave. It isn't safe for you here. Return only when you can restore Ut'hala."

Everyone stared aghast as she strode away, stepping so lightly through the bodies it was as if she didn't see them, and vanished behind a semi-shattered building.

Garon straightened. "She's right. We should leave."

Those stares then fell onto him.

"And leave her here?!" Rathen demanded in a strangled whisper.

"This is her home."

"Her home--*look around yourself!*"

"Her home is *dead,* Garon," Petra agreed in a similar hiss. "She has nothing left!"

But he shook his head, his grey eyes resolute. "She will draw too much attention. The Arana will be able to follow us all too easily with her in tow. We won't be able to go near any towns or cities without catching someone's eye, and it's as hard to mistake bronze skin as it is to completely conceal it. If anyone spots her even *outside* of the walls, people will assume the tribes are finally attacking."

While Petra began to argue, Rathen stepped in front of Anthis, barring his way, and shoved his palm firmly against his chest, eyeing him with unrestrained suspicion. "Where the hell are you going?"

"To make sure she's all right," he replied just as vehemently, wrenching away from his hand.

"No, you keep away from her. *I'll* go."

Anthis's fair eyebrows rose high above his incredulous eyes. "*You?* What makes you think she'll listen to you?"

"But she'll listen to *you?!*"

His green eyes were as sharp as daggers, and though Rathen saw the menace within them, he was less than underwhelmed. "You don't trust me anymore," Anthis told him levelly. "I get it. And do you know what? I don't care. I've done nothing wrong. I've picked apart my morals for years and acted in the best way I know how to, and I can walk with my head held high because of it. But if you would prefer to overlook the facts and focus on your own misinterpretation, *fine*. I really don't care. Regardless, *someone* needs to go after her." He turned to Garon.

"She *can't* stay here. What about when this tribe comes back?"

"They've killed everyone--"

"And they surely know they haven't killed *her*. Every village has a healer, that's what she's told me, and they *are* taught how to use their magic for attack and defence. Not to the level of the Order, but enough to put up a fight, and enough to exact vengeance. They know they didn't get her, and if they've killed every single person here, every *child* here, they're not going to let her slip by." The edge in his eyes had softened imploringly. "You cannot, under good conscience, leave her here alone!"

Anthis whirled while Rathen scoffed quietly behind him. "Yes," he hissed dangerously, "I know the meaning of 'good conscience'. As, some how, do you." But he pressed it no further. He straightened and squared his shoulders without a trace of the shame everyone else felt he should bear, and stepped to one side. "Go on. If you think she'd rather listen to you, go."

Rathen glowered at him a moment longer before shifting a tamer gaze onto Petra. "Go to Aria," he told her, "and wait there. Don't let her in the village, no matter what happens. And keep a close eye--"

"I know, Rathen. She'll be safe with me. These people were taken by surprise. I won't be."

He nodded. "I have no doubt."

The two then moved off, sparing neither Anthis nor the bodies another glance.

Anthis growled under his voice. The intolerance, the hatred - it was nothing he couldn't get used to. But at least Garon's ears weren't closed to him. "I hesitate to point it out," he began with a distinct lack of care as he folded his arms over his chest, "but you realise that, with the Arana possibly on our tail, her healing abilities could be needed at some point...?"

"I do," he sighed, "but I also know we're less likely to cross paths with them if we don't stand out at all."

"Ghosts see everything, Garon. They'll know where we are whether she's with us or not. Even if we changed our faces."

Garon cast him a sidelong look, one that would almost have been amused had there been any light in his eyes. "They're not seers, Anthis. They track, they watch, they listen, *that's* how they gather their intel. They don't have crystal balls."

"All I'm saying is that we could be better off *with* her than without. From a tactical perspective. Especially if Rathen has another of his turns." He shook his head and sneered in the direction the mage had gone. "We're lucky he's only had the one. But if that self-important git reacts like that to being out of control of a situation, then we're going to be more at risk of *him* than anyone else before too much longer."

"Mm..."

Anthis shifted uncomfortably at the inquisitor's hesitant tone, having hoped he might refute the point as he usually did, and absently followed his downward gaze in the hope of some visual reassurance instead. Instead he watched him repeatedly flex two fingers at his side. He frowned. "What's wrong with your hand?"

Rathen found her at the very edge of the village, sorting through a pile of windworn stones the size of dinner plates. They were shattered, raised and dropped with intentional force, but she was collecting even the tiniest fragments and diligently grouping them back together, giving them her absolute attention.

He approached her quietly, relieved that there were no corpses here to try in vain to ignore. She certainly heard him - sand was soft but far from silent beneath unpractised feet - but she didn't look around, and neither did he attempt to win her attention.

The stones, he saw as he stopped behind her, each bore carven patterns. They had surely once been intricate in design, but following years of the wind's assault, they'd been buffed away beyond recognition - though with the tribe's art so stylised, he was sure he wouldn't have understood them in such a small scale even had they been freshly etched. But two other details, at least, laid bare the significance of this odd collection: the number engraved with nothing more than swirling lines of wind, and the delicacy with which Eyila handled them.

It had, as Garon had guessed, been a religious assault, and the village's shrine to their wind goddess would have been a high priority for vandals.

He sighed to himself at her devotion to the task, unwaning even as she struggled to lift the largest stones which had survived unharmed due to their very size, but he didn't offer to help. Instead, he knelt down beside her, wondering what the shrine had looked like in its prime, and if it really had been as unimpressive as he imagined.

The silence soon became unbearable. "What do you do with your dead?" He asked softly, unable to think of anything else, and wished even before he'd finished that he hadn't.

"It has nothing to do with you. Leave."

But despite the acidic order, he didn't move, and despite his ongoing presence, she didn't ask again.

"The chief...he was your father, wasn't he?"

She pieced together five fragments with a particularly degraded image and set the collection aside. She seemed to be deciding whether or not to reply. "My uncle," she said eventually. "He raised me after my father died on a hunt. My mother in child birth."

"I'm so sorry."

She shrugged, and he didn't like it. "It's the fate of us all to die."

"Yes, but...not like this." His eyes burned into her with growing concern for her dispassion. "You can't stay here, Eyila."

"This is my home."

"*Was*." He watched her knuckles turn white as she clenched another fragment in her hands, and despite the emptiness he could see in her eyes as he leaned forwards, that subtle act eased him slightly. He challenged her carefully. "What will you do? Tidy up and rebuild by yourself? A healer with no one to heal? Or will you leave your home and find another tribe?"

Her head finally snapped towards him, and the emptiness in her eyes was overrun with rage. "I will *never* leave my home," she growled, "nor these sands. I will live here and survive as my people always have. I can hunt, I can trade with the caravans, I can--"

"You're being foolish. If you stay here, you'll die, either killed by the same people who killed everyone else, or through grief."

"I will not die through grief."

He watched her eyes as she spoke through her teeth. "Are you sure? Are you certain? Grief can only be cured by the people around you, no matter how few they might be. But if you're alone, your mind will betray you, you'll succumb to the darkest thoughts and doubts and you'll be torn apart by them. Believe me, I know. So I cannot, under good conscience, let you remain here by yourself." He suppressed the slightest snarl at that final choice of words.

But she laughed bitterly, again through barred teeth. "You know *nothing*. I am not grieving. Everyone I've ever known and loved has risen to join the Winds. The world is safer for their passing, and they will protect *me* for as long as it takes to reach the Frozen Gates." Her sour smile saddened him. "This is a *good* thing. A *good* thing. And you corrupted cityfolk could *never* understand that, not if you had one hundred moons to devote to trying. I am *not grieving!*"

He watched as she dropped the stone she had clutched so dearly, breaking in two as it struck another, and the tears finally began to fall in spite of her. He made no attempt to smile in comfort. He had enough experience with Aria to know when it would be taken as condescension. "Eyila," he said firmly instead, "trust me: you're grieving. And that is a good thing, too. If you were truly pleased for this, you would be a monster."

Her eyes pierced him. "Like you, you mean?"

They stared at one another for a moment, but Rathen made no outward show of his insult. He sighed instead and rose calmly to his feet. "Collect what we need for their last rites."

"I told you, it has nothing to do with you."

"I heard you. And I'm ignoring you. Get what we need."

"It has nothing to do with you!"

"Eyila--"

"*Get out!*"

He felt the brief rush of her magic the moment she raised her hands, but easily deflected the meagre attack she flung towards him, one which could have been stronger - though not strong enough - had she not been so frantic. She immediately prepared another, but he was much faster, and stepped forwards to catch her as she lost consciousness.

Garon and Anthis hadn't moved far from where Rathen had left them, but when Anthis, who had evidently been watching the path he'd taken very closely, saw him return with the white haired girl in his arms, he released an indelicate string of curses.

"*Wonderful* job," he drawled as Garon frowned in bewilderment. "She listened attentively then, did she?"

Rathen sent him a brief but sharp sneer. "I really don't think you would have fared any better." He found the nearest clearing away from the bodies and lowered her carefully to the ground. "We're seeing to the dead."

"B-but it's another culture's customs," Anthis stammered in a sudden panic, "if we--"

"Yes, yes, insult, wrath of gods, restless dead. It will be fine."

"He's right, Rathen."

The mage sighed. "I know that, which is why we will do our best. That has to count for something."

Anthis straightened defiantly. "No. *You* might not hold any respect for faith--"

"Oh I *do* hope you're not referring to that murderous club of yours as a 'faith'."

"You may not hold any respect for faith," he repeated over him, "but this matters to *her*. And that *does* mean something."

"Then *what* do you propose we do?! Leave them here and drag her off kicking and screaming?"

"It seems like you're already half way there."

"*What--*"

"She's told me about her people's beliefs," he said, finally disregarding him. "They're similar to pre-magic elves, but only the earthen tribes bury their dead. She said her people give their bodies back to nature in another way..." He thought for a moment while Rathen's furious eyes sought to set him alight. "Where's their shrine? A monument, a statue or something?"

"Back there--"

Anthis ran off, leaving Rathen to make a tart remark he chose not to hear, and shortly found the broken stones. He paid little attention to the disorganisation and spared no mind to wonder at its prior state. Instead he filtered through them deftly, lifting every piece without once spoiling the fragments, looking closely at every etching with a practised, speculative eye. It didn't take him long to find what he sought; as he'd expected, the act was engraved into the rock.

But a grimace soon edged over his face as the images took shape, though he admitted, reluctantly, that it made sense. The desert was a harsh place and its creatures had to travel far to find a meal...

He looked over the rest of the stones for certainty, then glanced around for anything else that might contradict it, but beyond stories of the winds and the typical tales of spirits and benevolent acts of Aya'u, there was nothing else that could be construed as funerary rites. It wasn't something he wanted to get wrong - in fact, it mattered greatly that he got it *right* - but there was simply no other way to interpret this single stone.

He took a deep breath and yielded himself to the matter, and when he returned, they looked dubiously upon his resigned expression. "There's not much we have to do."

After immediate and absolute refusals, he soon had them both helping him to unpile the bodies and lay them neatly side by side. They braced themselves as best they could against the smell that followed every disturbance, and kept their eyes fixed on the sand between the bodies or on the surrounding buildings to avoid the equally foul sights of stomachs and chests rent open. But they didn't cover the wounds. To do so, Anthis claimed, would be disrespectful. Coming from him, Rathen didn't trust it, but he slowly, sickly and secretly understood the connection. He just hoped that that perspective had been shared by the village as a whole...

By the time they'd finished the air had grown heavy, the sun was grazing the highest dunes, and no one had any desire to speak. Petra had come to find out what was taking so long, and after choking at the sight, even more excruciating now the scene was organised and the bodies countable, she had taken Eyila back to the edge of the village and became even stricter with how far she allowed Aria to pace.

After Anthis had shared some words - elven rather than Ivaean or the tribe's modified dialect, which he failed to translate to the emotionally exhausted – and spun the clay cylinders at the edge of the village, they left its remains to the beaks and claws of the desert, walking back out into the wild sands under a heavy silence with the last of the Ikaheka in tow. What she would say when she awoke was anyone's guess, but with the threat of a roaming and evidently violent tribe, one fiery-tempered girl's protests were the least of their concerns.

But as they made their way unguided towards the coast, bidden or not, they solemnly remembered Anthis's words. This was her darkness. Her life had become as murky as theirs. She had no one left. For now, at least, she belonged with them.

Chapter 49

Salus wiggled his fingers, marvelling again at the range of complex, tangled movements involved in even the simplest spells, and yet at just how fast Erran could infallibly form them. His own hadn't managed even half that speed all afternoon - but, as Teagan's mage had very delicately reminded him, he had only been trying for a few hours. Apparently it took 'time, practise and feeling' to reach such a level of competence and apply it in immediate situations, and though his lip curled again at the condescension he had *surely* imagined in the phidipan mage's words, he supposed he understood. Though he still resented the fact that he was being starting at a novicial level.

But despite his frustrating inadequacies, that small, smug smile he'd been trying to fight away since leaving the cells began once more to creep across his lips, and this time, he let it. He sighed in satisfaction and pressed his palms into the desk, ignoring the surrounding papers he should have been working on, and sat back in his seat, making himself quite comfortable.

He felt confident. Powerful. Even despite Teagan's apparent doubts and mistrust of the situation--

'No,' he reminded himself quite quickly, *'it wasn't mistrust.'* He was making the mistake of personifying a portian. Teagan was merely being rational, unbiased - rightly pointing out the things Salus had missed because he wasn't so pure-minded anymore. He hadn't been since he'd taken the position of Keliceran - something *else* he was indebted to Teagan for. He realised, not for the first time, how lucky he was to have him at his side, and as his eyes drew back to his splayed fingers, itching to twist them into the signs of spells, he knew Teagan understood that the country was in even safer hands.

Yes, he was lucky to have an advisor like him. An advisor...and a friend? He liked to think so, but in truth he had little idea what that meant. Two people who were often together, talking, doing business...joking? There were jokes, occasionally, and drinks. Sort of. Except only he seemed to supply the jokes, and the drinks were in his own home or celebratory in the office, all of which were occasions few and far between. He wondered absently if one could even befriend a portian. Though Teagan had only been phidipan when they'd met...

A knock against the door shook him out of his pointless musings, and he frowned towards it in puzzlement. It was late - but it was always late these days. He was barely sleeping thanks to those awful dreams, and rather than try, he preferred to work for as long as he could rather than subject himself to their torment.

"Come in."

Perhaps it was that very lack of sleep which prevented him from seeing things as easily as Teagan did. Perhaps, if he was well-rested, he might be more level-headed, less distracted.

He looked back up from his potent fingers as the door quietly clicked shut, and his heart immediately jumped into his throat. "Taliel!"

She stared at the wall behind him, and though she did flinch slightly at the exclamation, which he wished he hadn't loosened, she didn't otherwise react. "Keliceran," she began with the usual sturdy respect, "I received a message to report to you as soon as I returned from Adin."

"Well it..." he blinked, "it wasn't *urgent*..."

"Then I won't keep you."

"No, no," he half-rose from his seat in a curious panic as she turned back towards the door. "It's fine, please, by all means, take a seat. I...have too much work to do to go to bed just yet anyway."

"Then I shouldn't distract you."

"No," he rose further as she reached for the handle, but again she stopped and turned around with professional composure. "I...could also use a break."

"Would this meeting not constitute as work, sir?"

"No, it's not--I didn't want anything official...just..." he fought the redness from his cheeks, "just a chat, really."

The slightest frown flickered over her face. He may have imagined it, but at least she didn't turn away again. "Very well, sir."

"Salus, please." He smiled politely and gestured to a chair, ignoring how familiar the routine felt. Hopefully it would go better than their last 'chat'. She took the seat, and though she clearly intended to remain rigid and professional, her eyes flashed in surprise as she sank deeper into the cushioning than she'd expected. She quickly corrected herself as her cheeks flushed, and Salus could only smile. "I'm sorry, the chair's new."

She shuffled forwards so she didn't sink again. "What happened to the last one?"

Salus blinked. "It...broke." By his foot, then his hands, then the floor. He smiled nervously, then rose quickly again as a thought occurred to him, surprising her once more. "Would you like a drink? You've just returned, you must--"

"Thank you, yes. Ginger tea." She smiled sheepishly at her enthusiasm, provoking from him another smile. She must truly have been thirsty. He moved over to the frequently targeted and subsequently frequently replaced tea pot, freshly filled with hot water only half an hour before, and rifled through the drawers beneath it in hope that he had such a tea. Much to his surprise, there was an old jar marked 'gi-g-r' at the far end of the collection. He never touched it himself, but just as Arana House was always kept spotlessly clean, so was it kept freshly stocked, as if the few servants and cleaners who were permitted inside and followed by individuals of Teagan's choosing hadn't caught on to the fact that it wasn't actually the stately house of a surprisingly large and sombre noble family.

He brought her the cup and retook his seat, leaving his own to brew. Then silence hung. She didn't drink. He was about to ask what was wrong with it before he realised it was, of course, too hot to drink. She shortly put cup and saucer down on the small table beside her.

"Adin's evacuation is going smoothly?" He asked suddenly, desperate to escape the lull.

"Yes, perfectly well," she replied, startled. "All on schedule."

"Good..."

She nodded, and her eyes soon shifted onto the back wall once again. He sighed inwardly. She was uncomfortable. As was he. Which was ridiculous. Why should he be uncomfortable around a subordinate just because he wanted to have a casual conversation? After all, Teagan was little good for it, always picking apart statements meant as light sarcasm, or providing far too blunt responses when he needed a little delicacy. He was always so very matter of fact.

But Taliel, she *wasn't* so matter of fact. He could see some kind of joy in her eyes sometimes, she had the capacity to smile, to think, to be human, all while still being able to switch it off when needs arose. She would know when he was making a joke, and when he needed softer handling - she would tell him what he wanted to hear when the situation called for it. Because a white lie was harmless, while the truth...could be destructive. He knew that well as a leader of a faction for whom intelligence was a weapon.

And, quite possibly, as a human...

"Are you all right, sir?"

He blinked as Taliel shifted her eyes away from him, and he found a concerned, thoughtful tension in his face. He forced it to relax, and smiled. "Yes. Sorry, just lost in thought..." He sat up straight and reached for his tea, shaking off the discomfort. He had no reason to feel awkward. None at all. There was, at the very least, a desk between them.

"Was there something in particular you wished to talk about, sir?"

"Salus, please. And no, there..." he sighed as the discomfort returned in full force. He slumped deeper into his seat, defeated. "In truth, when I left that message, I just wanted some company."

Her eyebrows rose.

"I've not been sleeping well - again - and the war has been taking its toll. But," he smiled, and discovered that this one was difficult, "I'm all right now. You can leave, I'm sure you're tired and I don't want to keep you up."

Her eyes finally fell onto him, a suspicion deep within them. He felt his heart jump at their focus. "Forgive me," she said, though the formality in her tone had vanished, "but I believe you're lying."

Then Salus's eyebrows rose.

She sat back in her seat, cautiously, reached for her tea and made herself comfortable. "I don't know why you're choosing to come to me, but if my presence and advice can help you do your job, then as your subordinate, I have no right to refuse."

"You misunderstand," he said quickly, "this isn't an order--"

"I'm well aware of that, sir--Salus. I apologise. What I mean is that if I can help you to straighten out your thoughts and get a better night's sleep, I want to do it, for the good of everyone. And I assume that only I *can* - you wouldn't have called me here if Teagan or anyone else could do it instead." She smiled certainly. "You're not keeping me up."

He regarded her doubtfully, but found he didn't even want to *try* to argue the point.

"Is it the forest dream again?"

Something unstoppable compelled him to tell her everything. And she displayed no boredom, dispassion or condescension during or once he'd finished. Instead, she simply nodded. "Recurring dreams are the worst."

"You've had them?" He asked, surprised. "When you were younger? You said you struggled, for a time."

"You remember that? Yes, it was, but they can happen for any number of reasons. If you're worrying about something and you get stuck on a loop, if the matter doesn't get resolved or just seems to keep spiralling out of control, then it's only natural that your dreams will reflect that. And if you start panicking about them, worrying about going to sleep and having them again, you're even more likely to experience those same elements in your next dreams. But," she smiled encouragingly, "they're nothing to be afraid of."

"No, of course they're not, of course they're not...but they can be so..."

"I know. Everyone knows. Everyone has had a dream at some point in their lives that has terrified them so much that they've been afraid of falling asleep and suffering through it again. Some go as far as to avoid sleep altogether."

He nodded slowly, then noticed the suggestive glint in her eye. He chuckled in embarrassment. "Yes, I am guilty of that, I suppose. But how do you get past it? They seem so vivid, so *real*..." His face twisted in desperation. "They just won't stop. Even when I wake up, sometimes it feels like they just keep going for another half hour."

"Because you're lingering on them," she replied simply. "You have to just brush them off as nothing more than imagination, turn your mind away and focus on what the day brings instead. Concentrate on the things that matter. After a few days of redirecting your thoughts, you'll forget all about them."

"You seem so certain."

"Because I'm *right*."

He breathed a laugh and eased back in his seat. "Thank you."

"My pleasure. Salus."

He watched her as she raised the edge of the cup to her lips.

"Can I mention," she began after taking a soft sip, "that given all you've just said, you don't seem to be very tense right at the moment. Nervous, perhaps, but not tense."

He silently cursed himself. He thought he had it under control. "Well today's been a bit better than most."

"That's good to hear," she said, sipping quietly again. "Perhaps you'll sleep a little easier for it tonight."

His fists tightened. "Perhaps..." Excitement bubbled up. He had to show her.

He raised his hands and contorted his fingers as quickly as he dared, watching her all the while. She frowned in bafflement at the action at first, but astonishment swiftly set in, and as the orb of light appeared and outshone the office lanterns, she stared at the hovering body with an expression of dumbfoundment bathed in soft, blue light.

He read her eyes carefully, but he couldn't decide their nature. Even when they shifted slowly onto him, their astonishment unwavering, he couldn't decide what he saw. Suddenly, this didn't seem like a good idea.

"You did this?" She breathed, looking back onto the orb. "How did you do this?"

"You're not afraid, are you?" He asked, unable to bear her cryptic gaze. "I can control it, I promise you--"

"Afraid?" Though her eyes were still wide, her brow now furrowed as if the thought was preposterous. She was already reaching slowing towards it. "Why would I be afraid?"

"Because magic is a dangerous thing..." He watched her slender fingers move gracefully through the light, hesitant at first but soon enraptured, discovering at that moment himself that the orb had no solid core. His lips twitched into a smile, and relief settled. "It's a shame I couldn't have shown you anything more impressive..."

"This is impressive enough..." She looked through the light towards him as her fingers continued to swirl. "But *how* did you do it? I didn't think you possessed magic..."

"Apparently I did. The prisoner taught me to control it." He rose to his feet and moved around to the other side of the desk, leaning against it as he continued to watch her, but as he too became absorbed in the dancing glow, his thoughts began to wander. "I'll learn more," he promised himself quietly. "And then...then..."

Her eyes sharpened in caution. He didn't see it. "And then what?"

Teagan's doubt echoed in his mind. Salus didn't agree with it, but...what if Taliel did?

His gaze shifted and he smiled back at her, her eyes bright and interested. "And then I'll be able to do away with the candles and have lights as bright as daylight in here."

She chuckled. "Then you'll never get *any* sleep." She sat back, staring at the light until he dismissed it, and then found him staring at her with equal intensity. She smiled uneasily. "What is it?"

Salus hesitated. Her eyes were beautiful. Soft, but focused. "Can I ask you something personal?"

"Personal?"

"What would you say to someone if they told you they couldn't stop thinking about you?"

The teacup fell perfectly still, its edge hovering just inches from her lips, and a single, dying wisp of steam curled upwards to fog the surprise in her widened eyes.

He waited patiently, watching her closely, trying to read her first reaction before it could be replaced by instinctive phidipan control. But there was no change. From the moment he'd spoken she'd remained stunned and confused. There hadn't been even a momentary flash. It seemed that her walls truly had been lowered the moment she'd declared he was lying - she had honoured him with that. Her shock was genuine.

She slowly lowered the cup as she collected herself, the bone china clinking delicately against the saucer which she set just as carefully back onto the small side table. She didn't speak for a long moment, but her thoughts, moving faster than she seemed able to keep up with, were plain in her eyes. "Pardon?" She managed eventually.

'I have no reason to be embarrassed.' "For weeks now, I've been unable to get you out of my mind. I notice when you're not around, I'm *disappointed* when I find out you've been sent out on orders and there's no chance of bumping into you in

the halls, and when you *are* here, in this room with me, any tensions I have are subdued." He took a step towards her, the calmness of his tone tightening, but he refused to give in to his childish embarrassment and let it restrain him any longer. "I've not been able to relax even before this war started, and since it has, I've not been able to think straight because there are too many factors whizzing around for me to make the decisions I have to as easily as I should. But even though I'm filled with...such a...*paralysing* stupidity when I'm around you, you manage to make every tangled problem seem so clear, every solution so obvious! Taliel, I'm at my best when you're around!"

"This really doesn't seem appropriate." Her tone was firm, but she didn't shrink back from him, even as he took another heated step forwards.

"To hell with 'appropriate'! I've never thought of anyone as I do about you."

"You are being too bold."

"Perhaps, but I've been feeling all this for a long time and only recently did I begin to understand it!"

She shook her head in dismissal. "*Infatuation.*"

He took a final step and knelt quickly beside her, his eyes flicking fervently between hers. He regretted it, but he couldn't even think to hide it. "How can you know?"

"How can *you* know?"

In a second, his desperation fled. She analysed his eyes. She didn't think he could answer. But he could. "Because," he replied softly, certainly, "to reach my magic I had to delve deep into my subconscious. I waded through my emotions like mud. I have seen them all unfettered, felt them all, been overwhelmed by them all. And in those moments, I knew my emotions better than anyone else could ever know their own. I knew the difference between jealousy and envy, between shock and surprise, between regret and remorse. I couldn't mistake them, even if they seemed unfamiliar - and your face, your name, and your voice were among them. Among the most beautiful of them. I could not mistake that, either."

Their eyes were locked. His heart hammered, beating hard but steady, and though he inwardly held his breath, wondering just what she would say to that, say to *any* of it, to crush something he felt which was so alien but so definite, on the outside he appeared perfectly calm, perfectly patient.

But instead of ridicule, instead of insult, rage or denial, Taliel's beautiful brown eyes, ringed with copper, softened in defeat. Her lips parted to speak, but nothing eloquent came out. She stammered, and quickly gave up, staring into his blue eyes instead, searching for a clue for just how she should respond.

His mind turned blank under her gripping gaze. He leaned towards her, only slightly - not by manners or respect, but rather because a flood of nerves had rendered him suddenly unable to think or move. He had no clue what he was doing, if it was right or wrong, and a clamour of voices all began shouting in his mind, providing their own conflicting opinions to further complicate the matter.

He swallowed hard as he made his decision. He moved away, shrugging it off as a shift of his weight, and felt his heart lurch first in the greatest disappointment, then in surprise. The soft, warm lips he'd watched curve into a smile and sip the ginger tea pressed gently against his own. The slender fingers he'd watched weave through the handle of the teacup and tease the unnatural blue light traced softly over his stubbled chin. Her long, brown hair, disrupted by subtle waves, brushed over his arm. And her warm breath further heated his cheek.

Half of the voices in his mind had been stunned silent. The rest protested all the more to fill the void. But he found that ignoring them came easy.

He kissed back, clinging onto the moment with all his might, desperate for it not to end. But of course it did, and the moment that followed was the most confusing, fragile and expectant he had ever known. He couldn't bear it. "What does this mean?" He asked in the third.

She breathed a soft, bewildered laugh. "I don't...know..."

He nodded slowly at another great rush of disappointment. A moment ago, the silence had been almost comfortable, but now it seemed intrusive, judgemental. He could swear he felt a hundred pairs of eyes upon him.

He felt exposed. Foolish. He pushed himself back up in defeat and turned away from the woman, silently willing the ground to open beneath him. But again, her contact surprised him. He looked around, wide-eyed, as her fingers gently took a hold of his wrist, and he felt another foolish hope erupt inside him at the sight of her smile.

"It means," she said decisively with a gentle squeeze, "that if you need to talk to anyone again, you can depend on me."

Her fingers released him, his wrist slipping slowly out of her grip, and he was aware of how stupid his smile would be if he unleashed it. So he kept a tight hold over his facial muscles, concentrating so much on that that he forgot to respond. He watched her yawn, heard her apologise, and found himself wishing her a good night. And then she left.

He stood motionless in the middle of the room, staring unblinking towards the door. His mind had stalled again. But he smiled. He was happy. So very, very happy.

Taliel's hands only began to shake as she reached the foyer. She tightened her fists to ward it away and appeared otherwise composed, but her heart was racing, her mind riddled with conflicting thoughts. She felt disgusting - insubordinate and traitorous. Angry. At Salus for speaking so frankly, at Lord Malson for pushing her into the situation, and at herself for complying. She'd executed such orders before, but this...for the first time, she doubted her task. For the first time, it felt immoral. But...just like every other, she understood its importance.

She shook her head again, trying to chase the childish thoughts away. There were greater things to be concerned about.

Whether Salus had the best of intentions or not, the fact that he'd awakened his magic was a problem. An emergency meeting had already been held, the essence of which she'd been given as soon as she'd returned from Adin not an hour before. It had been brief with a unanimous agreement: they had to intervene. Carefully prepared pieces, she knew, were already being put into play, and messages were being sent to all their scattered assets. Everyone was being informed.

Everyone except the people most capable of making a difference. But the Order was in turmoil. Even if they were the most qualified to help, getting them involved would hinder their own efforts as well as the Arana's approved and classified work, which remained crucial to Turunda's safety regardless of the keliceran's mental state. They would need to know too many details about too many things, and with the Order's integrity in question, not even she was comfortable with the idea of shining the light of even a dying candle on any of the Arana's activity.

So it was all on them. They had failed to discourage him, to convince him that the prisoner was lying - the amount of time he'd devoted to the cells had left them little opportunity - and now he could form a spell by himself, albeit a meagre one, he would never give up on the tuition.

They had to go after the prisoner. Talk to him, have the Order invoke their right of custody - why they had yet to was a mystery - or perhaps go as far as to kill him if things really got so desperate.

But Taliel already knew what Malson would say. While the rest of their meagre little insurrection approached from other angles, he would again ask her to use Salus's affection for her to their advantage.

And while she would certainly agree, she privately found herself unwilling.

But it was for the good of all. She was a phidipan. She would not be paralysed by doubt. So she shed it, raised her head and walked taller through the building, making her way towards the dormitory for a well-deserved rest.

She stepped outside through the House doors and breathed the floral, late spring air, calling upon her training to rid her mind of troubles. It was as flawless as always. She was relaxed for almost a full minute before a large, brown moth fluttered down and flapped about in front of her, and her heart sank at the sight of the scroll of paper tied to its furry back. She expected it would drop further still as she read its contents.

But it didn't. Instead it jumped as if trying to clamber out of her mouth.

She folded the paper immediately, forcing away the steel rod that seemed to have been pushed through her shoulders with this newest reason to feel dirty, and tried with all her might to subdue the ridiculously immature racing of her heart as she set back off in search of a vacant bed.

Chapter 50

"Right back to the same routine!" Rathen roared in disbelief as they barrelled through the thin trees, shielding his face from the lowest branches that tried to rake his cheek as they whipped past.

"Well it's good to know the world hasn't forgotten us!"

He barely spared Anthis's tart remark a snarl. The three moved as fast as they could over the loose, sandy soil, only just managing to avoid the snaking reach of gnarled roots as they threw the briefest half-glances behind them, cursing the sun, the clouds, and all in the sky along with them as they went. The first sight of comfort and familiarity after three weeks in the desert, and no sooner had they dared to sigh in relief and marvel at the wonderful shape of leaves than an ear-piercing shriek had ripped through the air, and they were descended upon by a flight of harpies.

Rathen heard someone's foot catch behind him, then the waft of air from a single beat of powerful wings and the shrill cry of imminent victory. He gritted his teeth and formed a decisive spell, ignoring Garon's usual shouts for him to stand down, and a moment later the five feathered humanoids were buffeted up into the air and far beyond the cover of the trees.

Garon cursed in frustration even as he took immediate advantage of the lull to steer them off into denser forest. They expected their hunters to fall back upon them within a moment, having surely wizened to this trick by now, but they didn't reappear. None of them believed for even a second that they had been frightened off.

They slowed only as soon as they dared, Rathen and Anthis each fighting for their breath as quietly as they could while Garon listened closely to the air. Squawks soon rose nearby, but they moved no closer. They sounded distracted. Garon nodded to the south and the two followed, looping once more, wider, back in their original direction.

"Casting magic at them doesn't help," the inquisitor reminded Rathen sharply once the squawks had become distant and reduced to painful squeals, and their pace became a little less cautious.

"Well I fail to see what just running will do. They can track us - all too well, it seems. Not even three weeks in a desert shook them! They've probably been patrolling the border, waiting for us." He growled under his breath. "And all because--"

A rustle in the trees above brought them to a dead halt and their guard returned with force, but rather than a flurry of feathers bustling through the leaves, six muddy, child-sized squirrels came scurrying down the trunks instead.

All three sighed tiresomely.

"Of them." Rathen lowered his hands. "What do you want?"

"You're right, big 'uns ain't good at 'hello'."

"I told you."

The six ditchlings, armed with their usual makeshift spears and slingshots, the former very recently bloodied, surrounded the three and peered up at them with large, thoughtful eyes. Their gazes shifted in unison from one face to the next, their silent communication disturbingly evident, until one of them, whose hair either supported a bird's nest or was just that knotted, spoke what they all must have agreed upon.

"What was the desert like? Did you sink up to your whoseits in the sand?"

"The desert?" Anthis frowned. "How did you know we were...are there Arkhamas in the desert?"

The six blinked. "No..."

"...Then how did you know...?"

They peered slowly past them towards the east, where, beyond the edge of the trees, lay little but scrub and sand. Their eyes turned slowly back. "Where else would you have come from...?"

"Is there something you want?" Rathen sighed wearily, and their collective gaze flicked quickly onto him.

"We're here by coinkydink, mostly," another said as she leaned against her spear, her skin so pale that, joined with the paint, she almost perfectly blended in with the light-dappled soil. "But we saved your rears, so we reckon you owe us." She peered forwards, her eyes narrowing into silver-forested slits that just dared him to dispute it. "We 'ave *questions*."

The three looked uneasily from one to the other, but shortly saw little choice other than agreement.

Her gaze remained serious. "Did you find anythin' useful to yer job in that giant sandpit?"

"Why?" Rathen felt a sudden, ominous wave pass through his blood as he realised that it had been almost four weeks since they'd last had any news of Turunda, let alone any first-hand experience of its arcane suffering. "What's happened?"

She waved her hand vaguely despite the alarm in his eyes. "More of the usual, really. The Lady and her sisters get jealous when places get prettier than what they can make, then they leave, and we all 'ave to hunt 'em down again." With unnecessary theatrics, she turned her head and peered towards them with one wide, allusive eye. "But lately, the Lady's been getting mighty upset. Rather than keep leaving, she's been ob'iteratin' every place that outdoes her. They're startin' to break."

"Break? Do you mean the ground splits?"

"Exactly that, yep!" Said the first with the bird's nest as their faces turned a shade paler. "We been trying to apeese her, but she seems dead set on revenge. We figure it's this magic o' yours what's doing it, but it's all going out of control. She's really angry. Lots of us have gone to sleep in the mess what's left."

"Where?" He asked urgently.

They each thought for a moment, then began counting off on their fingers: "Greentop, The Ghost Patch, Wrenroot--"

"Wrenroot?" Anthis interrupted in a panic. "Is everyone all right?"

"No, not really, but they're still awake."

"And Nug?" Rathen added, unsatisfied and insulted on Aria's behalf by her casual tone.

"He's fine, he's fine." The girl waved it away with just as little concern. "So, did you find anything or not?"

"Nothing that will yield results right now."

The ditchlings exchanged mild looks of disappointment. "Thought as much," the boy replied. "But you did get *something*, didn't you?"

"Yes, but--"

"That's all we wanted to know. That and the whoseits. We heard sand is like water - *did* you have to swim?"

"...No..."

They nodded, apparently intrigued. "Weird. Well, we've all been itchin' about this magic busyness - we ain't been able to find out 'cause no one's been able to follow you for *ages*."

Rathen blinked. "Follow...? Are there usually di--*Arkhamas* following us?"

"No," he replied, casually again, "we just keep an eye. Check up on you every now and then. We got our own matters to take care of, you know! We can't be playing your shadows all the time!"

"Are you still being hunted?" Garon asked warily, but they laughed and waved the notion away.

"Na," a second girl replied, wearing a necklace of bird beaks - small birds. Too small even to be harpy chicks. They hoped. "We kill harpies, harpies kill us, and hoomans kill everyone. But it's okay, we're smarter than them. We've got all of 'em running and flapping about in circles. 'Course, we still don't know *why* hoomans are getting involved in summit what ain't their business." She leaned towards them suspiciously.

"We've already told you - or, others - that it's nothing to do with us," Garon explained quite firmly. "Humans aren't all connected."

"That really doesn't make any sense at all, but all right. Why do you *think* it's happening, then? What did we do to you but steal some pies and bread and run off with your washing? We ain't never *hurt* no one, not *really*." The rest nodded eagerly.

"Have your conflicts moved onto human land?"

"Oh, *all* land is 'hooman land' as far as you're thinkin'. But if you mean have we started throwing things at harpies on farms and outside your dens, then no. Near, maybe, but not *on*. That would be dumb. There's nowhere to hide from the sky on a farm, and if we tried to hide around your dens, you'd all point and shout and scream and make merry hell! Why? D'you reckon that's it?"

"Most likely. Your mischief upsets people, and with the war, your distractions could have severe consequences."

"Mm..." Deeply pensive frowns furrowed every pale brow. Rathen, Anthis and Garon watched them carefully, wondering what they were thinking, and what they were sharing. Finally, they all looked up with the same conclusion in their oversized eyes. "You're all so complicated." The first girl said flatly as the others once more nodded their whole-hearted agreement. "Can't seem to get *nothing* right where you big folks are concerned. Can't be outside your dens, can't be near 'em, can't be close enough to glimpse through a squint from the top of a tree!"

"Are things no closer to resolved between you?" Rathen asked, recalling Kienza's words to him about their own accidental hostility with the feathered terrors.

"Hah!" A second boy barked. "Resolved?! *How?* They dive on us, squawking and screaming, snatching us away! We ain't got a chance to sneeze or scratch our arses, never mind 'resolve' anythin'!"

"But we're awright, ain't we?" The second girl said, beaming mischievously around at her comrades. "No one's gonna get one up on us, not in the end!"

The shrill, metallic sound of bird call tore suddenly over the treetops. Immediately, everyone fell silent. All eyes turned searchingly towards the thin leaves as they lowered themselves in preparation to spring away, while the ditchlings readied their weapons and pressed themselves invisibly against the tree trunks.

A long moment passed under the oppressive silence before the ditchlings began to scurry away on an unspoken agreement. "We'll keep looking," the bird nest boy informed them in a whisper, "and if we find anything, we'll let you know."

"We're sure you will..."

The shriek came again, closer, but as the last of the ditchlings vanished among the trees, their crude voices rose in enthusiastic howls, and the harpies responded in fury.

The three waited until they were sure the cacophony was moving away from them, then took quick advantage of the ditchlings' distraction.

"The magic is getting worse," Rathen said needlessly as they slipped away.

"Of course it's getting worse," Garon growled. "But I didn't expect it to reach so far into Turunda already..."

"Could they be mistaken?"

Rathen shook his head. "No. They wouldn't be mistaken." His jaw tightened, feeling the growing weight of the rapidly increasing pressure he found himself trapped beneath. "We're running out of time..."

They hurried back to the small outcropping of stone that concealed their makeshift camp, additionally shadowed by a brief but dense cluster of trees, beneath which they found Petra standing diligently with her sword drawn and Aria stuck close beside her. Her sharp eyes flicked immediately onto them from her search of the leafy sky, but her relief evaporated once they'd assured her that the threat had passed. "Food?"

They shook their heads.

She sheathed her sword with a sigh and turned towards the bags set against the exposed clay wall, where she began rummaging through the preserved meats and soft, white cheeses they'd taken from the tribe. No one had been comfortable stealing from the reserves of the dead village, but it would have spoiled if left alone, and with a sea journey ahead of them, it would be a valuable asset. It was already curious that the earthen tribe hadn't taken it themselves when they'd attacked, but perhaps they viewed their diet with as much disdain as they did the wind goddess.

"How long is this doomed voyage of ours going to take?" She asked as she began to tear apart meagre morsels for another inadequate meal. Garon gave her a flat look of disapproval for yet again voicing her hopelessness for the sea passage, but she didn't see it.

"A week or so," he replied. "Maybe two. There should be enough to see us through. Even if we can't catch any fish."

"I don't think there *are* any fish. Boats always come back empty."

"Petra."

She rolled her eyes at his censure but otherwise said nothing.

"Where's Eyila?" Anthis asked softly, glancing around as he seated himself between two tree roots while Petra handed out the rations, ignoring the others as they shuffled away from him. They each followed Aria's finger as she pointed out through the trees and off into the sand. They saw the girl's form and could just about make out the bronze sheen to her skin in the dropping light. No one looked for too long, and only Anthis's cheeks reddened. "Has she...?"

"No. She's not said a word. She's just sat there, meditating."

"She's always doing that now..." Aria said sadly, settling down between Anthis and her father who pulled her closer towards him - or further from the other.

"She's not handling this well at all," Rathen stated with his own disapproval.

"She's trying to communicate with her people's spirits," Anthis explained. "That seems like a pretty normal response for someone like her, to me."

His lip curled at the cocksure tone he was sure he'd heard. "She's meditating *naked*. Is *that* normal?"

"She's not naked," Petra clarified primly "she's topless, and none of you should be looking so closely as to notice."

Anthis turned his eyes onto the salted oryx meat. "Perhaps it *is* normal practice and she was just being considerate of us before. It's understandable under the circumstances that she'd take any measures she could to try to reach out to them. Regardless of whether or not she'll admit that's what she's doing."

"She's not going to admit anything," she sighed. "She's not spoken for five days."

"Has anyone seen her eat anything?"

Everyone shook their heads.

Anthis rose to his feet.

"What are you doing?" Rathen asked quickly.

"You've got three guesses."

"Sit down."

"She has to eat something, and she's not going to do it by herself. *Someone* needs to make her - or," his eyes narrowed down at him, "do you think you're that person again?"

Rathen stared back steadily. "Leave her alone."

He hesitated, appearing to consider the demand, but rather than obey and sit back down or ignore him and approach her, he turned squarely towards the mage with crackling defiance. "Everyone? Or me?"

He matched his challenge. "You."

"I'm sick of this."

"Anthis, don't start," Garon warned, but the historian ignored him, green fire blazing in his eyes as they remained fixed sharply on the mage, watching closely for any and every reaction while he tightened his fists to steady his resolve.

"Where do you get off ordering everyone around?"

"What?"

"Do you still fancy yourself a sahrot? Still see yourself as a cut above everyone else, with your 'prodigy' magic? Your heroic honours? Because you must realise that *no one* remembers any of that. You're not here because of what you've done, you're only here because you're not linked to the Order anymore - you could just as easily have been left to rot wherever you've been hiding all these years! You're *not* as invaluable as you seem to think!"

"Anthis--"

"And yet *you* think you *are?!*" Rathen growled back, rising to his feet and cutting the inquisitor short. "How many other historians could have done this job with the right start? Even now, we could just take your notes, give them to someone else and leave you right here! 'Renowned historian' - you're arrogant, you're flighty, you're insane, and you're *not* invaluable either! We only need your notes!"

"Rathen--"

"I *am* the notes! After that fire, all we have left is what's in my head! So I'm afraid I have *become* quite invaluable. Quite *necessary*, in fact."

"I wonder if you would be so 'necessary' if I slammed your head into the floor and got it all out of there myself."

"That's enough!"

"I wonder if you would have to use your magic to achieve it."

Rathen's eyes flared. "Would you like to find out?"

Anthis smiled sickeningly. "Oh I would *love* to."

Rathen's taut, white fist flew towards him, but Anthis, by luck or by suddenly acquired skill, managed to avoid it with a swift backwards step. Rathen immediately swung for him again, and this time only missed because Anthis tripped over a root and fell to the ground just out of his reach. But when he leapt upon him for a third attempt, both of them ignoring the others' shouts for them to stop, Anthis firmly planted his boot in his chest and shoved him away with an unnaturally powerful push.

"*Magic,*" Rathen cackled acridly, rising easily back to his feet where he'd landed a few paces away, and responded in kind without a trace of reluctance. Anthis may have somehow used magic without casting any signs, but the mage formed the seals so quickly that Anthis similarly had no time at all to react. He was thrown back twice the distance, landing heavily in the dirt with a thump and a winded gasp, but before Rathen could take advantage of the result, his wrists were snatched and wrenched behind him, a knee struck the small of his back, and he was pushed swiftly to the ground. Anthis was restrained by Garon in the same instant, and as Rathen demanded that Petra release him, he finally heard Aria's young voice, racked by emotion, screaming above the clamour for them both to stop.

He looked around to her, shame engulfing him in a tidal wave as he finally caught up with himself, and found her big grey eyes looking desperately between the two of them. She was angry. She was confused. She was distraught. But most of all, she was incredulous. The wisdom she was too young to bear was shining through again, and both Rathen and Anthis squirmed under her furious gaze.

"Even an *eight-year-old* thinks you're acting like children," Garon spat. The addition of his authoritative tone made them feel even smaller, as well as the fact he presented. "Now pull yourselves together and keep away from each other. I'm *not* going to tolerate any more of this."

But Rathen couldn't help himself. "And what--"

"You don't want to know what I will do about it," he snarled. He yanked Anthis to his feet with shocking ease and shoved him off to one side of the camp, then stormed towards Rathen as Petra stepped off of him, moving instead to Aria's side, and threw him towards the other. "Go and cool off. Now."

Neither needed telling twice. Both spun on their heels and marched away.

Rathen paid little attention to where Anthis went. He'd have stayed for Aria, but he knew she didn't want to talk to him. Not because he'd frightened her, but because he'd disappointed her. And because that thought prompted shame to rise again like boiling water, he thundered off into the trees, growling to himself rather than listen to his own voice berate him.

There was a stream deeper in the forest. They'd heard its gurgle while attempting to hunt in the sparse, sandy forest, but harpies had attacked before they'd had the chance to reach it. If just to trick himself into thinking he was walking with a purpose rather than storming off to sulk, he decided to task himself with finding it, and when he did, he would wash the desert from his skin, drink as much as he could and just *relish* the fresh water, forgetting, for the moment, all the trials and desperate situations currently being thrust upon him, for it was very nearly all he could bear.

"Rathen."

His blood ran suddenly cold.

His legs halted as if the ground had reached up and ensnared him on the spot.

That voice... That unmistakable voice...

His head turned slowly, stretching the frozen, agonising moment. His heart thumped in his throat. His mind spun. Then his wide, uncomprehending eyes locked onto the figure standing not five paces away, so still as to have been mistaken for a tree.

The sound of hurried footsteps approaching from behind barely stirred his shock, nor the ring or flash of steel. And yet, he reacted immediately, though neither his body nor his voice felt like his own.

"*No!*" He found himself yelling as he stormed into their path. "Leave her!"

Petra's eyes flicked between him and the figure beyond, confusion just as evident in her eyes as it must have been in his. "Rathen?" She spoke slowly, warily. "What's going on?"

The light glinting over Garon's sword from beside her caught her eye as well as his, but her alarm and bewilderment only grew when she caught the mixture of recognition, dread and suspicion on the inquisitor's face. Rathen, too, slowly identified the myriad of reactions, and began to discover his own beneath the incapacitating shock.

Petra spared only a cursory glance behind them as Anthis came rushing in. "What is it?" She looked defensively back to the woman who stood a few feet beyond them, observing them all coolly. "Who is she?"

Defiance knotted further in his expression even as he cast another haunted, searching look towards her. But there was no mistake. There could never be any mistake.

He turned his challenge back upon the others. "She's my wife."

Chapter 51

Silence gripped the forest as his words hung in the air, persistently airborne like a falling downy feather. Everyone stared stupefied, their gaze shifting slowly between him and the unrattled woman he shielded, expressions frozen but for the steadily cascading and predictable chain of thought revealed in their eyes.

Rathen, however, had begun to rediscover his bearings, and as he cast another look of awe back around towards her, a soft, affectionate smile he could never have fought curved his lips and brightened his dark eyes. "Elle..."

She returned it, a beautifully soft, comforting smile, one that transported him back in time, brutally, wonderfully. There was a certain abashment within her warm, brown eyes, one that took him even further back, twenty five years, maybe more, and stirred within him even more distant memories. But there was a shame there, too, and a doubt of the wisdom of this moment, but though he found himself wondering the same thing, he decided, quite simply, that he didn't wish to think on it. He turned and approached her, half expecting her to vanish like a spectre of his past, but instead her smile broadened into one of relief at his acceptance and she eagerly left her place among the trees to meet him.

But another figure appeared suddenly between them. Garon, it seemed, had the same doubts of wisdom, but he was quite unaffected by the sentimentality that had silenced it within them. He fixed the woman with cold, sharp, calculating eyes before speaking with contemptuous suspicion. "How did you find us?" He growled. "What do you want?"

Her eyes, so beautiful only a moment ago, hardened under the brief interrogation and became suddenly unreadable. "I have information you need to hear."

"I'm sure you do," he sneered. He didn't need to look around to know that Rathen's hand was about to grasp his collar and wrench him out of the way. "Rathen, keep away from her."

As expected, he shoved him to one side and positioned himself once more between the inquisitor and his wife. His dark eyes were steel. "No. Put down your sword."

"Move. Now."

Menace edged Rathen's stare as he slowly raised his hand. "The sword."

The inquisitor met his gaze, but the intent within them was clear. Garon's frown tightened in disbelief. "Are you serious?"

"Dead serious."

"What's going on?" Petra asked from behind them, her tone rising in alarm. "Who is she? Really? Who are you?"

The woman's brown eyes softened as they flicked towards her and she offered a friendly smile, but Garon interrupted vehemently before she could speak.

"She's one of Salus's agents. A ghost."

Petra, and Anthis beyond her, paled. If it was possible, they fell even stiller.

"My name is Taliel," the woman amended, "I'm an Aranan operative, and you can trust me."

"You would say that."

"We *can*."

Garon's focus crashed back onto the mage, the anger and mistrust in his usually dispassionate grey eyes intensifying. The inquisitor was prepared for many scenarios, it seemed, but this encounter was not among them. "And you know that?" He challenged icily. "As a fact? As an absolute certainty? Because she has *certainly* lied before, her very profession demands it. As she has, no doubt, *directly* to you."

But Rathen remained steady. "I do. I trust her. Completely."

Garon snarled, then looked back towards the woman. "Prove it."

"How is she supposed to prove it?"

But she was already stepping past him. Swords had readied the instant she'd moved, their sharp edges angled towards her in a way that set Rathen's blood on fire, but he caught as she levelled a subtle but familiar scent, not one of perfume, but one of *her*. One that lifted his heart and tainted him with remorse as equally as her smile, but subdued him like an enchantment all the same.

Ignoring the blades, she handed the inquisitor a sealed sheet of parchment, who snatched it none too politely and immediately broke it open. Everyone watched impatiently, straining to see for themselves its contents or trying glean it from his reaction. But he was as unreadable as always. More so, in fact, and quite certainly due to the presence of a keen-eyed operative, even if she was paying his response very little attention.

He folded it back up and handed it tartly to Rathen, who noticed immediately the impression of the Crown's insignia within the broken white wax. "'Lord Elias Malson'," he read aloud. "I remember that name...the go-between for the Arana and the Crown?" He handed it back to Garon. "It has the Crown's official seal."

Garon screwed the parchment up with unnecessary drama and folded his arms tightly across his chest, clearly dissatisfied. "The Arana is an official body, and a deceptive one. This means absolutely *nothing*. We know you're after the artefact, so how can we know you're not trying to get information out of us?"

"For the simple fact that I will not speak of the matter."

"Someone like you wouldn't *need* to speak of it."

She smiled drily. "Nor will I use any crystal balls, probe any minds or question under duress."

Garon glared, unamused, but Elle ignored it. She straightened, raised her chin, flicked her brunette waves and let a severity fall over her. Rathen couldn't help smiling to himself. He had been on the receiving end of that look many times, and even seeing it from the sidelines, he felt a similar solemnity rise within himself. It was Elle, without a doubt.

"Salus is watching you," she told them plainly, looking from one face to the next as Anthis slowly joined them. "He's been following your trail for weeks, looking for the artefact, just as you have, and employed Tem Drassa to help him find it." Each reeled at the ease with which she'd revealed its name, but Anthis took a moment to scoff at the mention of his inferior colleague. Her eyes then fell onto him, and he took a wary half-step back as his voice caught in his throat. "And he's always kept a close eye on *you*, Mister Karth."

"We already knew that," Petra told her with the same caution.

"Yes, your inquisitor has been informed, but only of so much. Salus has been watching you *closely*."

"...How closely?"

"Closely enough to have snatched a bag." She looked suggestively towards Anthis, whose eyes brightened in relief as his shoulders sagged, the unseen weight they'd carried evaporating in an instant.

"But the fire..." He felt everyone's panic then focus upon him. "There is *nothing* in there that Salus *or* Drassa will make anything out of," he assured them urgently despite his foolish smile. "Not a thing."

"No," Elle agreed, "but his pet mage might." The concerned stares became suddenly ashen with horror. "A prisoner, arrested at Stonton," she explained. "Who has taught him to awaken his own magic."

"*What?!*" Their horror increased exponentially. "How--" Rathen's face dropped in grim realisation. "The magic. It's been strengthening dormant power in others, there--"

"*Partly.*" She offered him a apologetic smile. "His prisoner sensed the magic growing in him. Apparently it has always been strong enough to qualify him for tuition in the Order, but when he was learning to suppress his emotions, he suppressed his magic, too. He became a phidipan at sixteen, so when his magic would have awoken he was already shutting himself away. His magic must have gone with it. And now, just like all these new mages popping up like dandelions, his magic was strengthened to the point that he couldn't suppress it anymore. The mage sensed it and offered his help."

"Why would he do that?" Rathen frowned, bewildered. "Not only for the leader of the Arana, but for his *captor?*"

She shook her head, her hair bouncing with the movement. "Not for him, but for the sake of everyone *else*. Apparently, he's that powerful."

Rathen laughed nervously.

"I still don't understand," Petra frowned, lowering her sword a fraction. "I thought untrained magic was useless..."

This time Rathen shook his head, his expression twisted into something unreadable. "Mages aren't accepted into the Order based on the strength of their magic alone, but their...resilience. Their body's ability to contain, process and ultimately use it. Regardless of the strength of the magic, those with too little resilience can't keep the magic flowing as it should, rendering most of it inert. Those people can't be trained because their magic is more or less lifeless, and because their lack of resilience stops them from even being able to grasp it, let alone shape it. Mages who *can* use their magic have far greater resilience, but it still needs training. If a mage with an adequate balance of power and resilience isn't taught how to hone their control, their magic, in time, would overwhelm them or destroy them, injuring or killing others in the process. Like the mage in the desert, but...different... That's one of the reasons the Order patrols the streets of towns and cities as it does - they're looking for traces of awakening magic." He turned his uneasy gaze onto Garon and seemed reluctant to continue. "What do we do?"

The inquisitor looked to Elle. His eyes were no less suspicious, but they revealed a similar concern surfacing within him, one he was reluctant to acknowledge on the basis of who had encouraged it, but one he was professionally obliged to address. "If he *has* awakened his magic," he began dubiously, "it could be as severe as if he'd gotten a hold of the artefact. Quite possibly worse."

"In five days he's not learned to do more than form a light, boil water and move small things around. Ironically, the war has come to our rescue: it's been taking up most of his time. But he *has* awakened it, and with it he'll be able to use the artefact with his own two hands, directing it wherever he wishes on a whim, sparing no time for rational thought and reasoning." Her eyes, dark and grave, rested heavily upon each of them in turn, and each of them flinched under their weight. "You are Turunda's *only* chance at keeping the artefact out of his hands. If he recovers it and figures out how to use it - and with this mage of his, he very probably could..." She shook her head, and the momentary haunting in her face only hiked their dread. "I can't even begin to think about it."

Grimly, everyone else could.

The air grew heavy as they lost themselves in their thoughts, every scenario they envisioned growing steadily worse than the last. No one spoke for a long while.

But despite the density of the atmosphere, the gravity of the matter, and the smothering expectations being thrust upon them all - him above all others - Rathen couldn't help the drift of his gaze.

A gentle breeze rustled the surrounding leaves, pulling Elle out of her own reluctant thoughts. She must have felt his stare. She smiled at him, reading with ease the surprise he could feel on his face and the myriad of questions burning in his eyes.

The breeze came again, shaking the others back to the forest with shivers. But though their lips began to shape questions all at once, she smiled at them all too easily and turned away in dismissal. "That was all I had to say," she declared, her light tone indicating that her involvement in the matter was concluded, then turned to Rathen, gestured in the direction he had previously been storming, and excused them both over the top of their protests.

Garon flashed immediately in front of them, but Rathen eased him out of their way. "Enough, Garon," he said firmly, though not unkindly, then walked away by the woman's side, leaving the others without another thought as they stared after them, dumbfounded once again.

Elle cast a glance back towards them once they were in the darkness of the trees, but her attention was snatched by the wistful look on Rathen's face.

"I've had this dream before," he mused, peering up towards the dim evening light that crept in through the leaves. "It was..." he smiled to himself. "But you've never said anything about Salus having magic before."

"Perhaps it's an idea you're trying to hide from," she suggested lightly. "If it were all true, it would more than complicate matters, wouldn't it?"

"Mm..."

She watched him, raising an expectant eyebrow, and he soon looked around towards her. He considered her quietly for a moment, but a flash of sorrow, of regret, softened his eyes.

"I'm not looking forward to waking up."

She frowned sadly, her amusement escaping. "Rathen, this *isn't* a dream..."

"No," he sighed grimly, "it's half dream, half nightmare."

She reached out and grasped his hand, pulling him firmly to a stop and looked deep into his eyes. His heart jumped. The last time she'd looked at him so intensely, he'd just been given his sentencing. His jaw knotted and he squeezed her slender fingers. "I know it isn't a dream...but..." He shook his head as he groped for the words, searching desperately for a way to translate his impossibly tangled thoughts into a form they could *both* understand. His eyes weakened further in defeat. "It's been *eleven years*, Elle. Why did you come?"

"Because I had to," she replied softly. "I'm the only one among my colleagues who had *any* chance of convincing you to listen. Anyone else would have been attacked as soon as they'd spoken, as soon as they'd let slip any suggestion that they were involved with the Arana. But," she smiled that heartbreaking smile, "*you know me*, Rathen. So very well. And your inquisitor would have to know *of* me, at the very least - he'd have to know a lot about *you* to justify the risk of recruiting you." She watched the tension knot in his jaw as a hope began to die in his eyes. Her smile saddened as she understood. "Do you know how I found you?" He shook his head. "Because I've always known where you are."

He breathed a laugh, and though he surely tried to hide it, she could see that he was secretly satisfied. "You...yes, I suppose you would." But his expression became quickly tormented. "Then why didn't you...not even once--"

"Because," she replied softly again, "you were the one who left. Fled in the middle of the night."

Hurt pierced his eyes, but still she smiled, sadly and regretfully, and his heart dropped only further.

"Yes," she nodded, "I was upset. I was heartbroken and I was angry. If you had stayed for those final few days of grace, I would have left with you. I would have never left your side again. How could I? Neither of us understood what had happened to you, and the king had ordered you banished long before your wounds would have healed. With the aid of healers, you would have been fine, but I couldn't shake the possibility that it would happen again, and I couldn't bear to--" She bit her quivering lip and forced a smile. It would have convinced anyone else. "But I understood, in time, that you were trying to protect me. So though I tracked you down, I kept my distance, because you didn't just leave me behind, you left the *world* behind, and I didn't want to drag everything back along with me. It was enough to know you survived."

"Don't do that."

"What?"

His eyes glistened. "Be so understanding."

"Rathen," she smiled more easily, "as you say, it's been eleven years. I've had time to understand."

They stared at each other for a long while, switching between their own thoughts and trying to read the other's. Rathen's were plain: he felt unbearably guilty, he wished she would yell at him, release all she must have bottled up over the years. But hers, he was sure couldn't have been as they seemed. How could she look at him with such unfailing love and relief?

He flinched as she raised her hand and cleared his hair from his face, drawing it back from his temples and studying him with some small, almost-hidden anguish.

"You look old."

He breathed a laugh. "So do you."

"No," she replied matter of factly, "I don't."

He smiled, at last. "No," he agreed honestly, "you don't. You look no different at all..." He couldn't help himself. But there was no need to try. He leaned in and kissed her, firmly, desperately, and she responded in an instant. Out of nowhere, heat swelled between them, and every doubt, every question, every wonder and every regret fell away from them in their tight and familiar embrace, as if they had never existed, as if they had never been apart. They could feel each other's heart beat, and the heat of each other's quickening pulse only encouraged their passion.

Elle abruptly broke away and snatched him by the wrist, dragging him deeper into the forest, her copper-ringed eyes burning feverishly as he followed, and there, where their presence fell out of existence with no one around to notice them, they eagerly attempted to make a mark against a decade of lost love.

Chapter 52

"Don't leave."

She turned her head. Her tangled, rippling hair brushed her bare shoulder and offered him a fine view of her profile. But whether she sought to keep the delicate situation from growing worse or simply couldn't bear to see what lay in his eyes, her gaze didn't reach him. "I'll be back," she promised softly instead, reaching gracefully for her bustier which hung high upon a branch.

"With information."

Her expression twisted further at the cold resignation in his tone, and her eyes finally dragged themselves back to where he sat hunched upon a rock. Even in the darkness, it was impossible to miss the hard eyes that stared back at her, set beneath a frown so unyielding it could outlast a statue's smile, nor the sheer downward turn at the corners of his lips. He sat naked, physically and emotionally exposed, and yet the force behind his thoughts laid just as bare in his eyes made her shrink back an inch instead. She turned her eyes away. "Rathen, you must--"

"I do understand."

Neither spoke for a long while as she slipped back into her undergarments, and only then did she turn directly towards him, as if they offered some kind of armour. She smiled sadly, mirroring his stoicism. "I will come back."

"Would you still give up everything?"

"In a heartbeat," she replied with sudden ferocity. "But--"

"But you can't right now." He shook his head and sat forwards heavily. His tone hadn't changed, but at least he'd moved. "It's all right. I'm not going to ask you to. Not with things as they are. I just...wanted to hear you say it."

"I'm sorry--"

"You have a duty. I understand that. And whether I want it or not, so do I."

He didn't react as she approached him, nor when she rested his head gently against her breast, though he didn't fight the gesture, either. "When this is over--"

"Don't. We both know things aren't that simple."

She smiled in spite of herself. "Aren't they? You're overcomplicating things. As usual. But all right, I won't say it." She released him and stepped away, moving towards the rest of her clothes that had been strewn across the ground. He watched her go, dejected, but stubbornly made no attempt to stop her. But she didn't continue to dress, as he'd expected. Rather, she began fishing through one of her pockets. "I'll leave you with this, instead." She returned to his side and pressed something into his hand, closing his fingers tightly around it, and looked steadily into his eyes, trapping his gaze before he could discover what it was. "Have trust in yourself. You're smarter and more powerful than you give yourself credit for."

The corner of his mouth twitched. "You've said that before."

"And it irks me that I've had to say it so many times since." She turned away and only now began collecting her clothes. "Don't second-guess yourself. Trust your instincts. You've always had such good instincts - don't let them get clouded by other people's expectations."

"I don't understand."

She shot back a smile as she pulled her shirt over her head. "Because you're over-thinking it." She returned fully clothed and kissed him, both soft and deep, and he finally took her by the waist. He gripped her almost desperately, digging his fingers through her blouse, but when she made the first motion to move away, he released her without resistance. He knew that he wouldn't have let go at all if he'd hesitated for even a second, and he didn't want to feel her push herself away from him. At least this way, he could trick himself into thinking he had let her go on his terms.

She took slow but certain steps backwards, not once turning away from him, as though she was making the most of seeing him while she could, even though it had been her decision alone to leave. He watched her eyes all the while, and though they were just as reluctant as his, there was a promise in them, and he focused on that as she faded into the darkness and her voice drifted out through the night: "I will see you again."

For a long while, he stared at the spot where she had vanished, thinking of nothing at all. He moved only when a cold, night breeze prickled his skin, and remembered his hand clasped tightly around her token for nothing more than the ache in his palm. He loosened his grip, uncurled his fingers, and peered with certain hesitance between them.

As the morning sun glinted back from the simple golden band, he resented that that conversation was all he could clearly remember from last night's encounter. The rest had passed in an intoxicated blur, and though he'd tried desperately since she'd left him to recall all that had come before, his mind was still slow with the shock and exhaustion, both physical and emotional, and those last words were all that would return to him. His single solace was that the ring was proof he hadn't dreamt it.

He ran his thumb over its edge. He felt its weight. It was familiar, and yet tenfold heavier than he remembered. But that leaded density pressed not on his palm, but his conscience. She had kept his wedding ring for all this time, the one he'd left on the bedside table the night he'd left his life behind. The night he'd 'fled'.

No, not 'fled'.

'Yes,' he thought grimly, *'fled.'*

That was how she saw it, at any rate. And that, he found, was all that mattered.

He became slowly aware of eyes boring into him, and surreptitiously dropped the ring he'd shielded from nosy eyes back into his pocket. Relaxing his scowl as best he could, he looked to his side and smiled at Aria while she stared at him with unveiled suspicion.

"Petra said you were speaking to a friend last night," she informed him bluntly with no small degree of cynicism. "Who was it?"

"No one you know," he assured her softly.

Her frighteningly perceptive blue-grey eyes slighted further. "Someone from the Order, was it?" She barely gave him the chance to reply. She must have known he would evade the question with cleverly chosen words, neither lying nor telling the truth, nor really answering at all. "You've been keeping secrets. Don't look surprised, Daddy, I can tell. I know you better than anyone else. There's something you've wanted to say to me for *ages* now, I'm sure of it, but any time you almost do, you change your mind."

"Nonsense," he replied too quickly, smiling too brightly.

"Nonsense 'nonsense'," she retorted, then rose to her feet, her wood and whittling knife in hand. "But fine. I've not asked because I know you'll tell me when the time comes."

He frowned sadly. *'When the time comes.'* That would be today. How he loathed himself at that moment for his procrastination. He quickly forced it aside and did his best to offer her another smile as he reached out towards her. She frowned but accepted the hug, returning it tightly, then stared at him sadly when he held her by the shoulders. "I love you. You know that, don't you?"

Her frown deepened, but she didn't voice her thoughts. She nodded instead. "I love you too, Daddy..."

He rose to his feet and smiled reassuringly. "I'm going to the stream. Stay in Garon's sight, all right?" She looked back at him doubtfully, but nodded again, settling herself back on the soft, sandy ground in the inquisitor's clear line of sight from the bags he busied himself organising, as well as Anthis who sat on the far side with his books in his lap, suitably engrossed.

Rathen could feel her eyes tracking him as he left, but he didn't look back around. He was so conscious of it, though, that he jumped when he found Petra emerging from the trees on her way back to camp. And he knew very well why, because that guilt lingered, too.

"Thank you for looking after Aria last night," he said quietly when they drew level, trying unsuccessfully to hide from his own shame.

"It's all right." But there was a definite tone of disapproval in her voice, and it was one she seemed keen to express. "I'm surprised at you, Rathen. Leaving her to the rest of us like that. It was extremely irresponsible. What if something had happened to you?"

"Nothing would have happened to me."

"Oh," she cocked her head, feigned belief in her eyes, "well that's all right, then. Glad you can be so certain. I hope I gain that same foresight when I'm your age." She folded her arms across her chest, her eyes darkening in censure once more. "Rathen, she might be your...wife..." she said that with particularly colourful disbelief, "but you trusted her too easily. She's from the Arana."

"Yes," he replied lightly, belying his bristling. "She is. A phidipan."

She looked surprised, if even a little frightened. "Phidipan? She can...suppress her--"

"When she needs to. Yes, sometimes it was difficult to tell when she was hiding something when we were together - then I realised she was *always* hiding something. But I learned to tell when it was something I should be concerned about and I've always trusted her since. She's never given me reason not to."

He strode past her dismissively, pretending, poorly, to be unaffected by her suggestion, and she didn't attempt to stop him.

*

Once he'd returned an unreasonable half hour later, the group set off with Garon and his map at the lead. Petra remained near Eyila, keeping a careful but subtle eye on the silent tribal as she followed along, neither willing nor unwilling, walking in a daze as she did every day, and Rathen kept Aria close at his side, far away from Anthis. He held her hand more tightly than usual, prompting her to send occasional fretful looks his way. She distracted herself by staring beyond the visible horizon in search of the sea, a sight she was absolutely desperate to experience, and sniffed the air quite audibly as if she was afraid she might miss it if she wasn't so vigilant. In due time, the breeze grew stronger and carried with it the unmistakable scent of salt.

"You've not told her," Garon said quietly as Aria all but dragged her father to the head of the group in her haste.

"No," he replied resentfully.

"Rathen--"

"*I know*, dammit, I know."

"If you'd done it sooner, it wouldn't have to be so abrupt."

Rathen growled beneath his breath and relinquished his restraint against his daughter's enthusiasm, allowing her to pull him away. *'Assuming Kienza comes at all...'*

They reached the top of the extensive bank of sand ahead of the others, where Aria gasped in sudden awe and brought them both to a stop. Rathen expressed a similar sentiment.

The golden sands that had seemed so endless for so long were finally and abruptly cut short, halted by the encroaching blue ocean, a rippling, impassible body which truly stretched on forever where no giant swells rose to advance the horizon. Even beyond the natural crescent bay edged by pillars of limestone, the azure water was calm and lazy, and the few modest boats that rested at the jetty were as still as rock. The scene was so motionless and so tranquil that they could have been standing within the strokes of a grand painting.

Countless squeaks of excitement bubbled up beside him, and Rathen couldn't help a sad smile at Aria's uncontainable beaming grin as she stared, awestruck, at her first sight of the sea.

"I wonder how big it is," she breathed. "And what's in it--maybe there are selkies! Or sea monsters!"

"There are no sea monsters," Petra assured her grimly as she and the others stopped beside them. "There's *nothing* out there..."

Garon would have chastised her for this most recent pessimistic statement, but it seemed she was right. Though they looked and listened, stretching the reach of their eyes and ears across the vast expanse, there was not one single, obvious trace of life. There was no sight of even a lone sea bird soaring on distant winds, nor were there any calls from nests camouflaged in rocky nooks. The gentle rhythms of the waves weren't interrupted by fin or spray of whale or porpoise. Not even the scent of fish was present to wrinkle the nose. There was nothing at all but water and salt.

Suddenly, the thought of passing through a war zone felt all the more beguiling...

But their eyes fell heavily upon the boats ahead rather than the monotonous desert behind them, and among the four moored, one in particular caught their attention. But it was for more than its perfect fourfold size, its distinctly forest-brown if barnacle-crusted hull, the presence of masts rather than oars alone, or the fact that it was clearly not of simple but efficient tribal craft.

There was someone aboard it.

"*Kienza!*" Aria cried, sparing the strain of Rathen's eyes, and wriggled expertly out of his grip to rush down the sand towards the jetty, leaving him to follow at a hurry and swallow his sudden wash of dread.

The sylvan woman, adorned in her usual forested hues, rushed off of the deck and down the gangplank with an equally childish grin to envelop her in a hug, and Rathen couldn't help but smile at the enthusiasm they always shared. And her joy didn't change in the slightest when she turned her eyes onto him a moment later, snatching him immediately into an embrace as soon as he was close enough to reach.

But though he didn't protest, though he desired the contact, though he knew he was just as happy to see her, he hesitated. It was fleeting, not even a second; the briefest partial beat off of the expected time to wrap his arms around her in turn. But she noticed. She made no obvious reaction, but he knew she'd noticed.

And yet she still smiled with the greatest of affection when she released him, just as she always did, and he found himself returning it just as easily. There was nothing amiss in her emerald eyes; they were as entrancing and mysterious as they had always been, and he felt the guilt sitting at the top of his throat fractionally subside.

Aria unceremoniously tugged the bag off of her father's back while the others arrived behind them, but they were far beyond an awkward, partial beat to offer their greetings. And yet she didn't seem to notice this, either, and smiled fondly at each. Her gaze lingered on Eyila, however, whom he realised she had yet to meet, but she didn't stop and stare closely at the girl as she had the others. Instead, her smooth, perfect brow creased almost immediately in sympathy, and she made no attempt to speak to her. Rathen found that the girl's pale blue eyes were still glazed and peering far into another world.

And then Aria was suddenly between them again, pushing Rathen back towards the others, her sketchbook in hand and a deadly serious look in her eye. He wasn't going to protest.

She turned her back squarely towards them, opened the book in front of her face and presented the contents to Kienza alone. "Which one?"

The sorceress's expectant expression suddenly mirrored the child's severity, and she seemed to compare two pages with the greatest of dedication. She didn't pose the question anyone else would have. Instead she weighed her two options until her eyes began to linger longer on the left page, then pointed, declared 'that one' with the utmost certainty, and inclined her head at Aria's thanks as she snapped the book closed with finality. "That was my favourite, too."

With that matter dealt with, Kienza looked back to Rathen, ignored the puzzled looks of the others, and ushered him rather concisely towards an upturned fishing crate ten or so paces away. "Sit. Shirt off."

He knew better than to question or argue, though he flinched at her thoughtful grunt as he bared his back, and at the pressure of her fingers as she pressed them into the most painful of his lingering wounds. "The Ayavei girl did a fine job."

"Ayavei?" He flinched again at her enduring sigh.

"The girl from the wind tribe..."

"Ah." He nodded as he looked towards her. Petra still stood protectively nearby, her gaze never wandering far, and Anthis too, he noticed warily, spared her a moment of his otherwise absorbed attention from time to time. Eyila noticed none of it. "Is there anything you can do for her?"

"No," she replied regretfully, following his gaze. "She's grieving. I'm afraid that job falls to the rest of you."

"I thought so..." He hissed suddenly as she jabbed a finger into a particularly tender spot between his ribs.

"Oh stop it. She did well." He felt the hum of her magic and immediately found himself sitting straighter, only now aware of his previous protective, sideways lean. But as she moved around to examine his collarbones, he noticed the mild disapproval in her expectant expression. "So," she began mildly, "what happened?"

"I don't know."

"You lost control of yourself," she informed him. "But why? What happened?"

"There was a fire--"

"*Oh!* It must have been *catastrophic!* Did the flames take on the shape of a demon? Did it burn open the gates to the afterlife? Did it--"

"That's enough," he growled, but she only smiled in amusement as she directed her magic into another sore patch.

"Yes, you're quite right. So? What *actually* happened?"

His eyes slipped watchfully onto the historian. "Anthis Karth is a Sulyaxist."

She moved her left hand to his chest and began gently probing the joins between rib and sternum while her right continued to work over his shoulder, her brow softly knitted in concentration. It wasn't until she moved down to his hips that she finally looked up, but her eyes were wide and patient. "And?"

Rathen's eyes flashed. "*You knew?!*" He blinked at her incredulously. "...Of course you knew..."

"Of course I knew," she confirmed flatly. "And if he was a danger to you, I would have removed him myself right at the beginning. But," she began examining his legs with careful squeezing and prodding, "I don't expect you'll listen to me. You never do. So carry on giving the poor boy trouble. As if he hasn't already been struggling with it all his life. It's not like he has anything he needs to concentrate on right now, anyway - in fact he's probably grateful for having it on his mind."

Kienza rose to her feet and looked down at his evenly balanced body with satisfaction, all trace of sarcasm vanishing. "Better?" She smiled.

"Yes..."

"Good. Now," she raised her voice and turned back towards the others, finally acknowledging their belated greetings, and left Rathen to tentatively finger the areas her mysterious, unsigned magic had permeated. "You're setting out with the intention of walking into hostile land. You are aware of this, I presume?"

"It can't be helped," Garon replied rigidly, sparing no thought to wonder at how she'd found them nor how she'd deduced their heading. "Anthis says we need to get to Enhala."

"Um, about that," Petra interrupted hesitantly, "I thought Kasire and Ivaea were in talks..."

"In the very loosest sense of the phrase." Kienza sighed regretfully and folded her arms across her ample chest, shaking her dark curls wearily as a long-suffering mother would over two squabbling children. "The talks grew stale. Neither side were truly prepared to compromise so they made unreasonable demands of the other to avoid it. The Crowns eventually clashed, the talks descended into a back-and-forth of thinly veiled insults, then they finally gave up." She shrugged. "And then, war.

"You're right to go by sea. Crossing the border by foot isn't safe. Fortunately, Enhala is far west enough to be outside of the combat zone and is only a few days from the coast, so you won't have to venture too deep. And as for the Roquna itself," her arm cut a straight line through the air directly ahead of her. "As best you can. Pay attention to what's around you and you'll get where you need to go in the end."

"Do the stories have any truth?" Rathen asked, pulling his shirt back over his head as he joined them, but his brow flattened humourlessly when he found her looking back at him with precisely the impish grin he had expected after so foolishly vague a question. "'Every story has truth'," he said drily over the top of her. "But do the stories about fogs and looping straight lines out on the Roquna right there have any relevance to us?"

"Certainly," she smiled just as unhelpfully. "So do as I told you: *pay attention.*"

"Is this our boat?"

Everyone followed Anthis's gaze towards the vessel she had been waiting upon, and noticed together that not only did the boat bear the precise shade of tree-bark-brown that almost every Turundan forest wore, but its texture too. And lichen. They were not barnacles at all. Not one of them wondered aloud about the possible peril of wood worms.

"It is indeed!" She replied proudly.

Anthis regarded her carefully. "Will it protect us from...the fog...?"

She blinked at him. "If you're inside, I suppose it will 'protect' you from the fog..."

"So it's enchanted?"

"...It's a boat." She gave him a suddenly disapproving look, and he shrank shamefully beneath it. "Don't be ungrateful, Mister Karth. I could have left you to these dingies. Now hurry aboard. The sea won't stay so calm for long, and when you get out in the open, you'll be glad you have little current to contend with."

The group moved immediately on her order, walking without argument onto the simple wooden jetty and towards their most unusual vessel, keeping their doubts silent. Aria took Rathen's hand and began to pull him along eagerly when he didn't step on his own, but he resisted the encouragement. "Wait." He immediately regretted the slip of anger that compromised his intentionally soft tone, and his heart wrenched at the confusion in her eyes as she turned them up towards him. And for a moment he hated Kienza for answering his unspoken call, resented her impossible ability to know exactly when and where she was needed.

And she, he found, hadn't left with the others. Instead she stood a few feet away with far too much reluctance in her eyes. She knew exactly what he was about to do. But she must have agreed with it, for she didn't say a word.

Rathen sighed and knelt, turning Aria his full attention as he brought himself eye-level with her. She wasn't blind; she saw the weight behind the motion. Her confusion became tinged with the beginnings of panic and her eyes flicked with growing desperation towards Kienza for a clue. But she wouldn't meet her gaze.

"Listen to me, little one." He tried to force a smile, but his face refused to cooperate. He didn't have the strength of will to try for very long, and it took him a painfully long while to continue while he wrestled with his suddenly inadequate vocabulary. "You can't come with us."

She frowned, and half of her visible emotion was overwritten by simple confusion. "What do you mean?"

"I mean you can't come with us," he replied carefully, suddenly feeling the eggshells beneath his feet. "Not out to sea, not into Kasire. It's not safe for you."

"I don't understand...I've been everywhere else with you--"

"It isn't the same, Aria."

Her freckled frown deepened, and though she folded her arms in a manner more mature than her age would dictate, there was a certain wildness in her eyes. "*I* don't see how it's different."

"Sweetheart--"

"You don't want me around anymore, do you?"

His eyes flashed. "That is *not* true." He stared at her, watching the wildness grow, and wished, stronger than he ever had for anything in his life, that that old wisdom would spark within them and chase away her fragile innocence.

But it didn't. "It is!" She declared, her voice finally breaking. "You wouldn't send me away otherwise! Have I been getting in the way? Have I not been good?"

"Aria, it's nothing like that--"

"It *is!* I'm not helping enough, I'm getting in the way, I'm distracting you all - someone *always* has to look after me! But you don't *need* to! I can look after myself! You don't need to waste your time on me, just *let me stay with you!*"

Rathen could only watch her heart break in her eyes as his ability to speak abandoned him, and as he watched diamond tears gush into them, he felt them threaten to fill his, too. It was only through magic that he managed to ward them off. Because he understood how she felt all too clearly. She'd never been forced away from him before; this was quite possibly the worst thing she'd ever consciously experienced, and the weight of that thought only grew in intensity the harder he tried to fight it away. He could think only to take the doll he had made her out from her bag and clasp her hands around it.

"*Please,* Daddy!" She begged as her fingers tightened into it on reflex, her voice rising higher in her grief and certainly catching the attention of the others. She turned desperately to Kienza, her fair curls flicking wildly, pleading with her to tell him she could stay.

He finally tore his eyes away, wondering as he did so just how much he was failing her as a parent by giving up like this, but he was simply unable to bear it. He turned to Kienza, his resigned gaze deadened by his own grief, and yet she read it all too easily. He knew, because surprise seemed to physically strike her.

"*Him?*" She asked in a disbelief that belied the extent in her eyes. "Are you absolutely sure?"

"It's the safest option."

She studied him very carefully, but despite Aria's desperate pleas, he didn't waver. She soon straightened and nodded, and once he'd risen and taken Aria by the hand, which gripped his as tightly as if she were having a nightmare, they vanished.

The others stared openly at the spot they'd just been standing, but only Garon looked upon the empty space with regret.

The light had dimmed, the surrounding area darkened by the reach of walls and trees, and the air offered a welcome bite. Rathen wasn't sure if his nausea was a result of the teleportation, the sickening familiarity of his new location, the weight of the present situation or a mixture of all three, but he didn't care to think on it for long.

The house that stood before them at the head of the worn garden path hadn't changed much. The garden was overgrown, but only to the extent that it was tended to upon necessity rather than completely ignored, and the flowers that grew were certainly wild despite growing in coincidentally neat rows beneath the windows. But the windows themselves were clean, the curtains undrawn, and just beyond one, a small but fresh bowl of fruit could be seen sat upon a table. Someone occupied this house. Someone who had given up long ago and had learned to just 'make do'. Someone who existed, rather than lived. Someone Rathen could muster no compassion for.

Despite his screaming reluctance, he started towards the door. Aria cried openly beside him, making no attempt at restraint nor to keep him from moving, allowing herself through denial to be lead the few steps to the top of the path, and Rathen equally allowed her to vent her distress. The village wouldn't be disturbed by it; Kienza had prudently masked their arrival.

He knocked against the door as soon as it was within reach, pushing through his hesitation before it could truly ensnare him. He regretted it the moment his knuckles struck the wood. He resented it more than anything in memory, more, even, than when he'd abandoned his life a decade ago. This was far worse than that. Back then, he'd known the world would continue to turn without him, but Aria...she was his world now, just as big and yet infinitely more fragile, and he, in turn, was hers. And he was leaving her *here*.

She had grown suddenly quiet. Though she still sobbed and sniffed, she seemed more concerned about the door and what might lie beyond it. She was no doubt willing it not to open. As, for many more reasons, was he.

But it did - the hinge still creaked - and all too soon an old man with thin, white hair and deep-set, unfriendly eyes was standing before them, scrutinising his intruders in a manner that suggested he was unaccustomed to guests. There was no hint of recognition in his wrinkled face, not even the slightest suggestion, and though Rathen had expected to experience the same, he was surprised to find that, despite the wear of age, there was no mistaking him at all. "Ira."

"Yes?" The old man's voice creaked, just as haggard as his face, and he frowned cautiously, looking a little more slowly from face to unfamiliar face. "Can I help...you..." His white, wiry eyebrows rose high, revealing the true depth of his scowl, and he looked more closely at the man before him with a sudden vigour in his eyes. "Vastal's light...Rathen?"

But Rathen didn't respond. Satisfied that he had his attention, he turned away and knelt again in front of Aria who had fallen silent and paralysed in her dreadful apprehension, taking her small hands in his as comfortably as he could. Her hands and eyes latched onto him with a fearsome, steel grip. "Listen to me, little one," he said softly as she sniffled, leaving the old man to stare in foggy dismay. "I'm not doing this because I want to - this is the very *last* thing I want, and you must know that. But you have to trust me when I say that this *is* for the best."

"Where are we?" She demanded, though its effect was compromised by the shake in her voice.

"Redgrove. This is Ira's house. You're going to stay with him for a little while."

The alarm in her eyes intensified as they thundered back onto the old man, then once more in desperation onto Kienza. "No! No, I don't know him! I want to go with Kienza! Why can't I go with *Kienza?!*"

"It's not safe with her, either, sweetheart. I'm sorry. But she'll check in on you from time to time." He glanced up to her. "Won't you?"

"Of course, absolutely. As often as I can."

"*Why* isn't it safe with her?! I don't know him, I don't want to stay with him!"

"Rathen--"

He silenced the old man with a single black glance. "Because Kienza is investigating the magic herself."

"But that's what *we've* been doing!"

"It's not the same, she's going deep into dangerous places and neither of us want to put you in that kind of danger."

"Danger is danger!"

"No, Aria, it isn't!" He caught and squeezed her hands as she threw her doll to the ground, her frenzied eyes dragging him deeper into her despair, drowning him in the cascading sorrow he tried furiously to wade out of. "Please don't make this harder than it has to be, *please*."

"It's because I'm not helping enough, isn't it? I know it is! It's because I'm not useful!"

"That's not true."

"Name one time I've helped!"

"You subdued the ditchlings," he replied with confident ease. "They trusted us because of *you*, and since then have given us information we probably wouldn't have found on our own. But we're travelling into a *war zone*, Aria, and your safety is far more important to *all* of us than what good you could do, big or small." He managed the most fleeting of smiles. "You know Petra would flay me alive if anything happened to you."

Her eyes flashed in realisation, and he kicked himself for fanning the flames. "I've not even said goodbye to anyone!"

"You won't need to, you'll not be here any longer than you need to be. You'll be back with us all in no time. I promise."

"Rathen, What's going on?"

Fire sparked as a growl rumbled in his throat. He rose sharply to his feet, finally turning to face the old man who flinched beneath his sudden fury. "If there was *anywhere* else she could go, you had better believe that I would never even *consider* bringing her here." His voice was as low as the grave, and tinted by a menace that promised fulfilment. "But I have no choice - not that I'd expect you to understand." Ira appeared about to protest, but Rathen wasn't going to let him. "You failed me as a father when she died, carting me off to the Order as soon as you could so you could wallow in your own self-pity. But my mother can't die again, so you'll have no excuse to shirk your duties as a grandfather. And you won't. I'm not giving you the chance - not when this is the first thing I have *ever* asked of you, not when she *needs* you."

Ira's eyes, old, slow and moist, dropped briefly to the young girl, and though he managed to find his tongue, it provided him only the opportunity for a stammer. But Rathen had already dismissed him.

He shrugged the bag off of his back and pulled out the smaller sack that had been stuffed inside. "There is something you can do while you're here," he said softly as he handed it to Aria. "You've made a decision, haven't you? That's what you wanted to ask Kienza about last time, wasn't it? Which of your ideas she liked? Then you can finally start work on your artefact - in comfort, without distraction. You can stay in one place, with a hot meal every day and a soft bed every night, and give it the attention it deserves." He squeezed her hands, tightening her grip on the bag with encouragement, and somehow managed another smile. "Make me a masterpiece. Outshine the elves like I know you can."

Tears once again blurred her eyes as she threw her arms around him, and he embraced her tightly, so very tightly, kissing her tanned forehead as she cried against him, her tears soaking into his shirt. "I'm so sorry, little one," he promised her quietly, but she didn't manage to respond. She may have tried, but her sobbing overruled any attempt and strengthened her grasp around his shoulders as well as his heart.

"Daddy, please don't leave me here," he managed to make out, "please, please..."

"Aria, please trust me, I *will* come back for you."

"No, Daddy, no, *please...*"

She squeezed him desperately, and he knew that if he stayed there for much longer, he would give in. But he couldn't. For her own good, he couldn't.

He struggled out of her monstrous grip and turned her over to Ira, looking at him all the while with that same menace even as he spoke with a deceptive softness. "Look after her."

"Y-yes, of course."

Kienza finally stepped forwards from her respectful distance and silently extended a pouch of coins. The old man took it immediately, worsening the foul taste in Rathen's mouth by not even trying to refuse it. He gave no thought to the likelihood that it was an automatic reaction in his confusion and that he hadn't even noticed what it was. It took Rathen a long while to even realise that his eyes had barely left him at all, and that they had remained wide and disturbed throughout. But not the kind reserved for duress, nor for irritation. He looked as though he'd seen a ghost.

Rathen's shoulders dropped in understanding. "I'll answer your questions," he assured him, "next time. But for now, I need you to do this." Again he turned away before he could try to argue, but though Ira's eyes were confused and uncomfortable, he placed his hands gently on Aria's shoulders and eased her along to his side, speaking softly and keeping her from hurrying after him as Rathen stepped reluctantly out of her reach. He steeled himself against the lurch of his stomach and the words of the belittling voice in his head, and repeated to himself in as many ways as he could that this was the right thing to do.

Kienza knelt and hugged her for a moment, just as tightly as he had, and whispered something very close to her curl-covered ear. But whatever it was, it had little impact. Her eyes remained red, puffy, damp and torn between defeat and what truly seemed like hatred.

And though it tore holes into him, Rathen didn't permit himself to look away.

"I will come back for you," he assured her again, forcing as much promise into his eyes as he could. "I love you."

But she didn't say it back.

Rathen's teeth clenched together as he braced himself against her heartbreak, but still he didn't look away. Kienza joined him, her plump lips turned down in a perfect crescent, and after sparing him an evaluating moment, noting every thought that tumbled through his eyes, she cast her spell, ending his torment.

And Aria's quiet voice followed them.

Petra and Anthis uneasily watched the spot on the jetty where the three had vanished. They'd asked Garon where they'd gone, what they were doing and, most importantly, if they were coming back, but he hadn't answered. Neither could decide if he knew and was keeping secrets or if he was just as clueless as they were, but whatever the case, he waited silently beside the boat, his arms tightly folded, watching the spot just as intently. Neither of them saw the regret that took the place of their concern.

A few minutes passed and they reappeared without warning, the hum of magic briefly tugging on Eyila's mind just as it had the first, but she spared neither it nor them even a passing glance. But while Garon straightened and turned away, apparently satisfied by their return, there was one detail the others couldn't avoid noticing.

"Where's Aria?" Anthis asked in a restrained panic as Garon finally boarded, but he was given a sharp, silencing gesture in answer. They both looked back out towards the two mages, their alarm reluctantly quietening at Rathen's apparent composure, and realised that it had, of course, been his decision. And though they both found themselves in selfish disagreement with it, they equally knew that it was for the best. And in hindsight, one that should have come much, much sooner.

They stepped back from the bulwark and gave them their privacy, busying themselves with nonsense and pretending not to notice when they eventually made their way aboard. But despite appearances, they were acutely aware of Rathen's silence as he left Kienza's side at the top of the gangplank, and indirectly tracked him as he walked past them with a gaze almost as distant as Eyila's. He secluded himself just as she did, too, leaning against the bulwark at the far end of the boat and staring out over the water towards their heading as if eager to be away.

They cast silent looks towards Kienza, but she simply shook her head, and it took visible strength for her to smile as she sought to move the tension along. "I wish you luck," she said softly, "and remember," her sweeping gaze rested momentarily on the two distant casters, "pay attention. Don't trust in map and compass alone, and you will be fine." She smiled again, this time more easily, warmly and assured, and though the three's doubt remained at the notable lack of direct advice, warnings or instruction, they were at least slightly eased by her certainty.

"Thank you, Miss," said Garon with a formality that belied the curiosity he must surely have held, one which caused the others to equally restrain their questions, and he inclined his head politely, seeming suddenly quite eager to leave, himself.

Whether Kienza saw this and obliged or was simply finished anyway, she returned the gesture and began to issue brief farewells. But as she turned away from Petra, the duelist was struck by a sudden, urgent thought. One she would have expressed had the sorceress not then paused in front of Garon. "Look after him," she said quietly, a demand presented quite prettily as a request. He nodded his assurance, and Petra subdued her urgency as she watched him attempt to tighten his left hand at his side.

Until he shook it away and placed it lightly upon the edge of his scabbard to occupy it, and allowed the forest-clad woman to vanish from in front of him without saying another word.

His eyes passed briefly over her as he turned towards the rest of the ship, but he spared no explanation and quickly disregarded her questioning frown. "Let's go."

"Who's going to sail it?" Anthis asked, peering up at the masts and then back towards the wheel while Petra moved to the bow with an irritated stamp in her step.

"I will," Garon replied, then looked sternly at the historian's hesitance. "I know how to sail a cargo ship, and this isn't a large one. If all of you do as I ask *when* I ask, we'll be fine." He looked back towards Petra, whom he heard mutter beneath her breath, but she was too far for him to catch it. Again, he did his best to ignore her, as well as the clueless, niggling guilt he'd felt growing within him for the past few days whenever she crossed his sight.

Turning his mind away, he confirmed with a quick look across the deck that the ship had already been prepared. "Rathen, Anthis," he commanded as he took the wheel, "take up the oars. Petra, cast off the lines."

They both sent silent, doubtful looks towards the mage as they obliged, expecting some sharp response or to be simply ignored. But instead, he turned away from the calm, still sea and sat quietly on the rowing bench, his face strangely expressionless despite the increased depth of his lines.

Anthis warily took the seat beside him, but where the mage would usually have grunted, sneered or turned pointedly away from him, now he didn't seem to notice him at all. Anthis found he wasn't comfortable with that, either. "Ready," he declared hesitantly for the both of them, which Petra echoed as she pulled in the mooring line, and upon the inquisitor-captain's order, the men began rowing in perfect time, pushing off from the jetty and making towards open sea.

No one was sorry to see the land shrink behind them. Regardless of what riches the ruined temple had provided, little good had come from the rest. The sands were swollen with blood, tainted by massacre and haunted with mistrust, hatred and loss. It would be forever cursed in their memories.

And as for whatever lay ahead of them, on the treacherous sea or the battlefield that enveloped Kasire, it could surely be no worse than the events of this past tortuous, scorching month. Every one of them silently longed for the cleansing sting of the thick sea air.

Chapter 53

Salus glared down at the perfect golden circle, blinking slowly as his thoughts wandered. A sickening hopefulness lay as a blanket beneath them, and above, the sun that hung over the forest. A sun he could always see, unobscured, regardless of the thick canopy. Regardless of whether he was in the forest or not, or if his office ceiling had simply been replaced by it.

Yes, his dreams had changed again. His nightmares had receded a week ago, the night he'd grasped his magic, but they'd been replaced by those of yearning and desire once more, and the sensations had returned even stronger. They were under his skin, haunting him, taunting him, giving him the time to pick them apart, and he felt he could finally identify them - or perhaps they were merely accentuating his desperation to protect his country in its hour of need. Honestly, though, it didn't really matter. The thought that he finally understood them didn't offer him even a glimmer of comfort.

Instead he felt that the chain around his neck had been shortened. That the wildly barking guard dog had now been given a sharp, spiked collar, only to be staked further out of anyone's reach for fear it may actually frighten someone.

He possessed magic that he could barely use, like a child inheriting his father's greatsword, and he found that that made him angry - with himself above all else. For being so...normal. That despite his age, despite all the awful and necessary things he'd done in his life, he was just as helpless as anyone else. He needed the same instruction as any adolescent mageling, and his learning was limited, just as theirs was, by his own mental processes. Meanwhile, magic was tearing Turunda apart in the Order's trained hands, and he knew he could use his magic to *save* it if he only knew *how* to use it!

With tremendous effort, he forced away the tension in his shoulders. Under such conflicting thoughts, their impending victory over Skilan didn't offer any comfort, either. They were, ultimately, a simple matter. Magic was not. And neither, it seemed, was Doana.

He dragged his eyes away from the fried egg, shaking aside the ridiculous association and the lingering traces of dreams, but confusion gripped him for a moment as he forgot his surroundings. This wasn't his office.

No, thank goodness it wasn't. It was what should have been a drawing room, and he was taking his breakfast in there in a bid to escape his own prison. He practically lived in that office now, and he didn't like it. So he'd taken Taliel's recent suggestion to at least eat his meals somewhere else, and as she'd suggested the drawing room, he'd chosen the drawing room. It was as good a place as any - the morning sun reached in through the large windows to illuminate the expansive space, and he found that that had some kind of curious lifting effect on his mind, too.

But not enough.

His eyes turned sharply back onto Teagan, who waited patiently in the seat indirectly opposite, an untouched cup of tea standing on the small table between them. He made no reaction towards the severity of his stare.

"Kalokh has abandoned Skilan," the keliceran stated needlessly, the fact was no longer a revelation. "They've taken too many losses on their behalf. I'm certain they're relying on our victory to avoid a fallout from disloyalty and make an effort to reclaim their land."

"They have no love for Skilan," Teagan agreed, "but they won't aid us."

Salus sneered. "We don't *want* their help. How long would it be before they deserted us in turn? No, we're better off without them. Their withdrawal has done enough for us as it is. Skilan are feeling the loss, they were exhausted before this even started, and now that their spy in Moore's ranks has been discovered, each of their advantages have been lost."

Teagan's brow twitched in interest. "I was aware that we'd discovered the spy - was it who Malson suspected?"

He sneered again, though it was edged this time in suspicion. "No, but it was Rackson's subordinate. It's still too close..." But he shook the thought away. He had little mind to spare for Malson.

Salus pushed aside the remains of his breakfast, barely touched, and levelled his gaze. "If we target Skilan's mages, they'll be done for. The Order has severely reduced their numbers already, but I want *Aranan* mages to finish them off - I don't trust the matter to be left in the Order's hands, they've taken too many prisoners under the pretence of learning new techniques. How many mages do they really need for that? A handful, at best! They would all have been taught the same thing!" He raised his fork and plunged it into his food, bursting the golden egg yolk and crunching into the fried bread beneath it. Again, Teagan didn't react. "I don't want them getting their hands on *any* more. I don't want them to learn any more, or recruit any more. Our mages will go in from behind, there are too few left in Skilan's ranks to spare the attention to detect them, and they are permitted to use *any* means to obliterate them."

Teagan's face remained wooden. "'Any means'? They will be seen, of course."

"No," he growled, "*mages* will be seen. And any 'questionable' spells will be blamed, of course, on the Order. Our mages won't be identified."

"Is the Order not presently too unstable to be used as a scapegoat? It could worsen Turunda's internal situation."

"We will quell it." Salus sat back in his chair, unconsciously flexing his fingers. "With a sudden attack to wipe out their mages, Skilan will be shocked and scattered. Then Moore can attack them however he sees fit. In the mean time, we make one of our planted 'soldiers' a hero. Send out orders for each agent within the military to kill Skilan's general on the battlefield as soon as the chance presents itself."

"Moore will have issued--"

"And I want to make *sure* that it happens. Get the orders out."

Teagan passively inclined his head.

"As for the spy, he'll be in our cells within the hour and Nolan himself will rip out any information he has. I want to find out how he got in and what Skilan's status is beyond the war. We will crush them once and for all, and we won't be compromised while doing it. And," his lip twitched distastefully, "what, if anything, he knows about Doana." He shook his head and growled beneath his breath. Doana. *Doana.* How had this been able to get so far? How had he *let* it?! They had been nothing more than a trifle in the beginning, striking in small numbers and vanishing into the forests. But there had been something ominous in their last disappearance, and it seemed his unease was justified. In only two days, four substantial war camps had appeared out of nowhere in a variety of locations across Turunda, each sharing the single notable quality of providing a suitable battleground while being dotted with a range of natural landmarks which would certainly provide them with the advantage. Places and landmarks that only people familiar with Turunda's geography would know about. And as if their apparently acute knowledge of the land wasn't bad enough, their numbers had also been made evident. Somehow, they'd moved *half* of their military force into Turunda!

"How?!" He suddenly bellowed, barely startling the portian. "*How?!* How did we--how did *nobody* see?!--No matter, no *sodding* matter. We can deal with it. We can deal with it."

Salus shoved himself out of his chair, his breakfast finally forgotten, and began pacing around the bright, spacious and richly ornamented room. His thoughts swirled, drawing up his increasing exasperation like a waterspout. "We can deal with it." He forced his feet to stop and his mind to resist its spinning, and he snapped around towards his favoured. "Somehow," he began, his tone suddenly calm and considered despite his wild eyes, "Doana has been able to correctly identify and kill our planted operatives every single time, phaeacian and phidipan alike, and we've been unable to figure out how or find their counterparts because they've been too good at disappearing. Which means that this whole thing is a highly calculated manoeuvre, far more so than we've been giving them credit for. Given how successful they've been in creating chaos and, evidently, moving their sodding forces in undetected, they must have had movements well *beyond* even *this* stage planned out before they even began. And we've no doubt played into it with our every response." He clamped his teeth for a moment. "Doana. A land of mountains and terrace farmers, and it's a force to be taken seriously. *When* did they get so organised? How did we miss it?--And what happened to Voent?! For them to be *flooding* Turunda like this...!" He shrugged and spread his hands imploringly, lost for the words to make sense of it.

"It is possible," Teagan began calmly, "though unlikely, that they've discovered the identities of our people in both Doana and Voent and have been sending us false reports in their place all this time."

Salus snarled. "'Unlikely'," he snapped. "Everything they've done so far has been 'unlikely'." He shook his head and sighed tightly, fighting to collect himself again. "Then it's safe to assume that we're blind to their activities and to approach them as such. Don't trust any intel that doesn't come from an operative whose continued survival we can't confirm."

Teagan nodded his agreement, and Salus gave the chair a sharp kick without breaking his outward composure. "Once Skilan is dealt with, we can pour more resources into eradicating this infestation. They won't have the chance to reap any results from whatever ill-conceived master plan they've concocted over pipe weed and altitude sickness."

"And in the mean time?"

"In the mean time, we watch them. *Closely*. And close the borders. No one else gets in. Set a ring of fire all the way around the country if you have to! Then at least we'll know if someone's passed through it."

"And what about trade?"

A distasteful hiss slipped through his teeth. "This is *war*. Luxuries have to fall aside. Anything we *need*, we have." Salus folded his arms as his grimace deepened, emanating a grave darkness throughout the room. "Watch the camps," he said after a thoughtful moment, "work out which of them are real and which aren't - which are being honestly reinforced with men and supplies - then infiltrate and replace them - no more than two individuals. We can magically alter them to match the original soldiers, but no one high-profile. We don't have the intel to pull that off, but personal information can be picked up with only a little observation. It's never so closely guarded. Once Skilan is finished and our resources are opened back up we can provoke them, confirm which are actually prepared for combat and find out how they'll react when they're not in control; we can sabotage their supplies, prevent them from gathering from the surrounding land, and find some way to turn the advantage of their positions against them."

"That's Moore's area. Would we not be better off leaving it to him? He'd handle it quicker and more efficiently than we could."

Salus waved his words away, mumbling his consent, but his mind had clearly already been snatched away by other weighted thoughts. A wistful line drew his brows together. "There must be something I can do..."

"Your orders are well-considered--"

"To hell with 'orders'," he suddenly snapped, "I'm talking about *me*. There must be something *I* can do, personally, myself, *outside* the office!"

"We're not in the office."

Salus blinked. "I'm going to presume that was an attempt at a joke."

"Sir, forgive my bluntness, but you haven't the knowledge to do more than brew tea under a hovering light. At this point, there's nothing you *can* do."

He fought hard to restrain the heat of fury that followed the sickeningly honest statement. "Not magically, no," he conceded acridly, "but have you forgotten that I was once portian? I can--"

"And now, you are Keliceran." There was a flicker of something in Teagan's voice, a hard edge that compromised his usual indifference, and it stunned Salus for a moment. The portian, however, recollected himself easily. "You are our leader. It's too dangerous for you to step out onto the battlefield. You do more than well enough leading from here. Don't forget that it is, after all, your decisions that protect the country."

"*Not well enough!*" Salus roared. He slammed his fist into the top of a chair, but its rich and padded upholstery puffed an unsatisfying thump. "Look at what's happening around us! The Hall of the White Hammer only concern themselves with internal matters, the Order is trying to break the country from the inside, and the military is out dealing with what remains of Skilan! All prevention is left to us, and we're being torn in all directions trying to deal with it while our own countrymen work against us! We can't afford to hold *any* assets back!"

"You are not being held back, Keliceran. You're no longer allowing even the Crown to deny your actions."

But Salus had already dismissed his assurances. Teagan didn't understand. He should have known that by now, just as he should have expected his tiresome doubt. But it didn't matter, because he was right: he tended to the Crown's orders only because he agreed with them, but anything else, anything necessary that he wasn't officially tasked with, he saw to anyway. There was no longer any time to entertain the Crown with the days it took for them to make the big decisions, and too often lately those decisions had proven poor, with the lives of civilians, guards and soldiers needlessly lost as a result.

But he had nothing but desire, a need to protect Turunda and all its people with his own hands. He had no ideas - none fully-formed enough to act upon - and little opportunity to think any up. But when he did, he would enforce them immediately. That, he swore to himself.

The discordant chime of the old bell rang from a mile or so away in the city, humming through the air and seeping in through the open window. Salus instinctively glanced outside towards it, though it wouldn't have been visible even had there been no other stately houses around.

Denek would be expecting him.

He straightened and returned to the table without a word, tossed his cutlery and cold, ruined food back onto the tray, then righted his chair and tucked it back in, casting Teagan a polite nod in farewell before moving towards the door.

Once again his focus had clearly shifted; his mood swinging abruptly from rage to passive thoughtfulness as it was now prone to doing. Teagan watched him critically as he left, picking the fact apart, but neither of them caught the fine, tight line of disapproval on the portian's lips as he bowed his head in return, and neither did Teagan notice the unease which edged in every time Salus went to visit the mage. Instead he remained purely analytical as he rose to his feet and followed him out, maintaining a few paces' distance between them before branching off towards the stairs and, ultimately, the office. Because, once again, the duties of the keliceran fell to him while Salus learned to wield the latest of the Arana's assets. And what a great asset it would be. What power, what unstoppable, absolute things it could accomplish, what lives it could save, what wars it could deter.

...And yet, with every step, the small voice at the very back of his mind still felt the need to assure him that everything Salus did was for the good of the home and country they *both* sought to protect.

Muffled screams drifted through the narrow stone corridor, breaking up the otherwise dense silence that perpetually weighted the stale air. But the desperate cries went unnoticed by the guards and breakers, as they always did; only those few who maintained a more isolated residence paid them any heed. The doors and walls were just thick enough - or perhaps *thin* enough - to conceal any shape of words. Instead the screams arrived as nothing more than muffled agony and terror, revealing no trace of either defiance or defeat.

Salus, too, barely noticed them, just as he barely noticed the guards stand to attention as he passed. But as he stopped outside of the mage's cell, Denek's usual, arrogant smile landed immediately. He didn't bother to feign one in return. With a gesture, the nearest guard stepped forwards to open the gate.

"Just as cheerful as usual, I see," the mage sighed, rolling his eyes and wandering deeper into his cell as Salus stepped in behind him. "You'll get ill, you know."

"Because I don't walk around grinning like a fool?"

"Did your mother teach you nothing?" Denek stopped and turned back to face him, his fine lips already pursed in thought. "No, probably not, or you wouldn't be 'keliceran', would you?" He gestured vaguely for him to sit on the bare ground and settled himself in the spot opposite. "So," he began lightly as Salus obliged, "how are things?"

"Fine."

"And just as *social* as usual. You'll have to give me *something*, you're the only person here who talks to me." He gave him a suddenly half-cocked smile. "How's the lady?" His smile suddenly broadened as Salus's cheeks flashed red, but he held his tongue. Evidently, that involuntary reaction had been all he was after.

Salus glared but managed, somehow, to bite back his embarrassed irritation. The mage, satisfied with the confirmation of what could only have been a particularly astute assumption, straightened and took up the familiar position of relaxed attention, and Salus duly mirrored it. Without another word, the two slipped into the stupor that dominated their sessions, Denek's unusual consciousness linked, somehow, to Salus's, allowing him to keep track of his progress. It was a technique he greatly wished to learn himself - the Arana could surely benefit in some way from its usage.

But otherwise, an hour passed uneventfully, touching, turning and squeezing the light of the magic within him upon Denek's internal instruction, without any hint of his tutor's approval or frustration. Despite his definite presence, Salus felt so disconnected from him that he couldn't help - though actively hid - the certainty that he was being taken for a fool.

"Your control is improving," Denek said aloud after the silent suggestion that they take a break, surprising Salus for a moment, though that, too, he successfully hid.

"Good," he said instead. "Then you can teach me another spell."

"I said your control is *improving*, I never said your control was perfect." He gave him a sideways look of disapproval as he rose to his feet to stretch his long legs. "Don't rush ahead."

Salus growled as he followed. "This is *tiresome*. We do the same thing every day."

"And I said you're improving. You mustn't overlook the importance of this preliminary training, it's *vital* that you learn to feel your magic - to gain an understanding of how it moves through your blood, become familiar with its extents and learn to keep it subdued." Again, that irritating, haughty look of disapproval. "You are too passionate, and magic will take advantage of that."

"You speak as if it's sentient."

"And you speak as if you consciously created it." He folded his arms regally, but an imploring softness suddenly coloured his pale eyes, catching Salus momentarily off guard. "You can't rush this."

Even so, he easily kept the suspicion from his eyes. It wouldn't do to let him know he was on to his deception. "How much longer?"

"Salus, I know the spells you wish to learn. Trust me: you're not there yet. They're too complicated. You'll either injure yourself or apply the wrong signs and intentions and create something too powerful for you to control." And then, from nowhere, that superiority returned. "Do you want to protect Turunda, or be the cause of its destruction?"

Salus's teeth clenched. It was probably just as well he couldn't yet cast the kinds of spells he wished to, or at that moment, Denek would be little more than a pile of ash. "Very well," he managed tightly, retaking his seat. "Then we continue."

Denek studied him carefully, but Salus closed his eyes, eager to resume the task and caring little to know his thoughts. The mage slowly joined him on the ground.

Salus tightened further, however, at the sound of hurried footsteps, and waited impatiently for the approaching interruption.

"Forgive me," Teagan's confident voice rose from the corridor, loud and deep under the dull, menacing air, "Keliceran--"

But Salus was already rising to his feet, and stepped through the gate with weary patience. It clattered firmly shut behind him. "Go on."

"We've lost Karth and Koraaz."

A portian's lack of hesitance, he sharply reminded himself, should never be taken as a suggestion of severity. "*What?!*"

"They've set out towards the Roquna," he replied, quite unaffected, as usual, though his voice lowered against any eavesdropping prisoner-mages. "Enhala was their heading; they presumably intend to enter Kasire via the coast."

"Or have they found inspiration or made some other discovery in recent days? Tell Hower to get after them!"

"They took the only sea-faring vessel. As it is, they can't be tracked until they've made landfall." His voice dropped lower still as he glanced past him to the pale mage, who remained on the floor where Salus had left him, his eyes closed and expression neutral, as if he was in some kind of trance and quite unaware of the thickening atmosphere and sharp, hushed tones. "I suggest we continue to work with Lucinda and find what we need for ourselves. We have all of their notes and she's been able to translate both elven and Karth's--"

"*And if they've found something more?!* What use are these notes *then?!*"

"Sir--"

"*No,*" he hissed, managing, somehow, to shout while whispering. "They've been three steps ahead of us for *too long*. The artefact *cannot* fall into their hands! There will be no way to compete with them! Turunda will be *finished!* They're already tearing the land to pieces!"

"We know where they're heading--"

"*Think,*" he snapped, his eyes similarly darkening with unnatural menace. "You *think* you know where they're heading."

"Sir, they are nothing but a distrac--"

"Don't interrupt me."

Teagan stared at him, his lips abruptly closing and stiffening into a fine line as he watched the keliceran's face gain a wolfish quality, and he felt a familiar, irrational terror rise slowly from the pit of his being.

"I'm getting quite tired of all these reported failures," he told him tightly, his tone deceptively calm for such dangerous, dark eyes. "How *exactly* am I supposed to keep on top of the country's security if my own people can't do their jobs? If they can't even keep a *conspicuous* group of people in their *sights?* I can't issue orders without all the facts, *damn it*, and the Crown is constantly standing behind me, expecting immediate results! The military can't do what we do! The Hall won't! And the Order has already revealed their true damned colours! So tell me! Please! How am I supposed to keep this country safe if I can't use my own two hands and have to rely on all of *you to do it?!*" He stared at his favoured, his eyes penetrating the portian's, and Teagan stared back in absolute silence. His eyes were wider than usual, almost imperceptibly, but Salus took a small degree of satisfaction from it. He didn't notice the similar sideways gazes from the surrounding guards, nor that even the screams had stopped buffeting the walls. "Pull Hower out if he can't handle it. Send someone else. Get people out on that water, up along the Ronar Coast and get Karth away from them. We shouldn't have wasted our time with Drassa, we should have snatched Karth as soon as we'd found him. The Zi'veyn will *not* fall into the Order's hands."

He spun away from the silent operative without a word of dismissal, and stormed through the gate that creaked back open ahead of him, a beat later than it should have. But still he didn't notice the shock and fright on the face of that guard, nor his colleagues. He returned to his seat on the floor, opposite the curiously tranquil mage who appeared to have continued the session without him.

As he listened to Teagan's receding footsteps, he felt the tension that had coiled around every muscle in his body. The brief interaction had released in a moment all that he had successfully suppressed for days, and he knew it would be no simple matter to shut it back away.

But he tried. He gave shaking it off his very best effort, to relax and return to the task at hand. It was no sad matter that Denek was unwilling to teach him any further spells, but Erran had told him he needed to keep up this tedious training even if he was to teach him himself. And he knew that, while the kinds of things Aranan mages could teach him were on a whole other level to that of the Order, if it took the same preliminary training, he had no choice but to take it seriously.

But he couldn't help his eyes from flickering back open and looking closely, critically, at the mage sitting before him. He hadn't been interrogated for quite some time. He hadn't provided any information to begin with, and Salus hadn't wanted to risk him withdrawing his services once he'd discovered what lay within himself. But things were beginning to change; now he had his magic, he felt it might be worth the risk.

But not yet. Not just yet. He needed to make sure - from Erran - that he had learned from him all he needed before he burned that bridge...and there was bound to be a technique or two he could pry from Denek first. If the mage wished to maintain his own deception, he'd have to teach him something else soon or Salus would grow suspicious.

But the *mage* wasn't suspicious.

Indeed, Denek was unlike any of the other mages they'd held, and Salus had the strong impression that an interrogation would only be successful if he himself was present. Denek believed that he had been in full control of Salus's tuition - that all Salus had learned of magic had come from him. Which meant he underestimated him. And that could be used to their advantage.

As Salus's eyes closed, Denek's flicked open. Despite the poorly disguised conversation he'd easily overheard, his concerns were being pulled in quite an unexpected direction. Though at that moment his captor appeared physically normal, he knew as a fact that what he'd just seen hadn't been imagined. For a moment, at the height of his anger, Salus's skin *had* grown paler and the definite, all too familiar foreboding had crashed through the air around him like a tidal wave. His back had been turned to him, but each of his subordinates - even the portian - had stared at him as if he had physically become a monster, and when he finally turned away from them, Denek had caught as it receded the blackness that had filled even the whites of his eyes, and the definite sharpening of his features as they began to soften. They had been so mild and fleeting that there was no trace of them by the time he'd settled back down in front of him, but Denek knew he could never have missed something so familiar.

His sharp, perceptive eyes narrowed for a moment, his jaw knotted, then his lids finally lowered again.

Now he understood everything.

Chapter 54

The smell of smoke and alcohol hung heavily in the air, and even though the nearby bell tolled for only four in the afternoon, raucous laughter was already swelling from the tavern below. The Cockatrice had grown more lively in recent weeks, with war and magic driving people to drown their worries away, and with barmen's increased duties came an equal demand on the guards'. The laughter was frequently punctuated by a smash of glass or shattering of wood, few social concerns remaining to inhibit either rage or passion.

But though the public was too distracted to see who entered the tavern, nor where they went and with whom they spoke, these few still hid themselves away in the private room on the upper floor, its door concealed behind a curtain and blocked by a perpetual drinker, where their own concerns dwarfed the tensions outside.

Eight stood in silence, each lost in uneasy thought.

"All right," Malson began quietly, dragging the lost and distant gazes back onto him. "We can all agree that Salus's progress is alarming."

"He can't do much with his magic yet," Vari agreed tepidly, "but its presence is much stronger than it was a week ago, and what he *can* do, he can do well."

"And as for the artefact," a middle-aged phaeacian added, "call it shrewd planning or good fortune, but he easily obtained all of Anthis Karth's work and has an operative with a great deal of time on her hands assigned to picking it apart. He's losing nothing by keeping her focused on it."

Malson raised his hand. "One thing at a time." His eyes hardened decisively upon the phaeacian. "David: interference?"

"We're achieving little," he replied regretfully. "He's been isolating himself; no one delivers anything directly to him anymore, *everything* goes through Teagan. There's no opportunity to make any suggestions or try to lead his thoughts because he doesn't see the reports. Altering their information or delaying them only affects Turunda's security."

"Can Teagan himself be used?"

"No." The others nodded with equal certainty. "He's too loyal. Working as closely with him as he does, I'd wager he shares in Salus's mistrust of magic, and though he probably questions his sudden chasing of it, he's been convinced for too long that Salus knows what's best for the country. I have no doubt that he would die for him."

Again the others nodded, and Malson sighed as the possibility scratched itself from his mind. "He's portian. I didn't have much hope. In that case, hinder whomever is working on Karth's notes. Slow her down."

"Easily done."

"Good." He turned his lively and expectant gaze onto another young woman, one who bore a greater astuteness than most other phidipans. "Marie?"

"Interception is also proving fruitless," she replied promptly. "He has too many operatives out in the field and too much information coming in. The moths are being run ragged and we can't keep on top of it. By the time we've screened five reports, fifteen more have come in, and only one of those five contained anything we might want to keep from him. We risk delaying something truly urgent in our attempts to hinder his search."

"That's no matter. He's confusing himself by expanding his attention and resources so far. Leave him to it - it's no doubt already working for us if just for stretching him too thin. He's already close to breaking point." He looked, then, to Taliel. "What about hindering his other operatives?"

She looked at him slowly, her eyes returning from distant thoughts. "It's the same thing: too many, too far, doing too many things, and there are too few of us to handle it."

"Oy," Malson squeezed his eyes shut tight. "Well, at least he's given us *one* win."

A look of confusion passed around the room. "My lord?"

"He's assigned Jora here to keep an eye on me. At least we don't have to worry about any of this getting back to him, even if he is suspicious." He looked back up as that consideration eased their confusion, but a deeper frown had begun to etch itself into his brow. "But that could change all too easily if I don't tread more carefully... We need to embrace this little advantage while we can."

"Isn't that what we've been *trying* to do?" Jora asked, his young face shadowed in the same doubt that always plagued him in such meetings, but where it was usually met with disapproval or reassurance, now it seemed to be shared.

Malson nodded his own reluctant agreement. "'Trying', and getting nowhere." He puffed and folded his arms, clearing the clutter from his mind. "Forget the artefact for the moment - what about his magic? He has his prisoner and, as I understand it, an Aranan mage teaching him how to wield it?"

"If you're going to suggest recruiting Erran," Oliver said quite quickly, "you're wasting your time. He's too loyal. He's as bad as Teagan - in fact, if not for his magic, he would most likely have been promoted to portian years ago. It's only Salus's mistrust that stops mages from ranking beyond phidipan."

"And that may soon change, too."

The idea of emotionally void mages set another uneasy taint to the air. Oliver and Vari exchanged particularly concerned glances, knowing better than the others just what Aranan mages could do.

"Can we get him deployed?"

"No. He's a breaker. He's worked in the cells for the past three years, interrogating prisoners under Nolan, and with the kind of spells he could teach Salus, he's not likely to be let out of his sight. If push came to shove, Salus would still send out *any* other mage in his place."

"All right. Then this prisoner of his - Denek. Is there no way we can get to him?"

Oliver shook his head. "I'm still the only cell guard on your side, and there are always at least two others watching him. The breakers don't touch him any more, on Salus's orders, but that still doesn't help us much. I say it can't be done."

"We couldn't slip him something? A note? Information? He's fed, surely - could something not be delivered discreetly with his meals?"

"Well...yes, I suppose so - but what do you honestly think he can do for us?"

"A damn sight more than we can for ourselves," Malson growled regretfully. "When could a message be passed on?"

"I'm on rotation a few days from now," the mage replied, "I can do it, but what do you expect to gain from it? He's a prisoner, and despite his airs, he has no choice but to do what he's told. And if he were to try something extreme--"

"Then Salus would assume the Order to blame, not us."

Vari stared at him in surprise. "You want to use them as a scapegoat?"

"Scapegoats are the Crown's prerogative, but far from my preference. Which is why we will have to come up with a solid plan in the next few days."

Jora shifted his weight, the young man's doubt surfacing once more and again he voiced what all the others were thinking: "Is Denek really likely to help us, though? *Or* him, for that matter? Zikhon only knows what the Order is up to, but surely they don't *actually* plan to empower him like this...?"

"I don't know," the old man sighed. "But the fact is that it was Denek who told him about his magic, helped him to awaken it and is now helping him to understand and utilise it. I have absolutely no idea what the Order is up to either - the whole body is in confusion. Perhaps they *do* just want to distract him, or the chaos he could spread could be to their advantage, but whatever the case, they're going too far. He's learning, and he could grow to be a thorn in their side, too. Denek needs to be stopped."

"I suggest," David began soberly, "that if we can't come up with a plan to bring him to our side, we kill him. Poisoning his food would be no trial, and, of course, there'd be no risk of him refusing us. You're overlooking the possibility that we slip him a note and he then tells Salus of our intentions. He could have thrown his lot in with them for any number of reasons - we've just assumed that the Order's not taking custody of him was part of a bigger plan, but what if it wasn't? What if they betrayed him, and he's betrayed them in return?"

Malson's lips hardened reluctantly as the consideration he had already weighed countless times was finally spoken aloud. "The thought has crossed my mind..."

"...But?"

He shook his head doubtfully, drumming his fingers on his folded arms. "...But something about it doesn't strike me right."

"That's not as reassuring as you seem to think it is."

"It isn't, is it?" He smiled apologetically. "*But*, if we can't formulate a workable plan, we will have no choice but to dispose of him, whomever's side he's on. But *only* as a last resort. He has too much potential for us to handle him with haste."

Agreement rippled, some more assured than others, while the muffled sound of several glasses shattering outside intruded upon the strained silence, followed quickly by a mixture of drunken cheers and groans of defeat.

"How is our own search for this artefact progressing?" Malson asked, ignoring the ruckus ensuing in the tavern below, but Marie was already shaking her head.

"It's just as uncertain as Salus's. No one has any clear ideas, just educated guesses. And how far are they really going to get us? We don't have Salus's resources."

"His resources aren't doing much for him, though, are they?"

"David's right, but I'm afraid we have no choice either way but to make do and continue as we started. In the end, we'll only have failed if Salus gets to it first. We have to ensure that doesn't happen."

This time a reluctant silence was the only sign of agreement, and though he looked upon them all with as much reassurance as he could scrape together, he most certainly shared in their doubt. They had too little to work with, and while Salus's extensive resources weren't providing him with much in the way of results - indeed, even he was chasing Karth's shadow - a single discovery was all it would take to put him on top.

But then, the same could be said for them...

A stroke of confidence raised his chin, and he looked across the handful of discontented operatives with hard, resolute eyes. "Retract your efforts to delay or alter reports," he said decisively. "Otherwise, continue as you have been with the sole addition of planning a way to bring Denek to our side. Tell the others. No suggestion is too absurd. After all, this whole matter is quite out of the ordinary." He nodded in dismissal. "I'll reach out to you all again when it's necessary."

After the customary show of respect, they filtered out of the private room, leaving as a group that went completely unnoticed by the tavern patrons, so adept were even phaeacian skills. Taliel, however, didn't join them.

Malson stopped alongside her and considered her for a moment. She stood as she had throughout the meeting: her arms folded tightly, a light knot in her brow, her eyes distant and fretful. He had little doubt where her thoughts lay.

"I didn't want to ask in front of the others," he began quietly, his voice softened by a compassion that would befit any other old man, "but did Rathen believe you?"

She dragged her eyes onto him, but they had become suddenly sharp and attentive when they landed, and she straightened professionally, pushing aside her private thoughts with chilling success. "He did," she replied with a matching emptiness. "The others didn't, but that was to be expected. It won't be an issue. He'll either convince them in time, or give them no choice but to act on my information."

"Good." He watched her closely, and though no hint of her previous disturbance returned, he guessed it was taking more of her self-control to suppress it than it seemed. His lips twitched regretfully. "I'm sorry for ordering you to do this. It can't be easy."

"It's all right."

"Is it?" He felt a few of his own tensions ease as something flashed through her eyes. She was not unfeeling - she was not portian, and he hoped that Salus's interest in her would spare her that 'honour'.

She considered his encouraging smile with calculation, carefully deliberating her response until finally, and much to his relief, she gave in. "I...don't know. It's been so long...and to stand in front of him again like that, but for a reason like *this*..." She shook her head, her gaze growing distant again. "It...wasn't what I..."

But she looked back to him too soon, and the stony quality of her profession returned to her voice. "*None* of this is what I wanted. I won't bore you. The situation is severe."

His gaze became studious, and she made no attempt to hide from it. He then smiled sadly. "Very well. Good evening, Taliel."

"Good evening, my lord."

She stepped aside as he left, and for a moment, as the curtain fell back into place, she felt her control begin to slip. A rush of anger, remorse and despair flooded her body, seeping into her marrow, and she found herself deeply inclined to give in to the sudden and overwhelming compulsion to break everything in sight. The chairs would make for a satisfying target, and there was nothing quite like the irreversible shattering of large panes of glass - and just how easily could this old, sodden, sun-bleached drapery be torn?

But she was bitterly aware that, as enjoyable as it might have been to try, it wouldn't achieve a damned thing.

So she took a deep breath, choosing instead to regain her control - and regretted it immediately as a wave of nausea swelled in her throat from far too much dirty tavern air, leaving her sour and dizzy rather than subdued.

With a grunt of irritation, she left the room in defeat, almost ripping the curtain down anyway as she went, and stormed down the staircase to lose herself in the confusion of the tavern patrons as she made her way to the bar. She navigated through the bodies with little effort, artfully avoiding the wide-reaching elbows of drunkards looking for a reason to start a fight, and the boisterous dancing of oblivious couples to whom she managed not to shoot scornful looks. She was served promptly once she arrived despite the crowd of people still calling for attention, but the lascivious glances the barman gave her between his quick surveys of the writhing and smoke-filled hall explained the reason for that well enough. But she didn't respond to his hungry looks, and his attention was quickly stolen away by an uproar on the far side, where some unfortunate had blundered into an elbow trap.

She paid it no attention. She dropped onto the stool and stared deep into her mug of ale, succumbing to the engulfing cloud of unwanted thoughts without any effort to fight them off.

Of all people - of *all people* - why did *Rathen* have to be caught up in this? Why couldn't he have left well enough alone and remained in his odd little rock-house? Why couldn't he have grown truly bitter and given up on the world, like anyone else would have done? Fled to the mountains and forgotten any fact of war, monarchy and social burdens? Why did he have to take up the mantle of responsibility and turn *his* magic to the task? And *why*, of *all people* once *again*, did he have to be standing in *Salus's* way?!

'Because,' she thought with acrid affection, *'it's who he is.'* No matter what 'anyone else' would have done, *he* could never have turned his back on his country - not even if that country had betrayed him. He'd taken oaths when he'd joined the military wing - she had been there when he'd done so - and he hadn't spoken them lightly, and though his banishment had voided them, his heart had not. He had answered his country's call too many times before, and though he might presently think otherwise, though for anyone else it would certainly be the case, nothing had truly changed in him since then. He was absolutely devoted.

Did that make him noble, she wondered? Honourable? The model defender?

Or did it make him a fool?

'It makes him him.'

Her lips twitched briefly into a smile.

But why *now?!*

Her shoulders rounded even further as she slumped over the bar, and she raised her mug, almost snatching it from the sticky counter top, to trade her troubles for its comfort.

She fought off a gag at the first sour mouthful and slammed it back down, growling under her breath as the tavern slighted her again.

Damn Malson. She understood his reasons, but she deeply resented the position he'd put her in. Seeing Rathen again had knocked her sideways, unleashing powerful, juvenile emotions that had done nothing all day but cloud her judgement. She'd never begrudged her work before - but then, she'd never questioned her orders before, either. Not those of Malson, of Salus, nor of Elina who came before him.

...But this... None of those orders had ever involved--

"Vaesian red. I don't care which year - anything but the twenty-two."

Taliel froze in fright, while the barman merely laughed. "This ain't The Legionnaire, mate. My *clientèle* can't afford that perfume."

"Whiskey, then."

He grinned and shook his head quite unapologetically. "It's beer, ale or scrumpy. I'll have some bottom-shelf sauce at eight - it's not as strong as whiskey, but it'll sear off the walls of your throat just the same. Otherwise--"

"He'll have a beer."

Both men looked to Taliel in surprise, but she smiled back easily, having recovered from her own shock. Following no objection, the barman shortly shrugged and stepped away, leaving Salus to cock a quizzical eyebrow.

"I'd have said you'd be better off with water, but... Well, there's less likely to have been anything swimming in the beer..."

"And the ale?" He asked, peering into her mug before she pushed it an arm's length away from herself.

"You'd be better off with the water."

He breathed a laugh and a smile curved his lips, but it was fleeting. His expression was quick to sour again, and the thick, oppressive irritation which radiated from him like body heat suddenly incited within her a great desire to flee. She racked her brain for an excuse to leave, despite being well aware that he was too perceptive to believe anything she might come up with, and soon glanced towards him for a clue.

The severity of his eyes stalled her. They were quick, sharper than usual, but they weren't searching the glasses and hunting ornaments along the wall behind the bar as they appeared. They were keen with impatience, and though any other around them might dismiss it as an unpleasant daydream or a craving for drink, its truth was a thoughtfulness out of place in so common a tavern. Whatever was going on in his mind, it was clear it couldn't keep up with the thoughts he tried to balance like so many spinning plates.

She shifted uncomfortably. She was in little mood to entertain someone in so equally a frustrated and intolerant state as herself, but she found herself unable to turn away, and the longer she looked at him, the clearer it became that his desperation now flowed as a constant undercurrent rather than a periodic distraction.

He must have felt her eyes on him; she quickly looked away as his slipped onto her. "I had to get out of the office," he explained tightly.

"Well, this is where most people go to get away."

"I know. So I thought I'd try it..."

The barman returned and set a mug of thick amber liquid on the counter before him, at which Salus immediately grimaced. The barman responded with only the slightest chuckle and shake of his head, then moved off again to see to the demands of more reasonable customers.

"To be honest," he continued hesitantly, turning away from the offensive beverage to look at her instead, "I'd...hoped I might find you here."

"Oh?" She smiled, and his own features softened. "How did you know I'd be here at all?"

"I didn't. It was just...good fortune."

The two continued to smile at one another for an increasingly awkward moment, until Salus broke away with reddening cheeks. She didn't notice her own smile broaden in amusement, nor further still as he considered his beer in an attempt at nonchalance. She watched him reach tentatively for the handle, drag the mug towards himself, raise it, then think better of it and sink heavily instead upon the stool beside her, sighing in defeat. His face - bleak but not unattractive, she mused - dropped slowly back into its usual, tormented expression of dissatisfaction as his eyes rested on the tankard.

Pity forced her own smile away, and the returning reach of his frustration chased off the pleasantries. "Do you want to talk--"

"I'm tense." He spoke quickly, readily, as though he had only been waiting for her to ask. "I *cannot* wind down. Everything's building up, becoming more and more complicated - even the things that should be *simple* are being complicated by things that shouldn't even be related!" His fists, already balled up on the counter, tightened, turning his knuckles bone-white. "Things that should be an asset, should be a *strength*, are held back by the most...*trivial* of technicalities, and meanwhile the pressure just continues to build. I'm..." he shook his head helplessly. "I'm going to snap, I can feel it. I'm going to snap..."

Taliel said nothing as he stared into the dubious depths of his mug.

Words eluded her. She hadn't the first clue of how to respond. She wanted to - she *had* to - but what kind of answer was he looking for? What could she say that wouldn't sound insincere? She felt in need of comfort herself, her mind was in little place to provide it for someone else.

But she still found herself wrestling with ideas, and the reason was simple: she'd seen his walls come down before, but now they were nothing but rubble. All of a sudden, here was Salus, Keliceran, the head of the Arana, sitting in this less-than-savoury place, plagued by confusion and desperation and seeking her company to chase it away. And for the good of everyone, she couldn't shirk that responsibility. Things were too fragile - *he* was too fragile.

She straightened in her seat. She was *phidipan*. She'd been trained to shut away her guilt and childish emotions along with all the rest. She'd done it one hundred times before; now she would do it again. And, in the end, it didn't matter who was involved. These were her orders, and for Turunda's sake, she would see them through. And when she was finished...

Her eyes trailed back onto him. She watched his gaze draw further away, his frown loosen, and his mind become finally and totally swallowed by his thoughts like a drowned body giving up its last struggle and dropping beneath the surface of a lake.

Taliel rose decisively from her stool, dug into her pocket and dropped a few coins onto the counter before turning back to him with purpose in her suddenly lively eyes. He frowned back, puzzled and disappointed, but she didn't leave right away. Instead, to his visible curiosity, she smiled and extended her hand. "Come with me."

Towering beech and chestnut trees concealed what little light the late evening had to offer, and the thick, victorious darkness of the forest amplified its habitual chill and stillness. Nothing could be seen or heard moving within its grasp, but it was far from as empty as it appeared, the haunt of all kinds of clawed and taloned creatures whose watchful, unblinking gazes surveyed the comings and goings of the few authorised to tread within Blackbrush's dense confines.

But despite that fact, Salus's every step was hesitant, and his eyes flicked around uncomfortably from shadow to shadow as if searching for something that shouldn't be there. But there was certainly nothing - if there was, he wouldn't have been looking around so openly.

Taliel shook her head wearily as she walked slowly over the cluttered forest floor beside him. "*Relax.*"

"I *am* relaxed."

"You're absolutely not. Look, just breathe," she demonstrated the action for the fifth time, "and leave everything behind. I've told you, there's nothing out here but presence."

"Which still doesn't make any sense..."

"It makes perfect sense, you're just over-thinking it--" She stumbled suddenly at her own words, but Salus was quick to catch her. He looked down to locate whatever root had tripped her, but she shook it off and cursed aloud her own feet to dissuade him as she righted herself. He seemed to accept it.

"Then explain it to me," he said as they continued, intrigued, and waited patiently as she thought for a long moment to form an explanation that wouldn't require five more.

"Presence," she began slowly, "time...existence. Nothing but 'now'..." She cast him a musing look. "For example, you have no way of working out here, do you? No one to issue orders to, no reports to read, no meetings to attend. You have no entertainment, either - no books, no instruments, no pencils. No food. No distractions." She passed a brief, wide look over their surroundings and couldn't help a soft sigh of contentment. "*All* that is out here is *now.*"

Her eyes turned back to him when he didn't respond, and she found him watching her with interest and the slightest of smiles. "That's..."

"Profound?"

His smile widened. "A bit chilling - *but*...I think I like it. It's true escape... Though you did get one thing wrong."

She frowned. "Oh?"

"*We're* out here."

A laugh escaped as a smile curved her frown away. "What does that have to do with anything?"

Salus was suddenly in front of her, forcing her to a short stop as he blocked her path, but she didn't try to find a way around, nor shrink from the new kind of curiosity that intensified in his eyes. "It's a distraction," he stated plainly.

"Would you like me to leave?"

"I'd like to be distracted."

She considered him for a long moment, a soft frown once again playing on her brow. There was a confident weight to his words, but it was one she was sure was feigned. At that moment, he sought *only* distraction, something or someone to steal away his attention and silence his mind if only for a while. And something about that insulted her.

She hid behind a pleasant laugh, brushing the words away, and stepped past him to continue leisurely through the trees. He made no attempt to stop her, but disappointment didn't soften the keen edge to his eyes as they tracked her, and he shortly fell back in step alongside. They walked on in silence, acutely aware of each other's company even as they attempted to distance themselves for comfort, but Salus's watchful eyes were soon quietly analysing her again. "Can I ask you something?" She nodded her consent. "Does your work cause you stress?"

She trapped her reflex answer behind her teeth. The question wasn't as simple as it seemed. Posed when, where and as it was, it required careful thought, not obedience - a fact he confirmed with patience.

They reached one of the countless streams that engraved the forest floor, flowing around rocks and broken trunks and beneath ancient, cage-like roots, and they crossed it with a light jump.

"My work is necessary," she stated at last. "I'm aware of its importance, and if I notice the pressure, it never gets in my way. I'm phidipan. I can always shut it out."

"That's not what I asked."

Her eyes flicked towards him, noting the growing pressure of his gaze. "I know. But I'm not entirely sure what it is you want me to say..."

His lips parted, their corners turned downwards, and hesitation stayed his tongue for only a fleeting moment. Then he spoke without apology. "I want you to tell me that your work stresses you out. That the pressure gets too much sometimes, and that, once or twice, you have doubted your abilities or decisions on a task because of it. And that it happens to everyone. And that it doesn't make you any less competent, or cast shame on you, when it does." A wild and desperate spark ignited in his eyes, and he took a restrained half-step towards her. "Taliel, I feel...too much. I can't make sense of it. Some of it is good, like when I'm around you and I feel calmer, *happier*...but the rest...I can't concentrate. At night, I doubt my decisions - I *know* they were the right ones when I made them, but what if there had been a better choice, a simpler, quicker, more certain choice, but it just didn't occur to me? What if I could have saved even just a few more lives by issuing different orders? What if I could have eradicated Doana as a threat or even stopped Skilan's attack right from the *beginning* if I had just *chosen something else*--"

Taliel's lips silenced his growing exasperation. Surprise stalled him, but he was quick to overcome it. He returned the kiss eagerly, and his softness surprised her again, overriding her pity for his unending torment. Just like those few nights ago, she had expected his lips to be as rough and rigid as his temperament, but instead they were tender, pleasant. Enjoyable. The sad, sympathetic knot in her brow loosened as she leaned into his warmth against the surrounding chill, and he into her, and she felt the soft and uncertain pressure of his hand soon move onto her waist.

Shame surged through her like an explosion in a mine, stunning her back to her senses, and she suddenly heard the voice in the back of her head that had been screaming Rathen's name and the reason for her own tensions. Nausea was quick to follow, worsened by self-reproach, but somehow she managed not to push him away in disgust. She pulled away softly instead, and smiled reassuringly for both their sakes, desperately trying to regain control of herself. "*Everyone* has doubts," she promised him, successfully feigning composure. "*Everyone* wonders if they couldn't have done a better job if they'd gone about things in a different way, or if there wasn't an easier, safer or more convenient option. But only the people who let that doubt cripple them, who obsess and can't accept the choices they've made, become incompetent. The decisions *you* have to make are harder than most, but the fact that you make them and then turn your attention onto dealing with the next situation *proves* your strength." Her eyes, calmer now, gripped his troubled gaze. "These aren't concerns you need to burden yourself with. They're not weaknesses you will ever succumb to. You're too strong for that."

Salus didn't speak. He stared at her through a lingering flicker of surprise, weighing her words, searching them for any falsehoods or threads he could pull to unravel her sureties, perhaps out of self-pity or perhaps just to encourage her to kiss him again. She in turn maintained her confidence, trying at the same time to read his thoughts and silently assure herself that the kiss had been only to quell his rising desperation. And that it had been successful in doing so.

A breeze picked up around them, carrying the scent of damp moss and dirt from the wide river that cut through the forest a quarter mile away to water distant Kulokhar. In the still of the ageing evening and against the rustle of the disturbed leaves, they could almost hear its rush, along with the hoot of stirring owls and alarmed patter of the mice that hid from them. And if one concentrated, the scent of ripening apples from a nearby orchard and the wild lavender that grew beneath them, and the distant, lilting, territorial songs of unknown birds.

She noticed something change in Salus's pensive expression; a flash of realisation passed through his widening eyes, and a slight but visible jolt rocked his body, as if a thought had physically struck him. His gaze shifted briefly to the forest behind her and changed again, too quickly for her to be certain if it was recognition or fright, but when they returned to her they held a suddenly unmistakable longing. One powerful enough to freeze her heartbeat.

He closed the distance she'd put between them in a single, impulsive stride and pressed his lips against hers. She hadn't a moment to respond, and his sudden confidence, fuelled by something known only to him, confused and slowed her reflexes. But this kiss wasn't like the first, nor was it like the second, and not because it had been at his whim rather than hers. It was firmer, decisive, self-assured to the point that he believed there could be no repercussions. That it could just happen, that no one would see them, that they would both abandon their inhibitions and embrace one another, because what consequences could come from something the world didn't know about?

The kiss deepened, his force growing until he pushed her back a step. She staggered with the movement until her back found the trunk of a tree, unable to find the mind to resist, and he pressed himself still firmer against her. But she still didn't try to push him away.

His hand moved back to her waist and rested there with a permanence, and his other slipped behind her neck, his fingers entangling in her hair and pulling her closer. Her own sought the same hold even as that same voice resonated in her mind, screaming louder this time, determined to be heard. His touch was intoxicating, but this time she was aware of it, and she wouldn't succumb. The voice made sure of that, setting loose the reminder that it was Malson's wish and Rathen's safety that had put her in the path of its influence. Nothing more, for she felt nothing for him.

The pressure of the kiss increased as she ran her fingers through the back of his fair hair, and they breathed in the heat and scent of the other, moving ever closer, their lips parting for more.

If anything, she hated him. Salus had complicated everything. She had done all kinds of awful, necessary things for the sake of the country; she had stolen things, seduced nobles and royals for information, misled foreign authorities and planted seeds of dissent, endangering innocent people for the safety of her own, and even assassinated people of high status, ending their lives with clinical precision. Because that was her job. One she had entered into willingly. These were the things she had to do because so few others had the resolve to do them. And that had never bothered her before.

But it had never been personal before.

Rathen had never been involved before.

Salus's hand moved up from her waist while their lips remained locked, tracing her shape and pulling her away from the tree to glide back down her spine. He grasped her at the small of her back and pulled her torso against his, and she in turn dared to slip her arms under his and grip him by the shoulders, pressing her chest into him.

But it wasn't just Rathen.

Salus lived for his work. He had been portian from a young age, and with such mental retraining he could never have truly had anyone; the only closeness he'd have experienced would have been for the good of a task, the success of a mission, and he wouldn't have been Salus in those moments. Just as she hadn't been Taliel when such a duty had fallen to her. He'd have been whomever had been required.

He'd had nothing genuine. And now the repercussions were finally coming around. He had no release, and so had latched onto her to finally find it, and his intoxication, his poison, was seeping into her, bending her to his will.

She grunted into the kiss as her back struck the tree again, but still she didn't push him away. She didn't pull back as his tongue slipped over hers, and she didn't try to wriggle out of his powerful grip as his fingertips squeezed desperately into her flesh.

And then, without warning, he broke the lock, stepping back and leaving her staggered against the tree. She tried to recover her scattered bearings and work out what had caused him to stop, what accidental thought she had relayed through a half-second's hesitance she couldn't recall. But before she had the chance, she caught the question laid bare on his face, his eyes fogged by fire. He took another step backwards, posing the question again, and she followed in answer, grasping his hand in relief as he led her with haste back through the woods, taking paths and dubious shortcuts to avoid any over-inquisitive eyes.

She wouldn't let that poison grip her, but she would answer his needs. It was for the good of all. She provided Malson with an intimate resource, one that could discourage suspicion and lead him down other roads if their dissented group began to draw his attention; she could protect Turunda from an internal threat by advising Malson on his unorthodox plans, or perhaps even dissuade Salus from them herself.

And...it could be good for him, too.

They blustered through the trees, finally stumbling out onto the hidden gardens of the smaller, private building the keliceran called home, far from the sight of his all-seeing subordinates. He led her feverishly towards the back door, their footsteps, though rushed, silent even across the stone path, and remained so as they slipped inside and vanished from the moonless night.

No one under so much pressure should have to face it alone. And perhaps that's all this was: an obsession to protect because that was all he had to live for.

His lips found hers again the moment the door was closed, and they travelled softly across her cheek and down along her jaw. She tilted her head as he brushed her hair aside and began kissing her neck, and she felt him smile as a slight murmur escaped her at the delicate sensation. Encouraged, he tugged her away from the door and led her through the darkness to the staircase, which they ascended in a fervent, breathless stumble.

She pitied him. Even empathised. When Rathen had left, she had nothing but work and had thrown herself into it. But she'd never been weighed down by the same expectations that Salus was.

They reached the top and covered the hallway, and he paused not even to open the door. He kissed her again as he groped behind himself for the handle, and almost fell through when it gave way. But neither of them noticed. He dragged her inside and began pulling at her clothes, their lips parting only as she removed her shirt for him and his hands and lips began exploring her body instead.

Was this what came from such a loneliness? Could it truly destroy a person to such an end?

Or *was* this 'such an end'? Could the devastation go further?

He encouraged her back a step, and she felt the soft sheets brush against her legs as she took it. She let him lay her down upon the oversized, empty bed and strip her to her delicates, but she couldn't suppress the shudder that finally escaped her lips as he climbed on top and pressed his warm, bare skin against her.

She lost her grip on herself as he kissed down her body, succumbing to the exhilaration.

To make him feel better. To clear his mind.

Because the world knew nothing of the Arana. The world knew nothing of them. The world would *never* know.

Chapter 55

There was nothing around for miles to complicate the dead of night. There was no clamour of wild animals, no tangled perfume of damp wood, dew, flowers and earth, no flashes of lantern-light from nearby settlements or passing travellers. There was absolutely nothing. And that lack of variety, out in the middle of absolutely nowhere, painfully enhanced the simple elements that did manage to dog them, rendering them almost unbearable.

Salt permeated the air, present with every breath, never once varying in intensity. The predictable pattern of creaking wood groaned over the constant, droning sound of the waves. The monotonous rocking from side to side, gentle but tiresome in its inescapability, knocked the balance of one even already lying down.

Rathen pressed his pillow over his face, bracing himself against his lurching stomach, and tried to block it all out. It was thick and plump enough to deafen him, but the near-silence of the world was louder, and though its coverings, like the sheets, were unnaturally soft, not even they could tempt his weariness and lull him to sleep. He just couldn't escape the glaring fact that something vital was missing. His room was too quiet. Too empty.

Finally, he gave up. With a huff, he tossed away the pillow and kicked the sheets aside, threw on what clothing he could be bothered to and escaped the oppressive confines of his cabin to the dark, open deck above.

A breeze sharpened by salt stung his skin the moment he stepped out of the quarterdeck, but even so he felt his tensions ease at the change of scenery, and further still as he saw the ombre pass of azure to indigo on the north-eastern horizon. Dawn was closer than he'd guessed.

Relief loosened his shoulders as he moved out into the remaining starlight, a little more spirit beneath his feet, but he discovered right away that he wasn't alone.

Perched precariously upon the edge of the bow, Eyila had barely moved in the hours since he'd gone to bed. She remained directly in the path of the sharpened elements, and though she wore more against the sea's lingering winter chill than she had in the forest, she had since exposed more bronze skin in the night's privacy.

He'd have felt he was compromising that privacy had he not then noticed Anthis sat at the furthest end of the deck behind him, accompanied by his now pitiful collection of books. He was on shift that night, keeping an easy watch over their bleak, flat surroundings from up beside the wheel, a tiresome duty that had fallen to all of them after Petra had demanded in a frightfully unrefusable manner that Garon actually rested at night. But he was also positioned where he could keep a more subtle but ever-present eye on Eyila - something which made Rathen's skin itch. But despite his strangely paternal disapproval, even he felt it was still necessary that she wasn't let out of sight.

The young man visibly tightened at his arrival, but Rathen disregarded him. He was in no mood for hostility. He turned his back and approached the bow instead, where he leaned against the bulwark a respectful distance from the tribal girl and watched the prow cut through the waves.

The swells were small - they had yet to exceed two feet in height - and met the lichen-patched wood with a gentle wash at tediously regular intervals. The sound was just as anticipated.

He sighed in boredom, wishing not for the first time that Aria's voice might pipe up in song, and his grimace deepened when it didn't. "What I wouldn't give to be back in the desert," he grumbled quietly to himself.

His eyes flicked quickly towards Eyila, widening in alarm, but she didn't react to his foolish words. He apologised anyway, then asked if she'd eaten, but again she didn't respond. She didn't speak, grunt, turn or twitch. It was as if she'd encased herself within a glass box. In eight days, not one of them had managed to get any kind of reaction from her.

His frown softened in pity. He could only imagine what must be circling in her mind, and he hoped he'd never know for sure. She'd been away from her village when the massacre had happened, and while he doubted very much that she'd have been able to do a thing to stop it, she almost certainly held her absence to blame. She'd heard no last words, no dying wishes - she'd not even had the opportunity to *try* to save anyone, and as the tribe's healer, that must surely have been the final sting in the tail. She'd returned home excited for a festival, expecting to be welcomed, and prepared to recount what for her had been an adventure. But instead, she had found her whole world long since obliterated, as if her people and her home had been nothing more than flies caught in a spider's web.

She was too young for such a tragedy. Too young to be left all alone in the world, stranded with people she didn't know, who didn't understand her, who knew nothing of her culture...

Aria's beaming face suddenly shone in his mind. She, too, had been far too young, but in a merciful twist of fate had also been too young to understand it. Instead she'd pottered along, blundered into a garden and stuffed her face quite merrily with strawberries.

...What if something happened to him while she was away? Would she react the same way as Eyila? Would she take an unspoken vow of silence and stew in self-pity, thoughts of revenge, or grapple blindly with the mere struggle to move on? No one could tell which way Eyila's thoughts were leaning - could he guess where Aria's would go?

His heart jumped into his throat as his stomach made another dreadful lurch. Would she even find out that something had happened?

Yes, she would find out. If Kienza couldn't save them from whatever tragedy his imagination could conjure, she would tell Aria all she needed to know, and she would help her find closure. She wouldn't take a vow of silence, she wouldn't stew. She would move on, because she *wouldn't* be alone.

He sighed heavily and turned away from the water, shaking the dour thoughts from his head. He was in no mood for them - though he had little doubt that they'd return to plague him again in a few minutes' time. He felt Anthis's eyes on him, but as he met his gaze, the young man looked quickly back down to his books with an enduring grimace. Rathen's eyes narrowed.

Perhaps Eyila *was* recovering, but the hostility circulating around the ship discouraged her from trying to break through her shell. She could be forgiven for that since everyone else was succumbing to it. Against the realms of possibility, the two and a half days they'd spent on open water had been more agitated than four weeks in the desert. Though Rathen had been absorbed in his thoughts for the first day, he wasn't beyond noticing how severely they'd taken personal space for granted in the vast desert; trapped on this tiny boat, if they weren't in their cramped, bare cabins, they were sat on each other's laps. He'd wondered time and again if it had been Kienza's intention to drive them all to the brink of throwing themselves and each other overboard. After all, she could have made a bigger boat. She could, in fact, have made cabins five times larger on the inside than out. Having said that, she could have teleported them all straight to Enhala and done away with the need for a boat altogether.

He hung his head in shame for having only just realised it. But her hope of forcing them to bond and overcome the tensions that had risen to form walls of steel between them would be disappointed.

But...at least she hadn't left them to swing side by side in hammocks.

Over the past two days Petra had become increasingly brusque, and Garon seemed to fall victim more often than the rest. She snapped, she grunted, and she spent a little too much time tending her blades to the point that she was surely doing them more harm than good. Curiously, however, though Garon was just as commanding as always, he had become strangely if begrudgingly obedient towards her in return. It was a combination which led him to quite a narrow band of speculation, and no small degree of bewilderment.

Anthis spoke only to the inquisitor. He had little interest in trying to socialise with Rathen - a fact which Rathen found himself more irritated by than insulted - and Petra could barely tolerate his existence. Though he, like everyone else, did still try to chip away at Eyila's silence, believing for some obscure reason that a girl whose entire family had just been slaughtered would have any interest in talking to a murderer. Even if he was a murderer with morals.

Rathen's eyes trailed away from him in lingering thought, but he shook aside Kienza's echoing words. Despite the evidence, he had little desire to allow anyone to occupy his mind.

He moved away from the bow and headed back inside to collect his own work. There was little else to do, and with sleep eluding him, he wanted nothing more than to busy himself until breakfast. He settled at the port side of the ship where he could keep an eye on the approach of the sun, sitting upon a box that had been conjured with the boat which, knowing Kienza, was just an empty prop, and lost himself in his work. He got nothing at all done, and when the sun finally peeked over the horizon, a yawn rattled through his aching body.

He sneered with distaste. Typical.

"Uh-oh..."

Petra's quiet, dubious tone was quick to grasp attention, and as she hurried away from the edge of the ship and made urgently towards the helm, everyone else's suddenly skittish eyes set to careful scans of the horizon. But it was quickly apparent that there was neither ship nor beast out in the water, indeed no obvious cause for alarm anywhere in sight. Only the still, empty sea and clear blue skies they'd been surrounded by for days.

It wasn't until one drew his gaze back in that they finally noticed what had unsettled her.

Slowly at first, the colours around them had begun to dim. Blue and brown hues drained to duller tones so slightly that they each wondered if they weren't simply imagining it, but when the horizon began to mist away and Petra's usually vibrant hair turned a dark shade of steel, it became more difficult to mistake. At that point, the leeching happened faster.

Rathen and Anthis backed cautiously away from the greying bulwarks. There had been not even the slightest sign of a change in the weather, and yet from nowhere a fog had coalesced around them, forming a thick, dense cloud that engulfed the ship with a ravenous hunger and concealed the world absolutely just mere feet out from the hull.

Anthis glanced nervously towards the helm. "What do we do?"

"There's nothing we can," Petra called back, hopelessly. "The fog won't hurt us, it'll just spit us out in the direction we came from. I told you, we'll have to find another way. Or another lead..." Despite her resignation, Garon spotted a disturbed doubt in her hazel eyes, though they too were now rendered quite colourless.

A nervous silence blanketed the boat, the gloom muffling even the wash of the waves. No one moved beneath its weight, preoccupied with straining their senses to detect when their direction began to change - a slight tilt, a change of the breeze, a shift in the source of the weakened afternoon light. But there was nothing. Nothing but fog. Uneasy glances passed as they continued their efforts, until Rathen dared to step away, a sudden critical haste in his step.

The others watched in distraction as he moved to the furthest edge of the ship and peered keenly off into the fog. He said nothing, and no one asked, even as he snapped his head to the left to follow his curiosity, his expression twisted in concentration, tinged with disbelief.

They jumped as he spun around and hastened towards the helm, his eyes unnaturally wild. "To the left, *quickly*," he commanded, but his agitated step faltered before he reached them, his attention snatched suddenly to his right by another phantom. "No, right--left! *Left!*" He whirled back to the inquisitor in full expectation while he and Petra stared uneasily, and his desperate eyes flashed with urgency. "*Quickly!*"

"She did something to him," Petra murmured. "The woman."

"I don't think she did..."

They looked down towards Anthis, but Eyila stole their attention herself before they could follow his gaze towards her. Their concern doubled. Nothing had ever managed to break her meditation, and yet this time something had encouraged her to climb down from the bowsprit she'd been perched upon for the last three hours and lean far over the edge of the ship. And the fact that she stared just as attentively into the fog as Rathen, and with the same frantic look, did nothing to ease their minds.

"Turn right!"

Petra whipped back towards Garon as he began to turn the wheel. "What are you doing?!"

"They can sense something," he replied plainly, turning the ship to the left at Rathen's next conflicting order. "I doubt any of your sailors had mages on their ships, but we have two, and I'm not inclined to overlook something they're *both* picking up on."

"Right again. A little more..."

Petra murmured, far from assured as her troubled gaze slipped back onto the girl, whom she watched turn her head an eerie heartbeat before Rathen gave a matching adjustment. She folded her arms tightly across her chest. "There's no telling where we're going to end up..."

Rathen's eyes were ablaze beside her. "'Where we need to go'..."

After three minutes the abrupt corrections came more slowly, and Rathen soon fell silent and allowed the ship to straighten out.

"What's happened?" Petra finally asked, but he didn't spare an answer as he hurried towards the bow. His urgency had diminished, but it hadn't died, and again he began to scour the thick, surrounding cloud. Eyila moved up beside him, her expression equally charged.

The others began to stare closely in a futile attempt to discover their distraction for themselves, and so were quick to notice when the fog began to disperse. They held their breath and strained their eyes all the more, trying to see further than the cloud would have them in their impatience, and their hearts began to race.

But there was nothing there. Nothing but water and sky.

So why had neither mage stepped back from the bulwark?

"What--"

"Keep going," Rathen said just loudly enough for them to hear. "Straight ahead..."

Garon's lips tightened, but he didn't voice his doubts, just as he didn't address the weight of Petra's eyes as they lingered expectantly upon him, nor their growing alarm. Instead he let the boat carry on the gentle breeze and currents while his eyes remained fixed to the two at the head.

Rathen didn't feel the penetrating gazes. The magic was too strong to release his attention, too strange for his mind to let go of, and it encouraged a dubious fascination more befitting of Anthis than himself, especially as its source drew closer. But where was it? Beneath the waves? There was nowhere else it could be...

His eyes narrowed. No. He doubted that very much.

He squinted into a nearer pocket of emptiness, searching diligently for the edge of the spell chains to uncover some clue for what they concealed before it could spring upon them.

But it was already too late.

His hold slipped from the wood as he staggered backwards, the air knocked suddenly from his lungs, while Eyila leaned forwards with a startled gasp. It would have been the first sound he'd heard from her in a week, if he'd noticed it. But how could he notice it? Where a moment ago there had been an unbroken horizon and water stretching on forever, now...

A similar chorus of gasps whistled behind him as the ship continued to pierce through the spell like a slow-moving arrow, followed by the sluggish advance of astonished footsteps.

Not a quarter-mile out ahead, six islands had formed out of the waves, floating serenely, still and silent upon the cerulean water, their reaches shrouded in a tangle of emerald, peridot and malachite. The virile overgrowth was broken only by the bold contrast of near-white limestone, intrusions of weather-sculpted outcrops, some with sheer faces, others perfectly rounded - but the closer they sailed, the higher their nervous fascination rose, and as their keen and confused eyes grew sharper, the stone soon revealed ever finer angles and edges. The islands, the largest enough to support a large town, another barely the copse of trees that overran it, bore not outcrops of rock, but domes, towers and pavilions, and littered among them, as they peered even closer, houses carved directly into the interior cliffs. The incredibly expansive remains of a truly ancient city, unmolested by the elements despite standing abandoned in the middle of the Roquna Sea.

Anthis gasped once more in awe while Rathen and the others gawked, and began murmuring to himself about buttresses, capitals and pediments, a dull and half-whispered account that went ignored until 'Zikhon' passed his lips. Then their eyes tore away from the sight.

"A communal settlement," he breathed in astonishment, his voice barely rising. "The elves didn't regard Zikhon with fear or foreboding back then, remember?" His eyes roved hungrily over the still-distant masonry, and a stupefied smile crept over his lips. "Oh...it's so...*immense*... And it's old - look, the lines aren't straight. Magic didn't make them..."

"We should adjust course." Petra returned Anthis's startled look with an immediate glare and took a challenging half-step towards him. "We are trying to get to *Enhala*. Or have you forgotten?"

"Of course not," he replied quickly, his eyes darting briefly back towards Garon at the helm, "but it's along our route anyway, and this place has never been documented - if it had, I would know about it, as would many others, and this passage would have been redrawn and been busier than the Red Road. There's a greater chance of finding something in *there* than in Enhala!"

Petra's severe expression worsened. "How *very* convenient for you." She looked expectantly towards Garon while Anthis fought against shrinking back from her. "Well?"

Even from the far end of the ship they could see the calculations moving through his eyes. "Anthis could be right," he said with consideration. "This place was concealed behind a spell; it's not likely to have been stripped like Enhala. And it's still standing strong..."

"Yes," Rathen grunted dubiously. "*Remarkably* strong..."

The ominous shadow cast by the thought of stepping foot on an island dedicated to the God of Death joined with his scepticism and began to spread among them like a disease. It prickled the back of their necks while the breeze carried them closer to the dense, green cluster, and every gaze lingered heavily upon it.

The stone's details gradually became clearer and finer, and with them the delayed realisation that nothing was missing. No arch had collapsed, no wall had crumbled, no roof had caved in. No structure bore any damage at all. Despite Anthis's dating of several thousand years, the entire landscape could have been carved in the last fifty.

White statues also began to take shape, complete and uncountable inhuman forms the size of a man standing guard atop every other rock and hill, watching with eternal eyes the seas surrounding their hidden charge. But the haunting atmosphere worsened at the sight of them. And further still when more stepped up to join them.

Another, sharper bout of gasps suddenly spiked up across the deck, and Rathen frowned curiously at the abrupt and foul curses that punctuated it. But before he could question their alarm, a rush of heat flooded his body at the whispered mention of his name. Spoken with unmistakable horror.

He found himself suddenly frozen with dread, pinned beneath their heavy eyes as they drilled through to his core, unable to grasp the courage to even look behind him. His sight remained nailed to the still figures - their paper-white skin and black tattoos, their jet-black hair, their ribs and shoulders disproportioned from the rest of their long, lean bodies, and the terrible, thorn-like spurs at their shoulders and elbows. He couldn't tear his eyes away, and the longer he stared, the greater the terror that crept up his spine, a terror unreasonable but unsuppressable, absolute and primal in its roots.

He swallowed hard, fighting against whatever was trying to paralyse him from deep within his gut. There was something frightfully familiar about the magic in the air. Somehow he managed to suppress the nausea at the dreadful shame that it conjured, and his hand flicked for the comfort of one that wasn't there.

Another string of fetid curses drew their attention off of him, and Garon looked back with eyes sharp and wide as he spun the wheel in a full rotation to the left, then another to the right. They didn't need to ask what was wrong when the boat didn't turn. Their hope dwindled, and they looked in solemn silence towards the islands they hadn't yet reached and yet seemed unable to escape.

Some of the white figures melted back into the tangled forests while Garon continued his futile battle against the calm and unnatural current.

"What are we going to do?" Someone whispered, but no one had the courage to guess. And though a keen hope returned to snatch their breath away when their direction finally began to shift, they discovered with an even greater blow that it was not of Garon's doing. They skirted the second largest island, dragged among rocks and reefs without a bump despite the impossible squeezes, and a small quay emerged from around the head, little more than a flat reach of stone thrust out into the water to serve as a jetty. And it was lined with yet more of the frightful beings.

Rathen heard steel slide slowly over a sheath's locket as Petra drew her sword, and Garon behind them as he hurried down from the dead helm. Anthis, too, suddenly clutched a distasteful dagger, and Eyila had loosened her hands. But Rathen stood paralysed, rooted under his first clear look at them by helplessness and a terrifying thought, an instinctive understanding that burned in his gut and one he fought desperately against accepting. Every pair of onyx-black eyes pierced him alone, while gaunt faces, sharp and angular, curled into slight but monstrous snarls, freezing his already chilled blood. And all he found the mind to do was wish with all his might that the boat would just keep sailing.

But the unseen force that escorted the boat began to slow its lead, drawing them in perfect line with the stone arm. Their anxiety mounted as they tightened together, and as more joined the watchful crowd, moving among them with an oppressive authority, Rathen finally loosened his fingers.

But not all of these new arrivals were like the others, and incomprehension slackened their tensed muscles, tight sword grips and twitching fingers.

Where the beasts wore simple sarongs of neutral shades - and a few, they noticed among them, meagre chestguards concealing curiously feminine features - these three wore robes of silver adorned in details of the purest white and darkest black, covering quite human bodies. Their skin appeared just as white at first, but shone silver in the light just as Eyila's did bronze, and their black hair was tinged with a deep but definite shade of blue, pronouncing all the more the pale hues of their eyes.

But those eyes bore the same watchful acuity as the beasts around them, and their unmistakable hostility restored the five's frail courage.

Except for Anthis, who gawked anew.

"*Stop it*, you fool," Petra hissed as quietly as her anxiety would let her. "Don't antag--"

"No one mention a thing about the Zi'veyn." The historian shot them only the briefest look, but his eyes flared gravely despite their conflicting glitter of awe, and his demeanour was suddenly just as sharp and severe. "Nothing about the magic, Enhala, anywhere we've been - *nothing*."

"What is it?" Garon asked quietly from beside him, but any answer, even one delivered as quickly as his warning, was silenced by a sharp and brutal voice that rose from the land as the boat finally creaked to a dreadful stop.

They looked back to the three silver figures and hesitated as they picked over the words. It took a long moment for anyone but Anthis to realise they weren't of any living tongue.

"Das koruuz," he called back quickly, forcing his voice not to shake. "An feyk, val...uh..." He ignored the others' short, panicked glances. "Val...*anakhi!*"

Their eyes shifted expectantly back onto the gathering, among whom were shared equally uncertain looks. "Anakhaz fas voruul?"

"What are they saying?"

"They want to know who we are." He raised his voice again and answered, within which they each managed to at least decipher their names. But the woman at the head of the trio, sour with distinctly unwelcoming eyes, gave him only a brief response in a tone they were certain was tart. Anthis grunted uneasily and pushed himself away from the woodwork.

"Tell them we're sorry," Petra whispered, "that we didn't mean to come here and that we'll leave right away..."

But Anthis shook his head, and a rope landed over the side, tossed by one of the beasts. "We have to go with them. Don't argue, just do it."

"Who are they?" Rathen asked sharply, but again the eyes Anthis turned back upon them were both grave and excited.

"Elves."

He didn't delay in pushing out the gangplank and was the first to descend it, albeit tightly, while the others lingered behind, stalled in shock. Garon was the quickest to collect himself, his professionalism faithfully reasserted, and his stoic departure encouraged the others to follow if just for fear of being left behind.

Satisfied by their obedience, the woman turned without a word of explanation and began to lead them away. The two remaining took up the rear, notably blocking their return to the boat and fencing them immediately into a solid, single-file line, leaving them no choice but to tread the stone path as it climbed quickly into the thick forest. They were taken deep into the ominously tangled land with alarming speed, but none of them could spare that detail much fret.

Every one of them reeled. Their guard remained rigid and their eyes darted all around them, between every twisted tree and into every creeping shadow, and the world had suddenly become decidedly surreal. The oppressive terror that stifled their breath like a hot, damp cloth began to lift the further from the quay and the creatures they moved, but they were smothered instead by a rapid incredulity. Whether they believed the enthusiastic young man's conclusion or not - for blue hair and silver skin, there were no flashes of pointed ears - the stories they'd each been told as children began crawling unbidden from their memories; from tales warning of the brutality that came from the elves' misuse of magic and intelligence, to fables of elven spirits carrying naughty children away at night, dragging out their souls and eating them whole. They thought they'd outgrown the adolescent fears, but the twisting of their guts and beading perspiration begged to differ.

Their desperately flitting eyes caught unwilling glimpses of white bodies where the foliage thinned, and buildings hewn from whole stone stood timelessly in their depths, growing larger and grander than the last with every passing minute. But rather than beauty, rather than marvel, all that struck them was the haunting thought that they walked among ruins that hadn't yet fallen to disrepair, and extinct people who had yet to gasp their final breath. The question presented itself, though none dared to ponder it: had they passed though a barrier? Or had they passed through time?

Perhaps neither. More likely - and more appealing - it was a curious dream. Or a nightmare. They were being led like prisoners, and neither did the unnatural menace of the sentinels that watched their every movement dissuade that impression. Nor Rathen's unyielding dread.

Only Anthis, it seemed, was capable of looking beyond it. While they watched the woman at the lead with the severest mistrust, the almost outrageous zeal in his eyes as they darted all around shone through brighter and brighter with his every step, even despite the tightness that still bound his shoulders, as it did everyone else's. He gasped, he muttered, he chuckled giddily, and with every foolish, stifled sound he made, their muscles knotted only tighter.

After ten mentally exhausting minutes they found the edge of the forest, abrupt but natural as the dense fig trees gave way to a courtyard carved from the same white stone, and Anthis gasped aloud at the temple that rose in perfect elegance at its head. Intricately carved in images that could apparently only be appreciated by elf or historian, its grandeur would have astounded them, too, had its nature not been so imposing.

The robed woman stopped and turned sharply as she took the first step atop the stone, bringing them to a stumbling halt beneath her. The others moved up to join her, and together they cast their incisive and fractious glares from the slight but definite platform. She spoke again in the harsh language, the lines around her pouting lips revealing her seniority. All eyes shifted onto Anthis as he replied, his companions' consistently clueless but expectant, the others' dark with scrutiny.

And then those terrible, scrutinous eyes crashed upon Rathen, and he fought with all his strength not to take a step backwards. He parted his dry and sticky lips to speak as more harsh and alien words were spoken in his direction, but to his relief, Anthis replied in his stead.

But the woman's eyes, pastel-green, darkened even further upon the mage. "No human should have been able to do that."

The five stared back at the imperious figures, increasingly dumbstruck and far from sure what to make of them, but a flicker of hope kindled for the fact that, whatever or whoever they were, they clearly didn't want them on their land. But though they would have loved nothing more than to show themselves out, double time, something had caused them to lead the group into their inhospitable territory, and that stifled the flicker before it could offer any heat.

The woman turned to her companions and spoke quietly, but Anthis didn't catch enough of it to translate. As one of the three left with a bow of her head, she turned back to Rathen. "Your magic is unstable," she informed him clinically and without introduction, her speech clear and fluent. But Rathen only frowned.

"What?"

"Surely you are aware," she replied, an insincere smile curving her thin, unkind lips. "You cannot control your transformations - though of course that is no surprise for a fuhrahz."

He blinked uncertainly, and Anthis rubbed his nose. "Half-breed," he offered him very quietly.

Rathen's eyes flashed. "What do--"

"Please," she continued calmly, raising her slender white hand to punctuate her interruption, though a fire burned dangerously in her eyes. "Do not get distracted. A fuhrahz--"

"I have a name."

This time, she blinked, clearly taken aback by his own abruptness. "...My sincere apologies. Please..."

"Rathen Koraaz."

Immediately the expressions of both robed figures twitched with definite disdain, but the woman recovered with a polite smile. "Rathen *Koraaz*," she drawled needlessly, "your human side is out of sync with your...with the rest of you."

"You mean my magic?"

"No, your other half. Your..." Her expression twitched hatefully again. "Your elven heritage."

"My--"

"Please," her eyes seared once more despite her lingering, increasingly false smile. "Do not interrupt. You wear a band around your arm, do you not? And your mother gave it to you at a young age? As I suspected. To aid your human constitution. Usually they are only given to elven children for their first few years to help them learn control over their magic, but in your case...well, without it you would never have survived its awakening."

"It's a *do'osos*..." Anthis murmured, but her eyes did not even graze him.

The confusion that contorted Rathen's face only deepened. "B-but no other mage--"

"No other 'mage' is half elven. One twenty-sixth, at best."

He stepped forwards, increasingly exasperated by her own interruptions, while the others watched in dismay as their minds ticked slowly over their gathering and increasingly preposterous thoughts. "What are you saying? What do you mean?"

She muttered something coarse that prompted Anthis to glare, and closed her eyes for a moment. "Your mother was an elf." Her eyes flicked then to Anthis, who opened his mouth to speak while Rathen fell still and silent. "How can I be sure it's his mother? Because when an elf takes a human female as a mate, the gifts rarely survive in totality in the womb. But when a human male is taken, the matter is quite different - which is why such a union has been forbidden since the dawn of your kind. But," her gaze flicked back onto Rathen, now so still he seemed not to be breathing, "we will help you to control it."

"Why?" He said quickly, startling himself with his own voice.

"For the *single* fact that you bear Zikhoruikanax's gift, and by the rights of our faith, we absolutely cannot allow something so sacred to become corrupt and run wild. Unfortunately we cannot *stop* your transformations nor remove your ability to do so, such a thing is not possible. We can only teach you to control them. But first, the cuff's spell will have to be repaired - assuming you do not wish for your magic to consume you in the coming months."

His eyes were still lost and distant, but afflicted now with the grievous memory of the mage who lay seared in the desert. "I don't..."

"Then you will follow me."

"Wait--"

She spun towards Anthis, her unquenchable fire finally bursting into an inferno. "Enough of your questions! This is a place of praise and worship to our saviour, *not* a museum. We help your friend *only* because it concerns Him. There is no other reason." She straightened, the curl of her lip subdued, and turned to speak briefly with the remaining elf in perfect composure. "Thuvik will show the rest of you where you can eat and repose. You must be weary after being on the water for days. Rathen *Koraaz* will come with me."

Protests formed on their tongues as she curtly turned her back and started towards the temple, but their voices had been chased away. Even Garon paled.

Rathen swallowed hard and tightened his fists while Petra shuffled up beside him.

"You can't go with her," she insisted very quietly. "You have--"

"I have no choice."

The shortness of his tone silenced her, and she stared instead at the resolve that hardened his eyes. She felt something stir within herself as she watched him track the elf across the courtyard. Confidence. Summoned by the determination that had fallen over him from nowhere she could fathom. It wasn't clear what he thought of what the elf-woman had said - she wasn't sure what *she* thought of it, if she even believed it or this whole situation at all - but something had taken him over, something of his own making, something driven by necessity that he was compelled to answer.

She flexed her left hand, a habit she had yet to notice. He still had no clue of

Garon's injuries, but he was no fool. He didn't want to put anyone at risk, especially if that risk came from himself, and he had just been presented with a possible solution - likely the first such hope he'd had in his life. It didn't seem to matter who had presented it, nor where, nor why, nor even if it seemed remarkably and suspiciously convenient. He intended to grasp it. And she suspected that Aria was at the root of that resolve.

Petra said nothing as he started after her, leaving them behind without a word. Garon, too, stood taller as he watched in silence, and shortly turned his attention onto the waiting Thuvik and ordered the others to follow.

"What if something happens?" Anthis asked quietly as the only slightly less imposing elf led them away from the temple and around the edge of the courtyard. "He's our only real defence against--"

But Garon silenced him with a grunt, shifting his hand closer to his sword hilt. "We will just have to manage."

The silence of the temple was sheer, absolute. There was no rustle of movement as robed figures settled into positions of worship, there was no murmur of prayer from those already prostrated over the carven floor - there was not even a whisper of breath from those kneeling upon buckwheat cushions in a deep and distant trance of contemplation.

The only thing that seemed capable of shattering it at all were Rathen's very conscious footsteps.

He cringed as he trailed behind the woman, shrinking smaller as his every step echoed back five painful times louder and drew the irritated attention of every soul within, their pale eyes flashing upon him first in curiosity, then in disgust. He gave his very best efforts to stepping lighter, but such effort broke his regular gait and resulted in clumsy scuffs. He felt his cheeks grow hotter. He'd never felt so exposed in his life.

Magic could have muffled them, and the idea occurred to him anew every few seconds, but the following thought of displaying his powers in the presence of...and under such outraged eyes... No. Magic was not an option. And perhaps it wasn't his footsteps alone that disturbed them. He could sense the intense aura of magic from every individual with great clarity, so his own must have stuck out like a sore thumb. Especially if it was unstable enough to cause this belligerent woman concern...

He averted his sight to stare at the ground, his shoulders hunching under the unreasonable shame that had become so intense that he sickened even himself. But though he no longer even grazed another soul with his eyes, he was acutely aware of two bodies kneeling at the centre of the hall. Because they were not like the others. But despite their towering, jagged and horrifying appearance, they were more still and reverent in their bearing than any of the others, and the aura that radiated from the both of them was of perfect tranquillity. Not violence. Not hatred. Not terror. And they were the only two who didn't seem to notice him.

He dared a glance towards them, curiosity knitting his brow, but his shame didn't allow his eyes to linger.

Finally, they stepped through a door at the far end and the temple was shut away behind it, not a moment too soon. But the short corridor and adjoining alcoves that now lay ahead weren't empty, either, and he wasn't able to encourage himself to even level his shoulders. But at least here there was noise. Rustles, murmurs, breaths - even whispers.

He tried to ignore this newest wave of hateful glares and hurried up alongside his escort, matching her long stride and daring a thoughtful look. "How do you know about my transformations?" He asked as quietly as he possibly could. "Has word from Carenna--"

"Please." Impossibly, her tone became even sharper and crueller, and he stumbled as if the ice she'd spoken with had taken form on the ground. But at least she didn't turn her matching eyes upon him. "We are not interested in your people's petty business. I know about them because I felt the extent of your heritage, and I know they're out of control because the horror upon your friends' faces at seeing the kozahn was born of recognition, not of magic."

"Recognition?" He frowned, but as the woman sighed laboriously, that innate understanding that rocked him to his core, the undeniable truth he refused to face, returned with even greater force. And this time he couldn't ignore it. His expression dropped and haunted eyes widened. "That's..."

"What you become. An avatar of Zikhoruikanax. I'm not surprised you're unaware - in your uncontrolled state I doubt you would have comprehended your own reflection, if you'd stopped thrashing around long enough to catch it."

"But *why?*" He snapped incredulously, forgetting himself and drawing returning gazes. "What purpose could such an ability *possibly*--"

Like a hurricane, she whirled on him, stunning him in fear as a milk-green fire blazed again in her eyes, igniting within him the sudden comprehension that what he'd seen of their intolerance and thinly veiled hostility so far was not even a shadow of the malevolence they could truly exhibit. Her lip twitched acridly and she spoke through her teeth. "To maintain *peace*. But yours is imperfect, tainted by human blood, and it *causes* death rather than discouraging violence. That you should be able to do it at *all* is the greatest affront to us!" She took a step towards him, and he immediately stepped back. "You creatures view Zikhoruikanax with fear. Rather than accepting the inevitable and being humbled by mortal fragility, you view Him as a representation of something to try to flee and hide from! As the end of all things, as something dark and *evil!* You misunderstand and yet cast steel judgements, closing your mind to correction or consideration!" A sickening smile suddenly replaced her glower, and a humourless chuckle added further poison to her voice. "Perhaps your violent avatar *is* a fitting representation, if of your *own* Zikhon. For the one you've conjured bears no resemblance at all to Him."

The hatred in her eyes seemed to have stalled even time, and they were so dagger-sharp that he felt he'd been speared to the wall behind him. His heart hammered in his throat and his mouth had dried up again, and he only discovered that he was holding his breath when she finally turned away.

"Follow."

He didn't dare to hesitate. He stayed close, eager to at least escape the other eyes that fixed him, and was barely a half-step behind her when she turned into one of the side rooms. Three more elves were waiting within, but as each looked back expectantly, a definite foreboding darkened the air. His pace slowed, his heart began to race again as the door closed heavily behind him, and though no words were spoken, elven or otherwise, two of the three turned purposefully away. He looked reluctantly to the elf-woman for an explanation, but the words caught in his throat. She gestured towards stone seats, laid out just as in any cathedral's alcoves, and indicated for him to sit. He didn't want to. But he also knew he had no choice.

Uneasily, he selected the stool nearest to the door and tried to ignore his unsilencable mind as it skipped with ideas of what these people - people he suspected were unfathomably more powerful than he - would be capable of doing to him. Whether he was on his own or not.

One of the elves was suddenly beside him - one whose hair was arranged in a way that finally allowed him his first confirming glimpse of knife-sharp ears - and lifted Rathen's sleeve to reveal the silver band, two inches wide, that encased his right bicep. He didn't display his alarm at the elf's abruptness, and neither did the elf make any outward reaction to his probably blasphemous elven bindings, though his face seemed naturally harsh already. His own restraint slipped, however, as he felt magic swarm around the metal, and reminded himself brusquely that of course an elf wouldn't need to form signs to cast spells. Not even Kienza needed them.

Which meant that he would have no clue as to the nature of their spells, and no warning that they were coming beyond the fleeting disturbance in their aura a split-second before they cast them. And he could never defend himself with so little.

The woman turned back to him, prompting the man to move aside, and the two that had stepped away positioned themselves far enough to be out from underfoot but close enough to contribute - or to intervene. Their bodies were tensed in readiness.

He felt his panic claw up into his throat, but his body kept perfectly still while his mind ran rampant despite him, conjuring all kinds of ideas of what he'd let himself in for. But though his blood chilled with foreboding, skin prickled and beaded with anxious sweat, he knew casting a precautionary defence was not an option. He couldn't risk attacking them if their intent truly was harmless - all they'd been so far was sharp-tongued. In fact, he'd only witnessed a single spell.

The woman stood tall and stoic before him, maintaining a small but concerning distance, and gripped him with her cold and methodical eyes. Eyes he couldn't read.

The flood gates opened. Panic thundered through him like a tidal wave, the voice of reason shattering his mind with its cascading doubts and questions, stumbling over itself in the torrent, repeating its confusion over and over and over again.

But despite how many times it challenged what he was doing, forced its warnings and demands to run, run and keep running, he could only give it one answer: he was taking an obscene and desperate risk.

His body turned as rigid as the dead, but he forced himself to breathe. His presence alone had already insulted them; it would be all too easy to burn this bridge with rash actions, especially while the foundations had barely even been laid. Whether he liked it or not, if there was even the slightest possibility that they could provide him with the help they promised, he needed to take it. Which meant that he needed to trust them.

And trust that they were telling him the truth.

He gritted his teeth and clamped down on the fear that tried to move his lips, to squeeze from his throat desperate and futile questions. He knew he wouldn't understand the answers - and in some cases, he decided he would rather not know them one way or the other.

But one thing remained firm in the centre of his mind: if anyone could teach him to restrain the beast that lurked within him, a beast that could be born of nothing but magic, a beast that had slaughtered sixteen innocent people, and was a constant threat to his beloved Aria, it was an elf...

The woman pressed her slender palms together. He stifled his dread. She parted her lips and he held his breath. Her brief, tangled words cut through the air like a knife.

Pain tore through him like a fire over an alchemist's workbench. His mind flashed white with heat. The scream that ripped itself from his throat and scoured his flesh like the chemicals that fed the flame reached his ears as though from another world.

Chapter 56

Narrow shafts of sunlight trickled down through the canopy's young leaves, gracing the carpet of soft, emerald grass. Hundreds of tiny, reflective peach blossoms beaded the tips of delicate branches, amplifying the light, illuminating the small, verdant grove as though with starlight. The air was clean, fragranced by blossoms, hidden lavender and the subtle scent of wood only noticed on dewy mornings, and carried only the sound of a whispering breath tousling the highest leaves, and the gurgling of a small spring concealed somewhere among the roots. There was no trace of the vapid ocean, and the natural purity of the scene was interrupted only by a small shrine at the head of the clearing, carved directly into a stone thrust up by the earth, and a single standing wall chiselled from another. It was beautiful. Peaceful. It would have been the pinnacle of comfort and tranquillity had they been there by choice.

But rather than stumbling merrily upon it and pausing to take a serene lunch, the four had been led blindly, told nothing except that they weren't to wander, and then starkly abandoned with no real idea of where they were nor how long they could expect to be there.

Enough confidence had returned in the absence of any elven or eerie observers to bristle at the abruptness, but not enough to speak out against it, and certainly not to move more than a few paces from the precise spot they'd been dumped. It took almost half an hour before Garon dared more than four steps away to survey the area, and only when he returned did Petra begin a wary patrol as far as their unmarked boundaries allowed.

But though they were both deeply disturbed, they'd collected themselves for the good of all. The trees were dense, limiting visibility to only a few feet, and though the few beasts they'd seen along the coast were apparently passive, if repressive, their active preying on their minds coaxed them to watch the shadows all the closer. They'd seen only three since, and though each had been absorbed in some kind of meditation and kept as still as the stone they'd presumed hewn from, they two had experienced first hand the violent speed and strength that came from such a form. They were not prepared to take chances. If black eyes were staring back at them and their bearers decided to attack, they were more than capable of striking harder and faster than an arrow shot from the boughs.

Which left Anthis and Eyila with little choice but to trust in the swordsmens' expertise and try to occupy their minds. Eyila sat with her back to the chiselled wall and meditated, fully clothed despite the humidity trapped beneath the trees and the breeze it equally locked out. But her heart wasn't in it. She jumped at the slightest sound, be it their footsteps as they routinely passed her by, or one of Anthis's sudden exclamations. But she persisted in trying.

Anthis, meanwhile, had completely lost himself. He raced around the sparse grove like a puppy with his first bone, his initial wariness defeated by fascination as he ran back and forth between the stone forms, studying, comparing and studying again. His less than quiet enthusiasm even drew the attention of the occasional elf, but when they appeared through the trees to ensure he wasn't doing something obscene, he eagerly seized the opportunity to quiz them about, it seemed, *everything* he'd ever wished to.

Garon and Petra observed with concern from the corner of their eyes, their hands already glued to their hilts, but Anthis's own quizzical assault seemed to frighten each of them away before insult or trouble could arise. They ran off in moments without gracing him with any kind of response.

But there were, in time, a few it didn't seem to discourage. If not checking up on them, most came without a word or even a glance to kneel for a moment by the shrine - an effigy of Zikhon, they presumed, though it was too stylised for any but Anthis's eyes to interpret - before leaving without giving him a chance to begin. But a small handful, the youngest they had seen, approached the wall and made a show of looking closely at particular carvings while sending the four subtle but curious glances. Anthis blustered over to these scant few with similar lack of tact, but unlike the rest, they met his introduction quite eagerly, abandoning their obvious pretext. But, unfortunately - and to Garon and Petra's great relief - the two who dared to converse with him spoke only in elven and Anthis seemed unable to keep up, while the remainder either presumed as much from the start, or restrained themselves under orders or a recently-invoked cultural taboo.

But he, too, persisted, spurred on by those willing few, and while the elders who weren't as quick on their feet ignored him as he hounded them to the treeline, one particularly grouchy individual went so far as to send him to sleep on the spot to silence him. An action his companions found themselves in agreement with for the full hour he was out.

Though they had absolutely no warm feelings towards their unwilling hosts, they were surprised by the lack of respect and deference the historian showed them. Perhaps he was just as shocked as they were by the discovery and simply had no clue how to handle it. Reading of a people from the pages of dusty old tomes surely painted them in surreal colours.

But while the situation remained in the realms of a tantalising fantasy for Anthis, it was settling heavier and heavier upon the others. They were surrounded, undoubtedly, impossibly, by elves - black-blue hair, silver skin, pointed ears and haughty, though none they had yet noticed wore gloves - they were trapped on an island enveloped in spells, concealed from any who might rescue them or provide them an opportunity to rescue themselves, and they had lost Rathen, their single reasonable defence against the elves' vast and mysterious magic, with little idea of where he was, what he was doing, nor when he'd be back.

It was a numbingly helpless matter.

"It's been hours," Petra grumbled as her path crossed Garon's alternating route. She looked up towards the sky, then tutted vexedly to herself. After eleven glances, she should have learned by now that the sky was entirely concealed by the trees. There was no clue of the time. She knew only that they'd arrived at midday, but with the manner her stomach growled - uncannily like a bear - it must have been getting late. She grunted miserably. "So much for that mention of eating..."

Garon breathed a dry agreement, but a sudden chuckle snatched their eyes quickly back towards Anthis, who had finally found himself a capable conversation partner.

Petra's grip on her sheathed sword tightened. "Do you think it's wise to let him--"

"Probably not, no..."

She murmured uneasily as neither made any move to interfere. Then her disapproval shifted staunchly onto him. "Why didn't you ask Kienza to heal your arm?"

His expression flattened in boredom. "There was no time. She was already leaving."

"I doubt it would have taken long."

"It's not my place to make those kinds of demands of strangers."

She blinked as he started away from her, attempting to escape back to his rounds. "It--she wouldn't--"

"Will you just *stop* worrying about me?"

A laborious sigh rounded her shoulders, but she subdued the desire to throw offensive gestures at his back. "Oh, I'm not worrying about you," she drawled instead, her airy sarcasm purposely exaggerated as she began to trail along behind him. "Why *ever* would I worry? *Clearly* you know what's best for yourself."

"It isn't a hindrance."

"*No*, I'm sure, I'm sure. And you know, Rathen isn't suspicious at *all*. He thinks you're a man of metal, too. Unbreakable. That's why he hasn't gone off by himself to follow a mysterious and bitter old elf-woman who served him the perfect promises like gingerbread. Oh, wait!" She slapped her forehead while her eyes exaggeratedly widened. "He *did!*"

Her boots slipped and dug into the grass, stopping herself as quickly as she could as Garon spun swiftly on his heel to face her. "Why does this bother you so much?" He demanded through his teeth, his grey eyes hardening in irritation while a spark responded rapidly in her own. "What does my well-being have to do with you? You're always watching me or looking over my shoulder - why is that? What are you expecting? Are you just waiting for me to slip up again?"

The spark ignited as she held his fearsome gaze, and he prepared himself for the venomous retort she was sure to loose and braced against the temptation to stoop to whatever level she would pitch herself at.

But it didn't happen. Her lips tightened, she straightened, then turned and set back to her own rounds, leaving him standing in maddened confusion.

"No," she replied with perfect composure. "I'm not going in circles with you."

"We're only going in circles because you never answer me!"

Her brittle restraint snapped. "*Fine!*" She whirled after only three paces, blood red hair billowing while the volatility in her eyes swelled like a gusted flame, only adding to his disorientation. "*Because*," she flared, "you're a *strong* man. You're determined, you're intelligent, you're skilled with your blade - but you're *cursed* with everything else that comes with it! You're too proud to admit when you're wrong, when you're hurt, when you're *tired*, and you carry the weight of *everything* on your shoulders because you're so stuck in the White Hammer's mentality, even out here in the middle of *nowhere*, *miles* from any Hall, that you won't let yourself even *consider* sharing it. But guess what! We're *already* burdened by it! In fact, it's *worse* for us, because you act as though we have nothing at all to do with it, that it's *your* job to lead us in the right direction and *your* fault when things like *this* happen! As if you think we're useless, that we can't pull our own weight or contribute when things get tough. You put all that pressure on yourself! And maybe, at first, it *was* your fault when we got into trouble, you *did* slip up, but I *know* you've always made the best decisions you could *and* we always got out of it. But this merry little chase of ours has *long* since slipped out of your control! You could *never* have known what would happen! To *any* of us! So you can't keep hoarding the blame and carrying all the weight by yourself - you're going to *kill* yourself with that kind of pressure! And: your injuries are *not* badges of honour, either. They don't make you look strong or brave or weathered, they make you look like a *child!*"

Her voice reverberated through the charged air, ringing in their ears as she stared at Garon in exasperation while he stood still as ice, meeting her gaze with dark, rancorous eyes. Anger hardened the line of his jaw. "Are you done?"

And yet his tone was so indifferent. Her drive deflated like a punctured buoy, collapsing her shoulders, and her eyes softened with the downward turn of her lips. But just what had she honestly expected?

"I am," she sighed, defeated. "For good, I think." She turned away, but a sudden desperation, one familiar but still beyond his comprehension, speared through Garon's reason and forced his hand to grasp her wrist. She snatched it back vehemently. "No no," she said with that same insincere lightness that seemed again to strike him physically, "*you've* got to make sure we stay safe. I'm going to sit down because I'm tired, but I'm *sure* I can trust you to--"

"Petra, stop."

Surprise stuttered her feet as his fingers closed tightly back around her wrist, and that momentary shock was all he needed to drag her easily out of earshot and around the other side of the wall. He pressed her firmly against the stone and fixed her with severity. "Listen to me," he said gravely, a tone at which she immediately rolled her eyes, "when we get out of this place, you should--"

"Leave?" She finished wearily. "Why? So you've got one less burden to feel responsible for?" She shoved his hand away from her shoulder and matched his ferocity, squaring herself in defiance. "No."

He barred his teeth, jumped an exasperated step back and groped at the air as if he could catch some kind of understanding. "*Why?!*" He burst, infuriated. "*Why* is it so important that you stay with us? Why can't you just leave and go somewhere you're *not* in danger all the time? Is it because you think the Hall has information about your father? Because I don't have *anything* to tell you about Durhan!"

Sheer outrage flashed through her eyes, but she swiftly regained control. "It's more than that now."

"*Why?!* What in Vastal's name *is* it that's keeping you chained to us? To *me?!*"

She caught his left hand as they both flailed in frantic enunciation. "Because I don't trust you to make the right decisions for yourself."

"Seriously? *That's* worth endangering yourself for?"

Her gaze erupted anew into a hazel inferno, and he found his efforts to understand suddenly interrupted with a shock. "It is." She released his hand as sharply as she spoke, and it dropped heavily to his side. But Garon didn't scoff or look away in irritation. He was gripped by the sudden depth of her brown-green eyes, their constant, thoughtful if erratic warmth drowned by elements usually locked tightly away, rarely seen for more than a flash but now fully unleashed. In that moment, they screamed volumes. And yet he could only discern one impossible thing from their desperate, beseeching turbulence.

"And you seem to forget," she added, a touch calmer, already smothering the fire, "that I can look after myself. I've saved *your* arse twice already. Without me, you'd be worse off than a dead arm."

"It's not dead," he murmured.

"Well, it doesn't work properly, at any rate." An uncomfortable furrow disrupted the frustration in her brow as he continued to stare at her, his eyes coloured in growing bewilderment as though he'd only now truly seen her for the first time. But though her lips began to form a question, it didn't make it out.

"Why did you save me?" He asked her, softly despite his scowl.

"Because you'd have obviously been killed otherwise..."

"That's not what I mean. Why did you save me? You weren't with us the first time. In Carenna. You could have avoided it, you could have seen what was happening and gotten out clean. You didn't have to get involved."

"I was heading to the gate to join you - of course I didn't know you were actually planning to leave *without* me. And I *didn't* know what was happening, I just saw that you were being attacked and were clearly outmatched, so when I saw a chance while...Rathen was distracted, I took it."

"And I lured him far from the camp the second time. Out of earshot. None of you should have noticed..."

Though her lips parted again, this time it was her own voice that stalled her. Her cheeks flushed in embarrassment, her eyes darted away, but she shifted her weight and sighed in boredom in a bid to conceal it. But her facade instantly crumbled, unable to convince even herself.

She frowned quizzically as Garon took a tentative step towards her, but her eyes simultaneously livened with a nervous curiosity. She resisted shifting backwards under his intense gaze, lost and confused, baffled...and yet fully comprehending. Her folded arms slipped back to her sides, watching the heated perplexity double in his eyes as he stepped closer still, moving slowly, uncertainly, his confliction clear in every line on his face. But he didn't stop, and his stare didn't break.

Without thought, he leaned towards her. His heart raced, encouraged by the mixture of spices and rosehip, the red scent - *her* scent. He felt the heat of her breath as her lips parted in wonder, luring him closer...

They pressed against his an age before he was prepared. His heart erupted, and again his blundering thoughts were erased, emptying his mind to the sensations. A warmth he'd never truly felt; a scent he'd never breathed more hungrily.

But her pressure was softer than he'd expected. Her fire burned as it always did - he could almost feel its heat, hear its crackle - but only now did he discover the glass that lay above it. Encased, it flickered hot and fierce, close enough to sear him yet completely guarded. But that guard was fragile; it would take little to shatter and release her fury, and just as little to release her passion. And passion - volatile, benevolent, terrible and genuine - was woven into her every action, her every decision - her every reason.

How, he wondered, could he ever have been so blind?

Because he had never been looking for it.

He felt her fingers brush his skin, tracing the back of his hand. He turned his wrist to grasp them, but his hold was weak; his fingers refused to curl. In that moment he resented his injury more fiercely than he had anything else. Until she grasped his instead.

"*What?!*"

The sudden shout tore them away from each other as though lightning had struck between them, igniting a panic in their chests that burned away their fixation and reimposed their vigilance. Their hands immediately shot to their sword hilts while a haste burned beneath their feet, carrying them, alarmed and sheepish, back around to the grove it had risen from.

"*Learn* from it?!"

They came to a sharp stop, their dread twisting into confusion. Eyila still sat silently against the wall, her bronze face, paint disrupted by the damp air, contorted in an effort to keep her eyes shut tight and maintain her meditation, but of course it was impossible while the harshly-cut voice of an elf raged at Anthis, who stared back at him with similarly fevered disbelief.

"All you're doing by recording your mistakes is teaching your children that life goes on!" The elf continued with rigid confidence. "That it doesn't matter if they do something horrendous because time and life will continue regardless! That there are no long-term repercussions, they can just do as they wish!"

"*Nonsense!*" Anthis bellowed back. "These mistakes haven't *been* repeated! Our children learn of them, they hear the awful things that came from it all and they *don't* make the same mistakes!"

"No, they make *new* ones from the same desires! But such thoughts wouldn't even *occur* to them if there was nothing to plant the ideas! *We* manage to live peacefully, after all!"

Petra and Garon slowly lowered their swords, watching the exchange in bafflement.

"Oh, *certainly*," Anthis drawled, "in *ignorance*. But when one of you *does* get such an idea, there'll be nothing to discourage you! There are no past lessons to teach you right from wrong, only what your parents have told you about playing nice with the other children!" The elf opened his tightly-pursed mouth to retort, but Anthis wasn't finished. "There's *nothing* here for *anyone* to learn from! You can't be so short-sighted to think that dark ideas will *only* occur to people if something else plants the idea! You all think for yourselves, you're not...*bees!* Dark ideas are *inevitable;* they'll occur to *someone*, be it through hurt, hatred or the desire to be 'more', and when they do, there will be no records of your ancestors' mistakes to discourage anyone driven enough to strive for them! Or to discourage anyone else from agreeing with them and egging them along! *That* is how you repeat mistakes! *History serves a purpose!*"

There was such a seething electricity as the two stared daggers at one another that it seemed lightning might actually appear. Petra and Garon looked on in restrained caution, their swords half-raised despite knowing what little use they would be if the elf chose to turn to his magic to win the futile argument - but for the moment, he didn't move aside from the rise and fall of his elegantly embroidered shoulders with every smouldering breath. His skin had turned to shimmering rose, and his lips were pursed so very tightly that the pressure building up behind them might lead him to explode. Anthis, meanwhile, simply stared back in challenge.

In the tense silence, even Eyila opened one eye in suspense.

Then, the elf's lip curled, he snarled what was certainly a curse, spun around and stormed off, never once even grazing the others with his unnecessarily proud eyes.

"And will someone *please* bring us our belongings from the boat?!"

A joint breath was released once he was out of sight. "Helping relations?" Garon asked drily as he sheathed his sword and Anthis continued to leer into the trees where the elf had vanished.

"Unbelievable," he growled. "Arrogant little..." he strangled the air after him.

"After everything you've told us about elves, you're actually surprised?"

"Actually, yes." He gestured sharply towards the wall. "*They don't record their history.*"

"We're not here on a study expedition."

"No, you misunderstand," he scurried towards them, stifling his voice though it was no less squeezed by incredulity. "They have no records of *any* of it. We're not going to get a *thing* out of these people! They can't even tell me why they're here other than out of 'faith and veneration' for Zikhon, and that's all these bloody carvings dictate, too! They can't tell me what happened seven hundred years ago, they can't tell me where more of their people are, they can't--"

"They're living in seclusion," Garon reminded him slowly, "perhaps they just don't know."

But he shook his head adamantly. "Oh no. They would know. It's like the Arishan War. It's not something they'd forget. They would *all* have been affected - why else would we not have seen a *single* elf in seven hundred years?! Someone's gone through a lot of trouble to hide it all away!"

"Why does any of this matter?" Petra sighed.

"Because the Zi--" he caught himself quickly while the rest glanced about in caution. "*'It'* revolves around the fact. It's a pivotal component to the end of their history, of that I'm certain - but if these people have no records of any of it, it could mean that *'it'* has been destroyed as a final measure! Think about it! Why else would information have been scattered like this?! The renegades didn't want it *all* lost!"

"You're jumping to--"

"I really cannot *believe* their arrogance!" Anthis hissed on, spinning away from them and stomping into a pace. "*Imbeciles!* They're just as snobbish as they've always been, it's just a different shape - they might not be above *touching* things now, but rather than indulgent and superior, they're over-pious and *far* too assured of themselves! And they *really* believe that hiding from their past will avoid a repeat of their culture's degradation and *whatever* it resulted in! But it *won't!* They're too naturally curious - and *some* of them must be asking questions, otherwise that fool wouldn't have been able to give me such an assured excuse-- which, I might add, they've no doubt been fed in place of any *actual* answers. It's ridiculous! I doubt any single one of them *alive* even knows *why* it's all so forbidden! They're hiding in shame, but the shame isn't even *theirs! It's ridiculous!*" He stared at Garon, then Petra, and even down to Eyila in exasperation, as if hoping one of them might be able to explain it and set his utter lack of comprehension into order. But they could only look back in their own confusion, wondering, above all else, why it really mattered.

His eyes suddenly flashed again. "*And--*"

"Then how can it be that we *do* live peacefully, and have yet to repeat any of our ancestors' apparent mistakes?"

Blood ran cold at the interruption of another harsh voice. All four spun around, wide-eyed and guilt-ridden, to face the old elf who had entered the grove silently from behind them. His black-blue hair was arranged in a far less elaborate manner than most of the others they'd seen, favouring loose what others had worn in thick braids and braided again, and though his robes made up for that modesty in grandeur, his aged pastel eyes were lively and curious rather than lofty and dismissive.

But, still in the throes of furious conviction, Anthis's shock was quick to pass. "Because," he replied hotly, "I'd wager you've already made your greatest mistake. Why else would your people have suddenly vanished from across the world and left your cities and valuables to the hands of your lowly servants? Why else would you few regress to short post-magic times, to faith and simplicity? Why else would you have hidden all mention of it, even from your own kind, and been so convinced that just *hearing* about it could be so provocative that some might try to do it again, regardless of the outcome?"

Silent voices begged his tongue to cramp while tense, watchful eyes shifted onto the elf, who simply cocked his head and puckered his pale lips in thought. "My ancestors were undeniably ashamed of their people's actions, that much is true," he answered mildly, "so they concealed it, hid the fact away, ignored and denied it, and enforced a return to simpler times, placing a taboo upon the past." He left the shadow of the trees and began a slow and leisurely approach, prompting Garon to swiftly redraw his sword. But he paid no attention, and continued his considered response. "They wished for us to look forwards, only ever forwards, and to live peacefully in contemplation, to consider and accept the nature of eternity and fragility rather than striving for physical pleasures - the results of which, you see around you."

Anthis's eyes, surprised for a moment, narrowed suspiciously. "Yes, you're all so *very* enlightened. Aside from the conceit and irresponsibility."

"Anthis--"

He raised his hand, silencing the inquisitor's warning, and further fixated upon the impassive elf. "You even *admit* that your people have turned their backs on their history, as if you think that by ignoring it, it'll just go away. But it's not that easy to sever the ties to what you once were - you might be able to 'live peacefully in contemplation', but you've retained your misguided superiority, just as you retain responsibility for your ancestor's actions."

"Anthis--"

This time it was the elf's hand to interrupt. "You speak as if you have an inkling of what my ancestors did. I realise a great deal of our past has been chased down by a handful of your own kind - you, it would seem, number among them - but I can see a glimmer of cluelessness within the rage of your eyes. You have little idea, and no facts at all." He cocked his head thoughtfully again. "But regardless, what difference would it make if we faced the past and admitted responsibility? We cannot reverse it."

"You don't *have* to reverse it, you just have to know how to *prevent* it from happening *again!*"

The elf did not reply. He simply stared at Anthis for a long moment while the others watched with bated breath and rigid muscles, tight and ready to respond with a second's notice. But the elf's eyes were neither troubled nor malicious. They were studious.

They each jolted in surprise when he suddenly grinned, pronouncing the deep wrinkles around his eyes and mouth, and chuckled joyfully while Anthis glared back with even greater suspicion. "How marvellous!" He chimed, his grin widening as he hastened towards him, and grasped his hand before anyone's ready muscles could react, shaking it quite vigorously. "How marvellous indeed! My name is Eizariin - I'm sorry for my challenge, it was purely academic, I truly didn't intend to antagonise!"

"Academic?" The severity on Anthis's face waned in bafflement while Eizariin peered apologetically around at the others, and he quickly spun back, no less lively.

"Yes, I'm sorry - I can't help being curious. Not all of us are as unlearned as the majority would like to think, and that curiosity has gotten me into trouble all my life - but I've always felt it was worth it." He squinted with a shrewd smile. "I'm sure you can appreciate that." He abruptly released his tight hold on Anthis's hand before he could reply and hurried back towards the trees, leaving the others increasingly bemused while a small if dubious smile began to creep across the historian's face. The elf shortly returned with a basket. "I've brought you food--"

"At last!" Petra dashed away from Garon's side, caution a distant memory, and snatched the basket with little more than a fleeting glance of thanks.

"Yes, I thought as much," he chuckled, his black eyebrows rising. "I apologise for my people's 'hospitality'. You're the first guests we've had in...well, ever, I suppose. To say we're 'out of practise' would be an understatement."

"You're not a servant," Anthis surmised as he approached a little more carefully, though his intrigue had softened his caution, and he observed the intricacies of his richly embroidered robes with as much courtesy as his fascination would allow.

"Hmm? No, of course not. There are no 'servants' here, we're *all* Zikhoruikanax's devoted. But I thought you had probably been neglected and, I admit, I was quite curious about you - especially after seeing the ruffled manner in which some of the others left this grove..." His smile widened in amusement for a moment, but it didn't return to its usual state. Instead, it shrank, and his eyes dulled soberly. "But I don't share in their disapproval, unlike the others who 'hide from the past', as you so rightly put it. And I don't believe that Zikhoruikanax shares in it, either. He represents acceptance, not only peace and eternal rest, and if we cannot accept our past, how *can* we rest easily in the future?"

Anthis nodded slowly, his green eyes narrowing in slow, daring thought. He felt his stomach rumble, and though his gaze shifted momentarily towards the basket through which Petra rummaged, Garon stepped warily and, no doubt, hungrily towards and Eyila, too, turned her yearning eyes, he looked shortly back to the elf in absolute decision. "Eizariin," he began with excessive politeness, his eyes suddenly alight with a dangerous intrigue that verged on distraction, though one Garon was fortunately too preoccupied to notice, "I have spent my whole life learning about your people from fragments of books, scrolls and ruins, collecting half-broken and indecipherable memories, accounts and legends. *Never* have I thought that such an encounter with one of your kind would be possible." He placed his hand over his heart and bowed an inch in supplication. "I would be *beyond* honoured if you would share some of your knowledge with me."

The old elf hesitated for not even a heartbeat before his eyes brightened, touched by the same enthusiasm and the same devilish defiance. "I'd be happy to," he replied, glancing furtively towards the surrounding trees, "if I can be afforded the same honour."

Anthis's impish grin widened as he extended his hand in agreement. Eizariin shook it, short and eager, and quickly followed the young historian to the other end of the wall, out of earshot while the rest busied themselves with food, and with a clear view of potential eavesdroppers.

Chapter 57

The office was far too small for such a swollen silence. The immense pressure threatened to shatter the windows, and thickened the air in the meantime to the point of rooting in place everyone unfortunate enough to fall within its reach. Of course, few allowed their discomfort to show. Teagan stood, apparently composed, beside the desk in anticipation of the fast-approaching fallout, his hands clasped dispassionately behind his back while Salus sat slumped with his head in his palms, staring through the surface of his desk and the parchment cast askew upon it. Taliel stood just as motionless before him. It was the young boy beside her, surely no older than twelve, who was doing his best to keep his knees from knocking.

It took a long while before Taliel finally disrupted the atmosphere's rigid hold by quickly and quietly ushering the petrified phaeacian back out of the office. She was sure she heard the poor boy gasp for breath as he stepped outside into the vast and freeing corridors, but she spared him little pity, holding him firmly to blame for the bad news he'd delivered and whatever backlash was about to come from it.

The latch clicked shut, easing from her chest the slightest sigh of relief, and she turned purposefully back to the others, who had ignored the fuss, before the oppressive silence could ensnare her again. "Yoran survived in Fendale," she stated, clearly and calmly, "and Elisabet and Moroes will already be feeling through Orton. This is nothing we haven't handled before."

Salus looked up slowly as her soft, assured voice rippled through the stillness, dragging his hands down his face to meet her with eyes wide in hopeless thought. He lingered there for a moment, staring through her while his mind continued to spiral, but his eyes only emptied further as he began to process her words, disconcertingly offering no hint of their reception.

Taliel and Teagan both braced for an explosion; a caustic verbal assault, an attack upon the desk clutter, a chair hurled through the window. Given the circumstances, they decided that a combination of the three was the least they could expect. Their breath tightened the longer they were forced to wait.

But then, he nodded.

Teagan's eyes flicked momentarily towards Taliel, but his suspicion was as well-hidden as both of their surprise. Had she not been there, he had no doubts that Salus would have erupted into fury. But something, something about her, had stopped it.

He looked back to him, observing the rage that darkened his eyes and the consideration that caged it, and wondered just what power she held over him, where it had come from...and to what extent it had gripped him. For he was behaving stranger and stranger in her presence, and that presence was becoming increasingly frequent.

But...whatever her intentions, at least she was able to subdue him, and he needed a clear and composed mind now more than ever.

Teagan raised his chin and brushed the matter to one side. "Both attacks are connected, but what Fendale suffered in severity, Orton was similarly spared. No one died."

"But it still leaves a bitter after-taste," she observed. "Even with overpowering Skilan a success, to have a landmark like Fendale rent in two like this feels...ominous. We're divided between two wars; people will take this to heart."

"Such sentimentality serves no purpose."

Salus nodded slightly, his fingers laced over his lips. "She's not wrong, though."

"Perhaps," Teagan replied drily, "but the point is that the mage didn't die, either, which suggests he either wasn't committed or that they're changing tactics. The bottom line is that a perpetrator has survived to be caught and questioned."

"Unfortunately the guards apprehended him first and the Order will undeniably take custody." Salus rumbled in frustration and slumped back in his chair. "*Damn* the Crown. If they'd approved my request to station people among the guards' ranks in *every* town and village, we wouldn't be having this issue. We could have transferred him here straight away and at least delayed the Order's intrusion. Though I wonder if Malson even presented that request at all..."

"There is still time."

Taliel shook her head doubtfully. "To bring him here, yes, but will he even know anything? He may just be a puppet, a tool. It's true that the Order has usually been quick to take custody, but of all the mages Nolan and the other breakers *have* managed to interrogate, none have given us anything of any substance... sir?"

Salus's face had twisted into a pensive, calculating scowl, and his eyes pierced through the opposite door like an arrow through water, staring with such intensity he could have set it alight. But though he had surely only stopped listening mere seconds before, he was already too distant to notice the silence, nor their expectant eyes shifting onto him from the wall.

His fingers crept thoughtfully over his chin.

What she had said was true. Of all the mages they had captured, they'd had the chance to break only one in four, and none of them seemed to have any information to give them. They'd wanted to - the methods of Nolan and his team left little for even mages to defy - but all they'd dragged out of any of them was nonsense about studies. That was the trouble with scholars: learned men had fickle attention spans. If the elders, the high magisters, had given them the true reasons behind their tasks, they'd probably stopped listening long before they'd finished. Though that was no reason not to try dragging it from them. It was in their heads, somewhere, they just needed a firmer hand to help them remember it.

But true though her words may have been, they were defeatist. He wouldn't have entertained them at all had they not reminded him of a particularly strong card in his painfully sparse hand.

But...it was too soon. He'd decided that two days ago and little had changed since then.

His brow knotted tighter.

...Or had it? Teagan had said it - the Order could be changing their tactics. A less subtle approach would certainly lend a new shade of fear to their terrorism - but what if it went beyond that? What if such brash carelessness *wasn't* a tactic, but genuine confidence?

A sudden chill froze his heart.

What had they found?

His jaw knotted in resolution, and his fist dropped back to the desk with a thump. He was glad he'd pressured Erran to stop wasting his time with timid party tricks. 'Exercises' he had called them, to test the extent of his control. But when he'd pressed, that matter of control seemed suddenly obsolete. And it was also made clear that Denek had just been trying to keep him occupied after all.

Yes. It was time. It would have to be. He may have only a handful of spells under his belt, but now he could do more than merely 'brew tea under a hovering light', and even that was more than Denek was aware of.

"Sir?"

His eyes shifted back to the room and he sprang out of his chair, turning immediately to his favoured while Taliel stared with a mild and fleeting frown of confusion. His eyes, meanwhile, glinted with purpose. "Call Erran," he told him hurriedly, "have him meet us in the cells." Then he rushed out from behind his desk as Teagan obediently inclined his head and left to see to his cryptic task, lingering for only a moment beside Taliel. He looked at her with the same determination, only slightly softened by affection. "'Nothing we haven't handled before'," he said with a smile. "I need you to send word to Yoran, tell him I want Fendale evacuated to Morton as quickly as possible, before the Crown can issue an alternative. It's close enough and can bear the weight of more refugees. And tell him that I need everything he can give me on the mages that were stationed there, especially their contact with the rest of the Order - how often they received commands, their rotations, their field ratios."

"Of course," though her frown slightly deepened. "Would you like me to aid--"

"No," he said quickly, alarm sparking through his eyes. "Yoran can take care of the evacuation. You stay here."

"I can handle--"

"No." He felt a touch of guilt at the insult in her eyes, but though he knew fully well that she was capable of handling herself - she'd proven it countless times in a variety of ways - he couldn't silence the unease he felt at the idea of sending her to a town that had just been ripped in two by magic, divided by a chasm so deep that it had apparently swallowed whole buildings.

His eyes softened in apology. "Please, stay here."

She straightened, but the offence remained in her eyes, and as she inclined her head and shifted her gaze behind him in formality, he found himself equally bruised. But he had no mind to repair the matter. He spared only a muttered curse as she turned and left as coldly as any portian, then urged his mind onto much more important concerns, rushed out and down the opposing corridor, leaving the confines and irritations of the office behind him.

Chapter 58

"I can't believe it!" Such was Anthis's eighteenth mindless chirp in ten long minutes. But he seemed unaware of his incessant, giddy declarations as he scrutinised through torchlight the carvings on the latest wall to seize his fascination, until, quite without warning, he spun and darted away. Shadows shifted chaotically as he raced around with the single meagre flame, his unyielding enthusiasm coaxing another bout of tired groans while he chuckled stupidly to himself, and he covered the small, empty vault they'd been corralled into in a few short bounds, narrowly missing Petra as she wandered on another restless patrol. He didn't seem to notice. "I just can't *believe* it!" He spared them a bright but fleeting glance, as if they shared in his awe. "*Zikhon saved them!*"

"We know," Petra grumbled painfully, "you've told us *so* many times..."

But again he simply chuckled and shook his shaggy head as the wall stole back his airy attention. "*Zikhon* saved them! The God of *Death!* Who would *ever have thought?!*"

"No one, that's why no one's suggested it..."

"I *know!*"

Petra tutted and tore her eyes away from his foolish grin to spare her growing irritation, sending another involuntary but meaningful glance towards the back of Garon's head in the meantime. Barely a moment later she almost found herself beneath the careless historian's feet once again. She cursed after him, but he didn't notice that, either.

He ran his fingers over the carvings of another rounded wall, then dashed a few paces to his left, stopping short at another. But his eyes grew tainted by a hint of disappointment as they absorbed the cryptic shapes, and his energy faltered. "But I...still can't believe such an idealistic theory was right..."

"You're putting a lot of stock into the words of one man you've known for no more than a few hours," Garon noted clinically as he passed him on his own round, but Anthis shook his head, slumping in growing dejection.

"No, Eizariin was telling me the truth. He was holding a lot back, I have no doubt about that, but what he *did* tell me was honest. Feira, Nara, Doru - They're not...They're not *'faces'*, They're as real as Vastal and Zikhon...and Zikhon is far from the embodiment of darkness that we've painted Him to be. I knew the elves saw Him differently, but..." he gestured heavily to the walls around them, "only now am I really beginning to understand the extent... Eternal peace...'death'... Context; *one* mistranslation, *one* misinterpretation...that's all it took for us to debauch an entire religion we adopted as our own..." Haunted by his train of thought, he turned himself away from it to keep his mind from collapsing. "The, uh, the elves questioned the gods' power; they considered their own magic to be stronger and saw the gods as a threat to their supremacy, and for that, the gods destroyed them - even Vastal. Only...save me - only *Zikhon* opposed it. *None* of this is as black and white as we thought..."

Garon frowned dubiously, but decided not to voice his tumbling doubts. Petra, however, found herself unable to keep so still a tongue.

"I don't understand that," she snapped despite herself. "Wouldn't questioning Their strength be better than questioning Their existence? At least they were still acknowledging Them, which is more than can be said for a lot of our *own* people, and yet *we've* not suffered any ill consequences for it."

"Actually, no. If they'd questioned Their existence then it would have implied that the elves considered themselves the highest beings, and that would be that, matter settled. Only other mortals could have opposed them. But by continuing to acknowledge the existence of the gods and questioning Their power instead, they gave themselves a target and created a power struggle, even if the gods never actually participated in it."

"If the gods didn't participate, how did They wind up killing them all?"

Anthis hesitated. "Eizariin wouldn't go into detail on that. All he said was that they'd 'pushed theories further and further' - but I *strongly* suspect it has something to do with the Zi'veyn. We found mention of an artefact against humans and another against gods, didn't we? And while I still have no idea if they ever actually brought the last to life, I have no doubt in their arrogance that they thought about it - perhaps even *tried*. If they managed, or it seemed they were getting close, that could have alarmed the gods whether it would've worked or not. After all, I doubt they had much in the way to test it on..."

"I hate to stomp on your academic musings, but...the gods...aren't..." Petra paused for a long moment, searching for the most delicate manner of putting it, but shortly gave up and gestured to each of them instead. "They're *gods*. They can't be struck with blades or spells. What could the elves have done to Them? It would be like trying to attack an...*idea*."

"Except they had a doorway," he replied tartly. "Every site of magical magnetism - everywhere they built their homages, their temples, their shrines to the gods - were places where the veil between our world and the gods was at its weakest, which is presumably how they were gifted the magic in the first place. And while we still have no real idea of the extent of elven power, the gods *did*. As far as I can see, the gods would have eradicated *all* of them had Zikhon not disagreed. He saved only a handful, those He deemed to be uninvolved in the matter and untainted by their idealism--"

"Those faithful to Him, no doubt."

"Those faithful to *any* - although gods of creativity, nature and intelligence would have been completely overlooked when luxurious lives and the *ends* of them were their sole concerns, but even then it seems these 'faithful' were a dying breed by that point. But either way, He spared them the other gods' wrath, and that's why the *only* handful of elves in existence today are right here, on an island dedicated to Zikhon *alone*."

A notable quietness befell the room. Garon focused on the carvings of the oval walls as he passed them, Eyila remained as still as always, and Petra nodded slowly as she wandered past him again. "...What a lovely story," she said eventually. "Very colourful propaganda. Of course it completely clashes with *everything* the Temple teaches us. Remind me: from whom did we learn of the gods? Of Vastal and Zikhon? It was the elves themselves, wasn't it? Or did we just *dream* it all up ourselves?"

"I understand what you're saying, but I believe it. Humans were slaves and servants kept beyond arm's length; what little we learned from them we pieced together on our own. It's *far* from impossible that we misunderstood things. But there are elves *here*, nowhere else--"

"That we *know* of," she reminded him, "and *none* of them were alive when all of this supposedly happened, *seven hundred years ago*. And you said it yourself: they don't record their history. How could this 'Ayzareen' have uncovered all of this?"

"I agree with Petra," Garon announced, prompting the young man to bite back a retort and return to the walls, abandoning the matter with a roll of his eyes. "I'm glad you're making friends, but *don't* let your guard down."

"My guard is just fine."

"What did he want to know in return for all this?"

"Trivial things."

Garon cocked an eyebrow. "A little too convenient."

"Look," Anthis whirled, his eyes flaring as the inquisitor passed him. "I know you all think I'm being hasty or naive, but I *trust* Eizariin. I know his look. He's genuine - more so than most *human* historians I know. He's not driven by personal glory, he's driven by *passion*. We have nothing to worry about from him."

"That's the assumption that usually precedes betrayal."

Anthis growled and turned away again, absorbing himself back into the stone while muttering quietly beneath his breath.

Without warning, the vault's single door creaked open and snatched their fervid attention. They'd still been offered no word of Rathen - indeed the only official contact they'd had from the elves at all had been when they'd escorted them to another location for the night, by which point it had already been growing dark. Otherwise, they'd been explicitly neglected. They probably wouldn't have eaten at all if not for Eizariin because, despite Anthis's constant pleas, they still hadn't been brought any of their belongings, including what remained of the food they'd collected from the Ikaheka.

But though it wasn't Rathen who stepped inside, it was, at least, another delivery of food, and just in time to avoid a demonstration of nausea. By hunger, at least. Irritation was another matter.

The elf set the basket on the ground just inside with nothing more than a mild look of abhorrence, and left without a word. Petra sneered after her and collected it only once the door had closed, then again when she discovered that it contained little more than off-cuts of bread, bruised fruit and, most likely, washing water. But their stomachs churned too violently to turn their noses up at it.

Only Eyila didn't rise to collect her share. She sat in her usual straight-backed, cross-legged silence, but she was far from entranced in meditation. Instead her pale blue eyes were wide and potent. She'd been as such since they'd stepped into the vault, and with so much magic surely swarming around them, they found her sudden change unsettling. But her eyes were thoughtful rather than concerned, a fact only Anthis noted when he brought her her food. But he didn't ask her about it.

He set the wooden plate on the floor beside her, but eyed the red-green and brown-spotted apple dubiously. "Perhaps I'm crazy," he said softly, with a smile and to no one in particular as he exchanged it for his own, slightly less-mottled fruit, "but I don't think the elves think very highly of us." He rose back to his feet, sparing her the pressure to respond, and sought to continue absorbing the stories etched into the walls. They were scarce, meagre, and for them to have been dumped in this small and unimpressive room just as they had the grove, they must have held relatively little importance. It was no doubt an effort to keep their privacy from his prying eyes, but they had underestimated his fascination, and after all Eizariin had told him, he found he was deciphering them with a more considered eye.

"What do you believe now?"

The musical voice stalled his movement before he'd managed even a step, instilling the very same shock as the first time it had graced the air. His eyes fell back down to Eyila in surprise, just as the others interrupted their unenthusiastic eating to stare from opposite sides of the room, each wondering if they'd finally begun to imagine things.

Undecided, he blinked beneath her patient stare. "Sorry?"

"When you kill." The blood drained quickly from his face as though holes had been cut into his feet. But she continued, cold and undeterred. "Garon told me you believe you're delivering the souls of the people you kill to your god so He can use them to protect the world against Zikhon. But you've just discovered that Zikhon is a saviour, not a killer."

His gaze shifted towards the others, both of whom looked back at him just as expectantly, and he forced himself with great effort to recover from the shock, if just to shake their piercing eyes. "Well," he said, quiet and flat as he took a half-step away to return to the furthest walls, "Garon told you wrong."

"Then tell me right."

Her compelling voice halted him again. His retreat faltered, feet immovable even by his sudden if premature bridling, body frozen despite the heat of his defensiveness. But he found himself reluctant to overcome it.

He had little clue as to why. He knew no good would come of explaining his actions, the intricacies of his belief and the justification of its demands, and he found that she was the last person he wished to offer that explanation to. Her young mind was absorbed in death, trapped in it, but even had it not been he knew there was no way that she, a healer, could ever appreciate his position. And he had no desire to degrade her opinion of him any further.

And yet...she was also the only one who was giving him a chance to explain himself. The only one willing to listen. He found himself desperate to seize that opportunity - but to what end was she asking?

Anthis considered her for a very long moment. He ignored the judgemental gazes of the others while she fixed him with patience, and soon lowered himself back down beside her, slow and still quite undecided beneath his cascading thoughts.

"There is a...prophecy," he replied cautiously, wondering when his mouth had developed a mind of its own, "among Craitism, which states that the sulyax will come again - the 'end of times', in elven. It's said it will be the result of dying faith and the leading of selfish, violent and indulgent lives. It's widely believed in accordance with Craitic teachings that Zikhon will overpower Vastal in Their eternal struggle and finally lay waste to Her creations - us - just as He did the elves, and that we would know it had come when the world froze, gripped in ice and snow." He found her eyes hadn't dimmed. "The...Temple uses it to frighten people," he continued, no less doubtful as to the wisdom of doing so, "into living kind and peaceful lives, as we all rightly should, and maintaining faith in Vastal in order to keep Her empowered against Him. But there are...more and more who turn away from the temples to live for nothing but their own benefit. Many worry that it's the start of the sulyax, but there is a...small handful of us who are standing up to it, rather than rolling over and accepting it."

She nodded shortly. "Yes. You believe in the aid of a demigod. Vokaad."

His guarded frown flickered, still trying to decide to what degree mockery lay in her eyes. "Something like that."

"And you believe that by providing Him with particularly vigorous souls, He will use them to prevent this 'sulyax'. How?"

"...Definitively, I don't know. Some believe the spirits will form a guardian, others that they'll become a weapon. I believe they're..." his eyes shifted ever so briefly onto the others, who at least no longer *appeared* to be listening, "...forming a shield. And after everything I've heard today, I'm increasingly convinced. I don't see what kind of weapon or guardian could stand against *four* gods."

"But you believe that a shield will?"

Had that been curiosity, or scepticism? "It wouldn't have to fight, just withstand an assault. It's easier to brace than it is to attack..."

"Mm." Her gaze didn't waver in the silence, and though it had begun to seem more thoughtful than cynical, it still made him shift uneasily.

Petra's bitter laugh soon rose from nearby, and he decided he preferred the unbroken stare. "You're ridiculous!" The duelist hissed. "You spend your life uncovering facts, and yet all this time you've been sucked into a sick fairy story!"

He snapped towards her, his eyes darkening while a caustic retort readied on his tongue. But though she dared him with a raise of her chin, something barred his teeth before it. He returned to his previous position, turning his back more directly towards her, and found Eyila's eyes still fixed diligently upon him.

"But you believed Zikhon to be responsible for the disappearance of the elves," she continued, unperturbed. "You were wrong about that."

"Yes, but the prophecy itself has never said anything about gods by *name*. It was Craitic assumptions. And if it wasn't Zikhon that destroyed the elves but the other gods instead, then nothing has really changed."

"But does this not throw the Craitic beliefs into question?"

A crack formed in his brief, creeping victory. "...It does..."

"And if the Sulyax Dizan stems from it, does that not mean that it, too, is affected?"

"It has never been tied to the belief of two opposing gods, only the prevention of another--"

"But you follow Craitism too, do you not? Like most of your people? I've seen the talisman of Vastal around your neck."

"...I...do... But my research has made me long-aware that the elves regarded Zikhon differently to us, so I learned early on not to view Them as rigidly as everyone else. But my faith in the lessons and values it teaches has *never* waned - and it won't, whether Craitism has just been proven wrong or not."

"Mm."

He tried once more and even harder to read her thoughts, and only just managed to bite back the curse that jumped to the tip of his tongue as Petra remarked rancorously that killing was quite absolutely *not* among Craitic teachings.

Eyila, however, narrowed her eyes. "That's why you target the people you do, isn't it? Killers. People who have turned so far from what they should be that they're not 'people' anymore. You're working to make the world a better place before the sulyax can happen."

His green eyes brightened in hope, but with no clear difference to her sharp expression, he settled himself quickly, suddenly teetering on a knife's edge. "That's the way I see it," he replied softly, willing her, and the others, to understand that with all his might. "I assure you, despite the evidence, I find killing even people like that no easy thing."

Petra grunted. "Then maybe you should just *not* do it at *all*."

"No," Eyila said thoughtfully, "he should."

Anthis's eyes snapped onto her, as wide as the moon in his surprise, and both Petra and Garon's were quick to follow with the same immeasurable astonishment. Her own squinted further in consideration as she tilted her head, her straight white hair rolling over her shoulder. "There's nothing immoral about his motives."

"Then explain the *high!*" Petra squeaked, making the men flinch as she scrambled swiftly to her feet, her young face twisted in utter disbelief. "He's *rewarded* for it! It's not done out of the goodness of his rotten little heart, he's part of a *cult!* Morals, ethics - he *claims* them, but he still *kills people for his own benefit!*" She stared at her, then at Garon, begging them both to explain what she had misunderstood that allowed these two to take the matter so calmly.

Eyila, however, was still unrattled. "Would anyone's soul serve the purpose?"

"To varying degrees," he replied.

"And you would be rewarded for them all?"

"...To varying degrees."

"Then, do you also choose these people because of the reward?"

"*Of course he does!*"

Anthis didn't spare her a glance. He focused himself entirely upon Eyila, gripping her with honest eyes, tempering his tone to chase away any hint of mistrust, grasping what he hoped was a chance at understanding, as faint as it was. "I choose the people the world won't miss. Whose existences can absolutely be put to better use in death than in life. I take no shame in what I do, but make no mistake, I don't consider it an easy judgement to pass. I have *never* done it lightly and I am always fully aware of the consequences, for myself and for others who will be affected by it. But they all have prices on their heads. They would be killed by someone, and they'd continue to kill other people until that happened. And though they're *despicable*, they're also free-spirited, and souls with that kind of value mean I...have to 'deliver' less often."

There was no change to her eyes. "And the reward?"

He opened his mouth to speak, but this time his tongue resisted. Petra laughed bitterly.

Eyila, however, simply nodded. "You would be lying if you said it wasn't a factor, but you would hate yourself if you admitted it." Then her gaze finally broke, slipping onto her hands in her lap as her lips began to bow. But they curved upwards. Sadly, but upwards, and the disappointment that had replaced the pressure of her eyes upon him was in turn replaced by astonishment. "My people believe our spirits ride the Winds when they die, protecting the world until they reach the Frozen Gates."

"Yes, I remember..."

"*That's not the same!*"

Eyila met Petra's flaming stare with a brief, apologetic smile. "Only because my people didn't kill them," she replied softly, "and if they did, it wasn't for that purpose." Her piercing eyes then returned their grasp to Anthis. "You could take *any* lives and be rewarded for them. But you don't. You clean up the worst you cityfolk have created, facing them alone despite its dangers for the good of everyone else. I think that's noble."

"*What?!*"

She dropped her eyes again, her smile remaining so small as to be imagined while she cradled no doubt countless thoughts that would explain how she had arrived at such a preposterous conclusion. But she was prepared to reveal nothing, and further stunned them by looking back to Anthis with what could almost be considered a fraction of warmth. "I think I understand now," she said slowly, her fingers clasping absently around the oryx-horn pendant she'd taken from her uncle's body, and her gaze seemed to soften onto the very air around them. "And I appreciate your honesty."

"I--uh, you're...wel...welcome..." His eyes were too wide to blink and yet he still couldn't locate his bearings, so it was fortunate that the invasive creak of the door swinging open again spared him the need to speak.

With the ring of drawn weapons, everyone leapt sharply to their feet, food and quarrels forgotten as the air turned to lead and they fell once more under the scrutiny of pastel-green eyes. The elf-woman who had led them - Tekhest, Anthis had learned - strode in with the same contemptuous rigidity, a manner they suspected she wore even while she slept, and fixed each of them in turn. Her eyes spoke of nothing but mistrust.

"Where is Rathen?" Garon demanded, caring little for her disparagement as he positioned himself between her and the others. Her leer did not change.

"He'll be along. Though he is exhausted and needs his rest; his body and mind have been through more than you are capable of imagining. We have healed him, of course, but with his human constitution, he won't be very mobile so soon. You will have to stay here for a while."

Their concern was almost immediately replaced by a much more striking confusion as Rathen stepped in behind her, right as rain if a trace tired around the eyes. By the frown he shot her, it seemed he was just as baffled by her claims.

But Tekhest did nothing to address it. Her robes barely creased as she turned, casting an apparently cursory glance around the vault as she did so, no doubt noting every minuscule detail, and disappeared back out through the door, satisfied that the bare essentials of the matter had been relayed.

As they were shut back into darkness and the light of a single torch, all eyes fell quizzically onto Rathen, who offered them only an honest smile. "I'm fine." But the slight spring in his step as he made his way urgently towards the basket of food begged to differ.

Petra followed him closely. "What happened? You've been gone for ages and no one would tell us a thing..."

"They wouldn't tell me anything about you, either." He snatched out a helping without fussing over bruises or charred edges. "When I was *able* to ask." His tone was bleak, his tongue sharp, but there was an unnatural liveliness in his usually dark eyes that uneased the others more than had he returned with white skin turned silver and tapered ears. They watched as he tore ravenously into the bread.

"Rathen...what did they do to you?"

"They dragged that damned curse out," he spat with sudden vehemence, "over and over and *over* again. They didn't tell me what I had to do with it, no pointers, not even hints, *nothing*. They just cast some spell or something, recited some accursed nonsense and forced me in and out of it, no respite." He shook his head and snarled, but the brightness of his eyes hadn't dulled in the slightest.

"You don't seem like you've...transformed... Not even once..."

Rathen sighed wearily and leaned back against the wall, chewing the excessively crunchy bread with a little more composure. "They healed me," he said once he'd swallowed, "like she said. Better than Kienza ever has, actually. It's remarkable - I've never felt this good..." A smug smile flickered across his lips. "They underestimated my 'human constitution'."

"Or have they done something to you?"

"Like addled his brain?" Anthis interjected, for which he received fierce looks.

"You *are* awfully trusting of this," Garon agreed, but Rathen immediately shook his head, his eyes finally darkening.

"Oh I don't trust them one bit. They spoke elven the whole time, whispering and snapping and chuckling amongst themselves, they didn't once look at me with anything less than open contempt, they didn't stop to let me *eat*--"

"We noticed."

"*But*," he looked at them all earnestly, "they've proven that they *can* help me. And they're probably my only hope." Though they were expected, he bristled deeply at their dubious, uncertain glances. His tone blackened. "Yes, I get it. But not *one* of you can imagine the terror of knowing that at any moment you could completely lose all control of your body and mind. Or the guilt that comes with knowing that sixteen people had been *killed blindly* by your *own* hands while you recall *nothing* of it. Imagine discovering *second-hand* what you'd done while being given no explanation for it whatsoever, except the assurance that it could happen again in a moment's notice.

"That is what has been hanging over me for eleven years; it's ruined my life and robbed others of theirs, and *no one*, not even *Kienza*, has ever been able to tell me what it is or why it happens. And then Aria...she..." His eyes softened with grief, then hardened just as quickly, his misery lines intensifying. "*No one* is safe from me when it happens, and if it weren't for Kienza, or for Eyila, *I* wouldn't be, either. But these...*elves*, of all things...I believe they can *finally* change that. This is something only *they* understand, only *they* can do, and my mother...my *mother*..." he shook his encroaching disbelief away. He had no energy to wrestle with that claim. "*I* can do it, too. No one other than an elf can help me to get this under control and teach me to suppress it - and who's to say what *else* I could learn from them in the process? They're helping me to resynchronise with my magic, and that could help me to gain some greater understanding, the spell--"

"One thing at a time," Garon warned him.

Rathen suppressed a curl of his lip. "I know you're not inclined to believe it," he managed not to snap, though he could tell right away from their glances that his words were too soft. It was a scepticism he would have agreed with had he not spent the last ten hours in their unwilling but apparently necessary hands. But he sighed and let the matter go. "Look, at the very least, I have some small kind of control over my transformations now, and I understand why they happen."

"'Some small kind of control'?" Petra's young face furrowed. "Call me particular but that doesn't sound like enough."

"It isn't. I'm going back tomorrow."

"I question your wisdom."

Rathen's eyes widened in astonishment they darted across to Eyila, who had now fixed him with her familiar scrutiny. "The very first thing I was taught as a healer was to never try to heal someone absolutely. It compromises the body's efficiency to recover on its own, which could prove fatal. Instead, I was taught to use my magic to work *with* the body and help it to heal itself." Her pale eyes shifted towards the door. "But these supposedly learned elves don't seem to follow the same principles."

The bright relief in Rathen's eyes subdued solemnly. "It's worth the risk."

Her hold on his gaze was solid, but though she hunted relentlessly for the words to oppose him, she quickly came up empty. She had seen his transformation in the desert, and she had healed as much of the aftermath as she was able to. And at that moment she could see the crackling energy in his eyes, his drive, his desperate determination to finally control something wild within himself and put others, those dear to him and those unknown, out of the danger he posed.

Her bronze lips closed and she turned her eyes away. No, she couldn't argue. His reasoning was extreme, but sound. She, too, would rather put herself in harm's way if it would spare others...

"Don't worry about me," he said softly. "I'll be fine. I promise."

"You know, I don't think we really have a say in this." Anthis released the door handle. "They've locked us in, and I doubt even magic could break it. We're not getting out of here tonight."

"I bet you're *really* broken up about that."

He ignored Petra's latest scornful remark. "I'd be lying if I said no part of me was pleased, but I'd rather be on that endlessly rocking boat, rolling around in that tiny bed than stuck in here for a whole night." His eyes narrowed thoughtfully. "Though, if Eizariin returns, perhaps I can learn a little more about the sul--event that ended the elves. It could help us narrow our search - assuming he knows where we are..."

"Who is Eizariin?" Rathen frowned at the others, but the sudden crash of magic in the air knotted his tongue and launched him to his feet. Eyila's similar reaction to the otherwise unnoticed sensation froze the blood of the rest, and the only movement in the darkened room came from the bearer of frightfully wild, pastel eyes that surged towards them, surrounded by a face so white it reflected the moonlight that clawed in through the small, high windows.

Anthis stumbled back in a panic. "Eizariin--"

The elf's sharp eyes pinned him in place, turning blood to ice. "You're searching for the Zikrahlehveyn."

Chapter 59

Nolan nodded from the shadows. It was the slightest and subtlest of movements, but enough to encourage his subordinate's stiletto to deliver another sharp, shallow cut across Denek's shoulder blade. The bound and bloodied mage hissed, but gritted his teeth against anything more.

Salus, Teagan and Erran observed in silence from the edge of the chamber as the question was repeated again, calmly and clearly, but as with every other, the mage's grating voice offered only sarcasm. They hid their mounting irritation. It would do little good to give him any kind of satisfaction.

The interrogation had started three hours ago, and softly at Nolan's discretion, giving the mage the time to realise with every non-answer that his situation would only grow steadily worse. But though he'd been beaten limp by fist and blade - his lip and eye swollen, shoulder dislocated, leg certainly broken and his light skin a patchy mixture of berry-red, blue and purple - he had yet to give even an inch. That was not unusual for a mage, but Denek seemed particularly dedicated to obstinacy and smart-alec retorts, and his lack of surprise at the sudden removal of his 'untouchable' status baited them even more.

Salus's arms tightened across his chest. Denek had the answers - to the Order, to the artefact, and to everything in between. And he had been 'forgotten' by his colleagues for a reason, which they would drag out of him, too. It would just take persistence. Time. Patience.

But it was nearing midnight, everyone was waning, and Salus was fiercely aware that they were running out of time for that persistence, and he was personally running out of patience.

"How many more times? I don't know a damned *thing* about Karth or Koraaz!" The mage sneered with laborious effort as blood trickled from his brow. "For a speciality in intel-gathering, you're all *remarkably* inept. Tell me: how many threats *have* slipped past you because you've been too busy confirming the same fact sixteen times over?"

Like a fine, dry twig, that patience finally snapped. With menacing calm, Salus stepped away from the darkened wall, catching the mage's eye, whose broken lips tugged into a vile grin as the breaker stepped obediently to one side.

"Ah, the glorious Keliceran approaches. What an honour you do me! Or are you just tired of your lackey's ineptitude? I *do* hope you have different questions - this fellow's are starting to bore."

The mockery in the mage's eyes fanned Salus's contempt, but he remained the picture of professionalism. The thoughts and speculations of the others were hidden behind similar training as they tracked him from the shadows, but the pressure of their gazes forced his blood to course even hotter. He felt the burden of Erran's eyes the heaviest.

He stopped before Denek, who sat slumped in his bindings to a chair stained red and brown, and considered him for a long, deliberate moment. He was thinking little, but he watched Denek's eyes try to read the phantom thoughts he displayed in his own. His expression, a mocking sneer, the slightest pull at one corner of his lips, made it clear that he expected his ordeal to ease in Salus's inexperienced hands.

Salus suppressed his own identical smile. He would be disappointed.

He raised his hands, curiosity chasing the expectation from the mage's irksome face, and began to shape his fingers while Erran supervised surreptitiously from a distance. He did so slowly, taking care to avoid mistakes and conceal his own lack of confidence in the movements, but the combination was short, and there was no danger of Denek recognising its form. This spell, taught to him only the previous evening, was among the few of the Arana's own making; breakers' spells contrived and concealed from the Order's knowledge. And so the interest rather than panic that livened his face was both understandable and preferred. It made the shock of the pain that rattled suddenly down one side of his body all the more intense.

His muscles contracted, snapping him into a sideways hunch, and his voice, though stubbornly tight, rent a ragged howl more befitting of a beast than a man.

But Salus didn't smile in his satisfaction. He stepped closer as Denek raised his heavy head, turning him the blackest eyes, pained and confused, clearer and easier to read in his alarm than any common man's. "You," Salus began with a sedate and ominous certainty, his caustic disdain laid just as bare in his own, "will tell me what I want to know."

"Sorry, the what?" Anthis forced an innocent confusion into his eyes while the rest stared on, paralysed in horror. "I'm not...no, I'm afraid I'm not famili--"

His tongue pinned itself to the back of his teeth as the elf covered the distance between them in a flash, and his gaze frantically darted away, unable and unwilling to endure the wild eyes that dragged his secrets to the surface. He swallowed hard, and he was certain he heard the others do the same.

A bag was suddenly thrust into his hands. "You must find it."

Another wave of shock renewed their paralysis while Eizariin fixed him with fever. "The others want to stop you, but I can *help*--"

"Why?"

His eyes shifted impatiently to Garon, but they screamed a sudden and unmistakable shame. "Because," he continued, just as quickly, just as quietly, "the leaking magic plaguing the world is our fault. A few of us have been looking into it and searching for some way to stop it, others harbouring the same guilt as myself, but the krahvas, our elders, they absolutely *refuse* to acknowledge it; maintaining the secret of our existence is more important to them than correcting our past mistakes."

"*Leaking* magic?"

His increasingly urgent eyes then crashed on to Rathen - who seemed neither as shocked nor as nervous of his presence as the others - but though he hesitated, clearly reluctant in his tension to delve into the details, the spirit they'd seen in Anthis's eyes often enough won out in his. He sighed in defeat and spoke even quicker. "The ravein'okh was made as a testament to elven power - named

Khryu'vahz, Khry's Glory, after its creator - and it's a travesty. It was built *entirely* of magic and it is *potent*. The magic has been locked behind its walls for centuries, but there has been no one to maintain those walls nor their preservation spells. They're breaking down and fragmented spells are seeping out through the cracks, and it's the potency of that preservation which is responsible for so many spell chains remaining whole enough to function outside of it. But without their foundations, they're affecting *any* element rather than what they were designed to - imagine a chair was conjured and made more comfortable by a second spell. If the spell that formed the chair broke down enough for the chair to vanish, but the spell for comfort remained whole enough, it could replace 'chair' with something else - and if that spell escaped, that replacement could be something as simple as a rock, or as random as a river upstream of turbulent water." His wide eyes darted severely over each of them. "Do you understand that danger?"

"We've seen it first-hand," Garon replied, the others continuing to reel. "But why will your people not fix this if they know what's causing it?"

Anthis's expression creased distastefully. "Because they don't want their dear children to learn of their ancestors' mistakes."

Eizariin sighed heavily. "He is, I am ashamed to say, quite correct. The few who have been allowed to investigate were permitted only by the highest command we have, but they've been forbidden from acting upon it. I don't know what the krahvas intend to do, but at the magic's present rate, it will be far too late when they finally do it. As far as I can see, you truly are the world's only hope."

Something in the darkness snatched Rathen and Eyila's attention, and though Eizariin didn't follow their leftward gazes, his eyes glazed in the same, distant way. He returned to them immediately, his expression somehow even graver. "There's little time. I must warn you: your magic will respond to this place. There are spell chains already loose that have demonstrated the danger to mages. You must be vigilant, watch for any unusual behaviour."

"Will he be all right?"

"Yes." But his pastel eyes fell dubiously upon Eyila. "But she may not." Another distraction, a disturbance in the darkness, one the three non-mages realised could only have been magic. The elf forced another familiar bag into Garon's hands, and a third into Rathen's. "You must go."

"Where?"

"To Khryu'vahz and find the Zikrahlehveyn!" He hissed in exasperation. "I can send you there, but now the others know what you're up to, you *will* be hunted." He began herding them into as small an area as he could. "Rathen's magic will be able to open the door, but once you get inside, *you mustn't trust anything*. Keep your wits about you. Find the Zikrahlehveyn and get out. Then hide."

"But--"

"*No time!*" A bundle of scrolls suddenly appeared in his arms, which he thrust into Anthis's with an expression of promise and apology. "These will help. Now go! And good luck!" He smiled suddenly, a brief but honest flash directed wholly upon Anthis. "It was *truly* a pleasure to meet you."

The weak firelight vanished, and the narrow shaft of moonlight that had brushed them gently from the right blinded them head-on with the orb's sudden entirety.

*

None of the guards appeared to acknowledge the footsteps that echoed through the tunnel on his approach. But that wasn't unusual. Prisoners scurried fearfully to the furthest edge of their cells as he passed. That wasn't unusual either. And when he drew to a stop outside of one such barred alcove in particular, he received no kind of greeting from those standing straight and silent on its either side. And that, too, was completely ordinary.

The emptiness of that cell, however, was not.

Oliver looked quizzically to the nearest of those two guards. "Where is he?" He was graced only with a gesture, but that brief nod of the head towards a sealed door at the end of the corridor simultaneously answered that and every other question that would have followed. It also brewed a tingling dread in the pit of his stomach which snaked upwards into his heart.

It didn't show, of course.

He nodded his thanks, turned tidily and strode away, his footsteps no faster nor heavier than would be usual.

Only his white-knuckle grip on the food tray betrayed his alarm.

A shuddering gasp puffed free from broken lips, and a hateful, bloodshot glower fired from between loose, matted hair. But Salus remained unimpressed. "Why," he asked again, no less collected than the last, "does the Order want the artefact?"

Denek leaned over and spat the gathering blood at Salus's feet. His glare and menace remained unbroken until the same, simple movements of Salus's hand wrenched him sharply to the left, shocking from him another demoralising wail. "Why does the Order want the artefact?"

"Damned if I know," he growled tightly, but the gestures came again before he could brace for it. Every muscle in his back contracted, arching his body backwards until the chair threatened to dislodge vertebrae, and he howled again for the full, infinite moment it lasted.

"Why--"

"*It doesn't matter!*" He hissed, slumping forwards as he was released. "They couldn't use it if they tried!"

"'Couldn't'?"

"No! They don't have the magic for it!"

The spell came again.

"Why does the Order want the artefact?"

"*Gah!!* What is wrong with you?! *Listen to me! I'm telling you what I know!*" Salus's fingers twitched and a white flash of panic flared through Denek's veins. "The Zi'veyn," his fear said quickly, "it's an elven relic - it takes elven blood, elven magic to direct elven spells, including the spell inside it!"

"Oh?" The keliceran's hand stilled. "Then why does the Order want it? What could this undirectable spell do for it to enrapture them like this?"

"I don't know! Not for certain!"

Salus's eyebrow rose only the slightest in interest. "Are you sure?" Denek howled and jerked to the side again, but Salus held the spell for only an instant. The mage sagged and caught his breath in relief, but then his other side convulsed before his lungs could settle. This hold, too, was brief, and he slumped and gasped again. Then it came a third time.

He howled desperately. "It suppresses magic!"

"Good." Salus lowered his hand, at last. "That's the right answer."

Denek gritted his teeth in fury as his captor wandered leisurely to his other side, but he didn't vocalise the jibes and retorts that would usually have leapt off of his tongue. And Salus was no doubt aware of that.

"How do you know only elven magic can operate it?"

"Because elves *made* it," he hissed. "We know what it takes to make it work! No common mage among you could wield it!"

"No 'common' mage..." Salus continued to pace, keeping a subtle eye on him all the while, predicting and reading his reactions, his sneers, his flinches. "Koraaz is no common mage... Could it be used for anything else?"

"I don't know! *Gah!! I don't know!* I don't know how it was made or how to operate it! But it's not going to fall into your accursed hands *anyway!*"

"Oh?"

"No! We would never leave such a terrible, powerful thing where it could just be tripped over!"

Salus stopped and turned to face him. He looked down at the mocking grin revealed beneath his dark and tangled hair, and the hatred that thundered in his eyes. And that same sickening superiority, still present despite his split lip, brow and cheek, the blood, dried and fresh, coating his skin, and the irregular, haggard breath that came from rib damage. A superiority he had no right to.

His fist tightened and flew into the mage's bloodied cheek, landing with a wet thump. He was rewarded with little more than a grunt, but he wouldn't have taken satisfaction even from a scream. "You know where it is. Where has the Order hidden it? Why haven't they used it? Are they still trying to work out how?"

Exasperation crackled in the mage's eyes. "The Order doesn't *have* it! And they couldn't use it if they did! Only an elf or someone with elven blood could wield it - are you not *listening?!*"

"Mages have elven blood."

"*Ancient* blood!" He scoffed. "They've barely retained the magic!"

The two stared at one another, Salus's eyes pensive, Denek's ever-contemptuous. But the keliceran didn't raise his hands, though Denek's revolting glare dared it despite himself.

He stepped away, calmly, thoughtfully, and stopped in the darkness beside Teagan. Only when his back was turned did he let any trace of suspicion leak into his eyes, to which Teagan responded with a whisper of his curiously tinted voice. "Impossible."

But Salus shook his head, flexing his fingers, and stared with measure into the nearby blackness. "Nothing's impossible..." His body tightened. The chamber was plunged into silence but for the soft, irregular wheeze of breath being fought into submission, and his thoughts tumbled away before him.

It was a preposterous idea, one so absurd he didn't dare to put it into words, whose likeliness was thrown into question by the very fact that Denek was still there. He could have made his way out of the cells with minimal effort if that truly was the case...

But...those eyes. Salus didn't look around - he didn't need to. Those arrogant, pale eyes were ingrained into his mind. No average mage could have maintained that attitude under such duress...

The marionette, as the spell was affectionately known, may have been the limit of his own magical knowledge, but it was a spell that was easily amplified. Just as thrusting a fist and thrusting a blade took similar effort with drastically different results, with the slightest adjustment to the final gesture he could cause a spasm in the muscle, a cramp, or a blinding contraction so violent it burst blood vessels - an intensity impossible to predict by a mind hampered by stress. Erran had told him he had remarkable control over the detail, a fact Salus decided stemmed from his training as a portian, the result of a precise mind. And that precision, the spell's unpredictable severity, caused just as much torment as the spell itself. And Denek *was* suffering.

Wasn't he?

His attitude had changed when Salus took over. He'd offered nothing but sarcasm before he'd stepped forwards. Now, he was still sarcastic, it was true, but he also seemed more willing to speak. But was that only because of the spell?

No. Denek had underestimated him. Because of the meagre 'bond' that had formed like an old, frayed thread between them. And he was so sure of himself. He was *still* so sure of himself.

Those damned eyes...those damned, inhuman eyes.

Salus straightened and lowered his arms, easing the tightness in his jaw. Doubt swirled around him, but there was a pinpoint of certainty in his centre, one impossible to ignore. It was a preposterous idea - absolutely absurd. But it was so very unlikely that it should never have occurred to them, regardless of suggestion, regardless of evidence. And now that it had, it seemed horrifyingly obvious.

Denek was still there; he hadn't vanished and he hadn't fought back. He doubted the strength of his magical bindings, but...he was still there. Bloodied and broken. And sure of himself.

Salus turned and approached his prisoner. He remained the picture of serenity, even as those vile eyes turned back upon him, even as their malicious arrogance clawed at his temper, even as blood was spat again at his feet. And it remained unbroken as he raised his hands and cast the spell again. And again. And again.

No one looked away as the beaten man writhed, his body jerking and wrenching as if rabid. Neither did they close their ears to his desperate howls or curses. And neither did they show their own private disquiet at the keliceran's skill and free usage of the torturous spell.

Finally, he suspended the torment, and his chilling ease had at last given way to agitation. "Where is the Zi'veyn?" He demanded quickly.

Denek bared his teeth. "I'm not going to tell you."

"If only elves and their kind can use it, what difference does it make if I know where it is or not? Why don't you understand?! It's for the good of *everyone* that it's kept *out* of the Order's hands! Who knows what the high magisters plan to do with it?! I'm trying to *protect* Turunda!"

"You would lead it to *ruin!*"

His heart stopped and his composure fractured. *'You would lead this country to ruin.'* Elina's words bombarded his mind. They echoed sickeningly, reviving the rage that had filled him then, as he'd snapped the neck of his predecessor, returning with such force that he could have been back in that blinding, decade-old moment.

Heat surged through his body. His bones turned molten, his blood to pure fire. It didn't relent as his fist met Denek's pale cheek. It burned only hotter with every strike. His grunts of pain urged him on, but they were nothing compared to what he knew his magic was capable of drawing out from him. His spell, the trusty marionette, was cast over and over, twisting the mage into a dance of the possessed, and every howl, every terrible scream encouraged his fingers to contort again.

How dare he. *How dare he!* He didn't hear the words simultaneously bellowing from his own lips.

What right did *he* have to cast such judgement? Who was he? What did he know?! How *could* he know?! He had given up *everything* for his country, and *again* he was being told he would be its undoing! What gave him the right?! What gave *anyone* the right?!

"*Tell me where it is!*"

Salus bared his suddenly wolf-like teeth, but a ghoulish chuckle struggled out between Denek's screams. "Fuhrahz," he hacked, blood running down his chin, and he leered vehemently into the keliceran's black eyes, set within a harsh, gaunt visage. "I would never...tell you where it is... The world...would fall...all over again..."

"*Tell me!*"

The spells came faster, his movements sharpening in his fury. The chamber reverberated with cries of agony as Denek thrashed in his chair. But through his face's distressed contortions, smiles began to break, and his mindless cackling soon outweighed his howls. Infuriated, Salus's assault became faster still.

But blind rage couldn't smother the sudden tug on the edge of his senses; a familiar trace, a hum in the air, but one that was somehow different from anything memory offered.

Magic. Dangerous magic.

His spell expired, but his fingers didn't repeat it. A flash filled the room, small but dazzling in the darkness, and Salus had the time only to raise his hands in defence. But it was pointless.

The flash - the flash that had been coming for him - never struck.

The light burst, and the immediate crash of shattering wood was punctuated by the most terrible shriek, an awful cry, blood-curdling, and yet braced. And the laughter had stopped. When Salus's vision cleared he found the mage heaped upon the floor, the chair broken and scattered around him while he struggled to push himself up from his side, his hands still tightly bound behind him.

But confusion had silenced his rage and stunned the spinning of his mind. He turned around to the others, but where he had intended to find an explanation for the mage's spell casting despite his bindings, he found only four pairs of eyes staring back in paralysed terror. Even Teagan, portian, displayed something that resembled fright. But while at first it seemed their sentiments were in line with his own, when their eyes didn't shift from their lock upon him, he realised his mistake. Their terror was born of *him*.

Salus's frown worsened with his confusion until the same nail-scraping laughter, though choked and littered with retching, recaptured his attention.

He spun and grasped the mage by his shredded collar and a handful of long, knotted hair, snatching him to his feet. Another wincing grunt was forced from his lungs, but despite the threat in Salus's blue eyes, Denek continued to laugh.

"What was your grandmother's name?" He asked venomously, grinning like a viper.

Salus bared his teeth. "I have no family."

"Oh, if only that...were true. You look upon magic...with disdain, and yet--" he hacked suddenly, making no effort in exhaustion or politeness to turn his head as he freely coughed blood. "Yet you posses its roots...deeper than you would ever...dare to think..."

His exasperation intensified, but Teagan's soft and suddenly dumbstruck voice intruded from behind him before he could spit his amassing questions.

"Elven blood..."

Denek's foul grin widened. "He's got it."

"Don't try to distract me!" Salus suddenly yelled. "*Either* of you! Tell me where the Zi'veyn is or you *will* die here!" His blood boiled over as Denek responded with only a cackle once again, and he loosed his magic without restraint, all concerns forgotten. However he had done it, he would give him no chance at all to cast that unsigned spell again.

"Water..."

The guards ignored his rasping plea.

"W...water..."

They didn't turn. There was no need. He hadn't gotten up. He still lay on the floor of his cell where the breakers had dumped him on Salus's order. He hadn't managed even to roll over onto his back, though his seared and blackened hands played only a minor role in the fact.

"Dol...Dolunokh..."

A slight furrow formed in both of their brows, but still neither turned. "What?"

"There is...a door...in...Dolu...nokh..." He choked and whimpered pathetically. "The Zi'veyn...is there..." Another fit of coughing racked his broken body, and crimson spittle splattered the floor. "Please, water...water..."

A single look, brief but meaningful, passed between the guards, and after an unspoken exchange, one stepped away on silent feet. Denek's haggard, shredded breath was all that disturbed the silence until several pairs of urgent footsteps echoed their way down the corridor. They drew up level, and at the creak of the iron door, he pulled his tired eyes back open as far as the swelling would allow.

The keliceran's silhouette stepped inside, and he felt his rapid heart jump. He watched him drop into a crouch before him and study him with deceptive eyes. "Dolunokh?" He asked quietly. Denek nodded slowly, and Salus measured him with his gaze for another long moment, doing nothing as he choked. "Take us there. Elf."

Chapter 60

Silver blinded. Shards of violet tore the sky. Crackling and humming throbbed in the air. Thoughts stalled as chaos deafened the senses and tumultuous shifts of the land buckled knees, dropping Rathen to the tangle of up-heaved grass, jagged rocks and gnarled roots. His mind blurred as if his eyes were spinning in their sockets; primeval alarm and disorientation roared through his veins, conflicting with the oppressive, peaceful aura that wove into every terrible detail, seeking like a forest wisp to lure him to a gruesome fate.

But he knew better than to succumb to it.

He squeezed his eyes shut against the turmoil and forced himself back to his feet, but a sudden shudder beneath his left unleashed another hot surge of adrenaline. He barely managed to scramble away as the ground yawned open beneath him, a bellowed warning tearing from his lips, but as he found safety and turned to ensure the others', he found himself alone.

He spun around in a frenzy, wondering in the midst of his panic just who this Eizariin was and where in this most recent demonstration of brazen elven presumption he had sent them.

But he found no sign of the others, nor any clue as to where he was himself. Dizziness joined his confusion. He grounded his feet, forcing his spinning to stop, and focused himself on recovering his bearings and driving them back into place. "Garon!" The land shifted abruptly once again. He fought to stay on his feet and braced as a wind, one curiously alluring, struck him out of nowhere. "Anthis!" There were no answers. He began twisting in renewed agitation, searching for any sight of them, grasping all the while the single unlikely comfort of knowing that Aria had not been among them. "Petra!"

Again, he forced his panic to subdue. A door. He'd said there was a door.

But *where?!* There was nothing here! Trees stood shattered, raised, bent and tilted, crossing like wooden blades on a petrified battlefield, while the land around it either rose like welts or had been rent into chasms that even the unending flashes of lightning couldn't illuminate. Rocks torn free floated in the air, some mere pebbles, others the size of wagons, and travelled along random paths until they crashed into trees, which merely altered their relentless course. Orange glows rose from crevices in the distance, but he didn't dare to consider their source.

But there was no construction. This place, increasingly unrecognisable as belonging to any world he knew, had probably been nothing more than a sparse forest before this magic had obliterated it. Perhaps elven ruins had stood, but if so, they'd been torn apart beyond distinction and any lingering traces swallowed by the earth.

Nothing at all stood for a door to have been built into.

A petrifying thought began to creep up in the back of his mind, clawing its way forwards as his skin grew hot and clammy. This is what fate awaited Turunda if they failed.

A boulder twice his size hurtled through the air at frightening speed, which he noticed just in time to avoid with a hasty backwards jump. But as it crashed into and felled a tree, another, lighter realisation mercifully followed: if this magic was leaking from the 'place of magic', and the door to that place was indeed somewhere here...then he now stood at its source. Perhaps, if he could get inside, there would be something he could finally do...

'Find the Zikrahlehveyn and get out.'

He evaded another gaping chasm and shielded his eyes from another burst of purple lightning, feeling the hope sink before it could truly rise. He would have no opportunity. It would be too dangerous to spare the attention. If the magic was so destructive outside, then a place built of nothing but would be inconceivably worse, and as the only competent caster among them, he had a responsibility to keep the others safe from it.

Assuming he ever found them...

"Eyila!"

Then a voice, one broken by the winds and muffled by the air's dense hum, slipped through the discord. He called back and followed the answer, and soon a silhouette rose over the crest of up-heaved land and staggered against an uprooted tree.

"Garon!" Rathen ran towards him, ricocheting as he was grazed by another small but violent wind, and rushed to catch him as the inquisitor stumbled down the sheer slope. Somehow, he stayed on his feet, but his limp revealed that it had been more luck than skill.

"Where are we?" He asked as Rathen steadied him at the foot.

"I have no idea. Where are the others?"

Garon shook his head, then cast a surveying glance around them. "Where do we go?" He turned his eyes back upon him with purpose, no duller for the havoc of their surroundings nor his own apparent injuries, his limp joined now by a subtle clutching at his side. "Have you found the door?"

"Look around!" Rathen yelled over an eerily hollow crack of thunder. "There *is* no door!"

"There are no *buildings*. The place was built inside out from magic, the door could be just as intangible! The elf said you're the only one who can open it - you could also be the only one who can *find* it!"

"The magic is in *chaos*--"

"Then the magic of the door should be organised!"

Rathen growled over a rumble of the earth. "You assume it's still standing!"

"We wouldn't have been sent here otherwise - just search!"

His body stiffened, but he couldn't dispute the point. He closed his eyes, shutting away the world and Garon's dutiful calls to the others with his very best efforts, seeking out longer and longer spell chains amongst the ethereal rubble while fighting off his swelling panic and the unnatural tranquillity that permeated the violently thrumming air.

Salus's stomach turned, but his composure didn't break. He'd used the Arana's translocators in the past when urgent missions had demanded near immediate results, but the spell discs had been slow to work and the dematerialising sensation, he now realised, was quite comfortable. But the magic of elves - for Denek was indeed such a thing - was instantaneous and sent a flood of nausea through him like nothing else.

Fighting it away, he found himself and those few he'd ordered to follow standing under a foreign sky, filled with a full and blinding moon and streaked by amethyst lightning. The land around them was cataclysmic, but the worst of it was hidden by the darkness. Rage filled him; this was what fate awaited Turunda if he failed.

He stood taller and turned to the elf, ignoring the persistent tremors beneath his feet. "Where is this door?"

Denek, still brown-haired and white-skinned beneath the spell he was too weak to break, looked back at him in exhaustion. He would have been in a heap on the ground if Erran hadn't been holding him up, the only one among them even loosely capable of predicting and countering his magic. "It is hidden," he rasped.

"Then perhaps you ought to find it."

He swallowed dryly and looked around, but it was clear his glazed eyes were not what searched. He soon pointed eastwards towards a spot identical to where they were standing. They each peered, but there was nothing to see but splintered tree trunks.

But Salus didn't share the others scepticism. "A spell?" The elf nodded. "Then do what you must." He nodded to Erran, whose own eyes glazed with another sense's concentration while the elf focused himself upon the spot.

Salus's heart thumped so hard it could have shattered his ribs. Was he really so close? In a few moments, could the Zi'veyn really be his and out of the Order's reach forever? Could he truly, *finally* be about to foil the Order's plans to plunge Turunda into true chaos? Had he actually outmanoeuvred Anthis Karth? The thoughts sent a dizzying wave of butterflies through his stomach and he felt himself begin to sweat. Desperation mounted, and an overwhelming sense of peace begin to settle in his mind far too soon. But he embraced it, until his heart leapt into his throat at the collapse of the ground beneath his feet.

A crack had snaked from a nearby fissure and was widening impossibly fast. Stone, soil and grass crumbled under his weight like a trapped door, as though the earth had already been hollowed out beneath. He slipped. He dropped. He heard the startled yells of the two cell guards who followed. His own voice caught in his throat.

Something solid struck the bottom of his feet and his knees gave way beneath him. Before he knew it, he and the others had been returned to the surface, dumped on the shaking ground and left to scramble to their feet and escape the rapidly widening chasm on their own. Its direction suddenly veered and Teagan was next to fall, but Erran was just as quick to rescue him.

But despite the turmoil, Salus was not completely blind. Another familiar tug on his numbed senses turned him around just in time to leap away from the scything claws of a ferocious white beast. He had no opportunity to wonder at where it had come from as terror surged through his core; his blood burned, reflexes sharpened, and as it turned, tracking his movements with three times his speed, he felt a pang of helplessness. But he could not be helpless. He forced himself to dive away from its frightening agility, narrowly avoiding another rake of its claws, but it twisted into a pirouette, an inescapable, spinning mass of black and white thorns.

His eyes gaped in shock as blue fire exploded between them, engulfing the mass and leaving him unscathed. The beast howled raggedly, a blood-chilling sound, and its advance devolved into a frantic flailing.

Salus needed no time to understand the source of the flames. He leapt into the writhing fire, identified the creature's head, and snapped its neck with practised accuracy.

Then, finally, he breathed. Slowly, the world returned to a familiar pace, the cool flames extinguishing as his alarm passed, and the smoke was sucked away by a miniature cyclone, revealing beneath him the charred and smouldering remains of what once resembled a man.

He moved quickly as the ground shook again, but the split had trailed off in another random direction, and the others - Teagan, Erran and the two cell guards still well accounted for - had moved to safety a distance from the abyssal ledge. And all four stared at him with varying degrees of dubiety.

"We don't need him," Salus declared as he approached them. "The door is a spell. Erran can locate it."

"The spell will be of elven make," the mage pointed out carefully. "I can locate it, but I doubt I could do any more."

"Then I'll open it."

"Forgive me, Keliceran," Teagan then spoke up, "but if you *do* possess elven blood, it's only partial. There may not be enough for you to be able--"

"Well we'll never know until we try, will we?" Salus whipped away from him, his eyes venomous, and looked instead to Erran who yielded to his unspoken command, setting himself to locating the spell. It didn't take long before he stepped away. They followed close, trekking carefully over the narrowest cracks of the momentarily-still ground and dodging the paths of flying rocks, until they reached the same unimpressive spot Denek had indicated.

Then the duty shifted onto Salus. He closed his eyes and breathed to calm his fervoured mind, but while he concentrated, grasping his magic to search through the blinding, arcane jumble, doubts among the others began to rise. Salus felt them, too, but he also knew that he was right: until he tried, none of them would know for certain if he could do it. He had, somehow, deflected Denek's attack in the cells on instinct, and had summoned an obedient flame only moments ago - all without signs, all without thought. Only the elves were said to be able to cast spells so effortlessly.

And his grandmother - Salus knew nothing of her, nor of his parents, but Denek wouldn't have been so specific if *he* hadn't known something. Perhaps he could tell, could see the ratio of elf to human within him, and while Salus was disinclined to take so little to heart, at the same time, he couldn't fight the gut feeling that it was all absolutely true.

He reined in his growing impatience and refocused his mind, ignoring the cynical looks he could feel burning into the back of his head. He could do this.

The five scrambled through the bombardment of magically-infused elements, hands and arms shielding their eyes from the shredding winds while they followed Rathen's equally blinded lead, taking care over their every uneasy step.

They had been reunited one at a time; Petra first, no worse for wear, and Anthis who had suffered from the onslaught of aerial rocks just as Garon had, but where Garon walked on by himself, refusing any help, Anthis needed none. But Eyila hadn't been so lucky. A deep cut had scored her thigh while her torso had been lashed by what could only have been quickly-spinning tree roots, and she walked only with Petra's aid. But that was not all; she was distracted, sluggish and doe-eyed, and in no mind to heal the wound that bled with her every step. Petra had bound it as best she could, but whether the girl's sudden subdual was a result of another injury or the touch of the surrounding magic, no one could say. Ensuring someone kept close enough to watch her and support her struggle was decidedly best for either possibility, and all that could presently be done.

"This magic," Rathen guessed when Petra had asked what had scattered them. "It must interfere with spells. I expect it'll affect anything I cast, and the elf must not have compensated for it."

"Then how do you expect to open this door?"

His lips formed an even tighter line as he continued to lead them towards where he'd located the spell, which was indeed, as Garon suggested, more organised than the rest.

"Do you *know* how?"

"I'll figure it out."

"That--"

"I will figure it out." He stopped short, his eyes narrowing as his magic peered off into the distance between the shadows and criss-crossing trees. "Someone's here..."

Garon drew up beside him, his usual grip about the hilt of his sheathed sword tightening. "What?"

"Another mage..." Rathen shook his head, straining his senses further as a furrow of confusion edged in. "And..."

"...And?"

"...Two mages." He pushed off through the whipping wind once more, leaving the others to hurry behind his suddenly urgent pace and bite back their questions at what was certainly an incomplete answer. Because, deep down, draped in dread, they knew they didn't wish to know.

They skidded to a stop behind a mound of rocks, each silencing their awareness of the fact that they could come loose and fly off or turn molten at a moment's notice, and looked impatiently to Rathen, whose expression twisted in concentration.

"How far is the door?" Garon asked, to which the mage grunted and tossed his head, gesturing over the rocks. "And the mages?" Rathen simply nodded. No one asked him anything else. Instead they forced their own senses to sharpen, straining to hear any voices or footsteps, while Garon dared a skilful peek around the edge, keeping as low to the ground as he could. His voice was low, so quiet as to have been inaudible, but because the others didn't wish to hear it, it was all too clear. "Salus."

Eyes widened as panic squeezed their intestines. Salus - keliceran, portian, ghost...mage - a brutal, driven man who wanted the Zi'veyn as dearly as they did and was reportedly prepared to do anything at all to get it. And they each strongly suspected that murder was not beyond his reasoning.

"We'll be fine." But Garon's attempt at reassurance was poor. His jaw was knotted tighter than usual; he was clearly just as alarmed.

Eyes shifted heavily back onto Rathen, searching him for any sign of his progress as he analysed the spell, but his face was a perfect mask. It was only when he blinked and his gaze finally returned that they felt their heartbeats quicken in hope.

"I've got what I need," he informed them quietly. "It's a mess of broken spells and intentional distractions - there's even a trap in place over the top, probably the only surviving one of many - but now I've had a chance to pick it apart and follow the threads, I...think I can do it..."

"Are you sure? You were never a preserver..."

"I wasn't, but I was taught the basics just like everyone else, and these past few months, I've learned a little more." Shoving away his screaming doubt, he shifted his weight onto his knees to find a little comfort on the harsh terrain, if just to ease his concentration and provide a position he could quickly leap out of. Then he loosened his fingers.

The others rose to crouches and drew weapons where they were able, ready for what was surely going to draw the two mages' attention.

He took a deep breath. "Here goes nothing..."

Erran turned suddenly and stared off to the north. His eyes narrowed through the blackness and confusing streaks of light, searching for the source of the distinctly controlled disturbance in the arcanised air.

Teagan followed his gaze. "What is it?"

"Koraaz."

In an instant, Salus's eyes, closed in concentration, ripped open and burned violently into the distance. "*Where?!*" But before his tutor could reply, the treacherous earth jolted again and roared like an ogre. They grounded themselves, having grown used to the tremors, but this one grew quickly worse, tearing new cracks into the surface.

Erran gritted his teeth and sought to level or stabilise the ground, but though he cast his spells, the land would not heed the demands. "His spell is affecting the magic..."

"He's *trying* to make this place worse!"

"No." He looked gravely towards the keliceran. "He's trying to open the door."

His eyes erupted again. "*Stop him!*" Salus spun away and redoubled his efforts upon the accursed door, trying desperately to work out how to read its construction and just where he was supposed to push his own magic. Fury burned hot enough to sear the air, fed by disappointment and an inescapable foolishness. *What* had made him believe he could ever complete this task unhindered? Or unaided? He may have possessed magic but he had no idea how to use it, and he'd allowed himself to be distracted by it, and by the elf. And now he was in it up to his ears with no clue where to turn. And Koraaz was here, with Karth no doubt right behind him. And he had just killed the only one who could offer him any kind of guidance.

His teeth champed so hard they could have shattered. But he couldn't give up. He could never give up. The Order could not have it; they could not be allowed to obliterate Turunda like mages had Halen and Fendale. Turunda would not become *this*.

The land trembled again, but though he managed to steady himself for the first quake, he couldn't fight the next. Clumps of stone and soil exploded close by, striking them from the side while water burst from beneath, erupting from the earth in a geyser to fall back to the ground at half of normal speed. They braced against the pummelling, then dove away as previously soaring rocks began dropping so heavily from the sky that not even the immense and snaking winds could alter their paths. Before they could catch their feet again, the shaking landscape began rolling like water, tossing them about as if they stood within an ocean storm.

Torn from the indecipherable spells of the door, Salus felt the sudden release of magic, and his rage swelled in defeat.

Five figures appeared immediately in the darkness. He glimpsed no faces, but he knew who they were.

A great bellow ripped free from his throat, one so loud, so coarse that its power alone was enough to have filled his mouth with blood.

The air rent open. The land shattered like glass beneath the gaping black void. It crumpled and split, bucking Salus and the others several feet backwards with the force of its blast. They barely touched the ground; each leapt back up, Salus far faster than the rest, and raced immediately towards the ragged oval of darkness.

Turunda would not fall.

He would not be beaten.

All efforts were focused intently on scrambling up the steepening slope. The world was collapsing around them, and they blinded themselves to it desperately for fear of going mad, their eyes fixated instead on what could only be described as a hole in the night. In spite of the lack of wisdom for entering a world made entirely of degrading magic, they barely hesitated as they reached the top of the ledge. It seemed there was just as much to fear outside as within, but at least, inside, no threats were sentient. No threats would hunt them. No threats would actively try to kill them.

They all but threw themselves in.

But as Rathen approached to be the third to leap inside, a roar snatched his eye across the rend. Figures appeared, cresting the opposite peak, but only the first secured his attention.

White skin, black eyes, ferocious teeth and a deathly sunken face.

An immediate and dreadful understanding stalled his movements as Petra pulled Eyila up and past him, dragging her into the portal without sparing anyone a glance, and the inhuman, sepulchral cry came again to turn his blood to ice.

Somehow, he moved, launching himself off of the ground and away from his crumbling world, and with a backwards thought, squeezed the doorway closed behind him.

Chapter 61

Rathen didn't feel himself land, but the shock of the impact rattling through his bones promised him it had happened, and the chorus of concurring groans similarly assured that, this time, he hadn't landed alone.

So he wasted no time on a confirming glance, nor for his head to stop spinning, but even despite his urgency, it took a painfully long time to push himself to his feet. He struggled against his body which felt suddenly twice its weight, and after succeeding at a stagger, found it just as difficult to straighten. But in his frenzy, he wasted no thought on that, either.

He looked around critically while the others pushed themselves up with similar trouble, gathering his bearings in the low, golden light.

Wherever - or *when*ever - they'd ended up, it was sundown; the flaming sky was streaked with artistic wisps of cloud, pricked with the faintest stars, and its warmth was reflected and enhanced by the tell-tale buildings of gold, silver and ebon. But they were not a sight of promise.

No single building stood whole. Most were shattered, fragments of wall, roof and floor piled high on the ground at their side or floating in the air like the rocks that had careened around them only moments before. More worryingly, some structures appeared to have melted, their walls slumping inwards like molten glass.

He swiftly turned his eyes away to silence the thoughts of 'how', but the perfectly balanced wilds they fell onto instead was no more assuring. Streams and rivers flowed over the land, between overgrown gardens and decrepit buildings, until they rose suddenly into defiant arcs like ribbons curling away from the surface, and continued to meander through the air until whatever remained of their elevating spells caused them to drop abruptly into immature waterfalls.

And the nearby paths as he drew his gaze back in were just as hopeless. They rolled through the unnatural desolation like a maze, just as fractured, and shards of these, too, had rejected the powerful gravity. But unlike the orbiting debris of buildings, these stones hung suspended as though time had frozen the very moment the paths had exploded.

And while he could squeeze his eyes shut tightly against them, he could not escape the details which reigned absolute; above, beneath and woven intricately within it all, an ethereal music so light and clear it could have been playing inside his head, and peace, perfect peace. No tug at the edge of his senses, nothing to be fought against. It was infinite. Supreme. And beautiful. So terrifyingly beautiful.

He felt its influence and the madness it invoked begin to bubble unstoppably within him.

Rathen spun back to the others as they took in the sights with, he noticed, far less concern than they should have. "We have to hurry," he warned them sharply, speaking faster than his tongue could keep up with and snapping them immediately to attention. "Salus has elven magic - I saw it, he was half-transformed when we got in here and could open this door at any moment - he could be *seconds* behind us! We *have* to find the Zi'veyn!"

For the briefest moment, Garon stared back at him with completely exposed shock. He was quick to cover it, of course, and straightened despite his injuries to set a decisive pace. "Away from the door - quickly!"

"And then where?" Petra demanded, all but carrying Eyila as she and the others followed close. She looked hopelessly over the decomposing structures that spilled away before them, while a dense forest, no doubt impenetrable, fenced them in. "This place is a mess..."

No one answered. No one knew. But Rathen took the lead anyway, not permitting his eyes to linger on any one detail for too long, and narrowed his mind to a sliver. Garon shortly grunted in protest behind him, then came the rustle of paper. He cast back an intolerant look to find the inquisitor now laden with two bags and Anthis sorting through scrolls.

"Now isn't the time," he hissed, but Anthis merely shook his head.

"Eizariin wouldn't have given them to me if they weren't important. There might be a map or something to point the way - unless you'd rather stumble through this place blindly?"

Rathen growled, but provided no argument.

The winding path they'd chosen at random to carry them away from the door began to thin, and jagged black flagstones hung in their way. Rathen knocked one aside, which drifted slowly as if through syrup to settle in the air a foot or so to the right. The others, cautiously and curiously, did the same.

The path soon opened, the once elegant and ornate parlours giving way to equally neglected gardens, but movement ahead caught their attention and forced them rapidly into the hedges, where they held their breath and peered ever so carefully out from the thornless topiaries.

"Is it him?" Anthis whispered tightly in alarm, but Rathen shook his head as he watched the distant, slender figures skip and dance around together, notably untroubled by their aberrant surroundings. "...Is it an elf?" No one could decide if he'd sounded more or less panicked by his second assumption, but as another silver figure melted silently out from the greenery not three feet away, each felt their breath and muscles seize. They dared not a sound, not a motion, willing quietly within their minds that she wouldn't turn around.

But they must not have willed quietly enough.

She turned directly towards them, and their statuesque stillness was immediately obliterated as they staggered deeper into the leaves and twigs in sudden horror. But she didn't jump, shout, frown, nor even blink in mild surprise. She had no features at all with which to react. Her face was an endless black void. She was not real. It was only in that lull that they realised she was naked, and that her breasts and hips were still so very perfectly formed, as though more care had been taken over those such attributes than anything else. And by the way she giggled, the tinkling sound that floated from somewhere in the abyss where her face should have been, she had probably been devoid of any personality from the beginning.

She started towards Rathen, the closest, exaggeratedly swaying her hips with every slow and deliberate step, sending him stumbling further backwards into the foliage. Her flighty attention then slipped onto Garon, whose own retreat Petra hastened with a tug. The girl seemed undiscouraged, though it was difficult to tell.

Another giggle suddenly fluttered out from behind the unkempt topiaries, and as another faceless, silver beauty appeared, the first turned towards her instead and slipped her arms about her narrow waist. The pair didn't turn as they began skipping away, their existing fingertips tracing sensually over one another's bare skin and eliciting from the other gentle and provocative whimpers. All eyes tracked them, disturbed but unwillingly curious. The compelling display may have been successful in luring the men away had the young women been whole and a killer not been on their tail.

Another appeared as suddenly as the second, startling them again, and chased after the two with a giggle, her rear and curving back just as artfully constructed as the others' fronts. But her bare and slender foot caught something on the ground, and though she landed lightly, she didn't get back up.

The pair paid the motionless girl no attention, and soon lost interest in captivating their audience, turning and scampering away towards another fickle intrigue in another decaying garden.

Rathen didn't spare a moment to share in the stunned glances. He returned instantly to the path and hastened along its winding route as his urgency reasserted itself, and the rest were quick to follow for fear of being left behind and out of the mage's protection, for he was certainly their only chance of finding their way through and back out of the haunting place.

Anthis's attention shortly dropped back to his scrolls, and he soon grunted in thought. "Only elven magic can operate elven spells..." No one dared to turn their eyes away from their surroundings to send him their quizzical or impatient looks. "Which explains why no one has ever managed to make any elven relic work, even when magic has been clearly felt... It's not undetectable damage to the spells - not always, anyway - it's the magic used trying to activate them..."

"Elven magic..." Petra mused quietly, then turned a thoughtful gaze onto the back of Rathen's head. "Perhaps that's how he was able to affect the magic in the desert ruins..."

Anthis looked towards Garon, who was watching the mage with concentration, and dropped his voice even lower. "Does he *really* have elven magic?"

"So it would seem..."

Rathen gritted his teeth, but didn't inform them that he could hear them quite clearly, nor that their marvelling was unappreciated. Focused on his irritation, he didn't notice himself walking a little taller.

More ethereal bodies, both male and female, appeared in the distance as the gardens gave way once more to the glinting onyx city, where they frolicked with one another, enjoying beautifully composed music and the artistic workings of equally bare sculptors. Pavilions stood atop grand and towering pedestals, interconnected by elevated walkways, unreachable by the broken, winding staircases and yet ascended by some who seemed capable of travelling beyond their tangible edges, while a few that stood whole had been taken over by tumbling waters.

The others' quiet and easy gasps of awe only enhanced Rathen's unrest. The magic of this place was indeed potent, and though they'd not succumbed to the arcane taint at any of the ruins, now it seemed their resistance was beginning to crumble. How they'd managed to withstand the lure that had brought entire settlements like Loggerhead to a hypnotised stand-still continued to amaze him, but here the pull was immeasurably stronger, and he knew in the back of his mind, in a corner he daren't look, that even *he* should have fallen the very moment they'd plummeted inside. And yet he resisted - or his half-elven magic did.

Warily, he looked back towards Eyila, and his furrow worsened when he found exactly what he'd expected. While tension continued sparking beneath their feet even as they marvelled, she was the only one not to share in it. She stumbled along at Petra's side, her glazed eyes flitting about and following things no other could see, while a mixture of desperation and entrancement pinched the skin around them. Whatever steeled him against the poisonous lure was absent from her, but aside from escaping the place as soon as possible, he had little idea what they could do for her.

He looked back to the path, increasingly troubled, and his jaw tightened in further helplessness as it split off suddenly in several directions.

"Where do we go?" Petra asked as she and the others stumbled to a stop behind him, each looking at the dark slates as though seeing the path for the first time. But Rathen could only shake his head. He turned to assess the area, but there was nothing to lend any hint to a preferred direction, and his bearings, it seemed, had been left on the island. Nothing here had changed - not even the light. Eternal sundown.

His jaw knotted again and his spine turned rigid. He could almost feel their pursuers breathing down his neck.

Somewhere in this forsaken place, the Zi'veyn, the elven relic impossibly capable of directly affecting magic, was waiting for someone to collect and use it, possibly for the first time since its creation. And while it should have been a comfort to know that only one of elven blood could bend its power to their will, it seemed suddenly to be a curse. He was more painfully aware now than ever of the fact that it fell to him alone to repair its spell and turn it upon the magic that ravaged their world. If Salus managed to get to it first - and with the help of his captive mage and those magic-users under his command, he may well have better instruction than what Rathen had alone - he was just as likely to muddle through and repair it himself. And then...

He didn't dare to think. He knew only that they had to find it first, if just to keep it out of his hands.

But there was too much damned ground to cover to find the accursed thing, and that ground was too unstable and suspended for them to chance splitting up...

A long shadow shifted. Anthis stepped up beside him, his scrolls still open in his hands though he'd been paying them less and less attention, and surveyed the area himself. "Let's throw some logic at this," he began, clearly fighting against his wandering curiosity. "This place was built as a 'testament to elven power', yes? And its existence and location were kept a secret from almost every elf. The ones fortunate enough to be in the know would have been of the highest social status, which is always accompanied by some degree of arrogance. It's not a big leap to assume that they would have been arrogant enough to think the secrecy of the place was enough to make it safe - safe enough to store a mass weapon."

"We've already been told it's here," Garon reminded him.

"Yes - and likely not very well hidden, if even hidden at all."

The inquisitor blinked in realisation. "This place would have been enough..."

"That still doesn't tell us where we should start searching," Petra pointed out irritably, but Anthis only smiled. She sneered. He ignored it.

"We don't need to search. We need to go to the heart."

"And where would that be?"

The young historian pointed, far beyond the visible reach of any of the spilling paths and off towards a twisting spire, a structure that seemed in the sunset to be gilded in more gold than the surrounding onyx. But, like everything else in 'Khry's Glory', this 'testament to elven power', it was far from in one piece. In fact, almost a full quarter had broken away to float in the air alongside it, like the shards of the winding roads.

"A rickety old tower?"

Rathen grimaced. "I'm having flashbacks."

Garon, however, stepped past them and started down the path that seemed to head in its direction, stubbornly steeling himself against his limp and straightening from his sideways hunch. "Let's go."

Anthis was immediately behind him, releasing his dutiful hold over his focus, and though Petra and Rathen cast each other dubious looks, they could offer no alternatives. But Petra didn't remain quiet. "Something's been bothering me. The information about the artefact was scattered over at least two ruins - what if the artefact itself isn't here? What if these rebels got to it and stole it away? Or destroyed it? And that fact is stashed up in *another* ruin?"

But Anthis shook his head, even as his starry eyes returned to drinking in the strange world. "It's here," he replied absently as he watched four young women of varying completion enjoying a needlessly messy dessert in front of one mirrored parlour. "The rebels didn't get it. If they had, they would have left a much bigger mark on history; their legacy would be more than a few notes and scrolls locked away in dark holes..." He frowned for a moment and raised his hand to his temple. His head throbbed. The air was growing thin.

They struggled onwards, puffing as every step became suddenly more taxing than the last, as though in a single moment they'd travelled from the foot of a mountain to its peak and gained none of the visibility. But there was still no time to think on it.

Rathen looked up again to the burning sky. No time. And yet this place was timeless; nothing changed, but somehow grew ever stranger. He had no idea how long they'd been inside, nor how far behind them the door now lay, but with every passing moment the urgency of the others failed. Gasps began to rise more frequently with every turning they took, and Petra soon began to hum. Softly and absently, she sang along the incessant music that rotated in their heads like a never-ending music box, and Garon, too, eventually joined in. But Anthis fell further: three times he had wandered away from the group, twice for the lure of voluptuous figures and the perfectly sweet scents of fruit tarts, and once for a boutique filled with ornate trinkets, the magical functions of which were anyone's guess. If Eizariin had stashed a map within his scrolls, or directions, or even a nugget of advice, he wasn't going to find it.

But Eyila... The rest were so far gone that not even Petra noticed the mumbles and whispers as she staggered along at her shoulder. But Rathen heard them. And he saw the now absolute emptiness of her ice-blue eyes.

Eyila was no longer there.

And still he could do nothing but hurry them along. He couldn't risk casting a spell over her, not even one so simple as to discover the extent of the turmoil in her blood. He had no idea how it might affect her. And if her magic was responding to the arcanised air... He shook away the image of the burned corpse in the desert.

If her magic was responding, he'd rather not make it worse. He would just have to keep a closer eye on her. And if her situation worsened...he would have no choice but to intervene. If not to save her, then to save everyone else.

Despite his still-spinning head and the debilitating pressure of both gravity and responsibility, he increased his pace, and the others, when they noticed, followed suit.

The tower loomed. It was far bigger than they had first thought, all but piercing through the false sky, and its walls and frames truly looked ready to fail at any moment. As the rest stood and stared in a disconnected daydream, Rathen turned towards Anthis. The historian took his time to drag his eyes away from the sculpted claddings.

"You're sure?" He asked him gravely, but Anthis merely smiled and nodded before allowing his thin attention to float onto one of the strange, golden birds above them as it gave an unnaturally smooth aerobatic display, its jewelled feet and beak glittering in the unwaning light.

Rathen sighed hopelessly and turned back to the twisting spire. "This had better not take long..." With sufferance, he started up the fifty or so steps towards the enormous doors, leading the way around missing stones that had been replaced by pools of black he thought best not to touch, and gingerly pushed his way inside, gritting his teeth against the sound of broken rubble scraping across the floor.

Despite the reach of the low evening light, he wasn't hard for seeing. Inside, dozens of tiny flames floated at twice head height, illuminating the ostentatious decor like as many orange fireflies, and a few had drifted to engulf a wall lined with rich tapestries which brightened the atrium into day. He wondered for a distant moment if it had been burning for minutes or for years. The fire made no effort to spread, leaving the antique divans, tables and vases of freshly picked flowers untouched.

More outbursts of awe followed the far less cautious steps of the others as they wandered in leisurely behind him, and immediately they began to disperse and indulge their childish curiosity. Rathen was just as quick to round them all back up. "You're worse than Aria." He sighed and straightened, casting over them the same disapproving eyes that she would have been subjected to. "*All* of you, *try* to focus. This is no time *or* place to wander off." He looked pointedly towards Anthis again. "Where in this tower is the Zi'veyn most likely to be?"

"The top, knowing our luck," Petra muttered mildly, gazing up towards the distant ceiling which stood too far above them for their frescoes to be decipherable beyond a myriad of metallic colours. Rathen followed her gaze, cursing silently because, of course, that was bound to be the case.

Without warning, Anthis suddenly surged past him, evading his belated grasp as he snatched out towards his collar to pull him backwards, and barrelled across the lavish atrium with little care for the cracks and debris that tried to trip him up. Garon followed, though his pace was far more laggard than befitted him, and Petra sauntered along behind, Eyila hanging off of her as though she had become little more than luggage.

Rathen cursed and hurried after them, silently thankful once again that at least he didn't have to keep the mischievous Aria in his sights.

Finely gilded display cases lined the furthest wall, separated by pedestals bearing excessively large, ornate vases of the most unusually coloured and fragranced blooms, and watched over by a cavalcade of enormous, regal and distinctly contemptuous portraits. The elves' pastel eyes looked far too real, and Rathen did his best not to sneer back at them.

He also stubbornly restrained his awe as he peered briefly at the jewels and trinkets of typically extravagant design that filled each of those cases. Every piece was perfectly sized to fit in the palm of the hand, and all enrobed in spells. Even through the chaos that permeated the air, he could feel the hum and concentration of magic encased before him. Many of the trinkets were probably created entirely from spells, but what details he could pick from the mess were frivolous: music, intoxication, scents and sensations, some of which made him blush outrageously just by identifying them. But the tangle was so severe that just trying to follow a single thread quickly resulted in a headache, so he didn't waste his time for long.

Once again, he rounded the others back up, dragging them away from the exhibitions and towards the grandiose staircase at the furthest end, ignoring their protests and reminding them all the while of just why they were there. As he ushered Garon, the last to be collected, he found that Anthis had wandered away again.

Cursing colourfully, he stormed over to the small case the historian had returned to, standing quietly and nodding to himself as he peered indifferently through the glass with a benign purse to his lips. "This isn't a museum," Rathen reminded him, grasping him firmly at the elbow, but though he'd intended to, and quite unceremoniously at that, he didn't drag him away. He stared down at the lone, single trinket that rested inside the modest casing. The small, upturned pyramid that only just seemed to hold Anthis's flimsy attention. At the contours, accentuated by black and gold, that lured his eyes along the crown of thorns that arced into the centre of its broad, top surface. His gaze followed their points, and dropped into the golden lotus that unfurled beneath it before spilling over its dozen petals. He was quickly caught by the barbs protruding midway along each of the four edges, and guided down towards its jagged-cut tip.

He blinked, stunned and blind-sided, while Anthis grunted thoughtfully beside him. The historian cocked his head. "Smaller than I expected."

His irritation fled. Rathen tossed his elbow away and quickly probed the tiny trinket, and his disbelief only grew when he confirmed the nature of its surrounding spells. He shook his head as his eyes widened even further, and forcibly ignored the terror birthed by its very presence. "This is it, isn't it?"

"Mm. Seems to be..."

Rathen overlooked his disturbing mildness, along with the murmurs of wonder as the others gathered around them. If this was the Zi'veyn - if he could truly believe that such a small, unsuspecting thing could possibly be a weapon against all of elvenkind - then...the matter now fell to him.

With the greatest of effort, he forced his mind to clear, shaking away the shock at what appeared to be an actual result from their beyond unlikely quest, and focused into the magic as a petrified sweat began dewing his skin.

Dubiously, he levelled against the Zi'veyn's enrobing weave of spells, and discovered immediately that it was one thicker and more immense than anything he'd ever felt. That was not so surprising, but the extent of its degradation was. Despite the seven centuries that had led to the breakdown of almost everything else within this arcane place, each spell that protected the meagre little relic was still whole enough to function. And they were brutal, so much so that, had he not experienced the elven definition of 'helping' for himself, he would have presumed they were meant simply as a deterrent rather than actual punishment. Some boldly threatened physical pain - seared skin, blunt strikes and lacerations - while others dealt in mental torment, digging up one's most painful memories, or sucking away anything good and cheerful. But a few were far more intricate, resulting, when tripped, in a violent bio-chemical response that would cause the would-be thief's own magic to attack them. He didn't truly understand the workings of those, but something within him was assured that it was not something he *wanted* to comprehend, and certainly not to experience.

But, though he hunted, he found no alarms. Instead the shroud had been woven with hairpin triggers, fatally precise and even more sensitive now that certain chains had fallen away, and were almost certainly intended both to be triggered and to make disabling the defences even more difficult. The elves had had no wish for direct confrontation, instead it seemed potential thieves were left to see to their own undoing.

Rathen felt his blood begin to burn, and wondered for a moment if he hadn't tripped one of the snares just by looking at it. He recognised it as anxiety only when sweat began to trickle and nausea turned his stomach. But still something encouraged his hearing to sharpen and strain through the ever-present music for sounds of approach, but he couldn't decide if there was nothing, or if he just couldn't hear it.

He grunted belittlingly and refocused. The spells were complex, so much so that there had to be a quick and simple means of deactivating it in case the thing was needed. But he knew he had no time to discover it, and as his heart hammered, his attention slipped desperately beneath it and onto the Zi'veyn. A resentful hiss seeped through his lips. Its time-worn damage was repairable, and certainly minimised by its shroud, but if the intricacies of those protective spells were any indication, it would take far more to achieve than his limited knowledge could offer.

"Well?"

Startled, he snapped around to Garon, and the inquisitor looked back with a shadow of his usual steadiness. But at least some semblance of his dull and unappealing personality was still there. "Well what?"

"Can you fix it?"

He blinked. "Y-well, I--maybe--" He bit his lip. "Yes." He found he didn't want to hear any other answer, himself. "But not here. And not quickly. I need to...work it all out..." He looked disdainfully back to the small, glistening relic.

"Time isn't something we have a lot of."

Rathen glowered back at him. "You seem to forget that no mage has ever had to *reconstruct* a spell before. A *preserver* would have trouble with this, and you've--"

"Recruited a soldier. Yes." His grey eyes, softened by the magic's influence, sank to the Zi'veyn, and he cocked his head as distantly as Anthis had. "Will patching it not work?"

"No."

"Why?"

"Because of what it has to *do!* Impacting magic shouldn't even be *possible*; to even get *close* would take a solid spell, no holes *or* patches! The Order has never been able to flawlessly patch even the city walls!"

"All right, it's unknown ground," the inquisitor conceded too easily, "but you have elven magic. You were a child prodigy; your superiors felt your promise, felt the power in your blood. You have a better chance of achieving this than anyone else does..."

Rathen bristled but bit back his many possible retorts. "It's not something *any* mage has been trained to do, *least* of all me. Elven magic or not--"

"You have no choice but to do it."

"And it would help if I knew what, *precisely*, the spell was supposed to do!"

"Can you not work that out from what's left?"

His fists tightened at his sides, increasingly provoked by the officer's dreaminess, the easy confidence with which he spoke, and the fact that he was right on all counts. "Yes," he replied through his teeth, "but it will take time. But...but that will be all right. As long as we have the Zi'veyn, it will be all right..." His shoulders loosened ever so slightly, and he turned away from the case and the unyielding pressure that came from the very sight of the thing.

"Keeping it away from Salus is only part of the problem," Anthis murmured, absorbed in unreadable thoughts as he looked up at one of the paintings, an elf, gloved and adorned in outrageously ornate ebon filigree that made her moonlight skin even brighter. "I mean...the magic's only going to get worse..."

Rathen gave him a flat look. "You're not helping. Look, I've got notes, ideas for the spell - I have *no* clue if they will work, so I don't know what help they could be towards this thing, but it's all I've got. You're going to have to be patient."

"We don't have--"

Something snapped. "Don't you *dare* tell me what we don't have!" His bellowing voice filled the atrium as rage finally erupted in his eyes. "I am *well* aware of the situation - I wouldn't be here if I wasn't! Salus is after us, and now elves are *too*, apparently! So *shut up*, keep your helpful little reminders to yourself and let me do what you dragged me out here to do!"

"Perhaps," began Petra, untroubled by his outburst as she cast a half-wary glance back towards the enormous, carven doors, "we should actually *take* it first. Then we will have it, and then you can fix it."

Rathen hesitated as she looked back and offered a chillingly calm smile. "...That's the next prob--" His eyes flicked onto Eyila, certain he'd heard the melodious lilt of her voice. "Pardon?"

Her eyes, shockingly pale, as large as saucers and brimming with wonder and terror alike, drifted onto him from whatever had enraptured them. "Blanket..."

"Are you cold?" Petra asked her softly, but Rathen shook his head, his own eyes suddenly alight with a jumble of thoughts that cascaded like the unearthly waterfalls outside. He spun back to the case and stared, nodding and shaking his head, mumbling all the while as he filtered the thoughts and forced them into order. Then his lines smoothed and realisation settled. Even a smile tried to tug at the corner of his lips, though it didn't manage to take hold.

"An encasing spell?" Anthis murmured, still immensely distracted, this time by the contents of a neighbouring display. "Mm. A handful did that from time to time... Quite clever. Most would try to...uh...untangle the spells, piece by piece, and inevitably...trigger something... But who has the patience for that? Not a thief, nor a rightful owner..."

"The thief would snatch and stumble," Rathen nodded, "and the owner would have the release..." He ignored Anthis as he began mumbling about another relic nearby and returned to searching the chains. He breathed and slowed his hurried mind. He paid no attention to any one spell that had previously distracted him, as was all part of its design; instead he drew backwards, moving himself steadily away from the web to view it as a whole, and soon found a quilt where a moment before there had been hundreds of knotted threads.

There was little order to the string-ball-spells, but something bound them together. He could sense it. Something thin, like a skin over porridge, unnoticed until disturbed...and just as disgustingly simple.

A distant crash unsettled the air and snapped his brittle tensions. Pursuers or a collapse, his alarm jumped, but he steadied himself before he could trip over his thoughts. His eyes locked onto the golden-onyx trinket. He had what he needed to form a counterspell; there was no purpose in hesitating, and no time to try anything as advanced as the others seemed to expect of him. He had only moments, if that. Cancelling out the shroud as a whole was his only option.

And he had elven magic. That had to count for something.

His bearing shifted. His back straightened, drawing him to his full height, and he loomed over the unassuming pyramid, reflecting back its domination. He raised his hands, felt the thrum of magic coursing through his veins, heating his blood, and began twisting his fingers into a series of nimble and intricate signs. The blanket spell was no obstacle - any elf could have gotten around it. Its strength lay in its weakness; it was so subtle he had missed it, as certainly would any hasty thief. But now it had been revealed, now he'd found the lock and dislodged its catch with a hammer, it would *remain* no obstacle.

Finally, it was his turn to be useful.

His heart raced. He released his spell.

And his burning blood froze.

The air shook, filled with a cacophony of crashes, bangs and strange pops and jingles too loud and chaotic to process. It would have physically stunned them had the ground beneath their feet not turned to fluid, undulating like waves and forcing them to abandon all else and concentrate on maintaining their balance. But even that matter was more difficult than it should have been. The feeling of their own weight having doubled increased once again, and it seemed the heaving floor equally sought to drag them down if it couldn't trip them.

Rathen rooted himself against it, forcing his weight into the soles of his feet, and the others struggled in their own time to do the same. A window, huge and mosaicked in coloured glass, shattered beside them, sending fragments bursting both inwards and out, only to freeze suddenly in the air before striking anyone as though a pocket of time had stopped. The outside took immediate advantage; tree roots, creeping flowers and tamed streams spilled inside, quickly overrunning the crumbling atrium and transforming it into a sight more suited to Turunda's Wildlands.

"What did you do?!" Garon demanded, his voice sharp and furious over the clamour of destruction, and Rathen suspected in the moment he took to notice the alarm on his and Petra's faces that they were finally shaking off the atmospheric spells. But though he could make a guess, he couldn't find the courage to admit fault.

"This place is *ancient*," he shouted back instead, breaking the glass casing and snatching the small, inconspicuous and successfully disarmed pyramid, "it's been coming down for centuries!"

"Point blame later! We need to get out of here!" Petra adjusted her grip on the silent and delirious tribal and looked around desperately for any suggestion of safety. But no sooner had her eyes thundered onto the doors than they were covered by the wall above, which had slumped and melted down over them. It settled immediately; their exit was lost.

She spun back to Rathen, then to Garon, shooting them both fevered, helpless looks. Neither met her eyes; both held the same fatalism as they searched silently for an alternative.

As if in answer, another wall suddenly tore itself away, exposing the shifting world beyond as midnight spilled in - but it was not the cratered, silver moon that hung in the black sky, but the blinding and smooth-skinned sun, impossible to look at despite having been robbed of its strength. And among the darkness they began picking out pockets of deeper blackness, small voids like the door in Dolunokh, but no larger than a dinner plate.

With the dead light, more naked and faceless arcane beings came rushing in towards them, untroubled by the destruction and focused instead on wanton entertainment. But while before their bodies had been mostly intact, now they were missing limbs or whole chunks of their torsos, and their previously licentious giggling had become muffled, resonant bellows.

A few tripped and, like the first, didn't rise again, while the clumsy grasps of the rest were easily evaded. Fighting against the writhing ground, the group made their escape, only to stall again at the threshold. The air abruptly thinned and breathing came harder, but they were each still certain that the world outside wasn't as it had been when they'd reached the tower. The square that had stood before it had now become a lake, at the centre of which was not a grand fountain, but a single ornate dressing table. Around it, half of the parlours and carnal houses had been replaced by a myriad of irrelevancies - statues, dress mannequins, bird cages, lone doors, piles of throw pillows and even an ice sculpture - some standing upright, others upside down, and a few jutted sideways from trees and other impossible anchors. And the thick forest that encircled the city had moved up alongside to the right, despite the tower having stood a moment ago at its heart.

The tremors in the ground and air continued, shaking and shattering the illusory world. It melted and seeped, ballooned and burst; crumpled and expanded. Reformed and rearranged.

A terrible thought struck Rathen like the kick of a horse, but he didn't dare speak for fear of encouraging it.

Fortunately - perhaps - the shaping elements heard his mind's voice and provided both answer and solution. A short, splintered and yet oddly familiar path appeared at their feet, headed by dense, fencing trees, while another abyssal window ripped itself into existence between them.

The door.

There was no time to question their changing luck, and fortunately he didn't need to give Garon the urging glance. The inquisitor reached out and grasped Petra by the shoulder, and though she looked back at him with fierce doubt in her hazel eyes, she didn't hesitate for long. With a deep breath, straightening of her back and a short, resolute nod, she hurried towards it, trampling the debris of the tower walls and dragging Eyila along beside her.

They leapt inside, and were gone.

Garon turned to Rathen and gestured sharply for him to do the same, but as something pulled his gaze beyond him, his already severe expression worsened and a rich curse fell from his tongue. Rathen followed his sight. Anthis was still inside, lingering beneath the paintings and standing over another golden case. His entrancement, it seemed, hadn't broken.

Garon started towards him, but was stopped by a hand thrust firmly against his chest, hard enough to shove him backwards towards the void. "*I'll* get him," Rathen growled. "If the doorway closes, I can open it again."

Only the inquisitor's overbearing responsibility made him hesitate, but a single, dark look from the mage silenced it. He gave him Petra's same, resolute nod then turned and obeyed, saving himself with the cold comfort of logic.

Rathen turned his snarl onto the historian and rushed back inside. The heaving of the ground intensified, the roar in the air deafened, and the floor panels began to shatter and float. He ignored it, snatching up the bags they'd left in their haste along his way, just as he ignored the things that began to disintegrate around him - the walls, the decor, the women and the encroaching wild - that which disappeared into nothing as Khry's Glory began its final collapse.

He didn't dare look back to discover if the door was still there.

A sharp, piercing heat cut through Garon's leg. He was sure, for a moment, that he'd lost his foot, and so his priority in the instant he struck the writhing ground was not to protect himself from the jagged rock that only narrowly missed impaling him, but to grasp his ankle and make certain that his limb was still whole. It was; the matter was forgotten.

The tumultuous earth bucked, tossing him up and wrenching his attention at last onto his near-black surroundings. He twisted in the air, landing hard on his hands and knees, and spotted Petra close by, struggling to drag herself and her charge away from the epicentre. He was quick to follow.

The night sky was vast and alight with violet. Its characteristic darkness had been eradicated, as though the cataclysm ensuing around them had rewritten even fundamental physics, and the shifting, exploding light threw such maddened shadows that the landscape changed six times before they could blink.

But the charge and the rocks that hung in the air told them they had returned to Dolunokh. Not where they had left it, for the ground beneath them, though tearing and quaking, was not rent and crumpled, but if the door could move within that senseless place, then there was no reason it couldn't out here.

But the region was in a far worse state than when they'd left it, and after only three paces the ground under their feet disintegrated into fine dirt and pebbles, spread like water and rose quickly into a wave far larger than mathematically possible. It towered above and crashed upon them, lacerating their hands and faces like a sand-laden wind, and tried with all its might to sweep them away.

The turmoil of the magic, it seemed, had followed them out.

They managed, half-swimming, to escape the false and never-ending swell, and a moment later the land rumbled to a suspicious halt. Dubiously, they seized the opportunity to find their breath - but that opportunity was fleeting. They pressed themselves immediately against the dishevelled earth at the sound of frantic voices, and Garon dared a swift and artful peek around an upthrust clump of meadow. His jaw knotted at the sight of five obscure figures charging in their direction. "They're still here."

"But Rathen and Anthis aren't." Petra spared a look towards the pocket of air the three of them had just passed through, but stared instead directly up to the moon. Her eyes widened. There was no hole of nothingness to be found.

"He can open it again," Garon quickly assured her. "We'll find somewhere safe and wait for them."

But her eyes dropped to his ankle, which he clutched despite ignoring it. She saw the shred of his trouser leg, the blood that coated his skin, and the shard of ebon paving that he ripped free from his flesh and disintegrated quickly in his hand.

Then she recalled the dreadful, thundering boom that had followed the inquisitor's landing.

Her eyes tracked up to his with terrible comprehension, but he didn't meet them. "We'll wait for them," he said again, but the betraying wildness of his eyes was already confirming her fears.

"*Koraaz!*"

The sudden voice of fury itself resounded through the air, rivalling the cracks of thunder, and shocked them both to stillness. Garon snarled and pushed through it to his feet. "We have to move, *now*."

Petra eyed him in conflict, until the advancing cry howled again. He gave her no moment to hesitate. Keeping low, he bolted away, catching her in his shadow and dragging her along behind him. They spared no moment to hide from the relentless flashes of lightning, relying on its confusion to conceal them instead, and fixed their sights rigidly to the distance while the maddened cries continued to shake the riven night air.

"*I will protect Turunda with my own two hands! I don't need the Zi'veyn to stop you! But the Order will not have it!*"

They didn't dare a glance behind them into the flashing darkness, even as the

cries grew distant.
 "*I will find you, Koraaz!*"

Epilogue

A light knock came at the door. A timid knock, one that hesitated for a few long seconds after the ponderous footsteps had drawn to a stop outside. She'd heard them; she'd been listening for them. They came by every hour, no less often, paused just outside, then, usually, left again. But sometimes there was a knock, and softly spoken words. They'd only made her angry at first, even though she hadn't understood them through her sobs, but she'd never once responded.

"A-Aria," the frail, anxious voice finally followed. She didn't answer it, but she listened while glaring into the wooden door from across the room. "I...there's some...I've made you something to eat. I don't know if you'll like it...but..." He fell quiet, and for the second time she felt a curious pang of sympathy for the old man. But she held her tongue, and a short clatter of wood and clay soon interrupted the silence. "I'll leave it out here for you. Whenever you're ready... Aria, you must eat..." It sounded as though he was going to say more, and she found herself holding out for it. But he didn't. A slow and heavy retreat followed as hesitantly as his initial knock, and she listened to the footsteps cross the short hallway and carefully descend the staircase.

Aria hugged her knees, burying her face deeper into the freshly cleaned doll. She hadn't left the room since she'd arrived - her father's from when he was her age, the old man had said in a bid to comfort her through the door - so he'd brought her meals to her. But she never opened the door to them, and the smell of porridge, toast, eggs, stew - even a fruit tart - it all made her feel sick.

She felt a stronger wave of nausea pass over her as the aroma of another late fish supper drifted towards her little nose, but this time, punctuated by a deep, empty rumble, she knew for sure that it was hunger. But she still didn't want it.

She turned her head away in defiance and looked about the room instead.

It was enormous. Four beds could have been squashed into it, filling it from wall to wall. Her own could fit one and a half, she reckoned, and that had always been more than enough. And there were so many toys - a ball, a few blocks, a hobby horse and a wooden sword, the latter of which she kept close to her side for comfort. But there were no dolls. She found that strange. He played with dolls all the time with her.

She smiled to herself in amusement for a displaced moment, but her heart quickly plummeted. She sighed mournfully as her eyes drifted out through the dark window and watched a moth bump against the glass, hypnotised by the candle.

Two days had passed like weeks. Her eyes were raw and puffy, but she'd not cried for hours. She'd run out of tears, and instead a peculiar thoughtfulness had set in; she felt as if she was standing beside herself and watching her thoughts roll by. She wondered if that was what it was like to be grown up: to never have emotions get in her way and to consider things with perfect clearness, and for things to always make sense, and to always know exactly what to do, and to do it no matter how it might make people feel, if it really had to be done.

She still didn't understand why she was taken away, but it didn't matter anymore. Her father had given her something *so* important to do, and she'd been behaving like a silly little child instead of doing it and proving how useful she could be. Because, like him, like Anthis, like Garon and Petra, her job was important, and it was something only *she* could do. And her father would need it if he was going to save the world. And he *would* save the world. And she would have helped.

She straightened, dropping her knees to the blanket, and pursed her lips in resolution as she looked over the open book, knife and wood that were laid out in front of her. But her determination quickly slackened. The wood. She'd wanted something nicer than what she had for this arty-fact of hers, something special...something from home. Something to make her father happy.

Her dry eyes drifted back towards the window. Kienza hadn't been in yet. But surely she would be soon...Kienza wouldn't have forgotten about her. And when she arrived, she would ask her to fetch her some wood. And she would make something beautiful, something incredible, something not even the elves could have made. And she would do her father proud.

...Yes. Yes, she would wait. She would wait and make something glorious. And when she was finished, her daddy would come back for her, and they would be together again, and he would be proud, and he would save the world. And once he'd saved the world, she would never, ever have to leave his side again.

And in the mean time, she would eat. Because her job was so very important.

The story of The Devoted continues in *The Sah'niir*

Thank you. Truly. You have no idea what it means to me that you have read this far. Seriously. Not a clue.

I *really* hope you liked it.

If you did enjoy it, please consider taking a moment to leave a review – even just a few words - on Amazon, GoodReads, Google, Instagram, *whatever*. Even just a quick tweet. All authors rely hugely on the support and feedback of our readers, and this goes doubly for self-published authors.
We won't know what we're getting wrong if we're not told.

www.KimWedlock.com
@KimWedlock

Printed in Poland
by Amazon Fulfillment
Poland Sp. z o.o., Wrocław